Thomas Dick-Laude

The Wolfe of Badenoch

A historical Romance of the fourteenth Century

Thomas Dick-Laude

The Wolfe of Badenoch
A historical Romance of the fourteenth Century

ISBN/EAN: 9783743330382

Manufactured in Europe, USA, Canada, Australia, Japa

Cover: Foto ©Andreas Hilbeck / pixelio.de

Manufactured and distributed by brebook publishing software
(www.brebook.com)

Thomas Dick-Laude

The Wolfe of Badenoch

BY THE SAME AUTHOR.

THE GREAT MORAY FLOODS OF 1829. *With numerous Etchings by the Author. Third Edition. Price* 8s. 6d.

HIGHLAND LEGENDS. *Price 6s.*

TALES OF THE HIGHLANDS. *Price 6s.*

LOCHANDHU. *Reprinting.*

THE RIVERS OF SCOTLAND. *Reprinting.*

AN ACCOUNT OF THE ROYAL PROGRESS IN SCOTLAND IN 1842. *Out of print.*

THE

WOLFE OF BADENOCH

A Historical Romance of the

Fourteenth Century

BY

SIR THOMAS DICK-LAUDER, Bart.
Of Fountainhall

COMPLETE UNABRIDGED EDITION

LONDON: HAMILTON, ADAMS & CO.
GLASGOW: THOMAS D. MORISON
1886

PREFACE TO FIRST EDITION.

THE "WOLFE OF BADENOCH" was advertised in June, 1825, at which time it was ready for the press. Since then, certain circumstances, easily guessed at, have subjected it, with many a more important work, to an embargo, from which critics may possibly say it should never have been liberated. The author himself had forgotten it, until now that it has been unexpectedly called for; and this must be his apology for that want of revision which he fears will be but too apparent.

The author has been accused of being an imitator of the Great Unknown. In his own defence, however, he must say, that he is far from being wilfully so. In truth, his greatest anxiety has been to avoid intruding profanely into the sacred haunts of that master enchanter. But let it be remembered, that the mighty spirit of the magician has already so filled the labyrinth of romance, that it is not easy to venture within its precincts without feeling his influence; and to say that, in exploring the intricacies of these wizard paths, one is to be denounced for unwittingly treading upon these flowers which have been pressed by his giant foot, amounts to a perfect prohibition of all entrance there.

In the "WOLFE OF BADENOCH," the author has adhered strictly to historical fact, as far as history or historical character has been interwoven with his story. He has felt, indeed, that this scrupulosity has considerably fettered his invention; and, had circumstances permitted the public so to judge of his former production, some of the remarks thrown out upon it would have been spared.

[*Note to the present edition.*—The author of course refers here to Sir Walter Scott, at that time, one may almost say, inaugurating a new era in historical romance. The "WOLFE OF BADENOCH" was first published in 1827 under circumstances of disadvantage, from having to stand the contrast with the famous series of tales by the above distinguished author. It, nevertheless, passed successfully through this trying ordeal, and was most favourably reviewed in many, critical publications, some of which ranked it alongside the best productions of Sir Walter Scott. A still more certain and gratifying estimate of its worth was the favourable hold it took on public opinion, the work being extensively read and successive editions speedily called for.]

CONTENTS.

10 *CONTENTS.*

CHAPTER IX.

PAGE

CHAPTER X.

CHAPTER XI.

CHAPTER XII.

CHAPTER XIII.

CHAPTER XIV.

CHAPTER XV.

CHAPTER XVI.

CHAPTER XVII.

CHAPTER XVIII.

PAGE

THE

WOLFE OF BADENOCH.

CHAPTER I.

The Scottish Knights—Journeying Homewards—The Hostelry of Norham Towers.

It was in the latter part of the fourteenth century that Sir Patrick Hepborne and Sir John Assueton—two young Scottish knights, who had been serving their novitiate of chivalry under the banners of Charles the Sixth of France, and who had bled their maiden lances against the Flemings at Rosebarque—were hastening towards the Border separating England from their native country. A truce then subsisting betwixt the kingdoms that divided Britain had enabled the two friends to land in Kent, whence they were permitted to prosecute their journey through the dominions of Richard II., attended by a circumscribèd retinue of some ten or a dozen horsemen.

"These tedious leagues of English ground seem to lengthen under our travel," said Sir John Assueton, breaking a silence that was stealing upon their march with the descending shades of evening. "Dost thou not long for one cheering glance of the silver Tweed, ere its stream shall have been forsaken by the last glimmer of twilight?"

"In sooth, I should be well contented to behold it," replied Hepborne. "The night droops fast, and our jaded palfreys already lag their ears from weariness. Even our unbacked war-steeds, albeit they have carried no heavier burden than their trappings, have natheless lost some deal of their morning's metal, and, judging from their sobered paces, methinks they would gladly exchange their gay chamfronts for the more vulgar hempen-halters of some well-littered stable."

2

" Depardieux, but I have mine own sympathy with them," said Assueton. " Saidst thou not that we should lie at Norham to-night ? "

" Methought to cast the time and the distance so," replied Hepborne ; " and by those lights that twinkle from yonder dark mass, rising against that yellow streak in the sky, I should judge that I have not greatly missed in meting our day's journey to that of the sun. Look between those groups of trees—nay, more to the right, over that swelling bank—that, if I mistake not, is the keep of Norham Castle, and those are doubtless the torches of the warders moving along the battlements. The watch must be setting ere this. Let us put on."

" Thou dost not mean to crave hospitality from the captain of the strength, dost thou ? " demanded Assueton.

" Such was my purpose," replied Hepborne; " and the rather, that the good old knight, Sir Walter de Selby, hath a fair fame for being no churlish host."

" Nay, if thou lovest me, Hepborne, let us shun the Castle," said Assueton. " I have, 'tis true, heard of this same Sir Walter de Selby ; and the world lies if he be not, indeed, as thou sayst, a hospitable old knight. But they say he hath damsels about him ; and thou knowest I love not to doff mine armour only to don the buckram of etiquette ; and to have mine invention put upon the rack to minister to woman's vanity. Let us then to the village hostel, I entreat thee."

" This strange unknightly disease of thine doth grow on thee, Assueton," said Hepborne, laughing. " I have, indeed, heard that the widowed Sir Walter was left with one peerless daughter, who is doubtless the pride of her father's hall ; nay, I confess to thee, my friend, that the much-bruited tale of her beauty hath had its own share in begetting my desire to lodge me in Norham ; but since thou wilt have it so, I am content to pleasure thee, trusting that this my ready penance of self-denial may count against the heavy score of my sins. But stay ;— What may this be that lies fluttering here among the gorse ? "

" Meseems it a wounded hawk," said Assueton, stooping from his horse to look at it.

" In truth, 'tis indeed a fair falcon," said Hepborne's esquire, Mortimer Sang, as he dismounted to pick it up. " He gasps as if he were dying. Ha ! by'r Lady, but he hath nommed a plump partridge ; see here, it is dead in his talons."

"He hath perchance come by some hurt in the swooping," said Hepborne ; " Canst thou discover any wound in him ? "

" Nay, I can see nothing amiss in him," replied Sang.

"I'll warrant me, a well-reclaimed falcon," said Hepborne, taking him from his esquire; "ay, and the pet of some fair damsel too, if I may guess from his silken jesses. But hold— he reviveth. I will put him here in the bosom of my surcoat, and so foster the small spark of life that may yet remain in him."

At this moment their attention was arrested by the sound of voices; and, by the meagre light that now remained, they could descry two ladies, mounted on palfreys, and followed by two or three male attendants, who came slowly from behind a wooded knoll, a little to the left of the path before them. Their eyes were thrown on the ground, and they seemed to be earnestly engaged in looking for something they had lost.

"Alas, my poor bird!" said one of the ladies, "I fear I shall never see thee more."

"Mary, 'tis vain to look for him by this lack of light," said an esquire.

"Do thou thy duty and seek for him, Master Turnberry," said the second lady, in a haughty tone.

"A murrain on't!" said the esquire again; "this comes of casting a hawk at a fowl at sundown."

"I tell thee he must be hereabouts," said the second lady again; "it was over these trees that I saw him stoop."

"Stoop! ay, I'll be sworn I saw him stoop," said the esquire. "But an I saw him not dash his brains 'gainst one of those gnarled elms, my name is not Thomas, and I have no eyes for falconry. He's amortised, I promise thee."

"Silence, Master Turnberry," said the same lady again; "thou givest thy tongue larger license than doth well beseem thee."

"By the Rood, but 'tis well to call silence," replied the esquire, sulkily, "and to me too who did verily steal these two hours' sport of hawking for thee at mine own proper peril."

"Ay, stolen indeed were they on thy part, Master Turnberry," replied the same lady; "but forget not that they were honestly bought of thee on ours."

"Nay, then, bought or not," said the esquire, "the last nail's breadth of thy merchandize hath been unrolled to thee. We must e'en clip short, and haste us to Norham, else will Sir Walter's grey beard become redder than a comet's tail with ire. Thou knowest this has been but a testy day with him."

"Peace with thy impudence, sir knave," said the same lady hotly. "Dost thou dare thus to speak in presence of the Lady Eleanore de Selby? A greybeard's ire shall never——"

"Nay, talk not so," said the first lady, mildly interrupting her. "The honest squire cqueary hath reason. Though it grieveth me to lose my poor falcon thus, we must e'en give him up, and haste us to the Castle."

"Stay, stay, fair damsel," cried Hepborne, urging his steed forward from the hollow bushy path where he and his party had hitherto remained concealed, from dread of alarming the ladies, a precaution which he now entirely forgot in his eagerness to approach her, whose person and manners had already bewitched him. "Stay, stay—fly not, lady—your hawk—your falcon!"

But the sudden appearance of armed men had so filled the ladies with alarm, that they had fled at his first word; and he now saw himself opposed by sturdy Squire Turnberry, who being too much taken by surprise to catch the knight's meaning, and taking it for granted that his purpose was hostile, wheeled his horse round, and planting himself firmly in the midst of the path, at the head of the grooms, couched his hunting-spear, as if determined to prevent pursuit.

"What, ho! sir stranger knight — what seek ye, in the fiend's name?" demanded the squire, sternly.

"Credit me no evil," said Sir Patrick. "It galleth me sore that mine intemperate rudeness should have so frayed these beauteous damsels. Mine intent was but to restore the fair lady's lost falcon, the which it was our chance to pick up in this hollow way. He had ta'en some unseen hurt in swooping at this partridge, which he had nommed."

"Nay, by the mass, but I thought as much," said the squire.

"Tell the lovely mistress of this fair bird, that Sir Patrick Hepborne willingly submits him to what penance she may enjoin for the alarm he caused her," said the knight; "and tell, too, that he gave life to her expiring falcon, by cherishing it in his bosom."

"I give thee thanks in mine own name, and that of the lady who owneth the hawk," said the esquire. "Trust me, thy sin will be forgotten in the signal service thou hast done her. The bird, methinks, rouseth him as if there were no longer evil in him."

"Yea, he proyneth and manteleth him as if rejoicing that he shall again embrace his lady's wrist with his sengles," said the knight. "Happy bird! depardieux, but he is to be envied. Tell his fair mistress, that if the small service it hath been my good fortune to render her, may merit aught of boon at her hands, let my reward be mine enlistment in that host of gallant knights who may have vowed devotion to her will."

"Sir Knight," said the squire, "I will bear thy courteous message to her who owneth the falcon; and if I tarry not longer to give the greater store of thanks, 'tis that the Lady Eleanore de Selby hath spurred away so fast, that I must have a fiend's flight if I can catch her." And turning his horse with these words he tarried not for further parlance.

"'Tis a strange adventure, Assueton," said Hepborne to his friend, as they pursued their journey; "to meet thus with the peerless Eleanore de Selby at the very moment she formed the subject of our discourse."

"'Tis whimsical enow," said Assueton, drily; "yet it is nothing marvellous."

"Albeit that the growing darkness left me but to guess at the excellence of her features, from the elegance of her person," continued Hepborne, "yet do I confess myself more than half enamoured of her by very intuition. Didst thou observe that her attendant who talked so forwardly, though not devoid of grace, showed in her superior presence but as a mere mortal beside a goddess?"

"Nay," replied Assueton, "though I do rarely measure or weigh the points of women, and am more versant in those of a battle-steed, yet methought that the attendant, as thou callest her, had the more noble port of the two."

"Fie on thy judgment, Assueton," cried Hepborne; "to prefer the saucy, pert demeanour of an over-indulged hand-maid, to the dignified deportment of gentle birth. The Lady Eleanore de Selby—she, I mean, in the reddish-coloured mantle, she who wept for the hawk—was as far above her companion in the elegance of her air, as heaven is above earth."

"May be so," replied Assueton with perfect indifference. "'Tis a question not worth the mooting."

"To thee, perhaps, it may be of little interest," said Hepborne; "but I could be well contented to be permitted to solve it in Norham Castle. Why wert thou born with feelings so much at war with what beseemeth a knight, as to make thee eschew all converse with those fair beings, the sun of whose beauty shineth but to brace up the otherwise damp and flaccid nerves of chivalrous adventure?"

"Nay, thou mightest as well demand of me why my raven locks are not as fair as thine," said Assueton with a smile; "yea, or bid him who is born blind to will to see."

"By Saint Baldrid, but I do pity thee as much as if thou wert blind," said Hepborne. "Nay, what is it but to be blind, yea, to want every sense, to be thus unmoved with———"

"Ha! see where the broad bosom of Tweed at last glads our eyes, glistening yonder with the pale light that still lingers in the west," exclaimed Assueton, overjoyed to avail himself of so happy an opportunity of interrupting his friend's harangue.

"Yonder farther shadowy bank is Scotland—our country," cried Hepborne, with deep feeling.

"God's blessing on her hardy soil!" said Assueton, with enthusiasm.

"Amen!" said Hepborne. "To her shall we henceforth devote our arms, long enow wielded in foreign broils, where, in truth, heart did hardly go with hand."

"But where lieth the hamlet of Norham?" inquired Assueton.

"Seest thou not where a few feeble rays are shed from its scattered tenements on the hither meadow below?" replied Hepborne. "Nay, thou mayest dimly descry the church yonder, sanctified by the shelter it did of erst yield to the blessed remains of the holy St. Cuthbert, what time the impious Danes drove them from Lindisferne."

"But what, methinks, is most to thy present purpose, Sir Knight," observed Mortimer Sang, "yonder brighter glede proceedeth, if I rightly guess, from the blazing hearth of Master Sylvester Kyle, as thirsty a tapster as ever broached a barrel, and one who, if he be yet alive, hath hardly, I wot, his make on either side the Border, for knavery and sharp wit."

"Pray heaven his sharp wit may not have soured his ale," muttered Roger Riddel, the laconic esquire of Sir John Assueton.

They now hastened down the hollow way that led to the village and soon found themselves in its simple street.

"Ay," exclaimed Sang, "by St. Andrew, but old Kyle's gate is right hospitably open. I promise ye, 'tis a good omen for Border quiet to find it so. So please thee, Sir Knight, shall I advance and give note of thine approach?"

"Do so," said Hepborne, to the esquire. who immediately cantered forward.

"Ho! house there!" cried Sang, halting in the gateway. "Come forth, Monsieur, mine host of the hostel of Norham Tower. Where art thou, Mr. Sylvester Kyle? Where be thine hostlers, drawers, and underskinkers? Why do not all appear to do themselves honour by waiting on two most puissant knights, for I talk not of their esquires, or the other gentlemen soldiers of pregnant prowess, of the very least of whom it were an honour to undo the spur?"

By the time that Sang had ended his summons, the party were at the gate, and had leisure to survey the premises. A rude wall of considerable length faced the irregular street of the village, having the gateway in the centre. The thatch-roofed buildings within formed the other three sides of the quadrangular court. Those to the right were occupied as stables, and in those to the left were the kitchen, and various other domestic offices; whilst the middle part was entirely taken up by one large room, from whence gleamed the light of a great fire, that burned on a hearth in the midst, shedding around a common comfort on the motley parties of noisy ale-drinkers seated at different tables.

"What, ho! Sylvester, I say—what a murrain keeps thee?" cried Sang, although the portly form of the vintner already appeared within the aperture of the doorway, like a goodly portrait in a frame, his carbuncled face vying in lustre with the red flare of the torch he held high in his hand. "Gramercy, Master Kyle, so thou hast come at last. By the mass, but that paunch of thine is a right fair warrant for the goodness of thine ale, yet it will be well that it do come quicker when it be called for than thou hast."

"Heyday, what a racket thou dost make, gaffer horseman!" cried Kyle. "But the emptiest vessel doth ever make the most din."

"Tut, man, thou hast hit it for once with thy fool's head," replied Sang. "I am, as thou sayest, at this present, in very sober earnest, an empty vessel; yea, and for that matter, so are we all. But never trust me and we make not a din till we be filled. The sooner thou stoppest our music, then, the better for thine ears, seeing that if we be forced to pipe thus, and that thou dancest not more quickly to our call, thou mayest perchance lose them."

"By the mass, but thy music is marvellously out of tune, good fellow," replied the publican. "Thy screeching is like that of a cracked rebeck, the neck of which must be hard griped, and most cruelly pinched, ere its tone be softened. But of what strength is thy company?" continued he, whirling his torch around so as to obtain a general view of the group of horsemen. "By St. Cuthbert, I wish there may be stabling for ye all."

"Stabling for us all, sir knave?" cried Sang; "marry, thou dost speak as if we were a herd of horses."

"Cry you mercy, noble esquire," rejoined Kyle. "An thou beest an ass, indeed, a halter and a hook at the gate-cheek may serve thy turn, and so peraunter I may find room for the rest."

A smothered laugh among his comrades proclaimed Squire
Sang's defeat. The triumphant host ran to hold Sir Patrick
Hepborne's stirrup.

"By the Rood," cried the squire, as he dismounted, with a
good-natured chuckle at his own discomfiture—"by the Rood,
but the rogue hath mastered me for this bout. But verily my
wit is fasting, whilst his, I warrant, hath the full spirit of his
potent ale in't. Never trust me but I shall be even with him
anon."

"Master Kyle," said Assueton, to their host, as he ushered
his guests into the common room, "we should be glad to see
some food. The rising sun looked upon our last meal; so bestir
thyself, I pr'ythee, goodman, and let us know as soon as may be
how we are to fare."

"Room there, sirs, for two valiant knights," cried Kyle,
getting rid of the question by addressing himself to a party
seated at a table near the hearth; "room, I say, gentlemen.
What, are ye stocks, my masters?"

"Nay, treat not the good people so rudely," said Hepborne,
as some eight or ten persons were hastily vacating their places:
"there is room enow for all. Go not thou, at least, old man,"
continued he, addressing a minstrel who was following the rest.
his snowy locks and beard hanging luxuriantly around a countenance which showed all the freshness of a green old age; "sit
thee down, I do beseech thee, and vouchsafe us thy winning
discourse. Where is the chevalier to whom a bard may not do
honour?"

The minstrel's heart was touched by Sir Patrick's kind
words; his full hazel eye beamed on him with gratitude; he
put his hand to his breast, and modestly bowed his head.

"My time is already spent, most gentle knight," said he.
"Ere this I am looked for at the Castle; yet, ere I go hence,
let me drink this cup of thanks for thy courtesy. To thee I
wish tender love of fairest lady; and may thy lance, and the
lance of thy brave companion, never be couched but to conquer."
And so draining the draught to the bottom, he again bowed,
and immediately retired.

"So, Master Kyle," said Assueton to the host, who returned
at this moment, after having ascertained the country and quality
of his new guests, "what hast thou in thy buttery?"

"Of a truth, Sir Knight, we are now but ill provided for sike
guests," replied Kyle. "Had it been thy luck to have sojourned
here yestere'en, indeed, I wot ye mought ha' been feasted.

But arrives me my Lord Bishop of Durham at the Castle this morning; down comes me the seneschal with his buttery-men, and whips me off a whole beeve's carcase; then in pour me the people of my Lord Bishop—clerks, lacqueys, and grooms; bolt goes me a leg of mutton here—crack goes me a venison pasty there—gobble goes me a salmon in this corner, whilst a whole flock of pullets are riven asunder in that; so that there has been nothing from sunrise till sundown but wagging of jaws."

"Marry, these church-followers are wont to be stout knights of the trencher," said Assueton, with a smile. "But let us have a supper from what may be left thee, and that without more ado."

"Anon, courteous Sir Knight," said Master Kyle, with a grin. "But, as I was a-saying, there hath been such stuffing; nay, ye may know by the clinking of their cans that the rogues drink not fasting. By the mass, 'tis easy to guess from the seas of ale they are swallowing, what mountains of good provender they have to float in their stomachs. Why, yonder lantern-jaws i' the corner, with a mouth that opens as if he would swallow another Jonas, and wangs like the famine-ground fangs of a starving wolf—that same fellow devoured me a couple of fat capons single-head; and that other churl——"

"Have done with thine impertinence, villain, said Assueton, interrupting him; "have done with thine impertinence, I say, and let us straightway have such fare as thou canst give, or by St. Andrew——"

"Nay, then, sweet sir," replied the host, "there be yet reserved some delicate pig's liver for myself and Mrs. Kyle, but they shall be forthwith cheerfully yielded to thy necessities."

"Pestilence take thee, knave," cried Assueton, "couldst thou not have set them down to us at once, without stirring up our appetites to greater keenness by thine enumeration of the good things that are gone? Come, come, despatch—our hunger is beyond nicety."

Sir John Assueton now sat down to put in practice that patience of hunger, the exercise of which was one of the chief virtues of knighthood. As for Sir Patrick Hepborne, his attention was so entirely absorbed by a conversation that ensued at the adjoining table, to which the Bishop's people had retired, that he altogether forgot his wants.

"And was it thy luck to see the Lady Eleanore de Selby, Master Barton?" demanded one of the persons of the dialogue; "Fame speaketh largely of her perfections."

" Yea, Foster, I did indeed behold her," replied the other, who
seemed to be a person of more consequence than the rest.
" When I entered the Castle-hall this morning, to receive the
commands of my Lord the Bishop, she was seated between him
and her father. They were alone, and the old knight was
urging something to her in round soldier-like terms; but I
gathered not the purport of his speech, for he broke off abruptly
as I appeared."

" And is she so rare a beauty as folks do call her ?" demanded
Foster.

" Verily, so much loveliness did never bless these eyes before," replied Barton. " Yet was the sunshine of her face disturbed by clouds. Tear-drops, too, had dimmed the lustre of
her charms. But methought they were more the offspring of
a haughty spirit than of an afflicted heart."

" Nay, of a truth, they do say that she lacketh not haughtiness," observed Foster. " 'Tis whispered that she hath already
scorned some noble knights who would fain have wedded the
heiress of the rich Sir Walter de Selby."

" Nay, I warrant me she hath had suitors enow, and those no
mean ones," replied Barton. " What thinkest thou of Sir
Rafe Piersie, brother to the gallant Hotspur ? Marry, they say
that he deigns to woo her with right serious intent."

" Sayest thou so ?" exclaimed Foster ; " then must the old
knight's gold have glittered in the young knight's eyes, that a
proud-blooded Piersie should even him thus to the daughter of
him who is but a soldier of Fortune."

" Ay, and welcome, I ween, would the old knight's hard-won
wealth be to the empty coffers of a younger brother who hath
never spared expense," replied Barton.

" Yea, and high, I wot, mought Sir Walter's hoar head be
held with such a gallant for his son-in-law," observed Foster again.

" Trust me," said Barton, " he would joyfully part with all
the golden fruits he hath gleaned from Scottish fields, to see
this solitary scion from his old stock grafted on the goodly and
towering tree of Northumberland. But they say that the Lady
Eleanore is so hard to win, that she even scorns this high alliance ; and if I might guess at matters the which to know are
beyond my reach, I should say, hark ye, that this visit of our
Right Reverend Lord Bishop to Sir Walter de Selby, hath
something in it of the nature of an ambassage from the Piersie
touching this same affair."

" I do well know our Right Reverend Lord's affection for
that house," said Foster.

" Nay, he doth stand related to the Piersie in no very distant degree," replied Barton.

" Perchance this marriage treaty then had something to do with the lady's tears," observed Foster.

" Doubtless," said Barton. " But I mistake if she carrieth not a high brow that will be ill to bend. Her doting father hath been ever too foolishly fond of her to thwart her will, till it hath waxed too strong for his opposing. She will never yield, I promise thee."

" Then hath our Bishop lost his travel," said Foster. " But when returneth our Reverend Lord homeward ?"

" His present orders are for to-morrow," replied Barton.

" How sayst thou, Assueton ?" said Hepborne, in a whisper to his friend, after the conversation between the two strangers had dropped ; " how sayst thou now ? Did I right, think ye, to yield to thine importunity, to shun the hospitality of Norham Castle, that we might hostel it so vilely here i' the nale of the Norham Tower ? Dost thou not grieve for thy folly ?"

" Why, faith," replied Assueton, " to thee it may be cause of some regret ; and I may grieve for thee, seeing that thou, an idolater of woman's beauty, hast missed worshipping before the footstool of this haughty damsel. Thou mightest have caught a shred of ribbon from her fair hand, perchance, to have been treasured and worn in thy helmet ; but, for mine own particular part, I despise such toys. Rough, unribboned steel, and the joyous neighing of my war-steed, are to me more pleasing than the gaudy paraments and puling parlance of love-sick maidens."

" Nay, then, I do confess that my desire to behold this rare beauty hath much grown by what I have heard," replied Hepborne. " Would that thou hadst been less indolently disposed, my friend. We might have been even now in the Castle ; and ere we should have left it, who knows but we might have rescued this distressed damosel from an alliance she detesteth. Even after all these protestations to the contrary, thine icy heart mought have been thawed by the fire of her eyes, and the adventure mought have been thine own."

" St. Andrew forbid !" replied Assueton. " I covet no such emprise. I trust my heart is love-proof. Have I not stood before the lightning-glances of the demoiselles of Paris, and may I not hold my breastplate to be good armour against all else ?"

" Nay, boast not of this unknightly duresse of thine, Assueton," replied Hepborne. " Trust me, thou wilt fall when thine hour cometh. But, by St. Baldrid, I would give this golden

chain from my neck—nay, I would give ten times its worth, to
be blessed with but a sight of her."

"Ay," said Assueton, "thou art like the moth, and wouldst
hover round the lamp-fire till thy wings were singed."

"Pshaw, Sir Adamant," said Hepborne, "thou knowest I
have skimmed through many a festal hall, blazing with bright
eyes, and yet are my opinions as whole as thine. But I am not
insensible to woman's charms as thou art; and to behold so
bright a star, perdie, I should care little to risk being scorched
by coming within the range of its rays."

"Nay, then, I do almost repent me that I hindered thee from
thy design of quartering in the Castle," said Assueton. "Thou
mightest have levied new war on our ancient and natural foemen, by snatching an affianced bride from the big house of
Northumberland."

"Depardieux, but it were indeed a triumph, and worthy of
a Scottish knight, to carry off the Lady Eleanore de Selby by
her own consent from the proud Piersie," said Hepborne.
"But 'tis well enow to jest of."

Whilst this dialogue was going on between the two friends,
their esquires entered the place. Mortimer Sang, after recon-
noitring the different tables, and perceiving that there were no
convenient places vacant, except at that occupied by the attendants of the Bishop, went towards it, followed by his comrade
Roger Riddel.

"By your good leave, courteous gentlemen," said Sang, with
a bow, at the same time filling up an empty space with his
person; "I hope no objection to our joining your good company? Here, tapster," cried he, at the same time throwing
money on the table, "bring in a flagon of Rhenish, that we
may wash away the dryness of new acquaintance."

This cheering introduction of the two esquires was received
with a smiling welcome on the part of those to whom it was
addressed.

"Come ye from the south, Sir Squire?" demanded Barton,
after the wine had silently circulated, to the great inward
satisfaction of the partakers.

"Ay, truly, from the south, indeed," replied Sang, lifting
the flagon to his head.

"Then was I right, Richard, after all," said Barton, addressing one of his fellows. "Did I not tell thee that these strangers
had none of the loutish Scot in their gait?"

"Loutish Scot!" cried Sang, taking the flagon from his lips,
and starting up fiercely; "What mean ye by loutish Scot?"

Barton eyed the tall figure, broad chest, and sinewy arms of the Scottish esquire.

"Nay, I meant thee not offence, Sir Squire," replied he.

"Ha!" said Sang, regaining his good-humour; "then I take no offence where none is meant. Your Scot and your Southern are born foes to fight in fair field; yet I see no just cause against their drinking together in good fellowship when the times be fitting, albeit they may be called upon anon to crack each other's sconces in battle broil. Thine hand," said he, stretching his right across the table to the Bishop's man, whilst he poised the flagon with his left. "Peraunter thou be'st a soldier, though of a truth that garb of thine would speak thee to be as much of a clerk as an esquire; but, indeed, an thy trade be arms, I am bold to say, that Scotland doth not hold a man who will do thee the petites politesses of the skirmish more handsomely than I shall, should chance ever throw us against each other. Meanwhile my hearty service to thee."

"Spoke like a true man," said Roger Riddel, taking the flagon from his friend. "Here, tapster, we lack wine."

"Nay, Roger," said Sang, "but we cannot drink thus fasting. What a murrain keeps that knave with the——Ha! he comes. Why, holy St. Andrew, what meanest thou, villain, by putting down this flinty skim-milk? Caitiff, dost take us for ostriches, to digest iron? Saw I not hogs' livers a-frying for our supper?"

"Nay, good master Squire," said the flaxen-polled lad of a tapster, "sure mistress says that the livers be meat for your masters."

"Meat for our masters, sirrah!" replied Sang; "and can the hostel of Master Sylvester Kyle, famed from the Borders to the Calais Straits — can this far-famed house, I say, afford nothing better for a brace of Scottish knights, whose renown hath filled the world from Cattiness to the land of Egypt, than a fried hog's liver? Avoid, sinner, avoid; out of my way, and let me go talk to this same hostess."

So saying, he strode over the bench, and, kicking the rushes before him in his progress towards the door, made directly for the kitchen.

CHAPTER II.

The Host and the Hostess—Preparing the Evening Meal.

On entering the kitchen, Master Mortimer Sang found the

hostess, a buxom dame with rosy cheeks, raven hair, and jet-black eyes, busily employed in cooking the food intended for the two knights. Having already had a glimpse of her, he remarked her to be of an age much too green for so wintry a husband as Sylvester Kyle; so checking his haste, he approached her with his best Parisian obeisance.

"Can it be," said he, assuming an astonished air—"can it possibly be, that the cruel Master Sylvester Kyle doth permit so much loveliness to be melted over the vile fire of a kitchen, an 'twere a piece of butter, and that to fry a paltry pig's liver withal?"

The dame turned round, looked pleased, smiled, flirted her head, and then went on frying. Sighing as if he were expiring his soul, Sang continued,—

"Ah, had it been my happy fate to have owned thee, what would I not have done to preserve the lustre of those charms unsullied?"

Mrs. Sylvester Kyle again looked round, again she smiled, again she flirted her head, and, leaving the frying-pan to fry in its own way, she dropped a curtsey, and called Master Sang a right civil and fair spoken gentleman.

"Would that thou hadst been mine," continued Sang, throwing yet more tenderness into his expression: "locked in these fond arms, thy beauty should have been shielded from every chance of injury." So saying he suited the action to the word, and embracing Mrs. Kyle, he imprinted on her cheeks kisses, which, though burning enough in themselves, were cold compared to the red heat of the face that received them. Having thus paved the way to his purpose—

"What could possess thee, beauteous Mrs. Kyle," said he, "to marry that gorbellied glutton of thine, a fellow who, to fill his own rapacious bowke, and fatten his own scoundrel carcase, starveth thee to death? I see it in thy sweet face, my fair hostess; 'tis vain to conceal it; the wretch is miserably poor; he feedeth thee not. The absolute famine that reigneth in his beggarly buttery, nay, rather flintery (for buttery it were ridiculous to call it), cannot suffice to afford one meal a-day to that insatiable maw of his, far less can it supply those cates and niceties befitting the stomach of an angel like thyself."

Mrs. Kyle was whirled up to the skies by this rhapsody; Master Sylvester had never said anything half so fine. But her pride could not stand the hits the squire had given against the poverty of her larder.

"Nay thee now, but, kind sir," said she, "we be's not so bad off as all that ; Master, my goodman Kyle hath as fat a buttery, I warrant thee, as e'er a publican in all the Borders."

" Nay, nay, 'tis impossible, beautiful Mrs. Kyle," said Mortimer again—"'tis impossible ; else why these wretched pigs' entrails for a couple of knights, of condition so high that they may be emperors before they die, if God give them good luck ?"

" La, now there," exclaimed Mrs. Kyle ; "and did not Sylvester say that they were nought but two lousy Scots, and that any fare would do for sike loons. Well, who could ha' thought, after all, that they could be emperors ? An we had known that, indeed, we might ha' gi'en them emperor's fare. Come thee this way, kind sir, and I'll let thee see our spense."

This was the very point which the wily Master Sang had been aiming at. Seizing up a lamp, she led the way along a dark passage. As they reached the end of it, their feet sounded hollow on a part of the floor. Mrs. Kyle stopped, set down her lamp, slipped a small sliding plank into a groove in the side wall made to receive it, and exposed a ring and bolt attached to an iron lever. Applying her hand to this, she lifted a trap door, and disclosed a flight of a dozen steps or more, down which she immediately tripped, and Sang hesitated not a moment to follow her. But what a sight met his eyes when he reached the bottom ! He found himself in a pretty large vault, hung round with juicy barons and sirloins of beef, delicate carcases of mutton, venison, hams, flitches, tongues, with all manner of fowls and game, dangling in most inviting profusion from the roof. It was here that Master Kyle preserved his stock-in-trade, in troublesome times, from the rapacity of the Border-depredators. Mortimer Sang feasted his eyes for some moments in silence, but they were allowed small time for their banquet.

A distant foot was heard at the farther extremity of the passage, and then the angry voice of Kyle calling his wife. Mortimer sprang to the top of the steps, just as mine host had reached the trap-door.

" Eh ! what !" exclaimed Kyle with horror and surprise— " A man in the spense with my wife ! Thieves ! Murder !"

He had time to say no more, for Sang grappled him by the throat, as he was in the very act of stooping to shut the trap-door on him, and down he tugged the bulky host, like a huge sack ; but, overpowered by the descent of such a mountain upon his head, he rolled over the steps with his burthen into the very middle of the vault. More afraid of her husband's wrath than anxious for his safety, Mrs. Kyle put her lamp on the ground,

jumped nimbly over the prostrate strugglers, and escaped.
The active and Herculean Sang, rising to his knees, with his
left hand pressed down the half-stunned publican, who lay on
his back gasping for breath ; then seizing the lamp with his
right, he rose suddenly to his legs, and, regaining the trap-door
in the twinkling of an eye, sat him down quietly on the floor to
recover his own breath ; and, taking the end of the lever in his
hand, and half closing the aperture, he waited patiently till his
adversary had so far recovered himself as to be able to come to
a parley.

"So, Master Sylvester Kyle," said the esquire, "thou art
there, art thou—caught in thine own trap ? So much for treating noble Scots, the flower of chivalry, with stinking hog's
entrails. By'r Lady, 'tis well for thee thou hast such good store
of food there. Let me see ; methinks thou must hold out well
some week or twain ere it may begin to putrify. Thou hadst
better fall to, then, whiles it be fresh ; time enow to begin
starving when it groweth distasteful. So wishing thee some
merry meals ere thou diest, I shall now shut down the trap-door
—bolt it fast—nail up the sliding plank—and as no one knoweth on't but thy wife, who, kind soul, hath agreed to go off with
me to Scotland to-night, thou mayest reckon on quiet slumbers
for the next century."

"Oh, good Sir Squire," cried Kyle, wringing his hands like a
maniac, "let me out, I beseech thee ; leave me not to so dreadful a death. Thou and thy knights and all shall feast like
princes ; thou shalt float in sack and canary ; thou shalt drink
Rhinwyn in barrelfuls, and Malvoisie in hogsheads, to the very
lowest lacquey of ye. No, merciful Sir Squire, thou canst not
be so cruel—Oh, oh !"

"Hand me up," said Sang, with a stern voice, "hand me up,
I say, that venison, and these pullets there, that neat's tongue,
and a brace of the fattest of these ducks ; I shall then consider
whether thou art worthy of my most royal clemency."

Mine host had no alternative but to obey. One by one the
various articles enumerated by Sang were handed up to him,
and deposited beside him on the floor of the passage.

"Take these flagons there," said he, " and draw from each of
these buts, that I may taste.—Ha ! excellent, i' faith, excellent.
—Now, Sir knave, those of thy kidney mount up a ladder to
finish their career of villainy, but thy fate lieth downwards ; so
down, descend, and mingle with thy kindred dirt."

He slapped down the trap-door with tremendous force, bolted
it firmly, and replaced the sliding plank, so that the wretch's

shrieks of horrible despair came deafened through the solid oak, and sounded but as the moaning of some deep subterranean stream.

Master Sang had some difficulty in piling up the provender he had acquired, and carrying it with the flagons to the kitchen. There he found Mrs. Kyle, who, in the apprehension of a terrible storm from her lord, was sitting in a corner drowned in tears.

" Cheer up, fair dame," said Sang to the disconsolate Mrs. Kyle ; " thou needest be under no fear of him to-night. I have left him in prison, and thou mayest relieve him thyself when thou mayest. and on thine own terms of capitulation. Meanwhile, hash up some of that venison, and dress these capons, and this neat's tongue, for the knights, our masters, and make out a supper for my comrade and me and the rest as fast as may be. I'll bear in the wine myself."

Mrs. Kyle felt a small smack of disappointment to find that the so lately gallant esquire, after all he had said, should himself put such an office upon her ; but she dried her eyes, and quickly begirding herself for her duty, set to work with alacrity.

CHAPTER III.

The Knights Invited to Norham Castle.

ON the return of Mortimer Sang to the common room, he found that a new event had taken place in his absence. An esquire had arrived from the Castle, bearing a courteous message from Sir Walter de Selby, its captain, setting forth that it pained him to learn that Sir Patrick Hepborne and Sir John Assueton had not made experiment of his poor hospitality ; that their names were already too renowned not to be well known to him ; and that he trusted they would not refuse him the gratification of doing his best to entertain them, but would condescend to come and partake of such cheer and accommodation as Norham Castle could yield. An invitation so kind it was impossible to resist. Indeed, whatever Sir John Assueton might have felt, Sir Patrick Hepborne's curiosity to see the fair maid of the Castle was too great to be withstood. The distance was but short, and Sir Walter's messenger was to be their guide. Leaving their esquires and the rest of their retinue, therefore, to enjoy the feast so ingeniously provided for them by Sang, their horses were ordered out, and they departed.

The night was soft and tranquil. The moon was up, and her

3

silvery light poured itself on the broad walls of the keep, and
the extensive fortifications of Norham Castle, rising on the
height before them, and was partially reflected from the water
of the farther side of the Tweed, here sweeping wildly under
the rocky eminence, and threw its shadow half-way across it.
They climbed up the hollow way leading to the outer ditch, and
were immediately challenged by the watch upon the walls. The
password was given by their guide, the massive gate was un-
barred, the portcullis lifted, and the clanging drawbridge
lowered at the signal, and they passed under a dark archway
to the door of the outer court of guard. There they were surrounded by pikemen and billmen, and narrowly examined by
the light of torches; but the officer of the guard appeared, and
the squire's mission being known to him, they were formally
saluted, and permitted to pass on. Crossing a broad area, they
came to the inner gate, where they underwent a similar scrutiny.

They had now reached that part of the fortress where stood
the barracks, the stables, and various other buildings necessarily
belonging to so important a place; while in the centre arose
the keep, huge in bulk, and adamant in strength, defended by
a broad ditch, where not naturally rendered inaccessible by the
precipitous steep, and approachable from one point only by a
narrow bridge. Lights appeared from some of its windows, and
sounds of life came faintly from within; but all was still in the
buildings around them, the measured step of the sentinel on
the wall above them forming the only interruption to the silence
that prevailed.

The esquire proceeded to try the door of a stable, but it was
locked.

"A pestilence take the fellow," said he; "how shall I get
the horses bestowed?—What, ho!—Turnberry—Tom Equerry,
I say."

"Why, what art thou?" cried the gruff voice of the sentinel
on the wall; "what art thou, I say, to look for Tom Turnberry
at this hour? By'r lackins, his toes, I'll warrant me, are warm
by the embers of Mother Rowlandson's suttling fire. He's at
his ale, I promise thee."

"The plague ride him, then," muttered the squire; "how the
fiend shall I find him? I crave pardon, Sirs Knights, but I
must go look for this same varlet, or some of his grooms, for
horses may not pass to the keep; and who knoweth but I may
have to rummage half the Castle over ere I find him?" So
saying, he left the two knights to their meditations.

He was hardly gone when they heard the sound of a harp,

which came from a part of the walls a little way to the left of
where they were then standing. The performer struck the
chords, as if in the act of tuning the instrument, and the sound
was interrupted from time to time. At last, after a short prelude, a Scottish air was played with great feeling.

" By the Rood of St. Andrew," exclaimed Assueton, after
listening for some time, " these notes grapple my heart, like the
well-remembered voice of some friend of boyhood. May we not
go nearer ? "

" Let us tie our horses to these palisadoes, and approach
silently, so as not to disturb the musician," said Hepborne.

Having fastened the reins of their steeds, they moved silently
in the direction whence the music proceeded, and soon came in
sight of the performer.

On a part of the rampart, at some twenty yards' distance,
where the wall on the outside rose continuous with the rock
overhanging the stream of the Tweed, they beheld two figures ;
and, creeping silently for two or three paces farther, they sheltered themselves from observation under the shadow of a tower,
where they took their stand in the hope of the music being
renewed. The moonlight was powerful, and they easily recognized the garb of the harper whom they had so lately seen at
the hostel. He was seated on the horizontal ropes of one of
those destructive implements of war called an *onager* or *balista*,
which were still in use at that period, when guns were but rare
in Europe. His harp was between his knees, his large and expressive features were turned upwards, and his long white locks
swept backwards over his shoulders, as he was in the act of
speaking to a woman who stood by him. The lady, for her very
mien indicated that she was no common person, stood by the
old man in a listening posture. She was enveloped in a mantle,
that flowed easily over her youthful person, giving to it round-
ness of outline, without obscuring its perfections.

" By St. Dennis, Assueton," whispered Hepborne to his friend,
"'tis the Lady Eleanore de Selby. The world lies not ; she *is*
beautiful."

" Nay, then, thine eyes must be like those of an owl, if. thou
canst tell by this light," replied Assueton.

" I tell thee I caught one glance of her face but now, as the
moonbeam fell on it," said Hepborne ; "'twas beauteous as that
of an angel. But hold, they come this way."

The minstrel arose, and the lady and he came slowly along
the wall in the direction where the two knights were standing.

" Tush, Adam of Gordon," said the lady, in a playful manner, as if in reply to something the harper had urged, "thou shalt never persuade me; I have not yet seen the knight—nay, I doubt me whether the knight has yet been born who can touch this heart. I would not lose its freedom for a world."

"So, so," whispered Assueton, "thou wert right, Master Barton; a haughty spirit enow, I'll warrant me."

"Hush," said Hepborne, somewhat peevishly; "the minstrel prepares to give us music."

The minstrel, who had again seated himself, ran his fingers in wild prelude over his chords, and graduating into a soft and tender strain, he broke suddenly forth in the following verses, adapted to its measure :—

> Oh think not, lady, to despise
> The all-consuming fire of Love,
> For she who most his power defies
> Is sure his direst rage to prove.
> Was never maid, who dared to scorn
> The subtle god's tyrannic sway,
> Whose heart was not more rudely torn
> By his relentless archery.
>
> Do what thou canst, that destined hour
> Will come, when thou must feel Love's dart ;
> Then war not thus against his power,
> His fire will melt thine icy heart.
> Oh, let his glowing influence then
> Within thy bosom gently steal ;
> For sooth, sweet maid, I say again,
> That all are doom'd Love's power to feel.

"Why, Adam," exclaimed the lady, as the minstrel concluded. "this is like a prophecy. What, dost thou really say that I must one day feel this fire thou talkest of? Trust me, old man. I am in love with thy sweet music, and thy sweet song; but for other love, I have never thought of any such, and thou art naughty, old man, to fill mine ears with that I would fain keep from having entrance there."

"Nay, lady, say not so," cried Adam of Gordon, earnestly; "thou knowest that love and war are my themes, and I cannot ope my lips, or touch my harp, but one or other must have way with me. How the subject came, I know not; but the verses were the extemporaneous effusion of my minstrel spirit."

"Come, Hepborne," whispered Assueton, "let us away; we may hear more of the lady's secrets than consists with the honour of knights wilfully to listen to."

"Nay, I could stay here for ever, Assueton," replied Hepborne; "I am spell-bound. That ethereal creature, that enchantress, hast chained me to the spot; and wouldst thou not wish to have more of that old man's melody? Methought his verses might have gone home to thee as well as to the lady."

" Pshaw," said Assueton, turning away, " dost think that I may be affected by the drivelling song of an old dotard? Trust me, I laugh at these silly matters."

" Laugh while thou mayest, then," replied Hepborne; " thou mayst weep anon. Yet, as thou sayst, we do but ill to stand listening here. Let us away then."

When they reached the spot where their horses were tied, they found that the esquire who guided them to the Castle had but just returned with Master Turnberry, the equerry, whose state sufficiently betrayed the manner in which he had been spending his evening, and showed that the sentinel had not guessed amiss regarding him. He came staggering and grumbling along.

" Is't not hard, think ye, that an honest man cannot be left to enjoy his evening's ease undisturbed? I was but drinking a draught of ale, Master Harbuttle."

" A draught of ale," replied Harbuttle; " ay, something more than one draught, I take it, Master Thomas. But what makest thou with a torch in such a moonshiny night as this?"

" Moonshiny," cried Turnberry, hiccuping; " moonshiny, indeed, why, 'tis as dark as a pit well. Fye, fye, Mr. Harbuttle, thou must have been drinking—thou must have been drinking, I say, since thou hast so much fire in thine eyes; for, to a sober, quiet, cool-headed man like myself, Master Harbuttle, the moon is not yet up. Fye, fye, thou hast been taking a cup of Master Sylvester Kyle's tipple. 'Tis an abominable vice that thou hast fallen into; drink will be the ruin of thee."

" Thou drunken sot, thou," exclaimed Harbuttle, laughing, " dost not see the moon there, over the top of the keep?"

" That the moon !" cried Turnberry, holding up his torch as if to look for it; " well, well, to see now what drink will do— what an ass it will make of a sensible man ; for, to give the devil his due, thou art no gnoffe when thou art sober, Master Harbuttle. That the moon ! Why, that's the lamp burning in Ancient Fenwick's loophole window. Thou knowest he is always at his books—always at the black art. St. Cuthbert defend us from his incantations !"

" Amen !" said the squire usher, fervently crossing himself.

" But what a fiend's this?" cried Turnberry ; " here are two horses, one black and t'other white. I see that well enow, though thou mayn't, yet thou would'st persuade me I don't know

the Wizard Ancient's lamp from the moon. Give me hold of
the reins."

But as he stretched forth his hand to take them, he toppled
over and fell sprawling among the horses' feet, whence he was
opportunely relieved by two of his own grooms, who arrived at
that moment.

"Where hast thou been idling, varlets?" demanded Turnberry, as he endeavoured to steady himself, and assume the
proper importance of authority ; "drinking, varlets, drinking,
I'll be sworn—John Barleycorn will be the overthrow of Norham Castle.   See, villains, that ye bestow these steeds in good
litters, and that oats are not awanting.   I'll e'en return to my
evening's repose."

At this moment the lady, followed by Adam of Gordon,
came suddenly upon the group from a narrow gateway, at the
bottom of a flight of steps that led from the rampart, and were
close upon Hepborne and his friend before they perceived the
two knights.   The lady drew back at first from surprise, and
seemed to hesitate for an instant whether she would advance or
not.   She pulled her hood so far over her face as to render it
only partially visible ; but the flame of Master Turnberry's
torch had flashed on it ere she did so, and Hepborne was
ravished by the momentary glance he had of her beauty.   The
lady, on the other hand, had a full view of Sir Patrick's features, for his vizor was up.   The minstrel immediately recognized him.

"Lady," said the old man, "these are the courteous stranger
knights who came hither as the guests of Sir Walter de Selby."

"In the name of Sir Walter de Selby, do I welcome them
then," said the lady, with a modest air.   "Welcome, brave
knights, to the Castle.   But," added she, hesitatingly, "in especial am I bound to greet with mine own guerdon of good thanks
him who is called Sir Patrick Hepborne, to whose gentle care
I am so much beholden for the safety of my favourite hawk."

"Proudly do I claim these precious thanks as mine own rich
treasure, most peerless lady," exclaimed Sir Patrick, stepping
forward with ardour.   "Blessed be my good stars, which have
thus so felicitously brought me, when least expecting such bliss,
into the very presence of a demoiselle whose perfections have
already been so largely rung in mine ears, short as hath yet
been my time in Norham."

"Methinks, Sir Knight," replied the lady, in some confusion,
"methinks that thy time, albeit short, might have been better
spent in Norham than in listening to idle tales of me.   Will it

please thee to take this way? Sir Walter, ere this, doth look for thee in the banquet-hall."

" Lady, the tale of thy charms was music to me," said Sir Patrick ; "yet hath it been but as some few notes of symphony to lure me to a richer banquet. Would that the gentle zephyrs, which do now chase the fleecy cloud from yonder moon, might unveil that face. Yet, alas! I have already seen but too much of its charms for my future peace."

" Nay, Sir Knight," replied the lady, " this fustian is but thrown away on me. Thy friend, perhaps, may talk more soberly—Shall I be thy guide, chevalier ?" added she, addressing Assueton.

" No, no, no," interrupted Hepborne, springing to her side; " I'll go with thee, lady, though thou should'st condemn me to eternal silence."

" Here, then, lieth thy way," said the lady, hurrying towards the bridge communicating with the entrance to the keep ; "and here come the lacqueys with lights."

The squire, who had gone in before, now appeared at the door, with attendants and torches. Hepborne anxiously hoped to be blessed with a more satisfactory view of the lady's face than accident had before given him ; but as she approached the lights, she shrouded up her head more closely in her hood, yet not so entirely as to prevent her eyes from enjoying some stolen glances at the noble figure of Sir Patrick. She had no sooner got within the archway of the great door, however, than she took a lamp from an attendant, and, making a graceful obeisance to the two friends, disappeared in a moment, leaving Sir Patrick petrified with vexation and disappointment.

CHAPTER IV.

The Evening Meal at the Castle—The Minstrel and the Tourney of Noyon—Master Haggerstone Fenwick the Ancient.

Sir Patrick Hepborne was roused from the astonishment the sudden disappearance of the lady had thrown him into, by the voice of the Squire Usher, who now came to receive them.

" This way, Sirs Knights," cried he, showing them forwards, and up a staircase that led them at once into a large vaulted hall, lighted by three brazen lamps, hanging by massive chains from the dark wainscot roof, and heated by one great projecting chimney. A long oaken table, covered with pewter and wooden trenchers, with innumerable flagons and drinking vessels of the same materials, occupied the centre of the floor. About a third of its length, at the upper end, was covered with a piece of tapestry or carpet, and there the utensils were of silver. The upper portion of the table had massive high-backed carved chairs set around it, and these were furnished with cushions of red cloth, whilst long benches were set against it in other parts. The rest of the moveables in the hall consisted of various kinds of arms, such as helmets, burgonets, and bacinets—breastplates and back-pieces—pouldrons, vambraces, cuisses, and greaves— gauntlets, iron shoes, and spurs—cross-bows and long-bows, hanging in irregular profusion on the walls; whilst spears, pikes, battle-axes, truncheons, and maces, rested everywhere in numbers against them. The floor was strewed with clean rushes; and a dozen or twenty people, some of whom were warlike, and some clerical in their garb, were divided into conversational groups of two or three together.

Sir Walter de Selby, an elderly man, with a rosy countenance, and a person rather approaching to corpulency, clad in a vest and cloak of scarlet cloth, sat in *tête-à-tête* with a sedate and dignified person, whose dress at once declared him to be of the religious profession and episcopal rank.

" Welcome, brave knights," said Sir Walter, rising to meet them as the Squire Usher announced them ; " welcome, brave knights. But by St. George," added he, with a jocular air, as he shook each of them cordially by the hand, " I should have weened that ye looked not to be welcomed here, seeing ye could prefer bestowing yourselves in the paltry hostelry of the village, rather than demanding from old Sir Walter de Selby that hospitality never refused by him to knights of good fame, such as thine. But ye do see I can welcome, ay, and welcome heartily too. My Lord Bishop of Durham, this is Sir Patrick Hepborne, and this, Sir John Assueton, Scottish knights of no mean degree or renown." Sir Walter then made them acquainted with the chief personages of the company, some of whom were knights, and some churchmen of high rank.

After the usual compliments had passed, the Scottish knights were shown to apartments, where they unarmed, and were supplied with fitting robes and vestments. Sir Patrick Hepborne was happy in the expectation of being speedily introduced to the Lady Eleanore ; but, on returning to the hall, he found that she had not yet appeared, and he was mortified to hear Sir Walter de Selby give immediate orders for the banquet.

" These gallant knights," said he, " would, if I mistake not, rather eat than talk, after a long day's fast. We shall have enow of converse anon. Bring in—bring in, I say." And, seating himself at the head of the table, he placed the Lord Bishop on his right hand, and the two stranger knights on his left, while the other personages took their places of themselves, according to their acknowledged rank. Immediately after them came a crowd of guests of lesser note, who filled up the table to the farther extremity.

The entertainment consisted of enormous joints of meat, and trenchers full of game and poultry, borne in by numerous lac-queys, who panted under the loads they carried; and the dishes were arranged by the sewer, whose office it was to do so.

When the solid part of the feast had been discussed, and the mutilated fragments removed, Sir Walter called for a mazer of Malvoisie. The wine was brought him in a silver cup of no despicable manufacture, and he drank a health to the stranger knights; which was passed round successively to the Bishop and others, who sat at the upper end, and echoed from the lower part of the table by those who drank it in deep draughts of ale. Numerous pledges succeeded, with hearty carouse.

" Sir Walter," said Hepborne, taking advantage of a pause in the conversation, " the fame of thy peerless daughter, the Lady Eleanore de Selby, hath reached our ears : Shall our eyes not be blessed with the sight of so much beauty ? May we not look to see thy board graced with her presence ere the night passeth away ?"

" Nay, Sir Knight," replied Sir Walter, his countenance undergoing a remarkable change from gay to grave, " my daugh-ter appeareth not to-night. But why is not the minstrel here?" exclaimed he aloud, as if wishing to get rid of Hepborne's farther questioning; " why is not Adam of Gordon introduced? Let him come in; I love the old man's music too well to leave him neglected. Yea, and of a truth, he doth to-night merit a double share of our regard, seeing that it is to him we do owe the honour of these distinguished Scottish guests. A chair for the minstrel, I say."

A chair was accordingly set in a conspicuous place near the end of the hall. Adam entered, with his harp hanging on his arm, and, making an obeisance to the company, advanced to-wards the top of the table.

" Ay, ay, come away, old man ; no music without wine ; gene-rous wine will breed new inspiration in thee : Here, drink," said Sir Walter, presenting him with the mantling cup.

The minstrel bowed, and, drinking health to the good com-

pany, he quaffed it off. His tardy blood seemed quickened by
the draught; he hastened to seat himself in the place appointed
for him; and, striking two or three chords to ascertain the state
of his instrument, he proceeded to play several airs of a martial
character.

"Come, come, good Adam, that is very well," said Sir Walter, as the harper paused to rest his fingers awhile—"so far thou
hast done well; but my good wine must not ooze out at the
points of thy fingers with unmeaning sounds. Come, we must
have it mount to thy brain, and fill thee with inspiration.
Allons! Come, drink again, and let the contents of this cup
evaporate from thee in verse. Here, bear this brimming goblet
to him: And then, dost thou hear, some tale of hardy dints of
arms; 'tis that we look for. Nay, fear not for my Lord Bishop;
I wot he hath worn the cuirass ere now."

"Thou sayest truly, Sir Walter," said the Bishop, rearing
himself up to his full height, as if gratified by the remark; "on
these our Eastern Marches there are few who have not tasted
of war, however peaceful may have been their profession; and
I cannot say but I have done my part, thanks be to Him who
hath given me strength and courage."

Adam quaffed off the contents of the cup that had been
given him, and, seizing his harp again, he flourished a prelude,
during which he kept his eyes thrown upwards, as if wrapt
in consideration of his subject, and then dashed the chords
from his fingers in a powerful accompaniment to the following
verses :—

THE TOURNEY OF NOYON.

Proud was the bearing of fair Noyon's chivalry,
Brave in the lists did her gallants appear:
Gay were their damosels, deck'd out in rivalry,
Breathing soft sighs from the balconies near.
            Each to her knight,
            His bright helm to dight,
Flung her love-knot, with vows for his prowess and might:
            And warm were the words
            Of their love-sick young lords,
Mingling sweet with the tender harp's heart-thrilling chords.

But long ere the trumpet's shrill clamour alarming
Told each stark chevalier to horse for the strife;
Ere yet their hot steeds, in their panoply arming,
Were led forth, their nostrils wide breathing with life;
            Ere the lists had been clear'd,
            The brave Knollis appear'd
With his heroes, the standard of England who rear'd;
            But nor billman nor bowman
            Came there as a foeman,
For peace had made friends of these stout English yeomen.

As afar o'er the meadows, with soldiers' gear laden,
They merrily marched for their dear native land ;
Their banners took sighs from full many a maiden,
And trembled, as love-lorn each waved her white hand.
    But see from the troops
    Where a warrior swoops,
From the speed of his courser his plume backward droops ;
    'Tis a bold Scottish Knight,
    Whose joy and delight
Is to joust it in sport—or at outrance to fight.

His steed at the barrier's limit he halted,
And toss'd to his Squire the rich gold-emboss'd rein ;
Cased in steel as he was, o'er the high pales he vaulted,
And, bowing, cried, " Messieurs Chevaliers, prey deign
    To lend me an ear—
    Lo, I'm singly come here,
Since none of you dared against me to appear.
    One and all I defy,
    Nor fear I shall fly,
Win me then, if you can—for my knighthood I try."

Then a huge massive mace round his head quickly whirling,
He charged their bright phalanx with furious haste.
And some he laid prostrate, with heads sorely dirling,
And some round the barrier swiftly he chased.
    Where'er he attacked,
    The French knighthood backed,
Preux Chevalier le brave Jean de Roy he thwacked,
    Till his helmet rang well,
    Like the couvre-feu bell—
By the Rood, but 'twas nearly his last passing knell.

Then Picardy's pride, Le Chevalier de Lorris,
He soon stretch'd on the sand in most pitiful case,
And he rain'd on the rest, till they all danced a morris
To the music he played on their mails with his mace.
    Till tired with his toil,
    He breathed him a while,
And, bowing again, with a most courteous smile,
    " Adieu, Messieurs ! " said he,
    " Je vous rend graces, Perdie !
For the noble diversion you've yielded to me."

Then some kind parting-blows round him willingly dealing,
That on breastplates, and corslets, and helmets clang'd loud,
Sending some ten or dozen to right and left reeling,
He soon clear'd his way through the terrified crowd.
    O'er the pales then he bounded
    As all stood confounded.
To the saddle he leap'd—and his horse's heels sounded
    As he spurr'd out of sight,
    Leaving proofs of his might,
That had marr'd the bold jousting of many a knight.

Loud applause followed the minstrel's merry performance,
and Sir Walter de Selby called Adam towards him to reward
him with another cup of wine.

" But thou hast not told us the name of thy mettlesome
knight, old bard," said he.

Adam looked over his shoulder, with a waggish smile, towards Sir John Assueton.

" 'Twas a certain Scottish knight," said he, " one whose heart was as easily wounded as his frame was invulnerable—one who was as remarkable for his devotion to the fair as for his prowess in the field. It was whispered at Noyon that the feat was done to give jovisaunce to a pair of bright eyes which looked that day from the balcony."

" By St. Andrew, but thou art out there, goodman harper," cried Assueton, caught in the trap so cunningly laid for him by the minstrel ; " trust me, thou wert never more out in thy life. My heart was then, as it is now, as sound, entire, firm, and as hard as my cuirass. By'r Lady, I am not the man to be moved by a pair of eyes. No pair of eyes that ever lighted up a face could touch me ; and as to that matter, a—a—" But observing a smile playing over the countenances of the guests, he recollected that he had betrayed himself, and stopped in some confusion. The harper turned round to the host—

" Sir Walter," said he, " there never sat within this wall two more doughty or puissant knights than these. Both did feats of valour abroad that made Europe ring again. Sir John Assueton was indeed the true hero of my verses. As to his love I did but jest, for I wot 'tis well known he hath steeled himself against the passion, and hath never owned it. I but feigned, to draw him into a confession of the truth of my tale, the which his consummate modesty would never have permitted him to avow."

Sir Walter called for a goblet of wine—

" To the health of the brave knight of Noyon !" cried he. " Well did we all know to whom the merry minstrel alluded."

The health was received with loud applause, and compliments came so thick upon Assueton, that he blushed to receive them.

" Load me not thus, courteous knights, load me not thus, I beseech you, with your applause for a silly frolic. Here sits one," said he, wishing to turn the tide from himself, and tapping Hepborne on the shoulder—" Here sits one, I say, who hath done feats of arms compared to which my boyish pranks are but an idle pastime. This is the Scottish knight who, at the fight of Rosebarque, did twice recover the flag of France from the Flemings, and of whom the whole army admitted that the success of that day belonged to the prowess of his single arm."

This speech of Assueton's had all the effect he desired. Sir

Walter was well aware of the renown acquired by Hepborne upon that occasion, and there were even some at table who had witnessed his glorious feats of arms on that day. His modesty was now put to a severe trial in its turn, and goblets were quaffed in honour of him. He looked with a reproachful eye at his friend for having thus saved himself at his expense; and at last, to get rid of praises he felt to be oppressive, he signified to his host a wish to retire for the night. Accordingly the Squire Usher was called, and the two knights were shown to their apartments; soon after which the banquet broke up, leaving the Lord Bishop and Sir Walter in deep conference.

As Hepborne and Assueton passed up the narrow stair that led to the apartments appropriated to them, they were interrupted in their progress by a pair of limbs of unusual length, that were slowly descending. The confined and spiral nature of the stair kept the head and body belonging to them entirely out of view; and the huge feet were almost in Hepborne's stomach before he was aware. He called out, and the limbs, halting for an instant, seemed to receive tardy instructions to retire, from the invisible head they were commanded by, which, judging of the extent of the whole person by the parts they saw, must have been, at that moment at least, in the second storey above them. The way being at last cleared, the two friends climbed to the passage leading to their apartments. Irresistible curiosity, however, induced them to linger for a moment on the landing-place to watch the descent of a figure so extraordinary. It came as if measured out by yards at a time. In the right hand was a lamp, carried as high as the roof of the stair would permit, to enable the bearer to steer his head under it without injury, and the light being thus thrown strongly upon the face, displayed a set of features hardly human.

The complexion was deadly pale, the forehead unusually low and broad, and the head was hung round with lank tangles of black hair. A pair of small fiery eyes smouldered, each within the profound of a deep cavity on either side of the nose, that, projecting a good inch or two nearly in a right angle from the forehead, dropped a perpendicular over the mouth, almost concealing the central part of that orifice, in which it was assisted by the enormous length of chin thrust out in a curve from below. The cheekbones were peculiarly enlarged, and the cheeks drawn lankly in; but the corners of the mouth, stretching far backwards, were preternaturally expanded, and, by a convulsive kind of twist, each was alternately opened wide, so that, in turn, they partially exhibited the tremendous grinders that filled the jaws. It is not to be supposed that Hepborne and Assueton could exactly note these particulars so circumstantially as we have done; but the uncouth figure moved with so much difficulty downwards, with a serpentizing sort of course, that they had leisure to remark quite enough to fill them with amazement.

The apparition, clad in a close black jerkin and culottes, had no sooner wormed itself down, than both knights eagerly demanded of the Squire Usher who and what it was.

"'Tis Master Haggerstone Fenwick, the Ancient," replied he with a mysterious air.

"Nay," said Assueton, "he surely is fitter for hoisting the broad banner of the Castle upon, than for carrying the colours in the field."

"Why, as to that, Sir Knight," said the Usher, "he might i'faith do well enough for the banner; and he would be always at hand too when wanted, seeing that he rarely or ever quitteth the top of the keep. He liveth in the small cap-room, where he must lig from corner to corner to be able to stretch himself; yet there he sitteth night and day, reading books of the black art, and never leaveth it, except when he cometh down as now, driven by hunger, the which he will sometimes defy for a day or two, and then he descendeth upon the buttery, like a wolf from the mountains, and at one meal will devour thee as much provender as would victual the garrison for a day, and then mounteth he again to his den. He is thought to possess terrible powers; and strange sights and horrible spectres have been seen to dance about the battlements near his dwelling."

"Holy Virgin! and is all this believed by Sir Walter de Selby?" inquired Hepborne,

"Ay, truly," said the Usher gravely; "most seriously believed (as why should it not?) by him, and all in the Castle. But I beseech thee, Sir Knight, let us not talk so freely of him. Holy St. Mary defend us! I wish he may not take offence at our stopping him in his way to his meal. Let us not talk more of him. I bid thee good night."

"But tell me ere thou goest why we saw not that star of female beauty, the Lady Eleanore de Selby, at the banquet this evening?" demanded Hepborne.

"'Tis a fancy of her father's, Sir Knight," replied the Squire Usher, smiling; "and, if it may not offend thee, 'tis because he willeth not that the lady may marry her with a Scottish chevalier, that he ever doth forbid her entrance when any of thy nation are feasted in his hall."

"It irketh me to think that we should have caused her banishment," said Hepborne. "What, is she always wont to keep her chamber on like occasions."

"Yea," replied the Squire Usher, "ever save when the evening air is so bland as to suffer her to breathe it upon the rampart. She is often wont to listen to the minstrel's notes there. But there are your chambers, Sirs Knights. The squires of your own bodies will be with you in the morning. Sir Walter hath issued orders for the admission of your retinue into the Castle. And he hopes you will sojourn with him as long as your affairs may give you sufferance. Good night, and may St. Andrew be with you."

The two friends separated, and quickly laid themselves down to repose. The hardy and heart-whole Assueton slept soundly under the protection of his national saint, to whom he failed not to recommend himself, as a security against the incantations of the wizard. Nor did Sir Patrick Hepborne neglect to do the same; for these were times when the strongest minds were subject to such superstitions. But his thoughts soon wandered to a more agreeable subject. He recalled the lovely face he had seen, and he sighed to think that he had not been blessed with a somewhat less transitory glance of features which he would have wished to imprint for ever upon his mind.

"Why should her father thus banish her from the eyes of all Scotchmen? By the Rood, but it can and must be only from the paltry fear of his wealth going to fatten our northern soil. But I can tell him that there be Scots who would cheerfully take her for her individual merit alone, and leave her dross to those sordid minds who covet it."

Such was Sir Patrick's soliloquy, and, imperfect as his view of the lady had been, it was sufficient to conjure up a vision that hovered over his pillow, and disturbed his rest, in defiance of the good St. Andrew. Having lain some time awake, he heard the laborious ascent of the Ancient Fenwick to his dwelling in the clouds; but fatigue at length vanquished his restlessness, and he had been, for some hours, in a deep sleep, ere another and a much lighter footstep passed up in the same direction.

CHAPTER V.

Night at the Castle—The Friar's Visit to the Ancient.

THE Ancient Fenwick was sitting drawn together into a farther

corner of his den.   His everlasting lamp was raised on a pile of
manuscript volumes near him, that it might throw more light
on a large parchment roll that lay unfolded on the floor before
him.   His right elbow rested on the ground, and the enormous
fingers of his hand embraced and supported his head; while
his eyes, burning without meaning, like two small red fragments of ignited charcoal, could have been supposed to be occupied with the characters before them, only from the position of
his face, which was so much turned down that the tangled
hair, usually drooping from behind, was thrown forwards over
his ears.   He was so absorbed that he heard not the soft barefooted tread of the step on the stair, or as it approached his
den along the vaulted roof of the keep.

The person who came thus to have midnight converse with
him, stooped his head and body to enter the low and narrow
doorway, and halted with his head thrust forward within it to
contemplate the object he was about to address.

"Ancient Fenwick," said he, after a pause of some moments.

Fenwick started at the sound of the voice, and looked towards the little doorway.   A pair of keen eyes glared upon him
from beneath a dark cowl; and, plunged as he had been in the
mysteries of conjuration, it is not wonderful that he should
have believed that the Devil himself had appeared to further
his studies.

"Avaunt thee, Sathanas!" exclaimed he, speaking with the
alternate sides of his mouth, and drawing himself yet more up
into the corner—"I say unto thee, Sathanas, avaunt?"

"What?" said the figure, creeping into the place, and seating
himself on the floor opposite to him, "what! Master Ancient
Fenwick, dost thou wish to conjure up the Devil, and yet art
afraid to look on him?   I weened that thou hadst been a man
of more courage than to be afraid of a friar coming to thee at
midnight."

Fenwick made an exertion to compose himself, seeing his
visitor bore all the externals of a mortal about him.

"And what dost thou see in me," said he, in his usual harsh,
discordant, and sepulchral utterance, "that may lead thee to
think differently!"

"Umph, why, nothing—nothing now," said the monk, bending his brows, and throwing a penetrating glance from under
them into the Ancient's face; "nothing now, but methought,
for a conjuror, thou wert rather taken unawares."

"And who art thou, who thus darest to disturb my privacy?"
demanded Fenwick, somewhat sternly, and advancing his body

at the same time, from the more than ordinarily constrained attitude he had assumed.

The monk drew up his lips so as to display a set of long, white teeth, and raising his eyelids so as to show the white of his eye-balls, he glared at the Ancient for some time, and then slowly pronounced in a deep voice, " The Devil ! what wouldst thou with me now ?"

In a paroxysm of terror, Fenwick again drew himself up in his corner, with a force as if he would have pressed himself through the very wall; his teeth chattered in his head, and he sputtered so vehemently with the alternate corners of his mouth. that his words were unintelligible, except that of " Sathanas," frequently repeated. The monk relaxed his features, and, with a scornful laugh, and a look of the most sovereign contempt—

" So," said he, " thou must confess now that I proved thy courage to be in my power. I banished it with a look and a word. But 'tis not with thy courage I have to do at present ; 'tis thy cunning I want."

" Art thou then verily no devil ?" demanded the Ancient, doubtingly.

" Tush, fool, I am a poor monk of the order of St. Francis ; so calm thy craven fears, and listen to me." He paused for some moments, to give Fenwick time to recollect himself, and when he saw that the latter had in some degree regained his composure : " Now listen to me, I say. Thou knowest doubtless that the Bishop of Durham came to Norham Castle this morning ?" He waited for a reply.

" I did hear so," answered the Ancient, " when I went down to take food."

" Knowest thou what he came about ?" demanded the Franciscan.

" I know not, I inquired not," replied the Ancient.

" Then I will tell thee," proceeded the Franciscan—" Sir Rafe Piersie, brother to the noble Hotspur, has stooped to fix his affection on the Lady Eleanore de Selby ; he has deigned to court her for his bride, and has met with ready acceptance from her father. Not sufficiently sensible of this his great conde-scension, the lady has treated his high offer with neglect—with indifference. Her father, a weak man, though eager for so splendid an alliance, hath allowed himself to be trifled with by the silly girl, who hath done all she could to oppose it, though to the sacrifice of her own happiness. But Sir Rafe Piersie, being too much love-stricken, abandoneth not the demoiselle so easily. He therefore availeth himself of his ally the Bishop of

4

Durham, to urge, through him, his suit with the lady, and to
endeavour to stir up Sir Walter to a more determined bearing
with his daughter, should she continue in her obstinacy. I shall
not tell how I know, yet I do know, that the lady treated the
proposals of the Bishop, as well as the name and person of the
renowned Piersie, with contempt. His efforts to rouse Sir
Walter de Selby to the assertion of his rights as a father, have,
however, been more successful. The old man, who passionately
desireth great connexion, even became irritated against her
obstinacy. But Sir Rafe Piersie, wisely considering that a
peaceful religious pastor was not the fittest instrument for his
purpose, judgeth it right to put hotter and more efficient irons
in the work. Unknown to the Bishop, and unknown to every
one, therefore, he hath deputed me to seek thee and to urge
thee to aid his plans. Now, Master Ancient Fenwick, thou
hast the whole intricacies of the affair ; thou understandest me,
dost thou not ? "

The Franciscan paused for a reply, and tried to read the face
of him he was addressing ; but it was in vain he tried it, for.
except when very strongly excited by the passion of fear, or
something equally forcible, the features of the Ancient were at
all times illegible. After twisting and smacking the alternate
corners of his mouth, which was always his prelude to speaking,
and which even his actual utterance did not always go much
beyond—

"Well," said he, "and what can I do in this matter? What
can magic do in it ? "

"Magic !" exclaimed the Franciscan ; "pshaw, fool that thou
art, thinkest thou that thou canst impose upon me as thou dost
on the common herd of mankind ?—on one who hath dived into
the arcana of nature as I have done ? Thinkest thou that an
active mind like mine hath not searched through all the books
of these divinals—hath not toiled by the midnight lamp, and
worked with their uncouth and horrible charms and incantations ? Thinkest thou——"

"Hast thou so, brother ?" exclaimed the Ancient, eagerly
interrupting him ; "hast thou in truth studied so deeply ?"
Then throwing his body earnestly forward, "Perhaps thou wilt
clear up some small difficulties that have arisen in my path
towards perfection in the invaluable art."

The Franciscan paused. He saw at once that he had so far
mistaken his man. The Ancient, whilst engaged in deceiving
others, had also succeeded in deceiving himself, and was in truth
a believer in the art he professed. To undertake the barren

task of convincing him of his error was foreign to the Franciscan's present purpose; and seeing that Fenwick, in his eagerness
for an accession to his knowledge of magic, had mistaken the
contemptuous expressions he had thrown out against it for the
approbation and eulogy of an adept, he deemed it best to permit
him to continue in his mistake, nay, rather to foster it. He
therefore commenced a long and very mystical disquisition on
necromancy, answering all his questions, and solving all his
doubts, but in such a manner, that although Fenwick, at the
moment, firmly believed they were solved, yet, when he afterwards came to look back into his mind, he could find nothing
there but a vast chaos of smoke and ashes, from which he in
vain tried to extract anything tangible or systematic.

But this is not to our point. The Franciscan gained all he
wanted, in acquiring a certain ascendancy over his mind by
pretended superiority of knowledge—an ascendancy which he
afterwards hoped to bring to bear towards the object of his mission; and to this object he gradually led the Ancient back from
the wide waste of enchantment he had been wandering over.

"Thou art indeed much more learned in the sublime art
than I did at first suppose thee," said the Franciscan at length,
gravely; "thy study hath been well directed; and now that I
have poured the mere drop of knowledge I possessed into the
vast ocean flowing in thy capacious head, thou art well fit to be
my master. Some of those ingredients I talked of are of high
price; thou must buy them with gold."

"Ah!" exclaimed Fenwick; "but where shall I find gold to
buy them withal?"

The Franciscan groped in the canvas pouch that hung at
his girdle of ropes, and, drawing forth a leathern bag, with a
weight of broad gold pieces in it, he threw it down on the floor
between the Ancient's knees.

"There!" said he; "Sir Rafe Piersie sends thee that; 'tis to
secure thee as his friend. Use thine art magic in his favour, to
incline the haughty damosel to his wishes. Thou mayest do
much with her father. 'Tis well known that the old knight
looketh with awe upon thy powers. Thou art thyself aware
that thou canst bend him as thou wilt; he doth hold thee as
his oracle. Work upon his fears, then; work upon him, I say,
to compel this marriage—a marriage the which is so well calculated to gratify his desire of high family alliance. He is
ignorant that thou knowest of the negotiation; to find that
thou dost, when he supposes that it is only known to the chief
parties, will increase his veneration for thy skill. Exert thy

power over him; he is weak, and thou mayest easily make
him thy slave. Stimulate him to firmness, to severity, nay, if
necessary, to harshness with his daughter. Thou knowest 'tis
for his happiness, as well as for the happiness of the silly
damosel, that she should be coarted. Then do thy best to
screw him up to the pitch of determination that may secure
her yielding. I leave it to thyself to find out what schemes and
arguments thou must employ. The world lies if thou canst not
invent enow to make him do as thou wouldst have him. Remember, the Piersie is thy friend, as thou mayst do him proper
service. There are more bags of broad pieces in the same
treasury that came from. And now I leave thee to the hatching
of thy plans. Let them be quickly concerted, and speedily put
in execution, for your Piersie never was famous for patience.
Farewell, and may powerful spirits aid thee!"

The Franciscan gathered up his grey gown, drew his cowl
over his face, and, creeping on hands and knees to the door,
disappeared in a moment.

The Ancient remained for some minutes in stupid astonish- .
ment, with his back against his corner, and his vast length of
limbs stretched across the floor. He almost doubted the reality
of the vision that had appeared to him. He drew up his knees
to his mouth, and the leathern bag appeared. He thought of
the Devil as he seized it; and, as he poured the glittering gold
into his broad palm, he almost expected to see the pieces change
into dried leaves, cinders, slates, or some such rubbish. Twice
or thrice the thought recurred that it might have been the
Great Tempter himself who had visited him. The hour—the
place—the difficulty of anything mortal reaching him there,
through all the intricacies of a well-watched garrison—the great
knowledge displayed by the unknown—all contributed to support the idea that his visitor was something more than man.
Then, on the other hand, he remembered the friar's bare feet,
that were certainly human. He again looked at the broad
pieces of gold; they were bright, and fresh, and heavy as he
poised them. His confidence that they were genuine became
stronger, and he slipped them into the bag, and the bag into an
inner pocket of his black jerkin, resolving that they should be
the test of the reality of the seeming friar.

The Ancient had been for many years plunged in the study
of necromancy. His uncouth appearance, and awkward un-
gainly port, rendered him so unfit for the gay parade of war,
that Sir Walter de Selby had more than once refused him that
promotion to which he was entitled in the natural course of

things, and of which he had been very ambitious. This rankled
at his heart, and made him shun his fellows, slight the profession of arms, and take to those studies that, in so superstitious
a period, met with the readiest belief and reverence, and from
which he hoped to discover the means of gratifying both his
ambition and his avarice. His necromantic fame, increased by
tales hatched or embellished by the fertile imaginations of weak
and superstitious minds, rapidly grew among all ranks; and Sir
Walter de Selby was as firm a believer in his powers as the
meanest soldier under his command. He readily excused the
Ancient from all duty; so that, being thus left to the full and
undisturbed possession of that solitary cap-house he had himself
selected for his habitation, he became so immersed in his work
that he rarely left it, except when driven by hunger to seek
food. Living so entirely secluded as he did, it is not to be
wondered at that he had hardly seen a female face. As for
Lady Eleanore, he had never beheld her since her childhood,
until a few days previous to the time we are now speaking of,
when, having been led by some extraordinary accident beyond
the walls of the keep, he had met her by chance in the court-
yard; and the young lady was alarmed by the appearance of
the strange monster, who blocked up her way to the bridge, and
stood surveying her with his horrible eyes, that she fled from
him precipitately. It must be admitted, then, that he was but
little calculated to produce any favourable change on her mind
in behalf of Sir Rafe Piersie, unless, indeed, it were by the art
magic. With that brave old soldier of fortune, Sir Walter de
Selby, he was much more likely to be successful, since the chief
wish of his heart was that his daughter and his wealth should
be the means of allying him with some family eminent for the
grandeur of its name, as well as for its power and influence. It
was a grievous disappointment to him that he had had no son;
but as he had been denied this blessing, he now looked forward
to having a grandson, who might give him good cause to be
proud, from the high rank he should be entitled to hold in the
splendid galaxy of English chivalry. He was far from being
without affection for his daughter; yet his affection was in a
great measure bottomed upon these his most earnest wishes and
hopes; and of all this the Ancient, Mr. Haggerstone Fenwick,
was very sufficiently aware.

CHAPTER VI.

Making Love on the Ramparts.

WHEN Sir Patrick Hepborne and Sir John Assueton arose in the morning, they found their own squires and lacqueys in attendance. The busy note of preparation was in the Castle-yard, and they were told that the Bishop of Durham was just taking his departure.

The mitred ecclesiastic went off on an ambling jennet, accompanied by the knights and churchmen who had come with him, and followed by a long cavalcade of richly-attired atten-dants ; and he was saluted by the garrison drawn up in array, and by the guards as he passed outwards. He was, moreover, attended by Sir Walter and his principal officers, who rode half a day's journey with him. The two friends were thus left to entertain themselves until the evening. Assueton occupied himself in studying the defences of the place, whilst Hepborne loitered about the exterior of the keep, and the walls command-ing a view of its various sides, in the hope of being again blessed with a sight of the Lady Eleanore.

As he was surveying the huge mass of masonry, so intently that a bystander might have supposed that he was taking an account of the number of stones it was composed of, the lady appeared at one of the high windows on the side facing the Tweed. The knight had his eyes turned in a different direction at the moment, so that she had a full and undisturbed view of him, as he stood nearly opposite to her on the rampart, for some time ere he perceived her. He turned suddenly round, and she instantly withdrew ; but not before he had enjoyed another transient glimpse of that face which had already created so strong a sensation in his breast.

"Provoking !" thought Hepborne; "yet doth the very modesty of this angelic lady lead me the more to admire her. Unbending spirit, said that knave at the hostel ? She is as gentle as a dove. Would I could behold her again."

Sir Patrick stepped back upon the rampart so as to have a better view inwards, and he was gratified by observing that her figure was still within the deep window, though her face was obscured by its shade. He recognized the rose-coloured mantle she had formerly appeared in. He kissed his hand and bowed. He saw her alabaster arm relieve itself from the mantle, and

beheld the falcon he had rescued seated on her glove. She
stepped forward in such a manner to return his salute, that he
enjoyed a sufficient view of her face to make him certain that
he was not mistaken in the person. The lady pointed with a
smile to her falcon, kissed it, waved an acknowledgment of his
courtesy, and again retreating, disappeared.

As Sir Patrick was standing vainly hoping for her re-appear-
ance, the old minstrel, Adam of Gordon, chanced to come by.
Hepborne saluted him courteously.

" Canst thou tell me whose be those apartments that do
look so cheerily over the Tweed into Scotland ?" demanded he.

" Ay," said the old man, " 'tis, as thou sayest, a cheering
prospect ; 'tis the country of my birth, and the country of my
heart ; I love it as lover never loved mistress."

" But whose apartments be those ?" demanded Hepborne,
bringing him back to the question.

" Those are the apartments of the Lady Eleanore de Selby,"
replied the minstrel.

" Is it thy custom to play thy minstrelsy under the moonlight on the rampart, as thou didst yestere'en ?" demanded
Hepborne.

" Yea, I have pleasure in it," said Adam, with a shrewd
look.

" And art thou always so attended ?" demanded Hepborne ;
" is thy music always wont to call that angel to thy side whom
I last night beheld there ?"

" So thou dost think her an angel, Sir Knight ?" cried Adam,
with pleasure glancing in his eyes.

" I do," said Sir Patrick. " Already hath my heart been
wounded by the mere momentary glances to which chance hath
subjected me, and eagerly do I look for a cure from those eyes
whence my hurt doth come. She is beautiful."

" Yea," said old Adam, " and she is an angel in soul as well
as in form. But St. Andrew keep thee, Sir Knight, I must be
gone ;" and he hurried away without giving Hepborne time to
reply.

Assueton now came up, and Sir Patrick detailed to him
the occurrences we have just narrated, after which he walked
about, looking every now and then impatiently towards the
window.

" Would I could have but one more sight of the Lady
Eleanore," cried he ; " her features have already become faint
in my mind's eye ; would I might refresh the picture by one
other gaze." But the lady appeared not ; and he became vexed,

and even fretful, notwithstanding all his resolution to the contrary.

"Hepborne, my friend," said Sir John Assueton, "why shouldst thou afflict thyself, and peak and pine for a silly girl? A knight of thy prowess in the field may have a thousand baubles as fair for the mere picking up; let it not irk thee that this trifle is beyond thy reach. Trust me, women are dangerous flowers to pluck, and have less of the rose about them than of the thorn."

"Pshaw!" replied Heyborne, "thou knowest not what it is to love."

"No, thank my good stars," answered Assueton, "I do not, and I hope I shall never be so besotted; it makes a fool of a man. There, for instance, thou art raving about a damosel, of whose face thou hast seen so little that wert thou to meet her elsewhere thou couldst never tell her from another."

"It is indeed true, Assueton," replied Hepborne, "that I have seen but too little of her face; but I have seen enough of it to know that it is the face of an angel."

In such converse as this did they spend the day until the evening's banquet. Then Sir Walter exhibited the same hospitality towards his guests that had characterised him the night before; but he seemed to be less in spirits, nay, he was even sometimes peevish. Hepborne, too, being restless and unhappy, mirth and hilarity were altogether less prevalent at the upper end of the festal board than they had been the previous evening. The minstrel, however, was not forgotten, and was treated with the same personal attention as formerly; but he sang and played without eliciting more than an ordinary meed of applause. At last he struck some peculiarly powerful chords on the instrument, and as Hepborne turned his head towards him, in common with others, at the sound, old Adam caught his eye, and looking significantly, began to pour forth the following irregular and unpremeditated verse :—

'Twas thus that a minstrel address'd a young knight,
Who was love-lorn, despairing, and wan with despite,
What, Sir Knight, canst thou gain by these heart-rending sighs?
The hero ne'er pines, but his destiny tries,
And pushes his fate with his lance in the rest,
Whether love or renown be his glorious quest.
    Let not those who droop for Love
    Fly in grief to wild Despair,
    She, wither'd witch, can ne'er remove
    The cruel unkindness of the fair.
        Then with the gladd'ning ray
        Of Hope's bright star to cheer thee,

Do thou still press thy way,
Nor let obstructions fear thee.
True love will even bear
A hasty moment's slighting.
And boldly will it dare,
Nor ever fear benighting.
'Twill often and again
Return, though ill entreated ;
'Twill blaze beneath the rain ;
Though frozen, 'twill be heated.
When least thy thoughts are turn'd on joy,
　The smiling bliss is nigh ;
No happiness without alloy
　Beneath the radiant sky.
But haste to-night, to meet thy love
　Upon the Castle-wall ;
Thou know'st not what thy heart may prove,
　What joy may thee befal.

These seemingly unmeaning verses passed unnoticed by all at table except by Hepborne, on whom they made a strong impression. He was particularly struck by the concluding stanza, containing an invitation which he could not help believing was meant to apply to himself. He resolved to visit the ramparts as soon as he could escape from the banquet. This he found it no very difficult matter to accomplish, for Sir Walter was abstracted, and evidently depressed with something that weighed on his spirits ; so, taking advantage of this circumstance, Hepborne rose to retire at an early hour. His friend followed him, and, when left to the secresy of their own apartments—

" Assueton," said Sir Patrick, " didst thou remark the glance, full of meaning, which the minstrel threw on me to-night? or didst thou note the purport of his ditty ?"

" As for his glances," replied Sir John, "I noticed nothing particular in them ; your bards are in use to throw such around them, to collect their barren harvest of paltry praise ; and as for his verses, or rather his rhymes, I thought them silly enow in conscience. But thou knowest I do rarely listen when love or its follies are the theme."

" But I saw, and I listened," replied Hepborne. " By St. Denis, they carried hints to me that I shall not neglect. I go to take the air on the ramparts, and hope to meet the angelic Eleanore de Selby there."

" Art thou mad ?" said Assueton. " What can old Adam have looked or said that can induce thee to go on such a fool's errand ? Thou hast but fancied ; thy blind passion hath deceived thee."

" I shall at least put his fancied hints to the proof," said Hepborne, " though I should watch all night."

" Then I wish thee a pleasant moonlight promenade," said

Assneton. " I'll to my couch. To-morrow, I presume, we shall
cross the Tweed, and yede us into Scotland.   By St. Andrew, I
would gladly meet again with those well-known faces whose
smiles once reflected the happiness of my boyhood !"

" Go to-morrow !" exclaimed Hepborne, as if their so speedy
departure was far from being agreeable in the contemplation ;
" surely thou wilt stay, Assneton, if thou seest that thy so doing
may further my happiness ?"

" Nay," replied Assneton, " thou needst hardly fear that I
will scruple to sacrifice my own wishes to thy happiness,
Hepborne ; but I confess I would that my happiness depended
on some more stirring cause, and one in which we both could
join."

Here the friends parted.   Hepborne, wrapped up in a cloak,
stole gently down stairs, and slipping unperceived from the keep,
bent his steps towards that part of the ramparts where he had
formerly seen the lady.   To his inexpressible joy, he saw the
minstrel already on the spot.   There were two ladies in company
with the old man.   As Sir Patrick passed near the base of the
tower under which he and his friend had concealed themselves
the night before, a huge figure began to rear itself from under
it, throwing a shadow half-way across the court-yard.   It looked
as if the tower itself were in motion.   He stood undaunted to
observe it, as it gradually arose storey over storey.   It was the
Ancient Fenwick.   His enormous face looked downwards upon
Hepborne, and his red cinder-like eyes glared upon him as he
sputtered out some unintelligible sounds from the corners of his
mouth, and then moved away like a walking monument.

Whilst Hepborne's attention was occupied in observing the
retreat of the monster, who seemed to have secreted himself
there for no good purpose, the minstrel, and the two ladies who
were with him, had already walked down the rampart until they
were lost within the shade of a projecting building.   He began
to fear that they were gone, but he soon saw one of them, whom
he believed to be the attendant, emerge from the shadow and
retire by a short way to the keep, whilst the other returned
along the wall with the minstrel.   As they stopped to converse,
the lady leaned on one of the engines of war.   A breeze from
the Tweed threw back the hood of her mantle, and Hepborne
could no longer doubt it was the Lady Eleanore de Selby he
saw.   Her long and beautiful hair streamed down, but she
hastily arranged it with her fingers, and then came onwards
with Adam of Gordon.   Sir Patrick flew to the rampart and
sprang on the wall.   The lady was alarmed at first by his

sudden appearance, but perceiving immediately that it was Sir Patrick Hepborne, she received him graciously yet modestly.

"The soft and perfumed air of this beauteous night," said Hepborne, "and yonder lovely moon, lady, tempted me forth awhile ; but what bliss is mine that I should thus meet with her who, in softness, sweetness, and beauty, doth excel the Queen of Night herself !"

"Sir Patrick Hepborne, thou art at thy fustian again," replied the lady seriously. "This high-flown phrase of thine, well suited though it may have been to the pampered ears of Parisian damsels, sorteth but ill with plainness such as mine. Meseems," continued she somewhat more playfully, " meseems as if the moon were thy favourite theme. Pray Heaven that head may be right furnished, the which hath the unstable planet so often at work within it."

"And if I am mad, as thy words would imply," said Hepborne, smiling, " 'tis thou, lady, who must answer for my frenzy ; for since I first saw thee last night, I have thought and dreamt of thee alone."

"Nay, Sir Knight," said the lady, blushing, " methinks it savours of a more constitutional madness to be so affected by so short a meeting. We were but some few minutes together, if I err not."

"Ay, lady," said Adam of Gordon, significantly ; " but love will work miracles like this."

" 'Tis indeed true," said the lady, with a sigh ; and then, as if recollecting herself, she added, " I have indeed heard of such sudden affections."

"Ay," said Sir Patrick, "and that fair falcon of thine ! Depardieux, I begin to believe that he was Cupid himself in disguise, for ever sith I gave the traitor lodgment in my bosom, it hath been affected with the sweet torment the urchin Love is wont to inflict. My heart's disease began with thy hawk's ensayning."

"Nay, then, much as I love him," said the lady, "yet should I hardly have purchased his health, I wot, at the price of that of the gallant knight who did so feelingly redeem it."

"Heaven's blessings on thee for thy charity, lady," exclaimed Hepborne ; " yet should I rejoice in my disease were it to awaken thy sympathy, so that thou mightest yield me the healing leech-craft that beameth from those eyes."

"Verily, my youth doth lack experience in all such healing skill," said the lady.

"Nay, 'tis a mystery most easily learned by the young,"

replied Hepborne. "Thou dost possess the power to assuage, if not to heal, my wound," added he tenderly. "Let me but be enlisted among the humblest of the captives whom thine eyes hath made subject to thy will; and albeit thy heart may be already given to another, spurn not the adoration of one whose sole wish is to live within the sphere of thy cheering influence, and to die in thy defence."

"In truth, Sir Knight, these eyes have been guiltless of any such tyranny as thou wouldst charge them withal," replied the lady, artlessly; "at least they have never wilfully so tyrannized. As for my heart, it hath never known warmer feeling than that which doth bind me to him to whom I owe the duty of a daughter."

"Then is thy heart unenthralled," cried Hepborne in an ecstacy, in the transport of which he threw himself on one knee before her who had produced it. "Refuse not, then, to accept my services as thy true and faithful knight. All I ask is, but to be allowed to devote my lance to thy service. Reject not these my vows. Cheer me with but one ray of hope, to nerve this arm to the doing of deeds worthy of the knight who calleth himself thy slave. I swear——"

"Swear not too rashly, Sir Knight," said the lady, with a deep sigh, and with more of seriousness than she had yet displayed, "to one such as me, to one so obscure——"

"Obscure, lady!" cried Hepborne, interrupting her; "Hath not high Heaven stamped thee with that celestial face and form to place thee far above all reckonings of paltry pedigree? What, then, is that obscurity which may have dimmed the birth of so fair a star? What——"

"Nay," said the lady, interrupting him with an air of uncommon dignity and animation, "obscure though mine origin may be, Sir Patrick, yet do I feel within me that which doth tell me that I might match with princes."

"Lady, I well know thy high and justly-grounded pretensions," said Hepborne, in a subdued tone; "yet scorn not mine humble devotion."

"I scorn thee not, Sir Knight," said the lady, with combined modesty and feeling, and again sighing deeply; "it would indeed ill become me to scorn any one, far less such as thee; nor is my heart insensible to the courtesy thou hast been pleased to show to one who——"

"Thanks, thanks, most peerless of thy sex," cried Hepborne, gazing with ecstacy in her face, that burned with blushes even under the cold light of the moon.

"But in truth it beseemeth me not to stand talking idly with thee thus, Sir Knight," said the lady, suddenly breaking off; "I must hie me to my chamber."

"Oh, stay, sweet lady, stay—one moment stay!" cried Hepborne; "rob me not of thy presence until thou hast left me the cheering prospect of meeting thee to-morrow."

"I hope Sir Walter hath induced thee and thy friend to tarry some longer space in Norham; if so, it will pleasure me to meet theo again," said the lady, with a trembling voice.

"Then trust me I go not from Norham, betide me what may," cried Sir Patrick, energetically. "But tell me, lady, I entreat thee, when these eyes may be again blest with thy presence; give me hope, the which is now the food I feed on."

"Nay, in sooth, I can enter into no arrangements," said the lady, with yet greater agitation; "but," said she, starting away. "I have tarried here too long; in truth, Sir Patrick Hepborne, I must be gone; may the Holy Virgin be with thee, Sir Knight!"

"And may thou be guarded by kindred spirits like thyself!" cried Sir Patrick, earnestly clasping his hands, and following her with his eyes as she hastily retreated with old Adam.

Sir Patrick took several turns on the walls, giving way to the rapture which this meeting had occasioned him, and then hastened to regain his apartment, where he laid himself down not to repose, but to muse on the events of the evening.

"The minstrel was right," thought he; "the good Adam's prophecy did not deceive me. She admitted that her heart was free, and she confessed, as far as maiden modesty might permit her, that she is not altogether without an interest in me. She was pleased with the idea of our farther stay at Norham; and in her confusion she betrayed, that to meet me again would give her pleasure. And she shall meet me again—ay, and again; mine excellent Assueton's patience must e'en bear some days' longer trial, for go, at least, I shall not. Days, did I say? ha! but let events determine." With such happy reflections, and yielding to a train of the most pleasing anticipation, he amused himself till he fell asleep.

CHAPTER VII.

The Midnight Meeting in the Ancient's Chamber—Strange Proposal—A Dreadful Alternative.

It was past the hour of midnight, when all in the Castle had

been for some time still, save when the sentinels on the ramparts
repeated their prolonged call, that a footstep was again heard
upon the stair leading to the top of the keep.   It was the heavy,
slow step of Sir Walter de Selby.   He carried a lamp in his
hand, and often stopped to breathe; but at last he made his
way to the roof, and sought the aerial den of the monstrous
Ancient.   He went thither, deluded man, imagining that he
went of his own free will; but the crafty Ancient had taken
secret measures to insure his coming.

When the good old knight had sought the little private
oratory within his chamber, immediately after his attendants
had retired, he was fearfully dismayed by observing a blue lambent light flitting over the surface of an ancient shield that hung
above a small altar within a dark Gothic recess.   In that age of
ignorance, a circumstance so unaccountable might have shaken
the firmest nerves; but it had been the shield of his father, a
bold moss-trooper, and from him he had learned that this was
the ill-omened warning sign that was always said to appear to
foretell some dire calamity affecting him or his issue.   With
extreme agitation of mind he at once recurred to recent events
for an explanation of it.   During his ride with the Bishop of
Durham, that prelate had repeated the arguments he had employed the day before, particularly in the long conference they
had held after the banquet, to fortify him in the resolution of
pressing the Lady Eleanore into a marriage with Sir Rafe Piersie; and, indeed, Sir Walter's heart was so eagerly set on the
accomplishment of a union in every respect equal to his most
sanguine wishes, that little eloquence was necessary to convince
him of the propriety of urging his daughter to it by every
means in his power.   Nay, although she was his only child, and
that he so doted on her as to have got into a habit of yielding
to every wish she expressed, yet this was a point on which he
was very easily brought to adopt a determined line of conduct
with her.   She had somewhat provoked him, too, by the license
she had given her tongue in presence of the Bishop, when she
indulged herself in ridiculing the very august person he was
proposing to her as a husband; and the knight's passion at the
moment had so far got the better of his affection, that he spoke
to her with a degree of harshness he had never used before.
His after conversations with the Bishop had now brought him
to the determination of compelling the Lady Eleanore to a marriage so much to her advantage, and so flattering to his own
hopes of high alliance.   So firmly was he fixed in this resolution,
that, in a meeting he had with his daughter after his return from

accompanying the Bishop, he withstood all her entreaties, and steeled himself against all her grief, and all her spirited remonstrances.   After such an interview, it is not surprising that Sir Walter should have immediately supposed that the menacing prodigy, which now appeared before his eyes, had some reference to the purposed marriage of the Lady Eleanore.   On all similar occasions of threatened misfortune, he had been for some years accustomed to apply for counsel to the cunning Ancient Fenwick, whom he believed to possess supernatural powers of foretelling and averting the greatest calamities; nay, he had more than once been convinced of the happy effects of his interference in his behalf.   His impatience to seek him at present, therefore, was such that he could hardly restrain himself until he had reason to think that all eyes in the Castle were closed but his own.   He paced his chamber in a state bordering on distraction, stopping from time to time at the door of the oratory to regard the terrific warning, and wringing his hands as he beheld it still flitting and playing over the surface of the shield.

He was no sooner certain, however, that he might move from his apartment without risk of observation, than he seized his lamp, and, as we have seen, sought the lonely cap-house of the Ancient.   The small door of the place was closed.   So strongly were men's minds bound by the thraldom of superstition in those days, that the gallant Sir Walter de Selby, who had so often faced the foe like a lion in the field, and who would even now have defended the Castle of Norham to the uttermost extremity, yea, so long as one stone of its walls remained upon another—this brave old warrior, I say, absolutely trembled as he tapped at the door of the wretched Ancient Haggerstone Fenwick, who once formed his most common subject of jest. He tapped, but no answer was returned; he listened, but not a sound was heard.   He tapped again—and again he tapped louder.   He called the Ancient by his name; but still all was profound silence.   He hesitated for some moments, in doubt what to do.   At last he brought himself to the determination of pushing the door up.   He bent down on his knees to force it, and it yielded before his exertions; but the sight which met his eyes so appalled him, that he was unable at first to advance.

The Ancient Fenwick, to all appearance dead, lay stretched, with his arms and legs extended on the floor.   His face had the leaden hue of death on it; and a small orb, composed of a number of points of bluish lambent flame, like that so ominously illuminating the shield, flitted on his forehead—a book of necromancy lay open on the floor—his lamp burned on the usual pile of volumes—and, on a temporary altar, composed of several folios, raised one above the other against the wall, were placed a human skull, and thigh bones, and an hour-glass. Immediately over these a number of cabalistical figures were described with charcoal on the plaster; and a white rod seemed, from the position it lay in, to have been pointed towards them, and to have fallen from his hand, as if he had been suddenly struck down in the very act of conjuration.

Sir Walter was so overpowered with horror and superstitious fear, that some moments elapsed ere he could summon up resolution to creep into the place and examine the body more narrowly. He looked down on the hidous ghastly face, over which the magical flame still flitted. The small fiery eye-balls glared—but they were still; not a feature moved, nor was there the slightest sound or appearance of respiration. Scarcely bearing to behold such a spectacle, the old knight looked timorously around him, afraid that the demon, who had done this fearful work upon his disciple, might appear to annihilate him also. In truth his terrors so far overcame him, that he was just about to retreat hastily, when he observed a certain spasmodic twitch about the mouth, which soon afterwards became powerfully convulsed, writhing from side to side, and throwing the whole features of the countenance into the most fearful contortions. By degrees, the convulsion seemed to extend itself along the muscles of the body, arms, and limbs, until the whole frame was thrown into violent agitation; unintelligible sputtering sounds came from the alternate corners of the mouth; and Sir Walter quaked to hear the name of "Sathanas" often repeated energetically. At last, by a convulsion stronger than the rest, the head and body were erected, and, after a little time, the Ancient seemed to recover the use of his senses, and the command over his muscles, as well as of his powers of utterance.

"What, Master Ancient Fenwick, hath befallen thee?" exclaimed Sir Walter, in a voice almost indistinct from trepidation; "tell me, I beseech thee, what hath happened."

"My brain burneth," cried the Ancient, with a hideous yell, and striking his forehead with the palms of both hands, after which the flame no longer appeared. Then, after a pause, "Where am I?" said he, staring wildly around, "Where am I? Ha! I see I am again in the world of men. What?" exclaimed he, with surprise, on beholding Sir Walter, "art thou here? How camest thou to this place?"

"My friend," replied the old knight, "my excellent friend, I came to consult thee; I came to take counsel from thy super-human knowledge—thy knowledge gathered from converse with the spirits of another world."

"Another world!" exclaimed the Ancient, in a sepulchral voice—"in another world, didst thou say? Ay, I have indeed long had converse here, face to face, with some of its blackest inmates: but never till this night," added he, shuddering, "did I visit its fiery realms."

"Where hast thou been, then?" asked the knight, in a tone of alarm.

"In hell!" cried the Ancient, with a horrible voice that chilled the very blood in Sir Walter's brains. "Yes," continued he, "I have visited those dreadful abodes; but I may not tell their awful secrets. Some, it is true, I am permitted to disclose, if I can bring myself to speak of them—of things on which depend the fate of thyself and thy daughter, and deeply affecting thy country's weal,"

"What, good Ancient, hast thou learned, that may affect me or my daughter? I do beseech thee, let me straightway be informed. The blue fire burns on my father's shield to-night; some dreadful calamity impends."

"Ha! saidst thou so?" cried the Ancient, with a sudden start. "The blue fire, saidst thou? Signs meet then; prodigies combine to overwhelm thee."

"They do, indeed, most terribly," said the knight, shuddering with alarm.

"Their portent is direful," said the Ancient, groaning deeply.

"In mercy tell me by what means they may be averted," anxiously inquired Sir Walter.

"Nay," said the Ancient, with a desponding air, "'tis thyself who art bringing them on thine own head." Then, after a long pause—"Thou art about to marry thy daughter to the brother of the Piersie?"

"By what miracle knowest thou this?" demanded Sir Walter, in amazement.

"Ask me not by what miracle I know this," replied the Ancient, "after what thou hast thyself witnessed. Have I not been in the world below? Do I not know all things? Do I not know that Sir Rafe Piersie hath sought the hand of the Lady Eleanore?—that he hath been scorned by her?—that even the Lord Bishop of Durham's influence hath been employed by him to incline thee to the match; and that, overcome by his counsels, thou art about to compel thy daughter to accept of his hand? Yea, all this do I know, to the veriest item of the

5

conversation held between thee ; and now, canst thou doubt whence I have had this knowledge ?"

Sir Walter replied not, but groaned deeply.

"Sit down by me," said the Ancient, "and listen to me. 'Tis registered in the dread Book of Fate," continued he solemnly, "that if this marriage be concluded, consequences the most direful will result from it. First, thy daughter shall produce a son, of countenance so inhuman, that it shall be liker that of a wild boar than a man ; and the monstrous birth will produce the death of the mother. Then the child shall grow up, and wax exceeding strong, so that his might shall overmatch that of the most powerful men. But though his mind shall not ripen in proportion, yet shall his passions terribly expand them-selves; and, after murdering thee, from whom he shall have sprung, he shall gather unto himself a host of demons of his own stamp, and lay waste the fair face of England, cruelly slay-ing and oppressing its innocent people for the space of ten years, when he shall be at last overthrown by a Scottish army, which being brought against him, shall subdue and enslave our nation."

The white hairs of the aged Sir Walter bristled on his head as he listened to this dreadful prophecy. The scourge with which his country was menaced was worse, in his eyes, than even his own unhappy fate.

"Tell me, oh tell me, most excellent Ancient," said he, in the agony of despair, "tell me, I entreat thee, how this awful mass of approaching misery may be averted."

"There is only one way to shield yourself and mankind from the threatened curse," replied the Ancient tardily, and rather as if he felt difficulty in bringing it out ; "there is only one course to pursue, but it is such that, slave as thou art to the prejudices of the world, it is vain to hope that even the dread of these impending calamities will induce thee to adopt it."

"Talk not so, good Ancient, talk not so," cried the old knight impatiently, "There is nothing I would not do—Holy Virgin, forgive me !—there is nothing I would not do honestly to pre-vent this threatened curse from arising, to the destruction of my family and my country."

"Sayest thou so ?" said the Ancient, calmly shaking his head, as if in doubt ; "I will put thee to the proof then. It is written, as I have already declared, in the Book of the Fates of men, that this marriage shall take place, and that from it shall proceed this two-edged sword, to smite both thee and England, unless thou shalt bestow thy daughter on one whom—but thou wilt never condescend——"

" Nay," impatiently interrupted the knight, "better she should marry any honest man of good family than that she should be suffered to match so proudly only to be the mother of destruction to herself, to me, and to her country."

"Thou sayest well," calmly replied the Ancient; " but the Fates have not left the choice of her mate to thee or to her. Yet hear me patiently, and thou shalt know all. Thou art not ignorant that I have long abjured the pitiful affairs of men. 'Tis now more than fifteen years since, quitting their society, I have devoted myself to those studies by which thou hast more than once benefited. I have sacrificed all earthly prospects and enjoyments for the sake of that sublime knowledge which doth enable me to foresee and control coming events ; and it is to me a reward in itself so great, as to make every other appear despicable in comparison with it. But though I have forsworn the world, yet cannot I rid myself of attachment to thee ; my early feelings must tie me to thee and thine for ever. Thou hast had proofs of this devotion too often, to require me to repeat that it doth exist ; but I am now prepared to give thee a demonstration of it yet stronger than any thou hast hitherto received from me."

" Kind, excellent Ancient," exclaimed the grateful Sir Walter, " I well know the care with which thou hast watched over the welfare of my house ; I feel the magnitude of the debt I owe thee, and 'tis with gratitude I acknowledge it. What is it, I beseech thee, thou canst do ? "

" Yes," exclaimed the Ancient, with a show of much feeling, " yes ; I will sacrifice myself. I will come forth again into the haunts of deceitful and cold-blooded men. 1 will give up all I prize—my quiet, my solitude—to save thee and thine from the destruction that impendeth. On my part there shall be no failure, however at war with my habits and inclinations the sacrifice may be. 'Tis upon thyself, therefore—upon thine own decision—that thine own fate, and the fate of thy daughter, and of thy country, must depend."

" Name, name, I entreat thee, the terms ! " cried the anxious old knight; " name the conditions that I must fulfil ; tell me what I must do, and no time shall be lost in carrying it into effect."

The Ancient paused for some moments, during which he looked into the face of the knight with his fiery inexpressive eyes, and then, with slow and solemn, though harsh utterance— " I must espouse thy daughter, the Lady Eleanore ! " said he. " The Fates have willed it so; no other remedy doth now remain against the overwhelming destruction thou art doomed to behold."

This fatal declaration—this dreadful contrast to all those hopes of splendid alliance which had filled Sir Walter's thoughts, came upon him like a thunderbolt, and was perfectly annihilating. He could not stand the bitter alternative that was thus presented to him. Overcome by his feelings, he threw himself back among the straw composing the lair of the monster he had been listening to, and, covering his eyes with the palms of his hands, he, hardy soldier as he was, burst into a flood of tears.

A grim meteor smile of inward satisfaction shot over the pallid face of the impostor.

" Ay," said he, " no one can expect thee to match thy daughter with such as me. Better that she should give birth to ten thousand such demons as her fated marriage with the brother of the Piersie is infallibly destined to produce—better that she should die, and thou be cruelly murdered by the parricidal hand of thine inhuman grandchild, than that thou shouldst call such a wretch as me son. Thy determination hath been well taken : 'tis like a good soldier, as thou art, to brave the Fates. I thank thee, too, for mine emancipation from the vow I had resolved to subject myself to for thy sake. My time, and my quiet, and my solitude, shall be again mine own, and my darling studies shall receive no interruption."

" Is there no other alternative ? " cried the distracted father, rising with energy from the position he had thrown himself into.

" None ! " replied the Ancient. "But that thou mayest be ignorant of no tittle of what it so deeply concerns thee to know," continued he after a pause, " it is destined that if ever I do so espouse me, my son shall be the most perfect model of bravery and of virtue that ever England saw ; and that, taking the proud name of de Selby, he shall wax exceeding mighty, and, leading a small band of gallant youths, march into Scotland as a conqueror, until at last, dethroning the monarch of the North, he shall himself be proclaimed king of that country, and, uniting himself by marriage with the King of England, he and his posterity shall reign for twelve centuries. To look farther into futurity is denied ; but enow hath been told thee to point out the way that doth lie before thee. The space of three days and three hours is given thee to choose thy daughter's destiny. And now," continued the Ancient, putting out his hand to the hourglass, and solemnly inverting it ; " and now the stream of thy time beginneth to run ; see how the sand floweth down—a portion of it hath already glided away ; so will the rest, till the period assigned thee be irrecoverably gone. 'Twere better that thou shouldst retire to thy chamber, to weigh well the fates of thy daughter, for the balance of her destinies is in thine hand."

The impostor paused. The agitated mind of Sir Walter de Selby had eagerly grasped at the flattering picture which the Ancient had so cunningly reserved to the last, and which was so perfectly in harmony with every wish of the old man's heart. In his contemplation of it, he had almost forgotten the uncouth son-in-law destined to make him the grandfather of a hero, who was to raise the glory of his country's arms so high, and who was at last to become a King of Scotland. His pride was peculiarly flattered by the notion of the name of de Selby being retained to become eventually royal ; and he began to reason with himself as he sat, that it was but stooping to present humiliation in order to rise to the summit of human ambition. The crafty Ancient saw the working of his mind, from its operation on his honest countenance, as well as if he had been thinking audibly.

" Such proud prospects of an issue so glorious tempt not me," said he. " These dark volumes, and the retirement of this unseemly chamber, whence the stars can be most easily conversed with, are to me worth a world of such. But for thee, if thou demandest it of me, the sacrifice shall be made ; and shouldst thou make me the humble instrument of the salvation and exaltation of thyself and issue, it would," said he, with an affectation of extreme humility, " be no more, after all, than burying good seed in the soil of a dunghill, to see it buxion with the more vigour, shoot the more aloft, and rear its proud head far above the meagre plants on higher but more sterile spots. But it is matter worthy of grave thought. Yet judge me not as I seem —the poor, the wretched inmate of this owlet's nest. Why am I so ? Even because I despise all those gewgaws men esteem most valuable, and covet only that most precious of all jewels —the perfection of knowledge. Thinkest thou that it would not help me to all the rest, were it my pleasure to command them ? Thinkest thou that I could not command worldly wealth and honours, were I to fancy such baubles ? Wouldst thou have me conjure up gold ? Lo !—there !" said he, plucking the leathern bag from his jerkin, and emptying the shining contents of it on the ground, to the astonishment of Sir Walter ; " a little midnight labour would raise me up a hoard that might purchase the earth itself. But what is the vile dross to me ? Nay, I would not inundate the wretched world with that which hath already caused sufficient human misery. To pour out more would be to breed a more accursed scourge than e'en thy grandson Piersie will prove."

"Talk not of him," exclaimed the knight in terror; "the very thought of his existence is racking to me. I want not time for consideration on a point so plain. I do now resolve me on the alliance with thee. Sir Rafe Piersie comes to-morrow morning; I shall break with him abruptly—and then, my resolution being taken, my daughter must yield to the irresistible decrees of Fate."

With these words Sir Walter rose to his knees, and snatching up his lamp, scrambled hastily to the door, and stole softly down to his apartment. He looked with fear and trembling into the oratory, when, to his extreme relief, he saw that the ominous flame had left the fatal shield, and he retired to his couch in a state of comparative composure.

"So," said the Ancient, in grim soliloquy, after Sir Walter's footsteps had died away on the stairs—" so the hook is in thy nose, and thou shalt feel the power, as well as the vengeance, of him thou didst despise and make thy mock of. Thou didst thwart mine ambition; but my helm ere long shall tower amid the proudest crests of chivalry, and wealth and honours, yea, and the haughty smile of beauty too, shall be at my will. This is indeed to rise by mine abasement, even beyond the highest soaring of those early hopes which this man did so cruelly level with the earth. The thought is ecstasy."

CHAPTER VIII.

Arrival of Sir Rafe Piersie—The Challenge.

Sir John Assueton was early astir next morning, for his head was so filled with the remembrance of those friends and scenes of his youth, he now hoped to revisit after a long absence, that he was impatient to depart from Norham Castle. He had already given orders to the squires to hold themselves in readiness, and he had visited the stable, where Blanche-etoile neighed a recognition to his master, and was spoken to with the kindness of a friend. The knight then ascended the ramparts to enjoy a short promenade; and there he was soon afterwards joined by Hepborne, who came springing towards him, urged by an unusual flow of spirits.

"Good morrow, Hepborne," said Assueton; "I am glad to see thee so alert this morning. I have looked at our steeds;

they are as courageous as lions, and as gamesome as kids. They
will carry us into Scotland with as much spirit as we shall ride
them thither. After breaking our fast, and bestowing our meed
of thanks on the good old knight for his hospitality, we may yet
make our way o'er many a good mile of Scottish ground ere
yonder new-born sun shall sink in the west."

"Nay, my dear Assueton," said Hepborne, "what need hast
thou for such haste? Hadst thou some fair damsel in Scotland
—some lady bright, who, with her swan-like neck stretched
towards the mid-day sun, looketh day after day from her lofty
towernet, with anxious eyes, in the hope of descrying thee, her
true and constant Knight—hadst thou such a fair one as this,
I say, impatience might indeed become thee ; but what reason
hast thou, despiser of the lovely sex as thou art, to long for a
change of position ? By the Rood of St. Andrew, I begin to
believe that thou art no such woman-hater as thou wouldst pretend, and that all this seeming coldness of thine is nothing but
thy laudable constancy to some Scottish maid, who hath thine
early-pledged vows of love in keeping."

"Thou art welcome to rally me as it may please thee, Hepborne," replied Assueton, with a smile : "but, on the faith and
honour of my knighthood, I have not seen the maiden for whom
I would go three ells from my intended path, except for common
knightly courtesy, or to redress some grievous wrong. Nay,
nay, thou knowest my natural duresse—that my heart is adamant to all such weak impressions. Perdie, I cannot understand how any such affect the good, hardy, soldier-like bosom,
though I do observe the melancholy truth exampled forth, in
daily occurrence, with those around me. But I perceive thy
drift, my politic friend. To assail is the best tactique against
being assailed. Thou camest forth conscience-stricken, and being well aware that thy foolish fondness of this masquing
damosel of the Castle here would come under my gentle lash, to
divert the attack against thyself, thou dost begin to skirmish
against me. But I see well enow 'tis the Lady Eleanore's attraction that would keep thee here."

"It is e'en so, I candidly confess it," replied Hepborne. "I
candidly confess it, dost mark me ? so, throwing myself at thy
feet, I cry for quarter."

"Nay, an thou dost disarm me thus," replied Assueton, "I
can say no more."

"Oh, Assueton, Assueton, my bel ami," said Hepborne, en-
thusiastically, "I was the happiest of human beings last night.
I did indeed meet her on the ramparts. Old Adam of Gordon

was a good seer ; nay, perchance, though as to that I know not, he may have been Cupid's messenger. Yet, hold ! Depardieux, I do her most foul wrong in so supposing ; for she hath too much maiden modesty to have been guilty of so much boldness. But, be that as it may, her words—her looks—were kind and most encouraging. She did blushingly confess that her heart had known no other affection than that which she bears towards her venerable father. She half admitted that I was not altogether indifferent to her ; she did utter a hope that we should remain her father's guests for some longer space ; yea, and she even admitted that to see me again would give her pleasure. Then her accents were so sweet, and her demeanour so gentle—Oh, Assueton, she is in very truth an angel ! But what is all this to thee, thou Knight of Adamant ? I forgot that I might as well speak to the stones of these walls of amorets and love passages, as to Sir John Assueton."

" Thou art right, i' faith, Hepborne," replied Assueton ; "they say walls have ears, whilst I, in good earnest, may with truth enow be said to have none for such matters, since they do irk whenever the theme of love is handled in their hearing. Yet my friendship for thee bids me listen to thy ravings, and compassion for thy disease makes me watch the progress of its symptoms, as I should do those of any other fever. From all thou hast said, then, I would gather that thou wouldst fain loiter off another day or two, to catch fresh smiles and deeper wounds from the Lady Eleanore. Is't not so, Hepborne ?"

" In truth, Assueton," replied Sir Patrick, " her whole deportment towards me last night hath buoyed me up with hope, yea, and hath even led me to flatter myself that I am not indifferent to her, Scot though I be. At so critical a period, then, I cannot go, my dear Assueton ; and I am sure thy good nature will never allow thee to abandon thy friend in the crisis of his distemper."

" No, Hepborne," said Assueton, laughing, " I shall certainly not be so little of a Christian knight as to abandon thee when thine estate is so dangerous. Well, then, I must wait thy time, I suppose. But parfoy I must have some rounds of the tiltyard, were it but to joust at the quintaine, or Blanche-etoile and I too will lose our occupation. Wilt thou not take a turn with me for exercise ? But soft—I need not talk to thee of any such thing, for yonder comes the cause of thy malady."

" By St. Dennis, it is she indeed ! " exclaimed Hepborne : " that is the very mantle she wore. But who is that cavalier on whose arm she hangs so freely?" added he with a jealous tone and air.

"St. Genevieve! but he is a tall, proper, handsome knight," said Assueton.

"Pshaw?" said Hepborne pettishly, "I see nothing handsome about him; meseems he hath the air of a sturdy swineherd."

"Is not that the Lady Eleanore de Selby?" inquired Assueton of a sentinel who walked on the ramparts at some little distance from where the knights then stood.

"Ay, in truth, it is she," replied the man, stopping to look at her.

"And who may yonder knight be with whom she holds converse?" demanded Hepborne eagerly.

"By the mass, I know not, Sir Knight," replied the man as he turned to tread back his measured pace; "I never saw him before, that I knows on."

But notwithstanding the unfavourable remark which jealousy had made Hepborne cast on the stranger's appearance, he could not help secretly confessing that the knight with whom the Lady Eleanore had come forth from the keep, and on whose arm she was now leaning with so little reserve, was indeed very handsome, even noble-looking. An esquire waited for him at the end of the bridge, with two magnificently-caparisoned black horses. The lady seemed to be a drag on his steps, and to keep him back, as it were, with a thousand last words, as if with a desire of prolonging the few remaining minutes of their converse. On his part he displayed signs of the tenderest affection for her; and after they had crossed the bridge tardily together, she threw herself upon his mailed neck, and he enfolded her in his arms, both remaining locked together for some moments in a last embrace. The warrior then tore himself from her, and vaulting on his steed, struck the pointed steel into his sides, and galloped off at a desperate pace. The lady, leaning on the balustrades of the bridge, rested there a little space, and then turning slowly towards the door of the keep, disappeared.

The two knights commanded a full though distant view of this scene of dumb show, from the part of the rampart where they then stood. Assueton turned his eyes with compassion upon his friend to observe its effect upon him. He was standing like a marble statue, still gazing on the spot where it had been acted—his eyes fixed in his head as with apathetical stupor. At length, after remaining in the same attitude for several minutes, he struck his forehead violently with the palms

of his hands, and addressing his friend in hurried accents—
"Assueton, Assueton," said he, "didst thou see? didst thou
mark! Oh, woman, woman, woman! But it mattereth not.
Assueton, let our horses be ordered; I will forth with thee for
Scotland even now; ay, even now. Thou wert indeed right,
my friend; there is more of thorns than of roses about them
all. Thou wert wise, Assueton; but I am cured now—nay, I
am as sane as thyself. Our horses, Assueton—our squires and
cortege. Let us not lose a moment; we may despatch good
store of Scottish miles ere we sleep."

"Nay, let us not be guilty of doing violence to the courtesy
of knighthood," replied Assueton; "Sir Walter de Selby hath
used much fair hospitality towards us. It beseems us not to
leave Norham Castle without giving thanks to the good old
governor in person, and bidding him adieu. Besides, 'twere as
well, methinks, to go with less suspicious haste, lest we may be
misjudged; and, indeed, Sir Walter can have hardly left his
couch as yet."

"Ay, ay, true—thou sayest true, my friend," said Hepborne,
interrupting him keenly. "I had forgotten. Her father not
yet astir, and she taking leave of her lover so tenderly at such
an hour. Oh, damnable! He came, doubtless, last night, and
has been i' the keep without the old man's knowledge. So, all
her deep and long drawn suspires were but the offspring of her
fears lest her leman should break faith."

"Come, come, Hepborne, my bel ami, compose thyself," said
Sir John; "thou must not let this appear within; 'tis but a
short hour sacrificed to common civility, and then let us boune
us for Scotland."

"Thou sayest well, Assueton," said Hepborne, recollecting
himself after a short pause, during which he sighed deeply; "I
must endeavour to command myself; my passion too much
enchafeth me. The good old man hath indeed been to us kindness itself. How cruel that he should be so deceived in his
daughter! I pity him from the bottom of my soul. My wounds
will soon be healed—war-toil must be their confecture; but his,
alas! are yet to be opened, for now they do fester all unwist to
him, and when they do burst forth, I fear me they may well
out his life's blood. But come," added he, rousing himself,
"let's in."

They turned their steps towards the keep, but before they
had descended from the ramparts their ears were struck with
the sound of a bugle, and as they looked over the walls they
descried a long cavalcade of knights, esquires, grooms, lacqueys,

and spearmen, advancing with lances and pennons up the hollow way leading towards the outer gate of the Castle. The party soon came thundering over the drawbridge, and were saluted by the guards as they passed. At the head of the troop rode the proud Sir Rafe Piersie. The array of the very meanest of his people was magnificent; but his armour and his horse-gear shone like the sun, and glittered with the splendour of their embossments. They passed into the inner courtyard; loud rang the bugle of announcement, and the ear was assailed by the neighing of hot steeds, the clattering and pawing of impatient hoofs, the champing of foam-covered bits, the jingling of chains, and the clinking of spurs; whilst a rout of soldiers and grooms, with Master Thomas Turnberry at their head, ran clustering around them. The squires of the Castle, with the hoary seneschal and a host of lacqueys, came forth from the keep, and ushered in Sir Rafe Piersie and his suite.

Hepborne and Assueton soon afterwards followed, and, on reaching the banquet-hall, they found Sir Walter de Selby in the act of receiving and welcoming his newly-arrived guest, whose supercilious air, when addressing the plain, honest old soldier by no means prepossessed the two Scottish knights in his favour. Sir Walter introduced them to Piersie, and he received them with the same offensive hauteur. There is something in such a deportment that provokes even the humble man to put on haughtiness. Hepborne, from late events, was not prepared to be in the most condescending humour, so that he failed not to carry his head fully three inches higher than he had done since he became an inmate of the Castle of Norham. Nor was Assueton at all behind him in stateliness.

The table was covered with the morning's meal, and but little conversation passed during the time it was going on. Sir Walter de Selby seemed to be more reserved, and even less disposed to risk his words than he had been the previous night.

"I marvel much, Sir Governor," said Sir Rafe Piersie with a haughty sneer—"Methinks 'tis marvellously strange, I say, that thou hast as yet said nothing touching the object of the visit I have thus paid thee. Am I, or am I not, to have this girl of thine? Depardieux, there hath been more ambassage about this affair than might have brought home and wedded a queen of England. The damsel, I am informed, knew not her own mind, and thou were weak enough to suffer thyself to be blown about by her wayward whimsies; but my kinsman, the Bishop of Durham, tells me that, having at last brought thine own determination up to the proper point, thou art finally resolved

she shall be mine.   Marry, a matter of great exertion, truly,
to accept of Sir Rafe Piersie as a husband for Eleanore de
Selby ! ”

“My mind has indeed been made up, Sir Rafe Piersie,” said
the old knight, “ and would to Heaven, beausir, that it could
have been made up differently; for, certes, it doleth me sorely
to be driven to answer thee as I must of needscost do.   I
should not have broached this matter till privacy had put
the seal on our converse : but, since thou hast opened it, I am
forced to tell thee that, since I saw the Bishop of Durham,
obstacles have appeared which render it impossible for me to
give thee my daughter, the Lady Eleanore, to wife.   She is
affianced to another.”

“ So,” thought Hepborne, the ideas passing rapidly through
his mind, “ her father knows of the attachment between her
and the knight who left her this morning.   Then, perhaps, she
has been less to blame than I thought ; yet why were her words
and manner such, last night, towards me, as to mislead me into
the idea that I had reason to hope ?   Oh, deceitful woman, never
satisfied with the success of thy springes as long as there is a
foolish bird to catch.   So ! thou must have me limed to ?   But,
grammercy, I have escaped thy toils.”

Such were Hepborne’s thoughts ; but what Sir Rafe Piersie’s
were during the pause of astonishment he was thrown into, may
be best gathered from the utterance he gave them.

“ What is this I hear ? has a limb of the noble Piersie been
brought here to be insulted ?   Thou art a false old papelarde ;
and were it not for those hoary hairs of thine, by the beard of
St. Barnabas, I would brain thee with this gauntlet ;” and saying
so, he dashed it down on the board, making it ring again.

Hepborne and Assueton both started up, and stretched out
their hands eagerly to seize it.

“ Ah, thou art always lucky, Hepborne,” said Assueton, much
disappointed to see that his friend had snatched it before him.

“ Sir Rafe Piersie,” said Hepborne, “ in behalf of this good
old knight, whom thou hast so grossly insulted at his own board,
I defy thee to instant and mortal debate ; and in thy teeth I
return the opprobrious epithets thou didst dare to throw in his
face ; and here, I say, thou liest !” and with these words he threw
down his gauntlet.

“And who art thou ?” said his antagonist, taking it up :
“ who art thou, young cockerel, who crowest so loud ?   By St.
George, but thou showest small share of wisdom to pit thyself
thus against Sir Rafe Piersie.   But fear not, thou shalt have thy

will. Was thy darreigne for instant fight, saidst thou? In God's name, let us to horse then without farther parley. Let Sir Richard de Lacy here, and thine eager friend there, be the judges of the field; and as for the place, the Norham meadow below will do as well for thine overthrow as any other; thou wilt have easy galloping ere thou dost meet it. What, defy Sir Rafe Piersie to combat of outrance, and give him the lie, too! Thou art doomed, young man, thou art doomed; thine insolence hath put thee beyond the pale of my mercy. By the holy Rood, thou must be the young cock-sparrow the old dotard hath chosen as a mate for his pretty popelot, else thou never couldst have been so bold."

"I am not so fortunate," replied Hepborne, with calm and courteous manner.

"And what may thy name and title be, then?" demanded Piersie, with yet greater hauteur.

"My name," replied he, with a dignified bow, "is Sir Patrick Hepborne."

"Ha! then, by my faith, thou hast some good Northern blood in thee," replied Piersie; "thou art less unworthy of my lance than I did ween thou wert. Thy father is a right doughty Scot; and, if I mistake not, I have heard of some deeds of thine done in France, which have made thine honours and renomie to bud and buxion rathely. But 'tis a warm climate they have sprouted in, and such early and unnatural shoots are wont to be air-drawn and unhealthy; and albeit they may vegetate under the more southern sun, they are often withered by the blasts of the North as soon as they appear amongst us. But come, come, my horse, Delaval—my horse and gear, I say;" and, leaving the hall hastily, he sought a chamber where he might prepare himself for single combat.

CHAPTER IX.

The Combat—Departure of the Scots—Master Kyle Swears by St. Cuthbert.

HEPBORNE was not slow on his part, and in a very short time the Castle-yard was again in commotion, and grooms and esquires were seen running in all directions, bringing out horses and buckling on trappings. Hepborne's gallant steed Beaufront was led proudly forth from his stall by Mortimer Sang, and was no sooner backed by his master than he pranced, neighed, and

spurned the ground, as if he had guessed of the nature of the
work he had to do.   Attended by Assueton and their small
party of followers, Sir Patrick rode slowly down to the mead of
Norham, extending from under the elevated ground on which
the Castle stood, for a considerable way to the westward, between
the village and the bank of the Tweed.   Here he halted, and
patiently awaited the arrival of his opponent.   Piersie came in
all his pomp, mounted on a dapple-grey horse, of remarkable
strength, figure, and action.   Both horse and rider were splendidly arrayed, and his friends and people came crowding after
him, boasting loudly of the probable issue of the combat.   Sir
Walter de Selby came last, attended by some few officers,
esquires, and meaner people, and joined Hepborne's party, stationed towards one end of the field, Sir Rafe Piersie's having
filed off and taken post towards the other extremity of it.   Little
time was lost in preparation.   The two judges placed themselves
opposite to the middle of the space, and there the combatants
met and measured lances.

The bugle-mot gave them warning, so turning their steeds
round, they each rode back about a furlong towards their respective parties, and, suddenly wheeling at the second sound of the
bugle, they ran their furious course against each other with lance
in rest.   The shock was tremendous.   The clash of their armour
echoed from the very walls of the neighbouring Castle ; nor had
the oldest and most experienced men-at-arms who were there present ever seen anything like it.   Sir Patrick Hepborne received
his adversary's lance, with great adroitness, on his shield, at such
an angle that it glanced off broken in shivers ; yet the force was so
great that it had almost turned him in his saddle.   But he, on his
part, had borne his point so stoutly, so steadily, and so truly, that,
taking his adversary in the centre of the body, he tossed him entirely over the croupe of his horse.   Piersie lay stunned by the fall ;
and Sir Patrick, checking Beaufront in his career, made a circuit
around his prostrate adversary, and speedily dismounting, went
up to him, and kneeling on the ground beside him, lifted up his
head, and opened his vizor and beaver to give him freer air.   Sir
Richard de Lacy and Assueton came up.

"Sir Richard," said Hepborne, " thou seest his life is in mine
hands ; and after the bragging and insolent threats he used towards me, perhaps I might be deemed well entitled to use the
privileges of my victory, and take it.   But I engaged in this
affair only to wipe off the disgrace thrown on this good old
knight, Sir Walter de Selby, in whose hospitality I and my
brother-in-arms have so liberally shared ; and the blot having

been thus removed, by God's blessing on mine arm, I leave Piersie his life, that he may use it against me when next we meet in fair fight in bloody field, should the jarring rights of our two countries summon us against each other. But through thee, his friend, I do most solemnly enjoin him that, on the honour of a knight, he shall hold Sir Walter de Selby as acquitted of all intention of doing him any injury or insult in the matter of the marriage he contemplated with the Lady Eleanore, and that he think not of doing Sir Walter violence on that account."

For all this Sir Richard de Lacy immediately pledged himself in name of Sir Rafe Piersie; and the discomfited knight, who was still insensible, having been lifted up by his esquires, was straightway borne towards the Castle. As they were carrying him away, Mortimer Sang, who had by chance caught the dapple-grey steed, as he scoured past him on the field after his rider's overthrow, trotted up to the group leading him by the bridle. The worthy esquire had heard and treasured up the taunts and boasting of Piersie's people, as they were approaching the field.

"Hath any of ye lost perchance a pomely grise-coloured horse, my masters?" exclaimed he; "here is a proper powerful destrier, if he had been but well backed. Hast thou no varlet of a pricksoure squire who can ride him? Here, take him, some of ye; and, hark ye, let his saddle be better filled the next time ye do come afield."

Piersie's men were too much crestfallen to return his jibes, so he rode back to the group that surrounded the conqueror, chuckling over his triumph. The good old Sir Walter de Selby, his eyes running over with gratitude, approached Sir Patrick Hepborne, and embraced him cordially.

"The time hath been," said he, "the time hath been, Sir Patrick, when it pleased Heaven to permit me to reap the same guerdon of inward satisfaction thou art now feeling, and could the weight of a few years have been lifted from off this hoar head, by God's blessing, thou shouldst not have had this noble chance of gathering fame at the cost of Sir Rafe Piersie. As it is, I thank thee heartily for thy gallant defence of an old man, as well as for the generous use thou hast made of thy victory. Come, let us to the Castle, that by my treatment of thee, and Sir Rafe Piersie, I may forthwith prove my gratitude to the one and my forgiveness of the other."

"Thanks, most hospitable knight," said Sir Patrick, "I beseech thee in mine own name, and that of my friend, to receive our poor thanks for thy kind reception of us at Norham. But

now our affairs demand our return to our own country ; nay,
had it not been for this unlooked-for deed of arms, we had been
ere now some miles beyond that broad stream.　We boune us
now for Scotland.　Farewell, and may the holy St. Cuthbert
keep thee in health and safety.　We may yet haply meet again."

Sir Walter de Selby was grieved to find that all his efforts
to detain the two knights were ineffectual.

"Since it is thy will, then, to pleasure me no longer with
thy good company and presence, Sirs Knights, may the blessed
Virgin and the holy St. Andrew guide you in safety to your
friends ; and may you find those you love in the good plight
you would wish them to be."　And saying so, he again cordially
embraced both the knights, and slowly returned towards the
Castle with his attendants.

The bustle and commotion occasioned by the appearance of
the knights and their followers on the mead of Norham, the
sound of the bugle, and the clash of the shock, had brought out
many of the inhabitants of the village to see what was a-doing.
Amongst these was the black-eyed Mrs. Kyle, who came up to
Master Mortimer Sang, and laying hold of his bridle-rein—

" When goest thou for Scotland ?" said she anxiously.

" Even now, fair dame," said he calmly.

" Then go I with thee, Sir Squire," returned she.　" Let me
have a seat on that batt-horse ; I can ride right merrily there."

" Nay, my most beautiful Mrs. Kyle," replied Sang, " that
may in no wise be, seeing I am an honest virtuous esquire, not
one of those false faitors who basely run away with other men's
wives.　Thou canst not with me, I promise thee."

" Yea, but thou didst promise to take me," cried Mrs. Kyle,
a flood of tears bursting from her eyes, as she began to reproach
Sang, with a voice half-chocked by the violence of her sobbing.
" So false foiterer that thou art, I—I—I—I must be foredone
by thee, must I, after all thy losengery and flattery ?　Here
have I kept goodman Kyle all this time i' the vault, ygraven,
as a body may say, that I mought the more sickerly follow thee
when thou wentest.　Oh, what will become of me ?　I am but
as one dead."

" Why, thou cruel giglet, thou," cried Sang, " didst thou in
very truth mean to go off to Scotland with me, and leave thy
poor husband ygraven i' the vault to die the most horrible of
deaths ?　Did not I tell thee to let him out at thy leisure
and on thine own good terms ?　By the mass, a pretty leisure
hast thou taken, and pretty terms hast thou resolved to
yield him."

" Nay, judge not so hastily, good Sir Squire," replied Mrs. Kyle. " That I would boune me to Scotland is sure enow; but, as to leaving Sylvester Kyle to die a cruel death, Thomas Tapster here knows that I taught him the use of the sliding plank and the clicket of the trap door, and that Master Sylvester was to receive his franchise as soon as Tweed should be atween us. But what shall I do ? I can never go back to the Norham Tower again; goodman Sylvester will surely amortise me attenes when he doth get freedom."

" Squire," said Hepborne, " thou must e'en get thee back to the village, and make her peace with the bear her husband : we shall wait for thee at the ferry-boat."

" Nay, as for that matter," said Sang, " I must go back at any rate, for I have yet to pay the rascal for the excellent supper we had of him, and for the herborow of our party for the night we spent there. Come along then, Dame Kyle, I see thou art not quite so savage as I took thee to be."

They soon reached the hostel, and Master Mortimer Sang, dismounting from his horse in the yard, entered, and strode along the passage to the place where he knew the trap-door to be, and, sliding aside the plank that covered its fastenings, he hoisted up the lever.

" Sylvester Kyle, miserable lossel wight," cried he, " art thou yet alive? Sinner that thou art, I have compassion on thee, and albeit thou hast been there but some short space—small guerdon for thy wicked coulpe, seeing thou art in the midst of so great a mountance of good provender and drink, with which to fill thine enormous bowke—I condescend to let thee come forth. Come up, come up, I say, and show thy face, that we may hold parley as to the terms of thine enlargement."

A groaning was heard from the farther end of the place, and by and by Sylvester's head appeared above the steps, his countenance wearing the most miserable expression. Horrible fear of the agonizing death he had thought himself doomed to die had prevented him from touching food; but the anxious workings of his mind had done even more mortification upon him than a starvation of a fortnight could have accomplished. The red in his face was converted into a deadly pale copper hue, for even death itself could never have altogether extinguished the flame in his nose; his teeth projected beyond his lips, and chattered against each other from the cold he had undergone: and his eyes stared in their sockets, from the united effects of want and terror.

" Should it please me to give thee the franchise, thou

6

agroted lorrel, thou," said the Squire, "wilt thou give me thy promise to comport thyself more honestly in time to come, to have done with all knavery and chinchery, and to give thy very best to all Scots who may, in time to come, chance to honour thy hostelry with their presence ? "

" Oh, good Sir Squire," replied the host, " anything—I will promise anything that thou mayest please."

" Nay, nay, Sir Knave," cried Sang, " horrow tallowcatch that thou art—no generals—swear me in particulars—item by item, dost thou hear, as thou framest thy reckonings ? If thou dost not down goeth the trap-door again, and I leave thee here to meditate and ypend my proposal, until my return from the Holy Wars, whether I am boune. By that time thou wilt be more humble, and more coming to my terms. Swear."

" I swear, by the holy St. Cuthbert," replied the host, " that all Scots shall henceforth be entertained with the best meats and drinks the nale of the Norham Tower can afford, yea, alswa the best herborow it can yield them."

" 'Tis well," said Sang; " swear me next, then, and let the oath be strong, that thou wilt never again score double."

" Nay, Master Squire, that is a hard oath for a tapster to take ; 'tis warring against the very nicest mystery of my vocation," said Kyle.

" No matter, Sir Knave," said Sang, " I shall not have my terms agrutched by thee. An thou swearest not this, down thou goest, and I leave thee to settle scores with a friend of thine below, with whom thou wilt find the single reckoning of thy sins a hard enough matter for thee to pay."

" Oh, for mercy's sake, touch not the trap-door, Sir Squire, and I will swear anything," cried Kyle, much alarmed at seeing Sang's brawny arm preparing to turn it over upon his head.

" Well, thou horrow lossel," cried Sang, " dost thou swear thou wilt never more cheat, or score double ? "

" I do, I do," said the host ; " by the holy Rood, I swear that I will never cheat or score double again. God help me," cried he, after a pause, " how shall I eschew it, and what shall I do without it ? "

" Now, thou prince of knaves," cried Sang, " thou hast yet one more serment to swallow. Swear by the blessed Virgin, that thou wilt receive thy wife back into thy bosom, and abandoning thy former harshness towards her, that thou wilt kindly cherish her, and do thy possible to comfort and pleasure her, forgetting all that may have hitherto happened amiss between ye. I restore her to thee pure. She was not to blame for my being in the vault with her. The coulpe was all thine own. Thou madest me ravenous with hunger by thy villainous chin-chery. My nose, through very want, became as sharp in scent as that of a sleuth-hound. I winded the steam that came from the trap-door, yea, from the very common room where I sat. I ran it up hot foot, and descending the stair, I had but just begun to feast mine eyes with that thou hadst denied to my stomach, when thy pestiferous voice was heard. Thy wife is as virtuous and innocent as the child unborn. So swear, I say."

Master Sylvester Kyle shook his head wofully, and looked very far from satisfied; but he had no alternative; he swore as the squire wished him to do, and then was permitted to issue from his subterranean prison.

"And now, Sir Knave," said Sang, "do but note my extreme clemency. Thou wouldst have starved me, the knights, and our good company, because we were Scots, for the which grievous sin I did put thee in a prison full of goodly provender and rich drinks; whence I now let thee forth, with thy greedy carcase crammed to bursting, and thy whole person plump and fair as a capon. Do but behold him, I beseech ye, how round he looks. Now get thee to thine augrim-stones, and cast up thine account withal. Thou knowest pretty well what we have had, for thou didst give me the victuals and wine with thine own hand."

"Nay, good Sir Squire," said Kyle, glad to escape, "take it all, in God's name, as a free gift, and let us part good friends."

"Nay, nay," said Master Sang, "we take no such beggarly treats, we Scottish knights and squires. Come, come—thy reckoning, thy reckoning, dost hear? No more words; my master doth wait, and I must haste to join him."

Kyle, with his wife's assistance, and that of the pebbles or augrim-stones, by which accounts were usually made out in those days, scored up the first fair reckoning he had ever made in his life, and Sang paid it without a word.

"And now," said he, "let us, as thou saidst, Master Kyle, let us e'en part good friends. Bring me a stirrup-cup of thy best."

The host hastened to fetch a cup of excellent Rhenish. They drank to each other, and shook hands with perfect cordiality; and the squire, smacking the pouting lips of Mrs. Kyle, mounted his horse, and rode away to join his party.

As the knights and their small retinue were crossing the Tweed in the ferry-boat, Hepborne cast his eyes up to the keep of the Castle, towering high above them, and frowning defiance upon Scotland. A white hand appeared from a narrow window, and waved a handkerchief; and, by a sort of natural impulse, he was about to have waved and kissed his fervently in return.

"Pshaw!" said he, pettishly checking himself, for being so ready to yield to the impulse of his heart. The white hand and handkerchief waved again—and again it waved ere he reached the Scottish shore ; but he manfully resisted all temptation, and gave no sign of recognition.

As he mounted, however, he looked once more. The hand was still there, streaming the little speck of white. His resolution gave way—he waved his hand, and his eyes filling with tears, he dashed the rowels of his spurs against the sides of his steed, sprang off at full gallop, and was immediately lost amongst the oak copse through which lay their destined way.

CHAPTER X.

The Home of the Hepbornes—Remembrances of Childhood—The Old Wolf-Hound.

AFTER tarrying for a little while at the small town of Dunse, the two knights pursued their journey over the high ridge of Lammermoor, and early on the second day they reached Hailes Castle, the seat of the Hepbornes, a strong fortress, standing on the southern banks of the river Tyne, in the heart of the fertile county of East Lothian. At the period we are now speaking of, the varied surface of the district surrounding the place was richly though irregularly wooded ; and even the singular isolated hill of Dunpender, rising to the southward of it, had gigantic oaks growing about its base, and towering upon its sides, amidst thick hazel and other brushwood, wherever they could find soil enough to nourish them.

Sir Patrick Hepborne had been particularly silent during their march. The events which took place at Norham, and the conviction he felt that the Lady Eleanore de Selby had indirectly endeavoured to draw him into an attachment for her, when her heart either was or ought to have been engaged to another, made him unhappy. It was needless to inquire why it should have done so, since he was ever and anon congratulating himself on having escaped uninjured from the toils of one so unworthy of him. But the truth was he had not escaped uninjured ; he had "tane a hurt" from her, of a nature too serious to be of very easy cure. Assueton, who had never felt the tender passion, and who had consequently very little sympathy for it, had more than once complained of the unwonted dulness of his companion, who used to be so full of life and cheerfulness, and had made several vain attempts to rouse him, until at last, despairing of success, he amused himself in jesting with Master Mortimer Sang, who possessed a never-failing spring of good humour.

As they drew near the domains of Sir Patrick Hepborne the elder, however, a thousand spots, and things, and circumstances, began to present themselves in succession, and to force themselves on the attention of the love-sick knight, awakening warm associations with the events of his youthful days, and overpowering, for a time, his melancholy. To these he began to give utterance in a language his friend could not only comprehend, but participate in the feelings they naturally gave rise to.

"Assueton," said he, "it was here, in this very wood, that I took my first lessons in the merry art of woodcraft; in yonder hollow were the rethes and pankers spread to toyle the deer; and, see there, under yonder ancient tree, was I first planted with my little cross-bow, as a lymer, to have my vantage of the game. It was Old Gabriel Lindsay, then a jolly forester, who put me there, and taught me how to behave me. He is now my father's seneschal, if, as I hope, he be yet alive. He was a hale man then, and though twenty years older than my father, he had a boy somewhat younger than myself, who took up his father's trade of forester, just before I went to France. Alas, the old tree has had a fearful skathe of firelevin since last I saw it. See what a large limb hath been rent from its side. Dost see the river glancing yonder below, through the green-wood? Ay, now we see it better. In yonder shallow used I to wade when a child, with my little hauselines tucked up above my knees. I do remember well, I was so engaged one hot summer's day, when, swelled by some sudden water-spout or upland flood, I saw the liquid wall come sweeping onwards, ready to overwhelm me. I ran in childish fear, but ere I reached the strand it came, and overtaking my tottering steps, hurried me with it into yonder pool. I sunk, and rose, and sank again. I remember e'en now how quickly the ideas passed through my infant mind, as I was whirling furiously round and round by the force of the eddy, vainly struggling and gasping for life, now below and now on the surface of the water. I thought of the dreadful death I was dying; I thought of the misery about to befall my father and mother—nay, strange as it may seem, I saw them in my mind's eye weeping in distraction over my pale and dripping corpse, and all this was intermixed with flitting hopes of rescue, that were but the flash amidst the darkness of the storm. The recollections of the five or six years I could remember of my past childhood were all condensed into the short period of as many minutes ; for that was all the time my lucky stars permitted me to remain in jeopardy, till Gabriel Lindsay came, and, plunging into the foaming current, dragged me half dead to the shore. Full many a time have I sithence chosen that very pool as a pleasure bayne wherein to exercise my limbs in swimming, when hardier boyhood bid me defy the flood."

" My dear friend," said Assueton, " trust me, I do envy thee thine indulgence in those remembrances excited by the scenes of thy childhood ; they make me more eager than ever to revel in those that await me around my paternal boure. I shall be thy father's guest to-night ; but I can no longer delay returning to my paternal possessions, and in especial to my widowed mother, who doubtless longs to embrace me. I must leave thee to-morrow."

" Nay, Assueton, thou didst promise to bestow upon me three or four days at least," said Hepborne : " let me not then have thy promise amenused. To rob me of so large a portion of thy behote were, methinks, but unkind."

" I did promise, indeed," said Assueton, " but I wist not of the time we should waste at Norham. I must e'en go to-morrow, Hepborne ; but, trust me, I shall willingly boune me back again some short space hence."

Hepborne was not lacking in argument to overcome his friend's intentions, but he could gain no more than a promise, reluctantly granted, that his departure should be postponed until the morning after the following day.

" But see, Assueton," said Hepborne, " there are the outer towers and gateway of the Castle, and behold how its proud barbicans rise beyond them. As I live, there is Flo, my faithful old wolf-dog, lying sunning himself against the wall. He is the fleetest allounde in all these parts for taking down the deer at a view. What ho, boy, Flo, Flo! What means the brute, he minds me not?" continued Hepborne, riding up to him : " I wot he was never wont to be so litherly ; he used to fly at my voice with all the swiftness of the arrow, which he is named after. Ah ! now I see, he is half-blind ; and peraunter he is deaf too, for he seems as if he heard me not. But, fool that I am, I forget that some years have passed away sith I saw him last, and that old age must ere this have come upon him. 'Twas but a week before I left home, Assueton, that he killed a wolf. But let us hasten in, I am impatient to embrace my father, and my dear mother, and my sister Isabelle."

Loud rang the bugle-blast in the court-yard of the Castle. Throwing his reins to his esquire, Hepborne sprang from his horse, and running towards the doorway, whence issued a crowd of domestics, alarmed by the summons, he grasped the hand of an old white-headed man, who presented the feeble remains of having been once tall and powerful, but who was now bent and tottering with age.

"My worthy Gabriel," said he in an affectionate tone and manner, and with a tear trembling in his eye, "dost thou not know me? How fares my father, my mother, and my sister, the Lady Isabelle?"

The old man looked at him for some moments, with his hand held up as a pent-house to his dim eyes.

"Holy St. Giles!" exclaimed he at last, "art thou indeed my young master? Art thou then alive and sound? Well, who would hae thought, they that saw me last winter, when I was so ill, that I would hae lived to hae seen this blessed day!"

"But tell me, Gabriel," cried Hepborne, interrupting him, "tell me where are they all; I suppose I shall find them in the banquet hall above?"

"Stop thee, stop thee, Sir Patrick," said the old seneschal, "thy father and the Lady Isabelle rode to the green-wood this morning. There was a great cry about a route of wolves that have been wrecking doleful damage on the shepens; they do say, that some of the flocks hae been sorely herried by them; so my master and the Lady Isabelle rode forth with the sleuth-hounds, and the alloundes, and the foresters; and this morning, ere the sun saw the welkin, my boy rode away to lay out the rethes and the pankers. I wot, thou remembers thee of my son Robert? He is head forester now. Thy noble father, Heaven's blessing and the Virgin's be about him, did that for him; may long life and eternal joy be his guerdon for all his good deeds to me and mine! And Ralpho Proudfoot was but ill content to see my Rob get the place aboon him; so Ralpho yode his ways, and hath oft sithes threatened some malure to Rob; but as to that——"

"Nay, my good Gabriel," said Hepborne, impatiently interrupting him, "but where, I entreat thee, is my mother?"

A cloud instantly overcast the face of the venerable domestic; he hesitated and stammered—

"Nay, then, my dear young master, thou hast not heard of the doleful tidings?"

"What doleful tidings? Quick, speak, old man. My mother! is she ill? Good God, thou art pale. Oh, thy face doth speak too intelligibly—my mother, my beloved mother, is no more!"

The old man burst into tears. He could not command a single word; but the grief and agitation he could not hide was enough for Sir Patrick Hepborne. In a choked and hollow voice—

"Assueton," said he, "walk up this way, so please thee; there is the banquet-hall; I must retire into this apartment for some moments. If thou hadst known my mother—my excellent, my tenderly affectionate mother—my mother, by whose benignant and joy-beaming eyes I looked to be now greeted withal—thou wouldst pardon me for being thus unmanned. But I shall be more composed anon."

And with these words, and with an agitation he could not hide, he burst away into an adjacent chamber, where he shut himself in, that he might give way to his emotions without interruption.

It was his mother's private room. In the little oratory opening from the farther end of it, was her pric-dieu and crucifix, and on the floor opposite to it was the very velvet cushion on which he found her kneeling, and offering up her fervent orisons to Heaven on his behalf, as he entered her apartment to embrace her for the last time, the morning he left Hailes for France. He remembered that his heart was then bounding with delight at the prospect of breaking into the world, and figuring among knights and warriors, amidst all the gay splendour of the French Court. Alas! he little thought then he was embracing her for the last time. He now looked round the chamber, and her missal-books, with a thousand trifles he had seen her use, called up her graceful figure and gentle expression fresh before his eyes. He wept bitterly, and, seating himself in the chair she used, wasted nearly an hour in giving way to past recollections, and indulging in the grief they occasioned. At last his sorrow began to exhaust itself, and he became more composed. The cushion and the little altar again caught his eye, and, rising from the chair, he prostrated himself before the emblem of the Saviour's sufferings and the Christian's faith and hope, pouring out his soul in devotional exercise. As his head was buried in the velvet drapery of the pric-dieu, and his eyes covered, his imagination pictured the figure of his mother floating over him in seraphic glory. He started up, almost expecting to see his waking vision realized; but it was no more than the offspring of his fancy, and he again seated himself on his mother's chair, to dry his eyes and to compose his agitated bosom.

Though still deeply afflicted, he now felt himself able to command his feelings, and he left his mother's apartment to rejoin Assueton. At the door he met old Gabriel Lindsay, and he being now able to ask, and the hoary seneschal to tell, the date and circumstances of his mother's death, he learned that she had been carried off by a sudden illness about three months previous to his arrival. The firmness of the warrior now returned upon him, and, with a staid but steady countenance, he rejoined his friend.

"Assueton," said he, "if thou art disposed to ramble with me, it would give me ease to go forth a little. Let us doff our mail, and put on less cumbrous hunting-garbs and gippons, and go out into the woods. We may chance to hear their hunting-horns, and so fall in with them; else we may loiter idling it here till nightfall ere they return."

Assueton readily agreed; and both having trimmed themselves for active exercise, and armed themselves with hunting-spears, and with the anelace, a kind of wood-knife or falchion, usually worn, together with the pouch, hanging from the girdle-stead of the body, they left the Castle, with the intent of taking the direction they were informed the hunting-party had gone in. As they passed from the outer gateway, the great rough old wolf-hound again attracted his master's attention.

"Alas! poor old Flo," said Hepborne, going up to him, and stooping to caress him, "thou canst no more follow me as thou wert wont to do. Thou art now but as a withered and decayed log of oak—thou who used, whenever I appeared, to dart hither and thither around me like a firelevin."

The old dog began to lick his master's hand, and to whine a dull recognition.

"I believe he doth hardly remember me," said Hepborne, moving away; "he seems now to be little better than a clod of earth."

The old dog, however, though he had scarcely stirred for many months before, began to whimper, and rearing up his huge body with great pain, as if in stretching each limb he required to break the bonds that age had rivetted every joint withal, and getting at last on his legs, he began to follow Sir Patrick, whining and wagging his tail. Hepborne, seeing his feeble state, did what he could to drive him back; but the dog persisted in following him.

" Poor old affectionate fellow," said Hepborne, "go with me, then, thou shalt, though I should have to carry thee back. Assueton," continued he, " let us climb the lofty height of Dunpender, whence we shall have such a view around us as may enable us to descry the hunting-party, if they be anywhere within the range of our ken."

CHAPTER XI.

The Wolf Hunt—A Desperate Encounter.

THEY accordingly made their way through the intervening woods, lawns, and alleys, and ascended the steep side of the hill. From the summit, the beautiful vale of the Tyne was fully commanded, and the extent and variety of the prospect was such as to occupy them for some time in admiration of it. Hepborne discovered a thousand spots and points in it connected with old stories of his youth. He touched on all these in succession to Assueton, his heart overflowing with his feelings, and his eyes with the remembrance of his beloved mother, whose image was continually recurring to him. He made his friend observe the distant eminences in parts of Scotland afar off; and Assueton, amongst others, was overjoyed to descry the blue top of that hill at the base of which he had been born, and whither his heart bounded to return.

" Hark," said Hepborne, suddenly interrupting the enthusiastic greeting his friend was wafting towards his distant home —" hark ! methinks I hear the sound of bugles echoing faintly through the woods below ; dost thou not hear ? "

" I do," said Assueton, "and methinks I also hear the yelling note of the sleuth-hounds."

" That bugle-mot was my father's," said Hepborne ; " I know it full well ; I could swear to it anywhere. Nay, yonder they ride. Dost not see them afar off yonder, sweeping across the green alures and avenues, where the wood-shaws are thinnest ? Now they cross the wide lawnde yonder—and now they are lost amid the shade of these oakshaws. They come this way ; let us hasten downward ; we shall have ill luck an we meet them not at the bottom of the hill."

Hepborne was so eager to embrace his father, that, forgetting his friend was a stranger to the perplexities of the way, he darted off, and descended through the brushwood, leaving Assueton to follow him as he best might. Assueton, in his turn, eager to overtake Hepborne, put down the point of his hunting-spear to aid him in vaulting over an opposing bush. There was a knot in the ashen shaft, and it snapt asunder with his weight. He threw it away, and, guided by the distant sounds of the bugle-blasts and the yells of the hounds, he pressed precipitately down the steep, but in his ignorance he took a direction different from that pursued by Hepborne.

As he was within a few yards of the bottom of the hill, he saw an enormous wolf making towards him, the oblique and sinister eyes of the animal flashing fire, his jaws extended, and tongue lolling out. Assueton regretted the loss of his hunting-spear, but judging him to be much spent, he resolved to attack him. He squatted behind a bush directly in the animal's path, and springing at him as he passed, he grappled him by the throat with both hands, and held him with the grasp of fate. The furious wolf struggled with all his tremendous strength, and before Assueton could venture to let go one hand to draw out his anelace, he was overbalanced by the weight of the creature, and they rolled over and over each other down the remainder of the grassy declivity, the knight still keeping his hold, conscious that the moment he should lose it he must inevitably be torn in pieces. There they lay tumbling and writhing on the ground, the exertions of the wolf being so violent, as frequently to lift Assueton and drag him on his back along the green sward. Now he gained his knees, and, pressing down his savage foe, he at last ventured to lose his right hand to grope for his anelace ; but it was gone—it had dropped from the sheath ; and, casting a glance around him, he saw it glittering on the grass, at some yards' distance. There was no other mode of recovering it but by dragging the furious beast towards it, and this he now put forth all his strength to endeavour to effect. He tugged and toiled, and even succeeded so far as to gain a yard or two ; but his grim foe was only rendered more ferocious in his resistance, by the additional force he employed. The wolf made repeated efforts to twist his neck round to bite, and more than once succeeded in wounding Assueton severely in the left arm, the sleeve of which was entirely torn off. As the beast lay on his back too, pinned firmly down towards his head, he threw up his body, and thrust his hind feet against Assueton's face, so as completely to blind his eyes, and by a struggle more violent than any he had made before, he threw him down backwards.

The situation of the bold and hardy knight was now most perilous, for, though he still kept his grasp, he lay stretched on

the ground ; and whilst the wolf, standing over him, was now
able to bring all his sinews to bear against him, from having his
feet planted firmly on the ground, Assueton, from his position,
was unable to use his muscles with much effect.   The panting
and frothy jaws, and the long sharp tusks of the infuriated
beast, were almost at his throat, and the only salvation that
remained for him, was to prevent his fastening on by it, by
keeping the head of the brute at a distance by the strength of
his arms.   The muscles of the neck of a wolf are well known
to be so powerful, that they enable the animal to carry off a
sheep with ease ; so that, with all his vigour of nerve, Assueton
had but a hopeless chance for it.   Still he held, and still they
struggled, when the tramp of a horse was heard, and a lady came
galloping by under the trees.   She no sooner observed the
dreadful strife between the savage wolf and the knight, than,
alighting nimbly from her palfrey, she couched the light hunting-
spear she carried, and ran it through the heart of the half-
choked animal.   The blood spurted over the prostrate cavalier,
and the huge carcase fell on him, with the eyes glaring in the
head, and the teeth grinding together in the agony of death.

The bold Assueton, sore toil-spent with the length of the
contest, threw the now irresisting body of the creature away
from him, and instantly recovered his legs.   All bloody and
covered with foam as he was, he bowed gracefully to his preserver, and gazed at her for some time ere he could find breath
to give his gratitude utterance.   She was lovely as the morning.
Her fair hair, broken loose from the thraldom of its braiding
bodkins by the agitation of riding, streamed from beneath a
hunting hat she wore, and fell in flowing ringlets over the black
mantle that hung from her shoulder.   Her mild and angelic
soul spoke in expressive language through her blue eyes, though
they were more than half veiled by her modest eyelids.   Her
full fresh lips were half open, and her bosom heaved with her
high breathing from the exercise she had been undergoing, and
the unwonted exertion she had so lately made, and her cheek
was gently flushed by the consciousness of the glorious deed she
had achieved.

"Sir Knight," inquired she, timidly though anxiously, "I
hope thou hast tane no hurt from the caitiff salvage ? Thou
dost bleed, meseems ?"

"Nay, lady," said Assueton, at last able to speak, "I bleed
not ; 'tis the blood of the brute yonder.   Perdie, thy bold and
timely aid did rid me of a strife that mought have ended sorely
to my mischaunce.   Verily, thou camest like an angel to my

rescue, and my poor thanks are but meagre guerdon for the heroic deed thou didst adventure to effect it.   Do I not speak to the sister of my friend, Sir Patrick Hepborne?   Do I not address the fair Lady Isabelle?"

"Patrick Hepborne?" inquired she eagerly; "art thou, indeed, the friend of my brother?   Welcome, Sir Knight; thou art welcome to me, as thou wilt be to my father.   What tidings hast thou of my gallant brother?"

"Even those, I ween, beauteous lady, which shall give thee belchier," said Assueton; "my friend is well as thou wouldst wish him; nay, more, he is here with me.   We parted but now above yonder at the crop of the hill.   I lost him in the thickets on its side, just before I encountered with gaffer wolf yonder."

"Pray Heaven," said Isabelle, with alarm in her countenance, "that he may not meet with some of the wolves we drove hither before us.   Thou seemest to be altogether without weapon, Sir Knight; perhaps he is equally defenceless."

"Nay, lady," replied Assueton, "I broke a faithless rotten shafted hunting-spear ere I came down, and I lost my anelace from my girdlestead as I was struggling with the wolf.   Sir Patrick has both, I warrant thee, and will make a better use of them than I did.   Shall we seek him, so please ye?"

"Oh, yes," cried the Lady Isabelle joyfully; "how I long to clasp my dear brother in these arms.   But hold, Sir Knight," said she, her face again assuming an air of anxiety, "thou dost bleed, maugre all thou didst say.   Truly thy left arm is most grievously torn by the miscreant wolf; let me bind it up with this rag here."   And notwithstanding all Assueton's protestations to the contrary, she took off a silken scarf, and bound up his wounds very tenderly, even exposing her own lovely neck to the sun, that she might effect her charitable purpose.

"And now," said she," let's on in the direction my father took;   he and my brother may have probably met ere this.   Hey, Robert," cried she to a forester who appeared at the moment, "whither went my father?"

"This way, lady," said he, pointing in a particular direction; "I heard his bugle-mot but now."

"Charge thyself with the spoils of this wolf, Robert," said the Lady Isabelle; "I do mean to have his felt hung up in the hall, in remembrance of the bold and desperate conflict, waged without aid of steel against him, by dint of thewes and sinews alone, by this valiant knight; 'tis a monster for size, the make of which is, I trow, rarely seen."

"Nay, lady," cried Assueton, "rather hang up his spoils in

commemoration of thine own brave deed ; for it was thou who
killed him.   And had it not been for thee, gaffer wolf might,
ere now, have made a dinner of me."

"In truth, Sir Knight," replied Isabelle, "hadst thou not
held him by the throat so starkly, I trow I should have had
little courage to have faced him."

The lady vaulted on her palfrey, and Assueton, his left arm
decorated with her scarf, and holding her bridle with his right,
walked by the side of the palfrey, like a true lady's knight,
unwittingly engaged, for the first time in his life, in pleasing
dialogue with a beautiful woman.

Sir Patrick Hepborne, who thought only of seeing his father,
had rushed down the steep of Dunpender in the hope of meeting him somewhere near the base of the hill, for the sound of
the chase evidently came that way.   His old dog Flo had difficulty in following him ; and stumbling over the stumps of
trees, and the stones that lay in his way, he was at last completely left behind.   As Sir Patrick had nearly reached the
bottom of the steep, he too observed a large wolf making up the
hill.   The animal came at a lagging pace, and was evidently
much blown.   Hepborne hurled his hunting-spear at him without a moment's delay, wounding him desperately in the neck ;
and, eager to make sure of him with his anelace, rushed forward,
without perceiving a sudden declivity, where there was a little
precipitous face of rock, over which he fell headlong, and rolling
downwards his head came in contact with the trunk of an oak,
at the foot of which he lay stunned and senseless.   The wolf,
writhing for sometime with the agony of the wound he had
received, succeeded at last in extricating himself from the spear-
head, and then observing the man from whose hand he had
received it, lying at his mercy on the ground near him, he was
about to take instant vengeance on him, when he was suddenly
called on to defend himself against a new assailant.

This was no other than poor Flo, who, having followed his
master's track as fast as his old legs could carry him, came up
at the very moment the gaunt animal was about to fasten his
jaws on him.   His ancient spirit grew young within him as he
beheld his master's danger.   He sprang on the wolf with an
energy and fury which no one who had seen him that morning
could have believed him capable of, and, seizing his ferocious
adversary by the throat, a bloody combat ensued between them.

Hepborne having gradually recovered from his swoon, and
hearing the noise of the fight, roused himself, and, getting upon
his legs, beheld with astonishment the miraculous exertions his

faithful dog was making in his defence, and the deadly strife that was waging between him and the wolf. The fierce and powerful animal was much an overmatch for the good allounde, who had already received some dreadful bites, but still fought with unabated resolution. Hepborne ran to his rescue, and burying his anelace in the wolf's body, killed him outright. But his help came too late for poor old Flo, who licked the kind hand that was stretched out to succour and caress him, and, turning upon his side, raised his dim eyes towards his master's face, and slowly closed them in death.

Hepborne lifted him up, all streaming with blood, and, carrying him to a fountain a few paces off, bathed his head and his gaping wounds, with the vain hope that the water might revive him ; but life was extinct. Sir Patrick laid him on the ground, and wept over him as if he had been a friend.

The sound of the horns now came nearer, the yell of the dogs approached, and by and by some of the hounds appeared, and ran in upon their already inanimate prey. Immediately behind them came Sir Patrick Hepborne the elder, a powerful, noble-looking man, in full vigour of life, mounted on a gallant grey, and with a crowd of foresters at his back. He took off his hunting hat to wipe his brow as he halted, and though he displayed a bald forehead, the hinder part of his head was covered with luxuriant black hair, on which age's winter had not yet shed a single particle of snow. His beard and moustaches were of the same raven hue ; and his eyes, though mild, were lofty and penetrating in their expression.

" How now, young man," said he to his son, as he reined up his steed, " what, hast thou killed the wolf ? "

" My father ! " cried the younger Sir Patrick, starting up and running to his stirrup.

" My son ! " exclaimed the delighted and astonished Sir Patrick the elder ; and, vaulting from his horse, they were immediately locked in each other's arms.

It was some minutes before either father or son could articulate anything but broken sentences. The minds of both reverted to the overwhelming loss they had sustained since they last saw each other, and they both wept bitterly.

" My dear boy, forgive me," said the father ; " but these tears are—we have lost—but yet I see thou hast already gathered the sad intelligence. 'Tis now three months—Oh, bitter affliction !—but she is a saint above, my dear Patrick."

Again they enclasped each other, and, giving way to their feelings, the two warriors wept on each other's bosoms, till the rude group of foresters around them were melted into tears at the spectacle. Sir Patrick the elder was the first to regain command of himself, and the first use he made of the power of speech was to put a thousand questions to his son. The younger knight satisfied him as to everything, and concluded by giving him the history of his accident, and the glorious but afflicting death of his faithful old allounde.

" Poor fellow," said the elder Sir Patrick, going up to the spot where he lay, and dropping a tear of gratitude over him— " poor fellow, he has died as a hero ought to do—nobly, in stark stoure in the field. Let him be forthwith yirded, dost hear me, on the spot where he fell ; I shall have a stone erected over him, in grateful memorial of his having died for his master."

Some of the foresters, who had implements for digging out the vermin of the chase, instantly executed this command, and the two knights tarried until they had themselves laid his body in the grave dug for him.

" And now let us go look for Isabelle and thy friend Sir John Assueton," said the elder Sir Patrick. " Sound thy bugles, my merry men, and let us down to the broad-lawnde, where we shall have the best chance of meeting."

They had no sooner entered the beautiful glade among the woods alluded to by the elder knight, than the younger Sir Patrick descried his sister, the Lady Isabelle, coming riding on her palfrey, and his friend Assueton leading her bridle-rein. He ran forward to embrace her, and she, instantly recognizing him, sprang from the saddle into his arms. The meeting between the brother and sister was rendered as affecting by the remembrance of the loss of their mother, as that of the father and son had been. But the elder Sir Patrick having mastered his feelings, soon contributed to soothe theirs. The younger Sir Patrick introduced his friend Assueton to his father, and after their compliments of courtesy were made, the adventures of both parties detailed, and mutual congratulations had taken place between them—

" Come," said the elder Sir Patrick, " come Isabelle, get thee to horse again, and let us straightway to the Castle. The welkin reddens i' the west, and the sun is about to hide his head among yonder amber clouds ; let us to the Castle, I say. I trow we shall have enow of food for talk for the rest of the evening. We shall have the spoils of these wolves hung up in the hall, in memorial of the strange events of this day—of the gallantry of the Lady Isabelle, who so nobly rescued Sir John Assueton, and of the courage and fidelity of the attached old alloundc Flo, who so nobly died in defence of his master."

The bugles sounded a mot, and the elder Sir Patrick, with his son walking by his side, moved forward at the head of the troop. The Lady Isabelle sprang into her saddle, and Sir John Assueton, never choosing to resign the reign he had grasped, led her palfrey as before, and again glided into the same train of conversation with her which he had formerly found so fascinating. The foresters, grooms, and churls who formed the hunting suite, some on foot and others on horseback, armed with every variety of hunting-gear, followed in the rear of march, and in this order they returned to the Castle.

CHAPTER XII.

The Freaks of Love at Hailes Castle—The Tournament at Tarnawa announced.

THE affliction which had so lately visited the elder Sir Patrick Hepborne had made him avoid company, and Hailes Castle had consequently been entirely without guests ever since his lady's death. But it must not be imagined that the evening of the hunting day passed dully because the board was not filled. The sweet and soothing sorrow awakened by tender and melancholy reflections soon gave way before the joy arising from the return of Sir Patrick the younger. In those days letters could not pass as they do now, with the velocity of the winds, by posts and couriers, from one part of Europe to another; and, during Hepborne's absence, his father had had no tidings of his son, except occasionally through the medium of those warriors or pilgrims who, having fought in foreign fields, or visited foreign shrines, had chanced during their travels to see or hear of him, and who came to Hailes Castle to receive the liberal guerdon of his hospitality for the good news they brought. The elder Sir Patrick, therefore, had much to ask, and the son much to answer; so that the ball of conversation was unremittingly kept up between them.

The Lady Isabelle was seated between her brother and his friend Sir John Assueton, in the most provoking position; for she was thus placed, as it were, between two magnets, so as to be equally attracted by both. Her affection for Sir Patrick made her anxious to catch all he said, and to gather all his adventures; whilst, on the other hand, Sir John Assueton's con-

7

versation, made up, as it in a great measure was, of the praises
of his friend, intermixed with many interesting notes on the
accounts of battles and passages of arms her brother was narrat-
ing to her father, proved so seducing that she found it difficult
to turn away her ear from him.   Nor were Assueton's illustrations the less gratifying that they often brought out the whole
truth, where her brother's modesty induced him to sink such
parts of the tale as were the most glorious to himself.   As for
Assueton himself, he seemed to have become a new man in her
company.   He was naturally shrewd, excessively good-humoured,
and often witty in his conversation, but he never in his life
before bestowed more of it on a lady than barely what the
courtesy of chivalry required.   This night, however, he was
animated and eloquent; and the result was, that the Lady
Isabelle retired to her couch at an unusually late hour, and
declared to her handmaiden, Mary Hay, as she was undressing
her, that Sir John Assueton was certainly the most gallant,
witty, and agreeable knight she had ever had the good fortune
to meet with.

" But thou dost not think him so handsome as thy brother
Sir Patrick, Lady ?" said the sly Miss Mary Hay.

" Nay, as to that, Mary," replied the Lady Isabelle, "they
are both handsome, yet both very diverse in their beauty.   Thou
knowest that one is fair, and the other dark.   My brother, Sir
Patrick, and I, do take our fair tint from our poor mother.   Is
it not common for fair to affect dark, and dark fair?   My father,
thou seest, is dark, yet was my dear departed mother fair as the
light of day.   Is it unnatural, then, that I should esteem Sir
John Assueton's olive tint of countenance, his speaking black
eyes, his nobly-arched jet eyebrows, and the raven curls of his
finely-formed head, more than the pure red and white complexion, the blue eyes and the fair hair of my dear brother !
Nay, nay, my brother is very handsome; but algate he be my
brother, and though I love him, as sure never sister loved
brother before, yet must I tell the truth, thou knowest, Mary ;
and, in good fay, I do think Sir John Assueton by much the
properer man."

Hepborne had been by no means blind to that of which
neither his sister nor Sir John Assueton were, as yet, themselves
aware.   He saw the change on Assueton with extreme delight.
He enjoyed the idea of this woman-hater being at last himself
enslaved, and, above all, he rejoiced that the enslaver should be
his sister, the Lady Isabelle.   He longed to attack him on the
subject; but, lest he might scare him away from the toils before

he was fairly and irrecoverably meshed, he resolved to appear to shut his eyes to his friend's incipient disease. As he went with Sir John, therefore, to see him comfortably accommodated for the night, he only indulged himself in a remark, natural enough in itself, upon his wounded arm.

"Assueton," said he, "wilt thou not have thine arm dressed by some cunning leech ere thou goest to rest? ,Our chaplain is no mean proficient in leechcraft; better take that rag of a kerchief away, and have it properly bound up."

"Nay, nay," cried Assueton, hastily, "I thank thee, my good friend; but 'tis very well as it is. Thy sister, the Lady Isabelle, bound it up with exceeding care; and in these cases 1 have remarked that there is no salve equal in virtue to the bloody goutes of the wound itself. Good night, and St. Andrew be with thee."

"And may St. Baldrid, our tutelary saint, be with you," replied Hepborne, as he shut the door. "Poor Assueton," said he then to himself, with a smile, "my sister has cured one wound for him, only to inflict another, which he will find it more difficult to salve."

The next day being devoted to the gay amusement of hawking, was yet more decisive of the fate of poor Sir John Assueton. He rode by the side of the Lady Isabelle; and as the nature of the sport precluded the possibility of her using that attention necessary to make her palfrey avoid the obstacles lying in its way, or to keep it up when it stumbled, Sir John found a ready excuse for again acting the part of her knight; and, one-armed as he had been rendered by the bites of the wolf, he ran all manner of risks of his own neck to save hers. Hepborne was more occupied in regarding them than in the sport they were following. He rode after the pair, enjoying all he saw; for in the malicious pleasure he took in perceiving Assueton getting deeper and deeper entangled in the snares of love, and its fever mounting higher and higher into his brain, he almost forgot the toils he had himself been caught in, and found a palliative for his own heart's disease, producing a temporary relaxation of its intensity. Thus then they rode. When the game was on wing, the fair Isabelle galloped fearlessly on, with her eyes sometimes following the flight of the falcon after its quarry, but much oftener with her head turned towards Sir John Assueton, whilst Sir John's looks were fixed now with anxiety on the ground, to ensure safe riding to the lady, and now thrown with love-sick gaze of tenderness into the heaven of her eyes, for his had no wish to soar higher.

In the evening, the Lady Isabelle and her knight were again left to themselves by the father and son. Her brother's tales were less interesting to her than they had been the previous night, and though Assueton talked less of his friend, yet she by no means found his conversation duller on that account; nay, she even listened much more intensely to it than before. The younger Sir Patrick, towards the close of the night, begged of his sister to sit down to her harp, and when she did so, Assueton hung over her with a rapture sufficiently marking the strength of his new-born passion, and the little art he had in concealing it.

Having been asked by her brother to sing, she accompanied her voice in the following canzonette :—

> Why was celestial Music given,
>   But of enchanting love to sing !
> Ethereal flame, that first from heaven
>   Angels to this earth did bring.
>
> What state was man's till he received
>   The genial blessing from the sky ?
> What though in Paradise he lived ?
>   Yet still he pined, and knew not why.
>
> But when his beauteous partner came,
>   The scene, that dreary was and wild,
> Grew lovely as he felt the flame,
>   And the luxuriant garden smiled.
>
> Oh, Love!—of man thou second soul,
>   What but a clod of earth is he
> Who never yet thy flame did thole,
>   Who never felt thy witchery !

Assueton's applauses were more energetic, and his approbation more eloquently expressed at the conclusion of this song, than Hepborne had ever heard them on any former occasion. Though the theme was wont to be so very unpalatable to him, yet he besought the Lady Isabelle again and again to repeat it, and it seemed to give him new and increased pleasure every time he heard it. At last the hour for retiring came, and Hepborne inwardly rejoiced to observe a certain trembling in the voices of both Assueton and his sister, as they touched each other's hands to say good night.

Sir Patrick Hepborne the younger had no sooner accompanied his friend to his apartment than Assueton seated himself near the hearth, and put up his feet against the wall, where he fell into a kind of listless dream. Hepborne took a seat on the opposite side of the fire-place, and, after he had sat silently watching him for some time, in secret enjoyment of the state

he beheld him reduced to, the following conversation took place
between them :—

"Well, Assueton," said Hepborne, first breaking silence, and
assuming as melancholy a tone as the humour he was in would
permit him to use, "Well, mon bel ami, so we must part to-
morrow? The thought is most distressing. My heart would
have urged me to press thee to a farther sojourn with us at
Hailes; but thou wert too determined, and urged too many and
too strong reasons for thy return home, when we last talked of
the matter, to leave room for hope that I might succeed in
shaking thy purpose. I see that of very needscost thou must
go; nay, in good sooth, thy motives for departure are of a
nature that, feeling as I have myself felt, I should inwardly
blame thee were thy good nature to lead thee to yield to my
importunate entreaty. Yea, albeit thou shouldst consent to stay
with me, I should verily tine half the jovisaunce that mought
otherwise spring from thy good company; since, from the all-
perfect being I now hold thee to be, thou wouldst dwindle in
my esteem, and be agrutched of half the attraction thou dost
possess in mine eyes, by appearing to lose some deal of those
strong feelings of attachment for thy home, and for the scenes
and friends of thy boyhood, which thou hast hitherto so eminently displayed, and in which, I am led to think, we do so
much resemble each other. Having now had mine somewhat
satisfied, perdie, I could almost wish to boune me with thee,
were it only to participate in thine—were it only to see thee
approach the wide domains and the ancient castle of thine
ancestors—to see thee meet thy beloved mother, now so long
widowed, and panting to press her only child, her long absent
son, to her bosom—to watch how thou mayst encounter with
old friends—to behold the hearty shakes of loving souvenaunce,
given by thy hand to those with whom thou hast wrestled, or
held mimic tourney when thou wert yet but a stripling. Oh,
'twould be as a prolonging of mine own feelings of like sort to
witness those that might arise to thee. But the journey is too
long for me to take as yet; and besides, I cannot yet so soon
leave my father and Isabelle. Moreover, thou knowest that my
heart yet acheth severely from the wounds which it took at
Norham. Heigh ho! But, gramercy, forgive me, I entreat
thee, for touching unwittingly on the (by thee) hated subject of
love, the which, I well know, is ever wont to erke thee."

During this long address, Assueton remained with his heels
up against the wall, his toes all the time beating that species
of march that in more modern times has been called the devil's

tattoo, and with his eyes firmly fixed on the embers consuming
on the hearth.

"I hope, however, my dearest friend," continued Hepborne,
"that thou mayest yet be able to return to me at Hailes. Thine
affairs (though, perdie, thou must have much to settle after such
a succession, and so long an absence), thine affairs, I say, cannot
at the worst detain thee at home longer than a matter of twelve
months or so; after which (that is, when thou shalt have visited
thy friends in divers other parts) I may hope perchance to see
thee again return hither."

Assueton shifted his position two or three times during this
second speech of Hepborne's, always again commencing his
devil's tattoo on the wall; but when his friend ceased, he made
no other reply than—

"Umph! Ay, ay, my dear Hepborne, thou shalt see me."

"My dear Assueton," continued Hepborne, "that is but a
loose and vague reply, I ween. But, by St. Genevieve, I guess
how it is. Thou hast thoughts (though as yet thou wouldst fain
not effunde them to me) of returning to France in short space;
and thou wouldst keep them sicker in thy breast for a time, lest
peradventure I should grieve too deeply at thy so speedy abandonment of thy country."

"Nay, nay," said Assueton, hastily, "trust me I have no
such emprize in head."

"What then can make thee so little satisfactory in thy
reply?" said Hepborne; "surely 'tis but a small matter to grant
me; 'tis but a small boon to ask of thee to return to Hailes Castle
some twelve months or year and half hence? I doubt me sore
that thou hast been but half pleased with thy visit here; and
truly, when I think on't, it has been but a dull one."

"Nay," replied Assueton, eagerly interrupting him, "I do
assure thee, Hepborne, thou art grievously mistaken in so supposing. On the contrary, my hours never passed so happily as
they have done here; nor," added he, with a deep sigh, "so
swiftly, so very swiftly."

"'Tis all well in thee, Assueton," said Hepborne, "'tis all
well in thee to use thy courtesy to say so; yet, I wot well, 'tis
but to please thy friend. Thou knowest that my father hath
been so voracious in his inquiries into the history of my life
during my stay in France, that he hath never suffered me to
leave him, so that thou hadst neither his good company nor my
poor converse to cheer thee, but, much to my distress, thou hast
been left to be erked by the silly prattle and trifling speech of
that foolish pusel my sister Isabelle, worn out by the which, 'tis

no marvel thou shouldst now be thus moody, as I see thou art ; and to rid thyself of this dreriment of thine, it is natural enow that thou shouldst be right glad to escape hence, yea, and sore afraid ever to return here. But fear thee not, my friend ; she shall not stand long in thy way. She hath had many offers of espousal, on the which my father and I are to sit in counsel anon, that is, when other weightier matters are despatched ; and as soon as we shall have time to choose a fitting match for the maid, she shall forthwith be tochered off. She cannot, then, remain much longer at Hailes than some three or four weeks at farthest, to frighten from its hall my best and dearest friend. So that if she be the hindrance to thy return thither, make no account of her, and promise me at once that thou wilt come. By St. Baldrid, we shall have a houseful of jolly stalwart knights to meet thee there ; and our talk shall be of deeds of arms, and tourneys, till thy heart be fully contented."

This speech of Hepborne's very much moved Assueton. He shifted his legs down from the wall and up again at least a dozen times, and his tattoo now became so rapid, that it would have troubled the legions for whom the march may have been originally composed to have kept their feet trotting in time to its measure.

"Nay, verily, Hepborne," said he seriously, "thou dost thy sister but scrimp justice, methinks. The Lady Isabelle was anything but tiresome to me ; nay, if I may adventure to say so much, she hath sense and judgment greatly beyond what might be looked for from her age and sex ; there is something most truly pleasing in her converse—something, I would say, much superior to anything I have heretofore chanced to encounter in woman. But, methinks thou art rather hasty in thy disposal of her. The damosel is young enow, meseems, to be thrust forth of her father's boure, perhaps to take upon her the weight of formal state that appertaineth to the Madame of some stiff and stern vavesoure. Perdie, I cannot think with patience of her being so bestowed already ; 'twould be cruel, methinks— nay, 'twould, in good verity, be most unlike thee, Hepborne, to throw thy peerless sister away on some harsh lord, or silly gnoffe, merely to rid thy father's castle of her for thine own convenience. Fie on thee ; I weened not thou couldst have even thought of anything so selfish."

"Nay, be not angry, Assueton," said Hepborne, "thou knowest that they have all a wish to wed them. But 'tis somewhat strange, methinks, to hear thee talk so ; the poppet seems to have made more impression on thee than ever before was

made by woman. What means this warmth ? or why shouldst
thou step forth to be her knight?"

" 'Tis the part of a good knight," replied Assueton hastily,
" to aid and succour all damosels in distress."

" Nay, but not against a distress of the knight's own fancying, yea, and contrary to the wishes of the damosel herself,"
replied Hepborne.   " What! wouldst thou throw down the
gauntlet of defiance against thy friend, only for being willing to
give his sister the man of her own heart ?"

" And hath she then such?" exclaimed Assueton, his face
suddenly becoming the very emblem of woe-begone anxiety.

" Yea, in good truth hath she, Assueton," replied Sir Patrick.
" I did but suspect the truth last night, but this day I have
been confirmed in it."

" Then am I the most wretched of knights," cried Assueton,
at once forgetting all his guards ; and rising hastily from his
seat, he struck his breast, and paced the room in a frenzy of
despair.

Hepborne could carry on the farce no longer.   He burst into
a fit of laughter that seemed to threaten his immediate dissolution ; then threw himself on the couch, that he might give full
way to it without fear of falling on the floor, and there he tossed
to and fro with the reiterated convulsions it occasioned him.
Assueton stood in mute astonishment for some moments, but at
last he began to perceive that his friend had discovered his
weakness, and that he had been all this time playing on him.
He resumed his seat and position at the hearth, and returned
again to his tattoo

" So," said Hepborne—" so—ha, ha, ha !—so !—ha, ha !—
so !—Oh, I shall never find breath to speak—ha, ha, ha ! So,
Sir John Assueton, the woman-hater, the knight of Adamant,
he who was wont to be known in France by the surnoms of the
Knight sans Amour, and the Chevalier cœur caillou—who, rather
than submit to talk to a woman, would hie him to the stable, to
hold grave converse with his horse—who railed roundly at every
unfortunate man that, following the ensample of his great an-
cestor Adam, did but submit himself to the yoke of love—who
could not bear to hear the very name of love—who sickened
when it was mentioned—who had an absolute antipathy to
it, as some, they know not why, have to cats or cheese—who,
though he liked music to admiration, would avoid the place
if love but chanced to be the minstrel's theme ;—he, Sir John
Assueton, is at last enslaved, has his wounds bound up by
a woman, and wears her scarf—plays the lady's knight, and

leads her palfrey rein—rownes soft things in her ear, hangs o'er her harp, and drinks in the sweet love-verses she sings to him !"

"Nay, nay, Hepborne, my dearest friend," said Assueton, starting up, and clasping his hands together in an imploring attitude, " I confess, I confess ; but sith I do confess, have mercy on me, I entreat thee ; 'tis cruel to sport with my sufferings, since thou knowest, alas, too surely that I must love in vain."

" But, pr'ythee, ' why shouldst thou afflict thyself, and peak and pine for a silly girl ?'" said Hepborne ironically, bringing up against him some of the very expressions he had used to himself at Norham.   "'A knight of thy prowess in the field may have a thousand baubles as fair for the mere picking up ; let it not erke thee that this trifle is beyond thy reach.'"   And then rising, and striding gravely up to Assueton, and shaking his head solemnly—"'Trust me, women are dangerous flowers to pluck, and have less of the rose about them than the thorn.'   Ha, ha, ha !   Oh, 'tis exquisite—by St. Dennis, 'tis the richest treat I ever enjoyed."

" Nay, but bethink thee, my dear friend," said Assueton, with an imploring look; " bethink thee, I beseech thee, what misery I am enduring, and reflect how much thou art augmenting it by thy raillery.   Depardieux, I believe thou never didst suffer such pain from love as I do now."

" ' No, thank my good stars,'" said Hepborne, returning to the charge, and again assuming a burlesque solemnity of air and tone, " 'and I hope, moreover, I never shall be so besotted : it makes a very fool of a man.'"

" Well, well," said Assueton, sighing deeply, " I see thou art determined to make my fatal disease thy sport; yet, by St. Andrew, it is but cruel and ungenerous of thee."

" Grammercy, Assueton, I thought my innocent raillery could do thee no harm," said Hepborne; " methought that ' thou mightst be said to have no ears for such matters.'   But if thou in good truth hast really caught the fever, verily I shall not desert thee, ' my friendship for thee shall make me listen to thy ravings;' yea, and ' compassion for thy disease shall make me watch the progress of its symptoms.   Never fear that I shall be so little of a Christian knight as to abandon thee when thy estate is so dangerous.'   But what, I pr'ythee, my friend, hath induced this so dangerous malady ? "

" Hepborne," replied Sir John, " thy angelic sister's magnanimity, her matchless beauty, her enchanting converse, and her sweet syren voice."

" Ay, ay," said Hepborne roguishly ; " so 'twas her voice, her warbles, and her virelays that gave thee the coup-de-grace ? Nay, it must be soothly confessed, thou didst hang over her chair to-night in a most proper love-like fashion, as she harped it; yet her verses ' were silly enough in conscience, methought ' —and then, thou knowest, thou dost ' rarely listen to music when love or follies are the theme.' "

" Hepborne," said Assueton gravely, and with an air of entreaty, " it was not after this fashion that I did use thee in thine affliction at Norham.   Think, I beseech thee, that my case is not less hopeless than thine.   But who, I entreat thee, is the happy knight who is blessed by the favouring smile of thy divine sister, of the Lady Isabelle Hepborne, whom I now no longer blush to declare to be the most peerless damosel presently in existence ? "

" He is a knight," replied Hepborne, " whose peer thou shalt as rarely meet with, I trow, as thou canst encounter the make of my sister, the Lady Isabelle.   He is a proper, tall, athletic, handsome man, of dark hair and olive complexion, with trim moustaches and comely beard—nay, the very man, in short, to take a woman's eye.   Though as yet but young in age, he is old in arms, and hath already done such doughty deeds as have made him renowned even in the very songs of the minstrels. Moreover, he is a beloved friend of mine, and one much approved of my father, and he shall gladly have our consent for the espousal of my sister."

" Nay, then," said Assueton, in the accents of utter hope-lessness, " I am indeed but a lost knight, and must hie me to some barren wilderness to sigh my soul away.   But lest my disease should drive me to madness, tell me, I entreat thee, the name of this most fortunate of men, that I may keep me from his path, lest, in my blind fury, I might destroy him in some ill-starred contecke, and through him wrack the happiness of the Lady Isabelle, now dearer to me than life."

" Thou knowest him as well as thou dost thyself, my dear Assueton," said Hepborne.   " Trust me, he is one to whom thou dost wish much too well to do him harm.   His name is—Sir John Assueton."

" Nay, mock me not, Hepborne, drive me not mad with false hopes," said Assueton; " certes, thy raillery doth now exceed the bounds that even friendship should permit."

" Grammercy," said Hepborne, " thou dost seem to me to be mad enough already.   What ! wouldst thou quarrel with me for giving thee assurance of that thou hast most panted for ?

By the honour of a knight, I swear that Isabelle loves thee. 'Tis true, I heard it not from her lips; but I read it in her eyes, the which, let me tell thee, inexperienced in the science, and all unlearned in the leden of love as thou art, do ever furnish by far the best and soothest evidence on this point that the riddle woman can yield. Never doubt me but she loves thee, Assueton. She drank up the words thou didst rowne in her ear with a thirst that showed the growing fever of her soul. And now," continued he, as he observed the happy effects of the intelligence upon the countenance of his friend—" and now, Assueton, tell me, I pr'ythee, at what hour in the morning shall I order thine esquire and cortege to be ready for thy departure?"

" Hepborne," said Assueton, running to embrace him, " thou hast made me the happiest of mortals. Go! nay, perdie, I shall stay at Hailes till thou dost turn me out."

" But, my dearest Assueton," cried Hepborne, smiling, " consider thy mother, and the friends and the scenes of thy boyhood —consider what thou——"

" Pshaw, my dear Hepborne," cried Sir John, interrupting him, " no more on't, I entreat thee. Leave me, I beseech thee, to dreams of delight. Good night, and may the blessed Virgin and St. Andrew be thy warison, for this ecstacy of jovinaunce thou hast poured into my soul."

" Good night," said Hepborne, with a more serious air— " good night, my dear and long-tried brother-in-arms; and good night, my yet dearer brother by alliance, as I hope soon to call thee."

The meeting of the lovers on the next day was productive of more interesting conversation than any they had yet enjoyed; and although Assueton was, as his friend had said, a novice in the science and language of love, yet he caught up the knowledge of both with most marvellous expedition, and was listened to with blushing pleasure by the lovely Isabelle.

As the party was seated at breakfast, the sound of trumpets was heard followed by that of the trampling of horses in the court-yard, and immediately afterwards a herald, proudly arrayed, and followed by his pursuivants, was ushered into the hall.

" Sir Patrick Hepborne," said he, " and you, Sirs Knights, I come to announce to you and to the world, that on the tenth day of the next month, the noble John Dunbar, Earl of Moray, will hold a splendid meeting of arms on the mead of St. John's; and all princes, lords, barons, knights, and esquires, who intend to tilt at the tournament, are hereby ordained to lodge themselves within his Castle of Tarnawa, or in pavilions on the field, four days before the said tournament, to make due display of their armouries, on pain of not being received at the said tournament. And their arms shall be thus disposed : The crest shall be placed on a plate of copper large enough to contain the whole summit of the helmet, and the said plate shall be covered with a mantle, whereon shall be blazoned the arms of him who bears it ; and on the said mantle at the top thereof shall the crest be placed, and around it shall be a wreath of colours, whatsoever it shall please him. God save King Robert ! "

The herald having in this manner formally pronounced the proclamation entrusted to him, was kindly and honourably greeted by Sir Patrick Hepborne, and forthwith seated at the board and hospitably entertained, after which he arose and addressed the knight.

"Sir Patrick Hepborne," said he, " myself and my people, being now refreshed, I may not waste my time here, having yet a large district to travel over. I drink this cup of wine to thee and to thy roof-tree, with a herald's thanks for thy noble treatment. Say, shall the Lord of Moray look for thy presence at the tourney ? I know it would be his wish to do thee and thine particular honour."

"Of that I may judge by his sending thee to Hailes," said Sir Patrick courteously. " But in truth I cannot go. I must leave it to thee to tell the noble Earl how sorely grieved I am to say so ; but my heart ha' been ill at ease of late."

" Thine absence will sorely grieve the noble Earl, Sir Knight," replied the herald, " but, natheless, I shall hope to see thy gallant son, and the renowned Sir John Assueton, chiefest flowers in the gay garland of Scottish knights, who shall that day assemble at St. John's. Till then adieu, Sirs Knights, and may God and St. Andrew be with ye all."

The trumpets again sounded, and the herald, being waited on by the knights to the court-yard, mounted his richly caparisoned steed, and rode forth from the castle, again attended by all the pomp of heraldry.

" Assueton," said Hepborne, with a roguish air of seriousness, as they returned up stairs, " goest thou to this tourney ? "

" Nay, of a truth," replied Assueton, with his eyes on the ground. " I cannot just at present yede me so far. Besides, these wounds in my bridle-arm do still pain me grievously, rendering me all unfit for jousting."

" Then, as 1 am resolved to go," said Hepborne, " I do beseech thee make Hailes Castle thy home till my return, and play the part of son to my dear father in mine absence."

CHAPTER XIII.

Sir Patrick Hepborne's Departure for the North—Consternation at the Castle.

As the way was long, and the day of the tournament not very distant, Sir Patrick Hepborne the younger resolved to leave Hailes Castle next morning for the North, that he might save himself the necessity of forced marches. He accordingly made instant preparations for his journey; his father gave immediate orders for securing him a cortege as should not disgrace the name he bore; and his horses, arms, and appointments of every description were perfectly befitting his family and rank. When the morning of his departure arrived, he took an affectionate leave of his father and Assueton, who left the Castle with their attendants at an early hour, for the purpose of hunting together. The Lady Isabelle would gladly have made one of the party with her father and her lover, but, attached as she was to Sir John Assueton, her affection for her brother was too strong to permit her to leave the Castle till he should be gone. That he might enjoy her society in private till the last moment, Hepborne despatched his faithful esquire, Mr. Mortimer Sang, at the head of his people, to wait for him at a particular spot, which he indicated, at the distance of about a mile from the Castle; and he also sent forward the palfrey he meant to ride, for his noble destrier Beaufront was to be led by a groom during the whole march.

His fond Isabelle resolved to walk with him to the place where he was to meet his attendants, and accordingly the brother and sister set out together arm in arm.

Sir Patrick resolving to probe his sister's heart, adroitly turned the conversation on Sir John Assueton, and, with extreme ingenuity, touched on those agrémens and virtues which his friend evidently possessed, as well as on a number of weak and faulty points, both in person and manner, which he chose, for certain purposes, to feign in him, or greatly to exaggerate. In praising the former, the Lady Isabelle very much surpassed her brother; for, however highly he might laud his friend, she always found something yet more powerful and eloquent to say in his favour; but whenever Sir Patrick ventured to hint at any thing like a fault or a blemish, the lady was instantly up in arms, and made as brave a defence for him against her brother as she had done for him some days before against the wolf. This light skirmishing went on between them until they reached a knoll covered with tall oaks, whence they beheld the party, about to take shelter in the appointed grove of trees, on the meadow by the river's side, at a considerable distance below them.

"Isabelle," said Hepborne, taking her hand tenderly, "thou hast walked far enough, my love; let us rest here for an instant, and then part. Our converse hath not been vain. My just praise of Assueton, as well as the faults I pretended to find in him, were neither of them without an object. I wished ere I left thee to satisfy myself of the true state of thy little heart; for I should have never forgiven myself had I discovered that I had been mistaken, and that I had told what was not true, when I assured Assueton, as I did last night, that thou lovest him."

"Told Sir John Assueton that I love him?" exclaimed the Lady Isabelle, blushing with mingled surprise and confusion; "how couldst thou tell him so? and what dost thou know of my sentiments regarding him? Heavens! what will he think of me?"

"Why, well, passing well, my fair sister," said Hepborne; "make thyself easy on that score. He loves thee, believe me, as much as thou lovest him; so I leave thee to measure the length, breadth, height, and depth of his attachment by the dimensions of thine own. But as to knowing the state of thy heart—tut! I could make out much more difficult cases than it presents; for well I wot its state is apparent enough, even from the little talk I have had with thee now, if I had never heard or seen more. But, my dear Isabelle, after my father, thou and he are the two beings on earth whom I do most love. Ye are both perfect in mine eyes. I could talk to thee of Assueton's qualities and perfections for days together, and of virtues which as yet thou canst not have dreamt of; but I must leave thee to the delightful task of discovering them for thyself. All I can now say is, may heaven make ye both happy in each other— for I must be gone. And so, my love, farewell, and may the blessed Virgin protect thee."

He then threw his arms about his sister's neck, pressed her to his bosom, and, having kissed her repeatedly with the most tender affection, tore himself from her, ran down the hill, and, as she cleared her eyes from the tear-drops that swelled in them,

she saw him disappear in the shade of the clump of trees where
his party was stationed. A good deal of time seemed to be lost
ere the whole were mounted and in motion; but at last she
saw them emerging from the wood-shaw, and winding slowly, in
single files, up the river-side. She sat on the bank straining
her eyes after them until they were lost in the distant intricacies of the surface, and then turned her steps slowly homewards,
ruminating agreeably on her brother's last words, as well as on
the events of the preceding days, which had given her a new
and more powerful interest in life than she had ever before experienced.

"Oh, my dear brother," said she to herself, "thou didst indeed say truly that I do love him; and if thou sayest as soothly
that he doth love me, then am I blessed indeed."

It was courtesy alone that induced Sir John Assueton to
agree to Sir Patrick Hepborne's proposal of going that morning to the woodlands to hunt the deer. He went with no very
good will; nay, when his host talked of it, he felt more than
once inclined, as he had done with his friend about the tournament, to plead his wounded arm as an excuse for remaining at
home with the Lady Isabelle; and, perhaps, if it had not been
for absolute shame, he might have yielded to the temptation.
Hence he had but little pleasure in the sport that day, although
it was unusually fine; and he was by no means gratified to
find himself led on by the chase to a very unusual distance.
But to leave Sir Patrick was impossible. He was therefore
compelled, very much against his inclination, to ride all
day like a lifeless trunk, whilst his spirit was hovering over
the far-off towers of Hailes Castle. The deer was killed so far
from home, that it was later than ordinary before the party
returned.

"I am surprised Isabelle is not already here to receive us,"
said Sir Patrick, as they entered the banquet hall; "I trowed
she might have been impatient for our return ere this. Gabriel,"
said he to the old seneschal, "go, I pr'ythee, to Mary Hay, and
let her tell her lady that we are come home, and that we have
brought good appetites with us."

Gabriel went, and soon returned with Mary Hay herself, who
appeared in great agitation.

"Where is thy lady?" demanded Sir Patrick, with an expression of considerable anxiety.

"My lady! my good lord," said the terrified girl; "holy St.
Baldrid! is she not with thee then?"

"No," said Sir Patrick, with increasing amazement and alarm,

" she went not with us. We left her here with my son, when he rode forth in the morning."

" Nay, I knew that," said the terrified Mary Hay, " but— good angels be about us—I weened that her pages and palfrey might have gone with thee, and that she might ha' been to join thee in the woods, after having given her brother the convoy."

" Merciful powers! did she leave the Castle with her brother?" " Good Heavens! hath she never been seen since morning?" exclaimed Sir Patrick and Assueton, both in the same breath, and looking eagerly in the faces of the people around them for something satisfactory ; but no one had seen her since morning. Some of the domestics ran out to question those who had kept guard ; but though she had been seen as she went out with her brother, neither warder or sentinel had observed her return. Meantime the whole Castle was searched over from garret to cellar by Assueton, Sir Patrick, and the servants, all without success.

The consternation and misery of the father and the lover were greater than language can describe. Broken sentences burst from them at short intervals, but altogether void of connection. A thousand conjectures were hazarded, and again abandoned as impossible. Plans of search without number were proposed, and then given up as hopeless ; while all they said, thought, or did, was without concert, and only calculated to show their utter distraction. But matters did not long continue thus.

" My horse, my horse!" cried the agonized and frenzied father ; and " My horse, my horse!" responded Assueton, in a state no less wild and despairing.

Both rushed down to the stable, and the horses which yet remained saddled from the chase being hurriedly brought out, they struck the spurs into their sweltering sides, and, almost without exchanging a word, galloped furiously from the gateway, each, as if by a species of instinct, taking a different way, and each followed by a handful of his people, who mounted in recking haste to attend his master. They scoured the woodlands, lawns, and alleys, from side to side, and all around ; they beat through the shaws and copses, and hollowed and shouted to the very cracking of their voices. By and by, to those who listened from the walls, their circles appeared to become wider, and their shouts were no longer heard. Forth rushed, one by one, as they could horse them in haste, or gird themselves for running, grooms, lacqueys, spearmen, billmen, bowmen, and foresters, until none were left within the place but the men on guard, the old, the feeble, and some of the women. Even Mary Hay ran

out into the woods, beating her breast, tearing her hair, screaming like a maniac, and searching wildly among the bushes, even
less rationally than those who had gone before her.

Sir Patrick, as he rode, began, in the midst of his affliction,
to collect his scattered ideas, and, calling to mind what they
had told him of Lady Isabelle having gone to convoy her
brother, he immediately halted from the unprofitable search he
was pursuing, and turned his horse's head towards that direction
which they must have necessarily taken. He rode on as far as
the knoll where the brother and sister had bid adieu to each
other, and there being a cluster of cottages at the bottom of the
hill, he made towards one of them himself, and sent his attendants to all the others in search of information. From several
of the churls, and from their wives, he learned that his son had
been seen taking an affectionate leave of a lady whom they now
supposed to have been the Lady Isabelle, among the oaks on
the knoll, and that he had afterwards joined his party, waiting
for him under the trees by the river's side, whilst the lady
seemed to turn back, as if to take the way to the Castle. With
this new scent, Sir Patrick made his panting horse breast the
hill, and, assisted by his men, beat the ground in close traverse,
backwards and forwards, from one side to another, with so great
care and minuteness that the smallest object could not have
escaped their observation. They tried all the by-routes that
might have been taken, but all without success; though they
spent so much time in the search that darkness had already
begun to descend over the earth ere they were compelled to de-
sist from it as hopeless.

They returned towards the Castle, still catching at the frail
chance, as they hurried thither, that though they had been unsuccessful, some one else might have been more fortunate, and
that probably the Lady Isabelle had been already brought back
in safety. But unhappily the guards, who crowded round them
at the gate, and to whom both master and men all at once
opened in accents of loud inquiry, had no such heart-healing
tidings to give them. They obtained such intelligence, however, as had awakened a spark of hope. Sir John Assueton
had returned a short time before Sir Patrick, with the horse he
had ridden so exhausted that the wretched animal had dropped
to the ground, and died instantly after his rider had quitted
the saddle. He had called loudly for fresh horses and a party
of spearmen, and had then rushed into the Castle to arm himself in haste; and a number of those who had gone to search independently having fortunately by this time come in one by one,

8

some fifteen or twenty bowmen, spearmen, and billmen had been hastily got together, and provided with brisk and still unbreathed horses. Without taking time, however, to give the particulars of what he had gathered, or to say whither he was bound, Sir John had merely called out to the guard, as he was mounting, to tell Sir Patrick, if he should return before him, that he had heard some tidings of the Lady Isabelle, and that he would bring her safely back, or perish in the attempt; and after having said so, he had given the word to his men and scoured off at the head of them in a southern direction.

The miserable father was more than ever perplexed by this information. From the preparations Sir John had so effectually though hastily made, it was evident that the scene of the enterprise he went on was distant; and that it was not without doubt or danger, appeared from the few words he had let fall. Could Sir Patrick have had any guess whither to go, he would have instantly armed himself, and such men as he could have got together, to follow and aid Sir John Assueton; but such a chase was evidently more wild and hopeless than the fruitless search he had just returned from; and the pitchy darkness which by this time prevailed was in itself an insurmountable obstacle to his discovering the route that Sir John had taken. He was compelled, therefore, most unwillingly and most sorrowfully, to give up all idea of further exertion for the present; but he resolved to start in the morning long ere the first lark had arisen from its nest, and, if he should hear nothing before then that might change his determination, to ride towards England. He accordingly gave orders to his esquires to have a body of armed horsemen ready equipped to accompany him, an hour before the first streak of red should tinge the eastern welkin.

Old Gabriel Lindsay, his dim eyes filled with tears, and altogether unable to take comfort to himself, came to make the vain attempt to administer it to his master, and to try to persuade him to take some rest. But all the efforts of the venerable seneschal were ineffectual, and the heartbroken father continued to pace the hall with agitated steps among his people, despatching them off by turns, and often running down to the gate, or to the ramparts, whenever his ear caught, or fancied it caught, a sound that might have indicated Assueton's return.

CHAPTER XIV.

The Pursuit — Surprising the Camp.

But it is now time to state the circumstances of Assueton's search, as well as the cause of his abrupt departure. If Sir Patrick, on first starting from the Castle, had ·been so little master of himself as to lose time by galloping over ground where it was next to impossible his daughter could be found, it was not at all likely that Sir John and his people, strangers as they were to the neighbourhood, could make a better selection. But it not unfrequently happens that chance, or (which is a much better word for it) Providence, does more than human prudence in such cases. After making two or three wild and rapid circles through the woods in the immediate vicinity of the Castle, like a stone whirled round in a sling, he flew off at a tangent southwards, and accidentally hit upon a solitary cottage about a couple or more miles from the Castle, where he learned that a small body of English spearmen had halted that morning, and that the leader had made a number of inquiries about the late and future motions of his friend the younger Sir Patrick Hepborne, and himself. These were well enough known, for the arrival of their young lord had excited universal joy among the population of his father's estate; the coming of the herald, with Hepborne's departure, were also matters too interesting to escape circulation; and the churl of the cottage had told, without reservation, all the circumstances to the strangers. He also learned that the party had gone on to reconnoitre the Castle; and that afterwards, as the rustic was making faggots at some distance from his dwelling, he had seen them sweeping by towards England. Assueton could not elicit from the peasant whether it had appeared to him that the Lady Isabelle was with them, because the man had had but an indistinct view of them as they rode through the woodlands; but he and his people were agreed that these must have been the perpetrators of the outrage. His judgment, now that it had a defined object, began to come into full play. He saw that his own horse and the horses of his attendants were too much spent to enable him to pursue on the spur of the moment, and, had it not been so, that it would be vain to go on such an expedition so slenderly accoutred and accompanied. He therefore galloped back to the Castle as hard as the exhausted animal could carry him, fol-

lowed at a distance by his straggling men ; and there he made
those rapid preparations and that hasty outset which we have
already noticed.

The night became extremely dark before Assueton had gone
many miles ; but, luckily for him, Robert Lindsay, the head
forester, happened to be one of his company, for without him,
or some other guide equally well acquainted with the country
he had to travel over, his expedition must have been rendered
abortive.   Even as it was, he found difficulty enough in threading the mazes of the Lammermoors ; and although Lindsay
knew every knoll, stone, bog, flow, and rivulet that diversified
their surface, they made divers deviations from the proper line,
and were much longer in crossing the ridge than they should
have been if favoured by the light of the moon. Towards morning they judged it prudent to halt on the brow of the hills, ere
they began to descend into the lower and more level country, that
they might make observations by the first light, and determine
both as to where they were and as to their future movements.

As objects below them began to grow somewhat distinct,
they found that they had posted themselves immediately over
the hollow mouth of a glen, opening on the flat country, where
a rivulet wound through some green meadows ; and they soon
began to descry several tents, pitched together in a cluster, with
a number of horses picquetted around them.

" By'r Lady," said Assueton, " yonder lie the ravishers. Let's
down upon them, my brave men, ere they have time to be
alarmed and fly."

He gave his horse the spur, and galloped down the slope at a
fearful pace, followed by his party, and having gained the
level, they charged towards the little encampment with the
swiftness of the wind.   The morning's mist that hung on the
side of the hill, and the imperfect grey light, had prevented the
sentinels who were on the watch from seeing the horsemen approaching until they had descended ; but they no sooner observed them coming on at the *pas de charge*, than the alarm
was given and a general commotion took place among them.
Out they came pouring from the tents to the number of forty
or fifty ; and there was such a hasty putting on of morrions and
skull-caps, and seizing of weapons, and loosing of halters, and
mounting of the few that had time to get on horseback, and
such a clamouring and shouting, and so much confusion, as
assured Assueton an easy victory, though their numbers were
so much greater than his.   He came on them at the head of
his small body like a whirlwind, and before half of them had

time to turn out, he was already within a hundred yards of their position. A few of them, armed with spears, had formed in line before the tents, apparently with the resolution of standing his charge, and at the head of these was an old man, hastily armed in a cuirass. He stood boldly planted with a lance in his hand, though his head was bare, and his white hairs hung loosely about his determined countenance. Sir John Assueton was on the very eve of bearing him and his little phalanx down before the irresistible fury of his onset, when he suddenly pulled up his reins, and halted his men.

"Sir Walter de Selby!" exclaimed he with astonishment, and raising his visor, that he might the better behold him.

"Sir John Assueton!" cried Sir Walter, "I crave truce and parley."

"Thou hast it, Sir Walter," said Assueton, "but only on one condition, that I see not any one attempt to escape hence, or stir from the position he is now in, until all matters be explained betwixt us. Pledge me thine honour that this shall be so, and I shall parley with thee in friendship, till I shall see just cause for other acting. But, by the Rood of St. Andrew, if a single knave shall seek to steal him away, or to quit the spot of earth that now bears him, I will put every man to death, saving thee only, whose white hairs and recent hospitality are pledges for thy security. Advance, Sir Walter; I swear by my knighthood that thy person shall take no hurt from my hands, or from the hands of any of my people."

"Thou comest, doubtless," said Sir Walter, "to seek after the Lady Isabelle Hepborne, the fair sister of thy friend Sir Patrick Hepborne."

"I do," said Sir John Assueton, eagerly; "and, by the blessed Virgin, an she be not immediately delivered up scathless into my custody, I will put every man but thyself to instant death. Shame, foul shame on thee, Sir Walter, to be the leader in a foray so disgraceful as this. Is this thy requital to Sir Patrick Hepborne for—— ? But, hold—I will not in my friend's name cast in thy teeth what he himself would scorn to throw at thee."

"Nay, Sir John Assueton, judge not so hastily, I entreat thee. What didst thou see in my behaviour at Norham that should lead thee to suspect me of the foul deed thou art now so ready to charge me withal? Were I capable of any such, perdie, thou mightest well pour out all this wrath and wrekery on this old head of mine. Listen to me, I beseech thee, with temper, and thou shalt soon know that I have had no hand in this unknightly outrage, the which nobody can more deplore than I do. It was Sir Miers de Willoughby who carried off the lady—God pity me for being related to one who could so disgrace me! But on him be the sin and the shame of the act."

"Nay, Sir Knight," cried Assueton, hastily, "seeing that he did it in thy company, thou canst not, methinks, shake thyself free of a share of both. But where is the recreant, that I may forthwith chastise him? And where is the lady? By all the saints in the kalendar, if she is not instantly produced, I will make every man in thy troop breakfast upon cold steel."

"As God is my judge, Sir Knight," said Sir Walter, "as God is my judge, mine own afflictions weigh not more heavily on my old heart at this moment than does the thought that I have been in some sort, though innocently, the occasion of this outrage having been done against the sister of the very knight for whom, of all others, gratitude would make me think it matter of joy to sacrifice this hoary head to do him service. There are some honourable gentlemen here present who can vouch for me that, forgetful of mine own bereavement, and the direful consequences that may follow it, I had resolved to abandon my own quest, and to go forward this morning to Hailes Castle to inform Sir Patrick Hepborne in person of all I know of this ill-starred and wicked transaction; and if thou wilt but listen to me, I shall tell it thee in as few words as may be."

"But the lady, Sir Knight, the lady?" cried Assueton, in a frenzy; "produce the lady instantly, else the parley holds not longer."

"By mine honour as a knight," cried the old man," "she is not here."

"Not here!" exclaimed Sir John Assueton, "not here! What, hast thou sent her forward to Norham? By the blessed bones of my ancestors," said he, digging his spurs through mere rage into his horse's sides, and checking him again, till he sprang into the air with the pain, "I shall not leave a stone of it together. Its blaze shall serve to light up the Border to-night in such fashion that every crone on Tweedside shall see to go to bed by it."

"She is not at Norham, Sir Knight," said Sir Walter, calmly; "she is not in my keeping, I most solemnly protest unto thee."

"Where is she then, in the name of St. Giles?" cried Assueton. "Tell me instantly, that I may fly to her rescue. Trifle no more with me, old man; thou dost wear out the precious minutes. Depardieux, my patience is none of the strongest e'en now; it won't hold out much longer, I tell thee,

for I am mad, stark mad; so tell me at once where she is, or
my rage may overcome my better feelings."

"Nay, Sir John Assueton," said Sir Walter de Selby, with a
forbearance and temper that, old as he was, he could never have
exercised had it not been for the feeling of what he owed to Sir
Patrick Hepborne and the consciousness that present appearances warranted the suspicion of his having been accessory to
the outrage committed against the Lady Isabelle; "I beseech
thee, Sir John Assueton, command thyself so far as to listen to
me for but a very few minutes; hadst thou done so earlier,
thou hadst ere this known everything. Interrupt me not, then,
I implore thee, and thou shalt be the sooner satisfied. This is
now the third morning since—unfortunate father that I am—I
discovered the sad malure which hath befallen me, and that I
was bereft of my daughter, the Lady Eleanore, who had been
mysteriously carried off during the night. Certain circumstances——"

"Nay, but, Sir Knight," said Assueton, interrupting him,
"what is thy daughter to me? What is she to the Lady Isabelle Hepborne? Ay, indeed, wretch that I am, what is she in
any way to the point?"

Sir Walter de Selby went on without noticing this fresh
interruption.

"Certain circumstances led some of the people about me to
believe that thy friend, Sir Patrick, had had some hand in the
rapt, and that he, or some of his people, had returned at night,
and, by some unexampled tapinage, found means unaccountable
to withdraw my daughter from the Castle. In the frenzy I was
thrown into by mine affliction, I was easily induced to believe
anything that was suggested to me; and, getting together my
people in a haste, I——"

"So," cried Assueton, "I see how it is; a vile thrust of vengeance led thee to make captive of the Lady Isabelle. Oh, base
and unworthy knight!"

"Nay, indeed, not so," said Sir Walter, eager to exculpate
himself; "I have already vowed I had no hand in anything so
base. 'Tis true, I set out with the mad intent of besieging
Hailes Castle, and demanding the restoration of my daughter.
To this I was much encouraged by Sir Miers de Willoughby,
who happened to be at Norham at the time, and who offered to
accompany me. I got no farther than this place that night;
and having had time to reflect by the way on the nature of the
enterprise I was boune on, as well as on the great improbability
of so foul suspicion being verified against a knight of thy friend

Sir Patrick's breeding and courtesy, I resolved to proceed with the utmost caution, lest I should even give cause of offence where no offence had been rendered.   As the most prudent measure I could adopt, and as that least likely to excite alarm, I resolved to pitch my little camp in this retired spot, and to send forward Sir Miers de Willoughby, who readily volunteered the duty, towards Hailes Castle, to make such inquiry of the peasants as might satisfy me of the truth or falsehood of my suspicions; and this, thou must grant me, Sir John Assueton, was as much delicacy as could be observed by me, in the anguished and bleeding state of my heart for the loss of my only child, and the impatience which I did naturally feel to gain tidings of her."   Here the old man's voice was for some moments choked by his tears; and Sir John Assueton was so much moved by them that he spake not a word.   Sir Walter proceeded—

"De Willoughby returned here last night about sunset. He came to my tent alone, and he did tell me that, from all he could learn, he believed that my daughter had not been carried thither, either by Sir Patrick or any other person.   'But,' added he, 'be Sir Patrick Hepborne guilty or innocent of this outrage against thee, I have made a capture that will be either paying off an old score, or scoring the first item of a new account against these Scots, for I have carried off the Lady Isabelle Hepborne.'   Struck with horror, and burning with rage to hear him tell this, I insisted on her being instantly brought to my tent, that I might forthwith calm her mind, and take immediate steps to return her in safety, with honourable escort, to her father.   'Give thyself no trouble about her,' said the libertine, treating all I said with contempt, 'for ere this she bounes her over the Border, on a palfrey led by my people.'   I was thunderstruck," continued the old man; "and ere I had time to recover myself so far as to be able to speak or act, de Willoughby sprang to the door of the tent, and I heard the clatter of his horse's heels as he galloped off.   I was infuriated : I felt that he had basely made me the scape-goat to his own caitiff plans, which I now began to suspect were not of recent hatching.   I despatched parties in every direction after him, but all of them returned, one by one, without having gained even the least intelligence of him.   And all this is true, on the word of an old knight.   God wot how well I do know to feel for the father of the damosel, sith I do suffer the same affliction myself."

The old knight was overpowered by his emotions; and

Assueton, who had been at length prevailed on to hear his tale to an end, gave way at the conclusion of it to a paroxysm of rage and grief, which might have well warranted the by-standers in believing he was really bereft of reason. He threw himself from his horse to the ground, in despair. Roger Riddel, his esquire, a quiet, temperate, and, generally, a very silent man, did all he could to soothe his master; and even old Sir Walter de Selby, sorrowful as he himself was, seemed to forget his wretchedness in endeavouring to assuage that which so un-manned the Scottish knight.

After giving way for some time to ineffectual ravings, the offspring of intense feeling, and having then vented his rage in threats against Sir Miers de Willoughby, Assueton began by de-grees to become more calm, and seeing the necessity of exerting his cool judgment, that he might determine how to act, he was at length persuaded by Sir Walter de Selby to go into his tent for a short time, till the horses and men could be refreshed. Sir Walter had no disposition to screen his unworthy relative from the wrath with which Assueton threatened him; or, if he had, he conceived himself bound to make it give way to a sense of justice. He therefore readily answered the Scottish knight's hasty questions, and told him that it was more than likely that the lady had been carried to a certain castle belong-ing to de Willoughby, situated about the Cheviot hills.

Assueton's impatience brooked no longer delay. Accord-ingly, with a soul agonized by the passions of love, grief, rage, and revenge, he summoned his party to horse, and set off at a furious pace on his anxious and uncertain quest.

CHAPTER XV.

Norham Castle again—The Ancient's Divination—Sir Walter Bewitched—The Franciscan Friar to the Rescue.

SIR WALTER DE SELBY, who was enduring all the bitterness of grief that a father could suffer, whose only child, a daughter too, on whose disposal hung a whole legion of superstitious hopes and fears, had been rent from him in a manner so mysterious, broke up his little camp with as much impatience as Assueton had exhibited. But age did not admit of his motions being so rapid as those of the younger knight. He moved, however, with all the celerity he could exert, for he remembered the warning flame which had appeared on the fatal shield; and the very thought of his daughter's disappearance, with the frightful consequences which might result from her being thus beyond his control, filled his heart with horror and dismay.   He was also exceedingly perplexed how the wizard, Master Ancient Haggerstone Fenwick, could have so erred in his divination as to occasion him the fruitless and mortifying expedition into Scotland ; for Sir Walter, in the first fever of distraction he was thrown into by the discovery of his daughter's disappearance, had immediately made his way to the aerial den of the Ancient. The cunning diviner instantly recollected that he had seen Sir Patrick Hepborne going towards the rampart, where he had reason to know the Lady Eleanore de Selby had been walking, from which he was led to suspect an appointment between them. He was too artful to make Sir Walter aware of this circumstance, but, proceeding upon it, he enacted some hasty farce of conjuration, and then with all due solemnity boldly and confidently pronounced that Sir Patrick Hepborne had secretly returned, and, obtaining possession of the person of the Lady Eleanore, had carried her over the Border.

Some time after Sir Walter de Selby had gone into Scotland, however, a discovery was accidentally made that seemed to throw light on the disappearance of his daughter.   The mantle she usually wore had been found by a patrole, at several miles' distance to the south of Norham, lying by the way-side leading towards Alnwick—a circumstance which left no doubt remaining that she had been carried off in that direction.   But ere this could be communicated to Sir Walter on his return, his impatience for an interview with his oracle was so great that, putting aside all obstructions, he hastened to climb to the den of the monster on the top of the keep.

" What sayest thou, Master Ancient Fenwick ?" said the old man, as he entered the cap-house door, his breath gone with the steepness of the ascent and the anxiety of his mind ; " for once thy skill seemeth to have failed thee."

The Ancient was seated in his usual corner, immersed in his favourite study : a large circle was delineated on the floor, and in the centre of it lay the Lady Eleanore's mantle.

" Blame, then, thine own impatience and haste," said the Ancient.   " The signs were drawn awry, and no wonder that the calculations were erroneous ; but thou wert not gone half-a-day until I discovered the error ; and now thou shalt thyself behold it remedied   Dost see there thy daughter's mantle ?"

The old man instantly recognized it ; and, looking at it in silence for some moments, the feelings of a sorrowing and bereft parent came upon him with all the strength of nature ; his heart and his eyes filled, and burst into a flood of tears. He stepped forward to lift it up and imprint kisses upon it; but the stern and unfeeling Ancient called out, in a harsh voice,—

"Touch it not, on thy life, else all my mystic labours have been in vain. Stand aloof there, and, if thou wilt, be a witness of the power I possess in diving into secrets that are hid from other men."

Sir Walter obeyed. The Ancient arose and struck a light ; and having darkened the loophole window, he lighted his lamp and put it into a corner. He then approached the circle, and squatting down, he with much labour and difficulty drew his unwieldy limbs within its compass, and, kneeling over the mantle, he proceeded to mutter to himself, from a book of necromancy which he held in his hand, turning the pages over with great rapidity, and making from time to time divers signs with his forefinger on his face and on the floor. After this he laid his head down on the pavement, covered it with the mantle, and continued to mutter uncouthly, and to writhe his body until he seemed to fall into a swoon. He lay motionless for a considerable time ; but at length he appeared to recover gradually, the writhing and the muttering recommenced, and raising up his body with the mantle hanging over his head and shoulders, he exposed his horrid features to view. To the inexpressible terror of Sir Walter, the forehead blazed with the same appalling flame which he had seen it bear on the night of his long interview with the wizard.

"Seek thy daughter in the South," said the Ancient, in a hollow voice ; "seek her from Sir Rafe Piersie. Remember thy destinies. The balance now wavers—now it turns against thee and thy destinies. If but an atom of time be lost, they are sealed, irrecoverably sealed."

Quick as the lightning of heaven did the ideas shoot through the old man's mind, as the Ancient was solemnly pronouncing this terrific response. He remembered that Sir Rafe Piersie had left Norham, in a litter, the very day preceding the night his daughter had disappeared ; and it flashed upon him that some of the grooms had remained behind their master, under pretence of one of his favourite horses having been taken ill, and had afterwards followed him during the night. That they must have found means to carry the Lady Eleanore off with them, was, he thought, but too manifest. The very name of Piersie, when uttered by the Ancient, had made Sir Walter's blood run cold, from his superstitious belief of the impending

fate that was connected with it ; and the weight of his feelings
operating on a body oppressed with fatigue and want of sleep,
and on a mind worn out with the agitation and affliction it had
undergone, became too much for nature to bear.   He grew
deadly pale.   He made an effort to speak, but his tongue became dry and cleaved to the roof of his mouth, and his lips
refused their office ; an indistinct, mumbling, moaning sound
was all that they could utter—his cheeks became rapidly convulsed—one corner of his mouth was drawn up to his ear, and
he fell backwards on the floor in a state of perfect insensibility.

Fenwick became alarmed.   He started up with the ghastly
look of a newly-convicted felon, and the fear of being accused
of the murder of Sir Walter came upon him.   He crept towards
the knight, and raising him up, made use of what means he
could to endeavour to restore him to life ; but all his efforts
were unsuccessful.   Trembling from the panic he was in, he
then lifted the old knight in his arms, and with great difficulty
conveyed him down the narrow stair to his own apartment.
Horror was depicted in the faces of the domestics when they
beheld the hated but dreaded monster bearing the bulky and
apparently lifeless body of their beloved master.   A wild cry
of grief and apprehension burst from them.   The Ancient laid
Sir Walter on the bed, and, as the attendants stood aloof and
aghast, he took up a small knife that lay near and pierced the
veins of both temples with the point of it.   The blood spouted
forth, and the knight began to show faint symptoms of life.
Never negligent of any circumstance that might raise his reputation for supernatural power, the Ancient now began to employ
a number of strange necromantic signs, and to utter a jargon of
unintelligible words in a low muttering tone, laying his hand at
one time on the face, and at another on the breast, of the semi-
animate body, that he might impress the bystanders with the
idea of his magic having restored Sir Walter to life ; for, seeing
the blood flow so freely, he anticipated the immediate and perfect recovery of the patient.   But he was mistaken in the extent
of his hopes.   Sir Walter opened his eyes, stared wildly about
him, and moved his lips as if endeavouring to speak ; but he
continued to lie on his back, altogether motionless, and quite
incapable of uttering a word.

The dismayed Ancient shuffled out of the apartment, and
hastily retired to his lofty citadel.   A murmur of disapprobation
broke out among the domestics the moment he was supposed
to be beyond hearing.   They crowded about their master's bedside, every one eager to do something.   All manner of restora-

tives were tried with him, but in vain. He seemed to be
perfectly unconscious of what they did, and he lay sunk in a
lethargy, from which nothing could rouse him.

Sir Walter was the idol of his people and garrison. By degrees the melancholy news spread through the keep of the
Castle, and thence into its courts, barracks, stables, guardhouses,
and along its very ramparts, until every soldier and sentinel in
the place became aware of the miserable condition of their beloved Governor, as well as of the immediate share which Master
Ancient Haggerstone Fenwick, the sorcerer, had had in producing it. General lamentations arose.

"Our good Governor is bewitched!"—"The monster Ancient
hath bewitched him!"—"The villain Fenwick drew his very
blood from him to help his sorcery!"—"What can be done?"—
"What shall we do?"—"Let us send forthwith for some holy
man."—"Let us send for the pious clerk of Tilmouth Chapel;
he hath good lore in sike cases."

The suggestion was approved by all, and accordingly a horseman was instantly despatched to bring the clerk with all possible
haste. The messenger speedily returned, unaccompanied, however, by the pious priest of Tilmouth, who chanced to be sick
in bed, but who had sent them a wayfaring Franciscan monk,
of whose potent power against magic he had largely spoken.
The holy man was immediately ushered into the Governor's
apartment. Having previously taken care to inform himself
of all the particulars of the case, from the horseman behind whom
he had been brought, he approached the bed with a solemn air
and surveyed Sir Walter for some time, as if in deep consideration of his state and appearance, with intent to discover his
malady. He looked into his eyes, felt him carefully all over,
and moved his helpless legs and arms to and fro. Meanwhile
the officers of the garrison, the attendants, and even some of
the soldiers, were awaiting anxiously in the room, about the
door, on the stairs, and on the bridge below, all eager to learn
the issue of his examination.

"Sir Walter de Selby is bewitched," said the Franciscan
at length, "and no human power can now restore him, so
long as the wretch, whoever he may be, who hath done this
foul work on him shall be permitted to live. If he be
known, therefore, let him be forthwith seized and dragged to
the flames."

An indignant murmur of approbation followed this announcement, and soon spread to those on the stairs, and from them to
the soldiers in the court-yard below. Fortified by the spiritual

aid of a holy friar, the most superstitious of them lost half of their dread of the Ancient's supernatural powers.

"Burn the Ancient!" cried one.—"Burn Haggerstone Fenwick!" cried another.—"Burn the Wizard Fenwick!" cried a third.—"Faggots there—faggots in the court-yard!"—"Raise a pile as high as the keep!"—"Faggots!"—"Fire!"—"Burn the Ancient!"—"Burn the Wizard!" flew from mouth to mouth. All was instant ferment. Some ran this way, and others that, to bring billets of wood, and to prepare the pile of expiation; so that, in a short time, it was built up to a height sufficient to have burnt the Ancient if his altitude had been double what it really was.

This being completed, the next cry was—"Seize the Ancient —seize him, and bring him down!" But this was altogether a different matter; for although every one most readily joined in the cry, no one seemed disposed to lead the way in carrying the general wish into effect. The friar assumed an air of command—

"Let no one move," said he, "until I shall have communed with the wretch. I shall myself ascend to his den, and endeavour to bend his wicked heart to undo the evil he hath wrought on the good Sir Walter. But let some chosen and determined men be within call, for should I find him hardened and obdurate, he must forthwith be led out to suffer for his foul sorcery. Meanwhile let all be quiet, let no sound be uttered, until I shall be heard to pronounce, in a loud voice, this terrible malison, ' *Body and soul, to the flames I doom thee!* ' Then let them up without delay on him, and he shall be straightway overcome."

The Franciscan was listened to with the most profound deference, his commands were implicitly obeyed, and every sound, both within and without the Castle, was from that moment hushed.

CHAPTER XVI.

Raising the Devil—Delivered to the Flames.

THE Ancient Haggerstone Fenwick had been by no means comfortable in his thoughts after he had retreated to the solitude of his cap-house, and had in fact anticipated in some degree the effect which would result from the state of insensibility that Sir Walter had been thrown into. He was aware that the very mummery he had enacted over him, when he expected his immediate resuscitation, instead of operating, as in that event it would have done, to raise his fame as a healing magician, would now be the means of fixing on him the supposed crime of having produced his malady, and strengthened it by wicked sorcery. But he by no means expected that the irritation against him would be so speedy or so violent in its operation as it really proved, and he perhaps trusted for his safety from any sudden attack to the dread with which he well knew his very name inspired every one in the garrison.

He had crept into the farther corner of his den, where, in the present distracted state of his mind, it did not even occur to him to extinguish the lamp he had left burning, or to let in the daylight he had excluded. There he sat, brooding over the unfortunate issue of his divination, in very uneasy contemplation of the danger that threatened him in consequence, distant though he then thought it. A coward in his heart, he began to curse himself for having tried schemes which now seemed likely to end so fatally for himself. He turned over a variety of plans for securing his safety, but, after all his cogitation, flight alone seemed to be the only one that was likely to be really available. But then Sir Walter might recover; in which case he might still obtain the credit of his recovery, and his ambitious schemes be yet crowned with success. Thus the devil again tempted him; and he finally resolved to wait patiently until night, which was by this time at hand, and then steal quietly down to ascertain Sir Walter's state, and act accordingly. Should he find him worse, or even no better than when he left him, he resolved to go secretly to the ramparts, there to undo some of the ropes of the warlike engines that defended the walls, and to let himself down by means of them at a part where he knew the height would be least formidable, and so effect his escape.

Occupied as the Ancient was with these thoughts, although he had heard the clamours and shouts rising from below, yet, buried in the farthest corner of his den, they came to his ear like the murmurs of a far-distant storm ; and, accustomed to the every-day noise of a crowded garrison, they did not even strike him as at all extraordinary.

To divert these apprehensions which he could by no means allay, he opened one of his favourite books, and endeavoured to occupy himself in his usual study ; but his mind wandered in spite of all his exertions to keep it fixed, and he turned the leaves, and traced the lines with his eyes without being in the least conscious of the meaning they conveyed. He roused him-

self, and began reading aloud, as if he could have talked himself
into quiet by the very sound of his own voice. He went on
without at first perceiving the particular nature of the passage
he had stumbled on ; but his attention being now called to it,
he was somewhat horrified to observe that it contained the form
of exorcism employed for raising the devil in person. By some
unaccountable fatality, he went on with it, wishing all the while
that he had never begun it, but yet more strangely afraid to
stop ; until at length, approaching the conclusion, he ended with
these terrible words—*Sathanas, Sathanas, Sathanas, Sathanas,
Prince of Darkness, appear!*"

He stopped, and looked fearfully around him, as soon as they
had passed his lips. The door of the place slowly opened, and
the head of the very Franciscan monk who had formerly visited
him, the face deeply shaded by the projecting cowl, was thrust
within the doorway.

"I am here—what wouldst thou with me ?" said he, in a
deep and hollow voice.

The Ancient threw himself upon his knees, and drew back
his body into the corner. His teeth chattered in his head, and
he was deprived of speech. He covered his eyes with his hands,
as if afraid to look upon the object of his dread. He now verily
believed that he had been formerly visited by the Devil, and
that the Arch-Fiend had again returned to carry him away.
The Franciscan crouched, and glided forward into the middle of
the place.

"What becomes of him, lossel," said he, in a tremendous
voice, "what becomes of him who takes the Devil's wages, and
doeth not his work? What becomes of him who vainly tries
to deceive the Devil his master? Fool! didst thou not believe
that I was the Prince of Darkness?"

The terrified Ancient had now no doubt that he was indeed
the Devil; still he kept his hands over his eyes, and drew himself yet more up, in dread that every succeeding moment he
should feel himself clutched by his fiery fangs.

"Hast thou not tried to cheat me, wretch—me, who cannot
but know all things ?" continued the Franciscan.

"Oh, spare me, spare me! I confess, I confess. Avaunt
thee, Sathanas !—Spare !—Avaunt !—Spare me, Sathanas !"
muttered the miserable wretch, altogether unconscious of what
he uttered.

"Spare thee, thou vile slave !" cried the Franciscan with
bitterness, "I never spared mortal that once roused my vengeance, and thou hast roused mine to red-hot fury. Answer

me, and remember it is vain to attempt concealment with me. Didst thou not fail of thy promise to rouse Sir Walter de Selby to my purpose, as it affected Sir Rafe Piersie?"

"Oh, I did, I did—Oh, spare me, spare me, Sathanas!" cried the Ancient.

"Didst thou not rather stir him up to reject and spurn the noble knight?" demanded the Franciscan.

"Oh, yes, I did—Oh yes—Spare me, spare me!—Avaunt thee, Sathanas!—Spare me—Oh, spare me!"

"Spare thee!" cried the Franciscan, with a horrid laugh of contempt; "spare thee! What mercy canst thou hope from me? No, thou art given to my power, not to be spared, but to be punished. Thine acts of sorcery, which have murdered Sir Walter de Selby, have put thee beyond the pale of mercy, nor canst thou now look elsewhere for aid. Thou art fitting food for hell," continued he, with a fiend-like grin of satisfaction; and retreating slowly out of the doorway, and raising his voice into a shriek, that re-echoed from every projection and turret of the building, he pronounced the last fatal words, "*Body and soul, to the flames I doom thee!*"

An instantaneous shout arose from the court-yard below, and a clamour of many voices came rapidly up the stairs in the interior of the keep,

It quickly swelled upon the ear, and the clattering noise of many feet was heard approaching. Out they came on the platform of the keep, one by one, as they could scramble forth; and as the stoutest spirits naturally mounted first, the Franciscan was instantly surrounded by a body of the most determined hearts in the garrison.

"In on the servant of Sathanas," cried he; "in on the cruel sorcerer, who hath bewitched thine unhappy Governor, and who refuseth to sayne again; in on the monster, tear him from his den, and drag him to the flames. Fear him not; his supernatural powers are quenched. Behold!" and pulling a wooden crosslet from his bosom, he held it up to their view—"In on him, I say, and seize him."

The door was instantly forced open, and one or two of the boldest entered first; then two or three more followed, to the number of half a dozen in all, for the place could hardly contain more. The Ancient had now become frantic from terror, and his reason so far forsook him that he saw not or knew not the faces of those who came in on him to attack him, though many of them were familiar to him; he was fully possessed with the idea that a legion of devils were about to assail him, to drag him

9

down to eternal punishment. They sprang upon him at once
by general concert. The Ancient was an arrant coward; but a
coward so circumstanced will fight to the last, even against an
infernal host; and so he did, with the desperation of a maniac.
In the interior of the place, the scuffle was tremendous; the
very walls and roof of it seemed to heave and labour with its
tumultuous contents. The keep itself shook to its foundation,
and the shrieks, groans, and curses that came from within appalled the bystanders.

"Pick-axes, crows, and hatchets!" cried the friar; and the
implements were brought with the utmost expedition at his
command.

"Unroof his den," cried he again; and two or three of the
stoutest mounted forthwith on the flags of the roof, and by
means of the crows and pick-axes began to tear them up with so
much expedition, that they very soon laid the wood bare, and
following up their work of devastation with the same energy,
speedily and entirely demolished the roof, letting in the little
light that yet remained of day upon the combatants.

The ancient Fenwick was now discovered lying on his back,
his jaws wide open, his huge tusks displayed, and his mouth
covered with foam, while his opponents were clustered over him
like ants employed in overpowering a huge beetle. All their
efforts to drag him out at the door had been quite unavailing.
Though there were no weapons of edge or point among the combatants, many severe wounds and blows had been given and received, and blood flowed on the pavement in abundance. The
Ancient's teeth seemed to have done him good service after his
arms had been mastered and rendered ineffectual to him, for
many of his assailants bore deep and lasting impressions of his
jaws on their hands and faces.

"In on the savage wizard now, overwhelm and bind him,"
cried the Franciscan, with a devilish laugh of triumph.

At his word they scaled the roofless walls, and jumped down
on the miserable wretch in such numbers that the place was
literally packed. But the more that came on him the more
furiously the Ancient defended himself, kicking, and heaving,
and tossing some of them, till one of their number, laying his
hand on a huge folio, made use of his code of necromancy against
himself, and gave him a knock on the head that stunned him,
and rendered him for some time insensible. Taking advantage
of this circumstance, cords were hastily employed to bind his
arms behind him; and a set of ropes being passed under him,
he was with great difficulty hoisted from his den, and laid out at

length upon the platform of the keep. There he lay, breathing, to be sure, but in a temporary state of perfect insensibility.

Availing themselves of the swoon into which he had fallen, the assailants began to hold counsel how they were to get his unwieldy and unmanageable carcase down to the court-yard. To have attempted to carry it by the stairs would have been hopeless ; a week would have hardly sufficed to have manœuvred it through their narrow intricacies. The only possible mode, therefore, was to let him down by means of ropes, over the outside walls of the keep. Accordingly strong loops were passed around his legs and under his arm-pits ; and by the united exertions of some dozen of men, he was lifted up and projected over the battlements.

As they were lowering him down slowly and with great care, the wretched Ancient, recovering from his swoon, found himself dreadfully suspended between sky and earth ; and looking upwards, and beholding the grim faces of the men who managed the ropes scowling over the battlements, strongly illuminated by the light of the torches they held, he was more than ever convinced that they were demons, nor did he doubt that he was already in the very commencement of those torments of the nether world which he had been condemned to undergo for his iniquity. He shrieked and kicked, and made such exertions, that the very ropes cracked, so that he ran imminent risk of breaking them, and of tumbling headlong to the bottom. Afraid of this, the people above began to lower him away more quickly, and the darkness below not permitting them to see the ground, so as to know when he had nearly reached it, his head came so rudely in contact with it that he was again thrown into a state of insensibility.

The whole men of the garrison, both within and without the keep, having now assembled around him, a white sheet was brought out by order of the Franciscan, and he was clothed in it as with a loose robe. A black cross was then painted on the breast, and another on the back of it, from the charitable motive of saving his soul from the hands of the Devil, after it should be purified from its sins by the fire his body was destined to undergo. A parchment cap of considerable altitude, and also ornamented with crosses, was next tied upon his head ; and two long flambeaux were bound firmly, one on each side, above his ears. He was then carried to the pile of wood, and extended at length upon the top of it. The torches attached to his head were lighted, and the Franciscan, approaching the pile with a variety of ceremonies, set fire to it with much solemnity—a grim smile of inward satisfaction lighting up his dark and stern features as he did so.

"Thus," said he, "let all wizards and sorcerers perish, and thus let their cruel enchantments end with them."

The anticipation of the horrific scene which was to ensue operated so powerfully on the vulgar crowd around, that a dead silence prevailed ; and even those who, a few minutes before had shouted loudest and fought most furiously against the Ancient, now that they beheld the wretched victim laid upon the pile, and the fire slowly gaining strength, and rising more and more towards him—already hearing in fancy the piercing agony of his screams, and beholding in idea the horrible spectacle of his half-consumed limbs writhing with the torture of the flames —stood aloof, and, folding their sinewy arms and knitting their brows, half averted their eyes from the painful spectacle.

Up rose the curling smoke, until the whole summit of the broad and lofty keep was enveloped in its murky folds ; while the flames, shooting in all directions through the crackling wood, began already to produce an intolerable heat under the wretched and devoted man, though they had not yet mounted so high as to catch the sheet he was wrapt in. Life began again to return to him. He stretched himself, and turned his head round first to the right, and then to the left ; and, beholding the dense group of soldiers on all sides of him, their eyes glaring red on him, from the reflection of the flame that was bursting from beneath him, and being now sensible of the intolerable heat, and half suffocated with the gusts of smoke that blew about him, his belief that he was in the hands of demons, and that his eternal fiery punishment was begun, was more than ever confirmed. He bellowed, writhed, and struggled ; and his bodily strength, which was at all times enormous, being now increased tenfold by the horrors that beset him, he made one furious exertion, and, snapping the cords which bound his arms behind, and which, fortunately for him, had been weaker than they otherwise would have been, had those who tied them not believed that he was already nearly exanimate, he sprang to his feet and rent open the front of the white robe they had put round him. Down came the immense and loosely-constructed pile of faggots, by the sheer force of his weight alone, and onward he rushed, with the force and fury of an enraged elephant, overturning all who ventured to oppose him, or who could not get out of his way, the flambeaux blazing at his head, and his long white robe streaming behind him, and exposing the close black frieze dress he usually wore. The guards and sentinels at the first gate, aware of what was going on, and conceiving it impossible for human power to escape, after the precautions which had been taken, when they saw the terrible figure advancing towards them, with what appeared to them to be a couple of fiery horns on his head, abandoned their posts and fled in terror. Those at the outer gate were no less frightened, and retreated with equal expedition. But the drawbridge was up. Luckily for the Ancient, however, he, like many other fortunate men, was on the right side for his own interest on this occasion. Without hesitation he put the enormous sole of one foot against it—down it rattled in an instant, chains and all, and he thundered along it.

By this time the panic-stricken soldiers of the garrison had recovered from their alarm, and started with shouts after the fugitive, being now again as eager to take him, and much more ready to sacrifice him when taken, than they had even been before. On they hurried after him, yelling like a pack of hounds, and cheered to the chase by the revengeful and bloodthirsty Franciscan, their pursuit being directed by the flaming torches at his head ; and forward he strode down the hollow way to the mead of Norham, and, dreading capture worse than death itself, he darted across the flat ground, flaming like a meteor, and, dashing at once into the foaming stream of the Tweed, began wading across through a depth of water enough to have drowned any ordinary man; until at length, partly by swashing and partly by swimming, during which last operation the lights he bore on his head were extinguished, he made his way fairly into Scotland.

His pursuers halted in amazement. The whole time occupied in his escape seemed to have been but as a few minutes. Fear once more fell upon them, and they talked to one another in broken sentences and half-smothered voices.

"Surely," said one, "the Devil, whose servant he was, must have aided him."

"Ay, ay, that's clear enow," said another.

"He was stone-dead, and came miraculously alive again," said a third.

"Nay," said a fourth, "he came not alive again; 'twas but the Devil that took possession of his dead body."

"In good troth thou hast hit it, Gregory," said a fifth, with an expression of horror ; "for no one but the Devil himself could have broken the cords that tied his hands, or kicked down the drawbridge after such a fashion."

"Didst see how he walked on the water ?" cried a sixth.

"Ay," said a seventh, "and how he vanished in the middle o' Tweed in a flash o' fire that made the very water brenn again ?"

Having thus wrought themselves into a belief that the spectre they had been following was no other than the Devil flying off with the already exanimate body of Ancient Fenwick, they trembled at the very idea of having pursued him; and they crept silently back to the garrison, the blood in their veins freezing with terror, and crossing themselves from time to time as they went.

As for the Franciscan, he disappeared, no one knew how.

CHAPTER XVII.

Sir John's Pursuit in Quest of the Missing Lady—The Forester's Hunting Camp—Sir Miers de Willoughby's Border Keep.

SIR JOHN ASSUETON's fury and distraction carried him on with great rapidity, until he reached the banks of the Tweed, and his own horse, as well as the horses of his small troop of spearmen, were right glad to lave their smoking sides in its cool current, as he boldly swam them to the English shore. He tarried but short time by the way, to refresh either them or his men; and towards nightfall, found himself winding into a green glen, thickly wooded in some parts, opening in smooth pasture in others, and watered by one of those brisk streams that descend into Northumberland from the Cheviot hills.

The sight of those lofty elevations, now so near him, brought the object of his hasty march more freshly to his mind, too much agitated hitherto by the violence of the various passions that possessed it, to permit him to act or think coolly. But he began now to reflect that, although he had learned that the Castle of Burnstower, to which Sir Miers de Willoughby was supposed to have carried off the Lady Isabelle, lay somewhere among the intricacies of these hills, his rage and impatience had never allowed him to inquire farther, or to advert to the very obvious circumstance that the extent of the hilly range was so great that he might search for many days before he could discover the spot where it was situated. It was therefore absolutely necessary that he should avail himself of the very first opportunity which might occur of procuring information, both as to the Castle he was in search of, and the owner of it, of whom he had in reality as yet learned nothing. He rode slowly up the glen, therefore, in expectation of seeing some cottage, where he might halt for a short time to gain intelligence, or of meeting some peasant, from whom he might adroitly gather the information he wanted, without exciting suspicion as to the nature of his errand.

Fortune seemed to be so far favourable to him, that he had not ridden any great distance ere he descried a forester, standing under a wide-spreading oak, by the side of a glade, where the glen was narrowest. He had a cross-bow in his hand, and appeared to be on the watch for deer.

"Ho, forester," cried Assueton to him, "methinks thou hast chosen a likely pass here for the game; hast thou sped to-day?"

"Not so far amiss as to that," said the forester, carelessly leaving his stand, and lounging towards the party, as if to reconnoitre them.

"Dost thou hunt alone, my good fellow," said the knight.

"N—nay," said the forester, with hesitation; "there be more of us in company a short way off."

"Hast thou any cottage or place of shelter hereabouts, where hungry travellers might have a mouthful of food, with provender, and an hour's rest for our weary beasts?" demanded Assueton. "Here's money for thee."

"As to a cottage like," replied the forester, "I trow there be not many of them in these wilds; but an thou wilt yede thee wi' me, thou shalt share the supper my comrades must be cooking ere this time; and as for thy beasts, they canna be muckle to dole for, where the grass grows aneath their feet. Thy money we care not for."

"Thine offer is fair and kind, good forester," said Assueton; "we shall on with thee right gladly, and give thee good thanks for thy sylvan hospitality, such as it may be. Lead on then."

The forester, without more words, walked cleverly on before Sir John Assueton, who followed him at the head of his party. As they advanced a little way, the wooding of the glen became much more dense, and rocks projecting themselves from the base of the hills on either side, rendered the passage in the bottom between them and the stream excessively narrow, so that the men of the party could only move on singly, and were more than once obliged to dismount and lead their horses. The way seemed to be very long, and night came on to increase its difficulties. Assueton's impatience more than once tempted him to complain of it; but he restrained himself, lest his eagerness might excite suspicion that he had some secret and important hostile object in view, and that he might thus lose all chance of gaining the information he so much wanted. He kept as close as he possibly could to his guide, however, for he began to have strange doubts that he might be leading him into some ambush; and he had resolved within his own mind to seize and sacrifice him the instant he had reason to be convinced he had betrayed them.

After forcing their way through a very wild pass, where the rocks on both sides towered up their bold and lofty fronts, the glen widened, and the party entered a little gently-sloping glade or holme, bounded by the high and thickly-wooded banks, which here retired from the side of the stream, and swept irregularly around it. A blazing fire appeared among the trees.

"Ay," said the forester, "these are my comrades: I reckon we come in good time, for yonder be the supper a-cooking."

The party now crossed through the luxuriant pasture, that, moistened with the evening dew, was giving out a thousand mingled perfumes from the wild flowers that grew in it, and speedily came within view of about a dozen men, clad in the same woodland garb worn by their guide. Some of them were sitting about the fire, engaged in roasting and broiling fragments of venison; while others were loitering among the trees, or sitting under their shade. A number of cross-bows and long-bows hung from the branches, several spears rested against their stems; and these, with swords, daggers, and anelaces, seemed to compose the arms of this party of hunters. They appeared to have had good success, for six or eight fat bucks were hanging by the horns from the boughs overhead.

"Here is a gallant knight and his party," said their guide to a man who seemed to be a leader among them, "who would be glad of a share of our supper."

The person he addressed, and who came forward to receive Assueton, was a tall and uncommonly handsome man; and although his dress differed in no respect from that of the others, except that he wore a more gaudy plume in his hat, and that his baldrick, the sword suspended from it, his belt and dagger, and the bugle that hung from his shoulder, were all of more costly materials and rarer workmanship. But there was something in his appearance and mien that might have graced knighthood itself. He bowed courteously to Assueton.

"Sir Knight," said he, "wilt thou deign to dismount from thy steed, and partake with us in our woodland cheer? Here," said he, turning to the people around him, "let more carcases be cut up; there is no lack of provisions. Will it please thee to rest, Sir Knight?"

"I thank thee, good forester, for thy willing hospitality," said Assueton, alighting, and giving his horse to his squire; " I will rest me on that green bank under the holly busket there, and talk with thee to wile away time and beguile my hunger. This is a merry occupation of thine," added he, after they had sat down together.

" Ay," replied the forester, " right merry in good sooth, were we left at freedom to enjoy it. But, by the mass, that is not our case here, for there wons in this vicinage a certain dis- courteous knight, who letteth no one kill a deer on his ground that he may know of ; so we be forced to steal hither, at times when we may ween that he is absent, or least on the watch. The red and roe deer do much abound in these glens ; and, by the Rood, 'tis hard, methinks, that the four-footed game should be given by nature for man's food, and that he should be reft of his right to take it."

" And who may this discourteous knight be ? " said Assueton, wishing to feel his way with the stranger.

" His name," said the forester, " is Sir Miers de Willoughby, of a truth a most cruel and lawless malfaitor, and as bold a Borderer as ever rode through a moss. He rules everything here, and gives honest folks the bit to champ, I promise thee. Would that some such gallant knight as your worship might meet with him and humble him, for verily he is a scourge to the country."

Sir John Assueton inwardly congratulated himself upon his good luck in having thus so fortunately stumbled on a man, who, having himself suffered from de Willoughby's oppression, was manifestly so inimical to him : he felt much inclined to speak out at once, but he checked himself, and thought it wiser to proceed with caution.

" Is he so very wicked, then, this Sir Miers de Willoughby of whom thou speakest ? " said he to the forester.

" By the mass is he, Sir Knight," replied the forester. " He will soar ye from his Border-keep like a falcon, and pounce on any prey that may come within his ken ; and als he be so stark as to others using his lands for their honest and harmless occu- pation of hunting, by'r Lady, he minds not on what earth he stoops, if so be that there be anything to cluth from off its surface. 'Twas but some three days ago that he yode hence on some wicked emprise, for 'twas his absence that led us hither ; and this morning, as we lay concealed in these wood shaws, we saw him and his men ride by this very spot, bearing home with him some worthy man's gentle cosset he had stowne away."

Assueton perfectly understood the forester to have used the

word cosset—a pet lamb—in a metaphorical sense; but, to draw him on, he pretended to have taken him up literally.

"A cosset!" cried he, with feigned surprise. "A poor pet lamb was but a wretched prey indeed for so rapacious a lorrel as thou wouldst make this same Sir Miers to be, good forester."

"Nay, nay, Sir Knight," replied the forester, "I meant not in very simplicity a pet lamb, but a fair damosel, who looked, meseemed, as if she had been the gentle cosset of some fond father. 'Twas a damosel, Sir Knight, a right fair and beauteous damosel; and she shrieked from time to time in such piteous fashion, that, by the Rood, it was clear she went not with him willingly."

Assueton's blood boiled, so that it was with difficulty he could longer restrain his fury. He, however, kept it within such bounds as it might well enough pass for the indignation natural to a virtuous knight upon hearing of such foul outrage done to any damsel.

"Unworthy limb of knighthood," said he, "thus to play the caitiff part of a vile lossel? Show me the way to his boure, and by the blessed bones of the holy St. Cuthbert, he shall dearly rue his traiterie."

"Marry, 'tis no wonder to see a virtuous knight so enchafed at such actings," said the forester; "yet can the damosel be little to thee; and 'twere scarce, methinks, worth thy while to step so far from thy path. Had she been thine own lady, indeed——"

"Nay," said Assueton, hastily, but endeavouring to conceal his emotion, "thou knowest, good forester, that 'tis but my duty as a true knight to redress this foul wrong; and whosoever this lady may be, and wheresoever I may be bound, I must not scruple to step a little out of my way to punish so wicked a coulpe."

"Right glad am I, Sir Knight," said the forester, "to see thee so ready to do battle against this caitiff, Sir Miers, and full willing should I be to conduct thee to the sacking of his tower; but, in good verity, 'twere vain to go accoutred and attended as thou art. He keeps special good watch and ward, I promise thee, and he is too much wont to have his quarters beat up, not to be for ever on the alert. He hath scouts stationed all around him, in such a manner that no one may approach his stronghold of Burnstower by day or by night withouten ken, and he is straightway put on the alert long ere he can be reached. If those who come against him be strong and well armed, more than his force than overcome, then he hies him away to the fastnesses of his mosses and hills, where no one but the eagle may follow him, and leaves only his barren walls to the fury of the besiegers. But if the party be small, and such as his wiles may master, he is sure to lead them into some ambush, and to put every man of them to the sword. Trust me, were thou to go clad in steel, and with such a party of spearmen at thy back, he would take the alarm, and thou wouldst either have thy journey and thy trouble for thy guerdon, or thou and thy people might fall by cruel traiterie."

"Then what, after all, may be the best means of coming at him?" said Assueton; "for thou hast but the more inflamed my desire to essay the adventure."

The forester seemed to consider for a time—"In truth," said he at length, "I see no other way than one, the which thou wouldst spurn, Sir Knight."

"Name it," said Assueton; "depend on't, I shall not be over nice in this affair."

"Wert thou," said the forester, "and, it might be, no more than two of thy people, to venture thither in disguise, with one or two of us to guide thee, thou mightest peradventure pass thither without begetting alarm, and be received into the Castle as lated and miswent travellers, lacking covert for the night. But then all that would be but of small avail, for what couldst thou do with thy single arm, and so small a force to aid it?"

"Nay, good forester," said Assueton, "be it mine to see to that, and be it thine to bring me thither. Knights are but born to conquer difficulties, and, perdie, I have never yet seen that which did not, with me, give greater zest to the adventure I went upon. By the blessed Rood, I shall go with thee. Let us forthwith have our disguises, then, and these two men of my company," pointing to Riddel and Lindsay, "shall share the glory of mine emprise. So let us, I pr'ythee, snatch a hasty meal, and set forward without delay."

"By the mass, but thou art a brave knight," said the forester; "yet it doth grieve me to see thee go on so hopeless an errand. Nathless, I shall not baulk thee nor back of thy word; verily I shall wend with thee, to show thee the way thither. But I would fain persuade thee even yet to leave this undertaking untried."

"Nay," said Assueton, "I have said it, and by God's aid I will do it, let the peril be what it may; so let us use despatch if it so please thee."

Seeing that the bold and dauntless knight was resolved, the forester ordered some of the venison, that was by this time

cooked, to be set before Assueton, and some also to be served to
those who were to accompany him; and after all had satisfied
their hunger, Assueton doffed his armour, clad himself in a suit
of plain Lincoln green, such as the foresters wore, and, unperceived by any one, slipped his dagger into his bosom.   He then
openly girt his trusty sword by his side, and leaving orders with
his party to remain with the friendly foresters until they should
see him, or hear from him, he and his two people, who were
also disguised, mounted their horses, and set off under the guidance of the leader of the hunting party and two of his men,
whom he took with them, as he said, to bear him company on
his return.

CHAPTER XVIII.

The Horrors of the Dungeon.

THEIR route lay up the glen, and the darkness of the night,
with the roughness of the way, very much impeded their progress.   At one time they were led along the very margin of the
stream, and, at another, they climbed diagonally up the steep
sides of the hills that bounded it, and wound over far above, to
avoid some impediment which blocked all passage below.   Now
they penetrated extensive thickets of brushwood, and again
wound up among the tall stems of luxuriant oaks, or passed, with
greater ease to themselves and their weary horses, over small
open glades among the woods.   At length they began to rise
over the sides of the hills, to a height so much beyond any that
they had hitherto mounted, that Assueton thought the deviation
strange and unaccountable, and was tempted to put some question to his guide.

"Whither dost thou lead us now, good forester?" said he;
"thou seemest to have abandoned the glen altogether, and methinks thou art now resolved to soar to the very clouds.   I
much question whether garron of mosstrooper ever climbed such
a house-wall as this."

"Sir Knight," replied the forester, "I but intend to lead
thee over the ridge of a hill here, by a curter east.   The glen
maketh a wicked wide courbe below, and goeth miles about.
This gate will save us leagues twayne, at the very shortest
reckoning.   Trust me I am well up to all the hills and glens of
these parts, by night as well as by day."

"Nay, good forester," said Assueton, "I doubt thee not; but, by our Lady, this seemeth to me to be a marvellous uncouth path."

"T'other, indeed, is better, Sir Knight," said the forester; "but bad as this may be, 'twill haine us a good hour's time of travel."

Assueton was satisfied with this explanation, and the ground getting more level as they advanced, he soon discovered that they were crossing a wild ridge of moorland, and hoped that the impediments to a speedier progress would be fewer. But the way seemed, if possible, to be even more puzzling and difficult than ever. They wound round in one direction, and then went zig-zag to the opposite point of the compass; then they wormed their way through bogs and mosses—then stretched away Heaven knew whither, and then, making a little detour, they (as it seemed to Assueton) returned again in a line nearly parallel to that which they had just pursued. Hours appeared to glide away in this wearisome and endless maze, and Assueton's impatience became excessive.

"Good forester," said he, "methinks we are never to get out of this enchanted labyrinth."

"Nay, Sir Knight," replied the forester, "'tis an enchanted labyrinth in good soberness; for, verily, full many a goodly steed hath been ygraven in the flows that surround us. There be quaking bogs here that would swallow a good-sized tower. Nay, halt thee, Sir Knight, thou must of needscost turn thee this gate again."

"By St. Cuthbert," said Assueton, "meseems it a miracle that thou shouldst have memory to help thee to thread the intricacies of so puzzling a path, maugre the darkness that yet prevails."

"'Tis indeed mirk as a coal mine," said the forester, "but I look for the moon anon."

After better than half-an-hour more of such travelling as we have described, they at length wound down a very precipitous hill, where their necks were in considerable peril, and found themselves again in the glen, and by the side of its stream. As well as Assueton could guess, they had now travelled fully three or four hours, the greater part of which time they had spent on the high ground. The state of their horses, too, bore out his calculation, for they showed symptoms of great exhaustion, from this so large addition to the previous severe journey. They pushed them on, however, as fast as the nature of the ground would admit, the glen presenting the same variety of woods, glades, and thickets, as it had formerly done.

At length they came to a place where the hills approached on each side, and the glen narrowed to a wild gorge, where all passage was denied below, except for the stream, and they were consequently again compelled to ascend the abrupt banks by a diagonal path.   But they had no sooner gained the summit than the moon arose, and threw its silver light full over the scene into which they were about to advance.   Above the gorge, the valley was split into two distinct glens, or rather deep ravines, each pouring out its stream, and these, uniting together, formed that which they had so long traced upwards.   Above the point of their union arose a green-headed eminence, swelling from among the rich woods that everywhere clothed it, and all the other lower parts of the space within their view.   The round top of the eminence was crowned with a rude Border Tower ; and the whole was backed, a good way behind, by a semi-circular range of hilly ridges.   The moonlight shone powerfully on the building, the keep of which seemed to be of no great size, but very strong in itself ; and the outworks, consisting of massive walls defended here and there by round towers, showed that it was a stronghold where determined men might make a powerful resistance.

"Yonder is the peel of Burnstower," said the forester, pointing to it ; "thou must ford the stream there below, under the hill whereon it stands, and so make thy way up through the woods by a narrow path, that will lead thee to the yett.   I shall yet go with thee as far as the ford, to show thee the right gate through the water ; but I must then bid thee farewell, nor canst thou lack mine aid any longer."

"Good forester," said Assueton, "certes thou hast merited the guerdon of my best thanks for thine obliging and toilsome convoy.   When I join thee again, trust me they shall be cheerfully paid thee, together with what more solid warison thou mayest see fit to accept, in token of my gratitude.   Meanwhile, I beseech thee to take good charge of my brave men."

"Nay, fear me not in that, Sir Knight," said the forester ; "they shall be well looked after, I promise thee.   My men have doubtless already taken good care of them, and of their steeds too."

Having descended the hill, they pushed their way through the opposing brushwood, and reached the bank of one of the streams, immediately above the spot where it united itself to the other.   The forester indicated the ford to Assueton, and then took an abrupt leave, diving into the thicket with his two followers.

Assueton stood for a moment on the brink of the stream before he entered, and took that opportunity of telling his two attendants to be particularly on their guard, to watch his eye, attend to his signals, and be ready to act as these might appear to suggest to them. They were also to bear in mind that for the present they were to pass as equals. He then cautiously entered the ford, and, followed by Riddel and Lindsay, soon reached the farther bank.

They now found themselves on a low grassy tongue of land, which shot out between the two streams from the woods at the base of the eminence the Castle stood on, and which, though of considerable length, was nowhere more than a few yards wide. Along this they pushed their horses, as fast as the weary animals could advance. A few trees struggled down over it at the farther extremity, where it united itself to the base of the hill; and just as they had entered among these, all their horses were at one and the same moment tumbled headlong on the ground. An instant shout arose from the thickets on either side, and about a dozen men sprang from them on the prostrate riders; and, after a short and ineffectual struggle on their part, Assueton and his two attendants were bound hand and foot, and blindfolded. All this time not a word was spoken; and excepting the shouts that were the signal of the onset, not a sound was heard. But the prey was no sooner fairly mastered, than a loud bugle blast was blown from the thickets near them, and it was immediately answered by another, that rang through the woods at some distance. The horses were then extricated from the toils of ropes which had been so treacherously though ingeniously employed to ensure their prostration, and on regaining their legs, their late riders were lifted up and laid across them like sacks, and they were led by the villains who had captured them up the steep and devious ascent, through the thick wood to the Castle. The party then entered the gateway, as Assueton judged from the noise made in raising the portcullis, and the prisoners being lifted from their horses, were carried each by two men into the main tower.

Whither they took his two attendants, Assueton had no means of guessing; but he was borne up a long and winding stair, as he supposed to the top of the building, and then through several passages. There he heard the withdrawing of rusty bolts, and the heavy creaking of hinges; and, being set down on the floor of his prison, his arms and legs were unbound, his eyes uncovered, and he was left in utter darkness and amazement.

After sitting for some moments to recover from the surprise

occasioned by this sudden and unlooked for annihilation of all his plans and of all the hopes he had cherished from them, he arose, and, before yielding to despair, groped his way to the walls, and felt them anxiously all round. Not a crevice or aperture could he discover but the doorway, and that was blocked by an impregnable door, crossed and recrossed by powerful bars of iron, so that he saw no hope of its being moved by any strength of human arm, unassisted by levers or other such instruments. The walls and floor were of the most solid masonry in every part; yet he felt the balmy air of a soft night blow upon his face, and, on looking upwards, he could just descry a faint glimmer of light, that broke with difficulty through the enormous thickness of the building, by a narrow window immediately over where he then stood. This opening, however, was quite beyond his reach, being at least a dozen feet above him.

As he moved backwards to get from under the wall where the window was, that he might obtain a better view of it, his head came in contact with something hanging behind him. He turned round, but his eyes were not yet sufficiently accustomed to the obscurity, to enable him to discover anything more than that there was some dark object suspended from above. He put up his hands to ascertain what it was, and, to his inexpressible horror, felt the stiffened legs of a corpse, which swung backwards and forwards at his touch. Bold and firm as he was, Assueton started involuntarily back, and his heart revolted at the thought that he was to be so mated for the night. He retired to a corner, where he had discovered a heap of straw with a coarse blanket, and he sat him down on it; but it immediately occurred to him that this had probably been the bed of the unfortunate man who now dangled lifeless from the centre of the vault, and he could sit on it no longer. That the poor wretch had been put to death in the very chamber which had been his prison, seemed to argue a degree of hardened cruelty and summary vengeance in those in whose power he had now himself the misfortune to be, that left him little room to hope for much mercy at their hands.

Having moved to an opposite corner, nearly under the little window, he seated himself on the floor, and gave up his mind to the full bitterness of its thoughts. The first recollection that presented itself was that of the Lady Isabelle, torn from her home, her father, and himself, by an unprincipled and abandoned villain. His reflections on this painful theme banished every thought of his own captivity, as well as every speculation as to what its result might be, excepting, indeed, in so far as it might affect the fate of her who was now the idol of his heart. He ran over his past conduct, and seeing that he could now have no hope of being the instrument of her rescue, he blamed himself in a thousand ways. He accused himself bitterly for not having sent back a messenger from the place where he had met Sir Walter de Selby, to inform Sir Patrick Hepborne the elder of the intelligence he had obtained from the Captain of Norham; then unavailing regrets and self-accusations arose within him for having neglected to obtain more full information from Sir Walter, when he had it in his power to do so; but, above all, he cursed his folly for having abandoned his stout-hearted spearmen, who would have backed him against any foes to the last drop of their blood. He turned over the circumstances of his rencontre with the foresters, and, recalling the whole conduct of their leader, he now began to be more than half suspicious that they had played him false. This last reflection made him tremble for the fate of his people whom he had left with them; and remembering his guide's parting assurance, "that they should be well looked after," he felt disposed to interpret it in a very opposite sense to that he had put upon it the moment it was uttered.

He then again recurred to the Lady Isabelle. Why had he gone a-hunting on the day she was carried off, when he had been repeatedly warned, by something within his own breast, that he ought to stay at home with her? Alas! where was she now? The question was agony to him. Could she be within these walls? To know that she, indeed, really was so, would have been cheering to him even in his present state of desponding uncertainty, as it might have given him some frail hope of yet being of use to her. He listened for distant sounds. Faint female shrieks came from some part of the building far below. Again he heard them yet more distinctly; and, full of the maddening idea that they came from the Lady Isabelle, he started up, unconscious of what he was doing, flew like a madman to the door, and began beating it with his fists, screaming out, "Villains! murderers!" But his voice, and the noise of his furious knocking, returned on his ear with a deadened sound, and speedily convinced him that nothing could be heard from the lofty, solitary, and massive-walled prison in which he was immured.

With a heart torn and distracted, and almost bereft of reason, he paced the floor violently backwards and forwards. His ear then caught, from time to time, the distant and subdued shouts of merriment and laughter. These again stung him to fury.

10

" What !" cried he aloud, " do they make sport of her purity
and her misery ?   Villains ! demons ! hell-hounds !"   And he
again raved about his prison with yet greater fury than before,
a thousand horrible ideas arising to his heated and prolific
imagination.

At length he flung himself on the floor, utterly exhausted
both in body and mind by the intensity of his sufferings, and
lay for some moments in a state of quiet, from absolute inability
to give further way to the extravagance of action excited by his
feelings.   He had not been long in this state, however, when the
distant and faint chanting of a female voice fell upon his ear.
He started, and raising himself upon his elbow, listened anxiously
that he might drink in the minutest portion of the sound which
reached him.   Though evidently coming from some far-off chamber below, he distinctly caught the notes, which he recognized
to be those of a hymn to the Virgin, from the vesper service.
The melody was sweet and soothing to his lacerated soul.   Again
it stole on him.

" The voice," said he to himself, " that can so employ itself
must come from one who may be unhappy, but who cannot
suppose herself to be in any very immediate peril ; nor, if her
mind had been so lately suffering urgent alarm, could she have
by this time composed it so far as to be able to lift it to Heaven
in strains so gentle and placid."

Though immediately afterwards convinced of the folly of such
an idea, he, for a moment, almost persuaded himself that he recognized the voice of the Lady Isabelle Hepborne in that of the
pious chantress.   He threw himself upon his knees, and offered
up his fervent orisons for help in his affliction.   The voice came
again upon him—and again he fancied he knew it to be that of
her he loved ; but although he found himself, in sound reason,
obliged to discard all idea of the possibility of such a recognition, yet it clung to his broken spirit, and was as a healing balm
to it, in despite of reason.

It produced one happy effect, however, by causing his agonizing thoughts to give way, at last, to the immense bodily and
mental fatigue he had undergone.   He dropped asleep on the
bare pavement, notwithstanding the horrors that hung over him,
the uncertain fate that awaited him, and the complication of
misery by which he was oppressed.

CHAPTER XIX

Dawn in the Dungeon—An Appalling Sight—Rough Visitors.

Sir John Assueton's sleep was deep and uninterrupted until the first dawn of morning, when he awoke and rubbed his eyelids, having, for a moment, forgotten where he was, and all that had befallen him. The first object that presented itself when he looked upwards was the figure and countenance of the dead man, hanging almost immediately over the spot where he lay. The features were horribly distorted and discoloured, by the last agonies of the violent death he had died; the tongue was thrust out, and the projected eyeballs were staring fearfully from their sockets. The sight was appalling and heart-sickening.

He could now observe that the dress of the unfortunate man was that of a forester. The arms were rudely tied behind the back, and the body was suspended from a huge iron ring, that hung loose in an enormous bolt of the same metal, strongly built in vertically between the keystones of the vault, the height of which was very considerable. It seemed as if the wretched man had been dragged from his couch of straw to instant punishment, or rather perhaps murder; for portions of the straw yet littered the floor as if dragged along with him in his ineffectual struggles, and some fragments of it still adhered between his ankles, to the rough woollen hose he wore, as if retained there by the last dying convulsion that had pressed and twisted the limbs unnaturally together. Then the fatal rope was not like one intended for such a use. It was thicker than seemed necessary, and looked as if it had been hastily taken, as the readiest instrument for the murderous deed. After passing through the ring, where it was fastened by two or three turns, it stretched down diagonally to one corner of the place, where it lost itself in an immense coil. It had manifestly been hastily brought there, to effect the destruction of the unfortunate wretch, and afterwards left on the floor uncut, that it might not be rendered unfit for the purpose to which it had been originally dedicated.

It may seem strange that Assueton should have derived anything like pleasure from a spectacle so truly appalling; but it is nevertheless true, that a faint gleam of hope broke upon the miserable despair that had possessed him. He saw that the coil of rope was of sufficient extent to give him good reason to believe that, when untwisted, it might reach to the base of the

tower, at the top of which he was now confined, if he could only
detach it from what went upwards, and conceal it until night.
But how was he to sever it? He remembered that he had concealed his dagger in his bosom at the time he put on his disguise.
Those who seized and bound him had immediately deprived him
of his sword, but they had not suspected his being possessed of
any other weapon, and his dagger, therefore, had escaped their
notice. He drew it joyfully forth ; but just as he was about to
divide the rope, he paused, and observing that there were at
least fourteen or sixteen feet stretching diagonally between the
coil and the ring, he hesitated to cut it. To throw away so considerable a portion of it, when perhaps that very piece might be
essential to the preservation of his life, would have been the
height of imprudence ; yet, to get at that portion, there was but
one way, and this was so disgusting, and so repugnant to his
feelings, that the very idea of it made him shudder.

But liberty, and perhaps life depended on it ; and what will
not the desire of liberty and life compel human nature to
attempt? To him both were now more precious than ever, since
they might yet be the means of saving her without whom he
could value neither. He hesitated not a moment longer, but
screwing up his resolution to the revolting alternative, he laid
hold of the legs of the dead man, swung himself up from the
ground, and, catching at his clothes, at last got the rope within
his gripe, and thus continued to climb, hand over hand, until he
reached the fatal ring. Holding by one sinewy arm, he drew
forth his dagger, and was again on the eve of cutting the rope
close to the ring when prudence once more stopped him. He
had been from the first aware that it was absolutely necessary
to leave the dead body hanging, lest, when his jailors should visit
him, they might have their suspicions awakened by its removal.
What made him hesitate then, whilst hanging by one arm to the
ring and bolt to the arch in the vault, was the idea, that by
loosening the turns that were made in it, he might be enabled
to hoist up the body a few feet higher, then to fasten the turns
of the rope again, and thus gain so many more feet of rope. All
this, with immense fatigue of arm, he effected, and then dividing
the rope with his dagger, and descending to the floor, he lifted
up the large coil, and removing the straw of the bed, he hid it
underneath, covering it up with the greatest care. He was
fully aware of the possibility of its being missed from its place,
sought for, and removed from the concealment he had put it
into ; but it was also possible that the wretches who had
done the deed might not be among those who should come

to visit him, in which case its absence could never attract their observation.

He now sat down to consider and arrange his plans. He at once saw that it would be useless to attempt his descent while daylight remained, or, indeed, while the people in the Castle might be supposed to be still stirring, as, if he did try it then, he must do so with hardly a chance of escaping detection. To lessen the risk of being observed and seized, therefore, it was absolutely essential that he should postpone his enterprise until night. But then the risk of his rope being discovered before night crossed his mind : his judgment wavered, and he was filled with the most cruel and perplexing doubts. He remembered that the state of the moon, which left the earlier part of the night excessively dark, made that by far the most favourable time to risk his fate ; and he at length determined that, a descent in day-light being perfectly hopeless, he must be content to take his chance of the other alternative. But what was he to do if the rope should be missed, sought for, and detected? After some consideration, he resolved that in that event he would draw his dagger, spring unawares on those who might visit him, and so make a desperate endeavour to effect his escape, by striking down all that might oppose him.

But another and a different thought now occurred to him. What if the very first visit that might be paid him should be for the purpose of taking down the murdered body from the ring, only to hang him up in its place? Brave as he was he shuddered at the contemplation of such a fate. He had already often faced death in bloody field, led on by glory and the laudable thirst of fame ; but to be hung up like a dog by the hands of murderous ruffians in this lone chamber, far from every human ear or eye but those of his clownish and unfeeling executioners, who would take so small account of him, after witnessing his passing agonies, as perhaps to leave him, as they had done the wretch who had gone before him, till his place was wanted for a successor, and then throw his half consumed body into some unholy spot, over which his perturbed ghost might hover, seeking in vain for repose, this was to strip death of the fascinating drapery which men have contrived to throw over him, and to unveil all his terrors, But he steeled himself for the worst, and, resolving to wait firmly, and to act as circumstances might suggest, he determined that, happen what might, he would sell his life dearly, should he be reduced to the unhappy alternative of doing so.

With his mind thus wound up, he sat him down on the couch of straw, that he might appear unconcerned to any one

who might enter; and there he remained, waiting patiently for
the issue. He had been seated in this way about a couple of
hours, when he heard the heavy tread of feet approaching along
the passages. The key was inserted in the lock of the door,
and considerable force exerted before it could be turned.

"Be quick with you, old churl," cried an impatient voice;
"thou wilt be all day working at it."

The door half opened, and two or three heads were thrust in
at once. Seeing their prisoner calmly seated on the straw at the
farther wall, four men entered. One of these, a thick, squat,
large-headed old man, with a rough, cloddish, unfeeling countenance, and long, thick, grizzled hair hanging about it, was clad
in a close woollen jerkin and hauselines, appeared to be the
jailor, for several enormous keys hung from divers straps attached
to his leathern belt. He stationed himself with his back at the
door. The other three men were younger, but the expression
of their features betrayed such depraved and lawless spirits, as
might make them ready instruments to perpetrate any cruelty
or crime at the mere nod of a master. Their dress was similar
to that in which the murdered body was clothed. Two of them,
armed with short swords in their hands, placed themselves at
the door, in front of the old jailor, while the third, with a pewter-
covered dish under his left arm, an earthen jug of ale in his left
hand, and his naked sword in his right, advanced a little way,
and deposited the provisions on the pavement. Turning his
eyes round, he beheld the dead body hanging.

"Heyday, Daniel Throckle," said he, with a careless laugh,
to the jailor, "how camest thou to leave our comrade Tim Ord
here, to keep watch over this young man all night? By the
mass, methinks he was but a triste companion for him."

"'Twas none o' my doing, Master Ralpho Proudfoot; 'twas
Wat Withe that did the deed himsell. He got the key from
me, and thou knowest he doth not ever care overmuch, so he
gets his job done, whether the workshop be cleaned out or no.
He thinks that be none o' his business."

"Nay, but, fine fellow as he thinks himself, he may come
and take down his own rubbish for me," said Ralpho Proudfoot; "I clean out after no sike cattle, I promise thee. An
thou likest to do his dirty work thou mayest, seeing thou art
custodier of the place." Then, turning to Assueton, who had
sat quite still all this time, "Here, sir," said he, "is thy morning's meal—better eat it whiles it be hot—thou mayest not
have a many deal of sike like;" and as he said so, he threw his
eye sideways up towards the dead man. "Thou seest we be

sometimes rather more curt than courteous; thou canst not tell when it may be thy turn."

"Young man," said Assueton, composedly, and still without rising from his sitting posture, "canst thou tell me why I have been so traitorously seized and conveyed hither, and why I am thus immured, and treated like a foul felon?"

"Nay, as to being·treated like a felon, *young man*," replied Ralpho Proudfoot, evading his question, and laying particular emphasis on the words in italics, "meseems 'tis but ungrateful of thee to say so, seeing I have brought thee a dish of hot steaks, cut from the rump of a good Scottish ront; and then for ale, never was better brewed about the roots of the Cheviots, as well thou knowest, honest Daniel Throckle."

The jailor replied by a significant chuckle, indicating his perfect acknowledgment of Proudfoot's assertion.

"Well," continued Proudfoot, "we may e'en leave thee, *young man*, to the full enjoyment of this pleasing sunshiny day, such as thou mayest have on't through yonder window on high, for thou mayest see even less on't to-morrow." And, wheeling round, he was on the eve of departure, when he suddenly stopped—"But hold," said he, "had we not better ripe him, to see that he hath nothing of weapon sort about him? Come forward, young man; and do thou, old Daniel, approach, and feel his hide all over, as thou wouldst do a fat sheep fed for the slaughter. And who knows how soon it may be his lot? Approach, I say: we shall stand by here, and see that he doeth thee no harm."

Assueton perceived that resistance would be vain, and he also knew that it was unnecessary. Before they entered, he had taken the precaution to remove his dagger from his bosom, and conceal it among the straw near where he sat, yet in such a manner as he could have easily seized it had he seen any necessity for using it. He arose indignantly, and then, with assumed carelessness, submitted to be searched; not, however, without considerable inward alarm that they might not be contented with the mere examination of his person, but proceed to rummage the straw also. Should they do so, all his hopes were gone; but his heart kept firm, and he stood with so easy and indifferent an air, that the villains were soon satisfied.

"No, no," cried Proudfoot, "I see all is sicker. So a jolly morning to thee, young man. Come, lads, let us be trooping. We have work before us, as ye well know."

"Had I not better shake up his straw for him?" said one of the others; "he may not be used to make his own bed."

" Nay, nay," said Proudfoot, " he may learn to make it, then ; he can never learn younger, I ween.   Besides, hath he not Tim Ord there to help him ?—ha ! ha ! ha !   By St. Roque, but they will have pleasant chat together."

" Nay, Daniel Throckle," said the other man, " but thee shouldst come back ere long, and remove this grim mate from his dorture."

" Umph," said Throckle, as if in doubt ; " it's a plaguey long stair to climb, and I may not get hands to help me.   But, nathless, I'll see what may be done.   Wat Withe may per-aunter——"

" Come, come," cried Proudfoot, impatiently, " we are wanted ere this.   Off, I say—off ;" and with these words they all four left the prison ; the door was bolted and barred with the utmost precaution, and their heavy lumbering steps were heard retreating along the passages.   .

It was strange perhaps, but it was most true, that the shutting of the rusty bolts sounded almost as sweetly in Assueton's ear as if they had been opened to give him liberty.   The relief he felt at the retreat of the four men was so great, that, like a pious knight, he knelt down and offered up his heartfelt gratitude, in fervent thanksgivings to Heaven, that his plans were as yet unfrustrated.   He took up the food that had been left with him, and made a hearty and cheerful meal.   He then began turning in his mind the circumstances that were likely to occur to him before night, and again some cruel anticipations obtruded themselves.   Were Throckle to return to remove the body, perhaps it might be of little consequence ; but if, as he seemed to hint at when he was interrupted—if he should call in the aid of Wat Withe, as they had nicknamed the executioner, then all his schemes for escape must be ruined.   Nay, what if the coil of rope, the villain had so hastily taken, should happen to be wanted before night for the purpose it had been originally intended for ?   The thought was most alarming.   Assueton immediately removed the straw from it, that he might examine it narrowly, and his mind was very much relieved when he discovered that it was everywhere quite rough and new, as if it had never been used.   But still nothing presented itself to him, to rid him of the apprehension of the return of Wat Withe, who could not fail to mark the disappearance of the coil.   A thousand times during the day he fancied he heard steps approaching, and more than once he grasped his dagger to prepare for bloody work.   But it was all fancy.   The only sound he heard was that of the trampling of horses, the jingling of bridles, and the clattering of weapons, mingled with the voices of men, as if some party was riding forth.

CHAPTER XX.

A Dreadful Situation—Daniel Throckle the old Jailor.

THE time passed slowly and heavily until within about an hour of nightfall, when steps were again distinctly heard approaching Assueton's prison. Much to his relief, however, they seemed to be those of a single person; something was put down on the pavement on the outside; the bolts were tardily withdrawn, and the great head of Daniel Throckle alone appeared through the partially opened door, as if to ascertain in what part of the chamber his prisoner was, ere he should venture farther. Seeing Assueton seated as formerly, on the straw, he hastily pushed within the door-way vessels containing food and drink, as before, and instantly retreating, turned the bolts behind him, and departed without uttering a word.

Now Assueton's hopes beat high, and again on his knees he returned his fervent thanks to Heaven. He then determined to avail himself of the small portion of day-light which yet remained, to make everything ready for his escape.

Disgusting and revolting as it had been to him, on the first discovery of the murdered body, that it should have been left as his nightly and daily companion, he had now good reason to be glad that it had been so; for even if its removal had not occasioned the discovery of his appropriation of the coil of rope, without it he could have had no means of reaching the ring in the centre of the vault, the only thing within it to which he could have attached the end of his rope, and it would have been there only to have mocked his hopes.

After he had succeeded in making it fast, he had still an appalling difficulty before him; for the window was so high above the floor of the vault that it was quite beyond all reach. There was, to be sure, a small fragment of rusty iron, that projected an inch or two from the centre of the sole of it, like the decayed remains of a stanchion, that had once divided the space vertically within; but it was little better than a knob. It yet remained to be proved, therefore, whether he should succeed in throwing a part of his rope over this frail pin of iron, so as to furnish him with the means of pulling himself up to the window; and he lost no time in making the experiment. But this, so

absolutely essential part of his operations, he found most difficult
to effect.   He threw, cast, and jerked the rope, trying every
possible way he could think of; but the piece of iron was so
short that, although he often succeeded in throwing the rope
over it, he could never manage to make it hold.   The day-light
ebbed away fast, and still he laboured, but without success.   At
length he grew desperate, and threw the rope up time after time
with mad and senseless rapidity.   It became darker and darker
till pitchy night closed in, yet still he persevered in throwing
furiously and at random ; but it was the perseverance of despair, all attempt at skill being utterly abandoned.   At length,
when he had almost become frantic, it caught as he pulled back
after an accidental throw ; he felt it hold against him, and
keeping it down to the floor tight with one foot, to prevent it
from slipping, he laid the whole weight of the coil upon it, and
then, dropping on his knees, returned thanks to Heaven for his
success.   It was but a small matter throwing a coil of rope over
a projecting fragment of iron ; yet on that trifle depended all
his hopes, for by means of that small piece of iron alone could
he escape.

He now sat him down on the coil to wait patiently for the
hour when he might think it safe to make his bold attempt.

Judging at length that the night was sufficiently far advanced
for his purpose, he offered up a prayer for divine aid and protection, and tying the blanket of the bed around him in case of
need, laid hold of the rope and hoisted himself up by his arms,
until he had reached the window.   Having lodged himself
fairly in its aperture, he discovered that the wall was at least six
or eight feet thick.   He now laid himself on his side, with his
feet hanging inwards, and by slow degrees pulled up the rope,
until he got the whole coil deposited safely within the small area
of the window.   The space was barely sufficient to admit of his
creeping easily through.   Altering his position, therefore, and
advancing his feet, he wormed himself forward, when, just as he
expected to thrust them into the open air, he felt them suddenly
arrested by a vertical bar of iron.   His heart was chilled by its
touch.   He tried the width of the vacancies on either side of it,
but neither afforded space enough to admit of the passage of his
body.

Much disheartened by this unexpected obstruction, he withdrew himself, and with great difficulty again changed his position,
and advanced head foremost until he brought his hands near
enough the bar to feel it all over. It was much decayed by rust,
but yet by far too strong to be broken by the mere force of his

arm. After a little consideration, he drew his dagger, and making use of its point, worked away the lead and the stone where the lower end of the stanchion was inserted; and after labouring unceasingly for a considerable time, he found he had weakened the stone and removed the lead so much that he had some hopes of assailing it successfully with his feet. He was now, therefore, obliged to retreat again and change his position, so that he again projected his feet till they came in contact with the bar. Having fixed himself firmly in the place by means of his arms, that he might bring all his force to bear against it, he was about to strike violently at it with the soles of his feet when he remembered that the sound might be heard below. His situation made him fertile in expedients. He slipped forward a part of the blanket, and, adjusting two or three folds of it over the bar, he began to drive his feet furiously against it. It gradually gave way before them, and then it suddenly yielded entirely. He ceased working for an instant, and, to his no small alarm, heard a piece of the stone he had driven off fall in the court-yard below. He listened anxiously for a time, but no alarm seemed to have been excited. He again felt at the bar with his feet, and recommencing his attack upon it, after a succession of hard blows, he bent it so far outwards as to leave no doubt that he could pass himself through the aperture.

Commending himself to God, then, he slipped himself forward, and, committing his weight gently to the rope, he began his descent by shifting his hands alternately and slowly one below the other, always pulling out more and more of the coil of rope as he wanted it, until, the end of it being unwound, it fell perpendicularly below him. Still he went on descending till, to his no small dismay, he found that he had reached the last foot of his length. For an instant he hung in awful doubt. He cast his eyes below, but the night was so dark that the ground beneath was invisible, and he could not possibly calculate the height that yet remained. He thought for a few moments; and finally, resigning himself to the care of Providence, he loosened his grasp of the rope and fell. His fall was dreadful, and his death would have been certain had not his descent been interrupted by a fortunate circumstance. The blanket he had wrapped round him caught in the branches of a yew tree growing close to the wall, and although it did not keep its hold, yet the force of the fall was so much broken that he escaped comparatively uninjured.

He lay stunned for some moments under the tree; and then, recovering himself, he was about to rise, when, reflecting that he must proceed with caution, he crept silently forth from his covert, and listened to hear if there was any one stirring. All was quiet. He then moved forward, and dark as the night was, he could yet perceive the outer walls and towers of the building rising against the pale glimmer of the sky. His first step was to steal around the base of the keep, that he might reconnoitre it in all directions; and, as he did so, he passed by its entrance, which he found open. Wishing to examine farther, he went on listening, but all was silent around. At length, as he moved onwards to another side of the building, he descried a light breaking from a loop-hole window near the foundation of the keep, and heard the sound of human voices, with now and then a peal of boisterous laughter. He approached with extreme caution and silence, until he was near enough to see and hear all that passed within.

The place he looked down into appeared to be a sort of cellar, being surrounded with huge barrels placed against the walls, near one of which, on an inverted tub, sat the old jailor, Daniel Throckle, with a great wooden stoup of ale on his knee, and with no small quantity of the fumes of the same fluid in his brain, as was evident from the manner in which his eyes ogled in his head. Almost close by him stood a good-looking wench in conversation with him; and the group was lighted by a clumsy iron lamp placed on the top of one of the largest of the tuns.

"Coum, coum, Daeniel Throckle," said the girl, "thee hast had enow o' that strong stuff; that stoup but accloyeth thee. Blessed Mary! but thine eyes do look most fearsome askaunce already."

"Nay, nay, my bellebone," replied Throckle, "I mun ha' a wee drop more yet. Coum, now, do sit thee down, and be buxom a bit—a—a—. Thee knawest—a—that I loves thee dearly—he! he! he! Sit thee down, I say—a—a; sit thee down, my soft, my soote virginal!—By St. Cuthbert, there be not a he that yalt the gate through sun and weet—a—a—that—a—a—he! he! he!—that loveth thee more than I do.—Sit thee down, I say—a—a—and troll a roundel with me. Here ye, now, do but —a—a—do but join thy sweet voice with mine.—Nay then, an thou wont, I mun e'en—a—a—sing by mysell—a—a—

> O I am the man
> That can empty a can,
> And fill it again and again, ah!
> A—a—And empty and fill,
> And the barley-juice swill,
> Till a tun of the liquor I drain, ah!

A—a—Then it lightens mine eye,
    And my liard jokes fly,
And warms my old blood into pleasure.
    A—a—Then out comes my song,
    Trolling glibly a—along,
And merrily clinks in the measure.

Oh—a—a—a—And then should I see
    A sweet pusell like thee,
She catches mine eye, as I cock it ;
    And then at her, gadzooks !
    I throw such winning looks,
As soon turn both of hers in the socket.

A murrain on't ! how should I forget the rest on't !

So then I—a—a—then—a

The red fiend catch it, for I can't !—So, my bonnie mistress,
Betty Burrel, do thee—a—do thee sit thee down here, whiles I
but drink this single can of double ale ; and, sin' we canna sing
the rest o' the stave—a—a—sit thee down, and let me kiss
thee."

"Na, na, Daeniel Throckle," said the girl ; "thee knawest
thou'rt ower auld for me—thou'rt ower auld to be mate o'
mine"——

"Ower auld !—a—a—thou scoffing—thou scoffing giglet
thou !" cried Throckle ; "thou'll find me—a—kinder—a—thou'lt
find me kinder at least than that cross-grained, haughty knave,
Ralpho Proudfoot. A pestilent rascal !—Thou knawest—a—a—
a—thou knawest, I say, how ill he used thee—a—but last night
—no farther gone.   Did he not beat thee—a—yestreen—a—
till he made thee rout out like any Laverdale cow, when—a—
she hath been driven—a—across the Border—a—and hath left
her calf behind her ?"

"In troth, Daeniel Throckle," said the wench, " he did use me
hard enow, that's certain, now when a's done.   But rise thee up,
Daeniel.   Bethink thee, thou'rt a' that be left to guard the
Castle, and it be na mysel, and auld Harry Haddon standing
sentry at the yett.   Ise warrant he's asleep or this time :—And
what 'ud coum o' us an the prisoners were to break out ?"

"Phoo !" said Daniel, sticking one arm akimbo, and assuming the most ridiculous air of importance—" Phoo ! I would not
care that—a—a—snap of my finger, look you now, for—a—a—
for the whole bunch of 'em.   A stout, able-bodied—a—courageous—a—warlikesome—a—Southron like me—well fortified and
charged with potent double ale—against three lousy Scottish
louns ! Phoo ! I'd put 'em all down with my thumb.   But—a
—a—but look ye here, my bonnie Betty Burrel ; here they are

—a—a—all safe at my girdle. This mockel knave here," continued he, laying hold of the keys that hung from his belt,
" this mockel knave—a—I call Goliath ; he--a—a—he locks me
up and maketh me sicker—a—the tall dark wight—a—that
hath been put in durance in the hanging vault at the top o' the
keep : he's—a—he's fast enow, I warrant thee, and, ha! ha! ha!
hath got jolly company with him, I wot.   Poor Tim Ord, thou
knawest—a—was strung up for traitcrie ; and ha ! ha ! ha !—
sure I canna help loffen to but think on't ; ha ! ha ! ha ! ha ! he
hangs yonder aside the poor Scottish Knight they took yestreen
—a bonnie jolly comrade for him to spend the night wi', I trow."

" Poor Tim Ord !" said the girl, " thou gar'st mine heart creep
to think hoo hasty they waur wi' 'im."

" Hasty," cried Throckle, " ay, I trow, he lay not among his
straw an hour—a—till Wat Withe and his mates broke his
dreams, to send him to a sounder sleep, ha! ha! ha!   But—a—
a—'tis the gate, wench—a—'tis the gate that a' sike traitorous
faitours should yede them."

" But what key is that other wi' the queer courbed handle?"
inquired the curious Betty Burrel.

" Wilt thou—a—a—wilt thou gie me a buss, then, and I'll
tell thee ?" said Throckle.

Betty Burrel advanced her head within his reach.   Old
Throckle kissed her, and endeavoured to detain her, but, after
some little romping, she escaped.

" Tell me now," said she, " sin I gied thee the kiss."

" That courbe—hafted key," said Throckle, lifting it up ;
" that—a—a—I call—a—a—a—I call Crooked-hold-him-fast :
he locks the donjon vault at the end of the passage—a—the
passage aneath the stair.   There—a—there lies the tway rogues
wha were cotched i' the same trap wi' the wight in the hanging
vault.   This third key—a—this here is called Nicholas-nimble-
touch : he—a—he openeth the range of vaults on the north side.
They are tenantless ; but an the Knight and his bandon have
good luck, they may be filled ere the morn's night.   This—a—
this other key—a—I call Will-whirl-i'-the-wards—a : he opens
—a—opens the dark vault i' the middle, in which—a--in which
is the mouth o' the donjon pit."

" An' what be that sma' tiny key?" said Betty Burrel.

" That," said Trockle, " that—a—a--that is merry Mrs.
Margery-of-the-mousetrap, though—a–a—that is but an ill-
bestowed name, seeing that—a—a—it be's more of a bird-cage,
I wot.   But—a--a—Mrs. Margery keeps—she—a—she keeps
the door—a—the door of the ladies' room --the ladies' room off

the passage—a—the passage leading to the hall, thou knawest —a—thou knawest there be's a linnet bird there encaged. The Knight—a—the Knight can't at no rate make her warble—a— warble as he would ha' her. But she's but new caught—a— and she may sing another measure—a—ay, ay, and dance too, when he comes back again. Nay, but now I ha' told thee all— a—sweet Mistress Betty Burrel—a—sweet Betty, sit thee down —a—a—a—and sing—a—a—sing one roundel. Coum! here's to thy health, my—a—a—my bonny blossom."

He put the wooden stoup to his head, and drained it to the bottom.

" A—a—" said he then, attempting to rise and lay hold of Betty; "a—a—coum—a—a—sit thee—a—a—a—sit thee down —sit thee down—a—one roundel—one kiss—a—a—."

" Nay, nay," cried Betty Burrel, moving off; " I maun to my bed i' the kitchen, Master Throckle; I be wearisome tired and sleepy."

" Now, see," cried Throckle, standing up, " now see—a—see what it is—a—see what it is to be between liquor and love—a. Wise as thou art, Master Daniel Throckle, thou be'st but as the ass i' the fable between the tway haycocks—a.—Shalt thou after the Rownsyvall jade now?—or shalt thou—a—shalt thou have one stoup more—ay—one stoup more ?—Daniel, one stoup more will make thee—a—will make thee—a—one stoup the stouter. Coum, then—a."

He opened the spigot, and, holding the stoup with both hands, tried to catch the ale as it spouted forth, gallons of it spilling on the floor for the drops that entered the mouth of the vessel.

" A murrain—a—a—a murrain on it, I say—a. May I die —a—die of thirst—a—if the barrel be not dronkelew—a. It canna—a—a—it canna stand fast—a—a—stand fast only till I —a—a—till I fill mine stoup—a—a. But hold !—a—a—hold, I say—it runs over now—a—a—over now like a fountain. Oh ! I am the man—a—a—to empty a can—a—a—and fill it—a—a —(hiccup)—fill it again and again—ah !—a—a—so here goes."

And, leaving the spigot to run as it might, he put the stoup to his head, and drinking it out, staggered forward a step or two towards the door, and, losing his feet and his balance at the same moment, fell backwards with a tremendous crash on the pavement, where he lay senseless in a sea of ale that deluged the floor.

CHAPTER XXI.

Crooked-hold-him-fast—Making a Lantern of Burnstower Castle.

ASSUETON had no sooner witnessed the prostration of Master Daniel Throckle than he hastened round to the door of the keep ; and, having noted the part of the building where the cellar lay, he slipped down a stair, and, groping along a passage, was soon led to it by the light of the lamp. He entered hastily, and, unbinding the belt from the drunken beast's body, made himself master of the keys. He then seized the lamp, stole silently out by the door, and, taking the directions Throckle had so gratuitously given him, explored a passage at the end of which he found a stair leading upwards. Beneath it was the strongly-barred door of a vault. Having singled out the key called Crooked-hold-him-fast, he applied it to the door, and found it answer perfectly to the lock. He turned the bolt, and, to his no small delight his lamp showed him his esquire Roger Riddel and Robert Lindsay, both sound asleep on separate heaps of straw. He gently waked first one, and then the other : and, laying his finger on his lips, he cautioned them to be perfectly silent. The poor fellows were so confounded by their unexpected deliverance, that they rubbed their eyes, and could hardly believe that they were really awake.

"Bestir thee, but not a word," said the knight to them : "the Castle is all our own. There are but two men within the walls. One I have left in a cellar, senseless as a hog, rucking and wallowing in his ale ; from him we have nothing to fear, but the other yet standeth sentinel at the outward gate. So we must approach him cautiously ; and, when I whistle, pounce on him like falcons. But there is yet a woman in the place, whom we must first secure, to prevent all chance of alarm."

"Yea," said Roger Riddel gravely, "woman's tongue be's a wicked weapon."

The knight and his followers hastened to find out the kitchen, and, having peeped in, they descried Betty Burrel either asleep or pretending to be so ; and, remarking that the windows were strongly barred, so that she could not escape that way, they gently shut the door, and turned the key in the lock.

They now ascended the stair, and having set down the lamp, Assueton, to guard against all possibility of accident, took the large key from the door of the keep, as they passed out. They then stole towards the gateway, where, after prying about for some time, they discovered the watchful warder of the garrison, lying within a doorway, sound asleep, on the steps of the stair leading up to a barbican that overlooked the gate. Assueton immediately sprang on him, and threw the blanket over his head ; and, having taken the keys of the gate from him, they muffled him so completely up as to stop his utterance, and, crossing his arms behind his back, bound all tightly together with Master Throckle's leathern belt. They then hoisted the knave on the broad back of Roger Riddel, who marched merrily away with his burden, and deposited him in the vault, on the very straw from which he had himself so lately risen. Proceeding next to the cellar, they lifted up the drunken jailor, who, being perfectly senseless, had run no small risk of being drowned externally, as well as internally, by a flood of ale ; and, having carried him also to the vault, and put him among the straw that had been Robert Lindsay's bed, they turned Crooked-hold-him fast upon both of them.

Lighting another lamp, which they had found extinguished, the two squires then went to the stables to look for horses. Meanwhile Assueton ascended the stairs alone, to discover the ladies' chamber of which Throckle had spoken, and by attending to the description the jailor had given, soon discovered it. He tapped gently at the door ;—a deep sigh came from within ; —he tapped again.

" Who knocks there at this hour ? " said a female voice.

The voice made Assueton's heart bound with joy, for it was the voice of the Lady Isabelle Hepborne.

" Who knocks there ?—who comes thus to break the hour of rest, the only one I have been blest with since I entered these wicked and impure walls ? If it be thou, false and traitorous knight, know thou mayest kill, but thou canst never subdue me."

" Lady Isabelle," cried Assueton, in transport, " it is no traitor ; it is I, who will dare to call myself thy true and humble slave, thine own humble slave, thine own faithful knight, who, by God's blessing, has come to undo the bars of thy prison and to set thee free.

" Sir John Assueton," cried the fair Isabelle, overpowered by amazement and joy—" Sir John Assueton !—Blessed Virgin !— and how camest thou here ?—But thou art in dreadful danger. For mercy's sake—for my sake—I entreat thee not to speak so loud," continued she, tripping lightly towards the door, and whispering softly through the keyhole ; " speak not so loud, lest

11

thou shouldst be overheard and surprised by some of the caitiff
knight's cruel followers. I will brave all danger to fly with thee."

"Nay, fairest lady," said Assueton, "thou hast now but little
cause of dread. The Castle, and everything in it, is in my
power; but I am rather meagrely attended, and 'twere better
we should lose as little time as may be. I shall unlock thy
door, and keep watch for thee in the hall hard by, until thou
art ready to wend with me."

The knight accordingly passed into the hall, where he found
a long board, covered with the wrecks of feast and wassail, everything in the apartment betokening the riotous and reckless life
that was led by the libertine owner of the place. The walls
were hung round with arms of various kinds, and, to his great
surprise, he perceived the very armour he had worn, and which
he had left with his people when he changed his dress, together
with his shield, lance, and trusty sword, all forming a grand
trophy, at one end. He soon removed them from their place,
and speedily equipped himself like a knight as he was; and he
had hardly done so, when his eye caught the very baldrick and
bugle worn by the leader of the foresters who had acted as his
guide. He took them also down, and hung them from his own
neck, in memorial of the treachery he had suffered. He then
stood anxiously listening, nor did he wait long until he heard
the light step of the Lady Isabelle dancing merrily along the
passage. He flew to meet her, and the joy of both was too
great to be controlled. Yet they trifled not long to give way
to their feelings. Assueton gave his arm to the fair prisoner,
and they descended the stair together. On reaching the court-
yard, he found Riddel and Lindsay busy in the stable. His
squire was employed in putting the furniture and harness on
the very steed the knight had ridden from Hailes; but what
gave rise to most unpleasant speculation in the mind of Assueton, was the discovery that the horses and equipments of his
whole party were there. As he looked at the steeds and trappings of his brave spearmen, his heart sank within him at the
thought of the cruel death that treachery had probably wrought
on the gallant fellows who had used them. A palfrey was soon
selected and prepared for the Lady Isabelle; and the other
three horses being ready, Assueton ordered them to be led out.
Before they mounted, however, Roger Riddel, who never gave
himself the trouble of speaking except when he had something
of importance that compelled him to use his tongue, addressed
his master.

"Methinks, your worship," said he, "we should be the

better of a lantern to light us on our way till the moon
rises."

"Go seek one then," said Assueton; "but do not lose time,
for it is but a chance thou shalt find one."

"Fasten the horses to that hook, then, Bob," said Riddel to
Lindsay; "I shall want thee to help me to light it."

The two men went into the keep-tower together, where they
remained some time, and at length they came out, each bearing
a burden on his back.

"What, in the name of St. Andrew, bearest thou there?"
demanded Assueton.

"'Tis but the dronkelew jailor and the watchful warden," said
Riddel; "methinks they will lie better in the stable."

"Tut!" said Assueton peevishly, "why waste our time with
them?"

But Roger and his comrade deposited their burdens quietly
in the stable, and then returned again into the keep-tower, where
they remained so very long that Assueton lost all patience.   By
and by female shrieks were heard from within.   They became
louder, and seemed to approach the door of the keep, when out
stalked Roger Riddel with much composure, carrying Betty
Burrel like any infant in his arms.   The damsel, who was in
her night attire, was wrapped in a blanket, and was screaming,
kicking, and tearing the squire's face with her nails, like any
wild cat.   But the sedate Roger minded her not, nor did her
scratching in the least derange the gravity of his walk.

"This is too much, Riddel," said Assueton, losing temper:
"What absurd whim is this?   Is the Lady Isabelle Hepborne to
be kept standing here all night, till thou shalt find a new bed
for Betty Burrel?"

Roger turned gravely about, with the kicking and scratching
Betty Burrel still in his arms——

"Surely," said he, "Sir Knight, thou hast too much
Christian charity in thee to see the poor pusell burnt alive?"

"Burnt!" cried Assueton with astonishment; "what mean ye?"

But now came the explanation of all Roger had said and
done; for volumes of smoke began to burst from the different
open loop-holes of the keep, and to roll out at the door, sufficiently explaining what Roger Riddel had meant by a lantern.
The squire hastily deposited the kicking and screaming Betty
Burrel in the stable, to which there was no risk of the fire communicating, and locking the door, put the key quietly into his
pocket.   The Lady Isabelle and Assueton mounted, while the
squire and Lindsay went before them, to raise the portcullis and

open the gates ; and the whole party sallied forth from the walls, right glad to bid adieu to Burnstower. Their two attendants went before them, leading their own horses down the hill, and along the narrow tongue of land, towards the ford, lest there might have been any such trap in their way as they formerly fell into. But all was clear, and they got through the ford with perfect safety.

From the summit of the rising ground above the ford, that is, from the same spot where the moon had given Assueton the first and only view of Burnstower, on the night of his approach, they now looked back, and beheld the keep involved in flames. that broke forth from every opening in its sides, and forced their way through various parts of its roof. The reader is already aware of the grandeur of the surrounding scene, closely shut in all around by high backing hills, and the two deep glens with their streams uniting under the green-headed eminence, that arose from the luxuriant forest, which everywhere covered the lower grounds : let him conceive all this, then, lighted up as it was by Roger Riddel's glorious lantern, which, as they continued to look, began to shoot up jets of flame from its summit, so high into the air that it seemed as if the welkin itself was in some danger from its contact, and he will have in his imagination one of the most sublime spectacles that human eye could well behold.

The party, however, stopped not long to look at it, but urged onwards through the thickets and sideling paths of the glen. now losing all sight of the burning tower, and now recovering a view of it, as they occasionally climbed upwards to avoid some impassable obstruction below. At length a turn of the glen shut it altogether from their sight, and the place where it lay was only indicated by the fiery-red field of sky immediately over it.

Assueton resolved to follow the course of the glen, and in doing so he found that the forester had completely deceived him in regard to the path, that below having occupied about one-tenth part of the time which was consumed the former night in unravelling the mazes of the hill road. The moon now arose to light them cheerily on their way ; objects became more distinct ; and, as they were crossing a little glade, they observed a man running, as if to take shelter under the trees.

"After him, Riddel," cried Assueton ; "we must know who and what he is."

The squire and Lindsay charged furiously after the fugitive, and ere he could gain the thicket, one rode up on each side of him, and caught him. The knight and Lady Isabelle immediately came up, when, to their no small delight, they discovered that it was a trooper of Assueton's party, and, on interrogating him, they learnt that all the others were lodged safely among the brushwood at no great distance. The man was instantly despatched for them, and, when they appeared, the whole villainy of the pretended foresters was explained. The knight and his two attendants had no sooner left them than they were largely feasted with broiled venison, after which liberal libations of potent ale had been administered to them ; and they now firmly believed that the liquor had been drugged with an opiate; for, though the excessive fatigue they had undergone might have accounted for their being immediately overcome with drowsiness, yet it could have furnished no adequate explanation of their sleeping for the greater part of next day, as they had all done to a man, without once awakening. When at length they did arise from their mossy pillows, their horses and accoutrements, as well as the knight's armour, had vanished with the foresters, and nothing remained but part of the carcase of a deer, left, as it appeared, to prevent them from starving. In this helpless state the men were quite at a loss what to do. To advance with the hope of meeting their leader, even if he were not already the victim of a worse treachery than they had experienced, would have been vain ; yet, unarmed as they were, the brave fellows could not entirely abandon him, and after much hesitation, they had at last resolved, towards evening, to wander up the glen to see what discoveries they could make. They had got thus far, when the darkness of the night compelled them to halt until the moon rose ; and the man whom Assueton first descried had been sent out by the rest as a scout, to ascertain whether they were yet safe in proceeding.

Assueton's mind being now relieved as to the safety of the party, he resolved to send back Lindsay to guide the spearmen to Burnstower, that they might horse and arm themselves in the stables. Meanwhile, he proposed that he, the Lady Isabelle, and the squire, should halt in the thickets, near the spot where they then were, and wait patiently for their return.

" Stay," said Roger Riddel to one of the men, as soon as he had heard his master's arrangement, " stay, here is the key, and be sure thou shuttest the stable door after thee. Thou canst not mistake the way, even hadst thou no guide, for there is a lantern burning in the Castle of Burnstower that enlighteneth the whole valley."

CHAPTER XXII.

*Waiting for the Spearmen—The Lady Isabelle's Tale—
The Fight.*

THE party led by Robert Lindsay marched off, and Roger
Riddel proceeded to seek out a retired spot where the Lady
Isabelle might enjoy a little rest. A mossy bank within the
shelter of the wood was soon discovered, and the knight and his
fair companion seated themselves, whilst the squire secured their
horses at no great distance. Assueton was extremely desirous
to learn the history of the lady's capture, and she proceeded to
satisfy him.

As she was passing through the woodlands, on her return
towards Hailes Castle, after parting from her brother, she was
suddenly surrounded by Sir Miers de Willoughby's party, seized,
put on horseback, and carried rapidly off. She was compelled
to travel all that day and next night, halting only once or twice
for a very short time, to obtain necessary refreshment for the
horses and the people; and early next morning they arrived
with her at the Castle of Burnstower, where, although every
comfort was provided for her, she was subjected to confinement
as a prisoner. Sir Miers de Willoughby had taken every opportunity that so rapid a journey afforded, to tease her with offers
of love and adoration; and after they reached Burnstower he
had spent several hours in making his offensive addresses to
her. The lady had repulsed him with a spirit and dignity
worthy the daughter of Sir Patrick Hepborne, called upon him
boldly to release her at his peril, and made a solemn appeal to
Heaven against his treachery and baseness. At length she was
relieved of his presence by his being called on some expedition,
from which, fortunately for her peace, he did not return till a
very late hour, and she saw no more of him that night. But
next morning he came again to her apartment, where he compelled her to listen for some hours to addresses which she
treated with scorn and indignation. He became enraged, and,
in his fury, talked of humbling her pride by other means than
fair speeches if he did not find her more compliant on his
return from an expedition he was about to proceed upon. She
trembled to hear him; but fortunately his immediate absence
saved her from further vexation, until she was finally rescued
from the villain's hands by Sir John Assueton.

Having completed her narrative, the Lady Isabelle anxiously demanded a similar satisfaction from Assueton, who gave her all the particulars of his adventures, the recital being characterized by the modesty which was natural to him. The lady shuddered and trembled alternately at the perils to which he had been exposed on her account, and her eyes gave forth a plenteous shower of gladness and of gratitude when he had finished. He seized the happy moment for making a full declaration of his passion, and he was repaid for all his miseries, fatigues, dangers, and anxieties, by the soft confession he received from her.

After their mutual transports had in some degree subsided, Assueton called Roger Riddel from the spot where, with proper attention to decorum, he had seated himself beyond earshot of their conversation, and interrogated him as to what had occurred to him and Lindsay. Their story was short, and Roger, who was always chary of his words, did not add to its length by circumlocution.

"Why, Sir Knight," said he, "they carried us like bundles of straw to a drearisome vault, and locked us up in the dark. Next day came one Ralpho Proudfoot, with divers rogues—caitiff lossel had some old pique at good Rob Lindsay—swore he would now be ywreken on him—threatened him with hanging—and would have done it with his own hands then, but they would not let him till he got his master's warrant—swore that he would get the warrant and do execution on Rob to-morrow. So we got beef and ale to breakfast and supper, and slept till your honour wakened us to wend with thee."

Sir John now prevailed upon the Lady Isabelle to take a short repose, whilst he and Riddel watched over her safety. In a little time afterwards, Robert Lindsay returned at the head of his remounted cavalry. Assueton was now himself again, and, with spirits light as air, he and the lady got into their saddles, and proceeded slowly down the glen. To prevent all chance of surprise, Robert Lindsay preceded them with half the party as an advance guard, whilst Roger Riddel brought up the rear with the remainder.

The night was so far spent that day dawned ere they had threaded the pass that formed the entrance into the territory of Sir Miers de Willoughby. The sun rose high in all its glory, and threw a flood of golden light over the romantic scenery they were passing through. All nature rejoiced under the benignant influence of his cheering rays; a thousand birds raised their happy wings and melodious voices to heaven; nay, all vegetable as well as animal life seemed to unite in one general choir to pour out their grateful orisons. Nor did the souls of the lovers refuse to join the universal feeling. They each experienced inwardly a joy and a gratitude that surpassed all the power of expression, but which was, perhaps, best uttered in that silent, but not less fervent language used by the devout spirit, when, impressed with a deep sense of the blessings it has received, it rises in secret thanksgivings to its Creator. Each being thus separately occupied in thought, they rode gently on until they had cleared the defiles, and were entering the wider pastures, where the space in the bottom was more extended, and the trees that clothed the sides of the hills, or dropped down occasionally on the more level ground, grew thinner and more scattered.

As they were entering one of those little plains through which the stream they had followed meandered, they were surprised by the appearance of a party of armed horsemen approaching from the other extremity of it. Assueton immediately called forward his esquire.

"Riddel," said he, "we know not as yet whether those who come towards us may prove friends or foes; but be they whom they list, to thy faithful charge do I consign the care and protection of the Lady Isabelle; leave not her bridle-rein, whatever may betide. Take three of the spearmen, and let her be always kept in the midst. Should that bandon yonder, that cometh so fast, prove to be hostile, remember thou art in no wise to act offensively unless the lady be attacked; but be it thy duty, and that of those I leave with thee, to think only of defending her to the last extremity. I shall myself ride forward with the rest, to see who these may be."

The Lady Isabelle grew pale with alarm, partly because her lover was probably about to incur danger, but even yet more, if possible, because, in the knight who was approaching at the head of the troop, she already recognized the figure and arms of him from whose power she had so lately escaped.

"Blessed Virgin protect us," cried she, "'tis the caitiff knight de Willoughby who advanceth!"

"Is it so?" cried Assueton, his blood boiling at the intelligence; "then, by the Rood of St. Andrew, he shall not hence until I shall have questioned him for his villainy."

He stayed not to say more, but, galloping forward, he reined up his steed in the middle of the way, and instantly addressed the opposite leader.

"Halt!" cried he, in a voice of thunder; "halt, Sir Knight, if yet thou mayest deserve a title so honourable; for, of a truth, thou dost not, if thou art he whom I take thee to be. Say, art thou, or art thou not, that malfaitour Sir Miers de Willoughby?"

"Though I see no cause why I should respond to a rude question rudely put, yet will I never deny my name," replied the other, "I am so hight. And now, what hast thou to say to Sir Miers de Willoughby?"

"That he no longer deserves to be called a knight, but rather a caitiff robber," replied Assueton.

"Robber!" retorted the other; "dost thou call me robber, that dost wear my baldrick and bugle hanging from thy shoulder?"

"Thine!" replied Assueton; "if they be thine, 'tis well thou hast noted them so; I wear them as the gage of my revenge; and I have sworn to wear them until thou payest dearly for the wrong thou hast done to the virtuous Lady Isabelle Hepborne, for I speak not of the base treachery thou didst use towards myself."

"Nay, then," replied de Willoughby, "it seems thou art determined that we shall do instant battle. Come on, then."

And so saying, he put his lance in the rest and ran his course at Assueton. The Scottish Knight couched his, and, exclaiming aloud, "May God and St. Andrew defend the right," he put spurs to his horse and rushed at his opponent. They met nearly midway. Sir Miers de Willoughby's lance glanced aside from Assueton's cuirass, without doing the firmly-seated knight the smallest injury; but Assueton's point entering on one side, between the joinings of Sir Miers' helmet and neck-piece, bore him headlong from his saddle, and stretched him, grievously wounded, on the plain. Meanwhile, before Assueton had time to recollect himself, on came the party of de Willoughby, and, with the natural impression that he would dismount to put their leader to death, charged him *en masse*. His own spearmen rushed to his rescue, but, before they came, he had so well bestirred himself that he had prostrated three or four of the enemy. The battle now became general; but though the numbers were on the other side, yet the victory was very soon achieved by the prowess of Assueton and his people, who left not a man before them; all, save one only, being either thrown to the ground or forced to seek safety in flight.

That one, however, was Ralpho Proudfoot, who at the first onset had singled out Robert Lindsay, with a bloody thirst of long-cherished hatred. Their spears having been splintered in the shock, he had grappled Lindsay by the neck, and the latter seizing his antagonist in his turn, they were both at once dragged

from their horses. Rising eagerly at the same moment, however, they drew their swords and attacked each other. Some
of Lindsay's comrades having now no antagonist of their own
to oppose, were about to assist him.

"Keep off," cried he immediately, "keep off, my friends,
if ye love me; one man is enow, in all conscience, upon
one man; so let him kill me if he can, but interfere not
between us."

They rained down their blows upon each other with tremendous force, and the combat hung doubtful for a considerable
time. Proudfoot's expression of countenance was savage and
devilish. He tried various manœuvres to break through Lindsay's cool determined guards, but without effect; and, being
more desirous of wounding his adversary than of saving himself,
he received some severe thrusts. At length, as he attempted to
throw his point in on Lindsay's body, he received a cut from
him that laid his arm open from the shoulder to the wrist, and
at once rendered it useless. The sword dropped from his hand,
and, fainting from the loss of blood that poured from his other
wounds, he staggered back a few paces, and fell senseless on the
ground. The generous Lindsay, forgetting the brutal threats
Proudfoot had uttered against him, ran up to his assistance.

"He was my companion when we were boys," cried he; "oh,
let me save him if I can."

And so saying, he ran to the stream, filled his morion with
water, and poured it on Proudfoot's face. He then bathed his
wounds, and bound up his arm, and tried to staunch the bleeding from the thrusts he had given him. Nor were his pious and
merciful exertions unattended with success. Proudfoot opened
his eyes, and, his senses returning to him, he gazed with silent
wonder in the face of the man who had, a moment before, fought
so manfully against him, and who was now so humanely employed
in endeavouring to save his life, and assuage the acuteness of
his pains. His own villainous and cruel determinations against
Lindsay, which he had been contemplating, the having it in his
power to carry into execution that very night, now rushed upon
his mind. His conscience, long hardened by guilt and atrocity,
was at once melted by that single, but bright ray of goodness,
which darted on it from the anxious eye of Lindsay; and days
long since past recurring to his memory, he remembered what
he had been, and burst into an agony of tears.

Assueton had no sooner rid himself of his enemies than he
went to assist the wounded and discomfited Sir Miers de Willoughby; and on unlacing his helmet, discovered, to his no small

surprise, the features of the very forester who guided him to Burnstower.

The evidence of Sir Miers de Willoughby's villainy was now complete; yet was not the gallant Assueton's compassion for his hapless state one atom diminished by the discovery. The wound in his neck, though not mortal, bled most profusely, and he lay in a swoon from the quantity of blood he had already lost. The Lady Isabelle and the esquire now coming up, every means were used to stop the effusion, and, happily, with success, but he still remained insensible. Assueton therefore ordered his people to catch some of the horses of those who had fallen; and having placed de Willoughby, Proudfoot, and one or two others of whose recovery there seemed to be good hope, across their saddles, they proceeded charily onwards, and after some hours' slow travel, brought them safely to Carham, and lodged them under the care of the Black Canons of its Abbey.

Having rested and refreshed themselves and their horses there, they crossed the Tweed, and being impatient to return to Hailes, that they might relieve the anxious mind of the elder Sir Patrick Hepborne, they arrived there by a forced march.

The joy of Sir Patrick at the unexpected return of his daughter may be conceived. He had, as he resolved, gone in pursuit of Assueton, and had used every means in his power to discover the direction in which the Lady Isabelle had been carried; but all his efforts had been fruitless, and they found him in the deepest despair. It is easy to guess what happiness smiled upon that night's banquet.

CHAPTER XXIII.

Sir Patrick Hepborne's Journey North—Passes through Edinburgh—King Robert II.—The Wilds of the Highlands—The Celtic Host.

OUR history now returns to the younger Sir Patrick Hepborne, whom we left about to commence his journey towards the North. He had no sooner parted from his sister, the Lady Isabelle, and joined his esquire and cortege, under the trees by the side of the Tyne, than he espied a handsome youth, clad in the attire of a page, who came riding through the grove towards a ford of the river. He was mounted on a sorry hackney, carrying his valise behind him, and was guided by a clown, who walked by his bridle. The boy showed symptoms of much

amazement and dismay on finding himself thus so unexpectedly
surrounded by a body of armed men; and he would have
dropped from his horse, from sheer apprehension, had not Sir
Patrick's kind and courteous salutation gradually banished his
alarm.

"Who art thou, and whither goest thou, young man?" demanded the knight, in a gentle tone and manner.

"I am a truant boy, Sir Knight," replied the youth, in a
trembling voice; "I have fled from home that I might see
somewhat of the world."

"And where may be thy home?" demanded Sir Patrick.

"On the English bank of the Tweed," replied the boy.

"Ha!" exclaimed Sir Patrick, "and why hast thou chosen
to travel into Scotland, rather than to explore the Southern
parts of thine own country?"

"Verily, because I judged that there was less chance of my
being looked for on this side the Border," replied the boy.
"Moreover, the peace that now prevails hath made either side
safe enow, I hope, for travel."

"Nay, that as it may happen," said the knight. "But why
didst thou run away from thy friends, young man? Was it
that thou wert evil-treated."

"Nay, rather, Sir Knight, that I was over charily cockered
and cared for," replied the boy; "more especially by my
mother, at home, who, for dread of hurt befalling me, would
give me no license to disport myself at liberty with other
youths. I was, as it were, but a page of dames. But, sooth to
say, I have been long tired of dames and damosels, and knitting,
and broidery, and all the little silly services of women."

"Nay, in truth, thou art of an age for something more
stirring," replied Sir Patrick; "a youth of thine years should
have to do with gay steeds, and armour, and 'tendance upon
knights."

"Such are, indeed, the toys that my heart doth most pant
for," replied the boy; "and such is mine excuse for quitting
home. I sigh for the gay sight of glittering tourneys, and
pageants of arms, and would fain learn the noble trade of
chivalry."

"If thou hast no scruple to serve a Scottish Knight," replied
Sir Patrick, "that is, so long as until the outbreak of war may
call on thee to appear beneath the standard of thy native England, I shall willingly give thee a place among my followers;
and, by St. Genevieve, thou dost come to me in a good time,
too, as to feats of arms, being that I am now on my way to the

grand tournament to be held on the Mead of St. John's. So, wilt thou yede with me thither, my young Courfine?" The boy made no reply, but hung his head, and looked abashed for some moments. "Ha! what sayest thou?" continued the knight; "wilt thou wend with me, or no? Thine answer speedily, yea or nay, young man, for I must be gone."

"Yea, most joyfully will I be of thy company, Sir Knight," replied the boy, his eyes glistening with delight; "and while peace may endure between our countries, I will be thy true and faithful page, were it unto the death."

"'Tis well, youth," replied Sir Patrick; "but thou hast, as yet, forgotten to possess me of thy name and parentage."

"My name, Sir Knight," replied the boy, with some confusion and hesitation—"my name is Maurice de Grey—my father, Sir Hargrave de Grey, is Captain of the Border Castle of Werk—and the gallant old Sir Walter de Selby, Captain of the other Border strength of Norham, is mine uncle."

"Ha! is it so?" exclaimed Hepborne, with great surprise and considerable agitation—"Then thou art cousin to the La——? then thou art nevoy to Sir Walter de Selby, art thou? Nay, now I do look at thee again, thou hast, methinks, a certain cast of the features of his family. Perdie, he is a most honourable sib to thee. Of a truth thou art come of a good kindred, and if thou wilt be advised by me, sweet youth, thou wilt straightway hie thee back again to thine afflicted mother, doubtless ere this grievously bywoxen with sorrow for loss of thee."

"Nay, good Sir Knight, I dare not now adventure to return," replied the boy; "and sith thou hast told me of that tourney, verily thou hast so much enhanced my desire to go with thee, that nothing but thy refusal of what thou hast vouchsafed to promise me shall now hinder me."

"Had I earlier known of whom thou art come, youth," replied Sir Patrick gravely, "I had been less rash in persuading thee with me, or in 'gaging my promise to take thee; but sith that my word hath already passed, it shall assuredly be kept; nor shall thy father or mother have cause to regret that thou hast thus chanced to fall into my hands. Come, then, let us have no more words, but do thou dismiss thy rustic guide, and follow me without more ado."

The youth bowed obedience, and taking the peasant aside, gave him the reward which his services had merited, and, after talking with him for some little time, sent him away, and prepared to follow his new master. Meanwhile, Sir Patrick called

Mortimer Sang, and gave him strict charges to care for the
boy.

" Be it thy duty," said he to him, " to see that the young
falcon be well bestowed by the way. Meseems him but a
tender brauncher as yet; he must not be killed in the reclaiming.
Let him be gently entreated, and kindly dealt with, until he do
come readily to the hand."

All being now in readiness, the troop moved forward; and
Sir Patrick Hepborne, who wished to know something more of
his newly-acquired page, made the boy ride beside him, that
they might talk together by the way. Maurice displayed all
the bashfulness of a stripling when he first mixes among men.
He hung his head much; and although the knight's eye could
often detect his in the act of gazing at him, when he thought he
was himself unobserved, yet he could never stand his master's
look in return, but dropped his head on his bosom. The knight,
however, found him a lad of intelligence and good sense much
beyond his years, and ere they had reached Edinburgh, the boy
had perfectly succeeded in winning Sir Patrick's good affections
towards him.

On their arrival in the capital, Sir Patrick bestowed on the
page a beautiful milk-white palfrey, of the most perfect symmetry of form and docility of temper, and added rich furniture
of velvet and gold to complete the gift. He accoutred him also
with a baldrick, and sword and dagger, of rare and curious
workmanship—presents which seemed to have the usual effect
of such warlike toys on young minds, when the boy is naturally
proud of assuming the symbols of virility. He fervently kissed
the generous hand that gave them, and blushed as he did so :
then mounting his palfrey, he rode with the knight up the high
Mereat Street, to the admiration of all those who beheld him.
The very populace cheered them as they passed along, and all
agreed that a handsomer knight or a more beautiful page had
never graced the crown of their causeway.

Yet though the boy seemed to yield to the joy inspired by
the possession of these new and precious treasures, his general
aspect was rather melancholy than otherwise, and Hepborne
that very evening caught him in tears. He dried his eyes in
haste, however, as soon as he saw that he was observed, and
lifting his long dark eye-lashes, beamed a smile of sunshine into
the anxiously inquiring face of his master.

" What ails thee, Maurice ?" said Hepborne, kindly taking
his hand—" what ails thee, my boy ? Thy hand trembles, and
thy checks flush—nay, the very alabaster of thine unsullied

forehead partake of the crimson that overrunneth thy countenance. 'Tis the fever of home-leaving that hath seized thee, and
thou weepest for thy mother, whom thou hast left behind thee ;
silly youth," said he, chuckling him gently under the chin,
" 'tis the penalty thou must pay for thy naughtiness in leaving
them. Doubtless, thou hast made them weep too. But say if
thou wouldst yet return ? for if thou wouldst, one of mine
attendants shall wend with thee, and see thee safe to Werk ;
and——"

"Nay, good Sir Knight," cried the boy, interrupting him,
"though I weep for them, yet would I not return to Werk, but
forward fare with thee."

"Nay," said Hepborne, "unless thou shouldst repent thee of
thy folly, sweet youth, I shall leave thy disease to run its own
course, and to find its own cure. And of a truth, I must confess, I should part with thee with sorrow."

"Then am I happy," cried the boy, with a sudden expression
of delight : "Would that we might never part !"

"We shall never part whilst thou mayest fancy my company,"
said Hepborne, kissing his cheek kindly, and infinitely pleased
with the unfeigned attachment the boy already showed him.
"But youth is fickle, and I should not choose to bind thy vola-
tile heart longer than it may be willing ; for it may change
anon."

The boy looked suddenly to heaven, crossed his hands over
his breast, and said earnestly, "I am not one given to change,
Sir Knight ; thou shalt find me ever faithful and true to thee."

After leaving Edinburgh, Hepborne travelled by St. Johnstoun, and presented himself before King Robert the Second at
Scone, where he then happened to be holding his court. The
venerable monarch received him in the most gracious and flattering manner.

"Thy renommie hath outrun thy tardy homeward step, Sir
Knight," said His Majesty, "for we have already heard of thy
gallant deeds abroad. Perdie, we did much envy our faithful
ally and brother of France, and did grudge him the possession
of one of the most precious jewels of our court, and one of the
stoutest defences of our throne. We rejoice, therefore, to have
recovered what of so good right belongeth to us, and we hope
thou wilt readily yield to our command that thou shouldst remain about our royal person. Since old age hath come heavily
upon us, marry, we the more lack such staunch and trusty props."

"My Most Gracious Liege," said Hepborne, "I shall not be
wanting in my duty of obedience to your royal and gratifying

mandate. At present I go to attend this tourney of my Lord
of Moray's, and I go the more gladly, that I may have an opportunity of meeting with my peers of the baronage, of Scottish
chivauncie, whom my absence in France hath hitherto prevented
my knowing. Having your royal leave to follow out mine intent, I shall straightway render myself in your grace's presence,
to bow to your royal pleasure."

" By doing so, Sir Patrick," said the King, " thou wilt much
affect us to thee. We have of late had less of thy worthy
father's attendance on our person than we could have wished.
Mansuete as he is in manners, sage in council, and lion-hearted
in the field, we should wish to see him always in our train. But
we grieve for the sad cause of his retirement. Thy virtuous
mother's sudden death hath weighed heavily on him, yet must
he forget his grief. Let a trental of masses be said for her soul :
—he must bestir himself anon, and restore to us and to his
country the use of those talents, of that virtue and bravery with
which he hath been so eminently blessed, and which were given
him for our glory and Scotland's defence. If thou goest by the
most curt and direct way into Moray Land, thou wilt pass by
our son Alexander Earl of Buchan's Castle of Lochyndorbe.
Him must thou visit, and tell him that we ourselves did urge
thee to claim his hospitality."

Hepborne readily promised that he would obey His Majesty's
injunctions in that respect, and took his leave, being charged
with a letter for the Earl, from the King, under his private signet.

His route lay northwards, through the centre of Scotland.
As he journeyed onwards, through deep valleys and endless
forests, and over high, wide, and barren wastes, he compared in
his own mind the face of the country with the fertile regions of
France, which he had so lately left. But still, these were the
mountains of his fatherland that rose before his eye, and that
name allied them to his heart by ties infinitely stronger than
the tame surface of cultivation could have imposed. His soul
soared aloft to the summits of the snow-topt Grampians, where
the hardy and untameable spirit of Scotland seemed to sit en-
throned among their mists, and to bid him welcome as a son.

He made each day's journey so easy, on account of the tender page, that a week had nearly elapsed ere he found himself
in the upper part of the valley of the Dee. It was about sunset
when he reached a miserable-looking house, which had been
described to him as one accustomed to give entertainment to
travellers. It was situated under some lofty pines on the edge
of the forest. The owner of this mansion was a Celt; a tall,

stout, athletic man of middle age, clad in the garb of the mountaineers. Having served in the wars against the English, he
had acquired enough of the Southron tongue to enable Hepborne
to hold converse with him. The knight and the page (whom,
notwithstanding his injunction to Mortimer Sang, he had yet
kept always within his own eye) were ushered together into a
large sod-built apartment, where a cheerful fire of wood burned
in the middle of the floor. The squire and the rest of the party
were bestowed in a long narrow building of the same materials,
attached to one end of it. The night had been chilly on the
high grounds they had crossed, and the fire was agreeable.
They sat them down, therefore, on wooden settles close to it, and
the rude servants of their host hastened to put green boughs
across the fire, and to lay down steaks of the flesh of the red-
deer to be cooked on them.

Meanwhile the host entered with a wooden stoup in his hand,
and poured out for them to drink, into a small two-eared vessel
of the same material. The liquor was a sort of spirit, made
partly from certain roots and partly from grain; and was harsh
and potent, but rather invigorating. Hepborne partook of it,
but the page would on no account taste it.

"Fu?" said Duncan MacErchar, for that was their host's
name, "fu! fat for will she no drink?"

"He is right," said Hepborne; "at his age, water should be
his only beverage."

The host then went with his stoup to offer some of its contents to the knight's followers, most of whom he found less
scrupulous than the page. During his conversation with the
men, he soon learned who was their master; but he had no
sooner heard the name of Hepborne than he became half frantic
with joy, and hastily returned into the place where Sir Patrick
was sitting.

"Master Duncan MacErchar," said Hepborne to him as he
entered, "thou must e'en procure me some mountaineer who
may guide me into Moray Land. I be but a stranger in these
northern regions, and verily our way among the mountains hath
been longer than it ought, for we have been often miswent.
Moreover, I am altogether ignorant of thy Celtic leden, so that
when we have had the good fortune to meet with people by the
way, we have not been able to profit by the information they
could give us."

"Ugh!" cried MacErchar, with a strong expression of joy,
and rubbing his hands as he spoke; "but she'll go with her hersel, an naebody else can be gotten to attend her. Ugh ay, surely

12

she'll do that and twenty times more for ony Hepborne, and most of all for the son of the noble, and brave, and worthy Sir Patrick, and weel her part. Och ay, surely !"

"And how comest thou to be so very friendly to the Hepbornes, and, above all, to our family ?" demanded Sir Patrick.

"Blessings be upon her !" said MacErchar, "she did serve mony a day with her father, the good and the brave Sir Patrick, against the English, and mony was the time she did fight at her ain back. She would die hersel for Sir Patrick, or for ony flesh o' his."

Hepborne's heart immediately warmed to the honest Celt ; he shook him cordially by the hand, and MacErchar's eyes glistened with pleasure.

"Depend on it, Master MacErchar," said he, "my father shall know thine attachment to him."

"Ou fye," said MacErchar, "it would be an honour and a pleasure for her to see Sir Patrick again, to be sure !—ugh ay !" And he stopped, because he seemed to lack language to express all he felt.

"Thou livest in a wild spot here," said Hepborne ; "but thou art a soldier, and hast travelled."

"Ou ay, troth she hath done that," said Duncan, with a look of conscious pride ; "troth hath she travelled mony a bonny mile in England, not to talk o' Ireland, where she did help to take Carlinyford. Troth she hath seen Newcastle, and all thereabouts, for she was with the brave Archembald Douglas, the Grim Lord of Galloway. Och ! oich ! it was fine sport !—She lived on the fat o' the land yon time ; and, u-hugh ! what spuilzie !—ay, ay, he ! he ! he !"

"Thou didst march into England, then, with the French auxiliaries who came over to St. Johnstoun under Jean de Vian, Comte de Valentinois ?" demanded Sir Patrick.

"Ou ay, troth she was with the Frenchmens a long time," said MacErchar—"*Peut Parley Frenchy*, hoot ay can she. Fair befall them, they helped to beleaguer and to sack two or three bonny castles. Ugh ! what bonny spuilzie ! sure, sure !"

He laid his finger with great significancy against his nose, and, having first shut the door, he lifted a brand from the fire, and went to one end of the apartment. There he removed a parcel of faggots that lay carelessly heaped up against the wall, and, lifting a rude frame of wattle that was beneath them, uncovered an excavation in the earthen floor, from which he brought out a massive silver flagon, one or two small silver mazers, and several other pieces of valuable spoil ; and besides these, he produced a plain black bugle-horn, and two or three coarse swords and daggers.

"Troth she would not show them to everybody," said he; "but she be's an honourable knight, and Sir Patrick's son;—she hath no fear to show the bonny things to her. But she has not had them out for mony a day syne."

Hepborne bestowed due admiration on those well-earned fruits of Master Duncan MacErchar's military hardships and dangers. Though of less actual value to the owner than the wooden vessel from which he had so liberally dealt out his hospitable cup at meeting, yet there was something noble in the pride he took in showing them. It was evident that the glory of the manner of their acquisition gave them their chief value in his eyes; for it was not those of most intrinsic worth that were estimated the highest by him.

" See this," said he, lifting the plain black bugle-horn; " this be the best prize of them all. She took this hersel off a loon that fought and tuilzied with her hand to hand; but troth she tumbled him at the hinder-end of the bicker. Fye, fye, but he was a sorrowful mockel stout loon.—This swords, an' this daggers, were all ta'en off the loons she killed with her nain hand. —But uve, uve! she maunna be tellin' on her, though troth she needna fear Sir Patrick Hepborne's son. But if some of the folks in these parts heard of these things, uve, uve! they wouldna be long here."

Saying this, he hastily restored the articles of spoil to the grave that had held them, and putting down the wattle over them, he threw back the billets into a careless heap against the wall.

"Thy treasure is so great, Master MacErchar," said Hepborne, " that thou art doubtless satisfied, and wilt never again tempt thy fate in the field?"

"Hoot toot!" cried MacErchar, " troth she'll be there again or lang; she maun see more o' the Southrons yet or she dies. But uve, uve! what for is there nothing for her to eat?"

He then burst out in a torrent of eloquence in his own language, which soon brought his ragged attendants about him, and the best that he could afford was put on a table before Sir Patrick and the page. Cakes made of rough ground oatmeal, milk, cheese, butter, steaks of deer's flesh, with various other viands, with abundance of ale, appeared in rapid succession, and both knight and page feasted admirably after their day's exercise. Hepborne insisted on their host sitting down and partaking with them, which he did immediately, with a degree of independent dignity that impressed Sir Patrick yet more strongly in his favour.

CHAPTER XXIV.

*Savage-looking Visitors—Night in the Highland Hostelry—
Wolf-Dogs.*

As they sat socially at their meal, they were suddenly interrupted by the door being burst open, when two gigantic and very savage-looking men entered, in most uncouth and wild drapery. They were clothed in woollen plaids of various colours and of enormous amplitude, and these were wrapt round their bodies and kept tight by a belt of raw leather with the hair on it, leaving the skirts to hang half-way down their naked thighs, while the upper part above the belt was thrown loosely over the shoulder, so as to give their muscular arms and hairy knees the full freedom of nakedness. Their heads also were bare, except that they had the copious covering which Nature had provided for them, the one having strong curly black hair, and the other red of similar roughness, hanging in matted locks over their features and about their ears. The forests which Nature had planted on their faces, chins, and necks too, had been allowed to grow, untamed by shears; their legs were covered half-way to the knee by strips of raw skin twisted round them, and their feet were defended by a kind of shoes made of untanned hides. Each had a dirk in his girdle, and a pouch of skin suspended before, while across their backs were slung bows and bunches of arrows. In their hands they brandished long lances, and several recently-taken wolves' skins were thrown over their shoulders, but rather for carriage than covering. Five or six large wiry-haired wolf-dogs entered along with them.

MacErchar instantly started up when they appeared, and began speaking loudly and hastily to them in their own tongue, waving them from time to time to retire, and at length opened the door, and showed them the way to the other apartment.

"Who may be these two savage-looking men?" demanded Hepborne of his host as he entered.

"Troth, she no kens them, Sir Patrick," replied MacErchar, "she never saw them afore; but they tells her that they be's hunters from the north side of this mountains here."

"Live they in the way that I must needs wend to-morrow towards Moray Land?" asked Hepborne.

"Uch, ay," replied MacErchar; "but mind not that, Sir Patrick, for hersel will go wi' her the morn."

"Nay," said Hepborne, " that may not be, that is, if these men are to return whence they came, and that their road and mine run nearly in the same direction. Perdie, I cannot in that case suffer thee to yede so far with me unnecessarily, when their guidance might suffice. Thou shalt give them knowledge of the point I wish to reach, together with all necessary directions touching the places where we may best halt, and spend the night; and they shall receive a handsome guerdon from me when they shall have brought me and mine in safety to the Castle of Lochyndorbe, whither I am first bound."

"Uch-huch! of a truth she would like.to go with her," said MacErchar; "but troth, after all, she must confess that she kens but little o' the way beyond her ain hills there. Weel would it be her part to wend wi' her; but if yon loons ken the gate into Moray Land (as doubtless they have been there mony a time, and she does not mistake them) they will be better guides, after all. But what an she should ask some questions at them?"

"Thou hadst better do so," said Hepborne; "best ask them whence they come, and what parts of the country they know, before thou dost teach them the object of thy questions."

"Troth, and she's right there," said Duncan MacErchar; " this salvage loons are not just to lippen till; weel does she ken them; and, uve, uve! she maun tak special care to look sharp after them gin she should yede wi' them; they are but little chancy, in troth. But she'll call them in now, and see what the loons will say."

The two uncouth-looking men were accordingly brought in. They made no obeisance, but stood like a couple of huge rocks, immovable, with all their thickets and woods upon them. They even beetled over the tall and sturdy form of Duncan Mac-Erchar, who, though above the middle size, might have passed as a little man when placed beside those gigantic figures. Duncan put several questions to them in their own language, which they answered, but always before doing so, they seemed to consult each other's countenances, and then both answered in the same breath. They eyed the knight and his page from time to time, as the inhabitants of all secluded and wild regions are naturally apt to stare at strangers. After a good deal of colloquy had passed, MacErchar turned to Hepborne—

"Sir Patrick," said he, " these men ken every inch of the country from here to the Firth of Moray. Shall she now ask them if they be willing to guide her honour to Lochyndorbe ?"

"Do so, I beseech thee," said Hepborne, "and tell them I
will give them gold when they bring me thither."

MacErchar again addressed them in their own language. The
men seemed to nod assent to the proposals he made them;
and after a few more words had passed between them—

"Uch, Sir Patrick," said he, "they be very willing for the
job. They'll bring her there in two days. They say that she
must be off by sunrise in the morning."

This Sir Patrick readily undertook ; and Duncan MacErchar
having wet the treaty with a draught of the spirits from his
stoup, of which he poured out liberally to each, the men retired.
Sir Patrick Hepborne then signified a wish to go to his repose.
Two heather-beds, of inviting firmness and elasticity, were
already prepared at the two extremities of the chamber where
they were; and the knight having occupied the one, and the
page the other, both were very soon sound asleep.

About the middle of the night Sir Patrick was awakened
by a noise. He raised himself suddenly, and, looking towards
the door, whence it seemed to have proceeded, he saw that it
was open. One or two of the great rough wolf-dogs came
slowly in, looking over their shoulders, as if expecting some
one to follow them—and, making a turn or two round the expiring fire, and smelling about them for a little while, walked
out again. Hepborne arose and shut the door, and then threw
himself again within his blankets. He lay for some time awake,
to see whether the wolf-dogs would repeat their unpleasant intrusion ; and finding that there was no appearance of their
doing so, he again resigned himself to the sweets of oblivion.

He had lain some time in this state when he was a second
time awakened, he knew not how, but he heard as if there were
footsteps in the place. The fire had now fallen so low that he
could see nothing by its light, but by a glimmering moonbeam
that made its way in he saw that the door was again open. As
he looked towards it, he thought he perceived something like a
dog glide outwards. He started up, as he had done before, and,
going to the door, he again shut it ; and, that the wolf-dogs
might no more torment him, he piled up the rustic table he had
supped on, and some of the stools and settles against it. The
precautions he thus took were effectual, for the dogs were no
more troublesome to him all night; and the first interruption
his slumbers experienced was from the overthrow of the whole
materials of his barricado, and the exclamation of " Uve ! uve !"
that burst from Duncan MacErchar, who came for the purpose

of rousing him to prosecute his journey.   Hepborne explained
the cause of his having so fortified the door.

" Uch ay," said MacErchar, " they be's powersome brutes—
powersome brutes, in troth, and plaguy cunning.   I'se warrant
they smelt the smell of the rosten deer's flesh, and that brought
them in.   But they got little for their pains, the ragged rascals
—not but they are bonny tykes, poor beasts ! and troth, 'tis
better to have ane o' them in the house than the wolves themselves, that we're sometimes plagued with."

The host approached the side of Hepborne's couch, with his
everlasting stoup in his right hand, and the wooden cup in his
left, and poured him out of the spirits it contained.   The knight
sipped a little, and then MacErchar retired to see that his morning's meal was properly provided.   It was no less copiously
and comfortably supplied, according to his means, than the
supper of the previous evening had been.

At length Mortimer Sang came to receive his master's
orders ; and when Hepborne asked him how he and his people
had fared, he learned that they had been treated with every thing
the good host could procure for them.   Oats were not to be had
for the horses ; but, in addition to the grass that was cut for
them, Master MacErchar had himself carried a large sack of
meal to the stables and out-houses of turf, where the animals
had with some difficulty been forced in, and he had most
liberally supplied them with his own hands.   He went round all
the men of Hepborne's party, and gave each his morning's cup
of spirits.   In short, he seemed to think that it was impossible
he could do enough from his small means, for the knight and
every person and animal belonging to him.

When the horses were brought out, Hepborne called Mac-
Erchar to him, and offered him, from his purse, ten times as
much money as the value of his night's entertainment and
lodging would have cost.

" Uve ! uve !" said Duncan, sore hurt, and half offended ;
"uve ! uve ! Sir Patrick ! Hoot no.   What ! take money from
the son of Sir Patrick Hepborne, the son o' the noble brave
knight that she has followed mony a days !—take money from
his son for a bit paltry piece and a drink !—Na ! na !—Uve !
uve !—Ou fye ! ou fye !—na, na !—Troth, she's no just so poor
or so pitiful as that comes to yet.   Uve ! uve !   Surely !"

Hepborne at once saw the mischief he had done.   He would
have rather put his hand in the fire than have hurt feelings that
were so honourable to Duncan MacErchar ; and he almost began
to wish that his purse had been there, ere it had been the means

of giving pain to so noble a heart.   He did all he could, therefore, to remedy the evil ; for, putting his purse sheepishly into
his pocket, he called for the stoup of spirits, and, filling the cup
up to the brim, drank it off, to the health, happiness, and prosperity of Master Duncan MacErchar ; then shaking the mountaineer heartily by the hand—

"May we meet again, my worthy friend," said he ; "and
wherever it may be, let me not pass by thee unnoticed.
Meanwhile, farewell, and may the blessing of St. Andrew be
about thee !"

This courteous and kind behaviour completely salved the
wound Hepborne had so unwittingly inflicted.   Duncan was
overjoyed with it, and gratified beyond measure.   He tried to
express his joy.

"Och, oich !   God's blessing and the Virgin's blessing be
about her.   Och, och ! Sir Patrick ! uu-uch !   God's blessing
and the Virgin's blessing—and uch-uch !—and, Sir Patrick—
Sure, sure ! ou ay—uu—u !"

His English failed him entirely, and he resorted to that
language in which he was most fluent.   Hepborne mounted his
horse, and, waving him another farewell, rode on to overtake his
guides, who were standing on a distant eminence waiting for
him ; and as he receded from the humble mansion of Master
Duncan MacErchar, he for several minutes distinguished his
voice vociferating in pleased but unintelligible accents.

CHAPTER XXV.

Wild Scottish Bisons—Fight with a Bull—Cold and Fatigue.

SIR PATRICK HEPBORNE and the page, followed by Mortimer
Sang and the rest of the party, rode slowly on after their savage
guides, along sideling paths worn in the steep acclivities of the
mountains, by the deer, wild bisons, and other animals then
abounding in the wilderness of Scotland.   The fir forests appeared endless ; the trees were of the most gigantic stature, and
might have been of an age coeval with that second creation
that sprang up over the surface of the renovated and newly-
fructified earth, after the subsiding waters had left their fertilis-
ing mud behind them.   Long hairy moss hung streaming from
their lateral branches, which, dried by the lack of air and
moisture, occasioned by the increasing growth of the shade
above, had died from the very vigour of the plant they were

attached to. As Hepborne beheld the two mountaineers striding before them in their rough attire, winding among those
enormous scaly trunks, or standing on some rocky point above,
leaning against one of them, to wait for the slow ascent of
himself and party, he could not help comparing them with those
vegetable giants, and indulging his fancy in the whimsical notion
that they were as two of them, animated and endowed with the
powers of locomotion. The ground they travelled was infinitely
rough and varied in surface, hills and hollows, knolls, gullies,
rivers, and lakes ; but all was forest, never-ending forest. Sometimes, indeed, they crossed large tracks of ground, where, to open
a space for pasture, or to banish the wolves, or to admit a more
extended view around for purposes of hunting, or perhaps by
some accidental fire, the forest had been burnt. There the
huge trunks of the trees, charred black by the flames, and
standing deprived of everything but a few of their larger limbs,
added to the savage scenery around.

Before entering one of these wastes, in a little plain lying in
the bottom of a valley, where the devastation had been arrested
in its progress by some cause before it had been carried to any
great extent, their guides descried a herd of the wild bisons,
which were natives of Scotland for ages after the period we are
now speaking of. The animals were feeding at no very great
distance, and the mountaineers were instantly all eagerness to
get at them. Pointing them out to Hepborne, they made
signs that he and his party should halt. He complied with
their wishes ; and they immediately secured their dogs to the
trees, to prevent the risk of giving any premature alarm, and,
setting off with inconceivable speed through the skirting wood
that grew on the side of the mountain, were soon lost to view.
Hepborne kept his eye on the herd. They were of a pure milk-
white hue, and, as the sun was reflected from their glossy hides,
they appeared still more brilliant, from contrast with the
blackened ruins of the burnt pines among which they were
pasturing. At their head was a noble bull with a magnificent
mane.

As Hepborne and the page were admiring the beauty and
symmetry of this leader of the herd, noting the immense
strength indicated by the thickness and depth of his chest
with the lightness and sprightliness of his head, and his upright
and spreading horns, of a white rivalling that of ivory in lustre,
and tipt with points of jet black, they observed a fat cow near
to him suddenly fall to the ground, by an arrow from the covert
of the trees, while another having been lodged in his flank at

the same moment, he started aside, and bounded off in a wide circuit with great swiftness, and the whole herd, being alarmed, darted after him.   Out rushed the mountaineers from their concealment, and, making for the wounded cow, soon despatched her with their spears.

They then attempted to creep nearer to the herd, and even succeeded in lodging more than one arrow in the bull ; but as none of them took effect in a vital part, they only served to madden the animal.   He turned, and, ere they wist, charged them with a fury and speed that left them hardly time to make their escape.   They ran towards the place where Hepborne and his party were concealed, and, just as the knight moved forward into the open ground, they succeeded in getting up into trees.   Sir Patrick's manœuvre had the desired effect in check-ing the attack of the bisons, for they stopped short in the middle of their career, gazed at the party, and then, led by the bull at their head, again galloped off in a wide circle, sweeping round a second time towards the knight, and coming to a sudden stand beyond bow-shot.   After remaining at rest for some minutes, with their heads all turned towards the party, the bull began pawing the ground and bellowing aloud, after which he charged forward the half of the distance, and then halted.

Hepborne, seeing him thus detached from his followers, put his lance in the rest, and was preparing to attack him ; but just as he was rising in his stirrup, and was about to give his horse the spur, the page, with a countenance pale as death, and a hand trembling with apprehension, seized his bridle-rein, and looking anxiously in his face—

" Do not peril thy life, Sir Knight," said he—"do not, I beseech thee, peril thy life against a vulgar beast, where thou canst gain no honour ; do not, for the sake of the blessed Virgin—do not essay so dangerous and unprofitable an adven-ture."

" Pshaw," said Hepborne, vexed with the notion that the boy was betraying pusillanimity ; "is that the face, are those the looks, and is that the pallid hue of fear thou dost mean to put on as the proofs of thy fitness for deeds of manhood and warlike encounter ? "

The page dropped his head, ashamed and hurt by his master's chiding ; but still he did not let go the rein—

" Nay, Sir Knight," said he calmly, " I did but argue that thy prowess, shown upon a vile brute, were but lost.   Rather let me attempt to attack yonder salvage ; he better befits mine unpractised arm than thine honoured lance, which hath over-thrown puissant knights."

"Tush, boy," said Sir Patrick, somewhat better pleased to see the spirit that lurked in the youth, "thou art much too young, and thine arm is as yet too feeble to fit thee for en-counter with yonder huge mass of thews and muscles. Stand by, my dear boy, and let me pass."

He gave the palfrey the spur, and sprang forward against the bull. The page couched his slender lance, to which a pen-non was attached, and bravely followed the knight in the charge, as fast as his palfrey could gallop. The bull, seeing Hepborne coming on him, bellowed aloud, and, putting down his nose to the ground, he shut his eyes, and darted forward against his assailant. Hepborne wheeled his horse suddenly out of his way, and, with great adroitness, ran his lance through him as he passed him. But his manœuvre, though manifesting excel-lent judgment, and admirable skill and horsemanship, had nearly proved fatal to the page, whose palfrey, coming up in a straight line behind that of the knight, and seeing the bull coming directly upon him, sprang to the side, and by that means unhorsing the boy, left him lying on the ground, in the very path of the infuriated beast. In agony from his wound, the creature immediately proceeded to attack the youth with his horns. But the page having kept hold of his spear, with great presence of mind, ran its point, with the flapping pennon attached to it, right into the animal's eyes. The creature in-stantly retreated a few steps, and before he could renew his attack he was overpowered by the knight and his party, who immediately surrounded him, and was killed by at least a dozen spear-thrusts at once. A general charge was now made against the rest that still stood at a distance, crowded together in a knot; when the whole of them, wheeling suddenly round, galloped off with the utmost swiftness, and were lost in the depths of the forest.

Hepborne leaped from his horse and ran anxiously to assist Maurice de Grey, who still lay on the ground, apparently faint from the fall he had had, and perhaps, too, partly from the alarm he had been in. He raised him up, upon which the boy burst into tears.

"Art thou hurt, Maurice?" demanded Hepborne, with alarm.

"Nay," said the boy, "I am not hurt."

"Fye on thee, then," said Hepborne; "let not tears sully the glory thou has but now earned by thy manly attempt in so boldly riding to my rescue. Verily thou wilt be a brave lad

anon.   Be assured, my beloved boy," continued he, as he warmly
embraced him, " I feel as grateful for thine affectionate exertions
in my behalf as if I now owed my life to them.   But dry up thy
tears, and let them not henceforth well out so frequently, lest
thy manhood and courage may be questioned."

" Nay, Sir Knight," said the boy, "these are not the tears
of cowardice ; they are the tears of gratitude to heaven for thy
safety ; and methinks they are less dishonourable to me," continued he, with an arch smile of satisfaction, "since I see that
thine own manly cheek is somewhat moistened."

Hepborne said no more, but turned away hastily, for he felt
that what the boy said was true.   He had experienced very
great alarm for Maurice's life, and the relief he received by
seeing him in safety, operating in conjunction with the thought
that the danger the page had thrown himself into had been
occasioned by a mistaken zeal to defend him from the bull,
grappled his generous heart, and filled his eyes with a moisture
he could not restrain.

The two mountaineers proceeded to skin the animals, a work
which they performed with great expertness ; then cutting off
the finer parts of the flesh, and carefully extracting the tallow,
they rolled them up in the hides ; and each lifting one of them
on his brawny shoulders, proceeded on their journey, after allowing their hungry dogs to gorge themselves on the remainder.

The knight and his party were now led up some of those
wild glens which bring down tributary streams to the river Dee,
and they gradually began to climb the southern side of that lofty
range of mountains separating its valley from that of the Spey.
They soon rose above the region of forest, and continued to
ascend by zigzag paths, where the horses found a difficult and
precarious footing, and where the riders were often compelled to
dismount.   The fatigue to both men and animals was so great,
that some of the latter frequently slipped down, and were with
great labour recovered from the hazard they were thrown into.
At length, after unremitting and toilsome exertions, they found
themselves on the very ridge of the mountain group, from which
they enjoyed a view backwards over many leagues of the wild
but romantic country they had travelled through during the
previous day.

They now crossed an extensive plain, the greatest part of
which was covered with a hardened glacier, while two high tops
reared themselves, one on either side, covered with glazed snow,
that reflected the sunbeams with dazzling brightness.   The
passage across this stretch of table-land was difficult, the horses

frequently slipping and often falling, till, at length, they came suddenly on the edge of a precipice, whence they looked down into one of the most sublime scenes that nature can well present.

The long and narrow trough of the glen, bounded on both sides by tremendously precipitous rocks, rising from a depth that made the head giddy to overlook it, stretched from under them in nearly a straight line, for perhaps six or seven miles, being cooped in between the two highest points of the Grampians. The bottom of the nearer and more savage part of this singular hollow among the mountains was so completely filled with the waters of the wild Loch Avon, as to leave but little shore on either side, and that little was in most places inclined in a steep slope, and covered with mountainous fragments, that had fallen during a succession of ages from the overhanging cliffs. A detachment of pines, from the lower forests, came straggling up the more distant part of the glen, and some of them had even established themselves here and there in scattered groups, and uncouthly-shaped single trees, along the sides of the lake, or among the rocks arising from it. The long sheet of water lay unruffled amidst the uninterrupted quiet that prevailed, and, receiving no other image than that of the sky above, assumed a tinge of the deepest and darkest hue. The glacier they stood on, and which hung over the brow of the cliff, gave rise to two very considerable streams, which threw themselves roaring over the rocks, dashing and breaking into an infinite variety of forms, and shooting headlong into the lake below.

The sun was now sinking rapidly in the west, and night was fast approaching. The great elevation they had gained, and the solitary wilderness of alpine country that surrounded them, almost excluded the possibility of any human habitation being within their reach. Hepborne became anxiously solicitous for the page Maurice de Grey, who had for a considerable time been manifesting excessive fatigue. Their dumb guides seemed to stand as if uncertain how to proceed, and Hepborne's anxiety increased. He endeavoured to question them by signs, as to where they intended the party to halt for the night. With some difficulty he succeeded in making them understand him, and they then pointed out a piece of green ground, looped in by a sweep of the river, that escaped from the farther end of the lake. The spot seemed to be sheltered by surrounding pine trees, and wore in every respect a most inviting aspect. But if they had been endowed with wings and could have taken the flight of eagles from the region of the clouds where they then were, the distance must have been five or six miles. Taking

into calculation, therefore, the immense circuit they must make
with the horses in order to gain the bottom of the glen beyond
the lake, which must necessarily quadruple the direct distance,
together with the toilsome nature of the way, Sir Patrick saw
that Maurice de Grey must sink under the pressure of fatigue
before one-twentieth part of it could be performed. He was
therefore thrown into a state of the utmost perplexity, for the
cold was so great where they then were, that it was absolutely
impossible they could remain there during the night, without
the risk of being frozen to death.

One of the guides, observing Hepborne's uneasiness and
doubt, approached him, and pointed almost perpendicularly
downwards to a place near the upper end of the lake, where the
masses of rock lay thickest and hugest. The knight could not
comprehend him at first, but the man, taking up two or three
rough angular stones, placed them on the ground close to each
other in the form of an irregular circle, everywhere entire except
in one point, where the space of about the width of one of them
was left vacant; and then, lifting up a stone of a cubical shape,
and of much greater size, he placed the flat base of it on the
top of the others, so as entirely to cover them and the little area
they enclosed. Having made Hepborne observe that he could
thrust his hand in at the point where the circle had been left
incomplete, and that he could move it in the cavity under the
flat base of the stone, he again pointed downwards to the same
spot he had indicated near the upper end of the lake, and at
last succeeded in calling Hepborne's attention to one of the fallen
crags, much larger than the rest, but which, from the immensity
of the height they were above it, looked liked a mere handful.
The guide no sooner saw that the knight's eye had distinguished
the object he wished him to notice, than he turned and pointed
to the mimic erection he had formed on the ground, and at
length made him comprehend that the fallen crag below was
similarly poised, and afforded a like cavernous shelter beneath
it. At the same time he indicated a zigzag path that led pre-
cipitously down the cliffs, like a stair among the rocks, between
the two foaming cataracts. This was altogether impracticable
for the horses, it is true, but it was sufficiently feasible, though
hazardous enough, for active pedestrians. The guide separated
Hepborne and Maurice de Grey from the rest of the party, and
then, pointing to the men and horses, swept his extended finger
round from them to the distant green spot beyond the end of
the lake; and this he did in such a manner as to make the
knight at once understand he meant to propose that the party

should proceed thither by a circuitous route, under the guidance of his companion, whilst he should himself conduct Hepborne and his already over-fatigued page directly down to the Sheltering Stone below, where they might have comfortable lodging for the night. He further signified to Hepborne that the horses might be brought for a considerable way up the lake to meet him in the morning.

CHAPTER XXVI.

The Evening Encampment—Treachery.

So much time had been lost in this mute kind of conversation, that the night was fast approaching, and Sir Patrick saw that he must now come to a speedy decision. The plan suggested by the guide seemed to be the best that could be followed, under all the circumstances, and he at once determined to adopt it. At the same time, he by no means relished this division of his forces, and, remembering the caution he had received from Duncan MacErchar, he called Mortimer Sang aside, and gave him very particular injunctions to be on the alert, and to take care that his people kept a sharp watch over the mountaineer who was to guide them, and to be sure to environ him in such a manner as to make it impossible for him to dart off on a sudden, and leave them in the dark, in the midst of these unknown deserts. Had they once safely arrived at the green spot, where there was a temporary, though uninhabited, hunting-hut, and plenty of grass for the horses, he had no fear of his being able to join them with the page next morning; for the trough of the glen was so direct between the two points where they were separately to spend the night, that it was impossible to mistake the way from the one to the other. Mortimer Sang engaged to prevent all chance of the savage mountaineer escaping. He produced from one of the baggage-horses a large wallet, containing provisions enough for the whole party, which the good and mindful Master Duncan MacErchar had provided for them, altogether unknown to Hepborne. From it he took some cakes, cheese, butter, and other eatables, with a small flask filled from the host's stoup of spirits; these were added to their guide's burden of the flesh of the wild bisons they had slain; and, bidding one another God speed, the party, under Sang, with one of the Celts, and all the dogs, departed to pursue their long and weary way.

Maurice de Grey had sat all this while on the ground, very

much exhausted ; and when he arose to proceed he had become
so stiff that Hepborne began to be alarmed for him.   The poor
boy, however, no sooner remarked the unhappy countenance of
his master than he made an attempt to rouse himself to exertion,
and, approaching the edge of the precipice, he commenced his
descent after the guide, with tottering and timid steps, dropping
from one pointed rock to another, and steadying himself from
time to time as well as he could by means of his lance, as he
quivered on the precarious footing the rough sides of the cliffs
afforded.   The height was sufficiently terrific when contemplated
from above ; but, as they descended, the depth beneath them
seemed to be increased, rather than diminished, by the very
progress they had made.   It grew upon them, and became more
and more awful at every step.   The crags, too, hung over their
heads, as if threatening to part from their native mountains, as
myriads had done before, and to crush the exhausted travellers
into nothing beneath their ruins.   They went down and down,
but the lake and the bottom of the valley appeared still to
recede from them.   The way became more hazardous.   To have
looked up or down would have required the eye and the head
of a chamois.   A projecting ledge increased the peril of the
path, and the page, tired to death, and giddy from the terrific
situation he saw himself fixed in, clung to a point of the rock,
and looked in Hepborne's face, perfectly unable to proceed or
to utter a word.   There he remained, panting as if he would
have expired.   The knight was filled with apprehension lest the
boy should faint and fall headlong down, and the guide was so
much in advance as to be beyond lending his assistance, so that
he alone could give aid to the page.   Yet how was he to pass
the boy, so as to put himself in a position where he could assist
him ?   He saw the path re-appearing from under the projecting
ledge, a little to one side of the place where the page hung in
awful suspense, and, taking one instantaneous glance at it, he
leaped boldly downwards.   He vibrated for a moment on the
brink ; and his feet having dislodged a great loose fragment of
the rock, it went thundering downwards, awakening all the dor-
mant echoes of the glen.   He caught at a bunch of heath with
both his hands ; and he had hardly recovered his equilibrium,
when Maurice de Grey, believing, in his trepidation, that the
noise he had heard announced the fall and destruction of his
master, uttered a faint scream, and dropped senseless from the
point of rock he had held by.   Hepborne sprang forward, and
caught him in his arms.   Afraid lest the boy might die before
he could reach the Sheltering Stone, he shouted to the guide,

and, waving him back, took from him the bottle, and put it to the page's lips. The spirits revived him, and he opened his eyes in terror, but immediately smiled when he saw that Hepborne was safe.

Sir Patrick now put his left arm around the page's body, and, swinging him upwards, seated him on his left shoulder, keeping him firmly there, whilst, with his right hand, he employed his lance to support and steady his ticklish steps. The timorous page clasped the neck of his master with all his energy, and in this way the knight descended with his burden. Many were the difficulties he had to encounter. In one place he was compelled to leap desperately over one of the cataracts, where the smallest slip, or miscalculation of distance, must have proved the destruction of both. At length he reached the bottom in safety, and there the page, having recovered from his terror, found breath to pour forth his gratitude to his master. He now regained his spirit and strength so much, that he declared himself perfectly able to proceed over the rough ground that lay between them and the Sheltering Stone; but Hepborne bore him onwards, until he had deposited him on the spot where they were destined to halt for the night. The grateful Maurice threw himself on his knees before the knight, as he was wiping his manly brow, and embraced his athletic limbs from a feeling of fervent gratitude for his safety.

Sir Patrick now proceeded to examine the curious natural habitation they were to be housed in. The fallen crag, which had appeared so trifling from the lofty elevation whence they had first viewed it, now rose before them in magnitude so enormous, as almost to appear capable of bearing a castle upon its shoulders. The mimic copy of it constructed by the guide furnished an accurate representation of the mode in which it was poised on the lesser blocks it had fallen upon. These served as walls to support it, as well as to close in the chamber beneath; and they were surrounded so thickly with smaller fragments of debris, that no air or light could penetrate between them, except in one or two places. On one side there was a narrow passage, of two or three yards in length, leading inwards between the stones and other rubbish, and of height sufficient to permit a man to enter without stooping very much. The space within, dry and warm, was capable of containing a dozen or twenty people with great ease. It was partially lighted by one or two small apertures between the stones, and the roof, formed of the under surface of the great mass of rock, was perfectly even and horizontal. It presented a most inviting place of shelter, and

13

it seemed to have been not unfrequently used as such, for in one corner there was a heap of dried bog-fir, and in another the remains of a heather-bed.

The mountaineer carefully deposited his burdens within the entrance, and then set about collecting dry heather and portions of drift-wood, which he found about the edges of the lake; and he soon brought together as much fuel as might have kept up a good fire for two or three days.   Having piled up some of it in a heap, he interspersed it with pieces of the dry bog-fir, and then, groping in his pouch, produced a flint and steel, with which he struck a light, and soon kindled up a cheerful blaze.   He then began to cut steaks of the flesh of the wild bison, and when the wood had been sufficiently reduced to the state of live charcoal, he proceeded to broil them over the embers, on pieces of green heather plucked and prepared for the purpose.   Meanwhile the knight and the page seated themselves near the fire.

"How fares it with thee now, Maurice?" demanded Sir Patrick kindly, as he watched the cloud that was stealing over the boy's fair brow, and the moisture that was gathering under his long eyelashes, as he sat with his eyes fixed in a fit of absence upon the ground—"What ails thee, my boy?   Say, dost thou repent thee of thy rashness in having exchanged the softer duties and lighter labours of a page of dames, for the toils, dangers and hardships befalling him who followeth the noble profession of arms?   Trust me, thy path hath been flowery as yet, compared to what thou must expect to meet with.   Methinks thou lookest as if thy spirit had flown homewards, and that it were hovering over the gay apartment where thy mother and her maidens may be employed in plying the nimble needle, charged with aureate thread, or sowing pales upon their gorgeous paraments."

"Nay, Sir Knight," said Maurice de Grey, "my thoughts were but partly of those at home.   Doubtless they have ere this ceased to think of their truant boy!"   He sighed heavily, and tears rolled down his cheeks.

"But why dost thou sigh so?" demanded Sir Patrick, "and what maketh thy brow to wear clouds upon it, like yonder high and snow-white summit? and why weepest thou like yonder mountain side, that poureth down its double stream into the glen?   Perdie! surely thou canst not be in love at so unripe an age?   Yet, of a truth, those mysterious symptoms of abstraction and sorrow thou dost so often display, when thou art left alone to thine own thoughts, would all persuade me that thou art."

The page held down his head, blushed, and sighed deeply, but said nothing.

" Is silence, then, confession with thee, Maurice ?" demanded Hepborne.

The page wiped his streaming eyes, and raised them with a soft and melancholy smile, till they met those of his master, when he again sighed, and, dropping them with renewed blushes to the ground, " I am indeed in love," said the boy, " most unhappily in love, since I burn with unrequited passion. I did indeed believe, vainly believe, that I was beloved ; but, alas ! how cruelly was I deceived ! I found that what I had mistaken for the pure flame was but the wanton flashing of a light and careless heart, that made no account of the pangs it inflicted on mine that was sincere."

The page's eyes filled again, and he sighed as if his heart would have burst. Sir Patrick Hepborne sighed too ; for Maurice, whilst telling of his unhappy love, had touched his own case most nearly.

" Poor boy," said he kindly, and full of sympathy for the youth ; " poor boy, I pity thee. I do indeed most sincerely feel for thee, that thou shouldst have already begun, at so early an age, to rue the smart of unrequited or unhappy love. Trust me," continued the knight sighing deeply, " trust me, I know its bitterness too well not to feel for thee." And again he sighed heavily.

" Then thou too hast loved unhappily, Sir Knight ?" inquired the page earnestly.

" Ay, boy," said Hepborne sadly, " loved !—nay, what do I say ?—loved !—I still love—love without hope. 'Tis a cruel destiny."

" And hast thou never prospered in love ?" asked Maurice ; " hast thou never fancied that thou hadst awakened the warm flame of love, and that thou wert thyself an object adored ?"

" Nay, boy," said Hepborne, " thou inquirest too curiously. Yet will I confess that I have had vanity enough to believe that I had excited love, or something wearing its semblance ; but then she that did shew it was altogether heartless, and I valued the cold and deceitful beam but as the glimmering march-fire."

Maurice de Grey made no reply, but hung down his head in silence upon his breast, and again relapsed into the dream he had been indulging when Hepborne first roused him. The knight, too, ceased to have any desire to prolong the conversation. His mind had laid hold of the end of a chain of association, that gradually unfolded itself in a succession of tender remembrances. He indulged himself by giving way to them, and consequently he also dropped into a musing fit. Both were disturbed by their savage guide, who, having finished his unsophisticated cookery, now made signs to them to approach and eat.

Love, however fervent, cannot starve, but must give way to the vulgar but irresistible claims of hunger. The day's fatigue had been long, they were faint for want, and the odour of the smoking hot steaks was most inviting. They speedily obeyed the summons, therefore, and made a very satisfactory meal. Maurice de Grey had no sooner satisfied the cravings of nature, than, worn out by his exertions and overpowered by sleep, he wrapped himself up in his mantle, and throwing himself on the heather, under the projecting side of the huge rock, his senses were instantly steeped in sweet oblivion.

Sir Patrick Hepborne regarded the youth with envy. His own thoughts did not as yet admit of his yielding to the gentle influence of sleep. He tried to divert them by watching the decline of the day, and following the slow ascent of the shadows as they crept up the rugged faces of the eastern precipices, eating away the light before them. A bright rose-coloured glow rested for a time on the summits, tinging even their glazed snows with its warm tint; but in a few minutes it also departed, like the animating soul from the fair face of dying beauty, leaving everything cold, and pale, and cheerless; and darkness came thickly down upon the deep and gloomy glen. In the meantime the mountaineer had been busying himself in gathering dry heath, and in carrying it under the Shelter Stone, for the purpose of making beds for the knight and the page.

While the guide was thus employed, Hepborne sat musing at the fire, listlessly and almost unconsciously supplying it with fuel from time to time, and gazing at the fragments of wood as they were gradually consumed. His back was towards the entrance-passage of the place where the mountaineer was occupied, and the page lay to his right hand, under the shadow of the rock.

As Sir Patrick sat thus absorbed in thought, he suddenly received a tremendous blow on his head, that partly stunned him, and almost knocked him forwards into the flames. The weight and force of it was such that, had he not had his steel cap on it, his brains must have been knocked out. Before he could rise to defend himself, the blow was repeated with a dreadful clang upon the metal, and he was brought down upon his knees; but ere it fell a third time on him, a piercing shriek arose, and a struggle ensued behind him. Having by this time gathered his strength and senses sufficiently to turn round, he beheld the horrible countenance of their savage guide glaring over him, his eyeballs red from the reflection of the fire, his lips expanded, his teeth set together, and a ponderous stone lifted in both hands, with which he was essaying to fell him to the earth by a third blow. But his arms were pinioned behind, and it was the feeble page who held them. Hepborne scrambled to get to his feet, but, weakened by the blows he had already received, his efforts to rise were vain. The murderous ruffian, furious with disappointment, struggled hard, and at length, seeing that he could not rid himself of the faithful Maurice whilst he continued to hold the stone, he quickly dropped it, and, turning fiercely round on the boy, groped for his dirk. Already was it half unsheathed, when the gleam of a bright spear-head came flashing forth from the obscurity on one side, and with the quickness of thought it drank the life's blood from the savage heart of the assassin. Down rolled the monster upon the ground, his ferocious countenance illumined by the light from the blazing wood. In the agony of death his teeth ground against each other; his right hand, that still clenched the handle of the dirk, drew it forth with convulsive grasp, and, raising it as if for a last effort of destruction, brought it down with a force that buried the whole length of its blade in the harmless earth. Hepborne looked up to see from what friendly hand his preservation and that of the courageous boy had so miraculously come, when to his astonishment he beheld Duncan MacErchar standing before him.

"Och, oich!" cried the worthy Highlander, "Och, oich! what a Providence!—what a mercy!—what a good lucks it was that she was brought here!"

"A Providence indeed!" cried Hepborne, crossing himself, and offering up a short but fervent ejaculation of gratitude to God; "it seems indeed to have been a most marked interposition of Providence in our favour. Yet am I not the less grateful to thee for being the blessed instrument, in the hands of the Almighty, in saving not only my life, but that of the generous noble boy yonder, who had so nearly sacrificed his own in my defence. Maurice de Grey, come to mine arms; take the poor thanks of thy grateful master for his safety, for to thy courage, in the first place, his thanks are due. Trust me, boy, thou wilt one day be a brave knight; and to make thee all that chivalry may require of thee shall be mine earnest care."

Whether it was that the boy's stock of resolution had been expended in his effort, or that he was deeply affected by his master's commendation, it is not easy to determine; but he shrank from the knight's embrace, and, bursting into tears, hurried within the Shelter Stone.

CHAPTER XXVII.

Another Night Attack—A Desperate Encounter.

" By what miracle, good mine host," said Sir Patrick Hepborne to Master Duncan MacErchar—"by what miracle do I see thee in this wilderness, so far from thine own dwelling?"

" Uch ! uch ! miracle truly, miracle truly, that she's brought here; for who could have thought that the false faitours and traitrous loons would have led her honour this round-about gate, that they might knock out her brains at the Shelter Stone of Loch Avon ? An it had not been for Donald and Angus, her two cushins, that hunts the hills, and kens all the roads of these scoundrels, she would never have thought of coming round about over the very shoulders of the mountains to seek after them. But—uve ! uve !—where's the t'other rascals ? and where's her honour's men and beasts ? "

Hepborne explained the cause and circumstances of their separation.

" Uch ! uch !" cried MacErchar; " uve ! uve !—then, Holy St. Barnabas, I wish that the t'others scoundrels may not have them after all ; so she shall have more miles to travel, and another villains to stickit yet ! uve ! uve ! "

And then changing his tongue, he began with great volubility to address, in his own language, his cousins, who now appeared. They replied to him in the same dialect, and then he seemed to tell them the particulars of the late adventure, for he pointed to the dead body of the ruffian on the ground, while his actions corresponded with the tale he was telling, and seemed to be explanatory of it. The two men held up their hands, and listened with open mouths to his narration. He then took up a flaming brand from the fire, and, followed by his two cousins, proceeded to explore the passage leading into the chamber of the Shelter Stone, whence they soon returned with the burden of wolf-skins which the ruffian guide had carried. Duncan Mac-Erchar threw it down on the ground near the fire, and as it fell—

" Troth," said he, with a joyful expression of countenance— " troth but she jingles ; she'll swarrants there be's something in her. Sure ! sure ! "

With this he went on his knees, and began eagerly to undo the numerous fastenings of hide-thongs which tied the wolf-skins together, and which, as Hepborne himself had noticed, had been closely bound up ever since they started in the morning, though the other guide carried his hanging loose, as both had done the night before. The knots were reticulated and decussated in such a manner as to afford no bad idea of that of Gordius.

" Hoof ! " said Master MacErchar impatiently, after working at them with his nails for some minutes without the least effect; " sorrow be in their fingers that tied her ; though troth she needs not say that now," added he in parenthesis. " Poof ! that will not do neither ; but sorrow be in her an she'll not settle her ; she'll do for her, or she'll wonders at her." And, unsheathing his dirk, he ripped up the fastenings, wolf-skins and all, and, to the astonishment of Hepborne, rolled out from their pregnant womb the whole of the glittering valuables, the fruit of his English campaigns.

" Och, oich ! " cried MacErchar with a joyful countenance, forgetting everything in the delight he felt at recovering his treasure—"och, ay ! blessings on her braw siller stoup, and blessings on her bony mazers ; she be's all here. Ay, ay !— och, oich !—ou ay, every one."

The mystery of Master Duncan MacErchar's hasty journey and unlooked-for appearance at Loch Avon was now explained. His sharp-eared cousin, Angus MacErchar, had been loitering about the door at the time of the departure of the knight and his attendants in the morning, and had heard something clink-ing in the Celt's bundle of wolf-skins as he passed, but seeing no cause to suspect anything wrong, as regarded his kinsman's goods, he neglected to notice the circumstance until some time after they were gone, when he happened to mention, rather accidentally than otherwise, that he thought the rogues had been thieving somewhere, for he had heard the noise of metal pots in the bundle of one of them. Duncan MacErchar took immediate alarm. Without saying a word, he ran to his secret deposit, and having removed the heap of billets and the wattle trap-door, discovered with horror and dismay that his treasures were gone. It was some small comfort to him that they had not found it convenient to carry away what he most valued ; and he bestowed a friendly kiss upon the black bugle, and the swords and daggers that were still there ; but the whole of the silver vessels were stolen. What was to be done ? He was compelled to tell his cousins of his afflicting loss, that he might consult them as to what steps were to be taken. They

advised instant pursuit; but well knowing the men and their
habits, they felt persuaded that the thieves would carefully
avoid the most direct path, and guessed that, in order to
mislead their pursuers, they would likely take the circuitous
and fatiguing mountain-route by Loch Avon. Taking the advice
and assistance of his cousins, therefore, Master Duncan Mac-
Erchar set off hot foot after the rogues, and he was soon convinced of the sagacity of his cousins' counsels, for they frequently came upon the track of the party where the ground was
soft, or wet enough to receive the prints of the horses' feet; and
when they came to the ridge of the mountains, they traced them
easily and expeditiously over the hardened snow. It was dark
ere they reached the brink of the precipice overhanging the
lake; but Angus and Donald were now aware of their probable
destination, and the fire they saw burning near the Shelter
Stone made them resolve to visit it in the first place. They
lost no time in descending, the two lads being well acquainted
with the dangerous path; and no sooner had Master Duncan
MacErchar set his foot in the glen, than, eager to get at the
thief, he ran on before his companions. And lucky was it, as
we have seen, that he did so; for if he had been but a few
minutes later, both Sir Patrick Hepborne and Maurice de
Grey must have been murdered by the villain whom he slew.

Hepborne now became extremely anxious about the safety of
the party under the guidance of the other ruffian. For the
attack of one man against so many he had nothing to fear; but
he dreaded the possibility of the traitor escaping from them
before he had conducted them to their destined place of halt for
the night, and so leaving them helpless on the wild and pathless
mountain to perish of cold. He had nothing for it, however,
but to comfort himself with his knowledge of Sang's sagacity
and presence of mind.

Master Duncan MacErchar, with his two cousins, now
hastened to cut off a supper for themselves from the bison beef,
which they quickly broiled; and, after their hunger had been
appeased, the whole party began to think of bestowing themselves to enjoy a short repose. Before doing so, however,
Hepborne proposed that they should bury the dead body. This
was accordingly done, and from the debris of the fallen rocks a
cairn was heaped upon it, sufficiently large to prevent the
wolves from attacking it.

The page, wrapped in his mantle, was already sound asleep
within the snug chamber of the Shelter Stone, and Sir Patrick
lost no time in seeking rest in the same comfortable quarters;

but the three hardy Highlanders, preferring the open air, rolled themselves up, each in his web of plaiding, and then laid themselves in different places, under the projecting base of the enormous fallen rock, and all were soon buried in refreshing slumber.

It happened, however, that Duncan MacErchar had by accident chosen the spot nearest the passage of entrance. The fire had fallen so low as to leave only the red glow of charcoal ; but the night, which was already far spent, was partially illuminated by the light of the moon, which had now arisen, though not yet high enough to show its orb to those in the bottom of the glen. He was suddenly awakened by a footstep near him, and, looking up, beheld a dark figure approaching. With wonderful presence of mind, he demanded, in a low whisper, and in his native language, who went there, and was immediately answered by the voice of the other guide, who had gone forward with Hepborne's party, and who, mistaking MacErchar for his companion in iniquity, held the following dialogue with him, here translated into English.

" Hast thou done it, Cormack?"

" Nay," replied Duncan, " it is but now they are gone to sleep, and I fear they are not yet sound enough. What hast thou done with the party of men and their horses?"

" I left them all safe at the bothy," replied the other, " and if we had this job finished, we might go that way, and carry off two or three of the best of their horses and trappings while they are asleep, and we can kill the others, to prevent any of them from having the means of following us when they awake. But come, why should we delay now?—they must be asleep ere this ; let us in on them—creep towards them on our knees, and stab them without noise : then all their booty is our own."

" You foul murderer !" cried Duncan MacErchar, springing at him, his right hand extended with the intention of making him prisoner. The astonished ruffian stepped back a pace, as Duncan rushed upon him, and seizing his outstretched hand, endeavoured to keep him at a distance. Both drew their dirks, and a furious struggle ensued. Each endeavoured to keep off the other, with outstretched arm, and powerful exertion, yet each was desirous to avail himself of the first favourable chance that might offer, and to bury the lethal weapon he brandished in the bosom of his antagonist. The ruffian had the decided advantage, for it was his right hand that was free, while MacErchar held his dirk with his left. They tugged, and pushed stoutly against each other, and each alternately

made a vain effort to strike his opponent. The brave Mac-
Erchar might have easily called for help, but he scorned to
seek aid against any single man. They still struggled, frequently shifting their ground by the violence of their exertions,
yet neither gaining the least advantage over the other, when, all
at once, MacErchar found himself attacked behind by a new
and very formidable enemy. This was one of the great rough
wolf-dogs, which, having come up at that moment, and observed
his master struggling with Duncan, sprang upon his back, and
seized him by the right shoulder. The ruffian, seeing himself
supported, and thinking that the victory was now entirely in
his hands, bent his elbow so as to permit him to close upon his
adversary, and made an attempt to stab MacErchar in the
breast; but the sturdy and undaunted hero, in defiance of the
pain he experienced from the bites of the dog, raised his left
arm, and after receiving the stab in the fleshy part of it,
instantly returned it into the very heart of his enemy, who,
uttering a single groan, fell dead upon the spot. But the dog
still kept his hold, until MacErchar, putting his hand backwards, drove the dirk two or three times into his body, and
shook him off dead upon the lifeless corpse of his master.

"Heich!" cried he, very much toil-spent—"Foof!—Donald
—Angus—Uve, uve!—Won't they be hearing her?"

His two cousins, who had been fast asleep at the end of the
Shelter Stone, now came hastily round, making a great noise,
which roused Sir Patrick, who instantly seized his sword, and
rushed out to ascertain what the alarm was.

"Oich, oich!" continued Duncan, much fatigued, "oich! and
sure she has had a hard tuilzie o't!"

"What, in the name of the blessed Virgin, has happened?"
cried Hepborne, eagerly.

"Fu! nothing after all," cried Duncan, "nothing—only that
t'other villains came up here from t'other's end of the loch, and
wanted to murder Sir Patrick and his page; and so she grabbled
at her, and had a sore tuilzie with her, and sure she hath stickit
her dead at last. But—uve! uve!—she was near worried with
her mockell dog; she settled her too, though, and yonder they
are both lying dead together. But troth she must go and get
some sleep now, and she hopes that she'll have no more disturbance, wi' a sorrow to them."

"But, my good friend," said the knight, "thine arm bleeds
profusely, better have it tied up; nay, thy shoulder seems to be
torn too."

"Fu, poof!" said MacErchar carelessly, "her arm be's naething but a scart; she has had worse before from a thorn bush; and her shoulder is but a nip, that will be well or the morn."

So saying, he wrapped his plaid around him, and rolling himself under the base of the stone where he had lain before, he composed himself to sleep again, and the others followed his example.   The knight also retired to his singular bed-chamber, and all were very soon quiet.

As MacErchar had hoped, they lay undisturbed until daybreak, when they arose, shook themselves, and were soon joined by Hepborne from within.   The sun had just appeared above the eastern mountain-tops, and was pouring a flood of glory down among the savage scenery of the glen.   MacErchar and his two cousins were busily engaged in renovating the fire; and as Sir Patrick was about to join them, his ears were attracted by the low moans of a dog, which, beginning at the bottom of the scale of his voice, gradually ascended through its whole compass, and ended in a prolonged howl.   He cast his eyes towards the spot whence it proceeded—there lay the dead body of the ruffian murderer with the dog that died with him in his defence stretched across him stiff; and by his side sat two more of the dogs, that, having followed some chase as he came up the glen, had not fallen upon his track again until early in the morning, and had but just traced it out, when it brought them to his inanimate corpse.   There they sat howling incessantly over him, alternately licking his face, his hands, and his death-wound.   Their howl was returned from the surrounding rocks, but it was also answered from no great distance; and on going round the end of the Shelter Stone, he beheld another dog sitting on the top of the cairn they had piled over the dead body of the first man who was killed, scraping earnestly with his feet, and moaning and howling in unison with the two others.   Hepborne went towards him, and did all he could to coax him away from the spot; but the attached and afflicted creature would not move.   The howling continued, and would have been melancholy enough in any situation; but in a spot so savage and lonely, and prolonged as it was by the surrounding echoes, it increased the dismal and dreary effect of the scenery.   Hepborne called the MacErchars, and proposed to them that they should bury the dead body which lay exposed on the ground.   They readily assented, and approached it for the purpose of lifting and carrying it to the same spot where they had deposited the other; but Angus and Donald had no sooner attempted to lay hold of it, than both the dogs flew at them, and they were glad to relinquish the attempt, seeing they could

carry it into effect by no other means than that of killing the
two faithful animals in the first place, and this Hepborne would
on no account permit.

" Verily he was a foul traitorous murderer," said the knight ;
" but he was their master. His hand was kind and merciful to
them, whatever it might have been to others. Of a truth, a
faithful dog is the only friend who seeth not a fault in him to
whom he is attached. Poor fellows ! let them not be injured, I
entreat thee."

Some food was now prepared for breakfast, and Maurice de
Grey, who had made but one sleep during the night, was called
to partake of it. They repeatedly tried to tempt the dogs with
the most inviting morsels of the meat, but none of them would
touch it when thrown to them, and, altogether regardless of it,
they still continued to howl piteously.

Hepborne now resolved to proceed to join his party. Duncan MacErchar had already ordered his cousin Angus, who
was perfectly well acquainted with the way, to go with the
knight as his guide, and not to leave him until he should see
him safe into a part of the country where he would be beyond
all difficulty. Sir Patrick was much grieved to be compelled to
part with him who had been so miraculously instrumental in
saving his life. He took off his baldrick and sword, and putting
them upon Duncan—

" Wear this," said he, " wear this for my sake, mine excellent
friend—wear it as a poor mark of the gratitude I owe thee for
having saved me from foul and traitorous murder. I yet hope
to bestow some more worthy warison."

" Och, oich !" cried Duncan, " oich, this is too much from her
honour—too much trouble indeed. Fye, but she's a bonny
sword ; but what will hersel do for want of her? Ou, ay—
sure, sure !"

" I have others as good among my baggage," said Hepborne.

" But thou didst save two lives," said Maurice de Grey,
running forward, and taking Duncan's hand ; " thou didst save
mine twice, by saving Sir Patrick's. Receive my poor thanks
also, most worthy Master MacErchar, and do thou wear this
jewelled brooch for my sake."

" Och, oich !" said Duncan, " too much trouble for her—too
much trouble, young Sir Pages—too much trouble, surely ; but
an ever she part with the sword or the bonny brooch, may she
pairt with her life at the same time."

They now prepared themselves for taking their different
routes, and Hepborne reminding MacErchar of the injunction

he had formerly given him, to be sure to claim his acquaintance, wherever they should meet, and giving him a last hearty shake of the hand, they parted, and waving to each other their " Heaven bless thee ! " and " May the blessed Virgin be with her honour ! " set out on their respective journeys.

CHAPTER XXVIII.

Meeting the Wolfe of Badenoch—The Cavalcade.

HEPBORNE and his page proceeded slowly down the margin of the lake, preceded by their new guide ; and as they looked back, they saw the bright plaids of Duncan and Donald MacErchar winding up among the rocks, and appearing on the face of the precipitous mountain like two tiny red lady-bird beetles on a wall. The way towards the lower end of the lake was rough and tiresome ; but in due time they reached the place where the party had spent the night, and where they found Mortimer Sang looking anxiously out for their arrival. He had almost resolved to go himself in quest of the knight, for he had strongly suspected treachery, as his guide had more than once manifested symptoms of an intention to escape from them during the previous night's march, and had been only prevented by the unremitting watch kept upon him by the squire, and two or three of his most active and determined people, to whom he had given particular instructions. This circumstance, coupled with the subsequent discovery that the villain had gone off in the night, the moment he had found an opportunity of doing so, had made Sang so apprehensive of some villainy, that nothing would have kept him with the party so long, had it not been for the remembrance of his master's strict orders to permit no consideration whatever to detach him from them.

Poor Maurice de Grey was considerably fatigued, and required to be indulged with a little rest ere they could set forward. At length the whole party mounted and got in motion, and, taking their way slowly down the glen, under their new and intelligent guide, they soon found themselves buried in the endless pine forests. Game, both fourfooted and winged, of every description, crossed their path in all directions. Red deer, and roe deer, and herds of bisons, were frequently seen by them ; now and then the echoes were awakened by the howling of a rout of gaunt and hungry wolves, sweeping across the glen in pursuit of their prey ; and often the trampling of their horses' feet dis-

turbed the capercailzie, as he sat feeding on the tops of the
highest firs, while their palfreys were alarmed in their turn at
the powerful flap of his sounding wings, as they bore him rapidly
away.

Leaving the deeper forests for a time, they climbed the
mountain sides, and, crossing some high ridges and elevated valleys where the wood was thin and scattered, they again descended,
and began to penetrate new wildernesses of thick-set and tall-
grown pine timber; until, after a very long march, they arrived
on the banks of the rapid Spey, where they rested for a time,
to refresh themselves and their horses.   There Angus procured
a guide of the country for them, on whose fidelity he could depend, and, having received a handsome remuneration from Sir
Patrick, returned the way he came.

They now crossed the river by a broad ford, and began winding through the forests that stretched from its northern banks,
and continued gradually rising over its pine-covered hills.   The
day was approaching its close as they were winding along the
side of a steep hill, that rose over the head of a deep but narrow glen, surrounded by fantastic rocks shooting here and there
from amongst the oak woods that fringed its sides.   Sir Patrick's
attention was attracted by the sight of some white tents that
were pitched on a small level area of smooth turf in the bottom,
where it was divided by the meanders of a clear rill.

" She be the WOLFE OF BADENOCH yonder," said his guide,
pointing downwards with a face of alarm.

" The Wolfe of Badenoch !" cried Sir Patrick eagerly ; " what,
are those the tents of the Earl of Buchan ?" for he knew that
the King's son, Alexander Stewart, Earl of Buchan and Lord of
Badenoch, whom he was about to visit, had obtained that *nom
de guerre* from his ferocity.

" Ay, ay," said the guide, " she's right ; tat's the Earl of
Buchan—tat's the Wolfe of Badenoch.   Troth she's at the hunts
there.   Uve, uve !"

" Then, mine honest fellow," said Hepborne, " if those be indeed the tents of the Earl of Buchan, thy trouble with us shall
be soon ended.   Do but lead me down thither, and thou shalt
be forthwith dismissed, with thy promised warison."

The guide paused and hesitated for a time, his countenance
betraying considerable uneasiness and apprehension ; but at
length he began slowly to retrace his steps along the side of the
hill, and, turning off into a path that led down through the wood
over a gentle declivity, he finally brought them out into the
bottom of the glen, about a quarter of a mile below the spot

where they had seen the tents. As they issued from the covert of the trees into the narrow glade, the winding of a bugle-mot came up the glen, and Sir Patrick halted for a few moments, to listen if it should be repeated. By and by the neighing of steeds, and a loud laughing and merry talking, announced the approach of a crowd of people, who very soon appeared, filing round the turning of a rock.

"Mercy be about her! yon's ta Wolfe now," cried the guide, in the utmost trepidation; and, without waiting for reward or anything else, he darted into the adjoining thicket and disappeared.

At the head of the numerous party that advanced came a knight, mounted on a large and powerful black horse. And well was it indeed for the steed that he was large and powerful, for his rider was as near seven as six feet in height, while his body and limbs displayed so great a weight of bone and muscle, that any less potent palfrey must have bent beneath it. But the noble animal came proudly on, capering as if he felt not the weight of his rider. The knight wore a broad bonnet, graced with the royal hern's plume, and a hunting-dress of gold-embroidered green cloth, over which hung a richly ornamented bugle, while his baldrick, girdle-stead, hunting pouch, anelace, and dirk, were all of the most gorgeous and glittering materials. His boots were of tawny buckskin, and his heels armed with large spurs of the most massive gold. The furniture of his horse was equally superb, the bits in particular being heavily embossed, and the whole thickly covered over with studs and bosses of the same precious metal. His saddle and housings were of rich purple velvet, wrought with golden threads, and the stirrups were of solid silver.

But, accustomed as Sir Patrick Hepborne had been to all the proud pomp and splendid glitter of chivalry, he minded not these trifling matters beyond the mere observance of them. It was the head and face of the person who approached that most particularly rivetted his attention. Both were on a great scale, and of an oval form. The forehead was high and retreating, and wore on it an air of princely haughtiness; the nose was long and hooked; the lips were large, but finely formed; and the mouth, though more than usually extended, was well shaped, and contained a set of well-arranged teeth, of uncommon size and unsullied lustre. The complexion was florid, and the hair, beard, whiskers, and moustaches, all ample and curling freely, were of a jet black, that was but slightly broken in upon by the white hairs indicating the approaching winter of life. But the most characteristic features were the eyes, which would have been shaded by the enormous eyebrows that threw their arches over them, had it not been for their extreme prominence. They were fiery and restless, and although their expression was sometimes hilarious, yet they generally wore the lofty look of pride; but it was easy to discern that they were in the habit of being perpetually moved by an irritable and impatient temper, that was no sooner excited than their orbs immediately assumed a fearful inclination inwards, that almost amounted to a squint.

This knight, whom Sir Patrick immediately recognized, by the description he had often heard of him, to be Alexander Stewart, Earl of Buchan, the Wolfe of Badenoch, was about the age of fifty, or perhaps a few years younger. By his side rode a lady, clad in a scarlet mantle, profusely embroidered with gold, and seated on a piebald palfrey, covered with trappings even more costly than those of the horse that carried the Wolfe of Badenoch himself. She seemed to be approaching the age of forty, and was slightly inclining to *embonpoint*, fresh in face and complexion, and very beautiful. Behind them rode five gay and gallant young knights, the eldest of whom might have been about twenty. They were all richly apparelled, and accoutred in a taste somewhat similar to that of the elder knight who rode before them, and were mounted on magnificent horses, that came neighing and prancing along, their impatience of restraint adding to the pleasure of their youthful riders, especially of the younger, who were boys.

A large train of attendants followed, partly on horseback and partly on foot. These were variously armed with hunting-spears, cross-bows, and long-bows: and many of the pedestrians, who were coarsely clad, and some of them even barefooted as well as bareheaded, led a number of alloundes, raches, and sleuth-hounds, whilst others carried carcases of red deer and roebucks, suspended on poles borne between two, as also four-footed and feathered animals of chase, which had fallen victims to the sport of the day.

All this, which has taken so much time to describe, was seen by Sir Patrick Hepborne at a single glance, or at least he had sufficient leisure to make himself master of the particulars ere the cavalcade came up to him. As the Wolfe of Badenoch drew near, Sir Patrick dismounted, and, giving his horse to his esquire, advanced towards him, and paid him the respectful obeisance due to the King's son.

" Ha!" cried the Wolfe, reigning up his curvetting steed; " who, in the fiend's name, may this be?"

" My noble Lord of Buchan," said Hepborne, " I wait upon your Highness by the especial desire of His Majesty the King, your royal father.   Being on my way to Moray Land, to be present at the tournament to be held by the Earl of Moray on the Mead of St. John's, I passed by Scone, to pay mine humble duty at his Grace's Court after my return from France, where I have been for some of these late years ; and knowing mine intent of visiting these northern parts, your royal father did kindly bid me seek your well-known hospitality as I should pass into Moray Land.   Moreover, he did honour me so far as to charge me with a letter under his own signet, addressed for your Highness.—My name is Sir Patrick Hepborne."

The Wolfe fidgetted to and fro upon his horse, and displayed very great impatience until the knight had finished.

" Ha !" said he, the moment he had done speaking—" ha ! 'tis well.   By my trusty burly-brand, thou art welcome, Sir Patrick Hepborne.   Thy name hath a sweet savour with it for stark doughtiness in stiff stour, since thou be'st, as I ween, the son of the bold Sir Patrick Hepborne of Hailes.   By my beard, thou art welcome," said he again, as he stretched out his hand to him.   " As for the old man's letter, we shall see that anon when better place and leisure serve.   Know this lady, Sir Patrick," continued he, turning towards her who rode with him ; " she is the Lady Mariota Athyn (of whom peraunter thou mayst have heard), and mother to those five sturdy whelps who ride at my back, and who are wont to call me father.   But get thee to horse, Sir Patrick ; the feast waits for us ere this, and we can talk anon with our wine wassail.   If thou hadst done as much to-day as we have, and been as long from thy trencher, the red fiend catch me but thou wilt think more of eating than of talking.   Get thee to horse, then, and on with us, I say ; we are now but a short space from the tents.   To horse, then, to horse !"

Mortimer Sang brought up his master's steed, Sir Patrick vaulted into the saddle, and, being beckoned by the Wolfe to take his place beside him, immediately obeyed.   The Lady Mariota Athyn, who had eyed the handsome Maurice de Gray, gave him a condescending signal to come to her right hand, and in this order they rode up the glen, towards the place where the tents were pitched, the knight's party mingling as they went with that of Lord Badenoch, according to the various conditions of the persons who composed it.

14

CHAPTER XXIX.

The Wolfe of Badenoch's Hunting Encampment—Letter from King Robert—Arrival at the Wolfe's Stronghold.

THE spot chosen for the Wolfe of Badenoch's hunting encampment was beautiful. The little rill came welling forth in one great jet, like a copious fountain, from a crevice in the rocks that, rising like a mimic castle, terminated the glen at its upper extremity. The bright greens of the ivy, honeysuckle, and various creeping plants and shrubs that climbed over its surface, blended with the rich orange, brown, and yellow tints of the lichens that covered it. On the smooth flat sward, a little in advance of this, was pitched the pavilion of the Wolfe himself, with his banner waving before it. It consisted of three apartments, the largest of which, occupying the whole front, was used as the banqueting place, whilst the two others behind were devoted to the private convenience and repose of the Earl and the Lady Mariota.

To the right and left of this central pavilion were the tents of the five young knights. Of these the eldest, Sir Alexander Stewart, afterwards Earl of Mar, had all the violence of his father's temper; Sir Andrew, the second, was cool, crafty, and designing; and Walter, James, and Duncan, who were too young to have anything like fixed characters, had all the tricks and pranks of ill-brought-up and unrestrained youths, though Duncan, the youngest, had naturally rather a more amiable disposition than any of the others.

Besides these tents, there were several more on the two flanks, extending towards the extremity of the horns of the semi-circle, occupied by squires, and the principal people of the Earl's retinue. Within a rocky recess at one side, almost shut out from view by the embowering trees, a number of temporary huts were erected for culinary purposes, as well as for lodging the great mass of the lower order of attendants; and on the opposite side were extensive pickets, to which the horses were attached in lines.

The night dropped fast down on that low and narrow spot, and, as the cavalcade arrived, the people were already engaged in lighting a huge bonfire in the centre of it, quite capable of restoring an artificial day, and this immense blaze was to be kept up all night, partly for purposes of illumination, and partly to keep off the wolves. The Earl no sooner appeared, than all was clamour, and running, and bustle, and confusion. He halted in front of the tents—the bugles blew, and the squires and attendants ran to hold his stirrup. But he waited not for their assistance. Ere they could reach him he sprang to the ground, and lifting the Lady Mariota from off her palfrey, carried her into the pavilion.

"Sir Patrick," said he to Hepborne, as an esquire ushered him in, "thou must bear with such rustic entertainment as we have to offer thee here to-night. To-morrow we move to Lochyndorbe, where thou shalt be better bestowed."

Sir Patrick bowed; but he saw no lack of provision for good cheer as he cast his eyes over the ample board, which was covered with a profusion of silver utensils of all kinds, among which were strangely mingled pewter, and even wooden trenchers, and where there were not only silver flagons and mazers, but leathern black-jacks, wooden stoups, and numerous drinking-horns, the whole being lighted by a silver lamp that hung over the centre.

"What, in the fiend's name, makes the feast to tarry?" cried the Wolfe impatiently: "do the loons opine that we have no stomachs, or that we are blocks of wood, that we can stand all day i' the passes, and yet do at night without feeding? The feast, I say—the feast! Nay, send me that rascal cook here."

The cook, sweating from his fiery occupation, was instantly brought before him, trembling, carrying a stew-pan in one hand, and a long iron gravy-ladle in the other, with his sleeves tucked up, and clothed in a white apron and night-cap.

"Villain!" said the Wolfe, in a tremendous voice, "why are not the viands on the table? By all the fiends of the infernal realms, thou shalt be forthwith spitted and roasted before thine own fire, an we have not our meal ere I can turn myself."

The cook bowed in abject terror, and, as soon as he was beyond the tent door, ran off, bawling to his assistants; and in a few minutes, a crowd of lacqueys bearing the smoking-hot dishes came pouring into the pavilion, heaping the board with them till it groaned again.

"Blow the bugle for the banquet," cried the impatient Earl, seating himself at the head of the table. "Sit thee down, Mariota, on my right hand here; and do thou, Sir Patrick Hepborne, sit here on my left. The boys and the rest may find places for themselves."

"But where is thy gentle page, Sir Knight?" said the Lady Mariota to Hepborne. "I pray thee let him sit down with us.

Certes, he doth appear to be come of no mean blood. Make me
to know how the doced youth is hight, I do beseech thee?"

"Lady," said Sir Patrick, smiling, "he is called Maurice de
Grey, a truant boy of a good English house. His father is a
gallant knight, who governs the border strength of Werk. Tired
of soft service as a page of dames, he left his indulgent mother
to roam into the world, and chancing to encounter me, I adopted
him as my page. In truth, though young, he is prudent, and
perdie, he hath more than once showed a good mettle, and some
spirit, too, though his thewes and museles have hardly strength
enow, as yet, to bear it out."

"Oh, fye on thee, Maurice de Grey," said the lady, smiling
graciously on the page, as he entered among the crowd—"fye
on thee, Maurice, I say. Art thou so naughty as to wish to
shun the converse of women at thine age? Oh, shame to thy
youth-hed. Parfay, I shall myself undertake thy punishment,
so sit thee down by me here, that I may school thee for thy
folly and want of gallantry."

Maurice bowed respectfully, and immediately occupied the
proffered seat, where the lady did all in her power to gratify
him by putting the nicest dainties on his plate, and prattling
many a kind and flattering speech in his ear. Sir Alexander
Stewart placed himself next to Sir Patrick, and, though naturally
fierce and haughty in his air, showed every disposition to exert
hospitable and knightly courtesy towards his father's guest.
Below them, on both sides of the table, sat his brothers; and
the rest of the long board was filled up by the esquires and
other retainers, who each individually occupied the first room
he could find. For some time there was but little conversation, and nothing interrupted the clinking of knives upon the
trenchers but an occasional pledge called for by the Wolfe, who,
as he ate largely and voraciously, drank long draughts too, to
promote the easy descent of the food into his capacious stomach.
He continued to eat long after every one else at table had
ceased.

"Ha!" said he at length, as he laid down his implements of
carving; "quick! clear away those offensive fragments. Hey!
what stand ye all staring at? Remove the assiettes and
trenchers, I say—Are ye deaf, knaves?"

Every servile hand was upon the board in an instant, and the
dishes and plates disappeared as if by magic.

"Wine—Rhenish!—Malvoisie! Wine, I say!" vociferated
the Wolfe. "What, ye rogues, are we to perish for thirst?"

The silver flagons, stoups, and black-jacks were replenished with equal celerity, and deep draughts went round, and the carouse became every moment more fierce and frequent. The Lady Mariota Athyn rose to retire to her own private quarter of the pavilion.

"Young Sir Page," said she to Maurice de Grey, "wine wassail is not for thee, I ween; thou shalt along with my boys and me, thou naughty youth; thou shalt with me, I say. Verily, I condemn thee to do penance with me and my damsels until the hour of couchee. Come along, Sir Good-for-Nothing."

The page arose, and went with the lady and her three younger sons, but he seemed to go very unwillingly. In truth, he had received her little attentions rather coldly; so much so, indeed, that Hepborne had felt somewhat hurt at his seeming indifference.

After much wine had been swallowed, and a great deal of conversation had passed about hunting and deeds of chivalry—

"And so thou goest to this tourney of my brother-in-law, the Earl of Moray's, Sir Patrick?" said the Wolfe.

"Such is the object of my journey, my Lord," replied Hepborne.

"By St. Hubert! I have a mind to go with thee, were it only to show my boys the sport," replied the Wolfe. "But, by the thunder of Heaven! I am not over well pleased with this same brother-in-law. The old man, my doting liege-father, hath refused to add Moray Land to my lieutenantship, which now lacketh but it to give me broad control from the Spey to the Orcades; and, by my beard, I cannot choose but guess that Earl John hath had some secret hand in preventing him. My sister Margery denies this stoutly; but she would deny anything to keep fire and sword from her lord's lands. Yet may the hot fiend swallow me if I ween not that I have hit the true mark in so suspecting."

"By the red Rood, then, I would straightway tax him with it," said Sir Alexander Stewart.

"Nay, nay, meddle thou not, Sandy," said the Wolfe. "I lack not thine advice. This matter concerns not thee."

"Concerns not me!" exclaimed Sir Alexander, hotly—"by the martyrdom of St. Andrew, but it does though—it concerneth me mightily; yea, it enchafeth me to see thee, my father, pusillanimously suffer thyself to be agrutched and hameled in the extent of thy flight, an if thou wert a coistril hawk, to be mewed by any he of the mark of Adam."

"I tell thee, boy, thou art a silly fool," roared out the Wolfe, gnashing his teeth in a fury.

"If I am a fool, then," said Sir Alexander, in no less a rage, "I am at least wise enough to know from whom I have had my folly."

The ferocious Wolfe could stand this no longer. His eyes flashed fire, and, catching up a large silver flagon of wine, from which he had been going to drink, he hurled it at his son's head with so much celerity and truth of aim that had not Hepborne raised his left arm and intercepted it in its flight, though at the expense of a severe contusion, the hot Sir Alexander would never have uttered a word more. Heedless of the escape he had made, he rose to return the compliment against his father; but Hepborne, and some of those nearest to him, interfered, and with some difficulty the anger of both father and son was appeased. It was a feature in the Wolfe's character, and one also in which his son Alexander probably participated, that, although his passion was easily and tremendously excited on every trifling occasion, so as to convert him at once into an ungovernable wild beast, capable of the most savage and cruel deeds, yet there were times when he was not unapt to repent him of any atrocious act he might have been guilty of, particularly where his own family was concerned. He loved his son Alexander—with the exception of the child Duncan, indeed, he loved him more than any of the others, perhaps because he more nearly resembled himself in temper. After the fray had been put an end to he sat for some moments trembling with agitation; but, as his wrath subsided, and he became calmer, he began to picture to himself his son stretched dead at his feet by a blow from his own hand. His countenance became gloomy and oppressed; he fidgetted upon his seat, and at length starting hurriedly up—

"Depardieux, I thank thee, Sir Patrick," said he, taking Hepborne's right hand, and squeezing it heartily—"depardieux, I thank thee for having arrested a blow I should have so much repented—Alexander," continued he, going up and embracing his son, "forgive me, my boy; but provoke not mine ire in the same way again, I beseech thee."

"Nay, father," said Sir Alexander, "perhaps I went too far; but, by the mass, I was irritated by the thought that John Dunbar, Earl of Moray, should have got between thee and the King with his silky curreidew tongue."

"Right, boy," cried the Wolfe, relieved by finding a new outlet for his rage, and striking the table furiously with his fist as he resumed his seat—"right, boy: there it is. If I but find that my suspicions are true, by the beard of my grandfather his being my sister Margery's husband shall not save him from my wrekery. But, Sir Patrick," continued he, after a short pause, "so please thee, let me see the old man's letter thou wert charged with. Knowest thou aught of its contents?"

"No, my good lord," said Hepborne, taking the embroidered silken case that contained the King's epistle from his bosom. "His Majesty put it himself into my hands as I kissed his, to take my duteous leave, and here it is as he gave it to me."

The Wolfe glanced at the royal signet, and then, with his wonted impatience, tore up the silk, and began to read it to himself. His brow darkened as he went on, his teeth ground against each other, and his lip curled with a growing tempest. At length he dashed down the King's letter on the table, and struck the board with his clenched fist two or three times successively—

"Ha! see, Sir Knight, what it is thou hast brought me," cried he, in a fury so great that he could hardly give utterance to his words. "Read that, read that, I say. By all the fiends, 'tis well I read it not at first, ere I knew thee better, Sir Knight, or thou mightest have had but a strange reception. Read it—read it, I say!"

Hepborne took up the letter, and read as follows:—

"To the High and Noble, our trusty and well-beloved son, Alexander Stewart, Earl of Buchan, Earl of Ross, Lord of Badenoch, and our faithful Lieutenant over the northern part of our kingdom, from the bounds of the county of Moray to the Pentland Frith, these greeting—

"Son Alexander,—We do hope these may find thee well. It hath reached our ears that thou dost still continue to keep abiding with thee thy leman, Mariota Athyn. Though she, the said Mariota, be the mother of thy five boys, yet is the noble Lady Euphame, Countess of Ross, thy true and lawful wife; with her, therefore, it behoveth thee to consort, yea, and her it behoveth thee to cherish: yet are we informed, and it doleth us much that it should be so, that thou dost still leave her to grieve in loneliness and solitude. Bethink thee that thou yet liest under the threatened ban of holy Mother Church, and under the penalty laid on thee by the godly Bishops of Moray and Ross for having cruelly used her, and that thou dost yet underly, and art bound by their sentence to live with her in a virtuous and seemly manner. Let not gratitude permit thee to forget, also, that she did bestow upon thee rich heritages in land, and that it is through her thou dost hold thy title of Earl of Ross, which we did graciously confirm to thee. Return, then, from thy wicked ways, and cleave unto thy lawful wife, to her cherisaunce, as thou wouldst value our good favour, and as thou wouldst give jovisaunce to these our few remaining years of old. And so, as thou dost obey these our injunctions, may God keep thee and thine in health, and soften thine heart to mercy and godliness. So prayeth thy loving father and King,

"ROBERT REX."

Hepborne laid down the King's letter without venturing a single comment on it, and it was instantly snatched up by Sir Alexander Stewart.

"What!" cried he with indignation, after glancing it over, "is our mother, or are we, to be turned adrift from our father's house like ragamuffin quistrons, to beg our way through the world, to please a doting old man?"

"Nay, sooner shall I pluck out every hair of this beard from my face," shouted the Wolfe in a fury, and tugging out a handful of it unconsciously as he said so. "What! am I to be schooled by an old bigoted prater at my time of life, and to be condemned to live with a restless intriguing hag, who hath been the cause of so much vexation to me! The red fiend shall catch me then! Not for all the bishops in Mother Church, with the Orders four to boot, shall I submit me to such penance. But, by all the powers of darkness, the split-capped Bishop of Moray, Alexander Barr, shall suffer for this. He it is who hath been at the bottom of it all; he it is who hath stirred up the King; and by the infernal fires, he shall ere long undergo my wrekery. He hath been an eternal torture to me; but, by my trusty burly-brand, I shall make the craven, horrow lossel rue that ever he roused the *Wolfe of Badenoch.*"

He struck the table tremendously with his fist as he concluded. His calling himself by his *nom de guerre* was with him like Jupiter swearing by the river Styx. His people moved on their seats, put on stern brows, and looked at one another, as if each would have said, "Brother, we shall have something to do here." The Earl himself snatched up a flagon of Rhenish, and took a deep draught to cool his ire; then turning to Hepborne—

"I bid thee good night, Sir Patrick," said he; "thou hast no fault in this matter; good night, I say." Then turning to the rest—"See that Sir Patrick Hepborne have the best quarters

that may be given him.   Good night.   By all the fiends, the
white-faced hypocrite shall pay for it."   And so saying, he disappeared into the inner apartment of the pavilion.

Immediately afterwards, the page and the three younger
Stewarts came forth.   Sir Alexander still continued to fret
and broil with the fury which the King's letter had excited in
him ; yet he neglected not the civilities due to their guest.   He
gave orders that the youngest boy's tent should be prepared for
Sir Patrick Hepborne, and that his brothers, Duncan and
James, should occupy one tent for the night; and, leaving Sir
Andrew Stewart to see that the stranger Knight was properly
accommodated, he made an exit similar to his father's.

" 'Tis an unfortunate weakness," said Sir Andrew Stewart,
as he accompanied Hepborne to his tent, " 'tis an unhappy
weakness that so cruelly besets my father and my brother
Alexander ; half the hours of their lives are spent in temporary
frenzy.   It would be well for them if they could bridle their
passions."

Hepborne found it difficult to reply ; so changing the subject
adroitly, and thanking Sir Andrew for his courteous attention,
he bade him good night, and was glad to take refuge in the
quiet of the tent that had been prepared for him.   Being indisposed for sleep, he called his page, whose couch was in the outer
apartment, and, ere they retired to rest, their conversation ran
as follows :—

" Maurice," said the knight, " why didst thou show thyself so
backward in receiving the Lady Mariota's favours ?   She seemed
anxious to show thee all manner of kind attention, yet thou
didst repel her by thy very looks."

" Sir Knight," said the page, " I like not that woman ; she is
not the wife of the Earl of Buchan, and meseems it a foul
thing to see her sit in the seat of so honourable and virtuous a
lady as the Countess of Ross, queening it where she hath
no claim but the base one that may spring from her own
infamy."

" Thou art right, boy," said Hepborne, " thou art right, in
good truth ; but 'tis not for us to read moral lessons to our
seniors.   Where we see positive harm, or glaring injury, done
to any one by another, then it behoveth a true knight to stay
not his hand, but forthwith to redress the grievance at peril of
his life.   But though he is not to court the society of those who
sin grossly, yet cannot he always eschew it, and it falleth not
within the province of a knight to read moral lectures and
homilies to every one he meeteth that may offend against God's

laws; else might he exchange the helmet for the cowl. And, verily, he should have little to do but to preach, since the wickedness of man is so great, and so universal, that there is no one who might not call for his sermons; yea, and while zealously preaching to others, he would certainly fall into guilt himself. No, Maurice; let us take care to live irreproachably; then let us suffer no one to do tyranny or injustice to another; and having secured these important things, let us leave all else to a righteous God, who will Himself avenge the sins committed against His moral law. Yet do I much commend that virtuous indignation in thee; and if thy love should ever haply run smooth, as I sincerely pray that it may, I trust that thou wilt be a mirror of virtuous constancy."

The page clasped his hands on his breast, and, throwing up his eyes to Heaven, "Grant but that my love may yet prosper," said he, fervently; "grant but that, ye blessed Virgin, and the sun shall not be more constant to the firmament, than I shall be in the attachment to the object of my affection! But couldst thou be constant, Sir Knight?" added he, with a sigh.

"'Tis an odd question, boy," said Hepborne, laughing. "I think I know so much of myself as to say boldly that I could; and, verily, I would never mate me where I weened there might be risk of temptation to aught else. But, of a truth, I have not yet seen the woman of whom I might think so highly as to risk chaining my virtue to her side."

The page sat silent for some moments, and at length, turning to Hepborne, "I have seen knights," said he, "who did roune sweet speeches in the ears of foolish maidens, who did swear potent oaths that they did love them, and yet, when the silly pusels believed them, they would laugh at their facile credence, and then, leaping into their saddles, ride away, making mirth of the sad wounds they had caused. Say, Sir Knight, couldst thou do this?"

"Depardieux, mon bel ami Maurice de Grey," said the knight, laughing, "methinks thou hast made thyself my father confessor to-night. What meanest thou by these questions?"

"In truth, my dear master," said the boy, "I do but ask, that I may better myself by the wisdom of thine answers. How should I, an untaught youth, ever become an honour to knighthood, as I hope one day to be, save by thy sage precept and bright example?"

"Nay, then, sweet page," said the knight, kindly, "I shall

not deny to answer thee. In good sooth, I have never yet been so base, nor could I ever be guilty of so much wickedness."

The page's eyes brightened for a moment at the knight's virtuous assertion.

"There be women indeed," continued Sir Patrick, "to whom it is even dangerous for a courteous knight to address the common parlance of courtly compliment, without instilling into them the vain belief that their charms have wrought a conquest. Of such an innocent fault the folly of many maidens may have made me guilty. Never, save once, did I seriously love, and then, alas, I discovered that my heart had been affected by an unworthy object, so that I did forthwith tear myself from her."

"Unworthy, didst thou say, Sir Knight ?" cried the boy, earnestly ; "and who, I pray thee, could be so unworthy to thee?"

"Nay, my good Maurice," said Hepborne, "that were truly to ask too much. Were she as worthy as I did once esteem her, I would proudly publish her name to the world ; but after having said so much to her dishonour, and now that she cannot be mine, her name shall never more escape these lips whilst I think of her as I at present do, save when 'tis brought in accidentally by others, or when 'tis murmured in my secret despair. But what ails thee, boy ? Thou weepest. Tell me, I pray thee, why thou shouldst now be thus drent in dreriment ? What hast thou to do with my love-griefs ?"

"I but cry for pity, Sir Knight," said the boy. "Thy tale, too, doth somewhat touch mine own, and so doth it, peraunter, affect me the more. May Heaven in its mercy clear away those cruel clouds that do at present so darken our souls !"

"Amen !" said the knight fervently. "Then get thee to thy couch, Maurice, for I will to mine."

Sir Patrick Hepborne had already slept for a considerable time, when he was awakened by the clamour of voices. This, perhaps, would have excited little astonishment, had he not previously remarked the uncommon degree of quietness that had been preserved in the little encampment, the probable effect of the stern character and alert discipline of him who was at the head of it. He sat up, and leaning for some moments on his elbow to listen, he by and by heard the trampling of steeds, and the bustle of preparation, as if for a departure. He then called to the page, who answered him so immediately, that Hepborne suspected, what was really the case, that he had not as yet slept.

"What noise is that we hear, Maurice ?" said he.

"Methinks," said the page, "it is some party that sets forth.

Perhaps it may be one moiety of the retinue who go before, to prepare those of the Castle for the Earl's coming."

This very natural explanation satisfied Hepborne. He soon heard the noise increase, and the neighing and prancing of the horses, with the voices of many men, though their words were not intelligible ; then he heard a loud command to march, and the gallop of the troop died away upon his ear, and then again all was quiet, and his repose was uninterrupted until morning.

He was hardly dressed when Sir Andrew Stewart came courteously to offer the usual morning compliments, and to conduct him to the great pavilion.

" My father," said he, " hath been called on urgent business into Badenoch ; he left this yesternight, to ride thither sans delay : my brothers, Alexander, Walter, and James, also went with him ; but he left me here to do thee what poor hospitality I may until his return. To-day, with thy good leave, we shall hie us to Lochyndorbe, and to-morrow I hope he will be there to do the honours of the Castle in his own person."

This sudden departure of the Wolfe of Badenoch accounted to Hepborne for the disturbance he had met with in the night. The Lady Mariota received him graciously.

" But where is my handsome good-for-nothing page ?" eagerly inquired she. " Ah, there comes the naughty boy, I see. Come hither, Sir Scapegrace ; I trow I did school thee to some purpose yestreen ; but parfay, thou shalt have more on't anon. Come hither, I say. Verily, the young varlet hangeth his ears like a whelp that feareth the rod ; but i'faith I am not come to that yet,—though, never trust me," added she, laughing, " but thou shalt have it ere long, an' thou be'st not more docile. Sit thee down here, I say. And see now how, in hopes of thine amendment, I have carved for thee the tenderest and whitest part of this black grouse's breast ; yea, Sir Good-for-Nothing—with mine own fair fingers have I done it."

Maurice de Grey appeared more than half inclined to keep aloof from the lady, notwithstanding all her kind raillery ; but he caught his master's eye, and seeing that Sir Patrick seemed to wish that he should receive her notice with a good grace, he put on the semblance of cheerfulness, and took his seat by her accordingly.

The morning's meal passed over without anything remarkable, the lady devoting all her attention and all her trifling to Maurice de Grey, and Hepborne being engaged in conversation with Sir Andrew Stewart ; there being no one else present but the boy Duncan. Soon afterwards, orders were issued for the

encampment to break up, and the attendants to prepare themselves and their steeds for their departure.   Much time was lost
until all the necessary arrangements were made.   The sturdy
sullen loons were aware of the absence of the Wolfe, and revelled
in the enjoyment of the power, so seldom theirs, of doing things
leisurely.   Besides, all the most active and intelligent persons
of the suite were gone.   At length a string of little batt horses,
pressed from the neighbouring churls, were despatched with the
most valuable and more immediately necessary part of the
moveables, and a few more were left to bring up the tents and
heavier articles, when additional aid should arrive.

Meanwhile, the palfrey of the Lady Mariot♭ was brought
out, together with two others for her maids ; and the horses of
the rest of the party also appeared.   Hepborne assisted the lady
to mount, but though she thanked him graciously for his courtesy, she was by no means satisfied.

"That white palfrey of thine, Sir Page Maurice," said she,
" seemeth to have an affection for my pyeball; let them not be
separated, I pr'ythee.   Mount thee, and be thou the squire of
my body for this day.   Allons."

Maurice was obliged to comply, and rode off with the lady
at the head of the cavalcade, followed by her son Duncan, and
attended by the two damsels, who seemed, by their nods and
winks to each other, to imply something extremely significant,
yet understood by themselves alone.   Sir Patrick Hepborne rode
next, with Sir Andrew Stewart.   Their train was meagre compared to that which Hepborne had seen the previous evening ;
indeed, his own attendants formed by far the greater part of the
cortege that now accompanied them.   Their route was by the
same path that Hepborne had approached the glen, until they
reached the steep side of the hill overhanging the head of it,
whence he had first peeped into it.   They then continued onwards through the forest in the same northern direction in
which the guide was conducting the knight, at the time
he was diverted from his way by discovering the Wolfe's
hunting camp.

They travelled through a great and elevated plain, covered
by pine trees so thickly as almost to exclude the sun, and even
the hills that bounded it were wooded to their very tops.   At
length they turned towards an opening that appeared in the
hills to their left, and, winding over some knolls, began to catch
occasional glimpses of an extensive sheet of water, when the
dark green fir tufts, now and then receding from one another,
permitted the party to look beyond them.   In a short time they

reached the shore of the eastern end of Lochyndorbe, about four miles in length, and of an oblong form. The hills bounding it on the north and south arose with gentle slope. A considerable island appeared near the upper or western extremity of the lake, a short way from its southern shore, and entirely covered with the impregnable Castle, of the same name with the sheet of water surrounding it. In the vista beyond, a sloping plain appeared, with high hills rising over it. The whole scene was one continued pine forest, and as solitary and wild as the most gloomy mind could desire. A group of firs, more ancient and enormous than the rest, occupied a point of land, and were tenanted by a colony of herons; and the lonely scream of these birds, and their lagging heavy flight, added to, rather than enlivened the sombre character of the loch.

As they made their way up the southern shore, the enormous strength of the Castle became more apparent at every step. It was, in fact, a royal fortress, constructed for the purpose of sustaining regular and determined siege. It occupied the whole island to the very margin of the water, and its outer walls running, in long unbroken lines, from one point to another, in successive stretches, embraced a space of something more than two acres within them. On a low, round projection of land, immediately opposite on the southern shore, and within about two hundred yards of it, was situated an outwork, or sconce, erected for the purpose of preserving the communication with the terra firma, but yet of too little importance to be of any great benefit to an enemy that might chance to possess himself of it, or to enable him to do much injury to the Castle, even with the most powerful engines then in use—particularly as the massive walls opposed to it presented a straight, continuous, unbroken, and unassailable front. Here they found several large and small boats in waiting for them; but there appeared to be a great want of people to serve them.

" Methinks thou hast but a paltry crew for thy navy to-day, Master Bruce?" said the Lady Mariota to an old grey-headed squire-seneschal, who came to receive her.

" Madame," said he, " my lord the Earl sent orders here last night for the spears, axemen, and bowmen, to meet him early this morning on Dulnan side. About an hundred good men of horse and foot marched thither long ere the sun saw the welkin, so that we be but meagrely garrisoned, else thou shouldst have been received with more honour."

" Nay, then, since it is so," said the lady, " let us cross as we best may. That small boat will do for us, so lend me thine arm,

Sir Page Maurice." And immediately entering the boat, she made the youth sit beside her. Hepborne and Sir Andrew Stewart also embarked, and, leaving the horses and attendants to follow at leisure, were pulled rapidly towards the Castle by a couple of old boatmen. They landed on the narrow strip of beach, extending hardly a yard from the walls, and that only when the water was low, and were admitted through all the numerous and potent defences of the deep gateway, by the warder, and one or two men who kept watch. They then traversed the courts intervening between the outer and inner walls, which were defended at all the salient angles by immensely strong round towers, one of them completely commanding the entrance. Then passing onwards, they came to the inner gateway, through which they ascended into the central area of the Castle, forming a large elevated quadrangle, surrounded by the buildings necessary in such a garrison.

The Lady Mariota, still leaning on the arm of Maurice de Grey, led them into that part of the square occupied by the Earl's mansion, and soon introduced them into a banqueting-hall of magnificent proportions, hung round with arms, and richly furnished for the times we speak of, and where, notwithstanding the draft made that morning on the forces of the place, there was still a considerable show of domestics in waiting.

" Let us have the banquet immediately," said the Lady Mariota to the seneschal. " Sir Knight," said she, turning to Hepborne, " if our hospitality should lack its wonted comfort to-day, thou must lay it to the account of our late absence from the Castle ; and if it should want its usual spirit, it must be set down to the score of the Earl's absence. But to-morrow both these wants shall be supplied. Andrew, thou wilt see Sir Patrick Hepborne rightly accommodated. As for this naughty page, Maurice de Grey, I shall myself see him fittingly bestowed in a chamber near mine own, that I may have all proper and convenient opportunity of repeating those lessons I have already endeavoured to impress upon him. Come along then, good-for-nothing boy ; come along, I say."

The page cast an imploring look at his master, who regarded it not ; then hanging his head, he followed the Lady Mariota with an unwilling step, like a laggard schoolboy who dreads the ferula of his pedagogue ; whilst Hepborne was ushered to his apartment, where, having procured the attendance of the faithful Mortimer Sang, he proceeded to array himself in attire suitable to the evening.

CHAPTER XXX.

*The Castle of Lochyndorbe—An Evening Episode on the
Ramparts—The Wolfe's Raid on the Bishop's Lands.*

THE evening's banquet in the Castle of Lochyndorbe passed
away pretty much as the morning's meal had done in the hunting pavilion, that is to say, without anything very remarkable.
The Lady Mariota, still devoting all her attention to the page,
left her son, Sir Andrew Stewart, to entertain Sir Patrick Hepborne. Neither of the knights were disposed to quaff those
draughts of wine which the Wolfe of Badenoch himself seemed
to consider as essential to the comfort of life, and they soon
separated. Hepborne sat in his apartment for some time after
Mortimer Sang had left him, and then, falling into a train of
reflection on the events which had occurred to him since his
return from France, and perceiving that his clue of association
must be fully unwound ere he could hope to sleep, he walked
forth to enjoy the balmy freshness of the evening air, that he
might give freer vent to his thoughts.

He got upon the rampart that looked out over the broader
part of the lake, and as he entered on one end of it, he was confounded—he could not believe his eyes—but it certainly was
the figure of the Lady Eleanore de Selby that he beheld, leaning
against one of the balistæ near the farther angle of the wall.
The waning moon shed a dim and uncertain light; yet it was
sufficient to convince him that the figure he saw before him was
the same that had made so powerful an impression on his mind
at Norham. She was wrapped in a mantle, with her head bare,
and her beautiful tresses flowing down in the same manner he
had seen them when blown by the breezes from the Tweed; and
she seemed to look listlessly out upon the wavelets that flickered
under the thin and scanty moonbeam, as they lifted themselves
gently against the bulwark stones under the wall. Apparently
buried in thought, she was so perfectly without motion that he
began to doubt whether it was not a phantom he beheld; nay,
it was impossible she could be there in substance—she whom he
had left at Norham affianced as a bride. In those days of
superstition it is no wonder, therefore, that he should have believed it was the Lady Eleanore de Selby's spirit he saw, or, in
the peculiar language of his own country, her wraith. His
manly blood ran cold, and he hesitated for a moment whether

he ought to advance. The figure still remained fixed. Again the thought crossed him, that it might possibly be the Lady Eleanore, and love urged him to approach and address her; but then prudence came to caution him not to seem to see her, lest he might be again subdued, and forget what he had discovered at Norham. Thus tossed by doubt, until he could bear suspense no longer, both superstitious awe and prudence yielded to the influence of love, and, unable to restrain himself, he walked along the rampart towards the figure. It seemed not to hear his step—it moved not till he was within three or four paces, when it started at the sound of his steps, and, turning suddenly towards him, displayed the countenance of—the page, Maurice de Grey.

" Ah, Sir Patrick ! " said the boy, and instantly applying his taper fingers to his hair, he began twisting it up into a knot over his head, accidentally assuming, as he did so, the very attitude in which Hepborne had seen the lady when similarly employed on the rampart at Norham.

"Maurice de Grey ! " exclaimed Hepborne with extreme astonishment, " is it you I see ? Verily, thine attitude, boy, did so remind me of that in which I once beheld thy cousin, the Lady Eleanore de Selby, that for a moment I did almost believe it was really she who stood before me. I did never remark before that thou dost wear thy hair so womanishly long."

Sir Patrick's astonishment had been too great to permit him to remark the page's trepidation when first surprised by him, and before his amazement had subsided, Maurice de Grey had time to recover himself.

" 'Tis true," said he, " Sir Knight, that I have always worn my hair long, and put up in a silken net, being loth to cut it away, seeing it was the pride of my mother's heart; but, nathless, if thou dost think it unmanly in me to wear it so, verily it shall be cut off before to-morrow morning, that it may no longer offend thee. Yet I marvel much what could possibly make thee to think that my cousin, the Lady Eleanore, could be here in the Castle of Lochyndorbe ; or how hast thou perchance set thine eyes on her, so as to have so perfect a remembrance of her figure as thou dost seem to preserve ? I know that her father, Sir Walter, doth take especial care that she shall never be seen by any Scottish knight. Then by what accident, I pray thee, didst thou behold her ? "

Hepborne was considerably puzzled and perplexed by these naif questions from the page. To have refused to reply to them at all would have been the very way to have excited a thousand

15

suspicious in the boy's mind; he, therefore, thought it better to answer him, and he wished to do so in a calm and indifferent manner. But it was a subject on which he could not think, far less talk, with composure, and, ere he wist, he burst into an ecstacy of feeling that quite confounded the page.

"See her!" said he; "alas, too often have I seen the Lady Eleanore de Selby for my peace. Never, never, shall peace revisit this bosom. She is another's; yet, nathless, must this torn heart be hers whilst it shall throb with life." And saying so, he covered his face with his hands, and retreated some steps to hide the violence of his emotions; but becoming ashamed of having thus exposed his secret to the page, and made him privy to the extent of his weakness, he returned to the boy, and found him weeping bitterly, apparently from sympathy.

"Maurice," said Hepborne, calmly addressing him, "accident hath made thee wring from me the secret of my love, as chance did also make me tell thee yesternight, that I had cause to fear that the demoiselle who hath so deeply affected me was not in truth altogether what she at first appeared to me. As she is thy cousin, and so dear to thee as thou dost now say she is, I would not willingly allow thee to suppose that I have been estranged from her by mere caprice. I shall therefore tell thee that the Lady Eleanore de Selby did give me good cause to believe that my ardent protestations of love were not unpleasing to her; nay, she even held out encouragement to the prosecution of my suit; and yet, after all this ground of hope I did discover that she was affianced to another knight, in whose arms I did actually behold her, as they parted from each other, with many tears at the keep-bridge of Norham, on the very morning when I and my friend left the place. Her emotions were too tender to be mistaken. She it was who sported lightly with my heart, not I with hers, for, had she not been faithless, I would have sacrificed life itself for her love, and would have considered the wealth of a kingdom but as dross compared with the possession of a jewel so precious. Even as it is, I am doomed to love her for ever. I feel it—I feel it here!" said he, passionately striking his heart—"I can never, never cease to love her."

The page seemed petrified with the charge brought against his cousin. He grew faint, and staggered back a pace or two, until he was stayed by the support he received from the balistæ; then panting for a moment he was at length relieved by a flood of tears.

"Thou seest, Maurice," said Hepborne, "the facts are too damning. It would have been better for thee to have inquired less curiously. But what figure is that which cometh yonder from the farther end of the rampart ? "

" Blessed Virgin," cried Maurice de Grey, " 'tis my perpetual torment, the Lady Mariota. What shall I do ? Methought I had escaped from her importunity for this night at least."

" Why shouldst thou not be able to bear with her ? " said the knight ; " 'tis a part of thy schooling, young man, to submit to mortification, and, above all, to bear with unpleasant society, without losing a jot of thy courtesy, especially where women are in question."

"True, Sir Knight," said the page, half whimpering, " but the Lady Mariota hath actually made violent love to me. Oh, I cannot bear the wretch."

Hepborne could not help laughing at the ludicrous distress of the youth, and he had hardly time to compose himself ere the Lady Mariota came within speaking distance of them.

" So, so, thou art there, runaway ? " said she to the page, as she passed by Hepborne with a mere bow of acknowledgment, to get at Maurice, who retreated towards the balistæ with his head down—" so thou art there, art thou, Sir Scapegrace ? Thou art a pretty truant, indeed," continued she, hooking him under one arm, and giving him a gentle slap on one cheek. " But, thank my lucky stars, I have caught thee now, and verily thou shalt not again escape me. I'faith thou shalt have thy wings clipt, my little tom-tit ; I shall have thee tied to my apron string, that thou hop thee not away from me thus at every turning. I did but let thee out of my sight for an instant, and whisk I find thee at the very outermost verge of my circle. Nay, had it not been for these walls and waters, in good truth thou mightest have been beyond my search ere this. Come away, Sir Good-for-Nothing. Allons, make up thy mind to thy chain ; let me lead thee by it, and do not thou pull so."

" Lady," said Hepborne, " thou must have some mercy on the poor youth. He hath so lately escaped from female thrall at home, that as yet he can but ill brook anything that resembleth it. Leave him to me, I beseech thee. At present he joys in the newly-acquired society of men ; by degrees he will come to feel how much more sweet and soothing are the delights of women's converse, and——"

" Nay, nay, Sir Knight," said the Lady Mariota, interrupting him hastily, " I shall not yield my control over the renegado, I promise thee ; he shall with me this moment. Come, along, Sir Page Maurice—come along, I say. Thou art a pretty youth indeed ! I have searched for thee through every apartment, nay,

through every creek and cranny in the Castle ; and now that I
have found thee, by my troth, I shall not yield thee up so
easily. Come along, I say." And like a bitch-fox dragging
off an unhappy kid, so did the Lady Mariota drag away
the hapless Maurice de Grey, in defiance of his lagging step,
his peevish replies, his hanging head, his pouting lip, and the
numerous glances of vexation he darted from under his eye-
lashes at his tormentor.

Hepborne retired to his repose, half amused and half angry
with the persecution inflicted on his poor page. Early next
morning, Mortimer Sang came to him with a courteous message
from Sir Andrew Stewart, begging to know if it was his pleasure
to hunt for a few hours ; and Hepborne having cheerfully agreed
to the proposal, the two knights met alone at breakfast, and
then crossed to the mainland with their horses, hounds, hunting-
gear, and a few attendants, to scour the neighbouring forest
for deer.

As they were returning homewards towards evening, they
heard the echoing sound of bugles.

" 'Tis my father," said Sir Andrew ; " 'tis the Earl returning
with his party from Badenoch ; see, there they come, breaking
forth from yonder woodshaws."

It was indeed the Wolfe of Badenoch ; but he was now in a
very different array from that which he had first appeared in to
Hepborne. He was clad from head to foot in a complete suit
of bright plate armour, and his height and bulk seemed to be
increased by the metamorphosis. He rode at the head of a
gallant troop of well-mounted and well-equipped spearmen,
after which marched a company of footmen, consisting of pole-
axe-men, and bowmen. His sons, Sir Alexander, Walter, and
James, rode proudly by his side. The cavalcade went at a foot
pace, because a rabble of bare-legged and bare-headed tatterde-
malion mountaineers ran before them, armed with clubs, goads,
and pikes, and driving along a promiscuous herd of cows,
bullocks, sheep, and goats, of all different ages and descriptions,
which considerably retarded their march. A bugle-man preceded the whole, bearing aloft an otter-skin purse on the point
of a spear. His banner waved in the middle of the clump of
spears ; and in the rear of all followed a tired and straggling
band of men, women, and children, who were grieving loudly,
and weeping sadly, for some dire injury they had sustained, and
vociferating vain appeals in their own language to the stern
Wolfe, who, with his vizor up, and his brows knit, rode on
unheeding them.

Ere the parties met, the two boys, Walter and James, galloped up to meet their brother, Sir Andrew, and both began at once to shout out their news to him—

"Oh, brother Andrew, brother Andrew, we have had such sport!" cried the one.

"Nay, thou knowest not what thou hast lost, brother Andrew, by not being with us," cried the other.

"Father hath seized——" shouted Walter.

"The Earl hath taken possession of——" interrupted James.

"Tut, hold thy gabbling tongue, James, and let me tell," responded Walter.

"Nay, but I will tell it," cried James lustily.

"By the holy Rood, but I will not be interrupted," screamed out Walter.

"By the Bishop's mass, then, but I will tell out mine own tale in spite of thee," bellowed James; "the Earl hath seized, I say——"

"Confound thee, then!" roared out Walter in a frenzy, and at the same time bestowing a hearty thwack with the shaft of his spear across his brother's shoulders—"confound thine impudence, take that for thine insolence."

The no less irascible James was by no means slow in returning the compliment, and they began to beat one another about the head with great goodwill; nay, it is probable that their wrath might have even induced them to resort to the points of their weapons, had they been equal to the management of their fiery steeds; but the spirited animals became restive in the bicker, and plunging two or three times, the youths, more attentive to mauling each other than to their horsemanship, lost their seats, and in one and the same instant both were laid prostrate on the plain. Some of the followers of the hunting party caught their palfreys, and raised the enraged boys, who would have renewed their fight on foot had they not been held back.

"Oh, ye silly fools," said Sir Andrew, smiling coolly and contemptuously upon them; "as the old cock croweth, so, forsooth, the chicks must needs ape his song. Have done with your absurd and impotent wrath." And leaving them in the hands of the attendants, he rode slowly forward with Hepborne to meet his father.

"What!" demanded the Wolfe, laughing heartily, "were those cockerals pecking at each other?"

"Yea," replied Sir Andrew, "a trifling dispute between them, which I have quashed."

"Pshaw," replied the Wolfe, "by the beard of my grand-

father, but 1 like to see their spirit; let not thy drowsy control
quell it in them, son Andrew.   I would not have them tame
kestrels like thee, for all the broad lands of my father's kingdom; so leave them to me to tutor, son Andrew, dost hear?—
Sir Patrick," said he, turning to Hepborne, "I hope thou hast
not suffered in thine entertainment by mine absence?   I should
crave thy pardon, I wis, for leaving thee so suddenly, and perhaps so rudely; but I have let off my dammed-up wrath since
I last saw thee, and shall now be better company.   By this
trusty burly-brand, I have shorn off the best plumes from the
plump Bishop Barr; 1 have seized the fat lands he held in the
very midst of my Badenoch territory.   By the infernal fiends, I
swore that he should pay for his busy intermeddling in my
family affairs, and by all the powers of darkness and desolation,
I have faithfully kept mine oath.   I have hameled his pride, I
trow.   He shall know what it is to have to do with the Wolfe
of Badenoch.   He holds earth no more there.   These are the
custom-cattle of his lands, and there dangleth the rent and the
grassums gathered from his knave tenants.   Such of the churls
who were refractory I have driven forth, and put good men of
mine own in their room.   Begone with ye, ye screaming pewits,"
cried he, angrily turning towards the wretched train of men and
women who followed his party, and couching his lance as if he
would have charged furiously at them—" begone with ye, I say,
or, by the fires of the infernal realms, 1 will put every he
and she of ye instantly to the sword !"

The miserable wretches, without a house to go to, ran off
into the woods at his terrible threat, and the ferocious Wolfe
rode on with his party.   When they came to the water's edge,
the bugles sounded, and a boat being instantly manned by six
rowers, the Wolfe called to Sir Patrick Hepborne to go along
with him, and they were wafted across in a few strokes of the
oar, leaving Sir Alexander Stewart and his brothers to superin-
tend the embarkation of the booty.   All in the Castle was stir
and bustle the moment the owner of it appeared.   The oldest
man in it seemed to be endowed with additional muscular action
at the very presence of the Wolfe.   They were all ranked up to
receive him as he entered the gateway, and they followed him,
and darted off one by one, like arrows, in various directions, as
he gave his hasty orders.

CHAPTER XXXI.

The Lady Mariota and the Page—The Fury of the Wolfe.

THE Wolfe and Sir Patrick Hepborne had no sooner entered the banquet-hall than they were surprised by the appearance of the Lady Mariota, who approached them from a room beyond it, drowned in tears.

" Eh ! " cried the Wolfe, setting his teeth against each other; " ha ! *mort de ma vie*, what is this I behold ? Mariota in tears ? Say, speak, why art thou thus bywoxen ? What, in the fiend's name, is the matter ? Who hath caused these tears ? Speak, and by all the infernal demons, I will have him flayed alive."

" My Lord," replied the Lady Mariota, hiding her face in her kerchief, " I can hardly speak it—the page—the page Maurice de Grey——"

" Say, lady, what of him ? I beseech thee, what of him ? " cried Sir Patrick anxiously. " Hath any ill befallen him ? "

" Nay," said the lady ; " would that had been all I had to tell !—Oh, how shall I speak it ?—the wretch, taking advantage of my being left alone, dared to insult me. I fled forth from the apartment where I had unconsciously received him, and, having called the attendants, I had him secured, and he is now a prisoner in the dungeon."

Hepborne was petrified with horror and amazement at this accusation against Maurice de Grey.

" Ha ! " cried the Wolfe, " by my beard, thou didst bravely indeed, my girl.—The red fiend catch me, but he shall forthwith swing for it. A gallows and a halter there in the court-yard ! By all the grim powers of hell, he shall dangle ere we dine."

" Nay, nay, my Lord," said Hepborne, sternly yet calmly, " that may not be without a trial. The youth is mine, and I am thy guest. I demand a fair trial for him ; if he be guilty, then let him suffer for his coulpe ; but until his guilt be proved, depardieux, I shall stand forth his defender."

" By the holy Rood, but thou speakest boldly, Sir Knight," cried the Wolfe, gnashing his teeth in ire. " Art thou then prepared to fight at outrance for thy minion ? "

" My Lord," said Hepborne coolly, " I am here as thy guest. Whilst I am under thy roof I trust the common rules of hospitality will bind us both ; but shouldst thou rid thyself of their salutary shackles, I must prepare myself to do my best to resist

oppression, as a good and true knight ought to do. I ask but
fair trial for the boy, which, in justice thou canst not and wilt
not refuse me."

The Wolfe paced the room backwards and forwards for some
time with a hurried step, whilst the Lady Mariota sat sobbing
in a chair.

"Mariota," said he at length, "thou wert alone when the
page came to thee?"

"I was, my good Lord," replied the lady; "My damsels had
gone forth at the time he entered my chamber."

"Now, Sir Patrick Hepborne," exclaimed the Wolfe, "now
thou must of needscost see that all proof here is out of the
question.   Where can proof be had where there hath been no
witnesses?"

"Yea, my Lord," said Hepborne temperately, "what thou
sayest is true, in good faith; and it is also true that without
proof there can be no just condemnation."

The Wolfe began again to pace the room hastily, his eyes
flashing fire.

"What, Sir Knight," exclaimed he, "dost thou go so far as
to doubt the word of the Lady Mariota?   By the devil's mass,
but thou art bold indeed."

"I say not that I doubt the word of the Lady Mariota," replied Hepborne; "but were the Lady Mariota my sister, and
the page Maurice de Grey my greatest enemy, I would not
condemn him capitally on her simple saying."

"Mariota," cried the Wolfe in a rage, "leave the apartment;
get thee to thy chamber.   By the martyrdom of St. Andrew,
but thou dost beard me, Sir Knight.   Thou presumest on my
old dotard father's introduction of thee, and on the frail laws of
hospitality, which may indeed bind me to a certain point; but
beware thou dost push me beyond it, or, by my beard, neither
he nor they shall protect thee."

"Most noble Earl of Buchan," replied Hepborne, with perfect
temper and *sang froid*, "again I say, that all I ask is justice. To
that point only do I wish to push thee, nor do I fear but thou
wilt go so far.   I do confess, it seemeth somewhat strange to
me to hear so foul a charge against a boy who hath ever sought
to fly the Lady Mariota's advances.   Nay, 'twas but yesternight
that she came herself to seek him on the rampart, where the
youth held idle parlance with me; and though he tried to shun
her, verily these eyes beheld her as she did court him to go with
her, the which the boy did most unwillingly."

The Wolfe of Badenoch knit his brows, and strode two or

three times through the long hall, the arched roof ringing again
to the clang of his heel as he moved. He seemed to be pondering within himself what to resolve, an operation to the fatigue
of which he rarely ever subjected his mind, his general practice
being to act first, and then, if ever he thought at all, to think
afterwards. At length he stopped short in his career, opposite
to where Hepborne was standing, with his arms calmly folded
across his breast ; and, stretching out his hand to him—

" Sir Patrick," said he, " thou art right. I have perhaps been
a little hasty here. There is much in what thou hast said ; and
I honour thee for thy cool and determined courage and temper.
Listen to me then. If the page Maurice de Grey confesseth the
coulpe of which he is charged, thou wilt not call it injustice if
he be instantly ordered for execution. If he denies it, then let
him, or some one for him, do duel with me to-morrow, as soon
as light may serve us ; and may God and the Blessed Virgin
defend the right, and make his innocence clear if he be sans
coulpe."

"Agreed," said Hepborne. " I stand forth the boy's defender,
and will cheerfully appeal to wager of single combat in his
behalf. Let him straightway be sent for, then, and let him be
questioned with regard to his guilt or innocence ; all I ask for
him is full and free speech."

" He shall have it," cried the Wolfe ; " I swear by my beard,
he shall have full power to speak as he lists. Pardieux, 'tis
well we determined this matter one way or other forthwith, for
I long to dine."

" What is this I hear?" cried Sir Alexander Stewart, entering in a fury ; " what is this I hear ? My mother insulted by a
minion page ! By the ghost of my grandfather, the miscreant
shall die ere I eat a morsel. Why doth he not swing even
now ? What hath delayed his execution ? "

" Silence, Sandy," cried the Wolfe angrily ; " the matter is
already arranged without thine interference. The youth comes
anon to be questioned. If he confesses, the popinjay shall
straightway grace the gallows in the court-yard ; if he denies,
then is Sir Patrick Hepborne prepared to do battle in his cause
against me, by to-morrow's sun."

" Let that glory be mine, then, I beseech thee, my noble
father," cried Sir Alexander eagerly ; " I claim the right of
doing battle in defence in my mother's cause."

" Well, Alexander," said the Wolfe gruffly, " if it so please
Sir Patrick Hepborne, I scruple not to yield him to thee."

" My appeal," said Sir Patrick, " is against one and all who

may singly choose to challenge mine arm, and who may be
pleased to succeed one another in the single combat I am willing to wage in defence of the youth Maurice de Grey."

"Hey day!" cried the Wolfe; "gramercy, Sir Knight, then,
by mine honest and trusty burly-brand, thou shalt have thy
bellyful of it, and I shall not resign the first place to my son
Alexander. We shall tilt it first, so please thee. At sunrise
we shall bestir ourselves, and on the open lawnde beyond the
land sconce we shall try the metal of our armour and lance
heads. If thou escapest mine arm, Sandy may have thee, if he
likes; but the red fiend's curse upon it if it fail me. Ha! here
comes the prisoner."

The page Maurice de Grey now entered, wearing his
chains about his wrists. His countenance was placid and
composed, and he advanced with a firm step and undisturbed
manner.

"Knowest thou, Sir Page, of what coulpe thou art accused?"
demanded the Wolfe sternly.

"I do," replied the youth calmly.

"Dost thou admit or deny the charge the Lady Mariota
hath made against thee?"

"I most solemnly deny it," replied the page.

"Ha!" cried the Wolfe, "then is there no more to be said.
Let him be removed; and let everything be prepared for a
single combat to-morrow between Sir Patrick Hepborne and
me—the place to be the lawnde beyond the land sconce; and
the time, the moment the welkin sees the sun. 'Tis well 'tis so
soon settled. Now let us dine, Sir Patrick. We may be merry
companions to-night, though we be to fight like fiends i' the
morning. The banquet, I say—the banquet. Why dost thou
tarry with thy prisoner?"

"One word, I pray," said Maurice de Grey, now thrown into
extreme agitation by hearing that his master's life was to be put
in jeopardy for him—"I crave one word ere I go."

"My Lord," said Sir Patrick to the Wolfe, "I claim thy
solemn behote; thou didst promise free and ample speech for
the youth; hear him, then, I beseech thee."

"Well, youth, well," cried the Wolfe, very impatiently,
"what hast thou to say? Be quick, for time wears, and hunger
galls me; be quick, I say."

"I demand a private conference, noble Earl," said the page.
"I have something to unfold that will altogether change the
complexion of this case. If I do not make the Lady Mariota
clear me of all guilt, I hereby agree to hold myself as con-

demned to instant death, and shall patiently submit to whatever fate thou mayest award me."

"Nay, nay, dear Maurice," cried Hepborne anxiously, and
putting more faith in his own prowess than in anything the
page could urge to convince the Lady Mariota, of whose villainous falsehood in the foul charge she had brought against the
youth he had been fully convinced from the first—"nay, nay,
dear Maurice, rather leave the matter as it is ; rather——"

"By the bloody hide of St. Bartholomew," cried the Wolfe,
with evident joy, "but the boy shall have his way. We shall
thus have this mysterious affair cleared up, and settled forthwith,
instead of delaying till to-morrow. By the mass, but he hath
excited queer thoughts in my mind. But we shall see anon.
Come then, let him along with me, that I may show him to the
Lady Mariota's apartment. I swear by the Holy Rood, Sir
Patrick, that the youth shall have justice—justice to the fullest
extent of what he hath demanded. Clear the way, then, I say ;
come, Sir Page, come along ; thou shalt dance hither anon at
freedom, or thou shalt dangle it and dance it on the gallows-
tree below, where many as brave and stout a youth as thou hath
figured before thee. Come on, I say."

After the Earl and the page were gone, Sir Alexander
Stewart paced the hall in gloomy silence, his fiery soul boiling
within him, so that he could with difficulty restrain his rage.
Every now and then a stamp on the pavement louder than the
rest proclaimed the excess of his internal agitation. The cool
Sir Andrew sat him quietly down, without uttering a word, or
appearing to be much interested in the matter at issue. The
three boys had not yet come in, but a crowd of the retainers, who
were usually admitted to sit below the salt, stood in groups
whispering at the lower end of the hall. Sir Patrick Hepborne
had been rendered so unhappy by the turn the affair had taken,
and was so oppressed with distress, anxiety, and dread as to the
result, that he thrust himself into the deep recess of one of the
windows, to hide those emotions he felt it impossible to repress.
Not a word passed between the chief persons of the scene. The
time, which was in reality not in itself long, appeared to Hepborne like an age ; and yet, when at length he did hear steps
and voices approaching along the passage, leading from the Lady
Mariota's apartment into the banqueting-hall, brave as he was, he
trembled like a coward, lest the moment should have come too
soon for the unhappy page.

The door opened, and the Wolfe entered, frowning and
gnashing his teeth. Then came the page, freed from his fetters.

The Wolfe of Badenoch's red eye was disturbed from recent ire, which he seemed even yet to keep down with difficulty ; yet he laughed horribly from time to time as he spoke.

" Ha ! well," said he, " the page Maurice de Grey hath proved his innocence beyond further question. By the blood of the Bruce—ha ! ha ! ha !—but it is ridiculous after all. The red fiend catch me if I—but pshaw !—let us have the banquet," cried he, hastily interrupting himself in something he was going to say—" the banquet, I tell thee. Give me thy hand, Sir Patrick. Thou wert afraid to trust thy beauteous page with me, wert thou ?—ha ! ha ! ha ! Thou wouldst rather have fought me at outrance. By'r Lady, but thou art a burly knight ; but I like thee not the worse. Depardieux, but thou art safe enow in my hands ; trust me, thou shalt hear no more on't. Ha ! ha ! ha ! I confess that thy page is as innocent—I hereby free him from guilt. The banquet, knaves—the banquet. Ha ! the curse of the devil's dam on me, if I could have looked for this."

" What strange mystery is here ? " said Sir Alexander Stewart impatiently. " Where is the Lady Mariota, my mother ? "

The Wolfe had all this time been reining in his wrath with his utmost power; it was all he could do to curb it ; and it was ready to burst all bounds at the first provocation that offered.

" Better hold thy peace, Sir Alexander," cried he, darting an angry glance at him. " By the infernal flames, I am in no humour to listen to thy folly. I have pledged my sacred word as a knight to secrecy, and thou nor no one else shall know aught of this mystery, as thou callest it. Be contented to know that the boy Maurice is innocent."

" And am I to be satisfied with this ? " cried Sir Alexander. his wrath kindling more and more as he spoke ; " am I to remain satisfied with this, without my mother's word for it ? "

" Nay," said the Wolfe, hastily, " by the holy Rood, thou shalt have no word from thy mother to-night."

" No word from my mother ! " exclaimed Sir Alexander. " What ! dost thou treat me as a child ? By all the fiends, but I shall see her, though. Where is she ? Why doth she not appear ? By the holy mass, I must see her, and that instantly."

" By the martyrdom of St. Andrew, then," cried the Wolfe, gnashing his teeth, and foaming at the mouth from very ire— " by the martyrdom of St. Andrew, but thou shalt not see her. I have sent her to cool her passions in the dungeon to which she consigned the page ; and hark ye, son Alexander, if thou darest to prate any more about her, by all the fiery fiends of

Erebus, but thou shalt occupy the next chamber to that assigned her, there to remain during my pleasure. Ha! what sayest thou to that, Sir Alexander?"

"I say thou art a tyrant and a beast," exclaimed his son, boiling with rage; "and if thou dost not instantly liberate my mother, by all the powers of darkness, I will choke thee in thine armour;" and he strode across the banquet-hall in a frenzy, to put his threat into immediate execution.

"Halt!" cried Sir Patrick Hepborne, in a voice like thunder, as he stepped before the Earl, and planted himself directly in the assailant's way—"halt, Sir Alexander Stewart—halt, I say. Let reason come to thine aid, and let not ungovernable passion lead thee to lay impious hands on him to whom thou owest thine existence."

"Nay, let him come on," cried the Wolfe, his eyes glaring ferociously.

"Stand aside, Sir Patrick Hepborne," cried Sir Alexander, "or, by all the fiends of perdition, thou shalt suffer for thine interference; stand back, I say, and leave us to——"

"Nay," cried Hepborne, firmly, "I will not back; and by St. Baldrid I swear, that thou shalt do no injury to thy sire until thou shalt have stepped over my body."

"Sayest thou so?" cried Sir Alexander, his eyes flashing like firebrands—"then have at thee, Sir Knight;" and, catching up a truncheon that lay near, he wielded it with both hands, and aimed a blow at Sir Patrick's head, that would have speedily levelled a patent way for his fury over the prostrate body of the knight, had he not dodged alertly aside, so that it fell harmless to the ground; and then, with one tremendous blow of his fist, he laid the raging maniac senseless on the floor of the hall.

"Bind him," cried the Wolfe, "bind him instantly, I say, and carry him to the dungeon under the northern tower; he is a prisoner until our pleasure shall pronounce him free."

His orders were instantly and implicitly obeyed, and Sir Alexander was carried off, without sense or motion, under the charge of his jailors. Sir Patrick was shocked at the outrageous scene he had witnessed, in which he had been driven to interfere. Though satisfied of the justice of the Earl's sentence against his son, yet he was concerned to think that he had been instrumental in effecting it, and he conceived he was bound to endeavour to mediate in his behalf.

"Nay, nay," said the Wolfe hastily, "I thank thee heartily for the chastisement thou hast given the whelp. To loose him now, were to deprive him of all its salutary effects. By the blessed Rood, he shall lie in his dungeon until he comes so far to his senses as to make a humble submission both to thee and to me.—What! am I to be bearded at every turning by my boys?—The red fiend catch me, but they and the callet that whelped them shall down to the deepest abyss of Lochyndorbe, ere I shall suffer myself to be so disgraced by her, and snarled at by her litter."

Sir Patrick looked towards Sir Andrew Stewart for aid in his attempt to soften the Earl; but, cool and cautious, he had never stirred from his seat during the fray, and still sat there unmoved, turning a deaf ear to his father's stormy threats, and averting his eye from Hepborne's silent appeal.

"Come, come, the banquet, knaves," cried the Wolfe. "Why stand ye all staring like gaze-hounds? The red fiend catch me, but I will hang up half-a-dozen of ye like a string of beads, an we have not our meal in the twinkling of an eye!"

The lacqueys and attendants had hitherto been standing in silence and horror, but they were all put instantly in motion. The banquet appeared. The Wolfe ate more voraciously than usual, and swallowed deeper draughts of wine also than he ordinarily did; but it was evidently rather to wash down some vexation that oppressed him than from anything like jollity. His conversation was hasty and abrupt, and after drinking double his wonted quantity in half the usual time, he broke up the feast and retired to his apartment.

CHAPTER XXXII.

Maurice's Song—The Franciscan Friar—Excommunication.

As Sir Patrick Hepborne retired to his apartment, he called Maurice de Grey, to inquire into the mysterious means by which he had so effectually defeated the false charge which had been brought against him; but the youth hung his head in answer to his master's inquiries, and hesitated in replying to them.

"Sir Knight," said he at length, "there hath been a mutual promise passed on both sides, that neither the Earl of Buchan nor I shall reveal what did pass in the converse held between him, the Lady Mariota, and myself at our conference. I am therefore compelled to refuse thee that satisfaction which I should otherwise be glad to yield to thee."

With this answer Hepborne was compelled to remain satisfied, and the page being suffered to depart, he retired to rest.

Next morning the Wolfe and he met at breakfast, where were also Sir Andrew and the younger brothers, but the Lady Mariota, with her eldest son, Sir Alexander, were absent.

"My Lord of Buchan," said Sir Patrick, as they sat together, " I presume not to touch thee on the subject of the Lady Mariota, because, with regard to her, I can have no plea or right to interfere ; but wilt thou suffer me to entreat thee again in behalf of thy son Sir Alexander Stewart ? It grieveth me much that I should in any way have contributed to his punishment, however greatly he may have merited thy chastisement. Forgive me, I beseech thee, for being thus solicitous ; but as an especial boon granted to myself, I crave his liberation."

"Ha ! well, Sir Patrick," said the Wolfe, after listening to him with more patience and moderation of aspect than he usually exhibited ; " it is somewhat strange that thou and the child Duncan are the only two persons who have had the heart to make any appeal to me, either about my son Alexander or his mother." And as he said so, he darted an indignant and reproachful glance towards Sir Andrew, who, as if nothing amiss had occurred, had been talking of the weather, and of hunting, and was at that moment helping himself largely to venison pasty. " As for Sir Andrew there, he cares not who suffereth, so that his craven bouke be well fassed with food, like a kite as he is. True indeed is the saying, that misfortunes try hearts. But trust me, I thank thee as heartily for the tenderness thou hast displayed, as for the spirit thou didst show yesternight in checking that foolish boy Alexander. Let me but finish my meal, then, and I shall hie me straight to the dungeons of the prisoners, and observe in what temper they may now be, after a night's cooling, when I shall judge and act accordingly."

The Earl having gone in pursuance of this resolution, returned, after a considerable absence, followed by the Lady Mariota and his son. Both seemed to have been effectually humbled. The lady's face bore ample trace of the night of wretchedness she had spent. She curtseyed with an air, as if she hoped that the forced smile she wore would melt away all remembrance of what had passed ; and then, without saying a word, sidled off to her apartment. Sir Alexander Stewart came forward manfully. His brow still bore the black mark of Hepborne's fist that had prostrated him on the floor, " as butcher felleth ox," yet the blow seemed to have been by this time effaced from his remembrance.

" Sir Patrick," said he, stretching out his hand, " my father tells me that I owe my liberation to thee. Thou hast behaved generously in this matter. The Earl hath given me to know such circumstances as sufficiently explain his seeming harshness to my mother. I now see that I was hasty, and I am sorry for it."

Hepborne readily shook hands with the humbled knight.

"And now let us hunt," cried the Wolfe. "Horses and hounds there, and the foresters, and gear for the chase!" and away went the whole party, to cross to the mainland.

They returned at night, after a successful day's hunting, and the Wolfe of Badenoch was in peculiarly good spirits. The banquet was graced by the Lady Mariota, as usual, tricked out in all her finery, and wearing her accustomed dimpling smiles; and the Earl seemed to have forgotten that he had ever had any cause of displeasure against her. Instead of the marked attention she had formerly paid to Maurice de Grey, however, she now, much to his satisfaction, treated him with politeness, free from that disgusting and offensive doating which had heretofore so much tormented the poor youth. The Wolfe ate voraciously, and drank deeply; and his mirth rose with the wine he swallowed to so great a pitch of jollity, that he roared out loudly for music.

"Can no one sing me a roundelay?" cried he. "Mariota, thou knowest not a single warble, nor is there, I trow, one in the Castle that can touch even a citrial or a guittern, far less a harp. Would that our scoundrel, Allan Stewart, were here, but—a plague on him!—he hath gone to visit his friends in Badenoch. He could have given us romaunces, ballads, and virelays enow, I warrant thee."

"My Lord Earl," said the page modestly, "had I but a harp, in truth I should do my best to pleasure thee, though I can promise but little for my skill."

"Well said, boy," cried the Wolfe. "By the mass, but thou shalt have a harp. Ho, there!—bring hither Allan Stewart's harp. The knave hath two, and it is to be hoped he hath not carried both with him."

The harp was brought, and Maurice de Grey having tuned it, began to accompany himself in the following ballad:—

There was a damsel loved a knight,
   You'll weep to hear her story,
For he ne'er guess'd her heart's sad plight,
   Nor cared for aught but glory.

Lured by its bright and dazzling gleam,
   He left the woe-worn maiden,
Nor in her eyes beheld the beam
   Of love, from heart o'erladen.

She sigh'd ; her sighs ne'er touch'd his ear,
   For still his heart was bounding
For neighing steeds, and clashing spear,
   And warlike bugle sounding.

She wept ; but though he saw her tears,
   He dreamt not he had wrought them,
But ween'd that woman's idle fears,
   Or silly woes, had brought them.

He left her then to weep alone,
   And droop in secret sadness,
Like some fair lily early blown,
   'Reft of the sunbeam's gladness.

But love will make e'en maidens dare
   What most their sex hath frighten'd—
Beneath a helm she crush'd her hair,
   In steel her bosom brighten'd.

She seized a lance, she donn'd a brand,
   A sprightly war-horse bore her,
She hied her to the Holy Land,
   Where went her Knight before her.

She sought him out—she won his heart—
   Amidst the battle's bluster ;
As friends they ne'er were seen to part,
   Howe'er the foes might cluster.

But ah ! I grieve to tell the tale !
   A random arrow flying,
Pierced through her corslet's jointed mail,
   And down she fell a-dying.

He bore her quickly from the field,
   Through Paynim ranks opposing,
But when her helmet was unseal'd,
   Her maiden blush disclosing.

He cried, "Blest Virgin be our aid !
   What piteous sight appals me !
It is—it is that gentle maid,
   Whose lovely form still thralls me.

"Lift, lift those heavy drooping eyes,
   And with one kind look cheer me !"
She smiled like beam in freezing skies,
   "Ah, Rodolph, art thou near me?

"My life ebbs fast, my heart's blood flows,
   That long hath beat for thee, love ;
And still for thee my bosom glows,
   Though death's hand is on me, love.

"For thee in secret did I sigh,
   Nor ween'd that love could warm thee,
Nor that my lustre-lacking eye
   Could e'er have power to charm thee.".

"Nay, Angeline," cried Rodolph then,
   "I wist not that I loved thee,
Till left my home, and native glen,
   Remembrance of thee moved me.

16

"Let him who woos not health nor joy,
  Till lost are both the treasures,
My heart held love as childish toy,
  Nor cared to sip its pleasures.

"But follow'd by the form so fair,
  I saw it on each billow ;
I saw it float in empty air—
  It hover'd o'er my pillow.

"And e'en when hardy deeds I wrought,
  'Midst murderous ranks contending,
Thy figure ever filled my thought,
  Mine arm new vigour lending.

"And then the fame of deeds of arms
  Had lost all power to cheer me,
Save that, methought, its dazzling charms
  To thee might yet endear me.

"And have I pluck'd these laurels green,
  To deck thy dying brow, love ?
Oh, lift for once those lovely een,
  To hear my plighted vow, love ! "

"I'm happy now," she faintly said,
  "But, oh, 'tis cruel to sever ! "—
Upon his breast her head she laid,
  And closed her eyes for ever.

"Sir Page," cried the Wolfe, at the close of this ballad, "by
my knighthood, but thou dost sing and harp it better than Allan
Stewart himself, though thy lays are something of the saddest.
Meseems if thou didst ween that our mirth had waxed somewhat
too high, and that it lacked a damper. In sooth," continued he,
turning to Hepborne with an arch look, "thou art much to be
envied, Sir Patrick, for the possession of this lovely, this accomplished—ha ! ha ! ha !—this—this boy of thine—ha ! ha ! ha !—
this Maurice de Grey.—Come, Maurice, my sweet youth," said
he, addressing the page, "essay again to tune thy throat, and
let it, I beseech thee, be in a strain more jocund than the last.
Here, quaff wine, boy, to give thee jollier heart."

"Thanks, my noble Lord," replied Maurice de Grey, "I will
exert my poor powers to fulfil thy wishes without drinking."

And, taking up the harp again, he ran his fingers nimbly
over the strings, with great display of execution, in a sprightly
prelude, enlivening his auditors, and preparing them to sympa-
thize with something more in unison with the highly-screwed
chords of the Earl's heart, when he was suddenly interrupted
by the appearance of a new personage.

A tall monk of the order of St. Francis suddenly entered,
and, gliding like a spirit into the middle of the hall, darted

a pair of keen searching eyes towards the upper end of the festive board.

"What, ha! brother of St. Francis," cried the Wolfe of Badenoch, "what wouldst thou? If thou be'st wayfaring, and need cheer, sit thee down there at the end of our festive board, and call for what thou lackest."

The Franciscan stood mute and unmoved, with his cowl over his head, and his arms folded across his breast. The silver lamps threw a pale light upon his face, and his shadow rose gigantically upon the wall.

"Whence comest thou?—Speak!" cried the Wolfe, impatiently. "Are we to be kept waiting all night, till thou dost choose to effunde the cause of thy strange visitation?"

"Alexander Stewart, Earl of Buchan, and Lord of Badenoch," said the Franciscan slowly, and in a deep solemn tone; "Alexander Stewart, I come here as the messenger of the Bishop of Moray, to tell thee that the tidings of thy daring, outrageous, and sacrilegious seizure of the lands belonging to the Holy Church, have reached him: the cries alswa of the helpless peasants, whom thou hast ousted from their dwellings, have sounded in his ears. Thy cruelties are bruited abroad from one end of the kingdom to the other, and it is now time that thy savage career should be arrested. The godly Bishop doth, through me, his organ of speech, call on thee to give up the lands thou hast sacrilegiously seized in Badenoch; to restore the plundered herds and flocks, and the rents thou hast theftuously taken by masterful strength; to replace those honest and innocent peasants, who, resisting thy aggression, like true vassals, were, with their wives and little ones, driven from their homes and possessions by thee in thy brutish fury; and, finally, to make such reparation to Holy Mother Church, by fine to her treasuries, and personal abasement before her altars, as may stay her just wrath against thee. In default of all which, the Holy Bishop hath commanded me to announce to thee, that the lesser and greater excommunications shall go forth against thee; and that thou shalt be accursed as a vagabond on the face of this earth, and damned to all eternity in the next world."

The fiery and ferocious Wolfe of Badenoch was so utterly confounded by what he considered the unexampled audacity of this denunciation, that amazement kept him silent from absolute want of words, otherwise his limited stock of patience could not have endured the Franciscan till he had uttered the tenth part of his long speech. He gnashed his teeth, curled up his nose, and foamed at the mouth; and striking the table furiously, as was his custom when violently moved, he shouted out—

"Ha! Devils! Furies! Fiends of Erebus! What is this I hear? The Earl of Buchan—the son of a King—the Wolfe of Badenoch—to be thus insulted by a chough! Out, thou carrion-hooded crow! Thinkest thou to brave me down with thine accursed crawing? By the beard of my grandfather, but thou shalt swing twenty ell high, an thou voidest not the Castle of thy loathsome carcase in less time than thou didst ware in effunding one-fourth part of thy venomous and impudent harangue."

The monk stood motionless, in the same fixed and composed attitude he had at first assumed, altogether unmoved by these tremendous threats.

"Alexander Stewart, Earl of Buchan, and Lord of Badenoch," he again repeated in the same slow and solemn manner. "I call upon thee again to declare whether thou be'st disposed to submit thyself patiently to the healthful discipline of our Holy Mother Church? or whether thou be'st resolved that she shall cut thee off, like a rotten and diseased branch, to fall headlong into the pit where eternal fire shall consume thee? Already, ere this, hadst thou incurred her just vengeance by living in abominable adultery with Mariota Athyn, thy wanton leman, who now sitteth in abomination beside thee; and by the abandonment of thy leal, true and virtuous wife, whom thou hast left to mourn in a worse than widowhood. In addition to the solemn appeal I have already made, I am commanded to call on thee now to fulfil the sentence of the Bishops of Moray and Ross, to pay down two hundred broad pieces of gold as the mulct of thine offence, and forthwith to discharge thy foul and sinful mate, and recal to thy bosom her who hath the true and lawful claim to lay her head there. Wilt thou do these things, yea or not?"

This ripping up of the old feud not only redoubled the rage of the Wolfe of Badenoch, but roused that of the Lady Mariota and her sons. She burst into a flood of tears, a violent fit of sobbing followed, and she finally rushed from the banquet hall. The hot and fierce Sir Alexander was broiling with fury; but the Wolfe took the speech of him——

"Ha! so thou hast come to the kernel of this matter at last, thou ape of Satan, hast thou? Now I do clearly ken how far I was right in guessing at the tale-pyet that chattered in the ear of the King, my father. But, by the blood of the Bruce, I have revenged his impertinent meddling, by ousting him from the

roost he had in my lands ; and, by all the hot fiends of perdition, if he rouseth the Wolfe of Badenoch more, his neck shall
be twisted about.   Art content with my answer now, thou
hooded-carrion-crow ? "

"Alexander Stewart, Earl of Buchan, and Lord of Badenoch,"
said the Franciscan, with the same imperturbable gravity, firmness, and composure, " hast thou no better response than this to
make to the holy Bishop of Moray ?   Bethink thee well——"

"Scoundrel chough, begone ! " cried the Wolfe, interrupting
him.   "Thou hast already more than outstaid my patience,
which hath in itself been miraculous.   If thou wouldst escape
hence in safety, avoid thee instantly ; for if thou goest not in
the twinkling of an eye, may infernal demons seize me if thou
shalt have leave to go at all."

"Then, Alexander Stewart," said the Franciscan, "the
Bishop's curse be upon thee and upon thine ; for thou shalt be
an outcast from our Holy Mother Church, and——"

"And the red fiend's curse be upon thee and the split-
crowned Bishop ! " cried the Wolfe, interrupting him.   " Why
stand these kestrel rogues to see their lord, to see the Wolfe of
Badenoch flouted by that stinking and venomous weasel ! Seize
the vermin, knaves, and let him be tossed into the Water Pit
Vault ; if I mistake not, the loch is high enow at present to keep
him company there; but, let him sink or swim, I care not;
away with the toad, I say.   He may thank his good stars that ·
I gave him a chance for his life.   By the infernal host, I was
much tempted to string him up, without more ado, to the
gallows in the court-yard, that he might dance a bargaret for
our sport, sith he hath spoilt our mirth and music by his ill-
omened croaking.   Away with him, I say ! "

"Beware of touching the servant of Heaven," cried the firm
and undismayed Franciscan ; " whosoever dareth to lay impious
hands on me, shall be subjected to the same curse as the sacrilegious tyrant who sitteth yonder."

" Why stand ye hesitating, knaves ? " roared the Wolfe.   " Let
him not utter another word, or, by the pit of darkness, I shall
have ye all flayed alive."

The Franciscan's threat had operated too strongly on the
lacqueys to permit them to secure the monk with their own hands,
yet, afraid to risk their master's hasty displeasure, one or two of
them had not scrupled to fly off for the jailors and executioners
of the Castle, men who, like tutored bears, had neither fears nor
hopes, nor, indeed, thoughts of aught else but obedience to the
will of a master, engrafted upon their savage natures by early

nurture and long usage. Four or five of these entered as the
Wolfe of Badenoch was speaking. They appeared like creatures
that had inhabited the bowels of the earth ; bulky of bone and
muscle ; their hair and beards were long and matted, their eyes
inanimate and unfeeling, and their hands, features, and garments alike coarse and begrimed with filth, as if the blood of
their murderous trade still adhered to them.

"Ha ! ay ! there ye come, my trusty terriers ; seize that
polecat there in the cowl, and toss him into the Water Pit Vault.
Quick, away with him !"

The bold Franciscan had trusted to the sanctity of his character, but he had presumed too far on its protecting influence ;
these reckless minions of the Wolfe had him in their fell gripe
in an instant, and dragged him unresisting towards the door of
the banquet hall, as if he had been but a huge black goat.
There, however, his eyes happened to catch the figure and
countenance of the page, Maurice de Grey ; he started, and, in
spite of the nervous exertions of the ruffians who had him in
charge, he planted his feet so firmly on the pavement, that he
compelled them to halt, while he stood for a moment fixed like
a Colossus, darting a keen look at the page. The boy's eyes
sunk beneath the sternness of his gaze.

"Thou here !" exclaimed he with an expression of extreme
surprise ; "by what miracle do I behold thee here ? Would
that I had seen thee before—would that I had known——"

But the sturdy and callous knaves who held him, noticed
his sudden halt and mysterious speech no otherwise than they
would have done the voice or struggles of the goat we have
compared him to ; they only put forth a little more strength,
and, before he could get another word out, whirled him through
the door-way, and lugged him sprawling down the stair. Hepborne had been more than once on the eve of interceding for
the monk, but he saw that anything he could have said would
have been of little avail, amidst the general fury that prevailed
against him, and might have even provoked a more immediate
and fatal vengeance; so that all thoughts of running a hopeless
tilt in his behalf, against the highly excited ferocity of the
Stewarts, were abandoned by him for the present.

The Wolfe of Badenoch was too much unhinged in temper,
by the visit of the Franciscan monk, to be in a humour to prolong the feast.

"Caitiff ! carrion ! corby !" cried he after he was gone ; "the
red fiend swallow me, but the bold Bishop shall bide for the
return of his messenger. Ho ! bring me that stoup, knave."

He put the stoup of Rhenish to his head, and quaffing a potent draught from it, set it down on the table with a violent crash, and calling out, " Lights there—lights for the apart- ments," he broke up the feast.

CHAPTER XXXIII.

The Water Pit Vault—Friar or Devil, which ?

SIR PATRICK HEPBORNE went to his room, determined to leave Lochyndorbe next day, to proceed to Tarnawa ; so calling Maurice de Grey and Mortimer Sang, and intimating his inten- tion to both of them, he dismissed them for the night and retired to his repose.

A little past midnight, however, he was suddenly awakened by the page, who came rushing into his apartment in a state of intense apprehension, and sunk into a chair, overcome by his terrors.

" Holy St. Baldrid," exclaimed Sir Patrick, " what hath be- fallen thee, Maurice ? And of what art thou afraid ? Speak, I beseech thee, and tell me the cause of this strange alarm ? "

" Oh, Sir Knight," cried the boy, pale as ashes and ready to faint, " the friar—the monk—the Franciscan ! I was telling my beads by my lamp, as is my custom, being about to undress to go to bed, when one of the doors of my chamber opened slowly, and the figure of the Franciscan stood before me. My blood ran cold when I saw him, for methought murder was in his eye, and I fancied I saw the hilt of a poinard glittering from his bosom. I waited not to hear him speak, but snatching up my lamp, rushed through the farther door-way, and fled hither for succour."

" Pshaw, Maurice," said Sir Patrick, " verily thou must have dreamt that thou didst see the friar. How couldst thou see him, who was plunged by order of the stern Earl into the deep dungeon called the Water Pit Vault ? "

" Nay, Sir Knight," cried Maurice, " but he may have 'scaped thence, and may be now wandering about the Castle."

" Nay, verily, that were impossible," replied Sir Patrick ; " 'tis a terrible place ; I had the curiosity to peep into it, one of the times it happened to be open, as I passed by the mouth of it. It is so much below the level of the lake, that there is generally an ell's-depth of water in the bottom of it ; and its profundity is such, that without ropes, or a ladder, it were vain to hope to emerge from it, even were the heavy stone trap-door that shuts it left open to facilitate escape; nay, I tell thee it is impossible boy; believe me, the Franciscan stands freezing there, God help him, among the cold water, for the wretch cannot lie down without drowning. When I think of the horrors the miserable man was so hastily doomed to, I cannot help regretting that I did not make some attempt to soothe the Earl to mercy, though I have strong reason to fear I might have brought a more hasty fate on his head by my interference; but I shall surely use my endeavours to move my Lord of Buchan for the poor friar's liberation in the morning. Trust me, boy, it could in no wise be the Franciscan thou sawest; and by much the most likely explanation of thine alarm is, that thou hadst become drowsy over thy beads, and, dropping asleep, didst dream of the scene thou sawest pass in the banquet hall."

"Nay, nay, Sir Knight," cried Maurice de Grey, "it was the Franciscan, flesh and blood, or "—said he, pausing and shuddering, " or—it was his sprite."

"Tush, boy Maurice," said Sir Patrick, "in very truth, 'tis thy dreams which have deceived thee; and, now I think of it, by St. Baldrid, I wonder not that thou shouldst have dreamed of the friar, seeing that he looked at thee so earnestly; and then he seemed to know thee too. Pr'ythee, hast thou ever chanced to see him before ?"

"Not as far as I can remember, Sir Knight," replied the boy; " but sure I am I shall not fail to recollect him if I should ever see him again, which the blessed Virgin forbid, for there is something terrible in his eye."

"Tut, boy," cried Hepborne, " what hast thou to fear from his eye ? Methinks thou hast displayed a wondrous want of courage with this same peaceful friar."

"Peaceful !" exclaimed Maurice de Grey.

" Ay, peaceful," continued his master; " for a poor Franciscan friar cannot well be aught else than peaceful. Thou hast played but a poor part to run away from him, thou who didst attack the bison bull so boldly; yea, thou who didst so nobly wage desperate strife with the assassin who did attempt the life of thy master, at the Shelter Stone of Loch Avon. Why didst thou not draw thy sword, and demand the cause of his rude intrusion ?"

"Nay, Sir Knight," said the boy, shuddering, " he did verily appear something more than human."

" Well, well," said Hepborne, laughing, " I will but throw a cloak about me and go with thee to thy chamber, to see whether he may yet tarry there."

But when they went to the page's apartment they found not the slightest vestige of the friar; and Sir Patrick, with the wish of convincing the boy that he had been dreaming, laughed . heartily at his fears. But the youth resolutely maintained his assertion that he had not slept; and his master, seeing that the vision, or whatever else it might have been, had taken so strong a hold of the page's mind, that it would be absolute cruelty to compel him to sleep alone, admitted him into a small closet adjoining the apartment he himself occupied; and the boy's countenance showed that he was sufficiently grateful for the boon.

When Sir Patrick Hepborne met the Earl of Buchan at breakfast, he announced to him his determination to depart that day.

"Ha!" said the Wolfe, "by the mass, but it doleth me much that thou art going, Sir Patrick. Thou hast as yet had but small enjoyment in hunting, yea, or in anything else in Lochyndorbe. Thy visit hath been one continued turmoil. Since thou wilt go, however, by'r Lady, I will e'en resolve me to go with thee to this same tourney at Tarnawa. But I must think how to bestow the corby Franciscan friar ere I go; he cannot be left in the Water Pit Vault until I return hither, for one night of that moist lodging hath been enow to set many a one ere this to eternal sleep. I must look him out some drier, though equally secure place of dortoure."

"If I might not offend thee by the request," said Hepborne, "I would ask, as the last favour thou mayest grant me ere I go, and as it were to put the crown upon the hospitality thou hast exercised towards me, that thou wouldst give the poor wretch his freedom. Meseems it thou hast done enough to terrify him, yea, and those also who sent him; and the return of the ambassador with amicable proposals, may do more than all his sufferings, or even his death. Forgive these gratuitous advices, my Lord Earl, given in the spirit of peace and prudence, and with the best intention."

Hepborne's firmness, courage, and temper had in reality gained a wonderful ascendancy over the ferocious Wolfe, during the short space he had been with him; besides, he always managed to take the most favourable time for making his rational appeals. The Earl heard him to an end most patiently, and then pausing for a moment in thought—

"Well," said he, "Sir Patrick Hepborne, by the Rood, but there is something right pleasing in seeing thee always enlist thyself on the side of mercy—thou who so well knowest how to stand a bicker when it comes, and who refuseth never to place thyself in the breach when of needscost thou must. Well, we

shall see, then ; come along with me to the Water Pit Vault,
and we shall see what I can make of the hooded-crow.   He may
be more tame by this time, and peraunter he will croak less.
Come along with me, I say, so please thee.   Here, call the
jailor on duty—call him to the Water Pit Vault."

A lacquey ran to obey his commands, and Sir Patrick descended with him to the outer court-yard.   They found the grim
and gruff jailor standing ready to raise the stone at his lord's
command.   The vault was entirely under ground, the mouth of
it being immediately within the outer rampart, and opposite to
that part of the surrounding lake which was deepest.

"Raise the stone trap-door, knave," cried the Wolfe to the
man ; "we need not send for a ladder or ropes until we see how
the prisoner behaves."

The trap-door was lifted up with considerable difficulty by
the sturdy jailor, and all three cast their eyes downwards into
the obscure depth below.   It was some moments ere their sight
was sufficiently accommodated to the paucity of light to enable
them to see to the bottom.

"Ha ! what !" cried the Wolfe, "by the beard of my grandfather, but I see him not ; dost thou, Sir Patrick ?   Nay, by St.
Andrew, there is no Franciscan there, alive or dead ; for now I
can see even to the bottom of the ell-depth of clear water that
covereth the pavement.   Hey ! what ! by'r Lady, but it is
passing strange.   Knave," cried he, turning to the jailor, who
appeared to be as much confounded as the Earl and his guest,
"didst thou see him lodged here yesternight with thine own
eyes ? "

"I did put him down myself with a rope, so please thee, my
noble Lord," said the man.   The rest were called, and they all
declared they had assisted in lowering him, and in replacing the
stone over the mouth of the vault, and all were equally petrified
to see that the prisoner was gone.

"By all the powers of Tartarus," cried the Wolfe, "but this
passeth all marvel !   Of a truth, the devil himself must have
assisted the carrion corby ; and, by my beard, but I did suspect
that he was more the servant of hell than of heaven, as he dared
to call himself.   Ha ! well, if the wizard caitiff do fall into my
hands again, by all the fiends, but he shall be tried with fire
next, sith he can so readily escape from water."

Sir Patrick was not less astonished than the rest of those
who beheld the miracle.   He thought of the strange and
unaccountable appearance of the Franciscan to the page,
which he now readily believed to have been real, and he

shuddered at the narrow escape which the boy had made from murder.

The news of the friar having vanished from the Water Pit Vault soon spread like wildfire through the Castle, and many and various were the opinions concerning it. Some few there were who secretly in their own minds set it down as a miraculous deliverance worked in favour of the Franciscan, to defeat the impiety and sacrilege of the Wolfe of Badenoch, who had dared to order violent hands to be laid on a holy man ; but the greater part, who were of the same stamp with their master, thought as he did ; and some of them even went so far as firmly to believe that the Franciscan was in reality no monk, but the devil himself, disguised under the sanctified garb of a friar. The boldness he had displayed, and the sudden and irresistible halt he had made, in defiance of the power of the sturdy knaves who were dragging him away, confirmed them in their notions. Nay, many of them even declared that at that moment they had actually observed his cloven foot, pointed from under the long habit, and thrust like iron prongs into the flag-stones of the banqueting hall.

CHAPTER XXXIV.

The Wolfe of Badenoch and the Earl of Moray.

THE Wolfe of Badenoch having once made up his mind to accompany Sir Patrick Hepborne to the tournament of St. John's, allowed but little time to be lost by his people in preparation ; and his sons and their attendants, with his own splendid retinue, were speedily assembled on the lawn beyond the land sconce. Hepborne's more moderate cortège was also quickly mustered there, and in less than an hour the two leaders were at the head of their united trains, marching off with bugles sounding, and banners and pennons flying.

Leaving the lake by the same route by which Sir Patrick had approached it, they travelled northwards through the apparently ceaseless forest, that varied only in the undulations of the surface it grew upon, and in the trees it produced. The pines were very soon, in a great measure, exchanged for magnificent birches and oaks, spreading themselves far and wide over the country, and forming the vast forest of Drummyn. There they skirted the Findhorn, which thundered through the romantic chasm, yawning between confined and precipitous crags, until they found themselves on the summit of a bold cliff overhanging the river, from' the base of which it swept in one grand and broad line through the centre of a beautiful plain of about a mile in diameter, dividing it from south to north into two nearly equal parts. These were the Meads of St. John, and there the stream seemed gladly to slumber in a comparatively gentle current, after its boisterous and laborious passage downwards from its native mountains. Ledges of rock did indeed push themselves here and there from its enamelled margins, and served to diversify them, as did those groups of wide-spreading oaks of enormous growth, forming in most places a broad bowery fringe to either shore; but there was nothing to disturb the perfect continuity and level of the grassy surface of the meadows, except one or two bosky groves, carelessly planted by the hand of nature. The high banks retreating on both sides, to bend round and embrace the Meads, presented an irregularity of form and slope; while the forest, extending itself everywhere over the upper grounds, sent down some of its most magnificent representatives to grace their sides. About a mile or more to the left, perched on a gentle eminence, arose the venerable Castle of Tarnawa, looking far and wide over its woody domain. Towards the northern extremity of the Eastern Mead, stood the little chapel dedicated to St. John the Baptist, giving name to the lovely valley that now stretched in rich verdure beneath their eyes; and over the farther boundaries of the meadows appeared the fertile plain of Forres, the broad expanse of the Frith, and the distant mountain-range beyond.

But these, the mere ordinary and permanent features of the scene, though exquisitely beautiful in themselves, were at this time rendered tenfold more interesting by the animation that everywhere pervaded the Meads of St. John, where the whole population of the North had assembled. Midway down the long stretch of the river was erected a wide bridge, formed of enormous pillars and beams of wood, intended to give temporary passage between the opposite banks during the ensuing sports; and it was spanned above by several triumphal arches, which people were then employed in decorating with boughs of holly and other evergreens. A promiscuous and motley assemblage of booths, tents, log-houses, and huts, in number beyond all possibility of reckoning, were seen scattered like a great irregular village all around the base of those semi-circular banks embracing the eastern side of the Meads. These fragile tenements were occupied by the populace not only of the neighbouring town and surrounding country, but by many who had come from very distant parts of Scotland, some to establish a mart for their wares, others to exhibit feats of strength, or agility, or juggling, and the greater number, perhaps, to behold the spectacle, or assist in the labours incident to the preparation for it.

The lists were then erecting in the centre of the eastern meadow, while, on the western side of the river, were observed a number of pavilions, within the recess of a beautiful glade retiring among the wooded banks. These were brought thither by knights who came to attend the tournament, the accommodations in the Castle being quite unequal for more than a chosen few. Such as were already erected had each a banner or pennon flying before it, and others were pitching with great expedition. In the midst of the whole was the pavilion of the Earl of Moray, of much greater magnitude than any of those around it, while his banner unfurled itself to the breeze from the top of a tall pine fixed in the ground for the purpose.

Such were the most prominent objects, then, in the Meads of St. John; but the whole vale swarmed with living beings. Groups of men and horses were seen moving over it in all directions, and the very earth seemed in motion.

"By the Holy Rood," cried the Wolfe, "but it is a noble sight. Methinks my brother-in-law, Earl John, must have had his hands in the King's purse ere he could have ventured on such a show as this. Come, Sir Patrick, let us hasten to see how things may be in the Castle."

They followed a steep and winding path that led them down through the wood into the valley below, and quickly crossed the level ground towards the bridge. This they found guarded by a strong party of spearmen and archers. The captain on duty came forward—

"Sir Knights," said he courteously, "so please ye to honour me with your names and titles, that they may be passed forward to the Earl's pavilion for his inspection."

"Morte de ma vie," cried the Wolfe of Badenoch pettishly, "but this is ceremony with a vengeance. What! shall I not have liberty to approach me to mine own brother-in-law, until I shall have sent him my name! and am I, or is my horse, to be kept on the fret here until the return of a tardy messenger from yonder tents? What a fiend, dost thou not know me, Sir Captain? dost thou not know me for the Earl of Buchan?"

"My Lord Earl," replied the captain of the guard with perfect reverence, "I did indeed know the attence, but mine orders are so imperative, that albeit it doth indeed much erke

me to be so strict with thee, yet must I of needscost subject thee
to the same rule that hath been laid down for all."

To prevent further words, Hepborne hastened to give his
name and quality, and the number of his retinue, to the captain
of the guard; and observing the growing impatience of the
Wolfe, he managed to avert his coming wrath, by expressing a
desire to ride towards the lists, to see what was going forward
there, hoping that, by the time they had examined all the operations in progress, the passage of the bridge would be open to
them.

Having contrived to make the Wolfe waste nearly half-an-
hour in this way, Hepborne returned with him to the bridge,
where they were informed by the captain of the guard that the
Earl of Moray was coming in person to meet them; and
accordingly they beheld him riding across the bridge towards
them, followed by an esquire and a very few attendants. He
was unostentatiously dressed in a light hunting garb; his figure
was middle-sized, his complexion fair, and his countenance fresh,
round, and of a mild expression.

His horse's hoofs had no sooner touched the sod of the
meadow than he dismounted, and giving the rein to his esquire,
advanced to meet his brother-in-law. The Wolfe of Badenoch
leaped from his saddle, and moving one step forward, stood to
receive him. Sir Patrick Hepborne and the five Stewarts
having also dismounted, were at his back.

" Brother," said the Wolfe, after their first salutations were
over, " this is Sir Patrick Hepborne."

" Sir Patrick," said the Earl graciously, " I rejoice to see thee
here; welcome to thy country, and to these my domains; I
regret to understand that I must cast away all hope of seeing
thine honoured father upon this occasion, and I yet more grieve
at the cause of his present unfitness for mixing in sports in
which he was wont to shine as a bright star. Nevoys," continued he, saluting Sir Alexander Stewart and his brothers,
" I rejoice to behold ye thus waxing so stout; an ye thrive thus,
even the very youngest of ye will soon be well able to bear a
shock. What sayest thou, Duncan, my boy ? Your pardon,
Sir Patrick, for a moment, but I must speak a little aside here
with my brother, the noble Earl of Buchan ; I shall be entirely
at thy command anon."

The two Earls retired a few paces to one side, and Moray's
face assuming an air of great seriousness, he began to talk in an
under tone to the Wolfe of Badenoch, whose brow, as he listened,
gathered clouds and storms, which went on blackening and

ruffling it, until at length he burst out into one of his ungovern-able furies.

"Ha! by the beard of my grandfather, and dost thou think that I care the value of a cross-bow bolt for the split-crowned magpie?" cried he. "Excommunicate me! and what harm, I pr'ythee, will his excommunication do me? But, by'r Lady, he shall suffer for it. He has already had a small spice of what the Wolfe of Badenoch can do when he is roused, and, by all the fiends, he shall know more on't ere long."

"Talk not so loud and vehemently, I beseech thee, brother," said the Earl of Moray; "publish not the matter thus."

"Nay, but I will tell it," roared out the Wolfe; "I will publish the insolence of this scoundrel Bishop to the whole world. What think ye," continued he, turning round to his sons and Sir Patrick —" what think ye of the consummate impudence of the rascally Alexander Barr? He hath dared to void his im-potent curse on the Earl of Buchan and Ross—on the son of the King of Scotland—on the Wolfe of Badenoch. My brother here, the Earl of Moray, hath just had an especial messenger from the croaking carrion, to tell him the news of my excommunication; but the red fiend catch me, an I do not make him rue that he ever told the tale beyond his own crowing rookery. Ha! let us to the Castle, brother—let us to my sister Margery, I say. De-pardieux, but thou shalt see that the hypocritical knave's anathema shall be but as seasoning to my food. Trust me, I shall not eat or drink one tithe the less of thy good cheer for it."

"Most noble Earl of Buchan, and my most excellent brother," said the Earl of Moray, with a hesitating and perplexed air, "it erketh me sore—it giveth me, as thou mayest readily believe, extreme grief—to be compelled to tell thee that I cannot with propriety receive thee at present among the nobles who now house them within my walls, nor would the heralds admit of thy presence at the ensuing tournament, whilst thou liggest under the bann of the Holy Church, even were I bold enough to risk for thee the Church's displeasure against me and mine. Let me, then, I pray thee, have weight with thee so far as to persuade thee to ride straightway to Elgin, to make thy peace with the Bishop. Much as I have on my hands at the present time, verily I will not scruple to haste thither with thee, if thou dost think that I mought in any manner of way further an accom-modation, so that this dread reproach may be forthwith removed from off thee. We can then return together speedily, ere yet the matter shall have been bruited abroad (for, so far as I am

concerned, it is as yet a secret); and thou shalt then, much to
my joy and honour, take thy due and proper place by the side of
thy brother Robert, Earl of Fife and Menteith, at the head of
mine illustrious guests, and——"

"Ha! what!" cried the Wolfe of Badenoch in a fury;
"thinkest thou that I will hie me straight, to lout myself low,
and to lick the dust before the feet of that lorel Bishop, who
hath had the surquedrie to dare thus to insult me? By my
trusty burly-brand, I shall take other means of settling accounts
between us. But methinks he is right hasty in his traffic.
No sooner have I settled one score with him, than he runs me
up another in the twinkling of an eye. But, by all the furies,
he shall find that I shall pay him off roundly, and score him up
double on my side. And so, brother, thou dost think that I
carry such leprous contamination about my person, as may altogether unfit me for the purity of thy virtuous house? Gramercy for thy courtesy! But by the Rood, I do believe that
something else lurketh under all these pretences. Thou hast
seen my dotard father the King lately; thou hast held council
with him I ween; and, I trow, my interests have not been fur-
thered by the advices thou hast whispered in the Royal ear. I
still lack the best cantle of my Lieutenantship in lacking
Moray Land, and a bird hath whistled me that John Dunbar,
Earl of Moray, hath not been backward in urging the monarch
to refuse it to me. If this be so, Brother Earl——"

"I swear by my knighthood," cried the Earl of Moray earnestly interrupting him, and speaking at once with calmness and
firmness—"I swear by my knighthood, that whoso hath told
thee this, hath told thee a black falsehood; and I gage mine
honour to throw the lie in his teeth, and to defy him to mortal
debate, should it so please thee to yield me his name."

"Well spoken, brother John," cried the Wolfe. apparently
satisfied with the solemnity of the Earl of Moray's denial. "But
thou art pretty safe in thy darreigne; I did but suspect thee,
and, in sooth, appearances were infernally against thee. But I
must take it upon thy word and abide the event. Yet do I
know of a truth that thou wert with the King——"

"That do I most readily confess," replied the Earl of Moray
mildly. "I did indeed journey to Scone on my private affairs,
and, among other things, to crave His Majesty's gracious permission to hold this same tourney, and to petition for his royal
presence here. But State reasons, or infirmity, or perhaps both
causes conjoined, keep him back from us; nathless he hath sent
his banner hither to wave over the lists, to show that at least

we have his royal good-will with us. I most solemnly vow that I did never meddle or make with the King in any matter of thine."

"The red fiend ride me then," cried the Wolfe hastily, "but thy reception of me hath been something of the coolest. Methinks that, putting myself in thy case, and thee in mine, I should for thee have defied all the lorel coistrils that ever carried crosier. Ha! by'r Lady, 'tis indeed a precious tale to tell, that the Earl of Buchan was refused herborow within the Castle of his brother of Moray."

"Again I repeat that it doleth me sore," said the Earl of Moray, "that I should be compelled to put on the semblance of inhospitality, and, above all, towards thee, my Lord of Buchan, with whom I am so nearly and dearly allied. But in this case, were I even to set the Bishop's threats at defiance in order to receive thee, thou must be aware that it would only expose thee to certain disgrace; for, of a truth, thy presence would quickly clear my hall of all the noble guests who are to feast within its walls. Would, then, that I could incline thee to follow my counsel, and that thou wouldst be content to ride with me to Elgin, to appease the Bishop's wrath, that he may remove his Episcopal curse. We should be back here long ere cock-crow, and——"

"Thou hast had my mind on that head already, brother John," cried the Wolfe, interrupting him, in a rage. "By the mass, but it is a cheap thing for thee to make trade and chevisaunce of another's pride; but, by the blood of the Bruce, I promise thee, I shall give up no title of mine to swell that of the lossel drone of a Bishop; so make thyself easy on that score. What! to be trampled on by a walthsome massmonger, and then to go cap-in-hand, that he may put his plebeian foot on my neck! My horse there—my horse, I say. What stand the knaves staring for? I bid thee goode'en, my Lord of Moray. I'll to Forres then, to inn me, sith I may not put my leprous hide within thy pure and unsullied walls. God be with thee, Sir Patrick Hepborne;" and so saying he sprang into his saddle.

"But," said the Earl of Moray, "though I cannot receive thee at present, my Lord of Buchan, I shall be right glad to do all the honour I may to Sir Alexander Stewart and the rest of my nevoys."

"Gramercy for thy courtesy," cried the proud and fierce Sir Alexander; "sith thou dost hold my father as a polluted and pestilential guest, thou shalt have none of my company, I promise thee."

17

" Ha ! well said, son Alexander," shouted the Wolfe joyously ;
" well said, my brave boy ; by my beard, but thou hast spoken
bravely.   To Forres then, my merry men."

And without abiding farther parlance, the hasty Wolfe of
Badenoch, with Sir Alexander and the younger Stewarts, rode
off at a hand-gallop, followed by their retinue.   Sir Andrew,
however, remained quietly behind, and manifested no inclination
to accompany his father.

" And now, Sir Patrick Hepborne," said the Earl of Moray,
" I have to crave thy pardon for having been thus so long
neglectful of thee on a first meeting ; but, I trow, I need hardly
apologise, since thou hast thyself seen and heard enow, I ween,
to plead my excuse with thee.   This matter hath in very sooth
most grievously affected me.   It hath truly given me more
teene and vexation than I can well tell thee.   But I shall to
Forres by times i' the morning, and then essay to soothe my
Lord of Buchan into greater moderation and a more reasonable
temper than he hath just displayed.   Meanwhile the Countess
Margery doth abide for us in the pavilion.   Let us then hasten
thither, so please thee, for she will not leave it to go to the
Castle until I rejoin her, and verily it waxeth late, and the
nobles and barons will ere this be assembling in Randolph's
Hall."

The Earl now led the way across the bridge, and thence towards the pavilions.   As they approached the great one, before
which his banner was displayed, a group of squires, grooms, and
caparisoned palfreys appeared promenading in front of it.

" Yea, I see that her palfrey is ready," said the Earl ; " nay,
yonder she issues forth to meet us."

He dismounted, and Hepborne, following his example, was
straightway introduced by him to the Countess, who received
him with great kindness and courtesy.

" Nevoy," said she to Sir Andrew Stewart, who approached
to salute her, " I do most sincerely grieve at the cause of my
brother the Earl of Buchan's absence.   I hope, however, it will
be but short, sith I trust the holy Bishop Barr will not be inex-
orable, and that thy father will join our festivities ere long.   But
where are thy brethren ? "

" We shall talk of that anon," said the Earl, wishing to get
rid of an unpleasant subject ; " meanwhile let us not lose time,
for it waxeth late, and our presence at the Castle is doubtless
looked for ere now.   Get thee to horse, then, my sweet lady
spouse, with what haste thou mayest."

Hepborne advanced and gave his arm to the Countess, and

having assisted her into her saddle, the whole party mounted to accompany her to Tarnawa. During their short ride through the forest, Hepborne enjoyed enough of the conversation of the Earl and Countess to give him a very favourable impression of both. The lady, in particular, showed so much sweetness of disposition that he could not help contrasting her in his own mind with her brother, the savage and ferocious Wolfe, to make up whose fiery and intemperate character to its full strength, Nature seemed to have robbed her soft and peaceful soul of every spark of violence that might have otherwise fallen to its share in the original mixture of its elements. Sound reason and good sense, indeed, seemed in her to be united with a most winning kindness and sweetness of manner, and it was quite a refreshment to Sir Patrick to meet with society so tranquil and rational after that of the ever-raging and tempestuous spirits with whom he had been lately consorting. The Countess failed not to notice the handsome page, Maurice de Grey ; but her attentions to him were of a very different description from those of the Lady Mariota Athyn, which had so afflicted him at Lochyndorbe. She spoke to him with gentleness, and having been made aware of his family and history by Hepborne, manifested the interest she took in the boy in a manner so delicate that he was already disposed to cling to her as willingly as he had before wished to avoid the Lady Mariota.

As they approached the straggling hamlet, through which lay the immediate approach to the Castle, its inhabitants, as well as the peasants from the neighbouring cottages, were collected together. Men, women, and children came crowding about them for the mere pleasure of beholding the Earl and his Countess, and the grateful hearts of these poor creatures burst forth in showers of blessings on the heads of their benefactors.

" God bless the noble pair ! "—" There they come, God bless them ! "—" May the blessing of St. Andrew—may the holy Virgin's choicest blessings be about them ! "—" What should we poor folk do an 'twere na for them ? "—" What should we do if anything should come over them ? "—" Heaven preserve their precious lives ? "—" May Heaven long spare them to be a comfort and a defence to us all ! "—" God bless the noble Earl, and Heaven's richest blessings be showered on the angel Countess ! "

Such was the abundant and gratifying reward these noble and generous hearts received for well fulfilling the duties of the high station their lot had placed them in. They replied graciously to those simple but sincere benisons, and though in haste, the Countess more than once reined up her palfrey as she

passed along the lane they opened for her, to make inquiries
after the complaints, distresses, and wants of particular individuals ; and where the matter admitted of her relief, she failed
not to give an order to attend at the Castle at her daily hour of
audience.

CHAPTER XXXVI.

The Castle of Tarnawa—Distinguished Guests.

THE party now climbed the slope, on the summit of which the
Castle rose grandly before them ; and they were no sooner within
its outer defences than they found every corner of it alive.
Lacqueys and serving-men of all sorts, in all the variety of rich
attire, were seen running about in every direction.   Most of the
noblemen and knights had already assembled to prepare for the
tournament, and some of these, with their ladies and daughters,
were inmates of the Castle.   From the Earl of Moray's particular
regard and friendship for Sir Patrick Hepborne the elder, an
apartment was immediately assigned to his son ; yet those who
were favoured with lodgings at Tarnawa were but few in number compared with the many who were to be accommodated in
the pavilions erected on the margin of the Mead.   But as all
were expected to assemble at the daily feast at the Castle, tables
were laid for more than an hundred guests in Randolph's Hall,
where even a company of twice the number might have found
ample room—this grand monument of feudal times covering an
area of nearly an hundred feet in length.

A Squire Usher promptly attended to show Sir Patrick to
his chamber, where he unarmed, dressed, and perfumed himself ;
and when he had completed his attirement, the Squire Usher
again appeared to conduct him to the great hall.

" Nobles and chevaliers," cried a pursuivant stationed at the
entrance, " nobles and chevaliers, place there for Sir Patrick
Hepborne, younger of Hailes, a puissant knight, of good stock
and brave lineage, who but the other day overthrew the renowned
Sir Rafe Piersie in single combat, which was nothing to his deeds
of arms in France, for there——"

" Good pursuivant," said Hepborne, interrupting him, in an
under voice, as he poured a liberal largess into his cap, " thou
hast said enow—no more, I beseech thee." But the pursuivant's
tongue was rather oiled than gagged by the unusual magnitude
of his donation.

" Ay," cried he aloud, " a brave tree is known by its good

fruits, and gentle blood by its generosity. Well may ye ken a
noble hand by the gift that comes from it ; and well may ye ken
a gallant and well-born knight by his noble port and presence,
and by his liberal largess. Place there, I say, for Sir Patrick
Hepborne—place there for the hero of Rosebarque ! "

" Silence, I entreat thee," cried Hepborne, advancing with all
eyes upon him, to meet the Earl of Moray, who was approaching
to receive him.

The magnificent Hall of Randolph presented at that moment
one of the most brilliant spectacles that could well be conceived,
graced as it then was with some of the flower of Scotland's
chivalry, who, with their ladies and attendants, shone in all the
richest and gayest variety of silks, velvets, furs, and gaudy-
coloured cloths, blazing with gold and embroidery, sparkling with
gems, and heavy with curiously-wrought chains and other ornaments, while flaunting plumes fluttered about, giving a multiplied effect of motion, so that the whole area resembled one great
tide of gorgeous grandeur, that was perpetually fluctuating,
mixing, and changing.

" Sir Patrick," said the Earl to Hepborne, " I believe thy
sojournance abroad hath hitherto permitted thee to see but little
of our Scottish chivauncie. It will be a pleasing task to me to
make thee acquainted with such of them as are here ; and it
will give me yet greater jovisaunce to teach them to know
thy merits. Let me then, first of all, introduce thee to my
brother- in-law, Robert Stewart, Earl of Fife and Menteith,
who, though he be but the King's second son, is supposed, with
some truth, to have the greatest share of the government of
Scotland."

So saying, the Earl of Moray led Sir Patrick through the
dividing crowd, towards the upper end of the hall, where a platform, raised about a foot above the rest, marked it as the place
of honour. There they found a circle of knights surrounding a
tall majestic man of commanding presence, whose countenance
seemed to wear an expression of amiability, affability, and even
of benignity, apparently put on for the occasion, like the ornaments he wore, but by no means forming a part of his character.
His face was handsome, and Hepborne could just trace in it a
faint likeness to his brother the Wolfe of Badenoch ; but there
was a lurking severity about the eye which his gracious looks
could not altogether quench. He appeared to be highly courted
by all about him, and from the smiles that mantled over the
faces he successively looked at, he seemed to carry sunshine on
his brow, and to scatter joy wherever he threw his eyes. Hep-

borne only caught up the last of his words as he approached the group in the midst of which he stood.

——"And if it should so please my liege-father," said he to an elderly knight who stood bowing as he spoke,—"if it should so please my liege-father to throw the heavy burden of government on me, trust me, I shall not forget thy hitherto unrequited services. The debt thy country doth owe thee is indeed great, and thou hast hitherto been met with but small mountance of gratitude. But how cnorme soever the debt may be, it shall be faithfully paid thee should I have any control."

"My Lord," said the Earl of Moray, advancing, whilst the circle opened up to make way for him, "this is Sir Patrick Hepborne, whom I promised thee to introduce to thy notice."

"Thanks, my good brother, for this so speedy fulfilment of thy behote," replied the Earl of Fife. "Trust me, it giveth me exceeding joy to have this opportunity of knowing so valiant a knight, the son, too, of so brave and renowned a warrior, and one so sage in council, as the highly and justly respected Sir Patrick Hepborne of Hailes, who, to the great let and hinderance of his country's weal, hath kept himself too much of late from the bustle of State affairs. But now that thou hast returned to thy native soil, Sir Patrick, we shall hope to see thee bear a part of that fardel, which thy gallant father might have been otherwise called on to support alone ; for, if fame lie not, thy prudence bids fair to render thee as serviceable in the closet of council as thine arm hath already proved itself fit to defend the fame and rights of Scotland in the field."

"My Lord," said Hepborne, "I fear much that fame hath done me but a left-handed service, by trumpeting forth merits the which I do but meagrely possess, and that public expectation hath been raised high, only to be the more cast down."

"Nay, trust me, Sir Patrick, there is small fear of that," said the Earl of Moray.

"Fear !" said the Earl of Fife ; "I have had mine eyes ever on the branchers of the true breed, from whom Scotland and my father's house must look to have falcons of the boldest and bravest cast ; and none hath made promise of fairer flight than thou hast, Sir Patrick. True it is, that thou hast yet to be reclaimed, as the falconer would term it ; that is, I would say, thou hast yet to learn what game to fly at. But I shall gladly teach thee, for it will give me real joy to direct the views, and advance the fortunes, of the son of my worthy old friend Sir Patrick Hepborne."

"My Lord," said Sir Patrick, "I am indeed much beholden to thy courtesy——"

"Nay," said the Earl of Fife, interrupting him, "nay, not to me or my courtesy, I promise thee, but to thine own worth only; for if the good old King my father, and my brother John, should force the regency of this kingdom on me, the duty I owe to them and to my country will never suffer me to give place or office to any but those who are fit and worthy to fill them ; so thou hast to thank thyself and thine own good conduct, already so much bruited abroad, for the high opinion I have thus so early formed of thee, as well as for the desire I now feel to foster thy budding honours, and to bring out all thy latent talents for Scotland's behoof.

"I am overwhelmed with your Lordship's goodness," said Hepborne, bowing. "Trust me, mine humble endeavours shall not be wanting to deserve this thy kind and early good opinion, formed, as I am disposed to guess, for my revered father's sake, though thou art pleased to flatter me by assigning another cause."

"However that may be," replied the Earl of Fife, squeezing him warmly by the hand, "thou mayest rely on me as thy sincere friend, Sir Patrick.—Ho ! Sir John de Keith," exclaimed he, suddenly breaking off, and joining a knight who bowed to him as he passed by, "I shall have that matter we talked of arranged for thee anon.   The son of my old friend the Knight-Marischal of Scotland, and one for whom I have so high a personal regard, shall always command my most earnest endeavours to gratify his wishes.   Walk with me apart, I pray thee.   Thou knowest the money hath been——"

But the rest of his discourse was lost in a whisper, and Hepborne's attention was called off by the Earl of Moray, who introduced him to David Stewart, Earl of Stratherne and Caithness, another son of the King's, though by a second wife.   After a few expressions of mere compliment had passed between them, and the Earl of Stratherne had moved on,

"Lindsay," cried his noble host to a bold and determined-looking knight, who was elbowing his way through the crowd, with his lady hanging on his left arm, "Lindsay, I wish to make thee acquainted with Sir Patrick Hepborne, son of the gallant Sir Patrick of Hailes.—Sir Patrick, this is my brother-in-law, Sir David de Lindsay of Glenesk ; and this is his lady, the Lady Catherine Stewart, sister to my Countess.   Sir David is my most trusty and well-approved brother, and it would give me joy to see the bonds of amity drawn tight between you."

The lady received Sir Patrick's compliments most graciously; a cordial acknowledgment took place between the two knights; and Hepborne felt, that although there was less of protestation, there was a greater smack of sincerity in Lindsay than in the powerful Earl of Fife, who had said and promised so much.

"Welcome to Scotland, Sir Patrick," said he. "By St. Andrew, but I rejoice to see thee, for I have heard much of thee. What news, I pray thee, from foreign pa——"

The word was broken off in the middle, for ere he had time to finish it, to the great astonishment of his lady, and the no small amusement of Hepborne and the Earl, he suddenly struck himself a violent blow on the cheek with the palm of his right hand. A roguish laugh burst from behind him. Lindsay quickly turned round.

"Aha! Dalzell," cried he, "so it was thou, wicked wag that thou art?"

"'Tis indeed Sir William de Dalzell," said Lady de Lindsay, laughing; "he is always at his mad tricks. There now, do but see what he is about; he is actually applying the tip of a long feather from a peacock's tail to tickle the cheek of my sister Jane's husband, the grave Sir Thomas Hay of Errol."

"How doth he dare to attack the august cheek of the High Constable of Scotland?" said the Earl of Moray, with a smile.

"Nay, do but observe," said Sir David Lindsay, "do but watch, I beseech thee, what strange and uncouth grimaces our brother-in-law, the High and Mighty Constable, is making, as the fibres of the delicate point of the feather titillate the skin of his cheek. Ah! ha, ha, ha! by the mass, but he hath given himself as hard a blow as I did, thinking to kill the fly."

"And see," said the lady, "he hath suspected a trick; but he looks in vain for our waggish friend Dalzell, who hath dived like a duck and disappeared. Ha, ha, ha! see how strangely the High Constable eyes the solemn Earl of Sutherland near him, as if he half believed that grave personage was the perpetrator of the espiéglerie. 'Twould be rare sport if he should tax him with it."

"'Twould be a rich treat indeed," said Sir David Lindsay.

"Sir Patrick," said the Earl of Moray, "come hither, I pray thee. Yonder comes James Earl of Douglas and Mar, with his Countess the Lady Margaret Stewart, another sister of my Margery's."

"He is indeed a knight worth knowing," said Hepborne.

"This way, then, and I will introduce thee to him," said the Earl of Moray.

Hepborne followed his host towards that part of the hall where the bold and Herculean Earl of Douglas was making his way with his lady slowly through the assembled company, who crowded eagerly around him to offer him their compliments. His manner was plain and dignified, and he behaved with kindness and affability to all who addressed him, though, on his part, he did not by any means seem to court notice. When Hepborne was brought up to him by his brother-in-law, and his name made known, he gave him a good soldierlike shake by the hand.

"I am right glad to see thee in thine own country, Sir Patrick Hepborne," said he. "An I mistake not, some storm is a-brewing in England, that may cause us to want all the good lances which Scotland can muster. When King Dickon doth send these hawk-eyed ambassadors to talk of peace, depardieux, but I, for my part, am apt to smell war. My Lord of Fife sayeth that 'tis not so, and he is shrewd enough in common. I have mine own thoughts; but we shall see who is right, and that too ere many days are gone, an the signs of the times deceive me not."

"'Twere well that we young unschooled soldiers should have something to do, my Lord," said Hepborne, "were it only to keep our swords from rusting, and lest we should forget our exercises, and such parts of the rudiments of war as chance hath taught us."

"Thou sayest well, my gallant young friend," said the Douglas, his eyes flashing as he spoke, again shaking Hepborne heartily by the hand; "but thou art no such novice to forget thy trade so easily. Yet sayest thou well; piping times of peace are the ruin of our Scottish chivaunchie, and stiffen the movements of even the most experienced warriors. Such sentiments as these, seasoned with so much modesty, are but what I mought have looked for from the son of that knight of sterling proof of heart as well as hand, my brave old friend Sir Patrick Hepborne, thy father."

Sir Patrick was more than gratified by the expressions of respect for his father which he had heard drop from every mouth. The blush of honest pride, mingled with that of warm filial affection, rose more that once to his cheek; but it never before mounted with such a rushing tide of joy as it did when this short panegyric fell from the lips of the heroic Douglas. He was not permitted time to reply, for all were so eager to have one word, nay, one glance of recognition from the brave Earl, that his attention was rifled from Hepborne, and he was carried away before he could open his mouth to speak to him again.

" Dost thou see yonder group?" demanded the Earl of Moray as he pointed them out to Sir Patrick. "The elderly knight and dame are William de Vaux, Lord of Dirleton, and his lady. The fair damosel seated behind them is their daughter, the Lady Jane de Vaux, held to be the loveliest of all the maidens who have come to honour this our tournament. Nay, she is indeed esteemed one of the fairest pearls of the Scottish Court, and a rich pearl she is, moreover, seeing she is the heiress of her father's domains. The knight who lieth at her footstool, and sigheth enlangoured at her feet, effunding soft speeches from his heart, and gazing upwards with a species of adoration in his eyes, is the gallant Sir John Halyburton, who wears her favours, and bears her proud merits in high defiance on his lance's point."

" Let me entreat your Lordship, who are those knights who come yonder so bravely arrayed?" said Hepborne.

"Those," replied the Earl, "are the English knights who lately came on ambassage. He in the purple velvet is the Lord Welles ; that elder knight on his right hand, who showeth deportment so courteous, is the worthy Sir John Constable of Halsham and Burton, one who hath done good deeds of arms in his day ; he that is so flauntingly attired in the peach-blossom surcoat so richly emblazoned, is the gay Sir Piers Courtenay ; and immediately behind him is the stark Sir Thomas Fairfax of Walton. But stay, here comes my brother George, Earl of Dunbar and March. George," cried he, addressing his brother as he passed, "this is Sir Patrick Hepborne, whose father thou well knowest."

" I do," said the Earl of Dunbar, energetically squeezing Hepborne's hand, "and I shall not fail to receive the son of my dearest friend into my warmest affections for his father's sake. How left ye thy gallant sire ?"

This question was but the preliminary to a long and friendly conversation between Hepborne and the Earl of Dunbar, which lasted until it was interrupted by a flourish of trumpets and clarions, announcing the entrance of the Grand Sewer, with a white wand in his hand. He advanced at the head of a perfect army of lacqueys, who brought in the feast, and the company began to be marshalled to their places by the pursuivants.

CHAPTER XXXVII.

The Banquet at the Castle—Alarm—Forres on Fire.

THE banquet given daily by the noble Earl of Moray was in every respect befitting the rank and splendour of the company assembled to partake of it. On the raised platform, at the upper end of the hall of Randolph, a table was placed transversely, to which was attached, at right angles, a limb that stretched down the greater part of the pavement. One side only of the upper, or cross table, was occupied ; and opposite to the centre of it were seated the Earl and Countess of Moray, in full view of all their guests. With them sat the Earl of Fife, and all those who could boast of royal blood or alliance ; whilst both sides of the long table were filled up by the rest of the nobles, and knights, and ladies, who were marshalled according to their respective rank. The shield of each chevalier, with his coat armour emblazoned on it, was hung on a hook on the wall, opposite to the place occupied by him at table ; so that all might be known by their bearings.

Hepborne having been introduced to the party of William de Vaux, Lord of Dirleton, led off his lady to the festive board.

"Sir Patrick Hepborne," said the old knight to him, soon after they had taken their places, " perhaps thou art aware that thine excellent father and I were early friends ? yea, well did I know thee, too, when thou wert as yet but an unfledged falcon. Full often, perdie, hast thou sat on these knees of mine, and many a hair, too, hast thou plucked in frolic from this grizzled beard, the which was then, I'll warrant thee, as black as the raven's back. Thou knowest that my domains of Dirleton, and those of Hailes, stand within a fair degree of neighbourhood. Give me leave then to drink this cup of Malvoisie to the better acquaintance of friends so old."

"I have often heard my father give utterance to many a kind and warm remembrance of thy friendship for our house," replied Sir Patrick, as he prepared to return the Lord of Dirleton's pledge ; " and it giveth me extreme joy thus unexpectedly to meet with one who deigned to bestow notice upon my childhood, albeit I cannot recall the recollection of the countenance of him who vouchsafed it."

"Nay, thy memory was too young at the time, Sir Patrick, to have received permanent impressions of any kind," replied

the Lord of Dirleton ; " and as we were soon after driven abroad
by domestic affliction, thou never hadst any opportunity of seeing me after thou couldst observe and remember ; for when we
returned to Scotland again, we discovered that thou hadst gone
to the very country we had left."

"I did hear of thy name from those who considered themselves highly honoured by having enjoyed thy society during the
time thou didst make Paris thy residence," said Hepborne.

"Yea, we knew many there," replied the Lord of Dirleton,
"many who were worthy and amiable ; yet none, I trust, who
could dislodge the early and fixed Scottish friendships we had
formed. That between thy father and me was so strong in its
nature, that we longed to cement our families irrevocably together ; and I do well remember me, that when thou wert but
some two or three years old, and the Lady Dirleton had produced
her first child, a daughter, Sir Patrick and I did solemnly vow
that, with the blessing and concurrence of Heaven, thou and
she should knit us more closely by thy union, so soon as years
should have ripened ye severally into man and woman."

" Alas !" interrupted the Lady Dirleton, the tears swelling in
her eyes as she spoke—"alas ! it did not please Heaven to give
its blessing or its concurrence to our vows, or to lend its ear to
our many prayers and supplications for the fulfilment of our
wishes. A cruel fate deprived us of our infant daughter, and
made me a wretchedly bereft and grief-bywoxen mother. When
I saw thee——"

"Leave off this sad theme, I do beseech thee, Maria," said
the old knight, interrupting her, with eyes that streamed over
as fast as her own ; "'tis but unmeet talk, I wis, for a festive
scene like this. At some other and more fitting time, Sir Patrick
may be disposed to list the story, and to sympathise with our
dole and dreriment."

By this time the more substantial part of the banquet had
been removed, a profusion of lights had changed the dim twilight
of the place into more than day, and healths and brimming
goblets of wine were circulating. Each knight was called upon
to quaff a pledge to the bright eyes that held him in thrall ; and
this public avowal of his tender attachment was considered as a
sort of prelude to the more determined appeal he might be
afterwards disposed to make in support of her beauty and fame,
at the point of his lance in the lists. Some there were who,
when it came to their turn, bowed silently, and permitted the
cup to pass by them ; these, however, were few in number, and
were such as, from some private reason, wished to throw a veil

of delicacy over their attachment; but when Sir John Halyburton was called on, he arose from the side of the blushing Jane de Vaux, and boldly proclaimed his love and adoration of her to all present.

"I pledge this brimming mazer to the health of the peerless Lady Jane de Vaux," said he; "and as I now drink the cup dry for her sake, so am I prepared to drain my life's blood in her service."

A murmur of approbation ran around the festal board. When it had subsided,

"Sir Patrick Hepborne," said the Earl of Moray, "wilt thou vouchsafe to honour us with a cup to the fair enslaver of thine affections?"

Sir Patrick arose, and, putting his right hand over his heart, bowed gracefully, and then seated himself in silence. In the former instances, where knights had declined to speak, the Earl of Moray had passed them by without further notice, but he was himself so disappointed, and perceived disappointment so legibly written on the faces of the company after Hepborne's silent bow, that he could not resist addressing him again.

"What, Sir Patrick," said he, "hast thou then no lady-love, for the sake of whose bright eyes we may hope to see thee bestirring thyself sturdily in the lists?"

"My Lord Earl," replied Hepborne, risingly modestly, "it will give me joy to break a few spears, out of mere courtesy, with any knights who may esteem mine arm worthy of being opposed to theirs."

The Earl saw that it would be indelicate to press him further, and went on to the conclusion of his circle of healths. The choir of minstrels, who had already occupied the music gallery, had begun to make the antique Hall of Randolph resound with their pealing preludes, when their harmony was interrupted by a clamouring noise of voices from without; and immediately a crowd of squires and domestics of all kinds came rushing into the hall, exclaiming, "Fire, my Lord Earl of Moray, fire!"

"Where—where—where is the fire?" burst from every mouth; and the ladies shrieked, and many of them even fainted, at the very mention of the word.

"The town of Forres is blazing," cried half-a-dozen voices at once.

The utmost confusion instantly arose amidst the assemblage of nobles, knights, and ladies. Out rushed the Earl of Moray, and out rushed such of his guests as had no lady to detain them within. Hepborne, for his part, happened by accident more

than anything else, to follow his host up a staircase that led to
the battlements, which in daylight commanded a view over the
whole surrounding country ; but the landscape was now buried
in darkness, save where a lurid blaze arose at three or four miles'
distance in the direction of the eastern horizon, through which
appeared some of the black skeletons of the consuming tenements of Forres, or where the broad and full estuary of the
river reflected the gleam which cast its illumination even over
the houses of the seaport of the distant point, and the wide
ocean beyond it. Far off, shouts and yells arose from different
quarters of the circumjacent forest, as if from people who were
collecting, and hastening in dismay towards the scene of the
conflagration.

"Holy Virgin, defend us ! what can have caused so sudden
and unlooked-for a calamity?" cried the Earl of Moray, in a tone
of extreme distress.

"Meseems it can hardly be the result of accident," replied
Hepborne, "for the fire doth blaze in divers parts at once. Can
it have been the work of some enemy ?"

"Enemy !" cried the Earl, "what enemy can there be here ?
And yet it may have been done by some marauding band of
plundering peelers. Yet that seems impossible—it cannot be.
But let me not waste time here, when I can ride to the spot.
Ho, there, in the court-yard—my horse, d'ye hear ? " shouted he
over the battlements, and then rushed down stairs.

Sir Patrick followed him, with the determination of accompanying him to the blazing town. Both speedily donned their
riding gear and light armour, and sallied forth. On the terrace
they found a crowd of the nobles and knights collected together
in amazement. The Earl only stopped to throw out a few hasty
words of apology for so abruptly leaving his guests, and then,
accompanied by Hepborne, descended to the court-yard, vociferating loudly for their horses. In a short time both mounted
and galloped off, attended by a few horsemen, who threw themselves hastily into their saddles.

"Let us take our way by the Mead of St. John's," cried the
Earl, pushing his horse thitherward ; "we can cross the river
by the bridge, and we shall then be able to alarm the people,
who have there a temporary abode at present. Their aid will
be of much avail, if, as I fear, all aid be not already too late."

On they galloped through the dark alleys of the forest, every
now and then overtaking some straggler, who was hurrying on,
out of breath, in the direction they were going, shouting at
intervals to those who had outrun him, or who had lagged

behind him; but when they reached the Mead of St. John's, those plains, which were lately so full of animation, were now silent as death; not a human being seemed to have remained within their ample circuit; all had been already summoned away, some by anxiety to arrest the destruction of their houses and goods, others by the charitable wish to assist in subduing the conflagration, and others, again, by the nefarious desire and hope of an opportunity of pilfering, but the greater number by that universal human passion, curiosity.

"Let us hasten onwards to Forres, for there is no one here," cried the good Earl, after riding in vain over part of the ground, and knocking and shouting at most of the temporary erections on the Eastern Mead, as he swept past them. "This way, Sir Patrick; our road lies up this steep bank; I hope some good may yet be done by the united force of such multitudes. By St. Andrew, it was good they were here; and 'twill be a lucky tournament if it be the means of stopping this sad malure."

Sir Patrick followed him over some irregular hillocks, covered with the forest; and, winding amongst them, they entered a defile, where the trees grew thinner, giving place, in a great measure, to a natural shrubbery, composed of scattered bushes of furze, broom, and juniper. The fire had been all this time hid from their eyes, but it burst upon them through the farther opening of the defile in all its terrific grandeur, at about a mile's distance. The destructive element had now all the appearance of speedily gaining resistless dominion over the little town, for the several independent detachments of flame which had appeared in different parts of it, as they surveyed it from the Castle, had now run together, and united themselves into one great sea of red and overwhelming destruction, that heaved and tossed its tumultuous billows high into the air. The appalling blaze filled up the entire sky that was visible through the defile they were threading. Against the bright field it presented, a dark group of armed horsemen were seen standing on the path before them, where it wound from among the hillocks, their figures being sharply relieved against the broad gleam beyond. The Earl of Moray reined up his steed, but his previous speed had been such that he was almost upon them ere he could check him.

CHAPTER XXXVIII.

The Burning of the Church and Town of Forres.

" By'R Lady, but the bonfire brens right merrily," cried a stern voice, which they immediately knew to be that of the Wolfe of Badenoch.   " Ha ! is't not gratifying to behold ?   Morte de ma vie, see there, son Alexander, how the Archdeacon's manse belches forth its flaming bowels against the welkin.   By St. Barnabas, but thou mayest tell the very blaze of it from that of any other house, by the changes produced in it from the abundant variety of ingredients that feed it.   Thou seest the cobwebby church consumeth but soberly and meekly as a church should ; but the proud mansion of the Archdeacon brenneth with a clear fire, that haughtily proclaims the costly fuel it hath got to maintain it—his crimson damask and velvets—his gorgeous chairs and tables—his richly carved cabinets—his musty manuscripts, the which do furnish most excellent matter of combustion.   By the mass, but that sudden quenching of the flame must have been owing to the fall of some of those swollen down-beds, and ponderous blankets, in which these lazy church-men are wont to snore away their useless lives.   But, ha ! see how it blazes up again ; perdie, it hath doubtless reached the larder ; some of his fattest bacon must have been there ; meseems as if I did nose the savoury fumes of it even here.   Ha ! glorious ! look what a fire-spout is there.   Never trust me, if that brave and brilliant feu d'artifice doth not arise from the besotted clerk's well-stored cellars.   Ha, ha, ha ! there go his Malvoisic and his eau-de-vie.   The vinolent costrel's thirsty soul was ever in his casks ; so, by the Rood, thou seest, that, maugre every suspicion and belief to the contrary, it hath yet some chance of mounting heavenward after all.   Ha, ha, ha ! by the beard of my grandfather, but it is a right glorious spectacle to behold."

" My Lord brother-in-law," cried the Earl of Moray, in a voice of horror and dismay, as he now advanced towards the group, " can it be ?   Is it really thou who speakest thus ? "

" Ha, Sir Earl of Moray," cried the Wolfe, starting and turning sharply round, " what makest thou here, I pray thee ? Methought that ere this thou wert merry in thy wine wassail ? "

" Nay, perhaps I should have been so," replied the Earl of Moray temperately, " had not news of yonder doleful burning banished all note of mirth from my board. Knowest thou aught of how this grievous disaster may have befallen ?"

" Ha, ha, ha ! canst thou not guess, brother of mine ?" cried the Wolfe, with a sarcastic laugh.

"I must confess I am not without my fears as to who did kindle yonder wide-spreading calamity," said the Earl of Moray gravely ; " yet still do I hang by the hope that it was impossible thou couldst have brought thyself to be the author of so cruel, so horrible, so sacrilegious a deed. Even the insatiable thirst of revenge itself, directed as it was against one individual, could hardly have led thee to wrap the holy house of God, and the dwellings of the innocent and inoffensive burghers, in the same common ruin with the tenements belonging to those whom thou mayest suspect as being entitled to a share of thy vengeance. 'Tis impossible."

" Ha ! by the flames of Tartarus, but it is possible," cried the Wolfe, gnashing his teeth; " yea, and by all the fiends, I have right starkly proved the possibility of it too. What ! dost think that I have spared the church, the which is the very workshop of these mass-mongering magpies ? Or was I, thinkest thou, to stop my fell career of vengeance, because the beggarly hovels of some dozen pitiful tailors, brogue-men, skinners, hammermen, and cordwainers, stood in my way ?— trash alswa, who pay rent and dues to this same nigon and papelarde Priest-Bishop, who hath dared to pour out his veno-mous malison on the son of a King—on the Wolfe of Badenoch ! By all the infernal powers, but the surface of the very globe itself shall smoke till my revenge be full. This is but a fore-taste of the wrekery I shall work ; and if the prating jackdaw's noxious curse be not removed, ay, and that speedily too, by him that rules the infernal realms, I swear that the walthsome toad and all the vermin that hang upon him shall have tenfold worse than this to dree !"

" Alexander Stewart !" cried a clear and commanding voice, which came suddenly and tremendously, like that of the last trumpet, from the summit of the knoll immediately above where the group was standing. There was an awful silence for some moments ; a certain chill of superstitious dread stole over every one present; nay, even the ferocious and undaunted Earl of Buchan himself felt his heart grow cold within him, at the almost more than human sound. He looked upwards to the bare pinnacle of the rising ground, and there, standing beside a scathed and blasted oak, he beheld a tall figure enveloped in black drapery. The irregular blaze of the distant conflagration

18

came only by fits to illumine the dusky and mysterious figure,
and the face, sunk within a deep cowl, was but rarely and
transiently rendered visible by it, though the eyes, more frequently catching the light, were often seen to glare fearfully,
when all the other features were buried in shade, giving a
somewhat fiendish appearance to the spectre.

"Alexander Stewart!" cried the thrilling voice again;
"Alexander Stewart, thou grim and cruel Wolfe, when will the
measure of thine iniquity be filled up? Thou sweepest over fair
creation, levelling alike the works of God and man, regardless of
human misery, like the dire angel of destruction; the very green
of the earth is turned into blood, and hearts are rent beneath
every tramp of thy horse's hoofs: yet art thou but as a blind
instrument in the hands of the righteous Avenger; and when
thou shalt have served the end for which thou wert created,
verily thou shalt be cast into eternal fire. If thou wouldst yet
escape the punishment which speedily awaits thine atrocities,
hasten to bow, in penitence, before those altars thou hast dared
to pollute, and make full reparation to the holy ministers of
religion for the unheard of insults and injuries thou hast offered
them. Do this, or thine everlasting doom is fixed; death shall
speedily overtake thee, and thou shalt writhe amidst the ineffable
torments of never-ceasing flames."

As the voice ceased, there arose from the distant town a
strong and more enduring gleam of light, which rendered visible
every little broom-blossom and heath-bell that grew upon the
side of the knoll, and threw a pale, but distinct illumination
over the features of the figure.

"Holy Virgin! blessed St. Andrew! 'tis the mysterious
Franciscan," whispered several of the Earl of Buchan's attendants, as they crossed themselves, in evident alarm.

"Ha! is it thee, thou carrion chough?" cried the Wolfe of
Badenoch, recovering from the surprise and dismay into which
he had been plunged by so unexpected and fearful a warning
from one whom he had not at first recognized; "ha! morte de
ma vie," cried he, couching his lance, digging the spurs deep
into his horse's flanks, and making him bound furiously up the
slope of the knoll; "by all the furies, thou shalt not 'scape me
this bout, an thou be not a very fiend. Haste, Alexander, ride
round the hill."

"This way, villains," cried Sir Alexander Stewart instantly,
obedient to his father's command; "this way, one-half of ye, and
that way the other half. Let not the caitiff escape us; take
him alive or dead; by the mass, it mattereth not which."

Divided into little parties, the Wolfe's attendants spurred off to opposite points of the compass, in order to encircle the hill. The figure had already disappeared from the pinnacle it stood on, but the furious Earl of Buchan still pushed his panting horse up the steep ascent,' until he disappeared over the top. The Earl of Moray and Sir Patrick Hepborne remained for some time in mute astonishment, perfectly at a loss what to think or how to act. Shouts were heard on all sides of the hillock; but in a short time they ceased, and the individuals of the Wolfe of Badenoch's party came dropping in one by one, with faces in which superstitious dread was very strongly depicted.

"Didst thou see him?" demanded one. "Nay, I thank the Virgin, I saw him not," replied another. "Whither can he have vanished?" cried a third. "Vanished indeed!" cried a fourth, shuddering, and looking over his shoulder. "Ave Maria, sweet Virgin, defend us, it must have been.a spirit," cried another, in a voice of the utmost consternation.

"Hold your accursed prating," cried the Wolfe of Badenoch, who now appeared, with his sons clustered at his back, all bearing it up boldly, yet all of them, even the stout Earl himself, much disturbed and troubled in countenance. "Ha!" continued he, "by all that is good, there is something strange and uncommon about that same friar. I know not well what to think. I bid thee good-bye, brother-in-law; I wot, we part but as half friends; yet commend me to Margery. Sir Patrick Hepborne, when it pleaseth thee to come to Lochyndorbe, thou shalt be right welcome. Allons, son Alexander, we must thither to-night yet for our hostelry; so forward, I say;" and saying so, he rode away at the head of his party.

"Rash and intemperate man," cried the good Earl of Moray, in a tone of extreme distress and vexation, as he turned his horse's head towards Forres, "what is it thou hast done? Into what cruel and disgraceful outrage hath thy furious wreken driven thee. The very thought of this ferocious deed being thine, is to me more bitter than ligne-aloes. The noble and the peasant must now alike hold thee accursed for thy red crimes. Hadst thou not been my wife's brother, and the son of my liege lord the King, I must of needscost have done my best to have seized thee straightway; but Heaven seemeth to be itself disposed to take cognizance of thy coulpe, for in truth he was more than mortal messenger who pronounced that dread denunciation against thee."

The solemn silence with which these words were received by

Sir Patrick, showed how much his thoughts were in unison with those of the Earl.

" But let us prick onwards," cried Lord Moray, starting from his musing fit ; " every moment may be precious."

They had not gone many yards, when they heard the mingled sound of numerous voices, and found themselves in the midst of a great crowd of people of all ages, and of both sexes, who, idle and unconcerned, had taken post on the brow of the hill, and now stood, or lay on the ground in groups, calmly contemplating the rapid destruction that was going on in the little town, and giving way to thoughtless expressions of wonder and delight, at the various changes of the aspect of combustion.

" Why stand ye here, idlers ? " cried the Earl of Moray, riding in among them, and stirring up some of them with the shaft of his lance ; " come, rouse ye, my friends ; shame on you to liggen here, when ye might have bestirred ye to save the town ; come, rouse ye, I say."

" Nay, by the mass, I'll not budge," cried one. " 'Tis no concern of mine," cried another. " Nay, nor of mine," cried a third. " I do but come here to sell my wares at the tourney," cried a fourth.

" Depardieux, but every mother's son of ye shall move," cried the Earl, indignant at their apathy.

" And who art thou, who dost talk thus high ? " gruffly demanded one of the fellows, as he raised a sort of pole-axe in a half-defensive and half-menacing attitude.

" I am John Dunbar, Earl of Moray," replied the Earl resolutely ; " and by St. Andrew, if ye do not every one of you make the best of your way to Forres sans delay, and put forth what strength ye may to stop the brenning of the poor people's houses and goods, I will order down an armed band from the Castle, who shall consume and burn to tinder every tent, booth, bale, and box, that now cumbereth the meads of St. John. Will ye on with me now, knaves, or no ? "

" Holy Virgin, an thou be'st the good Earl," cried the fellow, lowering his pole-axe, " I humbly crave thy pardon ; verily we are all thine humble slaves. Come, come, my masters, run, I pray ye, 'tis the good Earl John. Fie, fie, let's on with him, and do his bidding, though we bren for it."

" Huzza for the good Earl John—huzza ! let's on with the good Earl of Moray," cried they all.

" Mine honest men," cried the Earl, " I want not thy services for nought. Trust me, I shall note those who work best, and they shall not go guerdonless ; and if ye should all be made as dry as cinders, by hard and hot swinking, ye shall be rendered as moist as well-filled sponges, with stout ale, at the Castle, after all is over."

"Huzza for the good Earl John! huzza for the good Earl of Moray!" shouted the rabble; and he rode off, followed by every man of them, each being well resolved in his own mind to earn his skinful of beer.

As the Earl and Sir Patrick were pushing up towards the ridge along which the town was situated, the shouts of men, and the dismal screams and wailings of women and children, arose from time to time from within it. The good nobleman redoubled his speed as he heard them, and the party soon reached the main street, the scene of confusion, misery, and devastation. The way was choked with useless crowds, who so encumbered those who were disposed to exert themselves, that little effectual opposition could be given to the fury of the fire. Amidst the shrieks and cries which burst forth at intervals from the mob, the Earl's ears were shocked by the loud curses on the Wolfe of Badenoch that were uttered by the frantic sufferers. But no sooner was he recognized than his arrival was hailed with acclamations of joy and gratitude, which drowned the expression of every other feeling.

"Here comes the good Earl"—"The Virgin be praised—blessed be St. Laurence that the Earl hath come"—"Ay, ay, all will go well now sith he is here"—"Stand aside there—stand aside, and let us hear his commands."

The Earl and Sir Patrick Hepborne hastily surveyed the wide scene of ruin, and were soon aware of its full extent. The manse of the Archdeacon, to which the incendiaries had first set fire, was already reduced to a heap of ashes. The priest who owned it had fled in terror for his life when it was first assailed; and the greater part, if not all the population of the little burgh having been employed on the Mead of St. John's in the preparations for the tournament, or in loitering as idle spectators of what was going on there, little interruption was given to the vengeful Wolfe of Badenoch in his savage work. He and his troop were tamely allowed to stand by until they had seen the residence of the churchman so beleaguered by the raging element, that little hope could remain of saving any part of it. He next set fire to one end of the church; and ere he and his party mounted to effect their retreat, they fired one or two of the intervening houses. Many of the tenements being of wood, and the roofs mostly thatched with straw, the fire spread so rapidly as very soon to form itself into one great conflagration, that threatened to extend widely on all sides. Still, however, it was confined to one part of the town, and there yet remained much to save. Hitherto there had been no head to direct, but the moment the Earl appeared all were prepared to give implicit and ready obedience to his orders. He took his determination in a few minutes, and, imparting his plan to Hepborne, they proceeded to carry it into instant execution.

The portion of the street that was already in flames had been abandoned by the people, the fire having gained so hopeless an ascendancy there that all efforts to subdue it would have been vain. The Earl therefore resolved to devote his attention to confining it within its present limits. He stationed himself within a few yards of that extremity which they had first reached, and, having ordered the crowd to withdraw farther off, he brought forward the useful and active in such numbers as might be able to work with ease, and he began to pull down some of the most worthless of the houses. Hepborne, in the meanwhile, called together a few hardy and fearless-looking men, and followed by these and Mortimer Sang, who was rarely ever missed from his master's back when anything serious or perilous was going forward, he proceeded, at the risk of life, to ride down the narrow street, between two walls of fire, where blazing beams and rafters were falling thick around them. His chief object was to get to the farther boundary of the conflagration, and he might have effected this by making a wide circuit around the town; but, besides gaining time by forcing the shorter and more desperate passage, the generous knight was anxious to ascertain whether, amidst the confusion that prevailed, some unfortunate wretches might not have been left to their fate among the blazing edifices.

He moved slowly and cautiously onwards, his horse starting and prancing every now and then as the burning ruins fell, or as fresh bursts of flame took place; and, steering a difficult course among the smoking fragments that strewed the street, or the heaped-up goods and moveables, which their owners had not had time to convey farther to some place of greater security, he peered eagerly into every door, window, and crevice, and listened with all his attention for the sound of a human voice. More than once his eyes and his ears were deceived, and he frequently stopped, in doubt whether he should not rush boldly through fire and smoke to rescue some one whom his fancy had caused him, for an instant, to imagine perishing within. His mind being so intensely occupied, it is no wonder that he could pay but little attention to his own preservation; and accordingly he received several rude shocks, and was at last fairly knocked down from his saddle by the end of a great blazing log, which grazed his shoulder as it descended from a house he was standing under. Mortimer Sang caught the reins of his master's horse, and Sir Patrick was speedily raised from the ground by the people who were near him ; and he regained his seat, having fortunately escaped with some slight bruises received from the fall, and a contusion on his shoulder, arising from the blow given him by the beam.

CHAPTER XXXIX.

Sir Patrick and the Earl at Forres.

Sir Patrick Hepborne had hardly recovered himself when, as he was passing a house to which the fire had but just communicated, he encountered a crowd of people rushing out, hastily attired in all manner of strange coverings. It was the inn of the burgh. Among those who came forth there was one gigantic figure, who ran against his horse like a battering-ram, and almost threw the animal on his haunches by the concussion. Ere Hepborne could recover himself the monster was gone ; but his attention was quickly diverted from this incident by the sound of a voice chanting irregularly in broken song, mingled with the notes of a harp. It came from the upper part of the building. The house, though extending a good way backwards from the street, was of two storeys only ; but as the flames were briskly attacking the lower part, no time was to be lost in making the musician leave it.

Hepborne sprang from his horse, and, hastening down a lane to the doorway, rushed up the narrow stair, and being led by ear towards the music, ran along a passage and entered an apartment over the gable next the street, where, to his utter astonishment, he beheld the minstrel, Adam of Gordon, seated on a stool, in his nightcap and under-garments, accompanying his voice by striking wild chords upon the harp, and looking upwards at intervals, as if seeking inspiration.

"Adam of Gordon !" cried Hepborne, in absolute amazement, "what dost thou here ? Quick, quick, old man ; thy life is in peril ; throw on thy cloak and fly with me ; the flames gain upon us !"

"Nay, Sir Knight," said the minstrel, "disturb me not, I beseech thee ; I do but work myself here into proper bardic

enthusiasm, that I may the better describe the grandeur of this
terrific scene. Trust me, this is the minstrel's golden moment;
let it not pass by unimproved." And saying so he again began
to strike on his harp, and to recur to his subject.

> The raging flame in fury swept,
> It seized their chamber where they slept,
> Along the wasting floor it crept,
>   Where locked in virtuous love they lay.
> She dreamt that on a bed of flowers,
> Beneath the cool and fragrant bowers,
> With him she wasted happy hours;
>   She waked—she shrieked! she swooned away!
> He quick uprose, in wild alarm,
> To snatch his love——

"Nay, Adam, this is absolute madness, for whilst thou art
composing thy ballad we shall both be brent. Haste thee, old
man. Hark! there was the crash of falling ruins."

"One stanza more, I entreat thee, Sir Knight; my brain is
hot with my subject.

> To snatch his love from threatening harm,
> He clasped her in his vigorous arm."

"Nay, then," said Hepborne, "I must of needscost enclasp
thee in mine, or we shall both perish;" and snatching up, with
one hand, the minstrel's drapery that lay beside him, he lifted
old Adam, harp and all, high in his other arm, and carried him
down the stair on his shoulder; whilst the bard, entirely occupied with his subject, was hardly conscious of being removed
from his position, and went on chatting and strumming—

> "He quick uprose, in wild alarm,
> To snatch his love from threatening harm;
> He clasped her in his vigorous arm,
> And rushed——

Holy St. Cuthbert, I'm choked! I'm—pugh!—ooh!"

A sudden stop was indeed put to his song by the smoke
through which Hepborne was condemned to force his way with
his burden, and the harp accompaniment was effectually silenced
by the flames which shot over them on either hand, and burnt
off the strings of the instrument. Hepborne bore the minstrel
bravely into the street.

"Where is thy steed, Adam?" demanded Hepborne, as he
set him down.

"In the stable behind," replied the minstrel, somewhat
brought to his senses by the danger which he now saw had
threatened him. Hepborne immediately despatched some of
those who were with him to fetch out the horse.

" Heaven bless thee for my safety, Sir Knight," said Adam ; " but now that I am beyond risk, if it so please thee I would gladly saunter through the burning town alone, to gather hints for the garniture of my ballad."

" Nay, nay, old man," replied Hepborne, quickly, " this is no place for thee. Here cometh thy little curtal nag—mount thee, straightway, and hie thee to Tarnawa with this man, who shall guide thee thither. There thou mayest inquire for a page of mine, called Maurice de Grey, who will quickly make thee known to my Lady the Countess of Moray ; she will be right glad to see any one of minstrel kind in these times of tournament. But stay," added Hepborne, laughing to observe the grotesque figure of the half-clad minstrel on horseback ; " Here, throw his cloak over him and hasten hence with him beyond danger.. Away, away from hence, or ye are lost," cried he, with increased rapidity of utterance ; and the group had hardly time to make their horses spring from the spot ere the front wall of a house, slowly cracking and rending, fell with a tremendous crash into the street, and they were divided from each other by the heaped-up debris. Satisfied, however, of the minstrel's safety, Sir Patrick now hurried on to the post which the Earl of Moray had assigned him at the farther extremity of the conflagration.

A considerable vacant space around the church had fortunately prevented the fire from spreading beyond it. The holy edifice itself was burning slowly, yet so little attention had been paid to it that the choir, which the incendiaries had first inflamed, was already almost consumed. Sir Patrick Hepborne immediately established two lines of people, extending between the church and a neighbouring well, so that buckets of water were conveyed with great rapidity towards it, and the supply in this way was so great that he soon succeeded in preventing the flames from spreading to the other parts of the building ; and their progress being once arrested, they at last began to sink of themselves from lack of combustible materials, and by degrees were altogether subdued by the crowds of active and well-directed men, who thought and talked of nothing but the Castle beer, and who worked to earn a skinful of it.

The sun had now risen on the scene of desolation. Toil-spent, and overwhelmed with grief at the misery which appeared around him, as well as vexation at the thought of how it had been occasioned, the Earl dismounted from his horse and sat himself disconsolately down on a stone by the side of the way. There Hepborne found and saluted him for the first time since their separation of the previous evening.

" 'Tis a grievous spectacle, my Lord Earl," said Sir Patrick, as he observed the affliction that was pourtrayed on his Lordship's countenance, " 'tis indeed a grievous spectacle ; but thou hast the pleasing gratification of thinking that, without thy timely presence here, the ruin must have spread itself wider, and that if it had not been for thy well-timed counsels and generous exertions not a house would have been remaining at this moment within the burgh."

" Alas ! " exclaimed the Earl, in a tone of extreme mortification, " grievous as the calamity is, I am less moved by it than with the tormenting reflection that it was the work of my wife's brother. 'Tis piteous, indeed, to listen to the lamenting of those helpless and innocent people, but their wounds may be speedily salved by the aid of a little paltry gold ; whilst those which the Earl of Buchan hath inflicted on the hearts of all connected with him by allowing a brutal thirst of revenge to make him guilty of an act so cruel and outrageous, must fester and rankle for many a day. What will the good old greyheaded Monarch suffer when the news do reach him ? Verily it doleth me sorely that by my marriage I should be sykered with one who hath the fear of God so little before his eyes. Yet must I not think of it. It behoveth me now to remedy the mischief he hath wrought, and to set about relieving the more immediate wants of the wretched people who have lost their houses and their all. Here, Martin," cried he to one of his esquires, " take these tablets ; seek out some one who is well informed as to the town and its inhabitants, and quickly bring me a careful list of the houses that have been burned, together with the name, sex, age, and condition of the inmates."

The squire hastened to obey the Earl's command. Several of the knights, his guests, who had followed him from the Castle, and who had given him good assistance in extinguishing the fire, now came about him, pouring out liberal congratulations on the success of his well-conceived and promptly-executed measures ; and while they formed a knot around him, they were in their turn surrounded by crowds of the lower sort of people, composed partly of the homeless sufferers, who were weeping and wailing for the calamity that had befallen themselves and their little ones, and pouring out curses against the ferocious Wolfe of Badenoch, who had brought all this misery upon them. But these execrations on the Earl of Buchan were not unmingled with blessings on the Earl of Moray for his timely aid, without which the speakers felt that they too might have been by this time rendered as destitute as their less fortunate neighbours.

Then many were the clamorous entreaties for charitable succour; whilst those indifferent persons, who had assisted in subduing the conflagration, were elbowing one another, and uttering many a broad and rustic hint of the reward they looked for. At length Martin appeared with his list.

"Here," said the Earl, aside to him, "into thy faithful hands do I confide this purse; 'tis for the more immediate relief of those poor people. Leave not the town until thou hast inquired into circumstances, and done all thou canst to secure temporary accommodation for those who have been rendered houseless. I shall take care to provide more permanent aid for them anon."

This order, though given in a half whisper, was caught up by some of those miserables, whose wretched and forlorn state had quickened their ears to every sound which gave them the hope of relief. The news of the Earl's humane bounty spread among them more rapidly than the fire had done over their possessions and property. Their gratitude burst forth in shouts:

"God bless the noble Earl of Moray!"—"Long live our noble preserver!"—"Heaven reward our kind benefactor!"—"If his brother, the wicked Wolfe of Badenoch, be a destroying devil, surely the good Earl of Moray is a protecting angel!"—"May the best gifts of the Virgin be upon him and his!"

The Earl called for his horse, and mounted amid the cheers of the populace.

"Let all those who lent me their friendly aid on this occasion forthwith follow me to the Castle," cried he, and, glad to escape from praises which, as they were bestowed on him at the expense of the brother of his Countess, gave him more of pain than pleasure, he turned his horse's head in the direction of the Castle, and rode off, accompanied by Sir Patrick Hepborne and the rest of the knights who were with him, and followed at a distance by a shouting and ragamuffin rabble, who were eager to moisten their hot and parched throats from the capacious and hospitably-flowing cellars of Tarnawa.

CHAPTER XI.

In the Countess of Moray's Apartments—Sir Patrick gets Quizzed.

The Earl and his friends had no sooner reached Tarnawa, than they retired, each to his own chamber, to enjoy a few hours' rest. Sir Patrick Hepborne made inquiry for his page, but the latter was nowhere to be found at the time; so, leaving orders that the youth should be in attendance, he gladly committed his wearied limbs to the comforts of his couch.

It was about midday when he raised his head from his pillow, and his first thought was to call for Maurice de Grey; but a lacquey informed him that the youth had not yet appeared. He sent the man for Mortimer Sang, and when the esquire came, he was much disappointed to learn that he had seen or heard nothing of the boy.

"Go then, I pr'ythee," said Sir Patrick, "and make diligent inquiry for the youth through the Castle, and when thou hast found him, send him hither without a moment's delay. Verily, it seemeth that he doth already begin to forget that I am his master."

Sang hastened to obey, but remained absent much longer than Sir Patrick, in his anxiety about the boy, could think reasonable. The knight walked hastily about the room, and at length becoming very impatient, he sent first one lacquey, and then another, after the esquire. At last Mortimer Sang returned.

"Well, where is Maurice de Grey?" demanded Hepborne.

"By the mass, Sir Knight, I can gain no tidings of him."

"'Tis very strange," replied the knight, with a look of much vexation. "I do much fear me that the youth is of a truant disposition; it was indeed that which gave him to me. He ran away from his paternal home, and from maternal care, united himself to my party, and how oft did he solemnly and hautently vow never to quit me until death should sever us! His present absence doth wear a very mysterious and suspicious aspect.— Hath the old Harper been seen?" demanded Sir Patrick, after a pause, during which he paced the room two or three times backwards and forwards.

"Nay, Sir Knight," replied the squire, "he hath not been visible."

"Depardieux, then they must have gone off together," replied Sir Patrick, with a tone of extreme dissatisfaction; "'tis most like that the minstrel, who must have known him before, hath aided, and perhaps been the partner of his escape. Yes, they must have been well acquainted, seeing that old Adam did so greatly frequent the English Border, and that he was so much esteemed by the Lady Eleanore de ——, I mean, by the page's kinswoman. Well, I shall feel the loss of the boy's company, for, sooth to say, his prattle did often beguile me of a dull hour. Truly, he was a shrewd and winning youth; but I am sore grieved to discover that he hath had in him such deceit, and so little feeling for the kindness I did ever show him."

With these words, the knight threw himself on the couch, altogether unable to conceal the chagrin and distress of mind he was suffering.

"Perdie, I should have been as a father to that boy," said he again ; " I should have made him a knight worthy of the highest place in the annals of chivalry. The youth seemed to value, yea, and to give heed to my counsels too ; nay, the admiration with which he looked up to me might have been almost considered as ridiculous, had it not been viewed as the offspring of extreme attachment. He spoke as if he imagined that I was all excellence, all perfection. What strange cause can have occasioned his so sudden abandonment of me, and that, too, without having given me the smallest warning or hint of his intention ? Did not I, more than once, tell him that I should be willing to aid his return to his friends, should he ever feel a desire to do so ? His escapade is an utter mystery to me. Ha! I have it," continued he, after a short pause of consideration ; " I trow, I have hit it at last. The youth hath some turn, nay, and, I wot, no mean one neither, for poesy and song ; moreover, he toucheth the harp with liard and skilful fingers ; and seeing that he is fond of change, he hath, 'tis like, taken fancy to become a troubadour, and so has exchanged me as his master for old Adam of Gordon. Well, well, why should I vex myself about a silly, careless, truant boy ?"

But Sir Patrick did, notwithstanding, vex himself most abundantly, and, nearly an hour afterwards, he was found, still lying in peevish and fretful soliloquy, by Mortimer Sang, who entered his chamber, with a message from the Countess of Moray, entreating his company in her apartment for a short conference. Sir Patrick hastily prepared himself to attend her, and was immediately ushered into her presence by a squire in waiting.

He found his noble hostess seated with the Lady Jane de Vaux, in the midst of her damsels, some of whom were employed in idle chitchat, others in singing, from time to time, to the harp or guitar, whilst the rest were assisting in an extensive work of embroidery. They were immediately dismissed on his entrance, and the Countess came forward graciously to receive him.

"I fear, Sir Patrick," said she, "that I may have perhaps broken in rather prematurely upon those hours of repose which the fatigue of yesternight's violent, though charitable, exertions had doubtless rendered as welcome as they were necessary. The Earl, my husband, was so overspent with toil when he returned this morning, that he was buried in slumber ere I had time to question him as to the cause of the calamity, or even as to its full extent. I was on the eve of entreating a few minutes' audience of thee at that time, that I might have my curiosity satisfied, but just as I was about to send my page to crave this boon of thine, thy page, Maurice de Grey, came hither, and informed me that thou also hadst betaken thee to thy couch. I have thus been compelled to champ the bit of impatience ever sithence ; but, impatient as I am, I shall not easily forgive myself if I have been the means of rudely disturbing thy needful refreshment."

"My page !" cried the knight with a mixture of surprise and eagerness, and made him forget everything else that the Countess had said to him ; "verily, I have been seeking and sending for my page during the greater part of the morning. I beseech your Ladyship, when was the little varlet here, and what could have induced him to be so bold as to intrude himself on the Countess of Moray ?"

"Nay," replied the Countess, with an air of surprise no less strong than that of Sir Patrick, "I did assuredly think that it was thou who didst order him to come hither. He came to introduce a certain minstrel to my notice, and in so doing to take the opportunity of paying his duty to me, by thine own desire, ere the old man and he should depart hence together."

"Depart hence !" cried Hepborne, with still greater astonishment, mingled with excessive vexation ; "depart hence, didst thou say ? So then the heartless boy hath really left me. Of a truth, when first I missed him, I did suspect that he and the minstrel had gone off together. Whither have they gone, I do beseech thee ? "

"Nay, that is indeed miraculous," replied the Countess ; "'tis indeed miraculous, I say, that thou shouldst not have known the page was going away ; for albeit he did not positively say so, yet did he so counterfeit with us that I for one did never doubt but that he came hither by thy very command to do his obeisance to me ere he should yede him hence. 'Tis a right artful youth, I'll warrant me. Nay, sir Knight, methinks thou hast good reason to congratulate thyself on being so happily rid of a cunning chit, who mought have worked thee much evil by his tricks. Of a truth, I liked not his looks over much——"

"Forgive me, noble lady," cried the knight, "I cannot hear the boy spoken of otherwise than as he may in justice deserve.

I saw not ever any trick or mischief in him ; on the contrary, he did always appear most doced in his demeanour and service. Moreover, he is a boy of most sensible remark, and more prudence of conduct than one might reasonably look for in a head so young and inexperienced; then as for his heart, it was warmer than any I ever met with in old or young. I trow he did prove to me more than once that his attachment to my person was something beyond mere pretence. Twice did he nearly sacrifice his life for me. What can have induced him to go off thus secretly? Had I been cruel to him he might have fled from me with good reason ; but I loved the boy as I should have loved a younger brother, yea, or a son, if I had had one. There was so much gentleness about him ; yet lacked he not a sly, sharp, and subtle wit."

"Yea, of a truth, he hath a wit," cried the Lady Jane de Vaux, archly ; "ay, and as you say, Sir Knight, 'tis indeed a sharp one. How the wicked rogue did amuse us by the rehearsal of thy loves, Sir Knight! [I do mean thy loves for his fair cousin, the beauteous Lady Eleanore de Selby. Ha, ha, ha! parfay, the varlet did stir up some excellent good-humoured pleasantry and merry laughter in us."

"In truth, his stories were most amusing," said the Countess ; "trust me, it is a smart and witty little knave as ever I saw."

"A most rare and laughter-stirring imp, indeed," cried the Lady Jane de Vaux ; "nay, the mere remembrance of him doth provoke me yet—ha, ha, ha !"

Sir Patrick Hepborne stood confounded and abashed, to find himself thus unexpectedly placed as a butt for the ridicule of the two ladies.

"My noble Countess of Moray, and you, beauteous Lady Jane de Vaux, you do seem to have vouchsafed me the honour of being your quintaine this morning—the targe against the which you may gaily prove the sharp points of your merry wit. Depardieux, my lot in being so selected is to be envied, not deplored ; and I must thank you for the distinguished preference you have deigned to show me. Yet cannot I but feel disappointment most severe, to discover thus that a youth, towards whom I was so well affected, should have requited my love so ill-favouredly. Of a truth, the wicked knave hath been most indiscreet. And yet meseems that I myself have been even more indiscreet than he, since the secret was altogether mine own, and I ought to have kept it better."

"In good sooth, we were much indebted to the imp for his information," said the Lady Jane de Vaux ; "for to be free with thee, Sir Knight, our stock of female curiosity, the which was raised highly by the public refusal of so renowned a chevalier to drink a pledge to his lady love, was beginning to be much an over-match for our limited store of patience. Our appetite for intelligence regarding the state of thy heart was waxing so great, that had not this boy of thine come to us this morning, to open his wallet and satisfy our craving, we might ere this have been dead of mere starvation. His visit here was quite a blessing to us."

"By St. Andrew, I am thunderstruck," cried the Knight, "Depardieux, the young caitiff hath indeed deceived me deeply in thus betraying the most sacred secret of my heart."

"Of a truth, thine unexampled constancy did deserve better treatment, Sir Knight," said the Countess, with a tone and manner tinged with a certain degree of asperity and sarcasm, which Hepborne hardly believed that amiable lady could have assumed; whilst, at the same time, she and Jane de Vaux exchanged very significant looks. With an effort to command herself, however, she turned the conversation rather suddenly towards the subject of the burning of Forres; and after gathering from Hepborne the general circumstances of that calamity, she, with more than usual dignity, signified to him her wish to be alone, and he retired to his apartment, to fret himself about the loss of his page, and the provoking circumstances by which it was accompanied.

CHAPTER XLI.

Rory Spears, the Earl's Henchman.

Sir Patrick Hepborne left the apartments of the Countess of Moray melancholy and unhappy. He retired to his own chamber, to ruminate on the ingratitude of his heartless page; and, when the hour of the banquet arrived, he went to the Hall of Randolph with a mind but little attuned to harmonize with its festivities. But it was more in unison with his feelings than he had anticipated. The Countess of Moray, who was by this time fully aware that the destructive fire of Forres had been kindled by her brother's hand, was unable to appear; and her example was followed by most of the other ladies. The Earl of Fife, too, and several other nobles and knights, were absent. The Earl of Moray was indeed present; but he was there only in body, for his thoughts seemed to be elsewhere. All his attempts to rally his spirits were unavailing, and the sombre air which hung upon his countenance speedily spread along the gay ranks of the festive board, to the extinction of everything like mirth.

In this state of things, the Earl speedily broke up the feast. He had serious thoughts of breaking up the tournament also, and these he privately communicated to his brother-in-law, the Earl of Fife; but that crafty politician objected to a measure which could only make his brother's outrage the more talked of; and he had a still stronger reason in his own mind, for he did not wish to be deprived of the opportunity, afforded him by the tournament, of gaining over friends to the party he was forming to strengthen his own power. It was therefore finally determined that next day it should be solemnly proclaimed by the heralds.

The Earl of Moray and his lady passed a sleepless night, turning in their minds how they could best repair the wrong done by their brother, the Wolfe of Badenoch. Early in the morning one of the Countess's favourite damsels, Katherine Spears by name, came to beseech an audience of the Earl for her father, Rory Spears. There was nothing extraordinary in this request, for the Earl was so much the friend of his people that he was ever ready to lend an ear to the complaints of the meanest individual among them. The man who now craved an interview was an old partizan of the Earl's, who had fought under his banner and at his back in many a battle, and who was employed in time of peace in hunting, hawking, and fishing.

As the Earl had a peculiar regard for Rory Spears, the damsel was ordered to send him up immediately to a small turret room, where his Lordship usually received people in his rank of life. Rory's heavy fishing boots were soon heard ascending the turret stair, and his bulky figure appeared, followed by a great rough allounde and one or two terriers. As Katherine showed him in, there was something peculiarly striking in the contrast between her sylphlike figure, delicate face, and ladylike air, and his Herculean mould and rough-hewn features, in which there was a strangely-mixed and contradictory expression of acuteness and simplicity, good nature, and sullen testiness. His huge shoulders had a natural bend forward, and a profusion of grizzled curls mingled in bushy luxuriance with the abundant produce of his cheeks, lips, and chin. On his head was a close red hood, that lay over his neck and back, and he wore a coarse grey woollen jerkin and hauselines, covered with an ample upper garment of the same materials, and of a form much resembling that constituting a part of the fisherman's garb of

19

the present day. In one hand he brandished a long pole with a sharp iron hook at the end of it, the bend of the hook being projected into a long pike, and the whole so constructed as to be equally serviceable as a hunting-spear or as a fish-clip. He stooped yet more as he entered the low doorway of the turret room, and had no sooner established his thick-soled boots upon the floor than he made an obeisance to the Earl, with his cap under his arm.

"What hath brought thee hither so early, friend Rory?" inquired the Earl.

"In good sooth, my noble Lord, I did think that the Castle mought maybe be lacking provender, wi' a' thay knights, grandees, and lordlings ilka day in the hall, an' so mony o' their people in the kitchen, so I did gather some of the knaves with their horse beasts, and I hae brought thee ower six fat deer, some wild pollayle, and a dozen or twa o' salmons, to help the buttery-man to fill his spense; 'tis no deaf nits, I rauken, that'll fill sae mony mouths."

"I thank thee, Rory," said the Earl; "it was indeed most considerate in thee; thy present is most welcome. How fares it with Alice, thy wife?"

"Fu' weel, my Lord Yearl," replied Rory; "troth I see no complaints about the woman. And how's a' wi' my Lady Countess?"

"A little indisposed to-day, Rory," replied the Earl gravely.

"Fie, fie! I'm sorry for that," said Rory; "I'se warrant feasting and galravaging mun agree but soberly wi' her Lady-ship's honour. By St. Lowry, but I'm no that mokell the bet-ter for it mysel when I drink ower deep."

"Too much drink is certainly bad, Rory, though the Coun-tess's indisposition hath nothing of that in it," replied the Earl smiling: "but a black-jack of ale can do thee but little harm of a morning, so get thee to the kitchen, that thou mayest have thy draught."

"Thanks, my most noble Yearl," cried Rory; "a black-jack full of ale—nay, I spoke of gallons; it will take gallons to gi' me an aching head, I promise thee; nay, one gallon, or twa gallons, peraunter, would do me but little harm. But that wasna just a' my business, my Lord; I hae something mair to speak to thee about. Wasn't thee wanting a cast o' hawks?"

"Yea, I did indeed much wish for some of these noble birds, the which our rocks are famed for rearing, good Rory," replied the Earl. "The King hath heard of the excellence of our falcons, and I have promised to send him a cast of them."

" Aweel, aweel, the King's honour shanna want them an' I can get a grup o' them," replied Spears; " and sae your Lordship may tell him frae me."

" Thanks, good Rory, for thy zeal," replied the Earl; " get thee then to the kitehen, and have thy morning's draught."

" But that was not just a' that I had to say to thine honourable Lordship," said Rory, still lingering.

" I do opine that thou lackest advice and assistance in some little matter of thine own, friend Rory?" said the Earl smiling.

" Troth, my noble Lord Yearl, thou art not far from the mark there; and yet it's not just mine own matter neither, though some few years mought peraunter ha' made it mine; but it's nobody's now but his who hath got it."

" Nay, now thou art somewhat mystical, Rory," said the Earl; " come to the point at once, I pr'ythee, and effunde thy whole tale distinetly to me, for my time is rather precious this morning."

" The short and the long, then, of this matter, my Lord Yearl, is, that my wife's mother hath been robbed of fifty broad pieces," replied Rory.

" What! old Elspeth of the Burgh? who can have done so foul a lareen?" demanded the Earl.

" Ay, good my Lord, just our old mother Elspeth," replied Spears. " The money was the hard earnings of her goodman, the smith, who, rest his soul, was a hard-working Christian, as thou mayest remember."

" And how did this wicked stouthrief happen?" inquired the Earl.

" By the mass, I will tell thee as speedily as may be, my Lord," replied Rory. " It was but the night before last, that is to say, the night o' the brenning o' the Brugh, that it did happen. The baflins lassie that looketh after old Lucky was sent out to bring her tidings o' the fire. Thee knawest that the poor soul downa easily budge from eild; and as she did lig in her blankets she hearden a heavy foot in the place; and when she got up she did find the kist opened, and the old leathern purse with her money gone."

" 'Tis a hard case, indeed," said the Earl; " and hast thou any suspicions, Rory?"

" Nay, for a matter o' that, I hae my own thoughts," replied Rory; " yet I canna say that I am just sicker anent it; but cannot thou do nought, my noble Yearl?"

" Do thou use all thine ingenuity to find out the thief," said the Earl; " I shall see what my people may be able to do to aid thee ; and if we discover the rogue, a court shall be summoned, and he shall straightway hang for his villainy."

"Thanks, my good Lord," replied Rory, making his obeisance preparatory to departure ; "verily I am much beholden to thee ; but an' we recover not the broad pieces, we shall gain little by the foiterer's neck being lengthened ; yet I'll see what may be done to catch him."

"Do so, Rory," said the Earl ; "thou shalt have the aid of some of my people, and I do wish thee success."

CHAPTER XLII.

The Lovely English Damosel.

"So," said Rory Spears to his daughter, as she saw him out into the court-yard of the Castle, previous to his departure, "my lady the Countess hath bid thee attend to a young English damosel, sayest thou ?"

"Yea, and she is one of the sweetest, as well as one of the loveliest damosels I did ever behold," replied Katherine, "and of temper and disposition most gentle and sunshiny. Of a truth, it is quite a pleasure to be with her ; I am already as if I had known her from infancy. She is so gently condescending with me, that I could live with her for ever."

"What, wouldst thou forget thy benefactress to cleave to a stranger ?" exclaimed Rory Spears, in a tone of reproach.

"Nay, verily, not so," replied Katherine. "The duty I owe the Countess, and, above all, the love and gratitude I bear her, are too strong to permit me ever to forget her ; but whatever my lady wills me to do, I am bound to do ; and I own I do feel grateful to her for laying no more disagreeable task on me than that of attending on one so truly amiable as this English lady."

"English leddy here, or English leddy there, what is ony English leddy, compared to the Countess of Moray ?" replied Rory Spears impatiently. "I like not newfangledness—I like not to see thee relish any one but thy noble mistress, to whom thou shouldst ever cleave. She hath made a woman o' thee, for the whilk may the Virgin's blessing be about her. She hath caused thee to be taught many things ; but let me not have the grief and vexation to find that thou hast forgotten the plain simple lesson o' hamely virtue, and right acting, and the kindly feelings that I did put into thy young heart when thou wert but as a wild kid o' the craigs, that is, when thou wert my bairn ;

for, from thy leddy lear and tutoring, thou art now far aboon a simple man like me. Yet dost ane honest warm heart, simple though it be, lift up him that carries it to be the make of the very greatest and wisest among the judges o' the land, and so I am even wi' thee, lassie, and enteetled to speak to thee, learned as thou art, and foolish though I be. Let not thy heart dance away after strangers."

"My dearest father, thou hast much misjudged me," replied Katherine. "This lady hath robbed me of no. title of mine affection for the Earl and Countess, whom I do most ardently love, yea, as second parents ; nay, I do love them hardly less than I do my mother and thee."

"Thou shouldst love them more, lassie," cried Rory, with great energy and emphasis. "Much as we may have claim to thine affection, what have we done for thee that may equal the bounteous blessings they have conferred ?"

"Thou art my father, and Alice is my mother," replied Katherine, seizing his rough horny hands, and looking up in his weather-beaten face and smiling affectionately. "Thou kennest thou didst put notions of virtue and of right acting, yea, and kindly feelings, into my young heart ; and do I owe thee nothing for sike gifts ?"

"Nay, Kate, thy lear hath made thee an overmatch for me," cried Rory, quite overcome, and, embracing his daughter with the tears pouring over his cheeks ; "God bless thee, my bairn— I fear not for thy heart ; but, by St. Lowry, I must away. My blessing rest with thee, Kate. Ho there, loons, hae ye redd your beast horses o' their burdens ?"

"Ou ay, Maister Spears," replied one of the men who came with him.

"Let's on, then," exclaimed he ; so, striking the end of his pole to the ground, and whistling shrilly on his dogs, he moved hastily out by the Castle gate at the head of his ragged troop.

CHAPTER XLIII.

Mustering for the Tournament—The Proclamation—
The Procession at St. John's Chapel.

THE lists were now finished, and the crests and blazoned coat-armour of such knights as meant to tilt were on this day to be mustered in the little chapel of St John's. Chivalry was to be alive in all its gaudy pomp. Hitherto the knights had loitered about idle, or wasted the hours in sighing soft things into the delighted ears of their lady-loves, or in playing with them at chess or tables. Some, indeed, had more actively employed themselves, in hawking or hunting, and others had formed parties at bowls; but now all was to be bustle and busy preparation in the Castle, both with knights and ladies.

By dawn of day, squires, pages, and lacqueys, were seen running in all directions. Armour was observed gleaming in the ruddy beams of the morning sun; proud crests and helms, and nodding plumes, and richly-emblazoned shields and surcoats, and glittering lances, and flaunting banners and pennons, everywhere met the eye. The Earl of Moray, who had much to direct and to decide on, was compelled to shake off the sombre and distressing thoughts that oppressed him, and even to use his eloquence with the Countess, to induce her to rouse herself from the grief she had been plunged into by the shame her brother, the Wolfe of Badenoch, had brought upon her. She also had important duties to perform; and the first burst of her vexation being now over, she exerted her rational and energetic mind to overcome her feelings, and to prepare for the proper execution of them.

To gratify to the fullest extent that fondness for parade which so powerfully characterised the age, and to render the spectacle as imposing as possible, the whole of the knights, with their respective parties, were ordained to appear in the Castle-yard, where, having been joined by the ladies, it was intended they should be formed into a grand procession, in which they were to ride to the Mead of St John's, to witness the herald's proclamation.

Sir Patrick Hepborne was early astir, and his attendants and horses were all assembled before the Castle-yard began to fill. In the midst of them waved his red pennon, bearing his achievement on a chevron *argent*, two lions pulling at a rose. The parade that Mortimer Sang had, with great good judgment, selected for them, was immediately opposite to the window of the apartment which he knew was occupied by Katherine Spears, whose melting eyes had much disturbed his repose, and had created no small turmoil in his bosom. Mortimer yet hoped to win his spurs, in which event, the daughter of Rory Spears, though he was reputed rich, might have hardly, perhaps, been considered a proper match for him. But Master Sang could not resist the fascination of Katherine's talk; and when in her company, he was so wrapped in admiration of her, that he invariably forgot that Rory Spears was her father, or that she

had ever had a father at all. The damsel, for her part, looked
with inexpressible delight on the soldier-like form of Squire
Mortimer, and listened with no less pleasure to his good-natured
sallies of humour, graced, as they always were, with much of
the polish of travel.

The sound of the trumpets, as the party of each respective
knight appeared within the arched gateway of the Castle's outworks, now came more frequent, and the neighing of impatient
steeds, provoking one another in proud and joyous challenge,
became louder, and the shrill voices of the pursuivants were
heard, proclaiming the name, rank, and praises of each chevalier
as he appeared. The sun shone out bright and hot, increasing
the glitter of the gold-embossed armour of the knights, and the
splendour of their embroidered pennons and banners, their
richly-emblazoned surcoats, and their horse-furniture, that swept
the very ground as the coursers moved.

As Sir Patrick Hepborne passed outwards, on his way to
descend to the courtyard, he found the Earl of Moray already
upon the terrace, arrayed in all his pride. Behind him stood
his standard-bearer, supporting the staff of his banner in an
inclined position, so that its broad silk hung down unruffled by
a breath of air, displaying on a golden field the three cushions
pendant, within a double tressure, flowered and counterflowered
with fleurs-de-lys *gules*.

"Sir Patrick," said he, "thou art yet in good time. If it so
please thee to tarry here with me for some short space, I will
endeavour to teach thee some of the names and titles of those
gallant chevaliers who are beginning to throng the yard of the
Castle below. Thou dost already know my brother, the Earl of
Dunbar, who standeth yonder, with his red surcoat covered with
argent lions rampant; and I have also made thee know him with
whom he holdeth parlance, who beareth an ostrich proper as his
crest, and who hath his surcoat emblazoned *gules*, with a fess
cheque *argent* and *azure*, to be the brave Sir David Lindsay of
Glenesk, my worthy brother-in-law. With him is the proud Sir
Thomas Hay of Errol, Constable of Scotland, who standeth alike
sykered to me. Thou seest he beareth as his crest a falcon
proper, and the silver cloth of his surcoat is charged with three
red escutcheons.

"But see how the noble Douglas's flaming salamander—
jamais arrière—riseth over the towering crests around him ;
and as he shifts his place from time to time, thou mayest catch
a transient glimpse of the bloody hearts that cover his *argent*
field. Yonder hart's head erased proper, attired with ten tynes,

and bearing the motto, *Veritas vincit*, tells us that the wearer is Sir John de Keith, son of the Knight Marischal of Scotland. His emblazonry is hid from thee at present, but peraunter thou art aware that his coat-armour is *argent* on a chief *or*, three pallets *gules*. Yonder surcoat of cloth of gold with three mascles on a bend *azure*, as thou mayest have already discovered, veils the armour of Sir John Halyburton, than whom no knight hath a firmer seat in saddle, or a tougher arm to guide his ashen spear. Thou seest he weareth the red scarf of his lady-love attached to the Moor's head proper, that grinneth as his crest amid the plumes of his helmet."

"I do know him well, my Lord," replied Sir Patrick; "it hath pleased him to admit me already into close friendship."

"Ha!" continued the Earl, "seest thou yonder knight, who rideth so gaily into the court-yard, with his casque surmounted by a buck's head couped proper, attired *or?* He is as brave a chevalier as ever spurred in field—Sir John de Gordon, Lord of Strathbolgy : his *azure* banner waves behind him, charged with three boars' heads couped *or*. That knight who beareth for his crest a sleuth-hound proper, collared and leished *gules*, and whose gold-woven surcoat is charged with three red bars wavy —he, I mean, who now speaketh to the Douglas as he leaneth on his lance—is his brother-in-law, Sir Malcolm Drummond. Next to him stands Sir Alexander Fraser of Cowie, known by his *azure* coat, and his three cinquefeuilles *argent*.

"Thou mayest know the Earl of Sutherland by the gravity of his air, as well as by his richly-embroidered red surcoat, displaying three stars within a border *or*, and the double tressure flowered and counterflowered with fleurs-de-lys of the field, marking his descent from King Robert the First. His helm beareth the cat sejant proper, with the motto, *Sans peur*. Behind him standeth Hugh Fraser, Lord of Lovat, with his crest, a stag's head erased *or*, armed *argent*, and his *azure* coat charged with three *argent* cinquefeuilles.

"Ha! ha! ha! there thou comest, thou mad wag, Sir William de Dalzell, with thine erect dagger on thy helm, and thy motto, *I dare*. Depardieux, thou mayest well say so, for, by St. Andrew, thou wilt dare anything in lists or in field. Thou seest, Sir Patrick, that his sable surcoat hath on it a naked man, with arms extended proper. That lion passant, guardant *gules*, doth ornament the silver surcoat of Sir Walter Ogilvie of Wester Powrie, Sheriff of Forfar and Angus ; and yonder golden coat, with the three red crescents, doth cover the armour of Sir William Seuton of Seaton. That *argent* lion rampant is the crest of Sir Robert Bruce of Clackmannan; thou seest his golden coat hath a saltire and chief *gules*. That crest, a boar's head couped *or*, marks Sir Gillespie Campbell of Lochow; and the unicorn's head, near it, is that of Sir William Cunninghame of Kilmaurs. My neighbour, Sir Thomas de Kinnaird of Cowbin, is easily known by his red surcoat, bearing a saltire between four golden crescents. He that holdeth converse with him, and hath three silver buckles on a bend *azure* on his silver surcoat, is Sir Norman de Leslie of Rothes. Behind him is Sir Murdoch Mackenzie of Kintail; his surcoat is hid from our view, but he beareth, on an *azure* field, a stag's head embossed *or*.

"Yonder knight, who rideth in at this moment, clad in a golden surcoat, blazoned with a bend *azure*, charged with a star of six points between two crescents of the field, is Sir Walter Scott of Rankelburn, as brave a Borderer as ever rode with his lance's point to the South. With him cometh a chevalier, whose crest is an erect silver spur winged; he is Sir John de Johnston, one of the guardians of the Western Marches. He who cometh after Sir John, bearing as his crest the bear's paw holding a scimitar, and who hath his red surcoat charged with a lion rampant holding a crooked scimitar in his dexter paw, is Sir James Scrimgeour, the Constable of Dundee, I wot a right famous knight. With him is a knight also clad in a red surcoat, but having three golden stars; that is Sir Henry Sutherland of Duffus.

"Yonder *sable* eagle displayed on the *argent* surcoat, doth distinguish the gallant Sir Alexander Ramsay, Lord of Dalwolsy; and that other knight in silver, with the three *sable* unicorns' heads, is Sir Henry de Preston of Fermartyn. He in the *azure* ——But hark, Sir Patrick, the trumpets sound—the procession is about to be marshalled—we must descend to the court-yard."

The trumpets had no sooner ceased than the voice of a pursuivant was heard—

"Oyez! oyez! oyez!—Let the standard-bearer of each noble and knight take up the parade which the herald did already assign to him, there to remain till he be duly marshalled."

Immediately the banners and pennons, which waved in numbers below, were seen moving in various directions through the crowd, and each became stationary at its fixed point, near the edge of the area of the court-yard. This was a preliminary arrangement, without which the herald would have found great difficulty in executing his duty. As it was, he and his assistants soon began to bring the most beautiful order out of the gay confusion that prevailed. The Earl of Fife, who was to represent the King, appeared, and the Countess of Moray, and all the ladies, gorgeously apparelled in robes of state, came forth from the Castle, and began to mingle their slender and delicate forms with the firm, muscular, war-proved, and mail-clad figures of the knights.

At length all were marshalled and mounted ; the court-yard shook with the shrill clangour of the trumpets and kettle-drums, and the neighing and prancing of the steeds ; and the shouts that began to arise from the vulgar thousands who were impatiently waiting without the walls, announced that their eager eyes were at least gratified with the appearance of the first part of the spectacle.

Forth came some mounted spearmen and bowmen, before whom the dense crowd began slowly to open and divide ; and then some half-dozen trumpets, with several kettle-drums and clarions, all riding two and two. These were followed by a troop of pages, also riding in pairs, and after them came a train of esquires, all gallantly mounted and armed, and riding in the same order. Between the pages and the esquires were some kettle-drums and trumpets as before. Then came the Royal Standard, preceded by a strong band of trumpets, kettle-drums, and clarions, and various other martial instruments, and guarded by some of the oldest and noblest of the knights, and such as had no ladies present to claim their attendance. The standard was followed by the Earl of Fife, who rode a magnificent milk-white charger, armed and barbed at all points, and caparisoned with regal splendour. On the present occasion he was here acting as representative of the King his father, and the pomp of his array was not inferior to what might have been looked for from a crowned head. Before him rode six pages and six esquires ; and eight more pages walked, four on each side of his horse, supporting the poles of a canopy of crimson velvet, covered with golden shields, bearing the lion rampant *gules.* His golden surcoat, and the drapery of his horse, were richly emblazoned with the rampant red lion, and his private banner that followed bore the full blazon of his arms. The Earl of Fife was attended by a number of elderly knights of noble blood, who acted as his guards.

After the King's representative came the trumpets of the heralds, followed by the pursuivants ; immediately after them appeared the heralds, in their crowns and robes ; and in the middle of the latter was Albany Herald, his horse led by a page on each side of him. He bore before him, on a crimson

velvet cushion, a helmet and sword of rare and curious workmanship, which glittered with gold, and sparkled with precious
stones. These were to be the prize of him who, by universal
consent, should best acquit himself in the lists; and the very
sight of them called forth loud shouts of applause from the
populace. Immediately after the heralds came the Marischal
and Speaker of the Lists, attended by the Marischal's men.

After these came the Earl and Countess of Moray, richly
attired, magnificently mounted, and nobly attended. They
were accompanied by the Lord Welles, and his suit of English
knights, to whom succeeded the married knights who had ladies
present, each riding according to his rank, with his lady by his
side, her palfrey being led by a page on foot. Before each
chevalier went his banner or his pennon, and he was followed
by his esquire, pages, and other attendants. Next came the
young or unmarried knights, also marshalled according to their
rank, each preceded by his banner or pennon, and followed by
his squire and cortège. But the youthful gallants were each
bound round the neck with a silken leash, which was held in
gentle thrall by the fair hand of a lady, who rode beside him on
a palfrey, led by a foot page. It is perhaps unnecessary to
mention that Sir John Halyburton's silken fetters were held by
the Lady Jane de Vaux.

After the knights came another train of esquires, who were
followed by pages and lacqueys; and, lastly, the procession was
closed by a considerable force of spearmen, bowmen, and pole-
axemen.

The head of the procession had no sooner appeared through
the echoing gateway, than the air was rent with the repeated
acclamations of the populace, who formed a dense mass, stretching away from the outworks in one uninterrupted mosaic of
heads and faces, until they disappeared beneath the shade of
the distant trees of the woodland. The paltry roofs of the
cottages in the straggling hamlet were clustered so thick that
they looked like animated heaps of human beings; and the
ancient single trees that arose here and there among the hovels,
were hung with living fruit. The agitation and commotion of
the motley and party-coloured crowd was very great, but it expanded, and consequently thinned itself, as the procession moved
on, the whole flowing forward like a vast river, until it lost itself
in the depths of the forest, where its winding course, and the
appearing and disappearing of its various parts among the boles
of the trees, with the brilliant though transient gleams produced
by the sunbeams, that pierced their way now and then down-

wards through accidental openings in the foliage, kindling up
the bright lance-heads and helmets, and giving fresh lustre to
the vivid colours of the proud heraldic emblazonments, lent an
infinite variety of effect to the spectacle.

Whilst they moved over the green sod, under the leafy
canopy of the forest, the tramp of the horses was deafened, and
the shouts of the populace were in some sort muffled ; but when
the procession issued forth on the Meads of St. John, the
affrighted welkin rang again with the repeated and piercing
acclamations of a multitude which went on increasing in numbers as they advanced, particularly after they had crossed the
bridge, and even until they reached the lists. The gates and
barriers were wide open, and the procession filed in.

The Royal Standard was now hoisted over the crimson-
covered central balcony, in which the representative of the
Sovereign was afterwards to take his place, and it was hailed
with prolonged cheers ; while the heralds, pursuivants, Marischal, and Speaker of the Lists, and the judges of the field,
having stationed themselves on a platform immediately underneath the royal balcony, the procession formed itself into a wide
semi-circle in front of it. Meanwhile the galleries surrounding
the lists were rapidly filled up by the populace, and all waited
the issue with breathless impatience.

The Albany Herald now advanced to the front of the platform, and, holding up the prize sword and helmet in both hands,
there was a flourish of trumpets and kettle-drums, which was
drowned by the deafening shouts of the spectators. This had
no sooner subsided, than Albany, having commanded silence by
means of the shrill voices of his pursuivants, thus began :—

"Oyez, oyez, oyez !—All ye princes, lords, barons, knights,
esquires, ladies, and gentlemen, be it hereby known to you,
that a superb achievement at arms, and a grand and noble tournament, will be held in these lists, within four days from this
present time, the acknowledged victor to be rewarded with this
helmet and sword, given by the noble and generous John
Dunbar, Earl of Moray. All ye who intend to tilt at this tournament are hereby ordained forthwith to lodge your coat-
armouries with the heralds, that they may be displayed within
the holy chapel of St. John the Baptist, and this on pain of not
being received at the tournament. And your arms shall be
thus :—The crest shall be placed on a plate of copper, large
enough to contain the whole summit of the helmet ; and the
said plate shall be covered with a mantle, whereon shall be
blazoned the arms of him who bears it ; and on the said mantle,

at the top thereof, shall the crest be placed, and around it shall be a wreath of colours, whatsoever it shall please him. Further be it remembered, that on the morning of the fourth day from hence, the arms, banners, and helmets of all the combatants shall be exposed at their stations ; and the speakers shall be present at the place of combat by ten of the horologne, where and when the arms shall be examined, and approved or rejected, as may be fitting and right. The chevaliers shall then become tenants of the field, and tilt with blunt weapons in pairs, and then the victors shall tilt successively in pairs, until they be reduced and amenused to two ; and he of the two who may the best acquit himself, shall receive from the hand of her whom he may proclaim to be the most peerless damsel, the prize of the helmet and sword.—God save King Robert !"

The herald's proclamation was received with a flourish of trumpets, clarions, and kettle-drums, and the continued shouts of the people. Silence being at length restored,

" Pursuivant," said he, "stand forth and deliver thee of the rules of the tourney."

The pursuivant obeyed the orders of his superior, and proclaimed the laws of the tourney item by item ; after which the trumpets and kettles again sounded, and the shouts of the populace were renewed. When they had died away, the heralds with their attendants again mounted, and then the procession moved round the lists in the order we have already described, and, issuing from the same gate at which it had entered, it proceeded slowly towards the adjacent chapel of St. John the Baptist, which it entirely surrounded, and then halting, under the direction of the heralds, it formed a wide circle about the beautiful little Gothic building that stood in an open grove of tall ash-trees.

" Oyez, oyez, oyez !" cried a pursuivant, " let the esquires of those chevaliers who mean to tilt at this tournament for the prizes given by the noble and generous John Dunbar, Earl of Moray, or who may, in any manner of way, desiderate to challenge others, or to leave open to others the power of challenging them to by-tilting for any other cause whatsoever—let their esquires now advance, and let the heralds have inspection of their crests and coat-armouries. He who shall fail to comply, and whose crest and coat-armour shall not be up before sunset, shall have no right to enter the lists as a tenant of the field in any manner of way whatsoever, except always as to pages or squires, to whom, for this day and to-morrow, the lists shall be open, to give all such an opportunity of proving their manhood. Advance, then, ye standard-men and esquires, that ye may deposit the gages which prove your masters to be gentlemen of arms, blood, and descent ; that ye may see their trophies erected, and stay and watch each by his master's achievement, to mark whosoever may touch the same, that his knight's honour may not suffer by his neglecting the darreigne."

In obedience to this order, each knight sent his standard-man, and an esquire or page, towards the chapel; and Sir Patrick Hepborne was about to send Mortimer Sang, when that faithful esquire dropped on his knee before him.

" Nay, my good master, I do humbly crave a boon at thy hands," said he ; " I do beseech thee let some other of thy people be chosen for this duty, sith I should at least wish to be a free man for this day and to-morrow, that I may do some little matter for mine own honour. By St. Andrew, if I may but bestir myself decently, it will not be amiss for thy credit, Sir Knight, seeing that a chevalier, whose personal renommie hath been already established, may be even well enough excused for amusing himself by taking pleasure in the well-doing of his horse, his hound, or his hawk."

" Friend Mortimer," replied Sir Patrick, " I do much rejoice that thou hast the glorious desire of reaping laurels so strong within thee. Trust me, I shall be no hindrance in thy way to fame, but rather I shall hold fast the ladder, and aid thee to climb and reach it. Thy time shall be thine own, and thou shalt be at full liberty to use thy discretion. I shall be much interested in thy success, and shall have small fear in thy commanding it ; so get thee to one of the armourers of the field, and fit thyself forthwith at my cost, in whatever thou mayest lack."

The squire threw himself on one knee, and, kissing his master's hand, warmly expressed his gratitude, and then hastened away towards the lists, to purchase from some of the armourers who had shops there, the pieces of which he deemed himself in want, and Hepborne, for his part, chose out another esquire to fulfil the duty of watching his achievement in the chapel.

The heralds having put everything in such order as might bear inspection, now came forth from the chapel, and marshalling the nobles, knights, and ladies into a foot procession, they led them through the enclosure to the western door, where they entered to behold the spectacle. The sight was most imposing. Along both sides of the nave, and all the way up to the screen of the choir, were placed stands, each covered by a plate of copper, on which stood the tilting helmet, surmounted by the wreath and crest of the knight. The helmet rested on the upper part of the mantle, so as to support it by the pressure of its weight, whence it was expanded with the lower part of it spread on the ground, in such a manner that the achievement emblazoned on it in dazzling colours was fully stretched before the eye. Behind it, on the right side, stood the squire or page who was appointed to watch it, and on the left stood the stand-ard-bearer, supporting the banner or pennon of his master.

"Advance, ladies, dames, and damosels," cried the herald in a loud voice, that made the groined roof re-echo; "advance and survey the helmets, crests, and coat-armouries, and see whether thou mayest peraunter descry the bearings of any traitor, mal-faitor, or reviler of the ladies; for if so be that such may be discovered by any, she shall touch his crest, and both it and his achievements shall be thrust hence, that he may have no tilting at this tournament. Advance, then, and the herald shall descrive them in succession; and if any other knight or achievement may yet appear this day before sunset, it is hereby reserved to the ladies to exercise their right on him, if they see fitting so to do."

The herald now led the knights and ladies in procession up the right side of the nave, around the transept, and returned down the left side of the nave; and having thus given them a general view of the whole, he led them around three times more, during which he accurately described the name and titles of each knight to whom the successive crests and achievements belonged. One or two achievements were touched by some of the younger knights, who wished to prove the firmness of their seat, before the day of tournament, by trial in a by-tilting, with some antagonist of their own selection, or against whom they wished to establish the superior charms of their lady-love; but the more experienced warriors, who had already well proved their lances elsewhere, reserved their efforts for the grand day when the tournament was properly to begin.

The ceremony of surveying the crests and coat-armouries being now over, the knights and ladies returned to their steeds, palfreys, and attendants, and the whole were soon again in motion, though not in the order or with the ceremony they had observed in their approach to the lists, and to the Chapel of St. John's. The procession was now broken up into parties, and the Earl of Moray and his Countess, leading the way with the Earl of Fife, all followed in gay disorder, with a less chastened pace and less formal air. The ladies had freed their knights from their temporary bonds, though they still held them by the mere

influence of their radiant eyes. The laughing Jane de Vaux
went on in the full enjoyment of her own triumph, and her face
reflected the smiles of her merry party, as she cantered joyfully
over the Mead after the Earl and Countess of Moray, to partake
of a collation spread under a large awning in front of the pavilions on the other side of the river.

Sir Patrick Hepborne's pleasure in this rural feat was damped
by the marked distance with which the Countess of Moray now
treated him. He fatigued himself with attempts to account for
a conduct so different from the kind and easy reception she had
given him at first ; and he was still more shocked to observe,
that even the Earl himself seemed to have adopted somewhat
of the same freezing exterior since he had last parted with him
in the court-yard. He tried to persuade himself that it was in
a great measure fancy in him, and that in reality it was to be
explained by the natural tone of dignity which the day demanded ; and with this explanation he was obliged to content
himself.

CHAPTER XLIV.

The Italian Armourer—The Knight of Cheviot.

" Ha ! Signor Andria Martellino, can it be ? Do mine eyes
deceive me, or is it really thou whom I do thus behold in
Scotland ? " cried Mortimer Sang, as he entered the temporary
shop of an armourer, erected at the back of one end of the lists;
" by the mass, I should as soon have looked to see our Holy
Father the Pope in these parts, as thee in the Mead of St.
John's."

The person the squire thus addressed was a tall, thin,
shambling, though athletic, black-a-viced looking man, whose
very appearance bespoke his long intimacy with ignited charcoal
and sulphurous vapours, and whose stooping shoulders argued
a life of bending over the anvil, whilst the length, swing, and
sinew of his arms betrayed the power with which he might still
be expected to assail the stubborn metal. As Sang spoke to
him he opened a wide mouth from ear to ear, so that the large
gold rings that ornamented their pendulous cartilages almost
appeared to issue from the corners of it, and replied with a grin
of immediate recognition.

" Eh ! Signore Mortimero Sang, how I am verri glad to see
dee. Dee be verri vell, I do hope ? E il vostro padrone, il

Cavaliere ?—Eh ! il Cavaliere Seer Pietro Hepborne, I hope he is good ?—sta bene ?—Preet vell, eh ?"

"Yes," replied Sang, "I thank God, he is well; he is here upon the field."

"Ha, ha !" returned the armourer, "Seer Pietro wid dee here ? Ha, I glad to hear dat. I glad to see heem. San Lorenzo, he alvays moss good for me. Sempre, sempre mi fa molto bene. He do me more vell dan all de oder Cavalieri in de leest at Paris; he break more shield, more breast-plate, more helmet of knight, dan all de oder who did joust. Dite mi, Signor Mortimero, dos he vant anyding in my vay? I have moss good armour, all made of right good Milano metal—tutta fabricata nella fabrica mia—all made in my vat dee do call vorksop. Dere, guardate, see vat a preet show. Aha !" continued he, as he opened a door that led from the temporary workshop, where his assistant workmen were labouring at the forge, into an inner place, where there was a grand display of armour, and weapons of all sorts and sizes, ready for immediate use; "dou mayest see I can feet il Cavaliere Seer Pietro vid anyding dat he may vant in my vay."

"Nay," replied Sang, "I do opine that Sir Patrick lacketh nothing in thy way; he is right well supplied with all necessary gear at present."

"Ah !" said the Italian, "I am verri sorri, verri sorri for dat. I glad to gif him armour for noding at all; he do cause me moss good vid the vicked blows he do give. Ha ! it vas vonder to see heem. I do make armour to stand against the blows of de Diavolo heemself—ma, for Seer Pietro—no; he cut troo anyding. I verri glad to arm heem for noding—si, Signor Mortimero, for noding at all."

"Eh ! sayest thou so, Signor Martellino, my master ?" exclaimed Sang, with a knowing look; "by the mass, but I am right glad to find thee so liberally disposed, yea, and all the more, too, that thou dost seem to have sike mountance of the very articles I do lack. By St. Baldrid, though Sir Patrick hath no need to put thy generosity to the preve in his own proper person, I shall do my best to pleasure thee, and shall strive so far to overcome my delicacy, and to yield me to thy volunde, as to coart myself to accept of a helmet and a complete suit of plate from thee on gift."

"Eh, cospetto ! no, no, no, Signor Mortimero, mio caro," hastily replied the Italian starting back, and screwing up his mouth, and shrugging his shoulders; "eh, povero me, quello non poso fare—I not can do dat. Ma, dou not intend vat I do

20

mean. I not do mean dee ; but I do mean il Signor Cavaliere Pietro Hepborne, il vostro padrone. It vas beem I do speak about."

"Nay, I do comprehend thee perfectly," answered Sang; "but as it is with my master's money that I must pay for what I may buy from thee, I was in full thought that thou mightest have been filled with jovisaunce thus to discover a mode of showing thy gratitude and regard towards him, by haining his purse, and giving that gratis the which he must otherwise lay out for so largely."

"Ha! Signor Mortimero caro," said Andria, "ma non m'intendete ancora; dou not intend vat I do say yet. Il Signor Cavaliere Pietro Hepborne e voi sono du persone; ha! don and dy master not von man. I do say (figurativamente) dat I moss glad to arm Seer Pietro, because he do vork moss mischief to de arms of de oder knights, so moss dat he more dan pay me by vat I sell to dem, for all vat I mote gif him. He do cut out good vork and good sell for me; ma voi siete vat you call an apprentiss in de joost. I give dee good armour! Ha, ha! it vould be all destroy in one leettel momento, and dou voud do leettel harm to dose dat mote be against dee. Ah-ha! dou voud destroy no von man's armour but dine own. Ha! dou hast de good coraggio, and de stout leems; ma, per Baccho, dy skeel is not like dat of dy padrone, Seer Pietro."

"Nay, as to that," said Sang, laughing good-naturedly, "thou mayest be right enow, Signor Andria; yet mescemed that the stream of thy generosity did run best when thou didst ween that no one thirsted. But I am glad to see thee so well provided with good steel plate, from the which I must now supply myself, sith that thou wilt not be generous; and though they be dear, yet of a truth I do ken that thy goods are ever of the best."

"Ah-ha! Signor Sang," answered the Italian, with an air of triumph, "adesso avete ragione—dou art right; la mia armadura è fabricata d'acciajo stupendissimo de Milano—vat dou voud call de best steel of Milano. Dere is not no von as do work in vat dou call steel as do know his trade better; dere is no armajuolo is so good as mine broder and me. Bah! Giacomo dere dost make so moss noise vid his hammaire dat I not see myself speak. Come dis vay, Signor Mortimero, com dis vay—come into dis appartamento, and I make dee see all vat do make thee vonder."

"Holy St. Andrew, what sort of men dost thou look to meet with in Scotland, when thou dost bring sike armour as that?" cried Sang, as he entered, and pointed to an enormous suit of plate armour that hung at one side of the farther wall of the place ; " why that must be intended for a giant."

" Ha, ha, ha, he ! so dou dost vonder already, Signor Sang," said the Italian ; " I did look for dy vonder, but I did not tink so dat I voud see dee vonder for dat ; I not tink but dou didst see dat in my store at Paris. I have had him verri long—ma no, I do remember dat 'tis not long since mine broder Giuseppe did bring him from our store at Milano. He and anoder I did sell yesterday morning vas make by mine broder Giuseppe, for de two ends of de store at Milano, for show. Dey look verri preet at de two ends of de appartamento dere, vere we did show de armour for sell. I never tink I sell von or oder, or dat I ever see von man dat mote be big enow to wear dem. But yesterday morning I have de good fortune to meet vid von Polypheme, who did come to me, vid von mout I fear he did eat me up. He did vant armour. Eh, morte, I do tink I did feet him ven none oder von man in Europe have done it but mineself. I make him pay vell ; ma, ven you see armourers like de broders Martellini—Andria me, e Giuseppe, mine broder—de first armourers in the vorld ? "

" True, true," replied Sang, " ye are both mighty men-at-arms, and ye seem to know it as well, too ; though, from what I know of ye both, ye do ken better how to make a sword than to use it. But come, we lose time. Hand me down that tilting helmet, that cuirass, and those vantbraces and cuisses. Let me see, I say, what thou hast got that may fit me for a turn or two in the lists. I must e'en try what I can do, an 'twere only to hack and destroy some steel-plate to win thy favour, and so screw up thy generosity, that I may earn a gratis suit from thee for my prowess one of these days."

" Aha ! Signor Sang, den must dou joost vid some knight dat vear de armour of dat donner Tedesche at de oder end of de leest," cried Martellino, with a sarcastic air of triumph ; " dat stupid Meenher Eisenfelsenbroken, dat do pretend to make de armour as good as me. Eh, he! quel bericuocolajo ! dat do make his breastplate of de bread of de gingaire, his vork vill split more easy ; ma, for dat sell by de Martellini, no, dou not break it so fast, caro Signor Sang."

" Perdie, if I can but meet with that same Polypheme of whom thou didst talk, I will at least try the metal of thy brother Giuseppe's plate."

While the squire was in the act of fitting himself with what he wanted, a new customer came into the front shop or forge, where the armourer's men were working strenuously, with heavy and repeated strokes, at a piece of iron that glowed at that moment on the anvil. It was Rory Spears.

" Hear ye me, lads," roared he ; " will ye haud yer din till I speak ? "

The hammers fell thicker and faster, for the men heard him not.

" Dinna ye hear me ? Haud yer din, I tell ye, till I effunde three words. Na, the red fiend catch ye, then—devil ane o' ye will stop. Haud yer din, I tell ye," shouted Rory, at the very top of his voice ; but if it had been like that of ten elephants united, it must have had as little effect as that of a weasel amidst such thunder. The furious grimaces and gesticulations that accompanied it were sufficiently visible, and the iron having now become cold, the men stopped of their own accord, and gave him an opportunity of being heard.

" Ay, by St. Lowry, I thought I should gar ye hear at length. Seest thou here, lad," continued he, addressing one of the men in particular, and at the same time holding out to him the strange amphibious weapon he usually carried, " seest thou here, my man ? my clip-gaud lacketh pointing ; try what thou mayest do to sharpen it."

The man understood not his words, but comprehended his signs, and nodded assent ; then pointing to the work they were busy about, he made Rory aware that he must wait until they had finished it.

" Ou, ay, weel-a-weel," said Rory, " Ise tarry here till thou be'st ready to do the job ; " and sitting down on a stool, he began peering about with his eyes in all directions.

The door of the inner apartment being open, he sent many a long look through the doorway, as Mortimer Sang and Andria Martellino crossed and re-crossed his field of vision. The squire at last appeared, fully armed cap-a-pie.

" Ha ! " said he, as he strode forth, well contented with himself, " ha ! this will do—this will do bravely."

" Ou, Maister Sang, art thou bound for the lists too," said Rory Spears.

" Hey, Master Spears, art thou there ? " replied the squire. " By'r lackins, I knew thee not at first. Yea, I am going to try my luck. What ! be'st thou bent thither alswa with thy gaud-clip ? "

" Na, na, not I," replied Rory. " I hae other fish to fry, I promise thee. I did come here but to get my gaud-clip sharpened. As I did sit yestreen watchin the salmons loupin at the ess, I did espy an otter creeping over the rock ; so I threw my gaud at the brute and speared him, but I broke the point on't, as thou mayest see here. Na, na, I can clip a salmon, or can toss a spear at a rae or red buck i' the forest, or it may be, at a man in the field; but I kenna about yere galloping and jousting."

"Signor Martellino, here is thy coin," said Sang, counting it out to him; "but remember thee thou didst owe me half a broad piece in change the last chevisaunce that did pass between us; I do mean the which thou didst forget to return me in our dealings at Paris, ere thou didst set out for Milan."

"Ah! signor, non mi recordo niente di quello," replied Martellino, with a knavish air of pretended forgetfulness.

"Nay, but by St. Bartholomew, thou must remember it," said Sang sternly. "I higgle never for thy price, but I shall have every penny that is lawfully mine own. It was in paying thee for a morion I had of thee; thou hadst not the change, and thou didst say I should have it next day; but when I did call, thou wert gone to Milan. By St. Barnabas, I will have mine own."

"Ah! si, Signor Mortimero," said the Italian, as if suddenly recollecting, and twanging his response obsequiously through his nose, accompanying it at the same time with a profound inclination of his body, "si, avete ragione davvero, I do now remember."

"'Tis well," said Sang, "take this then; I shall now go look for Polypheme. Master Spears, I bid thee good day;" and saying so, he walked out of the forge, and, taking the rein of his steed from the groom that attended him, mounted and rode off towards the chapel of St. John's.

As he approached the gate of the enclosure that surrounded it, he observed a countryman holding two sorry ill-equipped hackneys with one hand, and with the other an enormous heavy long-tailed coarse black waggon-horse, covered with saddle and trappings of no small value; yet, unfit as it seemed for tourney, it bore all the furniture necessary to a steed destined for the lists.

Squire Mortimer dismounted, and, tossing his rein to the groom, hastened into the Chapel, to see what new knight had arrived who could own so unseemly a courser. The crowds who had visited the interior to gaze at the achievements of the chevaliers, were by this time all gone to the lists, and the most perfect stillness reigned within the Chapel. The pages, esquires, and bannermen stood by the heraldic trophies of their respective knights, immovable as statues; and the only sound or motion

within the place proceeded from a herald who remained to
receive and put up the achievement of any knight who might
yet arrive before sunset, and to register his name and titles, and
who was at that moment employed in doing these offices for
him who called himself the Knight of Cheviot.

This colossal man in armour was standing opposite to the
place where his achievement was erecting.   On the helmet was
a furze bush, with the motto, "I prick full sore;" and the
blazon bore on a field-*vert*, a mountain *azure*, with the sun's disc
beginning to appear from behind it, *or*, and the motto, "I shall
shine."   The gigantic owner was leaning on a spear, the shaft of
which looked liker some taper pine-tree of good growth, than
any instrument that mortal might be supposed to wield.   The
vizor of his bassinet was down, and his face was hid so that no
one could judge of it or know it ; but the very shadow that he
threw over the length of the pavement of the transept, even
until it rose against the wall at the farther end of it, was enough
to have daunted the boldest heart.   Sang stood patiently, with
his arms folded, attentively surveying him, and the achievement that was rearing for him ; and no sooner was the arrangement of it completed than, clutching up the shaft of his lance
short in his hand, he bestowed such a thwack with the butt end
of it on one cheek of the tilting helmet of the Knight of
Cheviot, that he made it sound through the Chapel like a bell,
till all the squires, pages, and bannermen started to hear it.

"Who art thou," demanded the huge figure in a hollow and
indistinct voice—"who art thou who darest to challenge the
Knight of Cheviot to tilt before the day of tourney ?"

" I am Mortimer Sang, esquire of the body of the renowned
Sir Patrick Hepborne, younger of Hailes," replied he, "and
thus may the herald inscribe me, so please him.   Achievement
have I none at present, but a bold heart and doughty deeds may
yet win me a proud one.   I do crave the boon of a meeting from
thee, mighty Knight of Mountains, so soon as the lists may be
free for us."

" Am I, a knight, obliged to give ear to the challenge of an
esquire ?" demanded he of Cheviot.

"Sir Knight," said the herald, "such matchers are not without example, both for jousting and outrance.   But to-day and
to-morrow are set apart for giving license to all esquires and
pages of good report, who have fair reason to hope that they
may one day win their spurs, that they may challenge whom
they list."

"I could have wished some nobler antagonist to begin with,"

muttered the Knight of Cheviot ; " I could have wished that Sir Patrick Hepborne——"

"Dost thou refuse my challenge, then?" demanded Sang, striking the butt end of his lance against the other cheek of the helmet with greater force than before.

The Knight of Cheviot was silent and disturbed for some moments.

"Nay, Sir Knight," said the herald, "thou mayest not well refuse it, without forfeiting all right to tilting at this tourney."

"Then will I accept it," muttered the Knight of Cheviot, after a short silence of seeming hesitation. "What! must it be even now, saidst thou?"

"Ay, truly, as soon as the lists are clear for us," replied Sang coolly ; "for I take it some of them are hot at it by this time. I shall look to meet thee there forthwith, and I shall now hasten thither to secure us our turn."

CHAPTER XLV.

The Tournament.

THE Earl of Moray's sylvan banquet of refreshment was by this time over, the balconies and galleries were already filled with the knights and ladies, and the lists were surrounded by the populace, all eagerly beholding the numerous tilting matches going on between young knights who wished to exercise themselves, and prove each other's strength of arm, adroitness, and firmness of seat, or between squires or pages, who wished to earn their first harvest of fame. The sport had been as yet but indifferent. Most of those who had ridden against each other were novices, who afforded but a poor specimen of what the Scottish chivalry could do. The English knights, and, above all, the Lord Welles, were sneering to each other at the wretchedness of the exhibition, and every now and then throwing out sarcastic remarks against those who were engaged, whenever the occurrence of any slight piece of awkwardness gave them an opening for doing so. The Scottish knights who were within ear-shot of what dropped from them, were nettled at what they heard ; and had not the sacred character of an ambassador compelled them to keep down their emotions, the Lord Welles, or some of his suite, might have been called on to show, in their own persons, what Englishmen could do ; but, circumstanced as they were, none of the members of this diplomatic corps had considered it as necessary to put up his blazon in the chapel of St. John.

"Thinkest thou, Courtenay, that there is any chance of men appearing here to-day?" said the Lord Welles, in a voice that showed he little cared who heard him, or what soreness he might occasion. "In my mind those have been but women and boys who have been tilting for our amusement."

"Depardieux, thou sayest well, my lord," replied Sir Piers Courtenay, "for such woman's play and child's tilting did I never before behold. Our Cheapside shop-boys would make better work on't with their yard-measures. Then there is no fancy in their armour—a crude and barbarous taste, my Lord—yea, and a clownish and plebeian air about their very persons, too. Trust me, my Lord, I do not rashly venture on the grave and serious accusation I am now about to hazard, when I do declare, solemnly and fervently, that I have not seen one spur of the accurately proper fashion on any knightly heel in these Caledonian wildernesses."

"Ha, ha, ha. The nicety of thy judgment in such matters, Courtenay, is unquestionable," said the Lord Welles laughing.

A trumpet now sounded from one of the barriers, and was immediately answered from that at the other end of the lists. The voice of a pursuivant was next heard.

"Oyez! oyez! oyez! The good esquire Mortimer Sang doth call on the gallant Knight of Cheviot to appear to answer his challenge."

There was some delay for a little time, during which all eyes were thrown towards the barrier, where Mortimer was steadily bestriding a superb chestnut charger, with an ease and grace that might have led the spectators to suppose that the horse and man were but one animal. One of Sir Patrick Hepborne's pages, well mounted, attended him, to do him the necessary offices of the lists; and although his helmet displayed no crest, and that his arms were plain, and his shield without achievement, yet his whole appearance had something commanding about it, and all were prepossessed in his favour.

"That looks something like a man," quoth the English knights to each other.

"What a noble-looking presence! If he be only an esquire, of a truth he deserves to be a knight," went round among the spectators.

"How handsome he is, and how gallant-looking and warlike!" whispered the soft voice of Catherine Spears, who stood behind the Countess of Moray.

The pursuivant from Sang's barrier now repeated his challenge; a confused murmur soon afterwards arose from that at the opposite end of the lists, and by and by, the huge bulk of the Knight of Cheviot, mounted on his enormous charger, was seen moving like the mountains he took his name from, through an amazed group of wondering heads. The horse and man seemed to have been made for each other, and they looked like the creatures of a creation altogether different from that of this earth, and as if such inhabitants would have required a larger world than ours to have contained them.

"By'r Lady, but yonder comes no child, then," exclaimed Sir Miles Templeton, one of the English knights, who sat behind the Lord Welles.

"By St. George, 'tis an animated colossal monument," said the Lord Welles.

"If it be cast down, we cannot choose but have an earthquake," cried Sir Piers Courtenay.

"Who or what can he be?" said Sir John Constable.

"We shall doubtless hear anon," replied the Lord Welles.

"Hath not the brave esquire been rash in selecting so huge a monster for his *coup d'essai* in the lists?" said the Countess of Moray. "To what knight may he be attached?"

"To me, my noble lady," said Sir Patrick Hepborne from a place behind, where he had sat unnoticed by the Countess. "Trust me, he will acquit himself well—his heart is as stout as it is true."

"Sayest thou so, Sir Knight?" said the Countess, turning round and looking at him with some severity. "Then do I give thee joy that thou hast at least one leal heart in thy company."

"Oh, my lady," cried the alarmed Katherine Spears, "Squire Mortimer can never stand against yonder terrible giant. What will become of him? Holy St. Andrew protect us, I dare not look!"

"Nay, fear thee not, gentle damsel," said Sir Patrick, with assumed composure; "though yonder living tower look so big and so threatening, trust me I have no dread for friend Sang. He hath much good thew and muscle packed into reasonable compass, and they are nerved by a heart withal that nothing can danton. Fear ye not for Sang. By St. Baldrid, I begin to feel a stirring interest in this coming shock."

"May the blessed Virgin guard and aid him!" cried Katherine Spears, half covering her eyes.

The pursuivant at the end of the lists where the Knight of

Cheviot appeared, now responded to him who had given forth the challenge.

"Oyez! oyez! oyez! The gallant Knight of Cheviot is here, and ready to answer the darreigne of the good squire, Mortimer Sang."

"*Laissez les aller*," cried the herald from the platform under the Royal balcony; the trumpet sounded, and the barriers at both ends of the lists were immediately dropped.

The lists, as was very commonly the case in those times, were double; that is to say, they were divided towards the middle, for about two-fourths of their length, by a longitudinal barrier of wood of about four feet high. This was for the purpose of separating the horses of the combatants from each other, to save them from injury; for each knight, taking a different side of the wooden wall, ran his career close to it, and tilted at his adversary over it, without risk of the steeds meeting in shock, as in the undivided lists.

No sooner were the barriers withdrawn, than Mortimer Sang spurred his courser, sprang forward, and swept along like a whirlwind. The huge animal ridden by the gigantic and ponderous Knight of Cheviot was slow in getting into motion, and came on blowing and snorting, with a heavy lumbering gallop, that shook the very ground. The esquire had already ridden along one-half of the wall of division ere his antagonist had reached a third of the distance. His lance was firmly and truly pointed against the immense body that approached, and every eye was intently watching for the issue of a joust that promised to be unexampled in the annals of chivalry. Both steeds were steadily maintaining the line in which each had started. The enormous tilting-lance of the knight, as it came on, resembled the bolt-sprit of some vessel driven before the wind, and, blunt though it was, the annihilation of the esquire appeared certain to the spectators. The collision was within a few yards of taking place, when, to the astonishment of all, the Knight of Cheviot suddenly dropped his lance, and, seizing the bridle of his charger with both hands, exerted all his strength to pull him aside, and succeeded in making him bolt away from the thrust of his opponent. That it was an intentional effort and no accident was evident to every one. A general hiss, mingled with loud hootings broke, from the balconies and galleries. Mortimer Sang, exasperated at the shameful and cowardly conduct of him on whom he had so sanguinely hoped to prove his prowess, checked the straight course of his horse's career, and, sweeping around in a narrow circle, ran him at the wooden barrier, and, leaping him desperately over it, rode furiously, lance in rest, against the dastard Knight of Cheviot, who had hardly yet reined up his steed.

Shouts of applause followed this spirited manœuvre of Sang's. The base knight heard them, looked around, beheld the esquire coming, and began immediately to fly towards the gates of the lists. " Halt," cried Mortimer aloud, " halt, thou craven. What! fearest thou a blunt lance? Halt, thou mountain of Cheviot, halt, I say, that I may climb to thine uppermost peak to tweak thee by the nose, that I may pluck thy prickly crest from thy foggy head, and stick it beneath the tail of the draff-horse that beareth thee ; halt, coward, that I may forthwith blot out thy rising sun, that thou mayst no more dare to shine."

But the Knight of Cheviot stayed not to look behind him. His legs played upon the sides of his horse like some piece of powerful machinery, and he spurred off as if the devil had been after him, the animal exhibiting a pace which no one could have believed was in him. The marshalmen would have stopped him in his way to the gate, but to have essayed to arrest the progress of a huge rock, just parted from the summit of some lofty Alp, and spinning along the plain with all the impetus derived from its descent, could not have been a more irrational or more hopeless attempt, or one more pregnant with certain destruction to those who made it. The way was cleared before him ; but the gate was shut. Neither horse nor man seemed to regard the obstruction, however ; it appeared as if both were influenced by the same blind fear. They ran against it with so great an impetus, that its strong bars and rails yielded before the shock, and were strewed upon the plain. Away flew the fugitive across the Meads, and on Sang urged furiously after him. The shouts from the lists were redoubled. Down rushed crowds of the populace from the scaffolds, and away they poured with a hue and cry after the chase.

The flying giant had much the start of Sang, but the superior speed of the squire's well-bred courser was fast lessening this advantage. It was in vain that he attempted to double and wheel, for Sang, cutting sharply round, only gained the more on him. He stretched his course straight for the forest, but all saw that he must be speedily overtaken. Sang neared him, and couching his lance, planted himself firmly in his saddle. A single bound of his horse brought him within reach of the knight, and giving him an alert and vigorous push in the rear with his blunt weapon, he threw his unwieldy body forward on his horse's neck, so that, encumbered by the weight, the animal stumbled

a step or two, and then losing his fore legs, rolled himself and
hurled his rider forward upon the sod.

Ancient Æsop hath told us of a certain tortoise, that, being
carried into the clouds by an eagle, was dropped thence on a
rock.   It is easy to conceive how the various compartments of
the creature's natural armour must have been rent from each
other by the fall.   So it was with the Knight of Cheviot.   The
descent of such a mountain was no light matter.   Large as his
armour was, its various pieces were far from meeting each other
over the immense limbs and joints they should have enclosed ;
and the leathern latchets which laced them together being
somewhat aged, they, and even the rivets, gave way with the
shock ; and the fastenings of the helmet and of the different
plates bursting asunder, and there being no shirt of mail beneath
them, the Knight of Cheviot lay sprawling among the ruins of
his defences, in a black jerkin and hauselines.   The active Sang
would have been upon him in a trice, but, filled with astonishment, he reined up his steed and halted to wonder.   Nor was
superstitious fear altogether without its influence in arresting
him in his first intention of seizing the dastard impostor, who
had thus disgraced the name of knight, as well as the lists
in which he had dared to show himself, and of having him
dragged to that summary punishment inflicted on such occasions
by the laws of chivalry.   His eyes stared with an amazement
that was almost incredulous of the reality of what they beheld.
He whom he saw struggling on the ground was the wizard.
Ancient Haggerstone Fenwick, whom he had once accidentally
seen at Norham, and of whose supernatural powers he had then
heard enough to fill him now with temporary awe, at this his
unexpected appearance.   Sang raised his own vizor and rubbed
his eyes, and when he saw that it was really the face and figure
of the Ancient which he beheld, he for a moment suspected that
it was some demoniacal trick of enchantment that had been
played him to rob him of the fame he had hoped to earn.   Rage
got the better of every feeling of superstition.

"Ha !" exclaimed he, " be'st thou wizard or devil, I'll wrestle
with thee ;" and flinging himself from his horse, he strode
towards the struggling Knight of Cheviot.

But he was a moment too late.   Ere he could reach the
wizard, the latter had recovered himself sufficiently to scramble
to his legs ; and just as the squire was about to lay his fangs
upon him, he escaped with a sort of shuffling run, that grew as
he proceeded into an awkward striding gait that might have
done honour to a camelopard ; the plates of his armour hanging

to his body by frail tags, clattering and jingling as he flew, and spinning off at a tangent from his person, as the thongs successively gave way. The esquire pursued him as fast as he could, but his armour hampered him so much that he had no chance in a race with one who was loosely attired, and who was every moment lessening his weight by getting rid of some part of his steel encumbrances.

" Halt, coward !" cried Sang, puffing and blowing after him. " Ha, by St. Baldrid, 'tis in vain to follow him. An he were the Spirit of the Cheviots himself, who may step thee from one hill-top to another, he could not exert more alacrity of escape. He devoureth whole roods of ground at a stride as he fleeth. By the mass, see him ! he courses up yonder bank with his back-piece hanging down behind him, rattling like a canister at the tail of some mongrel hound. Body o' me, how it got atween his legs ; would that it had thrown him down. Ha ! now it hath lost its hold of him—and now the red fiend may catch him for me, for there he goes into the forest."

The squire returned slowly and sullenly to meet his page, who was by this time coming up. The huge dray horse of the Knight of Cheviot having regained his legs, was standing heaving his enormous sides like a stranded whale.

" 'Tis a cruel bite, Archibald Lees," said Mortimer Sang to the page ; " 'tis a cruel bite, I say, when a man thinketh he hath roused a lion, to find his game turn out but a stinking pole-cat after all. Get thee after the lurdon, and pick up the pieces of his armour, the which did drop from his scoundrel carcase as he fled."

" Methought, as I chanced to see him casing, that he would turn out to be some such vermin," replied the page, as he proceeded to obey the squire's commands.

Sang sat himself down for a little time to recover his wind, comforting himself with the idea that he had at least won a trophy of armour that would be valuable from its very rarity.

" I shall have them hung up in mine own tower," said he to himself. " As for the horse, he may fetch as much as may repay Sir Patrick for the advance he hath made for the arms I had of Andria Martellino. By mine honour, he hath a body and limbs that might pull a castle after them. He will sell right speedily to a wainman, ay, and that for a noble price too."

A crowd of the populace now began to approach the place where he was sitting, clamouring as they came along. At their head came Rory Spears, with his fish-clip brandished over his shoulder, and followed by a party of the marshal's men, bring-

ing along the Italian armourer in custody, whose face exhibited
an expression of extreme dismay and trepidation.

"Ay, ay, we shall soon ken whether the rogue speaketh truth
or no," cried Spears indignantly.   "He saith, if I mistake him
not, that Squire Sang knoweth somewhat of the matter.   We
shall see what he may hae to say for himsel when he cometh
before him.   Bring him along here."

"What turmoil is here, I beseech ye, my masters?" demanded
Sang.

"Ah ! Signor Mortimero," cried the Italian, with a deplor-
able face of terror; "a—a—ah ! It is moss joy for me to see
dee ; I ask dem to bring me to dee—dey no ondairstond me ;
ah, San Lorenzo !—dey do vant to hang me by de naik—dey do
accuse me of de steal."

"Well," said Sang, with a gruff laugh, as if the attempt at a
joke suited but ill with his present vexation and disappointment
at the issue of his combat, " by the mass, methinks thou mayest
be well enow content to be accused of steel in Scotland, for
there lacketh not in Paris those who did boldly affirm that thou
didst employ a much softer metal in thy warlike wares."

"Pah ! no, no, no, signor," exclaimed Martellino, in extreme
distress, " not acciajo, vat dou do call steel van metal—ma, de
steal, de rob ; dey do accuse me of steal a posse of gold, and as
dou art mine verri good friend, I did crave them to bring me to
dee."

"Nay," said Sang, "that is in truth a more serious matter.
An that be made out to be truly the case, thy neck will assuredly
be stretched, friend Audria, in spite of all that I may do to help
thee.   But sith thou hast come to me, I swear that I shall see
that thou hast fair play."

"Oh, Signor Sang, sarai il mio protettore," exclaimed the
Italian, with a gleam of hope in his anxious eyes.   "All dat I
do vant is de play fair.   If dou veelt listen to me, I vill make
dee ondairstond dat I no steal."

"Nay," said Rory Spears, coming forward, "I have no objection that he should be questioned by Squire Mortimer. St. Lowry
forbid that he sudna get justice.   Gif he be innocent o' the
coulpe, and can but make his innocence clear, we sall be saved
the trouble o' hooking him up afore the Yearl and his court. It
wad be but an evil turn to do a poor foreign deevil, to gar him
dree two or three days' jail, whan he hath done naething that
may call for sike a warison.   Question him, Maister Sang.
question him."

"If I am thus appointed preliminary judge," replied Sang,

mounting the dray-horse, " I shall get me on my sack here, that
I may sit at mine ease, and have mine eye on all that passeth
in court. Make way there ; clear the way for the prisoner,"
continued he, motioning to the crowd to form a circle round
him. " Who hath lost the purse the which he is accused of
having taken ?" demanded he.

" My wife's mother, auld Elspeth i' the burrows-town," replied
Rory, and he hastily recapitulated the meagre particulars he had
lately given the Earl of Moray.

" Ha !" said Sang, "and who accuseth Andria Martellino of
being the thief ?"

" Ich do dat, mynheer joodch," replied a squat, thick-set,
broad-faced, heavy-looking German.

' And who mayest thou be, friend ?" asked Sang ; "and what
mayest thou have to effunde that may throw light upon this
affair ? "

" Mine name ist Hans Eisenfelsenbroken, de grat Yarman,
dat mach de armou better nor nobody dat can mach dem so well.
Ich dit see de borse in de hond of dis him here mit mine own
eyes."

" A suspicious evidence," said Sang shaking his head gravely,
"a most suspicious evidence ; trust me, I shall tell no store by
it without strong corroboration. Hath the prisoner yet been
searched ?"

" Nay, there hath as yet been no time," replied the marshalmen.

" Let him be forthwith riped, then," said the esquire.

The marshalmen proceeded to execute his orders, and, to the
joy of Rory Spears, they very speedily drew forth from beneath
his gaberdine a leathern bag, containing a considerable weight of
coin.

" By St. Lowry, but that is my auld mother's money-bag,"
cried Rory Spears, eyeing it from a distance.

" Let me have it," said Sang ; "knowest thou thy mother's
money-bag by any mark ?"

" Yea," replied Spears, readily ; " it hath E. S. on the twa
lugs of it, and a cross on the braid side."

" Of a truth, this is the very bag," said the squire ; " the
marks are all here."

" Eh ! mine Got, did not Ich tell dee de troot, Mynheer
Spears ! I do know him to be a tafe. Ha, ha ! Er wird be
hanged, and Ich werde have all de trade Ich selbst !" cried the
rival German armourer, with a joy which he could not contain.

" Silence, fellow, and respect the court," cried Sang, in a

tone of authority. "Canst thou explain how thou hadst this leathern purse, Master Martellino?" continued he. "By St. Andrew, if thou canst not, it will go hard with thee."

"Ah, si, signor," replied Martellino, with a face of joy, "de page of dy vorship, de good Signor Lees, he happain to be vid me in my shop at de time after I did sell de great armour to de big gigante, and he did see him give to me de posse of gold dat is dere—van fifty broad piece of gold."

"That is thy mother's sum to a tittle," said Sang, addressing Rory. "But how camest thou to receive so much money from the dastard knave for a suit of armour?" continued he, putting the question to the Italian.

"He did bribe me to give him van of mine vaine horses, dat do carry mine goods," replied the Italian; "and he did give me de posse and de money and all."

Archibald Lees vouched for the truth of all this; and some one in the crowd, who had been in Forres during the fire, had remarked the uncouth and gigantic figure as it glided into the old bedrid woman's house; and having been struck with the strangeness of its appearance, had particularly remembered its passing speedily out again in great haste. Another remembered that the false knight and his two accomplices had lodged in a house of entertainment next door to Elspeth Spears' house; and it was even supposed by many that they had aided the conflagration, after it was begun by the Wolfe of Badenoch and his party.

All was now clear, and the upright judge proceeded to pronounce his decision.

"Let the money be forthwith told over, and let it, and the bag that holds it, be restored to Master Roderick Spears, as custos thereof for his aged mother. Let the armour, the which hath been gathered piecemeal from the plain, be restored to the rightful owner, Signor Andria Martellino; and let him have our judgment-seat also, sith it doth of right belong to him. I do hereby absolve him from all coulpe. Albeit he is sharp enow in a bargain, verily I believe he would hardly steal. As for thee, Mynheer Eisenfelsenbroken, I shall only say that thy zeal to further justice was rather of the eagerest, and mought have been more creditable to thee had not the culprit, against whom thou wert so ready to witness, been thy rival in trade. Thy conduct will doubtless have its weight with all good men. And now I dissolve the court," added he, jumping from the dray-horse, and proceeding to mount his own charger, which the page held for him.

The German went grumbling away, disappointed wickedness giving a blacker hue to his swarthy face.

" Ah, Signor Sang," exclaimed the Italian, coming up to him with tears of gratitude in his eyes ; " dou hast been mine good friend ; dou hast vin dine armour. Here is de money—here is de price thou deedst pay me. Take it back."

" What, fellow ! " cried Sang, jocularly, putting him by ; " what, wouldst thou bribe the hand of justice ? Wouldst thou soil that which should be pure ? Avoid, I tell thee, avoid ;" and, putting spurs to his horse, he rode off towards the lists, followed by the cheers of those who had witnessed the scene.

CHAPTER XLVI.

The English Ambassador and the gallant Lindsay.

By the time Mortimer Sang returned to the lists, he was disappointed to find that he had no chance left of establishing his reputation that night against a worthier antagonist. The Earl of Fife had already dropped his white wand, and orders had been issued for the clearance of the enclosure and shutting the barriers. The heralds had commanded the banners to be furled, and all were now on the move.

The gay groups of chevaliers and ladies returned from the lists in independent parties, some to the Castle, and others to their pavilions on the field, to prepare for joining the general assemblage at the banquet in the Hall of Randolph. The number of guests who met there at the usual hour was much greater than on any of the former occasions, many knights having arrived during the previous evening, or during that day, that they might have their heraldic blazons and trophies put up in the chapel of St. John the Baptist, to give them a right to tilt at the tournament. The Countess of Moray resumed her place beside her lord, at the head of the board. Sir Patrick Hepborne attended the party of the Lady of Dirleton, who, with her lord, showed him an increase of kindness each successive time they met ; but when he addressed the Lady Jane de Vaux, she seemed to have put on that frosty and chilling air which had given him so much vexation in the Countess of Moray.

The conversation naturally turned on the exhibition of the day, and was for some time confined to the various private dialogues in which it had sprung up. Praise fell on some few names—Sang's conduct, and his amusing chase were talked of

21

with commendation of him, and ridicule of his opponent, the impostor Knight of Cheviot, of whose robbery of the old woman's purse all were now made aware. Some young knights were mentioned with approbation, but the general feeling was, that the exhibition had been poor, and much more was hoped for from to-morrow.

By degrees the hum of voices that prevailed around the festive board began to subside beneath the interest that was gradually excited by a conversation now arising between the Lord of Welles and some of his English knights, on the one hand, and several of the Scottish chevaliers on the other; and, at last, so deep was the silent attention it produced, that every word of it was heard by all present.

"My Lord Earl of Moray," said the Lord Welles, "I feel much beholden to thee for having persuaded me hither from Scone; for, however tedious and tiresome mought have been the journey, it hath given me an opportunity of satisfying myself and my friends of the unbounded liberality and magnificence of thy hospitality, the which can be surpassed by nothing south of Tweed. But I hope thou wilt take no offence at the plainness of speech and honesty which I use, when I tell thee that had thy Scottish tilting been all the inducement thou hadst to offer me, I mought have as well staid where I was, as I should most assuredly have been but meagrely recompensed for the hardships and deprivations of my long and wearisome pilgrimage through so large a portion of your trackless Scottish forests and wastes."

"Nay, my Lord Welles," replied the Earl of Moray, "I care not what may have occasioned me the honour of thy presence at Tarnawa, enow for me is the satisfaction of its enjoyment, enhanced as it is by the gracious reception of what hospitality I may offer thee. Yet of a truth it erketh me to find that thou hast lacked that pleasure in the survey of the exercises of this day's jousting the which I had hoped to afford thee. Thou knowest that such meetings of arms are but rare with us in Scotland, and we may not look for that expertness the which doth distinguish the tourneys of more southern climes; yet had I hoped that thou mightest have been in some sort amused."

"Nay, perdie, I said not that I was not amused," cried the Lord Welles, with a sarcastic leer—"I said not that I was not amused; for amused I certainly was, and that exceedingly too; but amusement is not what I do ever look for in beholding the exercise of the lists. When I do lack amusement, I do hie me to view the tomblesteers, and those who do practise jonglerie; and indeed I did of a truth see many to-day who were very well fitted for shining among a corps of tumblers; and so I could not choose but be amused, yea even unto laughter, as I did witness the ingenious summersaults they performed. Yet looking, as I am ever accustomed to do, for firm sitting and well-addressed lances in the lists, depardieux, I could not but be disappointed that thou hadst nothing better to show me in behalf of Scottish chivalry."

"Thou knowest, my Lord Welles," said the Earl calmly, " that these were but the novices in arms, to whom the license of this day and to-morrow is given to exercise themselves withal. Judge not too hastily, I beseech thee, of our Scottish chivalry, of whom thou hast but as yet seen the feeble efforts of the braunchers."

"I should not wish to judge too hastily," replied the Lord Welles; "but if the young falcons show such poor courage of flight, parfay, I see not great hope of their ever winging well up to the quarry. If thy youthful knighthood of Scotland show no more bravely, depardieux, there is but little chance of much shining metal or skill being displayed among those who have grown tall under such awkward and unseemly practice."

"My most excellent Lord," said Sir Piers Courtenay, following up the speech of his principal, " my most sweet, excellent, and highly-respected Earl of Moray, I must be permitted to add to those remarks, the which it hath pleased the judicious and nicely-observant Lord Welles to effunde, that I did, to my inexpressible astonishment and dismay, yea, and almost to the doubting the accuracy of the observation of mine eyes, perceive, and I hope thou wilt forgive me for thus daring to divulge it, always believing that I do so without meaning offence, and giving me credence for the entertainment of the most perfect respect and consideration for your Lordship; I did verily perceive, I say, several grievous outrages on the established rules for the equipment of men and horses in those who did ride to-day. Three spurs did I observe that were too high set on the heels, by the fourth part of an inch at least; one did I notice of a vile fashion; one bridle-bit was all courbed awry; one dagger was worn nearly, though not quite, an inch too low; divers of the wreaths were ill adjusted on the helmets (the ladies," bowing round to them as he said so, " will pardon me for adventuring on criticism so nearly affecting them); some of the crests were an inch too high; and, to conclude, there were more than one surcoat ill cut. Now, I do crave thy permission to remark, most potent Earl, that he who doth neglect these highly essential,

though minute points of chivalry, cannot be expected to excel in
the greater and more obvious."

"I do hope, my noble Earl of Moray," said Sir William de
Dalzell roguishly—"I do hope that thou wilt exert thy power
and thine influence over the young and rising sprigs of Scottish
chivalry, that they may arm themselves more en regle ; but,
that they may strictly and correctly do so, it doth behove thee
to hunt out and catch that large ensample of good and well-
fashioned English knighthood the which did with such brilliancy
grace our Scottish lists this day—he of the Cheviot mountains,
I do mean, for I am credibly informed that he is of English
fabrication ; but I trow it will puzzle thee sore to find a Scot,
whether knight, esquire, or page, who can run with him ; yet
ought he natheless to be hunted out, caught, and exhibited for
the amelioration of our salvage nation ; yea, and after his death
he should be speedily embowelled, embalmed, and stuffed, to be
set up as a specimen of the rigid and scrupulous accuracy of
chivalric arming practised by English knights, to the securing
of the improvement of Scottish taste and the establishment of a
purer and more perfect description of it than hath hitherto prevailed in such matters, to the latest generation."

"Thou dost not call by the glorious name of knight that
impostor who assumed the character and name for some villainous purpose, and who had the lion's skin torn from his scoundrel
carcase ?" exclaimed the Lord Welles, with a haughty and indignant air.

"It mattereth not whether he were knight or no," replied Sir
William de Dalzell ; "of one thing we are all certain, and that
is, that he was ane Englishman."

"And are all Englishmen to be judged by the ensample of
such a craven as that ? one, too, who was hatched on the very
borders of Scotland ?" replied the Lord Welles, with a slight
expression of anger.

"Nay," said Sir David Lindsay of Glenesk, "nay, my good
Lord, not so ; but neither are the deeds of all Scottishmen to be
judged by the nerveless essays of a few untaught striplings. I
do beseech thee to suspend thy decision as to Scottish tilting
until our tourney doth commence, and I do give thee leave to
call us gnoffes if thou wilt, yea, tomblesteers, if so be thou dost
then think we deserve any such opprobrious epithets ; but if I
mistake not, thou shalt see enow to satisfy thee that thou
mayest meet with some in Scotland who may be an overmatch
for the best of thine English knights."

"Parfay, thou goest far, Sir David Lindsay," said the

Lord Welles, with a sneer; "meseems it thou knowest but little of the mettle of English chivauncie, to talk of it so slightingly."

"Nay, I went not farther than I did intend," replied the Scottish knight; "I trow I have seen good emptying of saddles in my day, and have encountered knights of all nations, and I am bold to say that were I to choose my champion it should not be from England he should be taken, while we have Scotsmen left to afford me good picking. At present, thanks be to God, we have whole armies of knights, any one of whom, so far from provoking an Englishman's mirth, will, by the very mention of his name alone, make any southern chevalier look grave."

"Nay, boast not, Lindsay," said the gallant Douglas, "we can prove enow by deeds to set us above vaunting."

"I vaunt not, my Lord Earl of Douglas," replied Sir David Lindsay; "yet when vaunts are the only weapons used against us, what can a man do?"

"Let words have no place, then," said the Lord Welles, with considerable eagerness, as well as haughtiness of manner—"let words have no place; and if thou knowest not the chivalry and the valiant deeds of Englishmen, appoint me a day and a place where thou listeth, and, depardieux, thou shalt have experience to thine edification."

"If it so please thee, then, to waive thy privileges, my Lord," quickly rejoined Sir David Lindsay; "if so be, I say, that thou wilt condescend to waive thy privileges, and that thou wilt vouchsafe to honour our lists with an exhibition of thy skill and nerve, by St. Andrew I will gladly meet thee to-morrow; yea, or if thou shouldst wish to eschew the encounter in thine own sacred person, of a truth I shall be well contented to take whichsoever of thy companions thou mayest be pleased to assign me. We shall at least be sure that the appearance of one English knight in the lists shall give a zest to the jousting which to-day's exhibition did so meagrely supply."

"I do beseech thee, my noble and most fair Lord," said Sir Piers Courtenay to the Lord Welles—"I do beseech thee, let me be the supremely felicitous knight who may appear under the banner of St. George to combat in honour of England."

"Nay, Courtenay," said the Lord Welles, "I can neither resign to thee the right I have obtained to the gallant Sir David Lindsay, nor can I submit to tilt now; but if Sir David will indulge me so far as to name some other time and place, verily, I shall pledge myself to give him the meeting, yea, and that, too, with as much good-will as he can wish for it."

" By the mass, I care not though thou dost make the meeting in England, or even in London itself," said Sir David Lindsay. " Let me have a safe-conduct from the English King for myself and party and I will not scruple to ride, yea, even to the farthermost point of thy southern soil in search of an antagonist so desirable."

" Let it be on London Bridge, then," said the Lord Welles.

" On London Bridge ! " muttered a number of the Scottish knights, as if they thought that it was but hardly liberal in the English noble to close so narrowly with the wide proposal of their champion.

" Yea, on London Bridge, or in thine own garden, if it so listeth thee, my Lord Welles," replied the staunch Sir David, without attending to the ejaculations of his friends. " Let us not delay to record the conditions."

" My word is enow for this night, I do trust," replied the Lord Welles, rising and offering his hand across the table to Sir David Lindsay, who took it in the most friendly manner. " To-morrow we may have the terms properly drawn up at greater leisure."

" So then, 'tis as it should be," said the Earl of Moray. " Let a brimming goblet be filled. I drink to the health of the Lord Welles and the health of Sir David Lindsay of Glenesk, and let both names float together in friendly guise on the same mantling mazer."

This double health was received with loud acclamations by all, and the goblets circulated briskly to do honour to it.

CHAPTER XLVII.

The Earl of Fife's Council Meeting—The Challenge between the Scottish and English Knights.

THE health had hardly well gone round ere the shrill notes of a bugle were heard, followed by a stir that arose in the court-yard, the noise of which even reached the ears of those in the hall. A messenger had arrived express, and a letter was speedily delivered to the Earl of Fife.

" Ha ! " said he, with an air of surprise, as he surveyed the impression of the signet attached to the purple silk in which it was wrapped ; and then hastily breaking it open, glanced rapidly over its contents.

All eyes were turned towards him with eager inquiry. An

expression of earnest attention to what he read was very visibly marked on his features.

" Your pardon, brother," said he, starting up at length, after a moment's thought ; "I crave your pardon, and that of this honourable company, but this letter is from my Royal father, and on pressing state affairs. I must of needscost break up the banquet sooner than thy wonted hospitality would authorize me to demand of thee, were the business of a less urgent nature ; but we must hold a council straightway to determine how we may best and most speedily fulfil the wishes of His Majesty. I shall wait thy coming in thy private apartment, and shall by and by hope for the attendance of such of the nobles and knights here assembled as may be required to aid our resolves."

Having said so, the Earl of Fife bowed graciously to the company with such a sweeping, yet particularizing glance, as left each individual in the firm belief that he had been especially distinguished by the great man's notice ; and, putting his hand into his bosom, he moved down the hall with all the appearance of being instantly absorbed in deep reflection.

The Lord Welles and his suite of English knights, darting very significant looks towards one another, sat a few minutes, and then rising, retired in a body. The Countess of Moray, and the rest of the ladies, also soon afterwards left the board, and sought their apartments, and the Earl of Moray instantly broke up the banquet, and hastened to join his brother the Earl of Fife, taking with him the Earl of Douglas and the Earl of Dunbar. Such of the Scottish nobles and knights, however, as conceived that their presence might be required at the expected council, continued to pace the ample pavement in small parties, or to stand grouped together in little knots, all exercising their ingenuity in guessing at the probable cause and nature of so sudden and unlooked-for, and apparently so important a communication. The most prevalent surmise was, that a war with England was to be declared, and the very thought of such a thing gave joy to every manly bosom. Suspicions of the prospect of a rupture between the two countries had begun to be pretty general of late ; and the circumstance of bringing down the English ambassadors to Tarnawa, was by some, who affected to be deeper read in such matters than others, interpreted into a fine piece of state policy to keep them out of the way, while preparations were maturing for the more powerful and successful commencement of hostilities on the part of Scotland. All were impatient to know the truth, and when a messenger came to the door of the hall with a roll of names, which he read over, calling

on those of the nobles and knights who were named in it, to
remain in the hall, and take their places at the board, at the
upper end of it, according to their rank, those who were so
selected could not well hide their satisfaction, while those who
were compelled to withdraw did so with extreme reluctance.

Sir Patrick Hepborne was overjoyed to find that he was to
be one of those in whom the Earl of Fife wished to confide. He
took his seat at the table with the rest, and the most profound
silence succeeded to the sounds of mirth and pleasure which had
so lately reigned within the hall. Whatever conjectures might
have escaped the lips of those around the board, whilst they
mingled carelessly with those who were idly speculating on the
probable purport of the King's message, they now considered the
seal of silence imposed on their lips, by their being selected as
councillors ; and accordingly they sat gazing at each other with
grave and solemn looks, calmly awaiting the arrival of the Earl
of Fife. Certain faces there were which betrayed something like
a consciousness of greater self-importance than the rest, as if
they either knew, or would have had others believe that they
knew, something more than those around them. But whatever
they knew or thought they ventured not to express it.

At length the Earls of Fife, Moray, Douglas, and Dunbar
appeared, and took their seats at the upper end of the table.
All eyes and ears were fixed in attention; and the Earl of Fife,
laying the King's letter and packet on the table, began to open
the business he had to communicate to them.

"My Lords and Gentlemen," said he, in a tone of voice
which, though audible enough to every one of them, was yet too
low to have found its way through any of the crannies of the
door at the farther end of the hall, " I shall be as brief as possible with you. Ye all know how great is my consideration for
you individually, so I trust that I have no need to waste time
in assuring ye of my love for ye all, or of the zeal with which I
am filled for promoting your respective interests. Highly sensible am I of the great blessing that hath befallen Scotland, in
raising up such store of wisdom and valour among her sons, as
I do know to exist in the persons of the noble lords and honourable knights by whom I have now the felicity of being surrounded ; and I do the more congratulate myself upon this
knowledge at the present time, seeing that the wisdom and the
valour I have spoken of must now be called forth into important
action. For, to withhold the news from you no longer, Scotland
is about to be, nay, more probably hath been already invaded—
a large army having hovered on the Eastern Marches, threaten-

ing the Merse with fire and sword, the which may have ere this been poured out upon them. Your good King, and my Royal father, hath sent this intelligence express from Aberdeen, where he now abideth, at the same time commanding our instant attendance there to counsel and advise him, and to receive his orders for our future conduct. We are, moreover, directed to lead thither with us all the strength of dependants we can muster, and to take such immediate measures as may ensure the instant gathering of those districts which are under the control of each of us respectively. A large force must of needscost be quickly got together ; it is therefore highly expedient that our vassals should be forthcoming with as little delay as possible, that they may be ready to unite themselves with the host wheresoever and whensoever it may assemble. Such of us as are wanted at Aberdeen must set forward to-morrow. These, then, are the matters and the commands which my Royal father sends you, and which I, as his organ, have been instructed to convey to you."

A murmur of applause ran round the table. Broken sentences burst from the respective knights, each shortly but pithily expressing the satisfaction he felt at the prospect of having something more serious than jousting to occupy him.

"I have yet one more communication to make, my Lords and Gentlemen, of which you must be the witnesses, and I need not say that I entreat you to be the silent witnesses of it. I must convey to the Lord Welles intelligence, which I am not without suspicion he hath been for some time anticipating, from his own private knowledge of events. I mean to crave an immediate conference with him here in your presence ; but it is my wish that no one whom I have here admitted to my confidence will talk to him, or any of the English knights, either now or afterwards of anything I have mentioned. I have to communicate to the Lord Welles the King's license for his departure, and I hope I do not ask too much when I beg that I may be left to do so entirely unassisted, and that nothing he or his shall say may provoke ye to speak. Silence will best accord with your dignity. Go, brother, my Lord Earl of Moray, so please thee, and entreat the presence of the Lord Welles among us, with such of his suite as he may list to accompany him."

The Earl of Moray hastened to obey his brother-in-law, and, during his absence, the Earl of Fife seemed to have retreated into his own thoughts. The knights who sat with him remained in still contemplation of him and of one another. The English envoy was received with dignified decorum.

" My Lord Welles," said the Earl of Fife to him after he was
seated, " I have now to perform a piece of duty to my King, the
which, as it regardeth thee, doth particularly erke me.   As thou
art thyself aware, I have this night received a letter from His
Majesty, and I have now to tell thee, that in it I am commanded
to inform thee that he will dispense with thy further attendance
at his Royal Court.   In so far as our personal intercourse hath
gone, I have good reason to regret that it is to be discontinued
so soon ; and the more so that it hath fallen into my hands to
snap it.   This parchment, which I have now the honour of presenting to thee, doth contain a safe-conduct for thee, and all
with thee, to return into thy native country by the shortest
possible route.   It doleth me much that we are to be so soon
reft of thine agreable society.   Yea, the removal of thy presence is most especially galling at such a time, when all was
prepared for making the days of thy stay in Scotland as light
as mought be.   Our coming tourney will be nought without
thee."

" My Lord of Fife, of a truth this is a most sudden and unlooked-for event," said the Lord Welles, with the appearance, if
not with the reality, of surprise on his countenance.   " Hath
any reason been assigned, the which it may be permitted thee
to utter to me ? "

" His Majesty's reasons, my good Lord, are not always given,"
replied the Earl of Fife, evasively ; " but thou knowest that it
is the part of a subject implicitly to obey, without inquiring too
curiously into the nature of the wires that may be on the stretch
to put him in motion ; and I must submit as well as others.
Hast thou had no communications lately from thine own court?"

" If thy coming tourney doth ever hold," said the Lord
Welles, altogether avoiding the home question of the Earl of
Fife, and glancing curiously into the faces of those around him,
" it will suffer little in its pomp or circumstance, I trow, from
my departure, where thou hast so great an assemblage of Scottish knights to give lustre to it , but if they should be called
away, indeed, by anything connected with my dismissal, it may
in that case dwindle, peraunter, and expire of very consumption
ere it hath been well born."

The Lord Welles's eyes returned from their excursion round
the table, without displaying signs of having gathered anything
from the firm Scottish countenances they had scanned.

" And when must I of needscost set forward, my Lord?"
continued the Lord Welles, addressing the Earl of Fife.

" A party of lances will be in waiting to-morrow morning by

sunrise, to guide and protect thee on thy way, and I do believe that thou wilt find that sufficient time hath been given thee in the parchment thou hast, to make the journey easy. Shouldst thou, peradventure, covet the provision of anything that may contribute to thy comfort or expedition, the which I may have the power to procure for thee, I do beseech thee to let me be informed, and it shall be mine especial care that thou mayest be gratified."

" Nay, my Lord Earl of Fife, I lack nothing," replied the Lord Welles.

" And now, then, my good Lord, I bid thee good night," said the Earl of Fife. "Farewell; it will give me joy again to meet with thee as a friend, until when may St. George be with thee."

" Receive our fullest thanks for all thy gracious courtesy," replied the Lord Welles.

The Earl of Fife now arose with the Earls Douglas, Moray, and Dunbar, and took his leave, with many condescending protestations. The Lord Welles and his friends loitered a little time after he was gone, and the Scottish knights having by this time risen from the council board, he mingled familiarly among them.

" This dismissal of mine is something of the suddenest," said he, in a general kind of manner, to a few of them who were clustered together. "Can any umbrage have been taken? Is it possible King Robert can mean to steal a march on His Majesty of England, and cross the Border ere he giveth him warning? or hath he already done so with an English envoy in his territories?"

He paused after each of these short interrogatories, as if in the hope of fishing out a reply from some one, which might instruct him in the extent of the information that had come from the Scottish Monarch; but no one exhibited either the will or the power to gratify him, and he adroitly changed to another subject.

" Ha! Sir David Lindsay," said he, turning round and addressing that knight, "let us not forget to settle the engagement and darreigne that hath passed between us."

" Nay, trust me, that shall not I," replied Sir David Lindsay; " I but waited until thou hadst concluded thy weightier and more pressing affairs, to entreat thee that we may enter into our articles of tilting now. I do hope that nothing may arise to baulk us of our sport."

" What, I beseech thee, can baulk us?" demanded the Lord

Welles slyly, and probably with the hope that he would yet catch what he had been angling for, by throwing this long line, and drawing it so skilfully round.

"Nay, I know not," replied Sir David Lindsay readily; "thou mightst have repented thee peraunter, and it would have sorely grieved me hadst thou wished to draw thy head from our agreement."

"Depardieux, thou needest be in no dread of that, Sir David; I am not a man of that kidney, I promise thee," hastily replied the Lord Welles, in some degree thrown off his guard by the gentle touch which Lindsay had given to his honour; "for whether it be in war or in peace thou shalt have a safe-conduct from King Richard, if I have the influence that I do believe I have; yea, a safe-conduct for thee and thine, that thou mayest on thy part fulfil thy behote. Let us straightway hasten to arrange and register the terms of our meeting."

"'Tis well thought of," said Sir David Lindsay; "let us have a clerk to put our mutual challenge in proper style, and distinct and lasting characters, that, each of us having a copy thereof, neither of us may mistake."

A scrivener was accordingly sent for, and the council board, again ordained to change the service it was destined to, now became a theatre, where the nicest points of chivalry and the minutest rules of tilting were canvassed at greater length and with more eagerness of debate than had been bestowed on the much more important business which had been previously gone through there. The superfine judgment of Sir Piers Courtenay in such matters was singularly pre-eminent; and his auditors were extremely edified by some long and very learned disquisitions with which he was pleased to favour them. At length everything was happily adjusted to the satisfaction of both parties, and written copies of the terms being signed and exchanged between the two principals in the proposed affair, they cordially shook hands and separated, with many chivalric and courteous speeches to each other.

Things were no sooner settled thus, than several Scottish knights pressed forward to entreat Sir David Lindsay that they might be permitted to bear him company when the time should be finally fixed. The first of these was Sir William de Dalzell, and another was Sir Patrick Hepborne. To these, and to Sir John Halyburton, Sir David Lindsay readily promised that places should be preserved, however limited a number the safe-conduct might be granted for; but he declined further promises until he could be sure of fulfilling them. The Scottish knights, who had been all too much interested in what was going forward to permit them to leave the hall until everything was finally adjusted, now hastened to call their esquires, and to make those private preparations for travelling which were not publicly to appear until after the departure of the English envoy and his suite.

CHAPTER XLVIII.

The Departure from the Castle of Tarnawa—The Alarm of War.

THE morning had not yet dawned when the court-yard of the Castle re-echoed to the tramp of the mettled steeds of the Lord Welles and the English knights, and their numerous retinue. The gay caparisons of the men and horses, and the gaudily embroidered banners they carried, flaunted and fluttered in vain amid the raw, grey, and chilling light that quenched their glittering lustre, and left them but meagrely visible. A body of Scottish lances, commanded by several trusty officers, stood ready to march with them as a guard, and the troop was of such strength as might overawe any undue curiosity they might display, as well as do them honour, or protect them from injury or insolence during their march through Scotland. The Earl of Moray was on foot to do them the parting civilities of a host.

"Forget not London Bridge," cried a loud voice from the window of a high turret that overlooked the court-yard. The Lord Welles and his knights were already in their saddles. They twisted their necks with some difficulty, so as to have a view upwards, and there they beheld the hairy bosom and sternly-comic features of Sir William de Dalzell, who, in his chemise and bonnet de nuit, had thrust his head and shoulders forth from a window.

"Fear not," cried the Lord Welles; "the meeting shall not fail on the side of England.

"Nor of Scotland neither," replied Dalzell, "if so be that fourfooted beasts can be had to carry our bodies to the muddy banks of thy stinking Thames. I bid thee bon voyage, my Lord, though, by St. Andrew, I envy thee not thine early morning's march; and so I'll to my couch, and court the gentle influence of Morpheus for some hour or twain, for contraire to all due course of nature, I see it threatens to snow."

With these words he threw into the air two large handfuls

of feather-downs, and instantly drew himself in.   The Lord
Welles was half disposed to take the matter up as an insult;
but the Earl of Moray, laughing good-humouredly as the artificial snow descended on the group, soon pacified his excited
indignation.

"Nay, mind him not, my Lord," said he—"no one among
us minds the jest of Sir William de Dalzell; and if we did,
perdie, we should gain little by the trial, for we should only
bring more of his humorous conceits on our heads.   His wit,
how rude soever it may seem, hath no meaning of harm or
insult in it."

The Earl allowed the Lord Welles and his knights to be
some time gone ere he began to summon his people about him,
and to issue his orders for an immediate march.   Sir William
de Dalzell was the first of the Scottish knights, his guests, who
appeared armed cap-a-pie in the court-yard, where the bustle of
the foregoing morning was soon more than renewed.   Two or
three hundred good men of the Earl's followers began to
assemble, with their horses and arms, in obedience to the
summons which had been secretly sent through the population
of the district during the night.   The rumour of the approaching
war spread from mouth to mouth, and rude jokes and laughter
followed its propagation, until the joyous clamour, becoming
louder and louder, began at last to swell till the welkin was rent
with the bursting shouts of the men-at-arms and soldiery, who
rejoiced at the prospect of having something more serious than
a tourney to do with.

Sir Patrick Hepborne sprang from his couch, and began to
busy himself for his departure.   As he moved across the floor,
his naked foot struck against something that felt like the head
of a nail, and was slightly wounded by it.   He stooped to ascertain what it was, when, much to his surprise, he discovered a
ring, with a beautiful emerald set in it, that had slipped into a
crevice between the planks, so as to leave the stone sticking up.
He immediately recognized it as having been worn by the page
Maurice de Grey.   It was of beautifully wrought gold, and, after
a more minute examination, he discovered some Gothic characters within its circle, which he read thus—

> Change never,
> Out love ever
> Thine Eleanore de Selby.

At the very name of Eleanore de Selby, Sir Patrick's heart
beat quicker.   He had no doubt that the jewel had dropped

from the finger of the page, probably the morning he left Tarnawa. He had already resolved to keep it carefully, in remembrance of the boy ; but the legend seemed to prove it to have been a gift to Maurice de Grey from his cousin the Lady Eleanore de Selby ; and the conviction that it had once been hers, all unworthy as she was, imparted to it a tenfold value, which he in vain attempted to struggle against. It seemed to have appeared miraculously to warn him never to forget her, and he resolved to treasure it as a relic of one who could never be his.

Meanwhile the court-yard resounded with the neighing of steeds and the din of arms, and the trumpets and bugles were heard to strike shrilly on the Castle walls, till its very turrets seemed to thrill with their hoarse clangour. It was chiefly thronged by some of the same knights, and some of the same esquires, pages, lacqueys, and steeds, whose painted surcoats of a thousand dies, whose armour glittering with gold and gems, and whose gorgeous attire and furniture, had reflected the rays of the sunrise of the previous morning. But the new-born orb of this day looked upon them in another guise. Though by no means devoid of splendour, what they now wore was more adapted for use than for ornament, and their very countenances displayed more of the fury of joy, and had put on an air of greater sternness, that sorted strangely with their uncouth jeers and laughter. The number of spearmen, bowmen, pole-axe-men, and men-at-arms of all descriptions, was now much larger ; and in addition to this variety of the motley crowd, there were several horse litters in attendance, and numerous batt and sumpter horses loading with the lighter baggage, whilst at the Castle gate appeared a small train of wains and wainmen, who were receiving the heavier articles that were to be transported.

One of the most active men in the midst of the bustle was Rory Spears, who, with a morion on his head, and a back and breast-plate donned instead of his fisherman's coat, was busily occupied assisting in and superintending the loading of the baggage.

"Father," said his daughter Katherine to him, as she at last obtained an opportunity of addressing him, whilst at the same time her eyes wandered to the adjacent spot, where Squire Sang was engaged in getting Sir Patrick Hepborne's party in order ; "would I could wend with thee, father !"

"Hey !" exclaimed Rory, turning suddenly round upon her, and at the same time poising a large package on his broad shoulder, and keeping it there with one hand, whilst with the other he brandished his gaud-clip, with singular energy of action ; "what ails thee, lass? Is the wench wud, think ye? Wouldst thou to the wars, sayest thou? Na, na, Kate; the camp be nae fit place for sike like as thee, I trow. What, expose thee, with all thy leddy learning and madame 'haviour, to be the hourly butt for the ribald jests of the guards, and the boozing companions of the sultering huts! By my fackins, that would be it indeed. Na, na! stay thee at home, lassie, and look to the Countess, and thy new young leddy; ay, and thy mother Alice, and the auld woman in the Brugh alswa ; and when I come back, my winsome grouse-pout, I'll bring thee some bonny-waully frae the wars. We shall ha' spulzie to pick and choose amang, I rauckon." So saying, he threw his right arm, gaud-clip and all, around his daughter's waist, and kissing her heartily and with much affection, hastened off with his burden.

He was no sooner gone, than Mortimer Sang, seizing one moment from the bustle of his occupation, strode across to where Katherine was standing, gazing in silent, abstracted, and melancholy guise, towards the pile of baggage heaped up on the ground, which her father's powerful arms had been rapidly diminishing. With the corner of her eye she marked the squire's approach ; but the fulness of her heart told her that she dared not look up, lest it should run over. Sang stood for some moments absorbed in contemplation of her, his eyes rapidly feeding his passion, and his passion slowly filling his eyes.

"Mrs. Katherine," said he at length, "ahem! Mrs. Katherine. Of a truth, it is a bitter and ill-favoured thing to be compelled to part with those with whom we have been happy. Verily, 'twas but yestre'en that you and I were right blithe together, and by this e'en there will be many miles atween us—ay, and who can tell, for a matter of that, whether it may ever again please Heaven to bring us together for even one such jolly evening—Heigho!"

Katherine could stand this no longer, but giving way to a burst of grief, hid her eyes in her apron, and being too much agitated to speak, and too much shocked at this her involuntary disclosure of her attachment to the squire, she ran off and disappeared into the Castle.

Sang brushed the mists from his eye-lids with the back of his hand, that his eyes might follow the fair vision as it flew. A Gothic doorway received it. He heaved up a sigh, that rose from the bottom of his heart, and again sunk heavily to the abyss whence it was raised, and stood for some moments gazing at the black void that no longer possessed her figure. Again his eyes were dimmed with moisture, again he cleared them, and again he sighed; and casting one look towards his men, who were standing idle in consequence of his absence, and another to the doorway, he seemed to stand fixed between the equal attractions of duty on the one hand and love on the other. A confused and half-smothered laugh roused him from his dream. It proceeded from the troopers and lacqueys of his party, who were all regarding him, and nodding and winking to each other. Stung with an immediate sense of the ludicrous appearance he must have presented his men, the balance of his will was overthrown at once, and he sprang off to rate them for their idleness.

"What ho, my masters, meseems as if ye had lost your main-spring, that ye stand so idle. By the bones of the blessed St. Baldrid, but I will baste your lazy ribs with my lance-shaft, an ye stand staring in that fashion; by all that is good I will make kettle-drums of yere bodies. Ha! I'll warrant me I shall alter your music, ay, and change these jokes and that laughter of yours into grinnings that shall make your fortunes at e'er a fair in Christendom. Go to, bestir yourselves, knaves." And following up this with a few well-directed hints of a more substantial description, laid across the shoulders and backs of those whom he conceived to be most deserving of his chastisement, they were all as busy as ants in a moment.

"Master Spears," said Sang to Rory, as he passed him accidentally, "it erketh me to learn that thou goest not with us."

"Not ganging with thee!" exclaimed Rory, with an expression of countenance partaking partly of surprise at the question, partly of doubt whether it was put seriously or in joke, and partly of the pleased anticipation of the proud triumph he was about to enjoy when he should have breath to pour forth his answer; "not ganging with thee, Master Sang! By St. Lowry, but I am at a loss to fortake thy meaning. What wouldst thou be at? Dost thou mean to say that I wend not with my Lord the Yearl? If thou dost, by'r lackins, but thou art as sore wide o' the mark as if thou hadst shot blindfold. I'd have thee to know, Sir Squire," continued Rory, raising himself up to his full height, sticking his left arm akimbo, and thrusting out his right to its utmost horizontal extent, his hand at the same time resting on the hook of his gaud-clip, the shaft of which was pointed to the earth, "I'd have thee to know, my

22

most worthy friend, Master Mortimer, and be it known to thee,
with all the due submission and respect the which I do bear
thee, that thy master, Sir Patrick, mought no more take the
field withouten thee, than my master, the noble Yearl of
Moray, would get into his saddle till he saw me at his back.
Trust me, though I cannot ride tilting as thou dost, nor loup
barriers, nor gallop after runaway Gogs, Magogs, and Goliaths
of Gath, in armour, as thou mayest, I can push as good a
thrust with a lance, when I take a grup o't in real yearnest,
against a chield that may be ettling to do me the like favour,
as I can yerk out this same gaud-clip i' my hand here, again a
rae or ane otter beast.   Na, na—the Yearl gang to the wars
withouten me !   No possible."

   " Nay, as to its being possible, Master Spears," replied Sang,
folding his arms across his breast with a waggish air, " trust
me, I can assure thee of the fact, seeing I did hear the Earl say
to his esquire that thou wert to tarry at Tarnawa, to wait on a
young English damsel, who might lack thy protection for a
certain journey she hath in contemplation."

   " Ha !" exclaimed Spears, who had stood in utter dismay as
Sang was speaking; " art thou sickerly assured of what thou
sayest, Squire Mortimer ?   My faith, things be come to ane
queer pass indeed, sin' they are gawin to transmew rough Rory
Spears into a squire of dames.   They will, nae doot, make a
tire-woman of him ere it be lang.   But, by my troth, I ken
mair aboot mewing of hawks than mutching of maidens, and
there is no sweet essence, oil, or unguent to me like the guff o'
a wolf, a tod, or a brock.   Aweel-aweel, the Yearl's wull sall
be my wull ; but this I will say, though it may be I should not,
that if ever it gaed contraire to the grain wi' me to do his
bidding, by St. Lowry, now is the very time.   But what maun
be maun be—that's a' I can say till't."   So shouldering his
gaud-clip, he slowly and sullenly retired into the Castle, his
utter disappointment and mortification being but ill concealed
by his drooping head, and his hair that hung loose about his
face from under his morion.

   Rory sought his Lord, and, notwithstanding the bustle of
business in which the Earl was immersed, he succeeded in
obtaining an interview with him, when, to his indescribable
horror, he discovered that all that Sang had told him was
correct.   His grudge at his daughter's present service now grew
into a dislike to her whom she served, who, besides her crime of
being an Englishwoman, no light one in his eyes, had also to
answer for his present humiliation.   The Earl paid him some

handsome compliments ou his fidelity, his good conduct, and his valour, the possession of which qualities had occasioned his selection as the person to be left at Tarnawa, to be in readiness for the honourable and delicate piece of duty which might be perchance required of him. But even these high commendations from the quarter most valued by him were insufficient to make amends for the mortification he felt at his disappointment, nor could they season the proposed duty so as to make it palatable to him.

"Aweel-aweel, my Lord Yearl of Moray, thy wull sall be my wull," was all that his Lordship could extract from Rory Spears.

After Mortimer Sang had arranged everything about the baggage of his party, and got the men and horses in proper order for the march, he took the opportunity of stealing away from them for a few moments, with the hope of obtaining a sight of Katherine Spears, whom he now discovered to be, even more than he had ever supposed, the ruling magnet of his heart. He found her drowned in tears.

"Fair Katherine," said he as he approached her with the utmost delicacy and tenderness, "why art thou thus grief-by-woxen? Knowest thou not that thy father tarrieth with thee at Tarnawa? Dost thou not already know that he goeth not with the host?"

"Yea, Sir Squire," sobbed Katherine, hastily drying her eyes at the sound of his voice, and vainly endeavouring to wipe away all traces of her sorrow; "yea, I did so learn this morning from my lady."

"For whom grievest thou, then, fair maiden?" demanded Sang. "Surely thou canst not be so oppressed at thoughts of the Earl's departure?"

"Nay, as to that, no," replied the artless girl. "It may be I shall partake in the woe of my Lady Countess. But I weep not for him. Nay, I weep not for any one now."

Mrs. Katherine spoke the truth. She certainly did not weep at that particular moment, but the exertion it cost her to restrain her tears becoming much more than she was equal to, their accumulation was too powerful to be withstood, and, overwhelming every dam and barrier that maidenly prudence and propriety had raised to confine them, they burst forth more violently than ever, and poor Katherine sobbed aloud as if her heart would have broken. If there were still any remains of resolution about that of the squire, it melted at once like the snow-wreath that lies in the direct course of some wide and resistless deluge of waters, which, as it is dissolved, mingles itself with and swells the very flood that creates its dissolution. He blubbered like an infant.

"Lovely Katherine," said he, sitting down beside her, and taking her hand with the utmost respect and tenderness—"most beauteous Mrs. Spears—my loveliest of all damsels, be composed, be comforted, I beseech thee; my dearest Katherine, my love, my only love, be composed and tell me—ah, tell, I entreat thee, whether I have any share in these precious drops? Tell me thou weepest for my departure, and those liquid diamonds that fall on my hand will be more prized by me than the purest gems that ever came from the East. Tell me but that I shall carry thy heart with me when I go, and I will leave thee mine in exchange for it, and swear on the honour and faith of a trusty esquire, to be thine, and thine only, for ever. What is glory, what is renown, what is the exalted rank of knighthood itself, without the possession of her we love? Say but thou wilt love me, sweet Katherine, and, when the war is at an end, I will return to claim thy hand, were it from the uttermost part of the earth. Say, do my hopes deceive me, or am I in very truth happy in being beloved by thee?"

Katherine's paroxysm of grief had been partially arrested, almost from the moment that Squire Mortimer had taken her hand so kindly, and begun to speak. She quickly became more composed as he went on; her cheeks became suffused with blushes, and showed beneath her tears like roses after a shower; smiles soon afterwards came to play over them like the sunbeams over the fresh and fragrant flowers; and, by the time that Mr. Sang had finished, the maiden's confusion, rather than her indistinct murmurs, gave the esquire all the satisfaction he could have wished. They swore eternal fidelity to each other, and, after a short and sweet conversation, and an exchange of some little love-tokens had taken place between them, they separated, to attend to their respective avocations.

By this time all was in order for the march. Already had several of the nobles and knights departed independently from the Castle; and those who remained, being of the Earl's kinsmen or connexions, were to guide their motions by his. He resolved to begin his journey immediately, being anxious to accomplish several miles of way ere the sun was yet risen to the height of his fury. The trumpets sounded; the clangour stirred up the hearts of both men and steeds, and they expressed their joy by stunning shouts and repeated neighings. But their shrill brazen voices were a death-knell to the departing joy of many a soft bosom that sighed within the Castle, and to none more than to that of Katherine Spears. Her nerves were subjected to no fresh trial of resolution, for the esquire's absence from his party, at the moment of starting, would have been inadmissible.

The trumpet brayed aloud, for the third time, its harsh summons, and the court-yard rang as the mailed horsemen leaped into their steel-cased saddles. The Countess of Moray was on the terrace with her maidens, waving many a sighing farewell to her gallant lord. The Earl gave the word, and, in company with his brothers-in-law the Earls of Fife and Caithness, his brother the Earl of Dunbar, the Earl of Douglas, Sir David Lindsay, Sir John Halyburton, the Lord of Dirleton, Sir Patrick Hepborne, and others, he rode forth at the Castle gate, followed by the whole column of march.

The troops which he headed were but a small portion of those whose attendance he could command as vassals, being only such horsemen as were ever ready to assemble at a moment's notice, to attend him on any sudden emergency. They now served him as a guard of honour in his journey to the King, and the charge of summoning and mustering the great body of his feudal force, and of despatching them under their proper officers, to join him where he might afterwards direct, was left to his Countess to carry into effect. The cavalcade filed off with a noise like thunder through the gateway, and part of them forming upon the natural glacis beyond, halted until the train of baggage wains had fallen into the line immediately in rear of the horse litters, in which the ladies travelled, and then they closed into the rear of the line of march. The whole moved on slowly through the little hamlet, now silent and deserted, except by its weeping women, its old men, and its children, and then wound into the depth of the forest. An opening among the trees gave them again a view of Tarnawa, and many was the head that turned involuntarily round to look once more at its grey walls, some of them, perhaps, though they little thought so, for the last time.

Sir Patrick lifted up his eyes, raised his beaver, and turned them towards the Castle. He beheld a bevy of white figures grouped together on a bartizan, and white scarfs or handkerchiefs were waving. He smiled in secret as the imagination crossed him that the motion of these was like that which had flashed upon his eyes from the keep of Norham. But his fancy had dreamt so, and the vision having been once engendered, continued to haunt him as he rode at the head of his small troop.

CHAPTER XLIX.

The Lord of Dirleton's Tale—The Bishop of Moray and his Clergy.

THE Earl of Moray led him and his little force through the Meads of St. John. That scene, lately so gay, was now considerably changed. Most of the pavilions on the hither meadow had been struck, and the knights who had occupied them had already left the ground with their people, whilst others waited to join the line of march. The temporary bridge was there to afford them a passage; but the demolition of the lists had been already begun under the superintendence of the pursuivants, and others of the heralds, to whom the property of the materials was an acknowledged perquisite. The inhabitants of the little town of tents and temporary huts were in humming motion, like a hive of bees that are about to swarm. All were preparing to depart with lamentations, their occupation being gone with the tournament that had assembled them; and pack-horses, and wains, and rude carts without wheels, that were dragged along the ground on the pointed extremities of the shafts projecting behind, were loaded with the utmost expedition.

The street of the burgh presented a different picture. Thither the news of the approaching war had not yet reached, and the townsmen rested with blackened hands and faces from their melancholy work of clearing out the burnt rubbish from the foundations of their houses, to gaze, and wonder, and speculate on the armed force. Loud were the cheers with which they greeted the Earl of Moray, and they were not tired with these manifestations of their gratitude to their generous lord until they had accompanied him for a considerable way beyond the eastern end of the town. At the distance of some five or six miles from Forres the Earl halted his men, just where the half-wooded and half-cultivated country gave place to a bare heath of considerable extent, and where the gentle breeze was permitted to come cool and unbroken against their throbbing temples, after they were relieved from the thraldom of their bassinets and morions; whilst the oaks that fringed the moor, and straggled into it in groups and single trees, enabled them to find sufficient shade from a now oppressive sun, to eat their morning's meal in comfort.

A pavilion was pitched for the reception of the nobles,

knights, and ladies, and, after partaking of the refreshment that
was provided under it, they wandered forth in parties to waste
the time beneath the trees, until the horses should have been
fed, and everything prepared for continuing the march.   Sir
Patrick Hepborne, having fallen into conversation with De
Vaux, the old Lord of Dirleton, wandered slowly with him to a
clump of trees at some distance, and they sat down together on
an old oak that had fallen by natural decay from the little grove
of gigantic trees that threw a shade over it.   The place was
sufficiently retired to promise security from interruption, and
Hepborne longed much to obtain from his companion the distressing history to which he and his lady had alluded on the
evening of their first meeting at Tarnawa.   He felt it difficult,
however, to hint at a subject of which he already knew enough
to satisfy him, that it could not fail to be productive of painful
emotions to his father's old friend, and he would have left it
untouched had not accident led to it.

"That blasted moor, where tree grows not," observed the
Lord of Dirleton, "and where, as thou see'st, the stunted heath
itself can hardly find food for life, amid the barren sand of
which its soil is composed, was cursed into sterility by the infernal caldron of the weird-hags who, by their hellish incantations,
did raise a poisonous marsh-fire to mislead Macbeth ; and did so
drag him down from the path of honour and virtue, to perish in
a sea of crimes his soul would once have shuddered at.   See'st
thou yonder huge cairn of stones?   Some men say that it marks
the very spot where the foul crones first met him, as, with his
associate Banquo, he did return victorious from the overthrow
of the Danes, who did invade Fife, and whose bravest leaders
he sent to eternal repose in St. Colme's Isle ; it was there, I
say, that tradition reporteth they did appear to him, when, with
the flattering tongue of the great Tempter, they did salute him
Thane of Glammis and of Cawdor, and alswa King hereafter."

"Tell me, I pray thee," said Sir Patrick, "what make these
soldiers who do so crowd towards the cairn?   Methinks some
of them on horseback, and some of them on foot, are riding and
running full tilt around it, as if in frolicsome chase of each
other."

The Lord of Dirleton was silent for some moments.   He
sighed, and, much to Sir Patrick's surprise, tears came into his
eyes.   He was deeply affected for some moments.

"Thou must of needscost marvel, Sir Knight," said he at
length, " to see me so much moved by a question the which is
so simple in itself, and the which did fall so naturally from thee.

But thy wonder will cease anon. Be it known to thee, that these men do run and ride in that manner, in compliance with a well-received belief, that to surround the cairn with three times three circuits, securely buys the happiness of him who doth so, for the space of three times three months. Peraunter thy marvel will now be enhanced, why I should have wept at the notice of a practice so apparently harmless; but that thine astonishment may forthwith cease, I shall haste me to tell thee the cause of these tears. I am not sorry that I have been led thus accidentally to the subject, sith I did well intend me to effund into thine ear, at first fitting time, the circumstances of that bereavement of the which, when I did once before obscurely hint to thee, thou didst then seem to wish to hear more."

The Lord of Dirleton paused, as if to recollect himself, and, after an effort to master certain feelings that agitated him, he began his narrative—

"It was about three months after the Lady of Dirleton had happily given birth to her first daughter, that I left her and her baby in full health, and soon afterwards travelled northward into these parts, with mine early friend, John Dunbar, Earl of Moray. We had been at Lithgow together, at the proclamation of King Robert, and I had yielded to my Lord's wishes, to bear him company for some few days at his Castle of Tarnawa. After a short sojournance in his hospitable hall, I reached this spot on my way homewards, and chancing to halt here, as we do now, I was told of the virtues of the Witch's Cairn. Bethinking me that it was good to secure nine months of happiness at so easy a price, I spurred my horse into a gallop, and began to course around it at full speed.

"I had already encircled it twice three times, and had begun the seventh round, when my horse was suddenly scared by the appearance of a haggard female figure that arose from among the docks and clot leaves in the middle of the heap, and glared fearfully at me. The animal started so unexpectedly aside that he threw me from the saddle, and I lay stunned by the severity of the fall. When my senses returned to me, I found myself in the hands of my people, who were busied about me under a tree. Convinced that it was some supernatural thing that had so strangely crossed me, and put a period to mine attempt to work against fate, I did eagerly demand of those about me what had become of the unsightly witch. All agreed that she had limped slowly away before their eyes until lost in the neighbouring wood; one or two there were who did ween her to be no other than some ancient shepherdess or nerthes-woman, who, wearied with watch, mought liggen her down to rest there, and who had been frayed from her sleep by the sounding tramp of my horse's gallop; but the rest were of my mind, that she was verily some evil witch, whose blasted form and eyne boded some dire malure.

"Sore oppressed with the belief of approaching calamity, I did hie me back to·mine own Castle of Dirleton, with a far heavier heart than I had left it, dreading drearily as I went that I should learn some dismal tidings when I should reach thither. But all was well; and as things went not in anywise awry for some time, I began to laugh in secret at my own apprehensions. Prosperity favoured me, indeed, in a somewhat unusual manner. For six months was I blessed by a train of good luck so unusual, that hardly a day passed without some happy or favourable occurrence; but this was the very cause of awakening new fears in me. If, said I, reasoning with myself— if the six withershin circles round the Witch's Cairn have had any influence in producing this marvellous coil of good fortune, what will happen when the spell-thread is unwound to the end, where it was so mysteriously snapped? This seventh moon must be pregnant with some dire affliction.

"I trembled for its approach. It began—several days of it had already stolen away—all was well, and I did again blush for my fears; but, alas! they were too soon realised. One evening Sarah, the nurse of our infant, was amissing with her charge. It grew late, and the Lady Dirleton became frantic with the most cruel apprehensions. She insisted on accompanying me out to search for the nurse and her babe. The alarm spread, and not only the domestics but the whole vassals, largely sharing in our affliction, turned out to aid us. All our efforts were in vain, for a dark and stormy night came on; and on that wide plain that stretcheth between the Castle and the sea, there was greater risk of the seekers losing themselves than chance of their finding the woman and the babe. The Lady Dirleton recklessly wandered until she was so sore toil-spent that she was carried to the Castle almost insensible. I did still continue my search in despair, in defiance of whirlwinds of sand and red glaring flashes of lightning. Faint and distant screams were heard by times ymeint with the blast. We followed in the direction they went in, as well as the mirkness of the night might permit us to do. Sometimes they would bring us down towards the shore of the sea, where they were lost amidst the thunders of its waves rolling furiously in on the beach. Anon we did hear them retreating inland, and we were led by

them, in a zig-zag course, hither and thither across the plain,
in idle pursuit. 'The child! the babe!—ha, the murderer!—
ha, blood, blood, blood!—murder, murder!—the child, the child!'
were the fearful words we caught from time to time, ymingled
with wild unearthly cries. Still we followed, and we shouted by
times; but our shouts were unheeded, albeit they must natheless
have been heard by the person whose voice reached our ears so
strongly.

"At length, after a harrassing night of fruitless following, the
voice died away from us, and we groped wearily and hopelessly
about until day did gloomily dawn upon us. We again wandered down towards the shore, and there descried a female
figure, with torn garments and dishevelled hair, running and
leaping about with wild and irrational action among the sand-
heaps by the sea side. I thought of the hag of the Witch's
Cairn, and my blood curdled within me.

"For some time we followed the figure, but almost with as
little success as we had before done in the darkness of night.
At length, by making a circuit around her, we came close upon
her, where she had seated herself on the top of a benty hillock.
It was Sarah, the nurse of our child. She rose wildly, by fits
and starts, and waved her arms high in the air, and gave streaming to the wind the infant's sky-blue mantle, the which was red
with blood-stains. Her eyes were fixed in vacancy, and she regarded us not as we approached her; but she screamed and
shrieked unintelligibly; and again she laughed loud and horribly at intervals. We rushed upon her, and then it was we
discovered that reason had been reft from her. Her eyes glared
wildly around on us all, but she knew no one, and no syllable
could now be extracted from her. It was too clear, alas! that
she had murdered mine infant in the sudden frenzy that had
seized her!"

"Blessed Virgin, protect us!" cried Sir Patrick Hepborne.
horror-struck with the Lord of Dirleton's story.

"She was the daughter of an old and much attached
domestic," continued de Vaux, "and she herself, devoted to us
as a daughter, loved the infant as her own. Nothing but
madness could have driven her to do a deed so horrible. Where
she had disposed of the body of the poor innocent we could never
discover, though our search for it was unceasing for some days.
As for the wretched Sarah, whom God had so visited as to make
her no longer accountable for her actions, she was brought back
into the Castle, and put under that needful restraint to the
which she was subjected for many years thereafter. When she

came to be examined more narrowly, some one discovered a dreadful gash on her right hand, as if given by a dagger, a circumstance the which did add to the heap of mystery the truth was buried under, and engendered full many a vague thought and idle surmise. I gave mine orders that some one should be for ever on the watch by Sarah, night and day, to catch up anything she might utter in her ravings, that might chance to illuminate the darkness that hung over this heart-breaking calamity. But albeit her voice was rarely silent for a moment, being unceasingly poured forth in elritch screams of laughter when she was in her wildest fits, or in piteous moaning and waymenting when she was low, yet did she rarely mould it into words of meaning. Full oft would she take up in her arms the mantle, the which she had never parted withal, and hush it with sad lullaby, as if the child had been within it ; and more than once, when thus employed, she was seen to clasp it in agony to her bosom, to look wildly on vacancy, and to stretch forth her arm, as if dreading the approach of some one, and fleeing into the darksome corner of her cell, she was heard to yell out, ' Murderer !—ha ! the babe, the babe !—help, murder !—blood, blood ! —my babe !'—and then she would lay open the mantle, and gazing into it with frenzy, would increase her screams to the very cracking of her voice, as if she had but that moment discovered that the infant was gone.

"Thou mayest right well conceive, Sir Patrick," continued the Lord of Dirleton, after a pause, during which he yielded to the emotions so powerfully excited by this recapitulation of the circumstances of this so terrible affliction which had befallen him—"thou mayest easily imagine, I say, what a deep, nay, fathomless tide of sorrow poured over the souls of the Lady Dirleton and me. We loathed the very air of the scene tainted by this dreadful tragedy. Anxious to escape from it, we hastened abroad, and strove, by mixing in the society of a new world, to blunt the pangs we suffered from the very souvenance of our home. I need say no more, I wis, but to crave thy good pardon, Sir Patrick, for drawing so hugely on thy patience by this long narration, the which, I do natheless opine, hath not been altogether uninteresting to thee, sith I have observed that thou hast, more than once, showed signs of thy friendly sympathy for our misfortune."

"In truth, my Lord, I am deeply affected by thy strange and melancholy history," replied Hepborne. "But what, I pray thee, hath become of Sarah, thy child's nurse, on whom so much mystery doth hang ?"

"After many years of confinement, Sarah's wudness did become more tranquil; it seemed as if it was gradually worn out by its own fury. Then did succeed the mantling and stagnant calmness of idiocy—and seeing that she was no longer harmful, she was, by slow degrees, permitted greater license, until at last she was suffered to go about at the freedom of her own will. But will she seemed to have none. Supported by the Lady Dirleton's charity, and tended by her order, she wandered to and fro in the neighbourhood of the Castle, like a living clod, hardly ever exhibiting even a consciousness of existence."

"And dost thou believe, my Lord," demanded Hepborne, " that the wudness of this poor afflicted wretch did verily work this sad malure to thee? Or didst thou never entertain aught of suspicion of crime against any who were more accountable for their deeds?"

"Ay," replied the Lord of Dirleton, after a pause; "ay, we had suspicions—horrible suspicions. My brother John, that is my half-brother, for he was the son of my father by a woman of low birth and infamous character, who, by sacrifice of virtue and afterwards by her cunning, didst circumvent my father, then an old man, and did induce him to patch up a marriage with her. After the death of my father she would fain have kept the same place she had done during his life; but as I had just then married me I could not insult my wife by the introduction to her notice of a woman so notourly infamous. I natheless did what in prudence I might for my brother, then a young man of some eighteen or twenty winters. I took him under mine own roof, where I in vain endeavoured to bring down his naturally haughty and unbending temper, and to restrain the violence of his passions. I had shown him an elder brother's kindness from very boyhood, and methought his heart did love me. But his wicked and infamous mother, stung with the disgrace of being refused admittance within our gates, so worked upon his young mind that she taught him to regard me rather as an enemy than as a benefactor. Forgetful of the anxiety I did ever display for the advancement of his fortunes and the improvement of his mind, he became impatient of reproof, and ever and anon he was guilty of the most gross and offensive insults to me, and yet more so to the Lady Dirleton, against whom his mother's hatred was more particularly inflamed. Such ungrateful behaviour did naturally beget much unhappy brawling, and high and bitter words often passed between us. At length his daring arose to such a height that he presumed to usher in his impure dam among the noble and honourable guests who assembled to witness the ceremonial baptism of our infant. O'ermastered by rage at the moment, and boiling with indignation, I forgot myself so far as to give him a blow; and I did hound both of them straightway forth with ignominious reproach from my walls. I saw not John ever again, yet I had good cause to fear that he——But hold! my wife and daughter approach; and, hark! the trumpets do sound for the march."

As the Earls of Moray, Fife, Dunbar, and Douglas, who led the line, were breaking through the oak forest through which they travelled for some time after leaving the halting-place, the proud towers of Elgin rose before them, and the tinkling of many a bell from its various convents and churches told them that its inhabitants were already aware of their approach. Soon afterwards the long train of a procession was seen winding down from the entrance of the town, and as they drew nearer they descried at the head of it the venerable Alexander Barr, bishop of the diocese. He was accompanied by his twenty-two canons secular, and various other members and servants of the Cathedral; and after him came a body of Black Dominican Monks, followed by the Grey Franciscan Friars, all marching in pairs. Ere the warlike body of nobles, and knights, and men-at-arms had reached the bridge, the procession had halted to receive them. The Bishop, in his episcopal robes, sat, patiently waiting them, on a well-fed milk-white palfrey, of sober and staid disposition, suited to his master's habits. The Earl of Moray hastened to dismount, and would have run to assist the Prelate from his horse. But there was no pride in the old man, and seeing the Earl's intention, he quitted his saddle with an agility hardly to be looked for from one of his years, and, hastening to meet his embrace, bestowed his willing benediction on him, as well as on the Earls of Fife, Dunbar, and Douglas, and those who followed them.

"My Lord Bishop," said the Earl of Fife, "verily I did scarcely look for this good countenance and gentle demeanour from thee, seeing how I am sykered to him who hath wrought the Church so much foul wrong. But thou well knowest——"

"Talk not of these matters, my Lord Earl of Fife, I beseech thee," cried the Bishop, interrupting him; "talk not of these matters now. We shall have ample leisure to discuss these painful themes ere the hour of couchee. Mount, I beseech thee, and let me now do what honour I may to the son of my King, and to his noble brothers-in-law, the gallant Earls of Douglas and of Moray, by escorting them to the Royal Castle. Thy messengers, my Lord," continued he, turning to Earl Moray, "did out-run my tardy hospitality; for ere I gathered tidings of thy coming, or could bestir myself to make fitting provision for thy reception, and for the banqueting of these nobles, knights, and ladies, thy preparations at the Castle were already largely advanced, else had I assuredly claimed thee and all as my guests."

"Of a truth, we are rather too potent a company to harass thee withal," replied the Earl of Moray; "and, as Constable of the Royal Castle here, it would ill become me to shrink from the fulfilment of its hospitality. Let us mount, then, and hie us thither."

All being again in their saddles, those composing the procession turned their faces towards the town, and began to move slowly onwards. The black crosses on the humble white gowns of the Dominicans or Black Friars, and the grey gown and cowl of the Franciscans—their meek and world-contemning countenances—their bare feet, the soft tread of which gave forth no sound—the humble banner of St. Giles, the tutelary saint of the town, who was represented in his pastoral habit, holding a book in his right hand, and a staff in his left, with the motto, "Sic itur ad astra," were all calculated to lead the mind far above the pomps of this vain world, and were strangely contrasted with the fierce and haughty looks of the warriors—their glittering armour—their nodding plumes—the yell of the bugles—and the proudly-blazoned surcoats, and shields, and banners, and pennons, which flared against the declining sun, as if their glory had been made to endure even beyond that of the blessed luminary itself.

They wound up the steep hill to the Castle, and there the religious orders halted in two lines, facing each other, until the gaudy war-pageant had passed inwards, with all its crashing clangour of instruments, and all its flash and glitter. The holy brethren then moved away in silence, disappearing in succession, like the waves that follow the foaming surges raised on the bosom of a lone lake by the fall of some mountain crag.

But there was one monk of the order of St. Francis there who staid not with his brethren to gaze with lack-lustre eye on the ranks of the warriors as they rode by. Deep excitation seemed suddenly to be awakened in him by some passing object. With an agitated air, he shrouded himself up in his grey cowl, and tightening his girdle of ropes about his loins, he mingled with the ranks of riders, and glided into the Castle.

CHAPTER L.

The Mystery of the Lady Beatrice—Arrival of the Nobles and Men-at-Arms at Aberdeen.

THE banquet, though sufficiently splendid, was tempered by moderation, and the guests broke up at an early hour, for the Bishop took an opportunity of signifying his wish to hold private council with the Earls of Fife, Moray, Douglas, and Dunbar, and one or two of the other nobles and knights whom he named. The hint was accordingly taken, and the accommodation of the Castle being too confined for a company so numerous, the Bishop of Moray consigned to the care of his canons the duty of providing fit lodging for such as might be compelled to go into the town. Though the apartments in the houses of these churchmen were small, yet were they most luxuriously furnished for the times to which this history refers.

As De Vaux, the Lord of Dirleton, was one of the few whom the Bishop requested to aid him with his advice, the former remained for some time at the Castle. His lady and daughter were therefore consigned to the care of a rosy-faced, tun-bellied canon, who was ready with his attendants to escort them to his antique mansion. As his lacqueys lighted them along under the covered arcades lining both sides of the streets, his gay smiles and gallant air sorted but indifferently with the solemn religious grandeur that was everywhere spread over this ancient episcopal town.

The subject of conference between the Bishop and the nobles was the late outrages of the Wolfe of Badenoch. The good Bishop was himself incapable of seeking vengeance, in as far as he as a mere man was concerned. But he was zealous for the interests of that religion and of that Church of which he was the minister; and being firmly resolved that neither should be insulted with impunity, he stated to the Lords and Knights his determination to go with them to Aberdeen, and to lay the matter before the King. To such a step no objection could be urged by those who heard him, and accordingly, after some conversation on other matters, which continued to a pretty late hour, the party broke up.

As the Lord of Dirleton was leaving the Castle, with the intention of finding his way to the house of the canon, whither his lady and the Lady Jane de Vaux had gone before him, he was suddenly addressed by some one from behind, who, in a distinct but hollow tone, whispered in his ear—

"Wouldst thou know aught of the fate of thy first-born daughter?"

"Ha! what canst thou tell me?" cried De Vaux, turning round with inconceivable eagerness, and addressing a Franciscan monk who stood behind him shrouded up in his cowl: "speak, I beseech thee, holy man, what hast thou to tell of my first-born daughter?"

"Dismiss thine attendants," replied the Franciscan calmly, "and follow me to the church of Greyfriars; there shalt thou learn all that I have to tell."

"Get thee to thy lodgings," cried the Lord of Dirleton to his people, "and leave me with this holy monk. I would have converse with him alone."

"My Lord," replied his esquire, "it were safer methinks to have thy people about thee; treachery hath many disguises—there may be danger."

"Talk not to me of danger," cried De Vaux; "leave me, as I do command thee."

The esquire bowed, and retired with the valets and lacqueys who had waited. The monk, who had stood aloof abiding his determination, now moved away, and the Lord of Dirleton followed him. The streets were deserted and silent, and the Franciscan staid not to speak, but glided so quickly along as to defy all attempts at conversation on the part of the knight who followed him. After threading through some narrow lanes and uncouth passages, the Lord of Dirleton was led by his guide to the door of the church of the Greyfriars, to which the monk applied a large key that hung at his girdle, and after letting himself and the knight in, he again locked it carefully behind him. The interior of the holy place was dimly illuminated by the few lamps that were burning here and there before some of the shrines, but the gloomy light was not even sufficient to dissipate the shadows that hung beneath the arch of the groined roof.

"Speak, quickly speak, father—in charity speak, and satisfy my anxiety," cried the old Lord of Dirleton, panting with the eagerness of expectation, combined with the breathlessness of exertion. "What knowest thou of the fate of my child?—Is she alive?—In mercy speak!"

The Franciscan shot a glance at De Vaux from under his cowl, and then strode slowly up the nave of the Church until he came opposite to a shrine dedicated to an image of the Virgin.

There he halted, and leaning against its iron screen with his back to the lamps, dropped his head on his bosom, and seemed lost in thought for some moments.

"Oh, speak," cried the Lord of Dirleton, following him—"Speak—does my child live? my child Beatrice?"

"Thy child liveth not," murmured the monk, in a deep sepulchral tone; "'tis of her death I would tell thee."

"Alas, alas! I did indeed fear so," cried the Lord of Dirleton, deeply affected. "I had indeed ceased to hope that she might be yet alive. Yet even to know her fate were something amid the sad obscurity which hath so long oppressed us. What canst thou tell me of her, holy father?"

"Thou hadst a brother," said the Franciscan, slowly and solemnly.

"Alas! I had. I had indeed a brother," cried De Vaux. "Then are my fears but too just. It was he then who reft me of mine infant. Oh, wretch, wretch, how couldst thou be so cruel!"

"It was he," cried the monk, with a peculiar energy of manner, whilst his eyes glared strangely from beneath his cowl as he spake; "it was thy brother, who, in revenge for the blow he received from thine hand, tore thine infant daughter from her nurse, and fled with her."

"Then may God in His infinite mercy forgive him!" cried De Vaux, clasping his hands together with strong agitation of manner; and, dropping on his knees before the shrine of the Virgin, he buried his face in his mantle, and gave way to his emotions.

"What! canst thou in truth forgive him, then?" cried the monk; "canst thou in sincerity pray for his forgiveness in Heaven? Wouldst thou not rather seek revenge against him—revenge, the which may ere long be put within thy power—revenge, to which even I might peradventure help thee?"

"And dost thou, the servant of Christ—thou who shouldst be the messenger of peace—dost thou become a tempter?" cried De Vaux, looking upwards at the monk with astonishment; "dost thou counsel revenge?—dost thou become a pander to the most malignant of human passions, so as to offer thyself to be the instrument who shall drag up my sinful, yet perchance ere this, repentant brother, to dree my vengeance?"

"'Tis well," replied the Franciscan coolly; "I did so speak but to prove thy virtue, the which I do find to be great. Forgiveness is the badge of our Christian faith, which it well becometh thee to wear; and thou hast the jewel of its highest

23

perfection, sith thou canst bring thy mind to forgive him who
was the murderer of thy first-born child."

"The murderer of my child!" cried the wretched De Vaux,
starting from his knees, and pacing the church, wringing his
hands. "Were my worst fears true, then? was my innocent
infant, my smiling cherub, was my Beatrice murdered? The
few words thou didst let fall had overpowered my first suspicions, and had already engendered hopes that my brother's
violence had at least stopped short of a crime so horrible. Murdered, saidst thou? Oh, most foul, most foul! He whom I did
love and cherish from boyhood as my son—yea, loved as the
issue of my own loins—in whose nurture I so interested myself,
and on whom I did propose to bestow large possessions—What,
the flesh of mine own father to murder my helpless babe!"

"Thy forgiveness is indeed of most marvellous and unexampled excellence," cried the Franciscan in a whining tone, the
true meaning of which could hardly be interpreted; "wouldst
thou, then, that thy brother should be brought before thee, that
he may receive full pardon at thy hands for the cruel coulpe he
hath committed against thee?"

"Nay, nay, nay," cried the wretched Lord of Dirleton with
rapid utterance, "let me not see him—let me not see him. I
loved the sight of him once as the darling son of mine aged
father—let me not see him now as the murderer of my child.
The taking of the life of my brother cannot restore that of which
he did bereave my Beatrice. As I hope for mercy from on high,
so do I forgive him. Let him then live and repent; let him do
voluntary penance, that his soul may yet meet with mercy at
Heaven's high tribunal; but let me not see him. Had he only
robbed me of my child, I mought peraunter have been able to
have yielded him my forgiveness face to face; yea, and moreover
to have extinguished all animosity by weeping a flood of tears
upon his bosom; for verily I am but as a lone and bruised reed,
and a brother's returning love were a healing balm worth the
purchasing. But the murderer of my child—oh, horrible!—let
me not see him."

The Franciscan drew his cowl more completely over his face,
and stood for some moments with his head averted, as if to hide
those emotions to which De Vaux's agitation had given rise.
Starting suddenly from the position he had taken, he sprang
forward a pace or two towards the Lord of Dirleton, and then
halted suddenly ere he reached him. De Vaux, wrapped up in
his own thoughts, was unconscious of the movement of the monk.
He threw himself again on his knees before the shrine of the

Virgin, and began offering up sincere but incoherent and uncon-
nected petitions, at one time for the forgiveness of his own sins,
at another for the soul of his murdered daughter, and again for
mercy and pardon from Heaven for the crimes of his brother.
The Franciscan, with his arms crossed over his breast, stood with
his body gently bent over the pious supplicant, absorbed in
contemplation of him, and deeply moved by the spectacle. A
footstep was heard—the Lord of Dirleton's ear caught it too at
length, and he arose hastily; but the Franciscan friar with
whom he had been holding converse was gone.

"Father," said the knight eagerly to a brother of the convent
who now approached him from an inner door, "tell me, I pray
thee, who was he of thine order who passed from me but now?"

"Venerable warrior," replied the monk with an air of surprise,
"in truth, I saw no one. May the blessing of St. Francis be
with thee. Peraunter thine orisons hath induced our Blessed
Lady to send some saint miraculously to comfort thee. Nay,
perhaps St. Francis himself may have been sent by the Holy
Virgin to reward thy piety for thus seeking her shrine at such
an hour. Leave me something in charity for our poor convent,
and her blessing, as alswa that of St. Francis, will assuredly
cleave to thee."

"Hath not one of thy brethren loitered in the streets until
now?" demanded the Lord of Dirleton.

"Nay," replied the monk, "I this moment left the dormitory,
where they are all asleep. Trust me, they are not given to
wander in the streets at such an hour as this; and no one else
could come hither, seeing that the door of our church is carefully
locked at night."

The Lord of Dirleton was lost in thought for some moments;
but, recollecting himself, he gave gold to the begging friar, who
received it meekly. He then craved the monk's guidance to the
house of the canon, where his lady and daughter were lodged;
and the holy man, taking a key from his girdle, unfastened the
door of the church, and De Vaux silently followed him, ruminating as he went on the mysterious interview he had had, as well
as on the sad story of his murdered daughter, the whole of his
affliction for whom had been so strangely and so strongly
brought back upon him.

In the morning, the march of the nobles, knights, and men-
at-arms was swelled by the presence of the Bishop of Moray,
attended by a large party of his churchmen and followers. The
whole body reached the ancient city of Aberdeen early on the
fourth day, and Sir Patrick Hepborne had reason to be fully

satisfied with the gracious reception he met with from King Robert. He was gladdened by a happy meeting with his father, and with his friend Assueton, who had come to attend on His Majesty.

"How fareth thine excellent mother, Assueton?" demanded Hepborne jocularly; "thou hast doubtless ere this had enough of her good society, as well as of thy home."

"Nay, of a truth, my dearest bel ami," replied his friend, "parfay my conscience doth sorely smite me in that quarter. Verily, I have not yet seen mine excellent mother. Day after day have I been about to hie me to her, to receive her blessing; but something untoward hath ever arisen to detain me; and just as I was about to accomplish mine intent, I was hurried away hither by the King's command. Perdie, I did never before think that I could have complained of the sudden outbreak of war; yet do I confess that I did in good earnest begrudge this unlooked-for call most bitterly."

"And hath love or filial affection the most to do in exciting thy complaint, thinkest thou?" demanded Hepborne.

"Um! somewhat of both, perhaps," replied Assueton gravely. "By St. Andrew, but I am an altered man, Hepborne. Nay, smile not; or rather, if it so pleaseth thee, smile as thou mayest list, for certes I am now case-hardened against thy raillery.

CHAPTER LI.

King Robert at Aberdeen— Duncan MacErchar again.

THE evening was beautiful, when the loyal inhabitants of Aberdeen, who, by their King's temporary residence among them, were rendered eagerly alive to every little movement regarding him, began to be aware that something was in contemplation, from observing a slender guard of spearmen marching forth from the Castle, and forming in single files at about a yard between each, so as to enclose an extended oblong space on the upper part of the street. The populace began to crowd towards the barrier of spears, in expectation of something interesting, and soon formed a dense mass everywhere behind it. The houses overlooking the spot began to be filled with guests, too, who were glad to claim acquaintance with their inmates, for the sake of procuring places at the windows, which were all of them quickly occupied, as well as every one of those antique and curiously applied outer stairs and whimsical projections that characterized the city architecture of the period.

Idle speculation became rapidly busy among the anxious gazers. All hoped they were to see the King, yet few thought the hope well founded; for the infirmities of age had so beset His Majesty that he was but little equal to undergo the labour of the parade attendant on his elevated rank, far less to endure public exhibitions of his person.

All doubt was soon put to an end, however. A distant flourish of trumpets was heard, and martial music followed, swelling and growing upon the ear as it slowly approached from the innermost recesses of the Castle. It burst forth with shriller clangour, and the performers presently issued from the Castle, preceding a grand procession of nobles, knights, and ladies, habited in the most magnificent dresses, followed by a small body of guards, in the midst of whom there was a splendid litter, having the Royal Arms, surmounted by the Crown of Scotland, placed over its velvet canopy. It was borne by twelve esquires, in the richest Royal liveries. Murmurs of self-congratulation and joyful greeting began to run around the assemblage of people; but when the litter was set down in the middle of the open space, and Robert II., their beloved monarch, the observer of justice, whose ears were ever open to the complaints of his meanest subjects, and of whom it was even commonly said that he never spoke word that he performed not—when the good King of Scotland was assisted forth from his conveyance, deafening shouts rent the air, and were prolonged unceasingly, till the lungs of the shouters waxed weary from their exertions.

The reason of the monarch thus taking the air before his people, was to give confidence to the good citizens of Aberdeen, amidst the exaggerated rumours of invasion, by showing himself so surrounded by his dauntless barons.

The infirm old King, plainly habited in a purple velvet mantle, lined with fur, and purple silk nether garments, with grey woollen hose, folded amply over them, for the comfort of his frail limbs, leaning upon his son the Earl of Fife, and partly supported by his much-favoured son-in-law, the Earl of Moray, took his broad hat and plume with dignity from his head, and, showing his long snowy hair, bowed gracefully around to the people, and then began to walk slowly backwards and forwards, aiding himself partly with his son's arm and partly with a cane, now stopping to converse familiarly with some of the ladies, or of the many nobles and knights by whom he was attended, or

halting occasionally, as if suddenly interested in some person or
thing he noticed among the crowd, and then again resuming his
walk with all the marks of being perfectly at home among his
people.   The show, if show it might be called, went not on
silently, for ever and anon the enthusiasm of the vulgar getting
the better of their awe for majesty, their voices again rose to
heaven in one universal and startling peal.   The gallant groups
of nobles and knights, who, by their numerous attendance on
the King, gave strength to the throne in the eyes of the people,
were also hailed with gratifying applause; and even some of
the more renowned leaders among them were singled out and
lauded by the plaudits of the spectators.   Among these the
Douglas was most prominently distinguished, and the good
John Dunbar, Earl of Moray, had his ample share.

How important do the smallest, the most pitifully trifling
circumstances of a King's actions appear in the eyes of his
people!   All those of his nobles or knights to whom Robert
chanced particularly to extend his Royal attention, were it but
for a minute, were noted by the shrewd observation of the
Aberdonienses as among the favoured of the Court, and many
a plan was hatched by individuals among the spectators for
winning their patronage.   Not a movement of His Majesty, not
a turn, not a look, escaped remark, and the mightiest results
were augured from signs the most insignificant.

It happened that Sir Patrick Hepborne was standing with
his father not far from the lower extremity of the open space,
when the King came up to them.   He had particularly noticed
both of them before; and the acclamations of the people, who
knew the deeds of the elder knight, and already loved the
younger for his father's sake, showed how much their hearts
beat in unison with this mark of their Sovereign's approbation.
But now the King had something more to say to Sir Patrick
the elder than merely to honour him in the eyes of the people,
with an appearance of familiarity.   He really wanted his advice
with regard to the proposed armament, and to have his private
opinion of certain matters ere the council should sit.   With
monarchs, opportunities of private conference with those they
would speak to, are difficult to be commanded without remark;
their actions, and the actions of those about them, are watched
too closely to permit them to be approached without begetting
speculation.   A politic King is therefore obliged to catch at
and avail himself of moments for business which are perhaps but
ill suited for it; and it is often in the most crowded assemblage
that they run the smallest risk of suspicion of being engaged in

anything serious. Robert, leaning on his two attendants, stood unusually long in conference with the Hepbornes. The fatigue and pain which he suffered in his limbs, by being detained in the standing posture for so great a length of time, was sufficiently manifest from the uneasy lifting and shifting of his feet, though his countenance, full of fire and animation when he spoke himself, and earnestly fixed in attention to what Sir Patrick Hepborne said to him in return, had no expression in it that might have led the spectator to believe that it was at all connected with the frail and vexed limbs that supported it, but which it seemed to have altogether forgotten in the intensity of the interest of the subject under discussion.

While the personages of this group were thus engaged, a considerable movement in that part of the crowd near them, followed by some struggling and a good many high words, suddenly attracted their notice. A momentary expression of anxiety, if not of fear, crossed the wan features of royalty. The Earl of Moray and the two Hepbornes showed by their motions that they were determined to secure the King's safety at the risk of their own lives; for, with resolute countenances, they laid their hands on their swords, and stepped between him and the point from which the danger, if there was any, must come, and to which their eyes were directed. The Earl of Fife acted independently. He made a wheel, which was difficult to be explained, but halted and fronted by the side of his father again, immediately in rear of the Earl of Moray and his two companions. The crowd, within a few yards of them, still continued to heave to and fro as if in labour, and at last a bulky figure appeared in the ancient Highland costume, and worming his way forward to the line of guards, immediately endeavoured to force a passage through between two of them. The two soldiers joined their spears to each other, and each of them grasped a butt and a point the more effectually to bar his progress. Undismayed by this their resolution, he in an instant put a hand on a shoulder of each of them, and raised himself up with the determined intention of hoisting himself over the obstruction. This action of his, however, was immediately met by a simultaneous and equally decisive movement on the part of the two guards. Just as he had succeeded in throwing one leg over the impediment, they, by a well-concerted effort, lifted him vigorously up, and horsed him upon the shafts of the coupled spears, amid the laughter of the surrounding populace. After some moments of rueful balancing upon his uneasy and ticklish saddle, during which he seemed to hang in dreadful doubt on which side he was to fall, his large body at last overbalanced itself, and he rolled inwards towards the feet of the King, and those who were standing with him. The whole was the work of a moment.

A loud murmur, mingled with the shrieks of " Treason— traitorie ! " arose among the anxious people ; and all bodies, heads, and eyes were bent towards the scene of action, in dread lest something tragical should follow. The two guards pressed forward to transfix the unceremonious intruder with their spears as he lay on the ground.

" Back," cried Sir Patrick Hepborne the younger, bestriding his body like a Colossus; " back, I say, this man must not be hurt ; he means no evil ; I will answer for him with my life."

" Secure him at least, Sir Patrick," cried the Earl of Fife.

" My Lord, I will be his security," replied Sir Patrick. " He is a good and loyal subject, and nothing need be apprehended from him."

" Is he not mad ? " demanded Fife, with some anxiety. " Methinks his eye rolls somewhat wildly. By the mass, I like not his look overmuch."

" Be assured, my Lord, I well know the man," replied Sir Patrick, stooping to assist him to rise.

" Out fie ! " cried Duncan MacErchar, who now stood before them, smoothing down his quelt, and blowing the dust with great care off a new suit of coarse home-spun tartan, that, with his rough raw-hide sandals, suited but ill with the splendid sword and baldrick that hung on him, and the richly-jewelled brooch that fastened his plaid ; " Och, oich ! Sir Patrick—ou ay, ou ay—troth, she be's right glad to see her honour again. Uve, uve, ye loons," continued he, addressing the two soldiers who had made so powerful a resistance to his entrance, " an she had kend that ye were going to give her sike an ill-faur'd ride as yon, and sike an ugly fling at the end o't, by St. Giles, but she would have crackit yere filthy crowns one again others like two rotten eggs. But, oich, is she weel ? " cried he, again turning eagerly towards Sir Patrick Hepborne the younger. " Troth she did hear of the gatherin', and so she e'en came down here to see if King Roberts was for the fechts. And oich, she was glad to see her honours again, and the ould mans Sir Patricks yonder : but, uve, uve, she has had a sore tuilzie to get at her."

" I rejoice to see thee, Master MacErchar," said Hepborne, hastily waving him away, under the strong impression of the necessity of ridding the King's presence of him, without a mo- ment's delay ; " but the present time and place ill befitteth for such recognition. Retire then, I do beseech thee, and seek me on some other occasion. Thou mayest ask at the Castle gate for mine esquire Mortimer Sang, whom thou knowest ; he will bring thee to me at such time as may be convenient for me."

" Uve, uve !" cried Duncan MacErchar, the warm sparkle gradually forsaking his eye, as Hepborne spoke, leaving him much abashed with a reception, for the coldness of which he had been little prepared ; " oit, oit—ou ay—surely—troth she'll do that. She's not going to plague her honour's honour a moment. She's yede her ways hame again to her nain glen as fast as her legs can carry her. That she will—surely, surely. But, by the blessed mass, had she but kend that she sould be any hinderance to her honour, she sould not have yalt so far to fartigue her with a sight of her. But she did bid her be sure to claim ken o' her in ony place, and before ony body."

" Yea, I did so," replied Hepborne, vexed to see that he still remained in the King's presence, and rather provoked at his boldness, not being aware that poor Duncan was perfectly igno- rant that one of the four persons before him was His Majesty— " I did indeed bid thee do so ; but verily I looked not for thine audacious approach before such eyes."

" And fat was Duncan MacErchar to mind fat other lord- bodies might be standing by, when her father, the noble Sir Patrick Hepborne, and at whose back she used to fight, was before her eyne ?" replied the Highlander, a little out of temper. " Uve, uve !—surely, surely, Sir Patrick Hepborne, that did lead her on to the fechts, is mokell more to her than ony lord o' them a'—ay, than King Robert himsel, gin she were here, as she's in yon braw box yonder. Sure she did ken hersel the bonny Earl John Dunbar there, right brave and worthy knight ; and feggs she kens that she's not the noblemans that will scorn a poor man. And as for that pretty gentleman, and that douce discreet auld carle in the purple silken hauselines and the grey hose, they may be as good as him peraunter, but surely, surely, they cannot be better. Na, troth, but they must be mokell waur than him, an they would be for clapping their hands on the mouth o' a poor man's gratitudes. But surely, surely," added he, " he be sorry sorry to have angered her honours."

" Thou dost altogether mistake in this matter, Duncan," said Sir Patrick the younger, much distressed to perceive the mutual misunderstanding that existed—" thou dost altogether mistake ; I am not offended."

" Hoot, toot—ay, ay—ou ay—sure," replied Duncan, with a whimsical look of good-natured sarcasm in his countenance.

"Troth, she doth see that she's not, neither the one nor the others, the same mans here, on the crowns o' the causey o' Aberdeen, that she was in the glen o' the Dee yonder. Hup up!—Troth, she did take a grup of her hands yonder, ay, and she did moreover drink out of the same cup with her, and a proud mans she did make Duncan MacErchar hersels. But, uve, uve!—she's with her neighbour lords and knights noo, and sike a ragged goat o' the hills as her nainsel is no to be noticed amang so many braw frisking sheep, with fine woo on their backs. But sith that she did make Duncan proud, troth she'll show her pride. Fient a bit o' her will force her nainsel to the kens o' mortal mans; so here's her bonny sword and braw baudrick," continued he, as he tried to take them off, "here's the sword and the baudrick she bore so lightly, but the which hae grown of the sudden over heavy for her backs. But the poor Sir Page's bonny brooch—oh ay! she'll keep it right sickerly, as it was kindly and gratefully gi'en."

"Nay, Duncan, keep the sword and baldrick, I beseech thee, and seek for mine esquire to-night," said Hepborne, much annoyed.

"Hoof, uve, no," replied the Highlander testily. "Sith she careth not to notice poor Duncan MacErchar before her father the ould mans (the Virgin's blessing be upon her!) and the good Earl of Moray, and that pretty gentlemans, and you discreet, well-natured, laughing auld carle in the grey hose and the purple hauselines yonder, troth she'll no seek to trouble her esquire. So here's her sword and baudrick, and she's yede her ways hame again."

"Nay, Duncan, I'll none of them," cried Hepborne, putting them back with the back of his hand. "Thou art strangely mistaken here. Trust me, mine is not the heart that can use an old friend, yea, and above all, one that did save my very life, with the coldness that thou dost fancy. But thou art now in the presence of——." He stopped, and would have added "of the King;" but at that moment His Majesty, who had richly enjoyed the scene as far as it had already gone, gave him such a look as at once showed him it was not his pleasure that it should be so speedily terminated. He went on then differently. "But thou art now in the presence of certain lords, with whom I am deeply engaged in discussing divers matters of most grave and weighty import, and deeply affecting the wellbeing of our country and the glory of our King; and of a truth I well know that thou dost love both over much to suffer thine own feelings to let, hinder, or do them prejudice in the smallest jot. Thou canst not take offence that I did seem to neglect thee for matters of such moment. By the honour of a knight I will take thee, brave preserver of my life, by the hand," continued he, seizing MacErchar with great cordiality, "I will take thy hand, I say, in the presence of the whole world, yea, an it were in the presence of King Robert himself. And as for drinking from the same cup with thee, what, have I not drank with thee of the sacred cup of thy hospitality, and thinkest thou I would refuse to drink with thee again? By St. Andrew, though rarely given to vinolence, I would rather swill gallons with thee than that thou shouldst deem me deficient in the smallest hair's-breadth of gratitude to thee for the potent service thou didst render me at the Shelter Stone of Loch Avon. Put on thy baldrick, man, yea, and the sword also, and think not for a moment that I could have been so base as to slight thee."

"Oich, oich!—oot, oot!—uve, uve!—fool she was—fool she was, surely," cried Duncan, at once completely subdued, and very much put out of countenance by these unequivocal expressions of Hepborne's honest and sincere regard for him. "Oit, oit! troth she was foolish, foolish; na, she'll keep the sword, ay, and the bonny baudrick—ay, ay, ou ay, she'll keep them noo till she dies. Uve, uve, she's sore foolish, sore foolish. Oich, oich, will her honour Sir Patrick pardons her? Troth, she's sore ashamed."

"Pardon thee," said Sir Patrick the younger, again shaking MacErchar heartily by the hand—"pardon thee, saidst thou? By St. Baldrid, but I do like thee the better, friend Duncan, for the proper pride and feeling thou didst show. Thy pride is the pride of an honest heart, and had I, in good verity, been the very paltry and ungenerous knight that appearances did at first lead thee to imagine me to be, by the Rood, but I should have right well merited thy sovereign despisal."

"Oich, oich," said Duncan, his eyes running over with the stream of kindly affections that now burst from his heart, and quite confused by his powerful emotions, "she's over goods—she's over foolish—out fie, surely, surely, she's over goods. God bless her honour. But troth, she'll no be tarrying langer noo to disturb her honour's honour more at this times; and, ou ay, she'll come surely to good Squire Mortimer's at night, to see if her honour's leisure may serve for seeing her."

"Nay, nay," said Hepborne, after consulting the King's countenance by a glance, to gather his pleasure, "thou shalt not go now. We had nearly done with our parlance, and the renewal of it at this time mattereth not a jot; so sith that thou

art here, my brave defender, perdie, thou shalt stay until I introduce thee to my father.   Father," continued he, turning to Sir
Patrick the elder, " this is a brave soldier who hath fought for
his King in many a stark stoure with thee.   I do beseech thee
to permit him opportunity to speak to thee, and peraunter thou
wilt all the more readily do so, when I tell thee that he did save
my life from the murderous blows of an assassin, the which had
well nigh amortised me, by despatching the foul traitor with a
single thrust of his spear."

"To hear that thou hast saved the life of my beloved son,"
replied Sir Patrick, advancing and taking MacErchar by the
hand, " were in itself enow to coart me to recognise thee as my
benefactor, though I had never seen thee before.   But well do I
remember thy brave deeds, my worthy fellow-soldier."

"Oich, oich," cried Duncan, dropping on his knees, and embracing those of Sir Patrick, but altogether unable to express
his feelings, " oich, oich—surely, surely—fat can she say?—
foolish, foolish —hoot, toot—ower big rewards for her—ooch—
ower good, surely—hoit, oit, Duncan will die hersel for the good
Sir Patrick—ay, or for ony flesh o' hers—och-hone—uve, uve,
she cannot speak."

"Yet did I never hear mortal tongue more eloquent," said
Sir Patrick Hepborne the elder, "sith that its very want of
utterance doth show forth the honest and kindly metal of the
heart.   But by St. Andrew, I do know the heart to be bold as
well as kind, seeing I forget not the actions of this heroic mountaineer in the field.   Where all are brave, verily 'tis not an easy
task to gain an overtopping height of glory; and yet less is it
easy in the lower ranks of war, where the individuals stand
thicker.   Natheless, and maugre all these obstacles to fame, did
this man's deeds in battle so tower above all others, that, humble as he was, I often noted them—yea, and he should have
been rewarded too, had I not weaned that he was killed in
doing the very feat for the which I would have done him
instant and signal honour.   What came of thee," continued Sir
Patrick, addressing MacErchar, who had by this time risen to
his legs, "what came of thee, my valiant mountaineer, after
thou didst so gallantly save those engineer-men and their engine,
when basely abandoned by the French auxiliaries, at the siege
of Roxburgh, whose retreat thou didst cover against a host of
the enemy by thy single targe and sword, until others were
shamed into their duty by thy glorious ensample?"

"Oich, oich—he, he, he!—a bonny tuilzie that," cried Duncan, laughing heartily, "a bonny tuilzie ; troth, she was but

roughly handled yon time. Of a truth, noble Sir Patrick, she did get sike an ill-favoured clewer from a chield with a mokell mace, that she was laid sprawling on the plain ; and syne, poo ! out ower her body did the English loons come flying after our men, in sike wicked fashion, that the very breath was trampled out o' her bodys."

"But how didst thou 'scape with life after all ? " demanded Sir Patrick the elder.

"Troth, after they had all trotted over her, the wind just came back again into her bodys," replied MacErchar ; "and so she got up till her legs, and shook hersel, and scratched her lugs, that were singing as loud as twenty throstle-birds ; when back came the villains, running like furies before our men, and whirled her away wi' them, or ever she kend, into the town. There she lay prisoners for mony a days, till she broke their jails, and made her way to the Highlands. But troth, she took her spulzie wi' her, for she had hidden that afore, and kend whare to find it again."

"Of a truth, the deed was one of the most desperate I did ever behold," said Sir Patrick the elder, recurring to Mac-Erchar's action to which he had alluded. "He planted himself against a host, and seemed doomed to certain destruction. 'Tis a marvel that he is alive."

Whilst Sir Petrick Hepborne and the Earl of Moray, who also remembered him, were holding some further conference with MacErchar, Sir Patrick the younger approached the King, and privately begged a boon of his Majesty, the particulars of which he specified to him.

"'Tis granted, Sir Patrick," whispered the King ; "but let it be asked of us aloud, that such part of the populace who may have been listening to what hath passed, may have their minds filled also with the wholesome ensample of their King rewarding virtue."

In obedience to Robert's command, Hepborne knelt before him, and addressed him in a loud and distinct voice.

"My liege, I do humbly beg a boon at thy Royal hands."

"Speak forth thy volunde, Sir Patrick Hepborne," replied the King ; "there are few names in our kingdom the which may call for more ready attention from King Robert than that the which hath ever been heard shouted in the front of his armies, and in the midst of the ranks of his discomfited enemies."

"The boon I do earnestly crave of your Majesty is, that you will be graciously pleased to bestow upon this gallant soldier, Duncan MacErchar, a commission in thy Royal Guard."

"He hath it," replied the King, "he hath it cheerfully at thy request, Sir Patrick ; and by the faith of a King, it doth right well pleasure us thus to exercise the happiest part of our Royal power—I do mean that of rewarding loyal bravery such as this man hath so proved himself to possess ; yea, and no time so fitting, methinks, for the exercise of this power ; for when war is beginning, we should show our people that we do know to reward those who do well and truly serve us."

"Kneel down, kneel down, I say, before Robert King of Scotland," said the Earl of Moray, slapping the astonished Mac-Erchar upon the back, as he stood bereft of all sensation on discovering in whose presence he had been standing and prating so much. He obeyed mechanically, whilst a shout arose from that part of the crowd who had heard all that had passed, and was caught up gradually by those farther off, who cheered upon trust long ere the story could spread among them. The King moved away ; but still Duncan remained petrified upon his knees, with his hands clasped, his eyes thrown up, and his mouth open, until Sir Patrick the younger showed himself his best friend by awaking him from his trance and leading him away, amidst the ceaseless shouts of the mob.

CHAPTER LII.

The Wolfe of Badenoch at Aberdeen—Father and Son.

DUNCAN MACERCHAR's intellect was so much confused by the unexpected discovery that he had been standing and talking before his King, a being whom he had always conceived to be something more than man, and whose image had floated like a spirit before his misty eyes, that it was some time ere Sir Patrick Hepborne could make him comprehend the good fortune that had befallen him. He then inquired eagerly into the nature and advantages of the situation which had been so graciously bestowed upon him by His Majesty ; and finding that he was to be an officer in that corps of stipendiaries who were always on Royal duty, with the best possible pay and perquisites, and superb clothing, he asked Hepborne, with some degree of earnestness, what became of the corps during the time of war.

"They never go to war, unless when the King appears in the field in person," replied Sir Patrick; " and of that I well wot there is but little chance during this reign."

"Uve, uve," cried MacErchar, with a look that showed he was but half satisfied; "and is she never to see the English loons again? Sure, sure, of what use will be the pay and the harness, an she must liggen at home while tothers folks be at the wars? And is she never to have the good luck to fight at the back of the good Sir Patrick again! Oich, oich, she would like full weel to see her down, and ane Englishman cleavin' her skull, and her mainsel wi' a pike in the body o' the chield—oich, hoich! it would be braw sport. Sure, she would rather fight for Sir Patrick, yea, and albeit she got nothing but cuffs and scarts for her pains, than sit wi' her thumbs across serving a king himsel, though she got goupins of gold for her idleness. Troth, she would die for Sir Patrick."

"And wouldst thou sacrifice the honour, yea, and the weighty emolument of a commission in the King's Guards, with all the fair promise of advancement the which it doth hold forth to thee, for the mere gratification of a chivalric self-devotion to my father?" demanded Hepborne, desirous to try him.

"Out ay—surely, surely, she would do that; and little wonder o' her, too, she would think it," replied MacErchar.

"Wouldst thou, then, that I do resign thy commission to the King, and that I do obtain for thee a lance among my father's spears?" asked Hepborne.

"Oich, oich!" cried MacErchar, rubbing his hands, and with his eyes sparkling with delight; "surely her honour is ower good—ower good, surely. But if her honour will do that same, oich, oich! Duncan MacErchar will be happy—oop, oop, happy. Troth, she will dance itsel for joy. Oit, she may need look for no more till she dies; God be good unto her soul then! Oich, will her honour do this for her?" demanded Duncan eagerly of Hepborne, and in his more than usual keenness, taking the knight's hand, and squeezing it powerfully; "will her honour do but this for her?"

"Verily, I shall at least do for thee what I can," replied Hepborne, heartily shaking his hand; "albeit so honourable a gift from thy King may not be lightly rejected. Yet will I do what I may for thee. Let me find thee with mine esquire to-morrow morning; thou shalt then hear the result of mine application to the King."

Hepborne was as good as his word. He craved an audience of the King, and, being admitted to his couchee, the good monarch was pleased with the singularly disinterested wish of the Highlander, and immediately signified his gracious pleasure that MacErchar should retain the commission in his Guards, whilst he should be permitted to follow the banner of Sir Patrick Hepborne to the wars. The old knight, who happened to be present, was much touched by Duncan's devotion to him, and very gladly admitted him among his followers, so that every wish of Mac-Erchar's heart was more than gratified.

As Sir Patrick Hepborne was quitting the Royal apartments, and as he was passing through a small vestibule feebly illumined by a single lamp, he was almost jostled by a tall figure, who, enveloped in an ample mantle, was striding hastily forward towards the door of the room whence he had issued, the metal of his harness clanging as he moved.

"Ha! Sir Patrick Hepborne," cried the Wolfe of Badenoch, for it was he—" by the blessed bones of my grandfather, but thou art right far ben already in the old man's favour, that I do thus meet thee ishing forth from his chamber at an hour like this; but thou art more welcome, peraunter, than his son the Earl of Buchan—Is the King alone?"

"By this time I do ween that he is, my Lord; for, as I left him, the Earl of Fife, the Earl of Moray, and my father, who had been in conference with him, were preparing to take their leave by another door, and the King was about to retire into his bed-chamber, with the gentlemen in waiting on his person."

"Ha!" said the Wolfe—"John Dunbar, Earl of Moray, saidst thou?—By my word, but he seemeth to be eternally buzzing about the King, ay, and he doth buzz in his ear too, I warrant me. Hast thou seen or heard aught of the Bishop of Moray being here?"

"The Bishop of Moray had an audience of His Majesty this very day, on his arrival," replied Hepborne; "and if I mistake not, he did take his leave, and hath already departed on his homeward journey."

"Ha! 'tis well," replied the Wolfe hoarsely, and gnashing his teeth as he said so. "Good night, Sir Patrick, I may, or I may not, see thee in Aberdeen at this time, for I know not whether I may, or may not, ride hence again anon." So saying, he passed hastily towards the door leading to the King's private chamber, to reach which he had several apartments to pass through.

The aged Robert, tired by the unusual fatigue he had that day undergone, was alike glad to get rid of business and of his privy councillors. Retiring into his bed-chamber, and laying aside the dignity of his high estate, his two attendants assisted him to put on his robe-de-chambre, and he immediately descended to the more humble level of a mere man, to which even the greatest and most heroic potentate is reduced by the operations of his valet. His legs had been already relieved from those rolls of woollen which had been employed to cherish and to support them during the day; and being seated in an easy chair of large dimensions, among ample crimson cushions, his pale countenance showed yet more wan and withered under the dark purple velvet cap he wore, from beneath which his white hair curled over his shoulders. Though his eyes were weak and bleared, their full and undimmed pupils beamed mildly, like the stars of a summer twilight. He had just inserted his limbs knee-deep into a warm foot-bath, which one of his people had placed before his chair, when a loud tap was heard at the door.

"Ha!" said the King, starting, "get thee to the door, Vallance, and see who may knock so late. By the sound, we should opine that either rudeness or haste were there."

Vallance did as he was ordered, and, on opening the door, the Wolfe of Badenoch stepped into the apartment, and made a hasty and careless obeisance before his father. The old King's feeble frame shook from head to foot with nervous agitation when he beheld him.

"Son Alexander, is it thou?" demanded Robert with astonishment. "We looked not to have our sacred privacy disturbed at so unseemly an hour, yea, and still less by thee, whose head, we did ween, was shrouded by shame in the darkness of thine own disgrace, or rather buried, as we had vainly hoped, amid the dust and ashes of ane humble repentance. What bringeth thee hither?—what hath"——He stopped, for he remembered that they were not alone. "Vallance, and you, Seyton, retire. Wait without in the vestibule; we would be private. What hath brought thee hither, son Alexander?" repeated he, after the door was shut upon them. "I wot thou art but a rare guest at our Court, and methinks that, infected as thou art at this present time, thou art but little fitted for its air."

Naturally violent and ferocious as was the Wolfe of Badenoch, he now stood before his father and his King, a presence in which he never found himself without being in a certain degree subdued by the combination of awe, early inspired into his mind by this twofold claim on his respect, and to which he had been too long accustomed, to find it easy to rid himself of it. The grim Earl moved forward some steps towards the chair where His Majesty was seated, and again louting him low, he repeated the obeisance which the venerable form of his parent and Sovereign commanded.

24

"My liege-father," said he at length, "I do come to pay mine humble duty to your grace, and——"

"Nay, methinks thou shouldst have bethought thee of humbling thy fierce pride before another throne than ours, ere thou didst adventure to wend thee hither," interrupted the King with indignation. "It would have well become thee to have bowed in humble contrition before the episcopal chair of our Right Reverend Bishop of Moray, yea, to have licked the very dust before his feet. Then, with his absolution on thy sinful head, mightest thou have approached the holy altar of God, and the shrine of the Virgin, in penitence and prayer ; and after these, and all other purifications, we mought have been again well pleased to have seen our reclaimed son mingling with the nobles of our Court."

"I do see that the Bishop of Moray hath outrode me," said the Wolfe of Badenoch, his eye kindling, and his cheek darkly reddening, the flame of his internal ire being rendered more furious by the very exertions he was making to keep down all external symptoms of it. "The Bishop hath already effunded his tale in the Royal car; but yet do I hope that thou wilt hesitate to condemn me, yea, even on the Bishop's saying, without hearing what I may have to declare in mine own defence."

"Son Alexander," said the old King mildly, and at the same time slowly shaking his head as he spoke, "we do fear much that thou canst have but little to tell that may undermine what the soothfast Bishop, Alexander Barr, hath possessed us of."

"He hath been with thee, then, my liege-father?" said the Wolfe, in a voice of eager inquiry, and at the same time biting his nether lip.

"Yea, the godly Bishop of Moray hath been with us this very day," replied the King. "He hath harrowed up our soul with the doleful tale of the brenning of our good burgh of Forres —of the great devastation of men's dwellings, goods, and mœubles, the which thy fury hath created—the sacrilege of the which thou hast been guilty in reducing God's house and altar to ashes, as also the house of his minister—the wicked and as yet unestimated sacrifice of the lives of our loving subjects, the which thou hast occasioned."

"As God is my judge, my liege," replied the Earl impatiently, "as God is my judge, there was not a life lost—credit me, not one life. The hour of the night was early when the deed was done ; yea, it was done openly enough, so that there was little chance of mortal tarrying to be food for the devouring flames. Trust me, my liege-father, I did secretly send to certify myself, as I can now truly do thee, on the honour of a knight, that not a life was lost."

" Nay, in truth, it must be confessed that the Bishop spake only from hearsay as to this head of charge against thee," replied the King, " and, of a truth, thou hast lightened our mind of a right grievous part of its burden by thy solemn denial of this cruel part of the accusation against thee. Verily, it was to my soul like the hair-shirt to the back that hath been seamed by the lash of penance, to think that flesh of ours could have done such wanton murder on innocent and inoffensive burghers. But yet, what shall we say to thy brenning of God's holy house —of the gratification of thy blind and brutal thirst of vengeance even by the destruction of his altars, and of the images of his saints ? "

" Nay, mine intent was not against the Church," replied the Wolfe, " but rage reft me of reason, and I deny not that it was with mine own hand that I did fire it; yet was it soon extinguished, and the choir only hath suffered. But," continued he, as he turned the subject with increasing irritation, " but had not an excommunication gone forth so rashly against me, yea, and poured out alswa by him who hath ever been mine enemy, the flood of my vengeance had not flowed ; and if it had swept all before it, by the Rood, but Bishop Barr himself must bear the coulpe of what evil it may have wrought."

" Speak not so horribly, son Alexander," said the King, with emotion. " Thine impious words do shock mine ear. Lay not blame to Bishop Barr for at last hurling upon thee the tardy vengeance of the Episcopal chair, which thine accumulated insults did loudly call for, long ere his long-suffering temper did permit him to employ them. Didst thou not outrageously and sacrilegiously ravish and usurp the lands of the Church in Badenoch ? and didst thou not refuse to restore them to the righteous possession of our holy Mother when called on so to do ? "

" Yea," replied the Wolfe of Badenoch, waxing more angry, and less scrupulous in his manner of speaking, as well as in his choice of terms, as his father thus began to approach nearer to the source of all his heart-burnings with the Bishop—" yea, I did indeed seize these lands, but, by the mass, it was not against the Church that I did war in so doing, but against mine insidious enemy, Alexander Barr, who did feed himself fat upon their revenues. And well I wot hath he worked for my vengeance. Hath he not poisoned thine ear against me ?—hath he not been ever my torment ?—hath he not been eternally meddling with my domestic, with my most private affairs?—hath he not sported with my most tender feelings?—hath he not done all that in him lay to rend the ties of my dearest affections?"

"Ah, there, there again hast thou touched a chord the which doth ever vibrate to our shame," replied the King, deeply distressed by the remembrance of the subject which the Wolfe had awakened. "That disgraceful connection with thy leman Mariota Athyn—'tis that which hath poisoned the source of all thine actings, and that hath thereby transmewed the sweet waters of our life into bitterness and gall. Did we not write to thee with our own hand, urging thee to repentance, and beseeching thee to dismiss thy sinful and impure mate, and cleave to thy lawful wife, Euphame, Countess of Ross? and——"

"Nay, my liege-father, I wot this is too old a wound to be ripped up now," interrupted the Wolfe of Badenoch, beginning to wax more and more ireful; "ha! by the Rood, but 'tis sore to bear—cruelly sore. I did come hither to complain of the evil usage, of the disgrace, of the insults which this upstart priest hath thrown on me, hoping for a father's lenient interpretation of mine actings; yea, and that some salve might have been put to the rankling sores this carrion hath wrought on me; but the croaking raven hath been here before me—he hath already sung his hoarse and evil-omened song in thine ear, and all that I may now say cannot purge it of the poison with which it has been filled. By my trusty burly-brand, but thou hast forgotten the mettle of thy son Alexander."

"Oh dole, dole, dole!" cried the old King, clasping his hands in bitter affliction at the obstinacy shown by his son; "what can be done with a heart which beareth itself so proudly, which refuseth to listen to the voice of reason, which despiseth a father's counsels, and which resolveth to abide in its wickedness."

"Wickedness!" replied the Wolfe fiercely, and enchafing more and more as he went on; "by the holy Rood, but I do think that the word is ill applied. Mesceems that to throw her off who hath borne me five lusty chields, and who hath stuck to me through sun and wete, would savour more of wickedness than to continue her under the shadow of my protection. Ha! by my beard, but the voice of reason—ha, ha, ha!—is like to be as much with me in this case as against me. Thank God, I have reason—yea, and excellent reason too—full, vigorous, and perfect reason—whilst thou hast thine, old man, far upon the wane. Whatsoever mountaunce of reason thou mayest have once had, by Heaven, thou dost now begin to dote. Yet what was thy reason in like matters when it was at the best? Didst thou not thyself live a like light life in thy youthhood, and dost thou school me for having followed thine example?"

"Oh, dole, dole!—oh, woe for my sins!" cried the old man, agonized by his son's intemperate accusation of him; "'tis bitter, I wot, to bear the reproach of a wicked and undutiful son. O, alas for my sins! yet sure, if I have had any, as the blessed Virgin knoweth, I do humbly confess them, and may her holy influence cleanse me from them; if I have had sins, surely I have dreed a right sore penance for them in having thee as an everlasting scourge to my spirit. God, doubtless, gave thee to me for the gracious purpose that thou mightest be as bitter ligne-aloes to purge away the disease of my soul; and may He sanctify the purposes of mine affliction! But what art thou, sinful wretch that thou art, who wouldst thus cast blame on thy father, yea, and ignominy on thyself? If I sinned in that matter, did I not awaken from my sin and repent me? did I not do all that mortal could do to salve the misery I had begotten? did I not——. But thou art a cruel and barbarous wretch, a disgrace and infamy to thy father—a diseased, polluted, and festering limb, the which should be cut off and buried out of sight."

"Old dotard," cried the Wolfe, his fury now getting completely the better of him, "talk not thus—I—I—I—ha!—provoke me not—thou hadst better——"

"Get thee to thy home," replied the King; "turn thy vile strumpet forth, and, above all, humble thyself in penitence before the good Bishop Barr, who, godly man, hath been unwearied in his pious endeavours to reclaim thee from thy sinful and polluted life. Lick the dust from the very shoes of the saintly Bishop of Moray; in his Christian mercy he may forgive thee, and thou mayest then hope for restoration to our Royal favour; but if thou dost not this, by the word of a King, I will have thee thrown into prison, and there thou shalt liggen until thou shalt have made reparation to God and man for all thine impurities and all thine outrages and sacrileges."

"Ha!" cried the enraged Earl of Buchan, half drawing his dagger, and then returning it violently into its sheath, and pressing it hard down, as if to make it immovable there were the only security against his using it; whilst, at the same time, he began to pace the apartment in a furious manner; "ha! what! confine the eagle of the mountain to a sparrow's cage? chain down the Wolfe of Badenoch to some walthsome den? threaten thy son so, and all for an accursed, prating, papelarde priest?

Old man," said he, suddenly halting opposite to his father, and
putting a daring hand rudely on each shoulder of His Majesty,
while his eyes glared on him as if passion had altogether
mastered his reason—" old dotard carle that thou art, art thou
not now within my grasp? art not thine attendants beyond call?
is not the puny spark of life that feebly brens in that wintry
frame now within the will of these hands? What doth hinder
that I should put thee beyond the power of executing thy weak
threats?—what doth hinder me to——"

He stopped ere he had uttered this impious parricidal
thought more plainly. The old man blenched or quailed not;
nay, even the agitation which he had before exhibited—an
agitation which had been the result of anger and vexation, but
not of fear—was calmed by the idea of approaching death; and,
pitying his son more than himself, he sat immovable like some
waxen figure, his mild eyes calmly and steadily fixed upon the
red and starting orbs of the Wolfe of Badenoch. The group
might have been copied for the subject of the martyrdom of a
saint.

" 'Tis the hand of God that hindereth thee, son Alexander,"
said the aged Monarch, slowly and distinctly.

The ferocious Wolfe could not withstand the saint-like look
of his venerable father. The devil that had taken possession of
Lord Badenoch's heart was expelled by the beam of Heaven
that shot from the eyes of the good King Robert. Those of his
son fell abashed before them, and the succeeding moment saw
the hard, stern, and savage Earl on his bended knees, yea, and
weeping before the parent of whom his ungovernable rage might
have made him the murderer. There was a silence of a minute.

" Forgive me, forgive me, father. I knew not what I did; I
was reft of my reason," cried the Wolfe of Badenoch, groaning
with deep agony and shame.

" Son Alexander," said the King firmly, yet as if struggling
to keep down these emotions of tenderness for his son which his
sudden and unexpected contrition had excited; " Son Alexander,
albeit the consideration that the outrage was done by the hand
of a son against a father doth rather aggravate the coulpe of the
subject against the King, yet as it doth regard our own Royal
person alone, we may be permitted to allow the indulgent affection of the parent to assuage the otherwise rigorous justice of
the Monarch. So far as this may go, then, do we forgive thee."

The Wolfe remained on the ground, deeply affected, with his
head buried within his mantle.

" But as for what the duty of a Sovereign doth demand of

us," continued Robert, " in punishing these malfaitours who do flagrantly sin against the laws of our realm, and those, above all, who do sacrilegious outrage against our holy religion and Church, be assured that our hand will be as strong and swift in its vengeance on thee as on any other ; nor shall these thy tears make more impression on us than thine ungovernable fury did now appal us. Doubt not but thou shalt feel the full weight of our Royal displeasure, yea, and thou shalt dree such punishment as befits the crimes thou hast committed against God and man, unless thou dost straightway seek the footstool of the injured Bishop of Moray. Nay, start not away, but hear us ; for thou shalt suffer for thy crime, unless thou dost straightway seek the injured Bishop's footstool, and, bowing thy head in the dust before it, submit thee to what penance he in his great mercy and wisdom may hold to be sufficient expiation for thy wickedness."

The Wolfe of Badenoch started up and again began to pace the room in a frenzy ; and as Robert went on he became more and more agitated by passion, gnashing his teeth from time to time, and setting them against each other, as if afraid to permit himself the use of speech, and with his arms rolled up tight into his mantle, as if he dreaded to trust them at liberty.

" Nay, never frown and fret, son Alexander," continued the King. " By St. Andrew, 'tis well for thee that thou didst come to us thus in secret, for hadst thou but had the daring to appear before us when surrounded by the Lords of our Court, verily our respect for justice must of needscost have coarted us to order thee to be forthwith seized and subjected to strict durance. As it is, thou mayest yede thee hence for this time, that thou mayest yet have some space left thee to make thy peace with the holy Bishop Barr ; for without his pardon, trust me, thou canst never have ours. And we do earnestly counsel thee to hasten to avail thyself of this merciful delay of our Sovereign vengeance, for an thou dost not speedily receive full absolution from the godly prelate whom thou hast so grievously offended, by the word of a King I swear that thou shalt liggen thee in prison till thou diest."

The Wolfe of Badenoch heard no more. He relieved his hands in a hurried manner from the thraldom in which he had imprisoned them—halted in his walk, and glared fiercely at the King—groped again at the handle of his dagger—threw up his arms in the air with frenzied action—dashed his clenched fists against his head—and then rushed from the Royal presence with a fury which was rendered sufficiently evident by the clanging of the various doors through which he retreated.

The King folded his hands, groaned with deep agony, looked up to Heaven, uttered a short petition to the Virgin to have mercy on the disordered and polluted soul of his unhappy son, and to beseech her to shed a holy and healing influence over it that might beget a sincere repentance; and then giving way to all the feelings of a father, he burst into tears, which he in vain attempted to hide from the attendants, who soon afterwards appeared.

CHAPTER LIII.

The English Lady's Departure from Tarnawa Castle—The Crafty Son of the Wolfe of Badenoch.

IT was more than a week after the departure of the Earl of Moray and his friends from Tarnawa that Rory Spears was ordered to attend the Countess of Moray to receive her instructions for the duty his master had left him at home to fulfil. He was called into the room, where the lady in whose service he was to be employed was sitting veiled; but the Countess had not more than time to open the matter to him when she was interrupted by a message from her nephew, Sir Andrew Stewart, who, with very opposite feelings to those of Rory, had found some plausible excuse for not going with the Knights to Aberdeen, and now craved a short audience of the Countess. The English lady arose and retired into the recess of a window, where Katherine Spears was plying her needle, and Sir Andrew was admitted.

"My gracious aunt," said he, "I crave thy pardon for pressing my unbidden services; but, I beseech thee, let me not be deprived of the highest privilege that belongs to knighthood; I mean that of being the prop and stay of beauty in distress. Thou knowest that I have some half dozen spears here. Be it my pleasing task, I entreat thee, to protect the lady through those difficulties and dangers that may beset her path. Trust me, she shall pass unscathed while I am with her."

"I am utterly astonished, nevoy," replied the Countess; "how, I pray thee, art thou possessed of the secret that any such emprise may be in hand?"

"Nay, it mattereth but little, I trow, how I know that, my noble aunt," replied Sir Andrew Stewart with a careless smile; "but, what may be to thee some deal more strange, peraunter, I do know the lady too.—Madam," said he, gliding gently past his aunt, and going up to the window, " I have only to tell thee that we have met at Lochyndorbe, to convince thee that I do not err; yet be not alarmed at what I have said; trust me, thou shalt find that I have over much delicacy and knightly courtesy about me rudely to withdraw the veil in which thou hast been pleased to shroud thyself. I come but to offer thee mine escort, and I do fondly hope thou wilt not refuse me the gratification of shielding and defending thee with this arm, amid the many perils that may environ thee in thy travel between Tarnawa and Norham."

" 'Tis gallantly spoken of thee, nevoy," replied the Countess; "and albeit I do hope that danger there may be none in this our own country of Scotland, seeing, I have reason to believe, that the tide of war hath already been turned from us; yet will it give me joy to be certiorated of the safety of this sweet lady, who will doubtless most cheerfully accept thy proffered courtesy."

The lady readily made her acknowledgements to Sir Andrew, and gladly availed herself of his protection. Katherine Spears, who was to accompany her as a female companion on the journey, was rejoiced, like all young persons, at the prospect of so speedily seeing a little of the world, especially as her father was to be with her, and she was going in the service of a lady to whom she was already so much attached. But old Rory, who had been standing aloof during the conversation, showed by his countenance that he was ill satisfied with the arrangement which had been made, as well as with every one about him. He turned on his heel to leave the place, brandishing his gaud-clip, and followed by a brace of large wolf-dogs in couples, and began slowly descending the stairs, letting down first one-half of his ponderous person and then the other in succession, each step he took bringing out a *humph,* as a break to the continuity of his audible grumble.

"Ay, by St. Lowry, wha wad hae thought it, humph—wha wad hae thought that Rory Spears, humph—the Yearl's hench-man, as a body mought say, umph—that Rory Spears, that mought be ca'd as necessar till his back as the hound to his heel, or the falcon to his wrist, humph—that Rory Spears, I say, suld hae been left behind at sike a time as this, umph—like a crazy old destrier, or ane crackit targe, humph—and to be turned ower to be the plaything to a silly bit lassie, umph—and an Englisher quean, too, mair's the wonder, hugh!—Ay, and to make matters better, she hirsels me off, too, like ane auld pair o' boots, to put faith in that kestrel, Sir Andrew Stewart, humph

—a kite frae an ill nest, umph—ay, and ane that she'll aiblins find is no that ower mukel to trust till, maugre a' his havers, umph !—Weel, I maun e'en do the Yearl's wull, and his leddy's wull ; but, troth, I sall gie mysel no unnecessar trouble wi' the lass, umph—aboon a', sith she hath chosen her ain champion, hugh !—And that fooolish glaikit thing Kate, too, umph,—she's smiling and smirking, when it wad better set her to be greetin', hugh !—Och sirs, sirs, it's a queer warld this. Whiew, whiew, Brand—whiew, whiew, Oscar," cried he, whistling to his hounds, as he gained the area of the Castle-yard; "come awa, my bairns, ye hae mair sense than half o' human fouk."

Next morning the beautiful milk-white palfrey, that had been the gift of Sir Patrick Hepborne to his page Maurice de Grey, stood ready caparisoned in the court-yard, along with those of the party who were to form the escort. The lady recognised him as she descended from the terrace, leaning on the arm of Sir Andrew Stewart, and her eyes ran over at sight of the noble animal. She stopped to caress him silently ere she mounted him, her heart being too full to permit her to trust her voice in speaking to him. As Sir Andrew Stewart aided her to rise into her saddle, the generous steed neighed a joyous acknowledgment of the precious burden he was entrusted with. The lady waved her hand to the Countess, who streamed her scarf from a window, in visible token of the prayers she was putting up for her safety; and the cavalcade rode slowly forth, the beauteous eyes of the Englishwoman so dimmed with tears that she saw not aught that was around her. She felt as if, in leaving Tarnawa, the last tie that had bound her heart to the object of its tenderest affections were dissolved, and it seemed to wither within her. She drew her mantle over her head and gave way to her feelings, so that even Sir Andrew Stewart saw that, to break in upon her by conversation, would have been an intrusion too displeasing to be risked by him. He therefore continued to ride by her side in silence ; and the example of the knight and lady spreading its influence over the party, not a word was heard among the riders.

The lady at last felt that common courtesy required her to exert herself to control her feelings, and with some difficulty she began to enter into conversation with Sir Andrew Stewart, who rode at her side. She was now able to reconnoitre her attendants, which she had not had strength or spirits to do before. Before her rode the minstrel, Adam of Gordon, who no sooner saw that the lady had given his tongue license by breaking the silence she had maintained, than he began to employ the innocent artillery of an old man's gallantry on the dimpling charms of the lovely Katherine Spears, who, by her merry replies, and her peals of laughter, showed that she enjoyed the well-turned compliments and high-flown speeches of the courteous and fair-spoken bard. Next came the spearmen, and a couple of lacqueys, and one or two other attendants; and last of all, wrapped up in a new fishing-garb of more than ordinarily capacious dimensions, with an otter-skin cap on his head, and his gaud-clip in his hand, rode Rory Spears, sulky and silent, on a strong, active little horse, whose ragged coat, here hanging down in shreds, and there pulled off bare to the skin, showed that he had been just rescued from the briers, brambles, and black thorns of the forest, which had been waging war against his sides for many a day. Rory was followed by a single wolf-hound, and his whole accoutrements were so far from being fitted for the important duty of convoy, to which he had been appointed, that it almost seemed as if he had purposely resolved it should be so from pure spite against his employment.

" Be'st thou for the hunts, Master Spears ?" cried the wife of a publican, one of the Earl's dependants, whom curiosity hurried to her door to gaze at the travellers as they passed.

" Na, na, Meggy Muirhead," cried Rory, checking his horse for an instant. " The hunts, quotha ! pretty hunts, truly. But hast thou e'er a stoup o' yill at hand ? for thou must know I am bent on a lang and tedisome journey—yea, and I do jalouse a right thirsty and throat-guisening travel, gif I may guess from the dry husk that my craig hath already been afflicted withal ?"

" Thou shanny want a drap o' yill, Master Spears," cried Maggy Muirhead, who ran in and brought out a large wooden stoup, that, as she swung it on her head, foamed over the brim with generous nut-brown, by which she hoped to extract some information from Rory ; " and where mayest thou be ganging, I pray thee ? to join the Yearl maybe at the wars, I'se warrant ?"

" Wars," cried Rory, " wars ! Gie me the stoup, woman." And dropping his reins, and sticking the shaft of his gaud-clip into his enormous boot, he stretched out both hands towards the double-handed stoup, and relieving mine hostess' head of the weight, he applied its laughing brim to his lips, and slowly drained it so effectually that she had no occasion to replace it there. " Haugh ; wars, saidst thou, Mistress Muirhead?" cried Rory again, as he held out the empty vessel, one handle of which the hostess now easily received upon a couple of her fingers, and kept swinging about as he was speaking—" wars ! look at me, am I girded for the wars, thinkest thou ? Na, I've c'en taen on to be tirewoman to yon black-e'ed Englisher leddy, and I'm to get a kirtle, and a coif, and a trotcosy, ere long. What thinkest thou of that, Mistress Muirhead?"

"Preserve me, the Virgin have a care o' us a'!" cried Mistress Muirhead in wonder, as Rory rode away; "wha ever heard tell o' sike a thing? The man's gaun clean wud, I rauckon."

Sir Andrew Stewart was unremitting in his attention to the lady, and all his speeches and actions were so cunningly tempered with delicacy, that she neither had the power nor the will to conceal her satisfaction at his treatment of her. He inwardly congratulated himself on the advance he supposed he was making in her good opinion, and with some consummate art began to pave the way for a declaration of the violent passion he had secretly cherished for her, and gradually drawing nearer and nearer to her bridle rein as they rode, whispered the warm language of love in her ear in sentences that grew more and more tender at every step they advanced. Being occupied with her own thoughts, she had the appearance without the reality of listening to all he said, and the enamoured knight, interpreting her silence into a tacit approval, seized the first favourable opportunity of addressing her in plainer language.

"Most angelic lady," said he to her, as he sat beside her alone under an oak, where they had halted for rest and refreshment, "why shouldst thou undertake this tedious journey? Why shouldst thou leave Scotland, where thou mightst be made happy? To permit beauty so divine, and excellence so rare, to quit the Caledonian soil, would be a foul disgrace to the gallantry of its chivalry. Deign, I beseech thee, to listen to my ardent vows; let me be thy faithful knight. The love thou hast kindled in this bosom is unquenchable. Oh, let me——"

"Talk not thus besottedly, Sir Knight," replied the lady, interrupting him hastily and rather sternly; "I may not honestly listen to any such. Gallantry may peraunter come with good grace enow from thy lips, but permit not thyself license with me, whose heart doth already belong to another, and who can allow these words of thine no harbour. I shall ever be grateful to thee for this thy courteous convoy, but I can never return thy love. Stir not then the idle theme again."

"Nay, loveliest of thy sex," said the silky Sir Andrew Stewart with strange ardour, "to keep thy heart for one who hath so vilely entreated thee, and that after thou didst sacrifice all to yield thee to his service, were neither just to thyself nor to me. Let me occupy that place in thy heart, so unworthily filled by one whose very bearing towards thee (rather that of a master than of a lover) did sufficiently betray how much those matchless charms had ceased to please his palled appetite. Let me then——"

"Sir Andrew Stewart," replied the lady with astonishment, mingled with a dignified expression of resentment, "I know not what falsehood may have conspired to conjure up so much unseemly boldness in thee ; for I cannot believe that thou, a knight of good report, couldst thus have ventured to insult me, unless on some false credence. What though my love hath been misplaced ? My heart can never change. Urge not, then, again a theme that must ever rouse my indignation."

A cloud passed across the smooth brow of Sir Andrew Stewart as he received this resolute rejection of his passion, but it speedily disappeared.

"Forgive me, beauteous lady," said he, after a pause, " mine unhappy passion hath indeed mastered my better reason. Kill me not with thy frowns, but lay my fault to the account of these thy stirring charms. Sith that I dare not hope for more advancement, I shall still be the humblest of thy slaves, for to cease to love thee were impossible."

After this decided repulse, Sir Andrew Stewart confined his attentions to those of mere courtesy. Towards evening, they began to descend into a narrow glen, watered by a clear river. The hills arose on both sides lumpish and vast, and the dense fir forest that covered them rendered the scene as gloomy as imagination could fancy. As they picked their way down the steep paths of the forest, they caught occasional glimpses of the lone tower of a little stronghold that stood on a small green mound, washed by the river on one side, and divided from the abrupt base of the mountain by a natural ravine, that bore the appearance of having been rendered more defensible by art."

"Behold the termination of our journey of this day," said Sir Andrew Stewart to his lady. " Thine accommodation, beauteous damsel, will be but poor ; yet, even such as thou mayest find it, it may be welcome after the fatigue thou hast endured."

They reached the bottom, and, crossing the ravine by a frail wooden bridge, climbed a short ascent that led them to the entrance of the little fortalice, that wore the appearance of having been lately demolished in some feudal broil; for the massive iron gate of the court-yard lay upon its side, half buried among the weeds. Many of the outhouses, too, were roofless, and bore recent marks of having been partly consumed by fire.

"Alister MacCraw," said Sir Andrew Stewart to an old man who came crawling forth from the low entrance at the sound of

the bugle, " so thine old dwelling yet standeth safe, I see.   I
trust it may afford us some better harbour than those roofless
barns and byres do show ?"

" In troth, not mokell better, Sir Andrew Stewart," replied
the old man ; " but stone vauts wunna brenn like thaken roof.
Troth, 'tis mokell wonders that the Yearl o' Buchan wouldna
gar mend them up, and put some stout loons to guard them,
sith he doth use to lodge here when he doth travel between
Buchan and Badenoch ; an yon bit gavels were mended, an yon
bit breach in the wa', yonder, and——"

" Nay, Alister, spare thy counsel for my father's ear," replied
Sir Andrew Stewart impatiently, " and forthwith proceed to
house us as best thou mayest.   Let us see how this lady may
be bestowed."

" Thou knowest there be no great choice of chambers," replied the old man, with a certain leering chuckle, which the
lady could not understand.

MacCraw had reason for what he said, for the simple plan of
the building was of three storeys.   That on the ground floor
contained one large vaulted kitchen, occupied by the old man,
with two small dark chambers.   A stair, ascending from a
central passage, running directly from the outer door, led to a
room occupying the whole of the second floor of the building,
from a farther angle of which a small stair wound up, within a
hanging turret, to a single apartment in the uppermost storey.

The lady was ushered by Sir Andrew Stewart into the
kitchen, where MacCraw busied himself in renovating the
embers on the hearth, and soon afterwards in preparing some
refreshment.   The knight spoke little and abstractedly, and
rising at last, he mumbled something about orders he had to
give, and abruptly left the place.

" Erick MacCormick," said he to his esquire, " I would speak
with thee apart."

The esquire followed his master without the walls.   " Erick,"
said Sir Andrew again, when he judged that they were beyond
all risk of being overheard, " I did try to move the lady to give
ear to my love, but she hath sternly rejected me, yea, and that
with signs of no small displeasure.   I burn with shame for the
blindness with which my passion did hoodwink mine eyes."

" Hath she indeed refused thee, Sir Knight ?" demanded the
esquire.   " By the mass, but with such as she is I would use
smaller ceremony, as a preface to mine own gratification."

" Ay, if we could without detection, Erick," replied Sir
Andrew.

" This is a fitting place, meseems," said the esquire.

" 'Tis as thou sayest, a fitting place, good Erick," replied Sir Andrew ; " but albeit I may put sicker trust in thee, yea, and peraunter in most of mine own men, yet were it vain to hope that I might effect my purpose without being detected by one of her followers."

" Fear not, Sir Knight," said the esquire ; " I trow we are strong enough to eat them both up."

" Nay, nay—that is not what I mean," replied Sir Andrew ; " but thou knowest, Erick, that I do put value on character and reputation. I have hitherto passed as a miracle of virtue, as a rare exception in the lawless family to the which I belong; nay, even in the ear of my grandfather the King hath my praise been sounded, and my name standeth in godly odour with the very Bishop of Moray himself. I must not sillily wreck the vessel of my fortunes, while 'tis blown on by gales so favouring."

" In sooth, it were vain to hope to have thine actions pass withouten the remark of her followers," replied the esquire.

" Her followers !" said Sir Andrew. " I would not adventure aught with her, unless I were secure that none but the most faithful of mine own instruments should have cause even to guess at my share in the matter. Were but that sly fox, Rory Spears, out of the way, methinks we might contrive to throw dust in the eyes of the maid and the minstrel."

" If Spears be all the hindrance thou seest," replied Mac-Cormick, " I beseech thee be not afraid of him. By St. Antony, but he cares not the value of a cross-bow bolt for her of whom he hath charge. I have had much talk with him by the way, and I will pledge my life that thou shalt win him to thy purpose with as much ease as thou mayest lure thy best reclaimed falcon. The old allounde is sore offended at being left behind by his master the Earl, to attend upon a damsel ; yea, and the damosel herself, too, seemeth to have done little to have overcome the disgust he hath taken at his employment. Trust me, Sir Knight, never hungry trout was more ready to swallow baited hook than old Rory Spears will be to pouch a good bribe, that may be the means of ridding him of so troublesome and vexatious a duty."

" Art thou sicker in thy man ?" demanded Sir Andrew Stewart, stopping short, after taking a turn or two in silent thought, with his arms folded across his breast.

" Nay, he did so effunde his ill humour to me by the way, that I will venture my life for him," replied the squire.

"Seek him out straightway, and bring him hither," said the knight.

CHAPTER LIV.

Sir Andrew's Deep-laid Plot—An Unexpected Arrival.

MacCormick proceeded in quest of Spears, and Sir Andrew Stewart continued to pace backwards and forwards upon the green sward outside the rampart wall, pondering how he might best open the negotiation. It was already dark; and, villain as he was, he felt thankful that it was so, for he had ever been accustomed to set so much value on outward reputation, that he was ashamed to lift the veil, even to him whom he was about to make an accomplice in his crimes. Footsteps were at last heard approaching softly, and Rory and MacCormick saluted him.

"Master Spears," said Sir Andrew Stewart, "this is a troublesome task the Earl hath imposed on thee."

"Task!" replied Rory, in a gruff ill-humoured tone; "I carena mokell how dour his tasks be, so he be present himsel for to see me fulfil them; but to cast his trusty servant frae his back—me, wha used to be tied, as I mought say, till his horse's curpin, and to tak a parcel o' young loons to the wars wi' him, is enow to break ane auld crazy heart like mine."

"'Tis indeed a bitter reproach on thee, Rory," said Sir Andrew, "and but little amended by the service thou art put upon. But what doth hinder thee to return? Surely I may save thee all this long and painful journey. My protection, methinks, may suffice for the lady."

"Na, na," replied Rory impatiently, being secretly nettled at the cheap rate at which his services were apparently held by the man he despised; "na, na—thy protection, Sir Andrew Stewart, that is to say, the protection o' thy stout lances yonder, may be a' weel enew; but I maun not at no rate be kend to slight the wull o' my lord the Yearl; and to leave the lass, and gang back afore the journey be weel begood—hoot, that wadna do at a'."

"Thou sayest true, Rory," replied Sir Andrew; "but thou knowest I have ever been a friend to thee, and I would fain do thee a good turn on this occasion. Methinks I have hit on a scheme for saving thee thy pains and travel, preserving thy good character for fidelity to the Earl, and, finally, putting a purse of gold into thy pouch."

"Ay!" replied Rory, in a tone of surprise. "By St. Lowry, an' thou canst make a' that good, thou wilt work marvels, Sir Andrew."

"Nay, 'twill need no conjurer," said Sir Andrew Stewart. "Keep thou but out of the way this night, and see that thou dost keep the old minstrel with thee. Thou canst not sleep in the lady's chamber, thou knowest, therefore it is but natural to leave the entire charge of her to me, who am to spend the night in MacCraw's kitchen. And then—d'ye mark me—if the lady should chance to disappear during the night, no one knowing how, the blame must of needscost fall on me alone. Thou mayest then yede thee back with thy daughter to the Countess to-morrow to tell the tale; nay, peraunter, I may go with thee to make all matters smooth, by the confession of my careless watch; and so thou shalt hie thee after the Earl, and may yet join his standard in the field. Dost thou comprehend me now, friend Rory?"

Rory stood silently pondering over the tempting proposal. Sir Andrew Stewart drew forth the purse of gold, and the broad pieces chinked against each other as he dangled it in his hand. Their music was most seducing.

"Give me the purse," said Rory at length.

"'Tis thine," cried the overjoyed Sir Andrew Stewart; "I know thee to be faithful, and I fear me not but that thou wilt earn it."

"I will do my best to deserve it," replied Rory.

"Quick, then, to thy duty," said Sir Andrew Stewart. "Be it thine to see that no one may approach the tower who might disturb our plans."

"The safety of my daughter Kate must be secured to me," said Rory.

"I am answerable for it," replied Sir Andrew Stewart. "If I can so arrange it, she shall be committed to thine own care; but if I should be defeated in this matter, she shall sleep in the highest chamber, where she may be out of the way. But, happen what will, her safety shall be mine especial care."

The conference being thus ended, Sir Andrew Stewart returned to partake of the meal which MacCraw had by this time prepared. A manifest change had taken place in his manner. His conversation was gay and sprightly, and he was so entertaining that the lady sat listening to him for some time after supper. At length the fatigue she had undergone began to overcome her, and she signified her wish to retire to rest. Katherine Spears, who had been out and in more than once during the

25

meal, now lifted a lamp to light her mistress upstairs to the principal apartment in the tower, which was destined to receive her.

"Katherine," said Sir Andrew Stewart, carelessly, after having
paid his parting evening compliments, " when thou hast done
with thine attendance on thy lady, MacCraw will show thee the
way to where thy father is lodged, where a bed hath been prepared for thee also."

" Nay, Sir Knight," replied Katherine, with uncommon
energy, " I will at no rate quit the tower, though I should sit
up all night by this fire."

"That as thou mayest list, my maiden," said Sir Andrew
Stewart, with the same tone he had already spoken in ; " I did
but wish to give thee the best harbour the place might yield.
But now I think on't, the high chamber may do well enow for
thee after all.   Here—drink thy lady's health in the remnant
of her wine-cup, ere thou goest."

Katherine did so, and then tripped up stairs before her mistress. She no sooner found herself fairly within the door of the
lady's apartment, than she shut it behind her, and began to look
eagerly for the bolt, and she exhibited no small dismay when she
saw that it had been recently removed.   Trembling with agitation, she then conducted the lady with a hurried step towards a
pallet-bed, which had been prepared for her in one corner of the
place, and seating her on the blankets—

" Oh, my lady, my lady," whispered she, half breathless with
alarm, " I fear that some foul treachery may be designed against
thee. Whilst thou didst sit at thy meal I didst step me up
hither to see thy couch prepared, and as I returned through the
lower passage, I overheard certain voices in the little vault to
the right—' When is it to be done ?' said one. ' It must not be
until late in the night,' replied another, 'for we must be sure
that she sleeps.' ' Ay, and her Abigail alswa,' said the first
man. ' Nay, I trust that she will be without the tower, for she
would spoil all,' said the other. Just then as I was listening,
the outer door of the tower was slowly opened, and my father's
head slowly appeared. He drew back when he saw me. I ran
out to him. ' Help, help, father,' said I to him in a whisper,
' or the lady will surely be the victim of treachery.' "

" And thy father," said the lady, stretching eagerly towards
her damsel—" what did thy father say ? "

" He laughed at me, lady," replied Katherine, hesitating—
" he laughed at my fears."

" But what were his words ?—give me his very words, I
entreat thee," anxiously demanded the lady.

"His words, lady," replied Katherine—"his words were but those of a bold man, who scorneth the fears of a weak woman. Trust me, he must be faithful, lady."

"Ay, Katherine, but his words—what were his very words?" asked the lady, with the same eagerness of manner.

"Nay, indeed, they were naught, lady," replied Katherine, "but thou shalt have them as they did drop from his very mouth. 'Tush! foolish quean,' said he in a tone of displeasure at what he did suppose to be my silly apprehension; 'where sould there be treachery, thinkest thou? But an there sould, tell thy lady that Rory Spears is ane auld fusionless doited dolt-head, as unfit for stoure and strife as for war-stratagem. What did cause his being left behind his lord the Yearl, but superannuation? The silly coof, Sir Andrew Stewart, guse though he be, is mair to be lippened till than Rory Spears. But get thee in, lass, and tend on thy mistress;' and so saying he opened the door of the tower, and shuffled me by the shoulder into the kitchen where thou didst sit at supper. In vain did I try to catch thine eye after I entered. But oh, sweet lady, believe not that my father can be traitor to thee."

"His words have spoken him to be anything rather than my protector," replied the lady, pale with alarm at what her maid had told her. "But," added she, with a forced smile, "thou hast redeemed his sin by nobly resolving to share my danger, when thou hadst the opportunity of escaping from it. As it is, I must prepare me for the worst. I have still a dagger, and weak as is mine arm, it shall do bloody work ere I do yield to such villainy; yet, after all, thou mayest have mistaken the words thou didst hear. Let us trust to God and the Holy Virgin, then, and, above all things, let us put up special prayers for protection from Her, who is purity itself."

The lady and her maiden knelt down together, and joined in earnest devotion, that was only damped at times as fancy led them to imagine they heard a soft tread on the stair, or a suppressed breathing at the door of the chamber. When their orisons were ended, they sat silent for some time. All was already quiet below, and an unaccountable and perfectly uncontrollable sleep, that seemed to bid defiance even to their apprehensions, was stealing insidiously upon them. Just at this moment Katherine Spears uttered a short and faint scream, and had nearly swooned away. The lady started up in a frenzy of alarm, and drew her dagger, when, much to her astonishment as well as to her relief, she perceived the large wolf-hound that had followed Rory Spears, which, having unceremoniously put

his cold nose into Katherine's well-known hand, had produced
the damsel's sudden panic. The lady and her attendant viewed
the unexpected appearance of this mute defender as an especial
interposition procured for them by their prayers. But the
scream, though scarcely audible, might have been heard below,
and they listened in quaking dread. All continued quiet underneath them. But, as they still listened, they distinctly heard a
heavy footstep cautiously planted, but, to their utter amazement, it came from above downwards. The lady grasped her
dagger more firmly, and wound up her determination to use it,
if need should demand it. The steps still came stealing down
the turret stair that communicated with the uppermost apartment, and at last the bulky form of Rory Spears, gaud-clip and
all, appeared before them.

"Heaven be praised!" murmured Katherine, as she sprang
to meet her father. "By what miracle of Heaven's mercy art
thou here?"

The lady stood aloof with her dagger clenched, still doubtful
of his errand.

"And what for needs ye ask?" said Rory to his daughter,
with a certain archness of expression quite his own. "Hath
not my Lord the Yearl o' Moray made a tirewoman o' me? and
was Rory Spears ever kend to be backward at his Lord's
bidding? Verily, it behoveth me not to desert mine occupation.
So I am here to do my new mistress's wark, I promise thee."

"May Heaven grant that thou mayest not have something
more cruel to do to-night than attend on dames," said Katherine
Spears; "yet verily thy coming is most providential, for assuredly we are sore beset with treachery."

"Ay, ay, I ken a' that," replied Rory; "and troth it was
the very thoughts o' a bicker that pat the pet out o' me, and
wiled me hither. But stap ye baith yere ways up the stair
there, and liggen ye down quietly, and leave me here to deal
with whomsoever may come."

"He is true to thee, after all, lady," said Katherine with
exultation.

"I rejoice to see that he is faithful," replied the lady; "may
St. Andrew reward him! Already are my fears banished, but
irresistible sleep oppresses me. I feel as if I had swallowed
some potent drug. I cannot keep my head up."

"Nay, Katherine nods too," said Rory; "by the mass, some
sleepy potion must have been mingled with your wine. Let
me help ye both upstairs; ay, there ye may rest in quiet,"
said he, as he set down the lamp and was preparing to leave

them, " and I'se leave Oscar with ye as a guard, for the loon
had nae business here, and wi' me he might spoil sport;" and
saying so, he tied up the dog beside them, and ere he had done
which both were in a profound sleep.

Having returned to the apartment below, Rory threw himself
down on the bed, and huddled himself up in the blankets, with
his inseparable companion the gaud-clip by his side, and there
he lay patiently to watch the event, until, the fire falling low on
the hearth, the darkness and his own drowsiness overcame his
vigilance, and he fell into deep oblivion.

He had not lain long in this state when the door slowly
opened, and the head of Sir Andrew Stewart appeared. Over it
there was a lamp, which he held up in his hand, so as to throw
a glimmer of light into the farther corner of the place. He
paused for a moment, and seeing the form of a figure within
the blankets, and observing that all was quiet, he withdrew the
lamp.

"She sleeps," whispered he to his esquire and the two men
who were with him; " the potion hath worked as it ought.
Approach the bed, yet be cautious; rude carelessness might
break her slumbers. Let her not be awakened while she is
within earshot of those within the place; ye may be less
scrupulous anon. Approach and lift her up in the blanket; her
weight can be but as that of an infant in such hands."

"No sike infant, I wot," muttered one of the men to the
other, as they strained to lift up the blanket with the enormous
carcase of Rory Spears in it.

" By the mass, but she is a load for a wain," said the other.

" Be silent, ye profane clowns," said Sir Andrew.

" St. Roque, how she doth snore ! " said the first, in a lower
voice.

" Silence, I say, villains," said Sir Andrew, " silence, and bear
her this way."

" Hold, hold, Murdoch, the blanket is slipping," said one;
" keep up your end, or we are done with her."

" Hout, she's gone," cried Murdoch, as his end of the blanket
slipped altogether, and Rory was rolled on the floor.

Though Rory had slept, his mind had been so fully possessed
with the action he had prepared himself to expect, that he had
dreamt of nothing else. He was no sooner rudely awakened by
the shock of his fall than his mind became full of his duty.

" Ha, villains," cried he, starting to his legs in a moment,
and roaring to the full extent of his rough voice, as he flourished
his gaud-clip around him in the dark like a flail ; " ha, caitiffs,

have I caught ye ?   What, would ye dare to lay impure hands
on the tender form of a lady of sike high degree ?   By St.
Lowry, but I'll settle ye, knaves."

All was now confusion.   The knight and his instruments
sought for the door with a haste that almost defeated their
object.   Precedence was by no means attended to ; and Sir
Andrew Stewart, being jostled aside, received a chance blow
from Rory's gaud-clip that prostrated him senseless on the floor.
The squire and the two men rushed down stairs, with Rory hard
at their heels, and were making towards the door of the tower
when it suddenly opened, and a party of horsemen appeared
without.

"Halt !" cried a voice like thunder, that instantly arrested
the flight of the fugitives, and sent them, crouching like chidden
curs, into the kitchen.   The light that was there showed the
terror and dismay of their countenance, and it also explained
the cause, for he who entered was the Wolfe of Badenoch.

"What rabble and uproar is this in the lone peel-tower of
Duneriddel ?" demanded he.   "Ha, Alister MacCraw, what
guests be these thou hast got ?   Ha, Erick MacCormick and
my son Andrew's people !   What a murrain hath brought thee
here, Master Esquire ?   Ha—speak.   Where is the worthy
knight thy master ? "

"My Lord—my master, Sir Andrew—my Lord—" replied
MacCormick, hesitating from very fear.

"Ha ! and Rory Spears too," continued the Wolfe ; "what
dost thou make here, old ottercap ?   Speak, and expound the
cause of this uproar, if thou canst."

"I will, my Lord," said Rory, "and that in sike short speech
as I well ken thou lovest to have a tale dished up to thee.   Sir
Andrew Stewart, thy son, did covenant wi' my leddy the
Countess o' Moray, thy sister, to convoy ane Englisher leddy
safe frae Tarnawa to Norham, and sure enew he brought her
here, being sae muckle o' the gate ; but having no fear o' God
or the Saunts afore his eyne, he did basely try to betray her,
just the noo, afore I cam doon the stairs there."

"Ha, hypocritical villain ! cried the Wolfe.   "By Saint
Barnabas, but I have long had a thought that his affected purity
was but a cloak for his incontinence."

"'Tis all a fabrication," cried MacCormick, who had now
recovered his presence of mind so far as to endeavour to defend
his master, though at the expense of truth ; "'tis fearful to hear
sike wicked falsehoods against thy son Sir Andrew Stewart."

"My Lord Yearl," cried Rory, taking Sir Andrew's purse of

gold from his pouch, "an thou believest that I do lie, here is a soothfast witness to what I have uttered."

"Ha ! my son Andrew's purse, with his cipher on it," cried the Wolfe, casting a hasty glance at it. "How camest thou by this, Master Spears ?"

Rory quickly told the Wolfe of the attempt made by Sir Andrew Stewart to bribe him from his duty, and shortly explained how he had watched his opportunity to creep up stairs unobserved, and to secrete himself in his daughter's apartment, together with the result.

"Foul shame on the sleeky viper," cried the Wolfe indignantly, after he had listened to Rory's abridgement : "But where hath the reptile hidden himself all this while ? By my beard, but he shall be punished for this coulpe." And so saying he seized upon a lamp, and rushing up stairs in a fury, beheld his son stretched on the pavement senseless, with a stream of blood pouring from his temple and cheek, which bore the deep impression of the hooked head of Rory Spears' gaud-clip.

"Hey, ha !" exclaimed the Wolfe, with a changed aspect, produced by the spectacle which his son presented : "by'r Lady, but Andrew hath got it. Fool that he was, he hath already been paid, I wot, for his wicked device. Ha ! the saints grant that he may not be past all leechcraft. Would that thou hadst hit less hard, old man. Though he be but the craven cock-chick of my brood, yet would I not choose to have his green grave to walk over."

"So please thee, my Lord, it was dark, and I had no choice where to strike," said Rory, with much simplicity of manner. "But fear not," added he, after carelessly stooping down to examine the wound, "trust me, 'tis no deadly blow ; moreover, 'tis rare that ill weeds do perish by the gateside. I'se warrant me he'll come to ; his breath is going like a blacksmith's bellows. But is't not a marvel, after all, to behold how clean I did put my seal upon his chafts, and it sae dark at the time ? I'se warrant he'll bear the mark o't till's dying day. Here, MacCormy, help me down the stair wi' him. Thou and I will carry his worship's body wi' mair ease than thou and thy loons wad hae carried mine, I rauckon. But hear ye, lad ; give not the lie again to any true man like me, or that brain-pan of thine may lack clampering."

The Wolfe of Badenoch was relieved by discovering, on examination, that there was good hope of his son's recovery ; and he employed himself and his people in using every means to bring it about. The whole night was spent in this way, but it

was only towards morning that Sir Andrew Stewart began to
show less equivocal signs of returning life, and even then he still
remained in a state of unconsciousness as to what was passing
near him.   The circumstance of the sleepy potion they had
drank accounted for the lady and her damsel having remained
undisturbed amid all the confusion that had prevailed.   But the
Wolfe of Badenoch, having occupied the morning in superintending the preparation of a litter to transport his wounded son
to his Castle in Badenoch, when all was ready, became impatient
to depart, and desirous to see the lady ere he did so.   Rory Spears
was accordingly despatched to awake her, and in a short time
she and Katherine appeared, with eyes still loaded with the
soporiferous drug they had swallowed.

"Ha, what!" cried the Wolfe with astonishment, the moment
the lady appeared; "by the beard of my grandfather, but I am
petrified.   Who could have dreamt that it was thou, my beauteous damosel?   By'r Lady, but it is strange, that whether thou
dost appear in the hauqueton or in the kirtle thou shouldst still
be harnessed by importunate love-suit.   But," continued he,
courteously taking her hand and kissing it, "it erketh me sore
to think that wrong so foul should have been attempted against
thee by a son of mine.   Thou hadst a claim for something better
at our hands, both for thine own sake and for that of Sir Patrick
Hepborne, a knight of whom the remembrance shall ever be
grateful to me.   Trust me, it giveth me pleasure to behold
lealty where tyrant Church hath tied no bands.   Thou hast
been basely deceived by him who undertook for thine honourable escort to Norham, and albeit I have reasons to think that
the proud Priest of Moray hath secretly obtained a power of
Royal troops to repossess him in his Badenoch lands, yet shall
not this knowledge hinder me from fulfilling for thee that
service which my traitor son hath so shamefully abused.   I shall
be myself thy convoy.   Let the croaking carrion-crow of Elgin
come if he dares; I have hardy heads, I trow, to meet him, who
will fight whether I am there or not.   Ha! by my grandfather's
beard, an he had not flown from Aberdeen with the wings of the
raven, he mought have been e'en now past giving me trouble."

"My noble Earl of Buchan, I do give thee thanks for thy
kind courtesy," replied the lady; "but I may in no wise suffer it
to lead thee to make sacrifice so great.   Trust me, I fear not for
the journey whilst I have this good man Rory Spears as mine
escort.   Under the guardance of one so prudent, brave, and
faithful as he has proved himself to be, I should nothing dread
to wander over the world."

" And I wad defend thee, my leddy, frae skaith, were it but frae the tining o' a single hair o' thy bonny head, yea, to the last drap o' bluid in my auld veins," cried Rory with great enthusiasm, being delighted to observe that his worth was at last fairly appreciated.

" Ha ! by my troth, but 'tis bravely spoken in both," cried the Wolfe. " Depardieux, I shall not venture to interfere where there is so great store of confidence on one side and fidelity on the other. But yet thou must take some pairs of my lances with thee, Rory, for thou art but slenderly backed, methinks."

Even this much both the lady and Master Spears were disposed to refuse; but on learning that the mountain range through which they must pass was at that time more than ordinarily infested with wolves, Rory changed his mind, and consented to take four able lances with him, to be returned when he should consider their services no longer necessary.

All being now arranged for the departure of the two parties, the Wolfe of Badenoch became impatient. He courteously assisted the lady to mount her palfrey, and, kissing her hand, bid her a kind adieu. He was about to leap into his own saddle, when he was accosted by Rory Spears.

" My Lord Yearl o' Buchan, seeing that thy son Sir Andrew, i' the litter yonder, hath not yet gathered his senses anew to tak the charge o' his ain cunzie, I here deliver up to thee, his father, this purse o' gowd he did gi'e me, the which my conscience wull at no rate let me keep, seeing that it wad in nowise let me do that the which was covenanted for the yearning o't."

" Nay, by St. Barnabas, honest Rory, but thou shalt keep the purse and the coin," cried the Wolfe, delighted with Rory's honesty ; " thou hast rightly earned it by thy good service to thy lady. I will be answerable to my son Andrew for this thy well-won guerdon, so make thyself easy on that score."

" Thanks, most noble Yearl," cried Rory as he pouched the purse, and mounted his ragged nag to ride after the lady, his countenance shining with glee. " By'r lackins, but this is as good as the plunder of a whole campaign against the Englishers."

CHAPTER LV.

*Travelling through the Wild Forest—A Dreadful Spectacle—
Arrival at the River Tweed.*

THE English damsel and her attendants travelled slowly by a
different route through the wild forest scenery of those mountains with which the reader is already sufficiently familiar.   So
much of the morning had been expended ere they set out, that
the length of their day's journey was considerably curtailed, and
the heaviness that still hung on the eyelids of the lady and
Katherine, from the drugged draughts they had swallowed, so
overcame them, that they were well contented to look for a place
of rest at a much earlier hour in the evening than they would
have otherwise done.   The information that Rory Spears had
gathered about the wolves made him also very ready to halt
betimes, that he might have sufficient leisure to fortify the
party against any chance of nocturnal attack from these ravenous animals, in a region where no human dwelling was to be
expected.

It still wanted nearly two hours of sunset when the cavalcade
was winding gently up the narrow bottom of a wild pass, that,
like a vast rent or cut in the mountains, divided the chain from
its very summit to its base.   From the close defile below, the
eye could hardly ascend the steep and even slope of the rocky
precipices to half their height, so closely did they approach on
either hand.   The pine forest, though still continuous, began to
grow thinner as they advanced, and Rory Spears, like an able
leader, was carefully scanning every point where he might hope
to discover a strong and convenient position for encampment.
At length one of the Earl of Buchan's troopers, well acquainted
with these wilds, showed him the upright face of a tall projecting
crag, at a great height above, where there was a small natural
cavern, and, accordingly, thither it was resolved that they should
ascend.

The ascent was long and arduous, but when they did reach
the spot, it was discovered to be admirably fitted for their purpose.   The rock rose smooth and perpendicular as a wall, and
in the centre of it was the mouth of the cavern, opening from a
little level spot of ground in front.   Rory began to take immediate measures for their security.   Broken wood was collected
in abundance, and a semi-circular chain of fires kindled, so as

fully to embrace the level ground, and touch the rock on either side of the cavern. Heather beds were prepared for the lady and her damsel under the dry arch of the cliff; and their hasty meal being despatched, they wrapped themselves up in their mantles, and prepared themselves with good-will to sleep off the stupifying effects of the narcotic. Rory meanwhile drew his cavalry within his defences, and having posted and arranged his watches so as to ensure the keeping up of the fires, he sat down with the rest to recreate himself with what store of provisions they had carried along with them.

The lady's sleep was so very sound for some hours that it bid defiance to all the merriment, the talking, and the music, that successively prevailed without. But at last it yielded to the continued twanging of the minstrel's harp, and she awaked to hear him sing, with great enthusiasm, the concluding stanzas of some tale, which he had been rhyming to those around him :

If minstrel inspiration wells
From yonder star-besprinkled sky,
To which my heart so strangely swells,
As if it fain would thither fly ;

Then on those mountain tops that rise
Far, far above the fogs of earth,
Thicker and purer from the skies
Must fall that dew of heavenly birth.

What marvel, then, my native land,
That heaves its breast to kiss high Heaven,
Hath fill'd my heart and nerved my hand,
And fresher inspiration given ?

Then if my heart a spell hath wove
More potent than of erst it threw,
And ye have wept its tale of love,
With rifer tears than once it drew,

Think not thou mayest the song reward
With thine accustom'd dearth of praise,
It comes from no weak mortal bard—
'Tis Scotland's spirit claims the lays !

Perfectly refreshed by her slumber, and cheered by the harper's strains, the lady arose from her couch, and stepped forth from the cavern to join her applause to the rudely-expressed approbation of Rory and his comrades. The air was balmy and refreshing, and she staid to hold converse with the good old minstrel.

" 'Tis a beautiful night, Adam," said she ; " see how the moonbeam sleeps on the bosom of yonder little lake far up the pass. How dark do these masses of pine appear when contrasted with the silver light that doth play beyond them on those opposite steeps; how deep and impenetrable is the shadow that hangeth over the bottom far below us, where all is silent save the softened music of the stream murmuring among the rocks. But hark, what yelling sounds are these that come borne on the breeze as it sigheth up the pass?"

"'Tis the distant howling of the wolves, lady," cried the harper; "methinks the rout cometh this way. An I mistake not, 'tis a ravenous pack of famished beasts that do pursue a deer or some other helpless tenant of the woods. Hark, the sound doth now come full up the bottom of the pass. List, I pray thee, how it doth grow upon the ear."

"I do hear the galloping of a horse, methinks," cried Rory Spears, who stood by.

"Holy Virgin, what dreadful screams were these?" cried the lady, starting with affright.

"St. Andrew defend us," said the minstrel, shrinking at the thought; "it may be some fiend o' the forest that doth urge his hellish midnight chase through these salvage wilds."

"Na, na, na," replied Rory Spears, gravely; "troth, I hae mair fear that it may be some wildered wanderer hunted by a rout o' thae gaunt and famished wolves. St. Lowry be wi' us, is't not awful?"

"Holy St. Cuthbert protect us," exclaimed the lady, after a pause, and shuddering as she spoke; "that cry, oh, that cry was dreadful; 'twas a shriek of terror unspeakable; fear of an instant, of a most cruel death, could have alone awakened it. Gracious Heaven, have mercy on the wretch who did give it utterance!"

"Hear, hear; holy St. Giles, how he doth cry for help!" said Rory Spears. "Hear again; 'tis awsome. St. Hubert be his aid, for weel I do trow nae mortal man can help him."

"Oh, say not so," cried the lady, with agonizing energy; "oh, fly, fly to his rescue; there may yet be time. Fly—save him—save him, and all the gold I possess shall be thine."

"Nay, lady," replied Rory, "albeit the very attempt wad be risk enew, yet wud I flee to obey thy wull withouten the bribe o' thy gowd; and the mair, that it wud be a merciful, a Christian, and a right joyful wark to save a fellow-cretur frae sike ane awsome end. But man's help in this case is a'thegither vain. Dost thou no perceive that the clatter o' his horse's heels is no longer to be heard? nay, even his cries do already return but faintly from far up the pass? And noo, listen—hush—hear hoo fast they do die away; and hark, hark—thou canst hear them nae mair."

"He hath indeed spurred on with the desperate speed of despair," said the lady; "but oh, surely thou mayest yet stop or turn his fell pursuers. Oh, fly to the attempt. Nay, I will myself go with thee. Hark, all the echoes of the glen around us are now awakened by their fearful howlings. Quick, quick; let us fly downwards—'tis but a mere step of way."

"Alas, lady," replied Rory, "to try to stop the accursed pack were now hopeless as to think to gar the raging winds tarry on the mountain side. These hideous howls do indeed arise from the shades beneath us; but had we the legs and the feet o' the raebuck, the ravening rout wad be a mile ayont us ere we could reach the bottom. Hark, hoo they hae already swept on. Already the cruel din frae their salvage throats doth become weaker; and noo—hist, hist!—it is lost far up the bosom of the mountains. May the Virgin and the good St. Lawrence defend the puir sinner, for his speed maun be mair than mortal gif he 'scapeth frae the jaws o' thae gruesome and true-nosed hounds. By my troth, an we hadna taken the due caution we might hae been a supper to them oursels at this precious moment—the Virgin protect us!"

"Oh, 'tis most horrible," cried the lady, as she rushed into the cavern, her mind distracted, and her feelings harrowed up with the thoughts of the probable fate of the unhappy traveller. She sunk on her knees to implore mercy for him from Heaven, after which she threw herself on her couch; but her repose was unsettled; and when she did sleep it was only to dream of the horrors her fancy had painted.

By the time the sun had begun to gild the tops of the mountains, Rory Spears was in action. The lady arose unrefreshed; and, after she and her attendants had partaken of a slight repast, they were again in motion. Descending by a steep and difficult, though slanting path, they gradually regained the bottom of the pass, and proceeded to trace it upwards in a southern direction. As they obtained a higher elevation the pine trees became thinner, and at length they reached to a little mossy plain, where they almost entirely disappeared. In the middle of this was the small sheet of water which had been rendered so resplendent in the eyes of the lady the night before by the moonbeams. It was a deep inky-looking pool, surrounded by treacherous banks of black turf.

"Is this what distance and moonlight made so bewitchingly beautiful to our eyes?" said the lady to the minstrel.

"Thus it doth ever chance with all our worldly views, lady," replied the old man. "Hope doth gild that which is yet at a distance, but all is dark and cheerless when the object is reached."

As they spoke the approach of the party disturbed a flight of kites and ravens, which arose with hoarse screams and croakings from something that lay extended amid the long heath near the water's edge. It was the skeleton of a horse. The flesh had been so completely eaten from the bones by the wolves that but little was left for the birds of prey. The furniture, half torn off, showed that the creature had had a rider. A few yards farther on a single wolf started away from a broken part of the bog. Rory Spears' gaud-clip was launched after him with powerful and unerring aim, and its iron head buried in the side of the animal, while at the same moment the quick-eyed Oscar seized the caitiff by the throat, and he was finally despatched by several lances plunged into him at once. They sought the spot whence the gaunt animal had been roused, and their blood was frozen by the horrid spectacle of the half-consumed carcase of a man.

It was of size gigantic; and although the limbs and body had been in a great measure devoured, yet enough of evidence still remained in the rent clothes and in the lacerated features of the face to establish beyond a doubt to the lady and the minstrel, who had known him, that he who had thus perished by so miserable a fate was the wizard Ancient Haggerstone Fenwick.

A leathern purse, with a few gold coins in it, was found in his pouch; and, among other articles of no note, there was a small manuscript book of necromancy, full of cabalistic signs.

The spectacle was too horrible and revolting for the lady to bear. She therefore besought her attendants to cover the wretched remains, and with Katherine Spears retired to some distance until this duty was performed and a huge monumental cairn of stones heaped over them, after which they again proceeded on their way.

The troopers belonging to the Wolfe of Badenoch were sent back as soon as Rory Spears judged they might be spared with safety, and nothing occurred during the remainder of the journey to make him regret having so parted with them. As the party travelled through the fertile Merse they found that which should have been a smiling scene converted into a wilderness of desolation. The storm of England's wrath had swept over it, and the rifled and devastated fields, the blackened heaps of half-consumed houses and cottages, around which some few human beings were still creeping and shivering, like ghosts unwilling to leave the earthly tenements to which they had been linked in life, brought the horrors of war fresh before them. The aged man and the boy were the only male figures that were mingled with those groups of wailing women that appeared. All who could draw a sword or a bow, or wield a lance, were already on their way to join the Scottish host, their bosoms burning with a thirst of vengeance.

As they were lamenting over the melancholy scene they were passing through—for even the English damosel deplored the ravages committed by her countrymen—their way was crossed by a troop of well-armed and bravely-appointed horsemen, which halted, as if to wait until their party should come up. Rory advanced to reconnoitre.

"Ha, Sir Squire Oliver," said he to the leader, whom he immediately recognized as belonging to the Lord of Dirleton, "can that in very deed be thee? Whither art thou bound in array so gallant?"

"Master Rory Spears," replied the squire with a look of surprise—"what, art thou too bound for the host?"

"Nay," replied Rory, mournfully, "I hae other emprise on hand just at this time. Goest thou thither?"

"Yea," replied the esquire, "I go with my Lord's service of lances to join the collected Scottish armies on their way to Jedworth. There will be rare work anon, I ween. Some English horses have been dancing over these fields, I see, but, by'r Lady, the riders shall pay for the sport they have had."

"Ha, their backs shall be well paid, I warrant me," cried Rory, flourishing his gaud-clip around his head, while his eyes sparkled with enthusiasm.

"Nay, fear not," replied the esquire; "the rogues shall feel the rod, else I am no true man. But St. Andrew be with thee, good Master Rory, I have no further time to bestow." And as he said so he gave the word to his men to move forward; the bugles sounded, their horses' heels spurned the ground, and their armour rang as they galloped briskly away, to make up for the time lost in the halt.

The lady and her attendants rode slowly on, but Rory lingered behind, to follow the rapid movement of the warlike files with an anxious eye; and when they wheeled from his view he heaved a sigh so deep that it was heard by the foremost of his own party.

"What aileth thee, Rory?" demanded Adam of Gordon.

"Heard ye not their bugles as they went?" replied Rory to him. "Was not the very routing o' them enew to rouse the

spirit o' a dead destrier, and dost thou ask what aileth me? Is't
not hard to be sae near the Yearl and yet to see as little o' him
or his men as gif they war in ane ither warld? is't not cruel for
a man like me to be keepit back frae the wark that best beseemeth him whan his very heart is in't?"

"And why shouldst thou be kept back from it, Rory, now
that thy duty to the lady is performed?" demanded the harper.

"Dost thou no see Kate yonder?" replied Rory sullenly.
"What is to be done with the wench, think ye? Sure I maun
e'en yede me back again to convoy the puir lassie safely to her
mother."

"If the care of Katherine be all thy difficulty, Rory," said the
lady eagerly, "thou mayest easily provide for her safety by con-
fiding her to me, on whom thy doing so will moreover be
conferring an especial gratification. Let her, I pray thee, abide
with me at Norham, whilst thou goest to the wars; and when
peace, yea, or truce doth happily come again, thou mayest forthwith reclaim her of me. Let me entreat thee, oppose not my
wishes."

Rory's rough but warm heart had been long ere this entirely
gained by the kindness, condescension, and beauty of the English
damosel. He could not have refused her request, whatever
difficulties it might have involved; but her present proposal was
too congenial with his own wishes, and her offer altogether too
tempting to be resisted.

"Troth, my leddy," replied he, with a tear glistening in his
eye, "when we first forgathered at Tarnawa, and when the Yearl
tell'd me that I was to be buckled till thy tail, I maun e'en confess I was in a sair cross tune at the news, for thou mayest see
it's no i' my nature to be governed by women-fouk, and gin the
truth maun be tell'd, it was wi' sair ill-wull I cam wi' thee.
But noo, by St. Lowry, I wad follow thee to the very warld's
end; troth, thou mayest e'en whirl me round and round with
thy pirlywinky; and so, though I am no just confidently sicker
that what I am doing is a'thegither that the which may be approven by my good dame at hame yonder, yet will I yield me to
thy wishes and mine ain. Kate shall wi' thee to Norham, and
I'll just tak a bit stride after the Yearl to see what he and the
lave are a-doing."

"But thou shalt thyself with me to Norham first, that I may
thank thee properly for the protection thou hast afforded me,"
said the lady.

"Nay, that may in nowise be, leddy," replied Rory; "I shall
see thee safe to the northern bank of Tweed; but I wot nae

Southern stronghold shall see me within its bounds, save as ane enemy, to do it a' the skaith a foeman can, and that I would fain shun doing to ony place that mought have thy good wishes."

After some farther travel the broad walls and massive towers of Norham Castle appeared before them, glowing with the slanting rays of the declining sun. A few steps more brought the Tweed in sight, and Rory Spears instantly halted.

" And noo I fear I maun leave thee, my leddy," said he, with an afflicted countenance, " for yonder's the Tweed."

The lady approached him, and, kindly taking his horny hand, gave utterance to the most gratifying expression of her strong sense of the services he had rendered her, and at the same time attempted to force a purse upon him.

" Na, na, my leddy, I'se hae nae gowd frae thee," said he ; " besides, I hae naething ado wi' gowd whare I'm gaun ; I'se get meat, drink, and quarters withouten cunzie, an' I'm no mista'en.—Na, na," continued he, as she pressed the purse upon him, " an ye wull hae it sae, keep it for Kate yonder ; she may want it, puir thing. May the blessed Virgin be thy protection, my bonnie bit lassie," said he to Katherine, as he turned about to her and pressed her to his breast.—" Hoot toot, this 'll no do —ye maunna greet, bairn," added he, as the tears were breaking over his own eye-lids. " Fear ye na I'll be back wi' thee ere lang, an I be spared. By St. Lowry, that's true, my leddy, ye maun promise me that if onything sould happen to hinder me frae coming back, ye'll see that somebody conveys her as safe to Tarnawa as I hae brought thee to Norham."

Katherine sobbed bitterly at the idea which her father had awakened. The lady readily promised him what he wished. Rory again pressed his daughter to his bosom, and, striking the side of his garron two or three successive blows with the shaft of his gaud-clip, he darted off, and was out of sight in a moment.

The lady, accompanied by Katherine Spears and the minstrel, slowly sought the bank of the Tweed. A signal was made for the ferry-boat, and they were wafted into England. At the gates of Norham Castle the lady was speedily known, and its friendly walls received her and her two companions.

26

CHAPTER LVI.

Old Acquaintances at the Hostel of Norham Tower—Great Gathering at Jedworth—The Council of War.

It was some days after the lady's arrival that five horsemen knocked at the gate of the hostel of the Norham Tower. They were clad rather as pilgrims than as warriors, and, arriving by the English side of the river, were judged to have come from the south. Matters had undergone a change since we had last occasion to notice the hall of Norham. Old Kyle had been gathered to his fathers, his buxom wife had wept her fair number of days, and, beginning to recover her spirits by the reflection that she was a well-looking and wealthy widow, her heart was already besieged by numerous lovers. Though under a woman's government, the police of the Norham Tower was at this moment more strict than usual. The war had made its mistress careful to rid it at an early hour every night of all straggling topers. There were certain privileged customers, indeed, to whom a more liberal license was granted, and of this number was Mr. Thomas Turnberry, the squire equerry.

As two of the strangers, of nobler mien than the rest, entered the common room, they found the esquire in the act of rising from table, with another man in whose company he had been drinking.

"A-well," said the latter; "I bid thee good e'en, Sir Squire. I'll warrant thou shalt not find better steeds between Tweed and Tyne than the two I have sold thee."

"Ay, ay, Master Truckthwaite," replied Turnberry with a sarcastic smile, "thy word is all well; yet would I rather trust the half of mine own eye than the whole of thy tongue in such matters. Good e'en, good e'en. A precious knave, I wot," added he, after the man was gone.

"Doth that varlet sell thee good cattle, Sir Squire?" said one of the strangers who had entered.

"Nay, in truth, he is a proper cheat," replied Turnberry. "But the villain had to do with a man who hath lived all his life in a stable, and one, moreover, who hath sober, steady. habits. Your drunkard hath ever but poor chance in a bargain with your sober man."

"Most true," replied the stranger. "Here, tapster; a flagon of Rhynwyn. Wilt thou stay, Sir Squire, and help us to drain it?"

" Rhynwyn!" exclaimed Turnberry ; "by St. Cuthbert, but
there is music in the very clink of the word. Nay, Sir Pilgrim,
I care not an I taste with thee ere I go; I am but a poor
drinker, yet hath honest Rhynwyn its charms."

" Ha," said Tom, after deeply returning the stranger's pledge,
" this is right wholesome stuff, I promise ye, my masters. 'Tis
another guess-liquor than old Mother Rowlándson's i' the
Castle."

"Thou art of the Castle, then?" said he who had always
spoken. "I drink to the health of thy gallant old captain, Sir
Walter de Selby."

"Thank ye, thank ye," replied Tom, taking the flagon.
" Well, here's to old Wat. Many is the ride we have had over
the Border together; and many is the hard knock we have both
ta'en and given, side by side. Trust me, there breathes not a
better man. His health, God wot, hath been none of the best
of late; so, with thy good leave, Sir Pilgrim, I'll drink to it
again."

"Hath he not a daughter?" demanded the pilgrim.

"Yea, that he hath," replied Tom—"an only daughter,
whose beauty hath been the talk of all Northumberland."

" Let us drink to her health, then," said the pilgrim.

" Here's to the Lady de Vere, then," said Turnberry, lifting
the flagon to his head to do justice to the health.

"The Lady de Vere !" said the pilgrim who had not yet
spoken, betraying an emotion that escaped Tom Turnberry, in
the long draught he was taking.

" Ay, the Lady de Vere," said Tom, taking the flagon from
his head. "'The Lady Eleanore de Selby is now the Lady de
Vere, as we have all heard at the Castle since two or three days
have gone by. Sir Walter would have fain had her marry Sir
Rafe Piersie, who courted her, but his haughtiness sorted ill
with her high and untameable spirit ; so she was contrarisome,
and ran away with a love of her own choosing some time
ago."

"And who might the lover be who bore away so rich a
prize?" demanded the pilgrim.

"Why, one of the Court lordlings, as we now learn, a Sir
something de Vere, a kinsman to the King's favourite, the
banished Duke of Ireland. He is but lately come from abroad,
it seems, for he is a foreign knight born, and being suspected as
coming on some secret mission to the King, it is thought that
he will rise high in his good graces. The poor ould soul, Sir
Walter, did live in grievous case until these few days bygone,

for he knew not until then what had befallen his daughter. But now that he hath learned who his son-in-law is, he hath somewhat raised his head. But fie on me," added the squire, after a long draught, that enabled him to see the bottom of the flagon, " I must hie me to the Castle ; and so good night, and many thanks, my civil masters. Trust me, I shall right willingly bestow a can upon you when ye do come this way again, if ye will but ask for old Thomas Turnberry, the esquire equerry."

The dialogue between Tom Turnberry and the two strangers had been over for a good hour, when another conversation took place a few steps from the gate of the inn, between Mrs. Kyle and one who considered himself a favourite lover.

" These be plaguy cunning knaves," said Mrs. Kyle ; " they thinks, I'se warrant me, that no one doth know 'em ; yet—but I shall say nothing, not I."

" I dare swear a man would need to be no fool who should strive to deceive thee, Mrs. Kyle," replied her companion, willing to draw her on a little.

" Me!" replied she ; " trust me, the old Fiend himself would not cheat me ; for instance, now, that saucy Sang there did no sooner show his face within the four walls o' the Norham Tower than I did straightway know him through all his disguises ; and so, having once nosed him, I did quickly smell out his fellow-esquire, and the two knights their masters."

" That was clever in thee, i' faith, Mrs. Kyle," replied her companion.

" Yea, but my name be not Margaret Kyle an I make no more out by my cleverness," said the dame. " But mum for that."

" Nay, thou knowest thou canst not be Margaret Kyle long, my bonny dame," replied the man.

" Fie thee now," replied she, " sure it will be long ere I do trust me to men again, after honest Sylvester, my poor dear husband that was."

" And what didst thou say they were here for ?" demanded her companion.

" Ye may trow they are here for no good," replied the dame. " I'll warrant me the seizing o' them will be a right brave turn ; but mum again, for he who is to take them this night did say as how none should ken nothing on't till the stroke should be strucken ; yea, and by the same token he did gie me kisses enow to seal up my mouth."

"And when did Sir Miers tell thee this?" demanded the man.

"Sir Miers!" replied Mrs. Kyle; "laucker-daisey, did I tell thee that it was Sir Miers? St. Mary, I had nae will tae hae done that. Hoot, toot, my lips hae no been half glued."

"And so thou dost say that Sir Miers is to surround the house to-night, and to take these same strangers?" observed the man.

"Yea, but of a truth I shouldna hae tell'd thee a' that; may my tongue be blistered for't," replied Mrs. Kyle; "for he bid me take especial care, aboon a' things, to let thee know nought on't."

"Nay, Mrs. Kyle," said the man, "but thou knowest thou dost love me over much to hide anything from me."

"O ay, for a matter o' that, I do love thee well enow," replied Mrs. Kyle; "but Sir Miers hath such pleasant ways with him,"

"Hath he?" replied the man carelessly. "Thou didst say, I think, that the attempt is to be made at midnight, and that thou art to be on the watch to let them in?"

"Nay, then," said Mrs. Kyle, "I did verily say no sike thing, I wot. What I did say was this, that Sir Miers is to be here an hour after midnight, and that John Hosteler is to let them in."

"Ay, ay, I see I did mistake thy words," replied the man. "Why, holy St. Cuthbert, thou wilt get a power of money for thine information."

"So Sir Miers hath promised me," replied Mrs. Kyle; "but what doth chiefly season the matter to my stomach is the spicy revenge I shall hae against that flouting knave Sang, and the very thought o' this doth keenly edge me to aid the gallant Sir Miers in his enterprise; yet, to tell thee the truth, the handsome knight might rauckon on as much service at my hands, yea, or more, when it mought please him bid me."

"So," replied her companion; "but come, I will see thee into the house, drink one cup of thine ale with thee, and so speed me to the other end of the village to Sir Miers. Who knows but I may be wanted after all to bear the brunt of this business."

By this time the two knights and their three attendants were the sole tenants of the common room, and this circumstance, coupled with the disguises they wore, led them to imagine that they ran no risk of discovery.

Robert Lindsay, who was the fifth man, took up a lamp, and sallied forth to look at the horses ere he should seek repose.

All was quiet in the court-yard, as well as in the various buildings surrounding it.   He entered the stable, but, though there
were main horses enow there belonging to the hostel, he saw,
with utter dismay, that the five steeds belonging to his party
were gone.   He turned to rush out of the stable to tell the
knights of this treacherous robbery, when the light of the lamp
in his hand flashed on the figure of a man, who was determinedly
posted in the doorway, as if resolved to oppose his passage.

"Ralpho Proudfoot!" exclaimed Lindsay in astonishment;
and then observing that he was fully armed, and that he carried a lance in his hand, whilst he himself had not even his
sword, he gave himself up for lost; but resolving to sell his life
as dearly as possible, he wrenched a rung from one of the stalls,
and planted himself in a posture of defence.

"Nay, thou needest look for no injury at my hands," said
Proudfoot; "this haughty spirit of mine, the which did once
make me thy determined foe because thou wert promoted above
me, doth now prompt me not to be outdone by thee in a generous deed.   I come to warn thee that an attempt on the liberty,
if not on the lives, of thee and those that be with thee, is to be
made, within less than an hour hence, by Sir Miers de Willoughby and a strong force.   The reward for taking prisoners of sike
note, together with the gold to be gotten for their ransom, is the
temptation to this enterprise.   Lose not a moment then in
rousing the knights, and warning them of their danger."

"But what hath become of our horses?" demanded Lindsay, not yet recovered from his surprise.

"It was I who removed them," replied Proudfoot.   "I took
them from the stable, after leaving the hosteller to sleep off the
heavy draughts of ale I made him swallow; they stand ready
caparisoned under the trees a few yards behind the inn.   Quick,
bring me to the knights, that I may show them their danger,
and teach them how to avoid it; not a moment is to be lost."

Without further question, Lindsay led the way to the common
room where the knights were lying.   They were soon roused,
and listened to Proudfoot's account of the plot against them
with considerable surprise; but they hesitated to believe him,
and were in doubt what to do.

"Nay, then, Sir Knights," said Proudfoot, "an ye will hesitate, certain captivity must befall ye.   Captivity, did I say?
yea, something worse; a base and black thirst of vengeance doth
move this treacherous knight against thee, Sir John Assueton.
I have reason to know that he hath ever cherished it sith thy
last encounter."

" 'Twere better to plant ourselves here, and fight to the death with what weapons we may have about us," said Sir Patrick Hepborne.

" Right, my friend," said Sir John Assueton, " we at least know and can be true to one another, and that of itself will give us victory."

" We shall be prepared for them," said Mortimer Sang, " and we shall make them fly before us by the very suddenness of our assault."

" How many De Willoughby spears are of them ?" demanded the taciturn Roger Riddel, with extreme composure.

" Some two dozen at the least, I warrant me," replied Proudfoot, " and all fully appointed."

" Bring they Norham Castle on their backs ?" demanded Riddel again.

" Nay," replied Proudfoot, " their leader hath kept his scheme to himself, that he may have the greater share of booty and ransom money."

" But Norham Castle hath ears," said Riddel again.

" Thou sayest true, friend," replied Proudfoot. " Were resistance to be made, the din of arms and the noise of the assault would soon bring out the garrison upon ye. Quickly resolve, Sir Knights, for the hour wanes, and they will be here anon. What can ye fear of traiterie from me ? Could I not have left ye to fall easy victims to Sir Miers de Willoughby's snare ?"

" So please ye, gallant knights, I will answer with my life for the truth of Ralpho Proudfoot in this matter," said Lindsay confidently.

" Nay, an ye fear me, ye shall all stand about me," said Proudfoot ; " and if ye do find me a traitor, your five daggers may drink my blood at once."

The minds of the two knights were at last made up, and they resolved to trust themselves to the guidance of Ralpho Proudfout. Armed with their daggers alone, they stole silently out in the dark, and were so planted by him behind the gate as to be prepared to rush out when the time for doing so should come. Ralpho Proudfoot cautioned them to keep perfectly quiet. To attempt to escape along the street of the village at that moment would have subjected them to certain observation : they were therefore to wait his signal, and to follow him. He placed himself, as he had said, in the midst of them, and set himself to listen for a sound from the outside.

They had not been long posted, when footsteps were heard

approaching very gently. There was then some whispering, and
a slight cough. Proudfoot immediately answered it.

"Art there, John ?" said a voice in an under tone.

"Yen," replied Proudfoot, imitating the language of the
hosteller, "but they be's still astir ; so when the yate be opened,
ye maun rush in like fiends on them, for the hinge do creak,
and they will start to their arms wi' the noise. Are ye a'
ready ?"

"We are," replied the voice without.

"Noo, then, in on them and at them," cried Proudfoot,
throwing the gate wide open, so as to conceal himself and his
companions behind it.

In rushed Sir Miers de Willoughby, at the head of a large
party of his men ; and out went Ralpho Proudfoot, with the
two Scottish knights and their attendants. The gate was hastily
locked externally ; the horses were quickly gained, and mounted
in the twinkling of an eye ; and Ralpho Proudfoot, who had
taken the precaution to have his steed placed with the rest, got
to saddle along with them. As they rode past the gate of the
hostel of the Norham Tower, the loud voices, and the execrations
of Sir Miers de Willoughby and his people, and the shrill screams
of Mrs. Kyle, told them that the failure of the plot had been
already discovered by the actors in it.

"So," said Ralpho, in half soliloquy, as he guided the knights
down the village street at a canter—"so, thou didst cease to
trust me, Sir Miers, me who hath been faithful to thee to the
peril of my salvation. By St. Benedict, thou shalt now find
that it would have been well for thee to have trusted me still ;
yea and thou didst tamper with her whom I would have espoused.
By the bones of St. Baldrid, but thou mayest mate thee with
her now an thou listest, for I am done for ever with her, with
thee, and with England, except as a focman."

The two knights made the best of their way until they had
got beyond the English march, and were fairly on what might
be termed Scottish ground. Armed men were still crowding in
greater or lesser bodies to Jedworth, where those who had by
this time assembled formed a large army. They were encamped
on what was then called the High Forest ; and thither the two
friends were hastening, and were already but a little way from
the position of the troops, when Sir Patrick Hepborne halted,
and thus addressed his companion—

"Canst thou tell me, Assueton, what may cause the mingled
crowd of squires, lacqueys, grooms, and horses, that doth surround the gates of yonder church ? Meseems it some convoca-

tion, and those varlets do wait the pleasure of some personages of greater note who are within."

"Thou art right," replied Assueton; "for to-day was fixed for a council of war to be held within that church, and it would seem that at least some, if not all, of the nobles and knights of the host are already met. Let us hasten thither, I beseech thee. I long to learn what is to be the plan of our warfare."

"I shall at least meet my father there," said Sir Patrick listlessly, and as if he cared for little else. "Do thou follow us, Lindsay, to take our horses, and then wait for us, with the esquires, under the spreading oaks of yonder swelling knoll."

On entering the church the two knights learned that they had arrived just in time for the opening of the business. The Earls of Fife, Douglas, Dunbar, and Moray were there, and indeed all the leading nobles and knights of Scottish chivalry; and the doors being closed, the assembly were soon deeply engaged in the gravest deliberations.

Whilst the council of war was so employed within the church, Mortimer Sang was lying at the root of an aged oak, holding conversation to, rather than with, Roger Riddel. Near them were the horses tethered and feeding, under the eyes of Robert Lindsay, and his old, though newly-recovered comrade, Ralpho Proudfoot, who were earnestly engaged in talking over many a story of their boyhood.

"What dost thou stare at so, friend Riddel?" demanded Sang, who observed his comrade stretching his neck so as to throw his eyes up the trough of a ravine down which stole a little rill, that murmured around the knoll where they were sitting; "what dost thou see, I say, friend Roger, that thou dost so stretch thy neck like a heron, when disturbed in her solitary fishing?"

Roger replied not, but nodded significantly, and pointed with his finger.

"Nay, I see nought," replied Sang, "save, indeed, a swinking churl, who doth untie and lead away a gallant and bravely caparisoned steed from yonder willow that weepeth over the stream."

Roger looked grave, and nodded again, and looked as much as to say, "A-well, and dost thou see nothing in that?"

"Nay, now that the knave hath mounted," said Sang, "he seemeth to ride like one who would make his horse's speed keep his neck from the halter. By'r Lady, he's gone already. Is the rogue a thief, thinkest thou, Roger?"

"Notour, I'll warrant me," replied Squire Riddel.

"By St. Baldrid, had we but thought of that sooner, we might have frayed the malfaitor, yea, or taken him in the very fact," said Sang. " But now we are too late to meddle in the matter."

"We are no thief-takers," replied Roger Riddel, with great indifference.

"Nay, now I think on't, he who would hang up his horse so in the Borders may be his own thief-taker for me," replied Sang ; " but look ye, friend Roger," continued he, after a pause, " who may that stranger be who cometh forth from the crowd armed and spurred, yea, as a squire ought, yet who walketh away as if neither groom nor horse tarried for him ? Stay— methinks he cometh this way."

The stranger looked around him, after getting rid of the embarrassment of the crowd about the church, and then moved quickly towards the knoll where the two esquires were sitting, and, passing quietly under it, without either looking at or speaking to them, made his way up the ravine in the direction of the willow-trees, where the horse had been tethered. The path he followed was so much lower than the ground whence they had observed the actions of the man who took the horse, that the stranger walked smartly on for more than a bow-shot, ere he came within view of the willow-trees. Then it was that he began to betray great confusion. He hastened to the spot whence the horse had been so lately removed, and finding that he was irrecoverably gone, he clasped his hands, looked up to heaven, and seemed to be lost in despair.

" Dost thou mark yonder man who did walk by here alone?" demanded Sang eagerly. " Behold how he doth show signs of distress, that would mark him to be the master of the horse which the thief took. I ween he be no Scottish squire, for he knew no one, and seemed to covet concealment as he did pass us by. An I mistake not, he will prove better worth catching than the thief would have done. Let's after him, Roger, that we may prove my saying."

Roger, though slow to speak, was quick to act. The two esquires seized their steeds, and throwing themselves into their saddles, galloped at full speed after the stranger. Startled by the sound of pursuit, he at first made an effort to escape, but. seeing how hotly he was chased, he lost spirit, and, shortening his pace, allowed them to come up with him.

"Whither wouldst thou, comrade ? and whence hast thou come ? and what dost thou, a spurred esquire, without a horse?" demanded Sang, in a string of interrogations.

" I do but breathe the air here," replied the man in great

confusion. "As for my horse, I do verily believe some villain hath stolen him from those willow trees where I had tied him."

"But why didst thou tie thy horse in this lone place ? and how comest thou thus unattended ?" demanded Sang again. "But, hey, holy St. Baldrid, is it thou, my gentle Clerk-Squire Barton ? When, I pray thee, didst thou leave the peaceful following of the godly Bishop of Durham, to mell thee with dangerous matters like these thou art now in ? By the blessed Rood, it had been well for thee, methinks, an thou couldst but have aped somewhat of the loutish Scot in thy gait, peraunter thou mightest have better escaped remark ? So, thou hast become a spy on these our Eastern Marches, hast thou ? By the mass, but thou must with us to the conclave. It doth erke me to speak it, mine excellent friend, but, by'r Lady, I do fear me that thou mayest hang for it."

"Talk not so, Squire Sang," replied Barton, with a face of alarm. "Trust me, I have seen nought—I know nought. Thou knowest we did drink together in good fellowship at Norham. Let me go, I do beseech thee, and put not an innocent man's life to peril, seeing that appearances do happen to be so sore against me."

"Sore against thee, indeed, pot-companion," said Roger Riddel, portentously shaking his head.

"Yea, appearances are sore against thee, Master Barton," re-echoed Sang. "Verily, we did behold thee as thou didst come forth from yonder church, where thou didst doubtless possess thyself of much important matter that did there transpire, the which it will be by no means convenient that thou shouldst carry in safety to those who may have sent thee hither. Better that thou hadst chanted thirty trentals of masses in the goodly pile of Durham for the soul of thy grandmother, ay, and that fasting, too, than that thou shouldst have set thy foot for a minute's space of time within yonder church this day."

"Let me go, good gentlemen, I do beseech ye," said Barton. "Squire Riddel, hast thou no compassion for me ?"

"Much," replied Roger; "Natheless, thou must with us, Squire Barton."

"Nay, in truth thou must with us without more ado," said Sang; "yet make thyself as easy as may be ; for, in consideration of our meeting at Norham, I shall do thee all the kindness I may consistent with duty, both now and when thou shalt be sent to the fatal tree, to the which I do fear thy passage will be short and speedy."

The English esquire shuddered, but he was compelled to sub-

mit; and he was accordingly led by his captors to the church,
where the council of war was assembled. The news of his
capture excited great interest and commotion among the knights;
and the Earl of Fife, who presided over their deliberations, had
no sooner learned the particulars of his taking than he ordered
him into his presence. Barton came, guarded by Mortimer
Sang and Roger Riddel. He had put on the best countenance
he could, but judging by the working of his features, all his
resolution was required to keep it up.

"Bring forward the prisoner," said the Earl of Fife. "What
hast thou to say for thyself, Sir Squire? Thou hast been taken
in arms within the Scottish bounds—thou hast been seen of
several who did note thine appearance at this our secret meeting—and there be knights here, as well as those worthy
esquires who took thee, who can speak to thy name and country. Whence art thou come? and who did send thee hither to
espy out our force, and to possess thyself of our schemes?"

"Trusting to the sacred office of my Lord the Bishop of Durham, I came but as a pious traveller to visit certain shrines,"
replied Barton. "Being in these parts, I wot it was no marvel
in me, the servant of a churchman so dignified, to look into the
church, and——"

"Nay, nay—so flimsy a response as this will by no means
serve," interrupted the Earl of Fife, who, though cool, calm, and
soft in manner, was in reality much more cruel of heart than
his brother the Wolfe of Badenoch himself, albeit devoid of the
furious passion so ungovernable in that Earl. "He doth but
trifle with our patience. Let a rack be instantly prepared, and
let a tree be erected without loss of time, whereon his tortured
limbs, whilst their fibres shall yet have hardly ceased to feel,
may be hung as tender food for the ravens. His throat shall
be squeezed by the hangman's rope, until all he hath gained by
his espial be disgorged or closed up for ever within it."

Barton shook from head to foot at this terrible sentence,
uttered with a mildness and composure that might have suited
well with a homily. His face grew deadly pale, despair grappled
at his breath, and he gasped as if already under the hands of
the executioner. His eyes, restless and protruded, seemed as if
anxious to shun the picture of the horrible death that so soon
awaited him. His lips moved, but they were dry as ashes, and
they gave forth no sound. Sang and Roger Riddel almost
regretted that they had been instrumental in bringing the
wretch there, though by doing so they had so well served their
country. They looked at each other with horror; but in such

a presence, and at such a time, Sang was condemned to remain as dumb as Squire Riddel. The good Earl of Moray had more liberty of speech, and he failed not to use it.

"Be not too hasty with him, my Lord," said he ; "he may yet peraunter be brought to give us tidings of the enemy. Let him but give us what information he can, under promise, that if it be found soothfast, he shall have no evil. Meanwhile, after he shall have effunded all that it may concern us to know, let him be delivered into the custody of the Constable of Jedworth, with him to liggen in strict durance, until we shall have certiorated ourselves by our own experience, whether the things which he may tell be true or false, with certification that his life shall be the forfeit of the minutest breach of verity. If he doth refuse these terms, then, in the name of St. Andrew, let him incontinent lose his head."

A hum of approbation ran around the meeting, and the Earl of Fife, though in secret half-chagrined that he had not had his own will, saw that in this point he must give way to the general voice.

"Thou dost hear thy destiny," said he to the prisoner ; "what is thine election ?"

"My Lord, seeing that I have no alternative but to yield me to dire necessity," answered the English esquire, with an expression of infinite relief in his countenance, "verily, I do most gladly accept your terms. As God is my judge, I shall tell thee all I know, without alteration, addition, or curtailment."

"Who sent thee hither, then ?" demanded the Earl of Fife.

"Being one to whom these Marches be well known, I was chosen by the Lords of Northumberland, and sent hither to learn the state of your enterprise ; as alswa to gather which way ye do propose to draw."

"Where, then, be these English Lords ?" demanded the Earl of Douglas.

"Sirs," replied the captive squire, "sith it behoveth me to say the truth, ye shall surely have it. I be come straight hither from Newcastle, where be Sir Henry Piersie, surnamed Hotspur, from his frequent pricking; and his brother Sir Rafe Piersie, yea, and divers other nobles and knights, flowers of English chivalry, all in readiness to depart thence as soon as they may know that ye have set forward into England ; for, hearing of the strength of your host, they do not choose to come to meet you."

"Why, what number do they repute us at ?" demanded the Earl of Moray.

"Sir," replied the esquire, "it is said how ye be forty thousand men and twelve hundred spears."

"What then may be their plan?" demanded the Earl of Fife.

"This be their plan, my Lord," replied the esquire: "If ye do invade England by Carlisle, then will they straightway force a passage for themselves by Dunbar to Edinburgh; and if ye do hold through Northumberland, then will they enter Scotland by the Western Marches."

As the English esquire Barton was thus delivering himself, the Scottish lords threw significant glances towards each other. Some further questions of less moment were put to him, and after he had answered to all with every appearance of perfect candour—

"Let him be removed into the strict keeping of the Constable of Jedworth," said the Earl of Fife. "His life and liberty shall be safe, provided his report shall in all things prove true, and for this I do gage my word in name of myself and all these noble lords and knights here present. Should he be found to have spoken falsely in the veriest tittle, he knoweth his fate."

After the prisoner was withdrawn under the charge of a guard, the Earl of Fife conveyed thanks to the two esquires for having so well fulfilled their duty to Scotland. The assembled lords and knights were overjoyed that the intent of their enemies should have been thus made so surely known to them, and a buzz of congratulation arose.

"This is all well, my Lords," said the Earl of Fife, after having again procured silence; "but let us now to council, I entreat you, that we may straightway devise how best to avail ourselves of the tidings we have gained. For mine own part I do opine that we should break our host into two armies. Let the most part, together with all our carriage, go by the Cumberland Marches and Carlisle, and let a smaller body draw towards Newcastle-upon-Tyne, to fill up and occupy the attention of the enemy assembled there. I speak under the correction of wiser heads," continued the Earl, bowing around him with great condescension, so as to excite a burst of approbation from those weaker spirits whom he daily flattered until he made them his staunch partisans—"I speak, I say, under the correction of wiser heads; yet meseems, from those unanimous applauses, my Lords, that you do honour my scheme of warfare with your universal support; and such being the case, I may now say, that whilst I do myself propose to lead the main army by the Western Marches, I shall commit the command of the smaller body to the brave Earls of Douglas, Dunbar, and Moray. For this last service, methinks, three hundred lances, and three thousand crossbows and axemen, may well enow suffice."

"By St. Andrew, but 'tis a fine thing to know how to keep one's head safe," whispered Sir William de Dalzell ironically to Sir Patrick Hepborne the younger; "what thinkest thou of him who shall shoulder ye a catapult to crush a swarm of dung flies, whilst he doth send out others to war on lions and bearded pards with a handful of hazel nuts. Depardieux, he who goeth by Carlisle may march boldly from one end of Cumberland to the other, with a single clump of spears at his back, ay, and take the fattest spoil too; but he who shall march to Newcastle will want all the hardy hearts and well-strung thewes and muscles he can muster around him, and is like after all to get nought but a broken head for his journey. Holy St. Giles, but 'tis well to take care of one's self."

By a little management, the opinion of the council of war was easily brought perfectly to coincide with the views of the Earl of Fife. But so great was the name of James Earl of Douglas, that it was in itself a host. The two brothers, George Dunbar Earl of Dunbar and March, and John Dunbar Earl of Moray, too, were so much beloved, that a puissant band of knights voluntarily mustered under their banners. Among these were Sir Patrick Hepborne, his son, and Sir John Assueton. Ere the assembly dissolved, it was determined that the armies should divide, and march on their respective routes early on the ensuing morning; and all was bustle and preparation accordingly.

CHAPTER LVII.

The Scots besieging Newcastle—The Fight on the Walls.

THE smaller force, under the Douglas, broke up from Jedworth, and set forward in high spirits, cheered by the good countenance and presence of their renowned commander. Their parting shouts were re-echoed from the sides of the surrounding hills, and were replied to with yet louder bursts of acclamation by the large army of which they had been so lately a portion. Their route lay through the wilderness of the forest which at that time covered the country, and they soon lost even the cheers of their departing comrades, that, mellowing by degrees, at last died away among the hollow valleys. On entering Northumberland, the Earl of Douglas allowed little time for pillaging the country, but stretched forward with the utmost expedition, so that he might carry on the war directly into the heart of the Bishoprick of Durham, before his movements could be made known to the Earl of Northumberland, who was at Alnwick, or to his two sons, who were at that moment patiently waiting at Newcastle, with the other English lords, for the return of their spy.

The Douglas was by no means one who could endure to make a mere empty show of invasion, for the purpose of creating a diversion that might smooth the way of his politic brother-in-law the Earl of Fife. His force was small indeed, but he resolved that it should do England as much harm as he could effect with it. Passing the River Tyne, therefore, at some distance above Newcastle, he spread his troops over the fair County of Durham, and began taking an awful, nay, a tenfold revenge, for the miseries which the Merse had so lately endured, at the hands of the English, by carrying devastation far and wide.

The news that the Scots were abroad at last reached Newcastle and Durham, and their numbers being exaggerated, these towns were filled with great consternation. They now learned the tale, indeed, from the evidence of their senses, for the smoke of the continued conflagration, creeping heavily over the country, and, carrying the smell of combustion along with it, poisoned the very air of both these places. Having reached the gates of Durham, the Douglas found them firmly closed against him ; so, after skirmishing there for some days, he pushed on, destroying everything in his way, even to the very gates of York, and leaving no town unburnt that was not sufficiently walled to require a regular siege.

Having thus more than made good a chivalric vow with which he had started, that he should see Durham ere he returned, and having already ventured farther into a hostile country than his small force warranted, he returned towards Newcastle, industriously perfecting any destruction that he had before left unfinished ; and having re-crossed the Tyne, at the same spot where he had passed it in his way southwards, he set himself down before the town on the side lying towards Scotland. The place was strongly garrisoned, and contained the flower of the chivalry of the counties of York, Durham, and Northumberland ; for as soon as it was fully known that the Scots were abroad, and that they had already passed onwards into Yorkshire, a general rising of the country took place, under the influence of Harry Piersie, lately appointed Keeper of the Northumbrian Marches ; and orders were even despatched to the governors of Berwick, Norham, and the other fortresses now in rear of the enemy, to join the general muster with what force they could spare without too much weakening their garrisons.

Sir Rafe Piersie had long ceased to think of Eleanore de Selby. His passion was like the summer-storm, violent in character, but short in duration. His father, the haughty old Earl of Northumberland, had heard of it, and had signified his unqualified displeasure that his son should have even thought of a marriage with the daughter of a mere soldier; while his elder brother, the lively and peppery Hotspur, had laughed and railed at him till he became tired of the very name of De Selby. Part of this feeling arose from an honourable cause. His conscience told him that he had permitted his violent temper to make him forget what was due to the courtesy of knighthood, and he now so deeply repented him of his conduct at Norham, where he had so grossly insulted his host, that the scene never occurred to his mind without bringing the blush of shame to his cheek. He longed for an opportunity, where, without debasing himself, he might prove these feelings to Sir Walter; and the issuing of the order for the Border Captains to appear at Newcastle being the first that presented itself, he immediately availed himself of it.

"Brother," said he to Hotspur, "as for Sir Matthew Redman of Berwick, he is a stout and able Captain, and in his own person a powerful aid. But what wouldst thou, I pray thee, with bringing the old Captain of Norham so far from home?"

"Dost thou fear to meet him, Rafe?" cried Hotspur, with a sarcastic smile; "or wouldst thou rather that I should send for his dark-eyed daughter hither?"

"Nay, nay, brother," replied Sir Rafe; "but methinks he is of years somewhat beyond the battle-field."

"Thou mayest do with him as thou listest, brother Rafe," replied Hotspur, who was too busy to waste time on such a matter; "but we must have his men."

Armed with Sir Henry Piersie's authority to do so, Sir Rafe despatched an especial messenger to Sir Walter de Selby, to assure him that it rejoiced him much to be the instrument of procuring his exemption from personal attendance at Newcastle, which to one who had already seen so many fields, must be rather irksome. The messenger found Sir Walter de Selby lately recovered from his bodily malady; for the death of the wizard Ancient and his villainy being now known to him, he

27

again enjoyed comparative peace of mind. But he was much
enfeebled by the shocks he had received. He heard the courier
to an end; and the moisture in his eye, with the nervous motion
in his closed lips, showed how much he was affected by it.

"Am I then deemed to be so old and worthless?" said he,
after a pause. "The time was when the Marches, neither East
nor West, could have turned out a starker pricker; yet was it
kind in Sir Rafe Piersie, after what hath passed between us, and
tell him, I beseech thee, that I so felt and received his message.
But it shall never be said that I am behind when others are in
the field; it shall never be said of old Sir Walter de Selby,
who hath worn the hauberk and morion from his cradle, that
he was afraid to die in knightly harness. No, no; let Tom
Turnberry prepare my war steed; I'll lead mine own spears to
Newcastle. To thee, my good Lieutenant Oglethorpe, do I
commit the keeping of old Norham. It is King Richard's now.
See that it hath no other master when I or King Richard
demand it of thee."

With these words, the brave old warrior gave orders for his
men to assemble immediately, and mounting, with the aid of his
esquires, he rode from the court-yard at the head of his force, on
a mettlesome horse, the fiery paces of which but ill suited with
his years; as he went, he joined feebly in the parting cheer
with which his brave bowmen and lances took leave of their
comrades.

It was the daring spirit of chivalry, more than any great hope
of taking the town, that induced the gallant Douglas to tarry
for two days before Newcastle. The most powerful thirst of
heroic adventure then prevailed, and those within the town
were as eager to rush beyond their ramparts to meet the assailants, as the Scottish knights were to assault them. Both days,
therefore, were occupied in a succession of skirmishes; and it
was a remarkable feature of this warfare, that it seemed to be
more regulated by the courtesy of the tournament, than guided
by the brutal and remorseless rage of battle. No sooner did a
body of lances show itself from within the Scottish lines, than
another of equal numbers appeared from behind the barriers of
the town, prepared to give it a meeting. Spurring from
opposite sides, the combatants encountered each other midway,
as if they had been in the lists. A desperate shock took place,
followed by a melée, in which prodigious feats of arms were
done, whilst the English from their walls, and the Scottish
troops from their temporary entrenchments, alternately cheered
their friends, as one or other side gained the advantage. But,

what was most wonderful, everything resembling atrocity appeared to be banished from the field, and mercy and generosity so tempered victory, that it was difficult to say whether the contest was greatest for glory in the skirmish, or for superiority in clemency, and every other noble feeling, after it was over.

On the evening of the first day, the Lord Douglas, to give the troops a breathing, ordered the place to be assaulted by means of scaling ladders, with the hopes of perhaps surprising it by a coup-de-main. The Scottish troops rushed to the walls with their usual hardihood, and Sir Patrick Hepborne and Sir John Assueton were found in the very front of the attack made by the Earl of Moray's division. Although they were provided with fascines and trusses of straw to throw into the ditch, yet the ladders were in general found to be too short for surmounting the walls. At one place, however, they were successfully applied; and the two knights, followed by their esquires and some few others, gallantly mounted in the teeth of the enemy, and fought their way into the town, driving the English before them; but being unsupported, owing to the failure of the escalade in other quarters, they were unwillingly compelled to retreat, which they and their followers did, bravely fighting with their faces to the enemy. Having gained the spot where they had climbed, the two friends planted themselves side by side firmly in front of it, to cover the retreat of those who were with them, and gallantly kept a whole host of foes at bay, until all who had entered the place with them had descended, except their trusty esquires, and two other individuals whom they had not leisure to note. The ladders had all been broken or thrown down in the confusion except one, and the English so pressed upon the little knot of Scotchmen that it appeared impossible for so many of them to escape.

"One desperate charge at them, Assueton," cried Hepborne. "Our safety depends on driving them back for a brief space's breathing. On them, brave Scots!"

The two knights raised a shout, in which they were joined by their fellow-combatants, and with one accord rushed furiously against the dense circle of English. The effect was tremendous. Many were overthrown by the vigorous blows of the knights and their assistants, but more by the press and confusion occasioned by the panic, excited by the belief that they were backed by a fresh assault of troops from without the walls. There was a momentary dispersion of them; but the individuals of the Scottish party were also separated from each other, and as Sir

Patrick Hepborne returned to the rallying point, he was grieved
to discover his friend Assueton lying wounded and helpless on
the ground. He immediately stooped, to endeavour to set him
on his legs, but he was unable to support himself.

"Leave me, dear Hepborne," said Assueton faintly; "thine
own safety depends on thy doing so."

"Leave thee, Assueton!" cried Hepborne with energy;
"nay, by St. Baldrid, if I cannot bear thee hence, I will perish
with thee. Clasp thine arms round my neck, my friend," added
he, as he lifted him up from the ground, and began carrying him
towards the walls. "Be of good cheer, and tighten thy grasp;
thou dost thereby lighten my burden."

As he moved off, the English returned, shouting upon his
heels, with Sang sullenly retreating before them.

"Succour, succour, my trusty esquire," cried Hepborne; " I
have a life here to preserve dearer to me a thousand times than
mine own."

Sang came up to him as he reached the top of the only
remaining ladder. To the esquire he hastily confided the care
of Assueton, and, turning on the foe, again drove them before
him, so as to give Sang leisure to descend with his burden ; and
then hastily returning to the spot where the ladder was, he discovered that it was broken, and saw Sang in the ditch beneath,
endeavouring to extricate himself and the wounded knight from
the bundles of straw and fascines among which they had fallen.
The enemy were fast gathering behind, and he had no alternative. Selecting a place where the heaps in the ditch were
highest, he sprang from the wall, and happily alighted almost
uninjured.

Whilst he and his squire were busily employed in lifting Sir
John Assueton from the ditch, their attention was attracted to
the walls above them, where a desperate struggle was going on
between two figures distinctly seen against the sky. But it was
of short duration.

"Uve, uve! an she wonnot let her go, by St. Giles, but she
shall go wi' her," cried Duncan MacErchar, who was one of
them ; and griping his enemy fast, he sprang with him over the
battlements.

Duncan had by no means time to be so select in the choice of
the spot where he was to alight as Sir Patrick Hepborne had
been. But he took care to leap with his antagonist before him,
and his doing so was the saving of his life, his fall being broken
by the body of the wretch who participated in it, and who was
crushed to death against the very bottom of the ditch, whilst

Duncan, though stunned, escaped with some considerable bruises, and immediately regaining his legs, assisted Sir Patrick and his esquire to carry off Sir John Assueton to the Scottish camp.

We have already apprised the reader that the brave knights were supported by two other individuals besides their esquires. One of these, it may be guessed, was the brave MacErchar. The other, when the little party was dispersed after their bold onset, unfortunately missed his way in attempting to return to the rallying point, and, being assailed by a crowd of his foes, was compelled to retreat before them, until he was stopped by a wall, under which he took shelter, and prepared himself for a desperate resistance.

"Yield thee, Scot," cried some of the first who came up to him. "On him—Seize him," cried a dozen of them at once.

"By St. Lowry, 'tis right well for ye Southrons to cry yield to ane honest Scotchman. But troth, I'll tell ye it's easier to say so to ane o' my country than to gar him do it, and mair, when ye speak to the henchman o' the Yearl o' Moray himsel'," cried Rory Spears; for it was he, no longer clad, indeed, in his fishing coat and otterskin cap, but armed as became the Earl of Moray's henchman, and wielding a long pole-axe instead of his gaud-clip.

"Take him alive," cried an officer who was present; "let not his life be taken, as you value your own. If he be of the Earl of Moray's household, we may be the better for knowing some of his secrets."

"Troth, ye'll hae ill taking o' me without taking my life too, my lads," said Rory, swinging his pole-axe so cleverly around him that no one was disposed to risk approaching him.

"In on him and take him, his ransom will be great," cried the officer; and thus encouraged, one or two of the hardiest did venture to attempt to close on him, but they paid dearly for their daring, being prostrated to right and left like so many nine-pins. The rest were so scared that they scrupled to approach him; and he might have kept them off long enough had not a man who had climbed on the wall behind him suddenly dropped down on his shoulders à califourchon, and brought him headlong to the ground.

"Well done, Tom Turnberry," cried a dozen voices at once, and in an instant Rory was overpowered, and hastily dragged down a stair and thrust into a dark dungeon under the ramparts, where he was left to his own reflections.

"Is there ony ither poor deevil like mysel' here?" demanded

Rory aloud, after he had in some measure recovered his breath; but finding that no one answered, he went to talk to himself. "Na—nae answer. A-weel, Maister Spears, thou art here, art thou, amang the foundations o' Newcastle? This is seeing merry England wi' a vengeance. Troth, after a', if this is to be the upshot, thou mightest as weel hae turned back frae Norham yonder. Thou canst be of nae satisfaction to the Yearl whiles thou art liggen here, I trow. And as to ony mair comfort or consolation in the wars, thou mayest e'en bid them good day, for thou'lt hae nae mair o' them, I'll promise thee. By my troth, an thou hadst not seen this day's fighting, thou mightest hae been as well liggen on the rocks at the Ess. A-weel, a-weel —it is most surprising how a man o' sense wull gae wrang at times. Hadst thou no been a fool, ye might hae let thae wud chields climb the wa's o' Newcastle themlanes, that is, takin' thy time o' life into consideration. By holy St. Mary, what wull become o' poor Kate? Hoot, the Leddy o' Norham wull surely see her sent safe back to Tarnawa; though in conscience I had rather been her guide mysel. I was a fool to leave the damosel. And then, St. Lawrence protect me, how I wull be missed at hame." The thought of his daughter, of his wife, and of his home, grappled Rory by the heart, so that he did nothing but sigh for some moments. "A-weel," continued he at length, "I maun say, after a', that albeit there is a great pleasure in fighting, it is but a fool-thing for God's rational creatures to be cutting ane anither's throats as if they war wild cats or wolf-beasts. What for sould I come a' the gate frae Findhorn-side to cleave the skull o' some poor honest deevil o' the Tyne here, against whom, as I hope for mercy mysel, I hae no decent or wiselike cause o' quarrel? War is a fool-thing; but I wull say there is some pleasure in't, after a'."

"Ay!" said a long yawning voice from a deep recess in the dungeon.

"St. Lowry defend us, wha's that!" cried Rory.

"One Roger Riddel," replied the voice.

"What hast thou been doing, that thou hast been so long silent?" demanded Rory.

"Sleeping," answered Roger.

"Thou art esquire to that brave knight Sir John Assueton, if I err not?" said Rory.

"Thou art right," replied Roger.

"And how, in the name of St. Andrew, camest thou here?" demanded Rory.

"By being taken," replied Roger.

"Thou wert on the ramparts with us to the last," said Rory.

"I was," replied Roger.

"By St. Giles, but it was a noble escalade, comrade, an we had only been well backed," cried Spears with enthusiasm.

"Noble," cried Roger in the same tone.

"Didst thou mark how the knaves fled afore sax o' us?" cried Rory. "Sax against twa hundred o' them at least."

"Nay, three hundred, brother," replied Roger.

"Ay, faith, that may be," said Rory; "I'll no dispute as to that. There might be three, ay, or four hundred o' them, for I had no great leisure to count them. But this I ken, neebour, that an it hadna been bigget ground, thou and I souldna hae been here."

"No, that I'll promise thee," replied Roger.

"Where art thou, comrade? Gi'es thy hand; we fought like brave chields thegither," cried Rory in great glee, and groping about for Squire Riddel. "Thou art a prince of brave fellows."

"And thou art a very king," replied Roger, shaking him heartily by the hand.

"'Tis a pleasure to meet thee, though it be in this dungeon," cried Rory. "Would we had but some yill to wet our friendship. St. Lowry grant that we had but a wee sup yill."

"Ay, would indeed we had a drop of ale," re-echoed Roger with a deep sigh.

At this moment steps were heard descending, a light glimmered faintly for a moment through a chink beneath the door, and the key being turned, the round, rosy visage of Master Thomas Turnberry, the squire equerry of Norham, appeared within it. He entered, bearing a lamp in his hand, and was followed by an attendant, who carried an enormous pasty, that had been just broken upon, and a huge stoup of ale.

"So!" said Master Turnberry; "put thee down these things, and let the gentlemen eat and drink. Having put a man into captivity by mine own hard riding, I do think it but consistent with charity to see that he starveth not. Yea, and albeit I am but a soberish man myself, yet do I know that there be others who love ale; and having mortal bowels of compassion in me, I have pity for the frailties of my fellow-men."

"Sir," said Rory, lifting the vessel with great readiness from the ground, "an thou hadst been St. Lowry himsel, thou couldst not have ministered to my present wants more cheeringly. I

drink to thee from the bottom o' my soul——Hech!" cried he,
after having swallowed half the contents of the vessel, with the
nicest measurement, and most scrupulous justice to him who was
to come after him; "hech, 'tis most invigorating to the very
spinal marrow. It must be allowed that ye do brew most excellent nut-brown to the south o' the Tweed."

"Excellent, indeed, judging by its good sale," cried Roger
Riddel, looking into the flagon before he put it to his head;
then nodding to Master Turnberry, he drained it to the
bottom.

"By'r lackins, but ye have good go-downs, my masters," cried
Turnberry, taking the flagon, and raising the bottom of it, so as
to show that it was empty, and at the same time betraying some
disappointment. "Methinks I could ha'e ta'en a drop of ale
myself. But there be more where this came from. See that
the gentlemen lack for nothing," said he, turning to the
attendant. "And so, good night, my merry masters."

It was about the middle of the ensuing day that Rory
Spears was sitting indulging in soliloquy, Roger Riddel having
retired to the farther part of the vault, where he had thrown
himself down, and buried himself among the straw, to sleep
away the time.

"I hae sat for days by mysel, as a relay to watch for the
deer," said Rory—"ay, and I hae lien for weeks by my lane,
watching the saumonts loupin', without hearing voice save the
water-kelpy roarin' in the Ess—yet was I never sae tired as I
am at this precious moment, sitting in this hole, wi' a bit chink
yonder aboon just enew to let a poor deevil ken that it's day-
light, and that he mought be happy thereout i' the sun. As for
that chield, Roger Riddel there, my ain Oscar would be mair
companionable, I wot. He lies rucking and snorting there as
composed as if he were in the best hostel in a' bonny Scotland.
As St. Lowry kens, I wad be content to be in its warst,
rather than whaur I am. Holy St. Mungo, the chield hath
buried himsel like a very mouldiwort; I can see nought but
his nose. A-weel, an I could only gie owre thinking o' Alice.
and Kate, and the Yearl o' Moray, I mought peraunter sleep
mysel."

As he was stretching himself along the bench where he had
been sitting, with the resolution of trying the experiment, he
was disturbed by a coming step. The door opened, and an
officer entered in great seeming haste.

"Thou art a body attendant of the Earl of Moray, art thou
not?" said he, glancing at Spears.

"Yea, I am the noble Yearl's henchman, as I mought say," replied Rory.

"Doubtless thou knowest well the person of the Lord Douglas?" said the officer.

"Ay, weel do I that," replied Rory; "and mair, he hath a great good-wull to me, for mony is the time we hae hunted thegither. Is he not my master the Yearl's brother-in-law?"

"Follow me then without loss of time," said the officer; "Sir Henry Piersie would have conference with thee."

Rory said no more, but joyfully obeyed; and the officer, too much occupied with his errand to investigate things closely, and having no suspicion that the place contained two prisoners, tripped up the stair that led from the dungeon, leaving the door open behind him.

Master Roger Riddel was not asleep; he had only dosed, to save himself the trouble of forming replies to the incessant talk which Rory had carried on; on peeping out from his straw after the officer and his fellow-prisoner had left him, and seeing the door of the dungeon wide open, he slowly raised himself up, walked out of the place, and ascended the short winding stair, from the top of which he quietly emerged into the pure air. With the utmost composure, he then struck into one of the lanes that led from the walls, and walked coolly down a street, through crowds of anxious individuals, all of whom were too busily occupied with anticipations of glory or defeat, to notice a man in the attire of a squire, of whom there were many. Following a crowd that was pressing forwards, he reached the gate. There was a muster at the barriers.

"Where are thy weapons, Sir Squire?" demanded a spearman as he passed by.

"Lend me thy lance, good fellow," said Roger; "I am in haste—here be money to get thee another."

The man gave him the spear, took the money, and thanked him; and Roger went on. At the gate stood three horses held by a single groom. Roger went boldly up to him.

"Thou waitest thy master, friend?" said he in a tone of inquiry.

"Yea; and what be that to thee?" replied the fellow surlily.

"Because I have got an angel for thee, and I would know if thou be'st the right man," replied Riddel.

"Give it me straight, then, good master," said the man, eagerly.

"Nay, that will I not, neither straight nor crooked," replied

Riddel ; " that is, not till I know thy master's name from thee, that I may know whether in very deed thou be'st the man I do look for."

" 'Tis Sir Robert Ogill that be my master," replied the man.

" Then art thou the very good fellow I would speak with," said Roger. " Give me that roan as fast as may be, and this angel here is the token thy master Sir Robert sent thee. I ride on business of his to the barrier.

Without more ado, and without interruption from the groom, he leaped into the saddle, and riding by the guards at a careless pace, got beyond the barriers, and put his horse to speed for the Scottish camp. A shout was raised among a party of spearmen who were forming without, and some dozen or two of them spurred after him ; but he had gained so much start of them, and his horse was so good, that he escaped in spite of all their exertions, and got fairly within the lines occupied by his countrymen.

CHAPTER LVIII.

Combat between Douglas and Hotspur—The Fight for the Pennon.

As the Earl of Douglas was sitting in his pavilion, in conversation with his chaplain, Richard Lundie, on the second day of his being before Newcastle, a squire in waiting announced to him that one of Lord Moray's men wished to have a private interview with him.

" Give him entrance speedily," said the Douglas, " his business may be of moment. He seeth me in private when he seeth me alone with him who knoweth mine inmost soul."

The squire bowed and retired, and immediately returned to introduce—Rory Spears.

" Rory Spears !" exclaimed the Douglas ; " what hath brought thee hither, and what hath my brother of Moray to tell my private ear through thy mouth ? Thou art not the messenger he is used to send between us for such affairs. Were it a matter of wood or river craft, indeed, we might both recognize thee as a right trusty and merry ambassador ; but at this time we have other game upon our hands. What hath Lord Moray to say ?"

" My Lord Yearl o' Douglas, naebody kens whaur gowd lies till it be howkit out," replied Rory, with an obeisance. " Albeit that thou and the Yearl o' Moray, my noble master, have never yet discovered my talents that way, it proveth not that I do lack them. He who is stranger to the soil may chance to divine that, the which he who owneth it hath never dreamt of ; and he——"

"What doth all this tend to, Rory Spears ?" demanded the Earl of Douglas, interrupting him rather impatiently. "Trust me, though I may have trifled with thee at Tarnawa, this is no time for such idlesse."

"Bide a wee, my Lord Yearl, bide a wee," said Rory, with great composure ; "call it not trifling till thou art possessed of the value of what I have to effunde unto thee. I was going to tell thee that he who doth own a man like me, ay, or a horse beast, for instance, may ken less o' his qualifications than he who doth see him but for a gliff."

"But what hath all this to do with thy message from Moray to me ?" cried the Douglas.

"Nought at all, my Lord Yearl," replied Rory, "for I hae no message frae him. But," added he, assuming an air of unusual importance, "it hath much to do, I rauckon, with the embassage the which I am at this moment charged with by the Hotspur."

"The Hotspur—thou charged with a message from the Hotspur !—How can that be ? Quick—try not my patience longer ; where hast thou encountered the Hotspur ?" exclaimed the Douglas eagerly.

Rory proceeded to give the Earl a sketch of the history of his capture, as well as of his being sent for by Sir Harry Piersie.

"He told me, my Lord Yearl o' Douglas," continued he, "that he heard I confessed mysel to be ane esquire o' the Yearl o' Moray's. I didna daur to contradick Hotspur, the mair because I am in a manner the Yearl's henchman. 'I hae made yelection o' thee,' said he to me, 'as the fittest man for my job amang a' the Scottish prisoners in Newcastle. Thou art to bear a message of importance frae me to the gallant Douglas. Tell him Hotspur hath had the renommie o' his prowess rung in his lugs till the din hath stirred up his inmost soul and made his very heart yearn to encounter sae mokell bravery. Yet hath my evil fortune so willed it,' quoth he, 'that though I have sought him unceasing for these two days, yet have I never had the chance to meet him hand to hand.'"

"Nay, and God wot, I have not been wanting in my search after the noble Hotspur," replied Douglas with energy. "But what said he more ?"

"'Get thee to the Douglas, Sir Squire,' said he to me.

'Tell him that I do entreat him, for the love he bears to chivalry, that he may so order his next assault that I may not fail to meet him in person. Be the manner and terms of our en counter of his own fixing, and let him trust to the word of a Piersie for their fulfilment on this side, as I shall to the unbroken faith of a Douglas. Bear this to him, Sir Squire, and take thy liberty and this golden chain for thy guerdon.'"

" Bravo, Harry Hotspur !" cried the Douglas, rising from his seat, whilst his eyes flashed fire from the joyous tumult of his heroic spirit ; " bravo, brave heart ! trust me thou shalt not lack thy desire. Quick—let me hasten to reply to the gallant Piersie's challenge with that promptness the which it doth so well merit. My most faithful and attached Lundie," continued he, addressing his chaplain,—" get thee to the provost, if thou lovest me, and use thy good judgment to choose me out from among our English prisoners one who may be best fitted for being the bearer of mine answer. Let him be an esquire, for we would rather surpass than fall short of Hotspur's courtesy."

" Nay, an ye would surpass the courtesy of the gallant Hotspur," said Rory, who stood by, " ye maun e'en send him a knight, for he did send thee ane esquire,—ay, and ane esquire with a golden chain round his craig."

" Right," cried the Douglas in the fulness of his joy—" right, Squire Rory Spears ; for esquire thou shalt hereafter be, sith it hath pleased Harry Piersie to make thee so. And if a knight is not to be had, by St. Andrew I'll make one for the purpose of this embassage."

" Hear ye, Maister Ritchie Lundie," cried Rory ; " I take thee witness that my Lord the Yearl o' Douglas hath allowed me the rank the which the noble Hotspur did confer on me when I did act as his ambassador. Let not this escape thy memory."

" Fear thee not, Rory Spears," said the Douglas ; " I shall myself see that thine honours shall be duly recognized."

Lundie soon returned with an English esquire, selected from among the prisoners. The Earl of Douglas made Rory repeat over in his presence the message of which he had been the bearer from Hotspur.

" And now, Sir Squire," said Douglas, " thou hast heard the wish of that gallant leader, the noble Hotspur. Be thou the bearer of mine answer. Tell Sir Harry Piersie that for a man to have oped his eyes at noon-day without beholding the light of heaven would have been as easy as to have had ears without their being filled with the renowned achievements of the flower of English chivalry. The Douglas burns to meet him ; and that time may in no wise be lost, but each forthwith have his desire, tell him that the Douglas will be on the field anon with fifty lances. Let Sir Harry Piersie come forth with a like number at his back, and let this be the understanding between the parties, that both escorts halt within view of each other, and that both knights singly run a career with grounden spears at the outrance, the knights to be left to themselves. Be thou, I say, the bearer of these terms and conditions; but ere thou goest vouchsafe me thy name."

"My name is Thomas Scrope, so please thee, my Lord," replied the esquire.

"Within there," said the Douglas; "call in my knights and officers. And now, Sir Squire," said he, after the pavilion was filled, and he had given some necessary orders, "kneel down on this cushion, that before this brilliant knot of Scottish chivalry I may do due honour to him who is to bear my message to the Hotspur." The English esquire obeyed. The Douglas ordered a pair of golden spurs to be buckled on his heels by the hands of the two eldest Scottish knights present. They then belted him with a magnificent sword, a gift from the Earl, who immediately bestowed on him the accolade, saying—

"I dub thee Knight, in the name of God and St. Michael; be faithful, bold, and fortunate. And now rise up, Sir Thomas Scrope."

Astounded and confused with this unlooked-for honour, the newly-created knight but awkwardly received the congratulations which poured in on him from those present. The Douglas himself conducted him to the door, where a noble horse, fully caparisoned, awaited him.

"Get thee to saddle, then, Sir Thomas Scrope," cried he, "and tarry not till thou hast possessed the Hotspur of our reply to his message. Say more—that if he liketh not the terms let him name conditions of his own, to the which I do hereby agree par avance; and let me have them forthwith, for in an hour hence I shall be in the field in front of these lines. God speed thee, Sir Thomas."

"Might it not have been better, my Lord," said Richard Lundie, after they were again alone, "might it not have been better to have taken a new sun to gild so glorious a combat? The day is already far spent."

"Yea, it is so," replied the Douglas; "but to-morrow we move hence from this idle warfare, and I would not willingly go without proving the metal of the gallant Hotspur, so 'tis as well that his impatience be gratified."

The bruit of the coming encounter spread like wild-fire through the camp, and the whole chivalry within its circuit pressed forward to be admitted of the chosen band who were to witness the onset of the two bravest knights in Christendom. Lord Douglas's difficulty was how to select so as to avoid giving offence, and he required all his judgment to manage this. Sir Patrick Hepborne had the good fortune to be one of those who were admitted into the honourable ranks.

When the gay little cohort of mounted lances were drawn forth in array, and the Douglas's banner was displayed, the stout Earl sprang on a powerful black war-horse, that had neighed and pranced whilst he was held by two esquires, but that became quiet and gentle as a lamb when backed by his heroic master. The whole Scottish line turned out to gaze, and shouts of applause arose that re-echoed from the walls of Newcastle. Immediately afterwards Sir Harry Piersie appeared before the barriers of the town, mounted on a milk-white steed, and as Douglas, even at that distance, could perceive that his escort was of similar strength and description to his own, he had the satisfaction of thinking that the terms he had proposed had been accepted. The fortifications were soon covered by the garrison, who crowded to behold the combat, and the Scottish cheers were loudly returned by the English. A trumpet call from the Piersie band was instantly returned by one from that of Lord Douglas, who immediately gave the word for his knights to advance, whilst he rode forward so as to gain a position about fifty yards in front of them, that he might be the better seen by the opposite party. Having brought up his escort to a point sufficiently near (as he judged) for the arrangement agreed on, he halted them, and ordered them to remain steady, whilst he continued to approach until he came within a due distance for running his course against Hotspur, who had also come forward a considerable way before his attendants.

The trumpets from both bands sounded nearly at once, as if by mutual consent—both knights couched their lances—their armed heels made the blood spring from the sides of their coursers—and they flew like two thunderbolts towards the shock. Anxious suspense hung on both sides as they were stretching over the field, and the silence of the moment was such that the full crash of the collision entered every listening ear, however distant. Loud and exulting cheers from the Scottish lines, which, though they came so far, altogether drowned the uncouth sounds of dismay that ran along the walls of Newcastle, proclaimed the success of the Douglas, whose resistless arm, nerved with a strength that few men could boast, bore the no less gallant Hotspur clean out of his saddle, though, owing to his adroitness in covering his person against his adversary's point, he was hardly if at all wounded.

The band of English knights who attended him, forgetting the nature of the combat, as well as the express orders they had received from Piersie, saw their adored leader on the green sward, and thinking only of the jeopardy he lay in, began shouting—"Hotspur, Hotspur, to the rescue!" and ere the bold Douglas could well check the furious career of his horse, he was in the midst of a phalanx of his advancing foes. Abandoning his ponderous lance, he grasped the enormous mace that hung at his saddle-bow, and bestirred himself with it so lustily that three or four of the English chevaliers were in as many seconds dashed from their seats to the earth, in plight so grievous that there was but little chance of their ever filling them again. But the throng about the hero was so great, and their blows rained so thickly and heavily upon him, that his destruction must have been inevitable long ere his own band could have reached him, had not the noble Hotspur, whom some of his people were by this time carrying hurriedly away, called out to the knights of his party in a voice of command that was rarely disobeyed—

"Touch not the Douglas—harm not a hair of his head, as ye would hope for heaven. What, would ye assault at such odds the brave Douglas, who hath relied on the word of a Piersie? Shame, shame on ye, gentlemen. Your zeal for Hotspur's safety came not well at this time for Hotspur's honour. Trust me, his life stood in no peril with so chivalric a foe."

Awed and ashamed by these chiding words, the English knights fell back abashed, and made way for the valiant Douglas, who emerged from among them like a hunted lion from among the pack of puny hounds who have vainly baited him.

"Halt! chevaliers," cried he, rising in his saddle, and raising his right arm, as he in his turn addressed his own band, who were pouring furiously down on the English knights, shouting, "Douglas, Douglas, to the rescue!" "Halt," cried he again, "halt, in the name of St. Andrew! Let the gallant Hotspur retreat in peace. I blame not him for this small mistake of his trusty followers, the which, after all, was but an excusable error of affection. And as for thee, Piersie, I thank thee for thy courtesy. Depardieux, thou hast proved thyself to be brave as honourable and honourable as brave. Can I say more? By the honour of knighthood, thou hast proved thyself to be Harry

Piersie, and in that name all that is excellent in chivalry is centred. The chance hath been mine now; it may be thine anon, if it do so please Heaven. Get thee to refresh thyself then, for we shall forthwith beat up thy quarters with a stiffer stoure than any thou hast yet endured."

"Douglas," cried Piersie, who was by this time remounted, "Douglas, thou art all, and more than all that minstrels have called thee. Farewell, till we again meet, and may our meeting be speedy."

With these parting words, the two leaders wheeled off their respective bands.

Immediately after the Earl of Douglas had returned to the camp, a council of war was held, and, after a short deliberation, preparations were made for instantly assaulting and scaling the fortifications. The army was drawn out from its entrenchments and was led to the attack arranged in three divisions. The Earl of Douglas, attended by the little chosen band of knights who had that day vowed him their special service, led on the central body directly against the barriers. The right and left wings, commanded by the Earls of Dunbar and Moray, marched on steadily, to attempt the storm of the walls at two several points on each side of the gates, in defiance of a heavy shower of arrows from the English bowmen, mingled with some weightier missiles from the balistæ, which sorely galled them, and which they could but ill return with their cross-bows. Each of these flanking divisions covered the approach of a number of wains, laden with hay and straw collected from the neighbouring country; and so soon as they had come near enough to the fortifications, a signal was given, the wains were brought suddenly forward, and hurled one over another into the ditch, so as in many places to fill it up, and admit of the ladders being raised against the wall with great success. The Scottish soldiers rent the air with their shouts, and wielding their destructive battle-axes, rushed like furies to the escalade. But the English were so well prepared, and defended themselves so manfully that they beat back the assailants at every point, and soon succeeded in setting fire to the combustible materials in the ditch, by throwing down lighted brands, so that all hope of forcing an entrance in that way was soon at an end.

Meanwhile the Douglas forcibly assaulted the wooden barriers that defended the entrance to the town; and Piersie and his chivalry, who were immediately within them, no sooner heard the war-cry of "Douglas, Douglas! jamais arriere!" than, collecting themselves into one great body, they rushed out on the Scottish forces with so resistless an impetus, that nothing could withstand the fury of the stream.   Douglas and his troops were borne away like trees of the forest before some bursting torrent.   But no sooner had the English spread themselves out upon the plain like exhausted waters, than the voice of the · Scottish hero was heard above all the clang of the battle, cheering his men to the charge, and his superb figure, exalted on his black courser, was seen towering onwards against the slackening foe, gathering the firmest Scottish hearts around him as he went.

The English now in their turn gave back ; but Harry Piersie, recovered from his stunning fall, mounted on a fresh roan, and, surrounded by the brave knights by whom he was formerly attended, restored their courage both by his voice and example. Shouts of " Piersie, Piersie ! " and " Douglas, Douglas ! " arose from different parts of the field, and were re-echoed from the walls.   At length the two leaders caught a glimpse of each other amid the volumes of smoke that, tinged by the setting sun, were rolling along the ground from the blazing straw, which the descending damps of evening now hardly permitted to rise into the air.

" Ha, Douglas, have I found thee at last ? " cried Piersie, turning towards him.

" Trust me, 'twas no fault of mine that we met not sooner, Harry Piersie," cried Douglas, spurring to encounter him with his mace, his lance having been shivered in the melee.

There was time for no more words.   Piersie ran his lance at the Douglas as he came on, who with wonderful dexterity turned it aside, and catching it in his hand, endeavoured to wrench it from his owner.   Piersie's embroidered pennon was waving from the spear head.   Douglas snatched at it, but his adversary disappointed him, by forcing up the point, and each retaining his grasp, they were now drawn together into close contact.   The little silken trifle, utterly worthless in itself, glittered like a child's bauble over their heads ; but if it had been a kingdom they were contending for, they could not have been more eagerly set on the contest.   Each forgetful of the defence of his own life, put forth all his strength and skill, the one to obtain what he considered so glorious a prize, and the other to keep what he thought it would be so disgraceful to lose, and what, moreover, he so much valued, for the sake of her whose taper fingers had interwoven its golden threads.   The struggle was strong, but it was short in duration, for the iron hands of Douglas snapt the slim ashen shaft in twain, and in an instant he held up

28

the broken lance, and waved the pennon triumphantly over his head.

"The Piersie's pennon! recover the Piersie's pennon!" was the instant cry, and the English crowded to assist Hotspur, led on by Sir Rafe Piersie.

At that moment a body of Scottish lances, headed by Sir Patrick Hepborne, came pouring down in tremendous charge, shouting "Douglas, Douglas!" and dividing the two combatants as they swept onwards, they bore away the Piersies and the English before them to the very barriers, where the press of the combat was so hot, that they were soon compelled to retreat within their palisadoes, and to close up their defences. The partial breathing of an instant ensued, during which Douglas looked eagerly for Hotspur, and at length having descried him over the pales—

"By St. Andrew," he cried, rising in his stirrups, and again waving the captured pennon high in the air, "I have good reason, Harry Piersie, to be thankful for the glorious issue of this bicker. Trust me, I value this pennon of thine above all the spoil of Newcastle, nay, or of an hundred such towns. I shall bear it with me into Scotland, fair Sir, in token of our encounter; and in remembrance of thy prowess, I do promise thee it shall grace the proudest pinnacle of my Castle of Dalkeith."

"Be assured, Douglas," replied Piersie courteously, though with manifest signs of great vexation, "ye shall not bear it over the Border; nay, ye shall not pass the bounds of this county till ye be met withal in such wise that ye shall make none avaunte thereof."

"Well, brave Sir," replied the Earl of Douglas, "it shall be set up before my pavilion this night; so come thither to seek for thy pennon, and take it thence if thou canst; till then, farewell."

The Lord Douglas turned away, proudly bearing his trophy; and the night was now approaching, and all hopes of succeeding in the assault being at an end, he ordered the retreat to be sounded, and collecting his forces, he retired behind his trenches.

The Scottish troops were no sooner withdrawn than Hotspur, smarting under the stinging disgrace of the loss of his pennon, summoned a council of war, in which he bravely proposed to lead on the English troops to a night attack against the Scottish entrenchments. This proposition was warmly supported by Sir Rafe Piersie, who participated largely in his brother's injured feelings; but an opinion prevailing among the English knights that the Earl of Douglas's party was but the Scottish vanguard, and that the large army, of which they had heard so much, was hovering at no great distance, ready to avail itself of any imprudent step they might take, very generally opposed his wishes.

"Sir," said the prudent Seneschal of York, who was present, and who seemed to speak as the organ of the rest, "there fortuneth in war oftentimes many chances. Another day thou mayest gain greater advantage of Earl Douglas than he hath this day won of thee. Let us not peril the cause of England for a paltry pennon, when the power of Scotland is abroad. Who knoweth but this empty skirmish of theirs may be a snare to lure us out to destruction? Better is it to lose a pennon than two or three hundred brave knights and squires, and to lay our country at the mercy of these invading foemen."

Though some of the young and impetuous, and even the old Sir Walter de Selby, showed symptoms of being disposed to support the plan proposed by the Hotspur, yet this prudent counsel was so generally applauded, that, though boiling inwardly with indignation at their apathy, he was compelled to yield with the best face he could, while his lip was visibly curled with a smile of ineffable contempt for what he considered their pusillanimity.

"What a hollow flock of craven pullets, brother Rafe!" said he, giving way to a burst of passionate vexation after the council had broke up, and they were left alone. "What, a paltry pennon, saidst thou, Sir Seneschal? May thy tongue be blistered for the word! Depardieux, were it not unwise to stir up evil blood among us at such a time, I would make him eat it, old as he is, and difficult as he might find the digestion of it. Oh, is't not bitter penance, brother Rafe, for falcons such as we are to be mewed up with such a set of grey geese? By Heaven, it is enough to brutify the noble spirit we do inherit from our sires. What will the Douglas, I pr'ythee, think of Harry Hotspur, now that after all his vaunts he cometh not out to-night to give him the camisado in his tent, and to pluck his pennon from the disgraceful soil in the which it doth now grow so vilely? But, by St. George, though I should be obliged to go with no more than our vassals, I will catch the Douglas ere he quits Northumberland, and I will have my pennon again or die in the taking of it."

The Douglas was well prepared to give Harry Piersie a welcome had circumstances enabled him to have paid his visit to the Scottish camp before they broke up from Newcastle. The

sentinels were so stationed that the whole army would have
been alarmed and under arms in a few minutes. His sleep was
therefore as sound as if he had been in his own Castle of Dalkeith, though he slept in his armour, that he might be ready to
meet the foe on the first rouse.

"Well, my trusty esquires," said he to Robert Hart and
Simon Glendinning, as they came to wait on him in the morning,
"doth Harry Piersie's pennon still flutter where these hands did
place it yesternight?"

"Yea, my good Lord," replied Glendinning, "thy challenge
hath gone unheeded."

"Nay, then, we bide no longer for him here," said Douglas ;
"an he will have it now, he must come after us to take it.   Are
my Lords Moray and Dunbar astir?"

"They are, my Lord," replied Hart.

"Go to them, then, Robert, and tell them, that with their
leave we shall march anon.   But, by St. Andrew, there shall
be no appearance of unseemly haste.   Let the sun, that saw the
Piersie's pennon planted yesternight ere he did go to bed, be
suffered to look upon it for some time after he be well risen
again, so that we may not be accused of being more dexterous
in carrying off our prey than bold in defending it."

The little Scottish army broke up from their encampment
with as much composure as if they had been in a friendly
country, and marched leisurely off with loud cheers.   Harry
Piersie was on the wall, and his blood boiled at the very sound.

"By the holy St. Cuthbert, they mock me," cried he, his face
flushing with anger ; "ay, an well may they too," continued he,
striking his forehead.   "Oh, I could leap over these walls from
very despite.   By the mass, their numbers are naught ; see how
small their columns appear ; already the last of them are gone ;
oh, is it not enow to drive me to madness !"—and, dashing his
mailed foot to the ground, he turned away to gnaw his nails
with vexation.

After taking two or three turns with his brother along the
rampart, he suddenly called for an esquire, and ordered him to
procure some intelligent scouts ; to these he gave orders to
follow the Scottish line of march, and to bring him frequent and
accurate intelligence of their numbers, their route, and all their
actions ; and, having taken this precaution, he and Sir Rafe
Piersie continued to pace the walls by themselves, giving vent,
from time to time, to their indignation and disappointment, in
abrupt sentences addressed to each other.   During that day and
the evening following it, large reinforcements of troops poured

into Newcastle, from different quarters of the circumjacent country; and the stronger Hotspur found himself, the more impatient he became to make use of his strength.

" Ay, ay, see where they come; see where they come, brother Rafe," said he in a pettish tone. " But what come they for, an we have them not in the field? Depardieux, from the careless guise and strutting gait of some of these butter-headed burghers, and clod-pated churls, meseems as if they came more to parade it in a fair than to fight."

" If we can but get them once into the field," said Sir Rafe Piersie, " by all that is good, we shall teach the knaves another bearing and another step."

" Ay, marry, would that we but had them in the field, indeed," replied Hotspur; " the very smell of battle hath a marvellous virtue in it, and doth oftentimes convert the veriest dolt into a hero. Of such fellows as these men, one might make rare engines for recovering a lost pennon, yea, as of finer clay. Would we but had them at the proof. But a plague upon these cautious seniors of the council, methinks my patience was miraculous; nay, in truth, most miraculous, to hear that old driveller talk of my paltry pennon, and not to dash my gauntlet in his teeth for the word."

" Nay, I could hardly keep my hands down," cried Sir Rafe Piersie. " Methinks our blood must be cooling, or else even his age should have been no protection."

" 'Tis better as it is, Rafe," replied Hotspur; " but why tarry these scouts of mine? I shall fret me to death ere they return. Why are we not blessed with the power of seeing what doth pass afar off? Had I this faculty, how would mine eyes soar over the Douglas and my pennon!"

In such talk as this the brothers wasted great part of the night. The impatient Hotspur was kept in suspense until next morning, when, much to his relief, the arrival of the wearied scouts was announced to him. He ordered them instantly into his presence, and having closely interrogated them, he soon gathered from them all the intelligence he wanted.

The Earl of Douglas had marched slowly and circumspectly, and although his little army had sufficiently marked his course, by plundering and burning whatever came in its way, the troops had not been suffered to spread far to the right or left. They halted at Pontland, and took and burnt the town and castle, making prisoner of Sir Aymer de Athele, who defended it. Thence they marched to Otterbourne, where they encamped, apparently with the intention of besieging the castle of that

name next day. The scouts also brought certain information
that the Scots did not amount to more than three thousand
men-at-arms, and three or four hundred lances, and that the
main body of the army was nowhere in the neighbourhood, but
still lying indolently on the Western Marches. Full of these
particulars, Hotspur, with a bounding heart, again summoned
the council of war, and bringing in his scouts, he made them tell
their own story.

"What say ye now, gentlemen?" cried he with a triumphant
air; "was I right, or not? By the Rood, I was at least wrong
to listen to the cold caution of some few frozen heads here; for,
an I mistake not the general voice of the council yesterday was
with me. We mought have spared these Scots many a weary
mile of march, I ween. By St. George, they were a mere handful for us, a mere handful; not a man of them should have
escaped us; ay, and such a price should they have paid for the
ruin they have wrought on these fine counties, that Scotland
should have quaked for a century at the very thought of setting
foot across the Border."

"Frozen heads, didst thou say, Sir Harry Piersie?" demanded
the Seneschal of York calmly; "methinks that thy meaning
would be to accuse those frozen heads of being leagued with
frozen hearts; but let me tell thee, Hotspur, where snow is shed
on the poll we may look for a cool judgment; and if a cool, then
probably a wise judgment."

"Pshaw!" said Hotspur, half aside to his brother; "this
fusty utterer of worn-out saws and everyday wisdom goadeth me
beyond all bearing; yet must I temper mine answer. Trust me,
I meant not to impeach thine ordinary judgment, Sir Seneschal,"
continued he aloud, "though I do think that it did for once err
grievously in our yesterday's council. But let us not talk of
this. I am now here to tell ye, gentlemen, that, by the faith I
owe to God, and to my Lord my father, go who list with me, I
shall now go seek for my pennon, and give Lord Douglas the
camisado this night at Otterbourne; yea, by St. George, though
I should do it without other aid than that of my brother
Rafe, and the faithful vassals of the Piersie. What, am I to put
up, think ye, with the loss of my pennon, and the disgrace of
our house and name? By heaven, though it were but a hair's-
breadth of the hem of my Lady's mantle, the Douglas should
not carry it into Scotland. But if disgrace doth attend the losing
of Hotspur's pennon, depardieux, let it be borne by those who,
calling themselves his friends, will not yield him their help to
retake it; for Hotspur is resolved to wipe off shame from him-

self—he will follow his pennon to the Orcades, yea, pluck it from their most northern cape, or fall in the attempt. Disgrace shall never cleave to Hotspur."

"No, nor to Rafe Piersie neither," cried his brother. "Let those who fear to follow stay at home. We shall on together, hand in hand, and seize the pennon, though grim death held its shaft; yea, paltry as it may be thought, it shall be the sun on whose beams our dying eyes shall close. Let us on then."

The loud murmurs of applause which arose from among the younger knights manifested how much they sympathized with the feelings of the Piersies. But the old Seneschal of York again put in his word of prudence.

"Gentlemen," said he, "I see that, in speaking as I must do, I shall have but few to agree with me, yet must I natheless freely speak my mind, more especially as I do perceive that those knights who, like myself, have seen more years of warfare than the rest, do seem disposed to think with me. I must confess, that, albeit some potent reasons do now cease to war with your opinion, mine is but little altered. Meseems it still is an especial risk to move so far from garrison after an uncertain enemy, for a mere shred of silk and gold."

"A shred of silk and gold!" exclaimed Sir Walter de Selby. "What, dost thou not think that all England is disgraced by this triumph of the Scottish Douglas over the Hotspur? And dost thou regard nought but the shred of silk and gold? Talk not of the old ones, I pray thee, Sir Seneschal of York. Trust me, old as is Sir Walter de Selby, he shall never rest idle whilst gallant deeds are adoing to wipe off a foul stain from the name of England. Be it death or victory, he shall have his share on't."

"Thy hand, my brave old soldier," cried both the Piersies at once.

"Thou shalt go with us," exclaimed Hotspur; "though thine years might have well excused thee leaving thine own Castle of Norham, yet hast thou come hither; yea, and thou shalt now forward with us to the field, were it but to show how the noble fire of a warlike soul may burn through the thickest snows of age."

"Nay, then," said the Seneschal of York, "thou shalt see, Sir Harry Piersie, that albeit I do advise caution, yet shall I do my part as well as others, when my words do cease to avail aught; yet would I fain have thee tarry until thou art joined by the Bishop of Durham, who is looked for with his force this night."

" What, while we can muster eight thousand good soldiers without him, and six hundred gallant lances? Shall we wait for the Bishop, and so permit the Scots to 'scape from our vengeance? Nay, nay, let's to horse, my brave friends; my heart swells at the thought of reaping so glorious a field. Let's to horse without delay, if your blood be English."

Hotspur's call was hailed with loud approval, and the brave though cautious Seneschal, seeing that it was in vain to urge more, joined heartily with the rest in getting the army under arms, and in hastening the march.

The Scots had begun to sound their bugles at an early hour that morning, and to assault the Castle of Otterbourne, and they wasted the whole of the day in unsuccessful attempts against it. A council of war being held in the evening, it was found that there were cautious heads among the Scotch as well as among the English knights. Some of those who spoke were of opinion that they should abandon all further attempts against the Castle, and march forward towards Scotland. But the Earl of Douglas opposed this.

" What, my brave Lords and Knights of Scotland," cried he with energy, " would ye give Harry Piersie cause to say that we have stolen this pennon of his? Let us not creep away with it like thieves in the dark; nay, rather let us show these Southerns that we do earnestly covet their promised visit to us. Let us, I pray ye, tarry here for some two or three days at least; we shall find occupation enough in beleaguering and taking of this Castle hard by, the which is assuredly pregnable to bold and persevering men, and will yield us the more honour that it be strong. Then shall Hotspur have leisure to bethink himself how he may best come to fetch his pennon; and if it should so list him to come, depardieux, he may take my banner too, if he can."

The old and the cautious hardly in secret approved this counsel; but so much was the heroic Douglas the idol of all, that his wishes were of themselves enough to determine the resolution of those who heard him. Measures were accordingly taken for securing the army against surprise, and for rendering their camp as strong as circumstances would allow; and seeing that they were to remain for so much longer a time than they at first imagined, the soldiers hastily threw up huts, composed of sods and branches of trees, to give them better shelter. The baggage-wains and baggage, with the wainmen, sutlers, and other followers of the army, were stationed so as to block up the approach to the camp; and their position was so defended by morasses and woods, flanking it on either side, as to render it almost unassailable. At some distance from this, the troops were encamped on the slope of a hill, and the wooded rising grounds on either hand contributed to form defences which left it open to attack nowhere but in front, and even there only after the outwork formed by the baggage at a distance in the meadow below should be broken through.

Earl Douglas said little to those around him, but made his various dispositions with the cool and skilful eye of an expert commander. He surveyed the ground with thoughtful attention, as the sun was setting bright on the hill. It glanced upon Piersie's pennon, that fluttered as if idly impatient of its captivity beside the large banner of Scotland, the heavy drapery of which, drooping to the ground in ample folds, hung in silent and majestic dignity, unruffled by the gentle evening breeze. He thought on the Hotspur and his threats—on the violence and impotence of man's passions—on the actual insignificance of the object which had so stirred up himself and Harry Piersie, compared with the number and value of the lives of those who might soon be called on to fight for it to the death. He mused on the peaceful quiet that now hung over the scene, and of the change that in a few short hours it might undergo ; on the change, above all, that might affect many of those brave hearts which were now beating high with the pulses of life, eager to return to their native soil, and to fulfil schemes of future happiness, never, perhaps, to be realized.

"There is something solemn and grand in the stillness of this lovely evening," said the Douglas at last to the Earl of Moray, who was with him. "The parting radiance of day in yonder western sky might make us fancy that the earth was yblent with heaven. Why might we not pass to that long-wished-for country on those slanting rays of glory, without intervening death, or the penitential pains of purgatory ?"

"'Tis a whimsical conceit, brother," replied Moray with a smile ; "but why, I pray thee, are thy thoughts so employed at a time like this ?"

"I will tell thee," said Douglas gravely. "I know not why it is, but my memory hath been at this time visited by the recollection of a strange dream I once had, and which, long forgotten, doth now arise to me afresh with all its circumstances. Methought I was sitting on a hill side, when, all at once, I beheld a furious battle on the plain of the valley below. One side was led by a figure the which I was conscious bore striking resemblance to mine own. He rushed to the fight, but was quickly

pierced with three lances at once, and fell dead on the field.
Dismay began to fasten on his army, and defeat appeared
certain, when the dead corpse of the knight arose, and, towering to a height ten-fold greater than it had when alive,
moved with the solemn step of the grave towards the foe. The
shout of victory arose from those who were about to yield,
and their enemies were dispersed like chaff before the wind,
when the giant figure and all vanished from my fancy's eye."

"Strange!" cried Moray, his attention grappled by this
singular communication from the Douglas.

"Thou canst never believe me to be a driveller, Moray,"
continued Douglas, without noticing his brother-in-law's interruption, "far less one whom the approach of death may affright.
Death must succeed life, as the night doth follow the day, and
we who can know little how much of our day is gone, must be
prepared to couch as decently when and where the night doth
overtake us."

"Nay, Douglas," said Moray, again interrupting him, "I well
wot that those grave sayings of thine are anything but the
offspring of a quailing heart; I know that they are begotten by
thy dauntless and well-grounded courage that doth accustom
itself to survey death at all times, in thought as well as in field,
till thou has converted his grim image into the familiar figure
of a friend. Yet why should such thoughts find harbour with
thee now? Harry Piersie, if he do come at all for his pennon,
will hardly be here to-night."

"I think not of the Piersie," said Douglas, taking Moray's
hand, and warmly pressing it between his, while a tear glistened
in his manly eye, "I think not of the Piersie or his pennon; but
promise me now, when mine hour hath come, and I shall have
gloriously fallen in battle, as I well trust may be my fate, that
thou wilt yield thine especial protection, and thy love and
cherisaunce, to my widowed Margaret. I need not tell thee
what she hath been to me. Our brother-in-law Fife is cold, and
calculating, and politic, yea, and heartless. He doth aim at the
Regency, and he will doubtless gain his end. Margaret is his
much-loved sister while she is the proud wife of Douglas; but
trust me, little of her brother's sunshine will fall upon her
widow's weeds. Be it thine, then, to be her prop and comfort.
I well know that the warmth of thy Margery's love will go hand
in hand with thee. I am a man, Moray—we are both men—
why should we be ashamed of a few tears shed at a moment
like this?"

"Nay, but Douglas, why shouldst thou talk thus?" said

Moray. "Fate may call for my life first, and then thou wilt have those duties to perform for Margery the which thou dost now claim from me for her sister."

"Nay," replied Douglas, with ominous seriousness of aspect. "Yet be it so," said he, after a pause; "do thou but listen to my sad humour. Mine attached Lundie doth well deserve thy care; see that he do meet with that advancement his piety to God and his devotion to me hath so well merited. And then as for my gallant Archibald, my brave esquires Hart and Glendinning, and my faithful shield-bearer Hop Pringle, they have already carved out a shining reputation for themselves; yet do thou never let it be forgotten that they have been faithful followers of the Douglas."

"Canst thou believe that the name of Douglas can ever lose its potent charm?" exclaimed the Earl of Moray with energy, yet deeply affected; "or canst thou doubt that to me thy will must ever be a sacred law? But why should we now talk of matters so sad?" continued he, endeavouring to rally his own spirits as well as those of Douglas; "the banquet doth abide us in thy pavilion yonder, and the lords and knights of Scotland do doubtless wait for thee there, in obedience to thine invitation."

"I had forgotten," said Douglas, resuming his usual cheerful countenance. "Let us then attune our spirits to mirth and joyous manly converse, sith we have discussed these melancholy themes. Allons, let us to the banquet—such banquet as the rude cookery of the field may furnish."

It was at this time that Rory Spears, having collected a little knot of friends about him, thus addressed them—

"Captain MacErchar, and you most worthy esquires, Masters Mortimer Sang and Roger Riddel, yea, and you, brave Robin Lindsay and Ralpho Proudfoot, and the rest, who are nobly ettling to rise by your deeds as others hae done afore ye—ahem —panting after that most honourable honour and dignified dignity of an esquire, I do hereby invite ye all to go down wi' me to the baggage-camp and sutlerages, whaur we may find comfortable and cozy houf in a braw new bigget sodden hostel, yereckit for the accommodation o' Dame Margaret MacCleareye's yill-barrels and yill-customers, and there, at my proper expense, to eat the bit supper I bid her prepare as I came up the hill, and to drink till ye hae weel wet the honours, the which, descending on mine unworthy head from the gallant Hotspur (whose health we shall not fail to drink, albeit we may yet hope to hae the cleaving o' his skull), have been approven of by our noble Lord of Douglas, and by mine especial dear Lord of

Moray, for both of whom we are not only bound to drink to the
dead, but to fight to the dead."

"Oich, hoich, Maister Spears, surely, surely—he, he, he!"
cried MacErchar.

"Bravo, Master Spears, I shall willingly go with thy squireship," cried Sang; "nay, and never trust me an I do not my
best honour to thine entertainment."

"Squire Spears, I am thine," cried Roger Riddel; and the
rest all heartily joining in ready acquiescence in his invitation,
they followed Rory joyously down the hill in a body.

CHAPTER LIX.

The Battle at Otterbourne.

RORY SPEARS was presiding with joyous countenance over the
supper to which he had invited his friends—the more solid part
of the entertainment had been discussed—and the ale jug had
already performed several revolutions, to the great refreshment
and restoration of the strength of those who partook of it, when
the jovial companions were suddenly disturbed in their revelry
by a very unusual cry from some of the sentinels posted along
the line of entrenchment that protected the baggage-camp.
The hilarious esquires and men-at-arms were silenced in the
midst of their mirth, and sat looking at one another with
eyes of inquiry. But they sat not long so, for the cry was
repeated, and ran rapidly along the chain of sentinels.

"By St. Lowry, it's the English, as I'm a Christian man!"
cried Rory Spears. "My troth, it was maist ceevil of the
chields to wait till we had souped; natheless, it erketh me to
think that they carried not their courtesy so far as to permit
us to drink but ae ither can. Yet, by the Rood, we shall have
at it. Here, Mrs. MacCleareye—d'ye hear, guidwife?"

"Phut, tut!—oich, hoich!—fye, fye, let us awa, Maister
Spears," cried Duncan MacErchar. "Troth, she'll no wait for
us, the Southron loons."

"Hark again," cried Sang; "by all that is good, they will be
in on us in the twinkling of an eye."

"Let's out on them, then, without further talk," cried Rory,
brandishing his battle-axe. "Troth, I wad maybe hae had
mair mercy on them an they had gi'en us but time for ae ither
stoup; but as it is, let's at them, my friends, and let them take
care o' their heads."

"Pay for the supper and yill, Master Spears," cried Mrs. MacCleareye, thrusting herself forward.

"This is no time, woman, to settle sike affairs," cried Rory.

"Better now, I trow, than after thou art amortized by the sword o' some Southron thrust through thy stomach, Master Spears," said Mrs. MacCleareye. "Pay to-day, I pray thee, and have trust to-morrow."

"Nay, of a truth, we have no time to stand talking to thee, good woman," cried Rory impatiently; "had it been to drink mair yill, indeed, I mought hae tholed it; but, holy St. Barnabas, an thou dost keep us much longer there will be guests in thy hut who will drain thy casks without filling thy pockets. Let me past: Rory Spears' word, though that of ane esquire only, is as sicker as that o' the best knight in the land. Thou shalt be paid after the scrimmage. Nay, I'll no die, woman, till thou be'st paid, so fear thee not—and stand out o' my gate, I tell thee."

With a turn of his wrist, Rory shoved Mrs. MacCleareye aside. She was jostled by Sang, who followed; and her round and rolling person was fairly run down by MacErchar, who was pressing hastily after them. The rest sprang impetuously over her. The cries now came more distinctly upon them, mingled with the clash of weapons.

"The English, the English!—Piersie!—The English!" were the words now distinguishable.

"To the trenches, my friends; not a moment is to be lost," cried Mortimer Sang.

"Blow, blow!" cried Roger Riddel; and Rory putting to his mouth an old hunting bugle that hung from his shoulder, blew a shrill and potent blast, that awakened the very echoes of the hills.

"Let us disperse ourselves through the baggage-lines, and rouse up the wainmen and varlets, and the other camp followers," cried Rory Spears, after taking the bugle from his mouth.

"Thou art right, Rory," said Sang; "we may do much to support the guard. Let Riddel, and I, and some others, hasten to the entrenchments, to keep up spirit among those who may now be fighting, with the hope of speedy aid, and do thou and the rest quickly gather what force ye may, and straightway bring them thither. The point of assault is narrow. If we can keep back the foe, were it but until the main body of the army be alarmed, should our lives be the forfeit, they would be bravely spent, for we might be the saving of Scotland's honour this night."

"Ralpho Proudfoot, companion of my youth," cried Robert Lindsay, kindly, "we have striven together for many a prize; now let our struggle be for glory."

"Away, away," cried Sang; and he and Riddel sprang off to the trenches, followed by Lindsay and Proudfoot, whilst Rory hied him away at the head of the others, all blowing their horns, and shouting loudly through the lines, as if the whole Scottish army had been there, and ready to turn out. The huts were soon deserted. Such as they met with in their way they collected together, and armed as fast as they could with whatever weapons lay nearest to hand; and in a very short time these few intelligent and active heads had assembled a force, neither very numerous nor very well appointed, it is true, but, when headed by men so determined, amply sufficient to defend a narrow pass between marches for a considerable time, especially against assailants who were awed by the conviction, favoured by the darkness, that they were attacking the camp where the whole Scottish army were lodged.

While things were in this state in the baggage camp, the banquet in the pavilion of Lord Douglas was going on with all that quiet and elegant cheerfulness of demeanour beseeming a party chiefly composed of the very flower of Scottish chivalry. The talk was of the love of the ladies, and the glories of tilts and tournaments. Sir Patrick Hepborne was seated between Sir John Halyburton and Sir William de Dalzel. With the former of these knights he recalled some of the circumstances of their friendly meeting at Tarnawa, and the Lady Jane de Vaux was not forgotten between them. Sir William de Dalzel changed the theme to that of the challenge which had passed between the Lord Welles and Sir David Lindsay. Then Sir David Lindsay himself and several others joining in the conversation, it gradually became general around the board. Sir William de Keith, the Marischal of Scotland, displayed his consummate learning on the subject of such challenges between knights; and Sir John de Gordon, Lord of Strathbolgy; Sir John Montgomery; Sir Malcolm Drummond, brother-in-law to the Douglas, as well as to the Scottish champion, who was the person most concerned in the debate; Sir Alexander Fraser of Cowie, and many others, spoke each of them ably as to particular points. The Douglas himself then delivered his judgment with clearness and precision, and the attention with which his words were listened to showed how valuable they were esteemed by those who heard them. After this topic was exhausted, the Earl was indefatigable in ministering to the entertainment of his guests by ingeniously drawing forth the powers of those around him ; and his deportment was in every respect so much more than ordinarily felicitous, and so perfectly seasoned by graceful condescension, that all at table agreed he never had charmed them more, and that, as he was the hardiest warrior of all in the field, and the most resistless lance in the lists, so was he by far the most accomplished and witty chevalier at the festive board.

The rational happiness of the evening was approaching its height, and the Douglas was occupying universal attention by something he was saying, when, to the surprise of every one, he suddenly stopped in the middle of his sentence, and turned up his ear to listen.

" Methought I heard a bugle-blast from the baggage lines," cried he, with a flash in his eye that denoted the utter extinc- tion of every other thought but that of the enemy.

" Perdie, I did hear it also," cried the Earl of Moray ; " nor was it strange to me. Methought I did recognize it for one of Rory Spears' hunting-mots. He doth feast his friends to-night at the sutlerage, in honour of his newly-acquired squireship ; so, peraunter, he doth give them music with their ale."

" Ha, heard ye that ? " cried several of the knights at once.

" Nay, there be more performers than one there," cried the Douglas, rising quickly to gain the outside of the pavilion, whilst the whole of the knights crowded after him.

" 'Tis dark as a sightless pit," cried some of them.

" Yea," cried the Earl of Douglas ; " but dost thou see those lights that hurry about yonder ? Trust me, there is some stir- ring cause for the quickness of their motions."

" Hark ye, I hear distant and repeated cries," said the Earl of Dunbar. "Hark, a horse comes galloping up the hill. Hear ye how he snorts and blows ? I'll warrant the rider hath hot news to tell."

" The English !—the English in the baggage-camp !—Piersie and the English ! " cried the rough voice of a wainman, who made towards the light in the pavilion, mounted on a bare- backed and unharnessed wain-horse, that heaved its great sides as if it would have burst them.

" Arm, arm, chevaliers," cried the Douglas in a voice like thunder ; " arm ye in haste, and turn out your brave bands without a moment's let. Mine arms—mine arms, my faithful esquires. My horse, my horse ! "

All was now hurry, bustle, and jostling; cries, orders, oaths, and execrations arose everywhere. Horses were neighing, and steel was clashing, and every one tried to buckle on his armour as fast as he could. Meanwhile Douglas, with Moray near him, stood calm and undismayed, putting one question after another rapidly to the varlet who brought the alarm, until he had gained all the information he could expect from him.

" By the Rood, but thy new esquire Rory Spears hath well demeaned himself, brother Moray," said Douglas. " He and those with him have done that the which shall much avail us if we but bestir ourselves. Let us arm then, and get the line formed. I did well mark the ground, my friend. By skirting the woods upon our right, and if the moon will but keep below the hill-tops long enow, we shall steal down unseen upon the enemy, and pour out our vengeance on his defenceless flank. May St. Andrew grant that thy gallant squire may but keep his own until then. Haste, haste, Glendinning. Where is Robert Hop Pringle, my brave shield-bearer ? Haste thee, Hart, mine arms and my horse. Ha, Archibald," cried he to a young man of noble carriage who was passing him at the moment; "get thee my standard, my son ; thou shalt bear my *jamais arriere* to-night. Part with it not for thy life ; and bastard though thou be'st, show thyself at least to be no counterfeit Douglas. Quit it not even in death, boy."

From time to time the shouts of the combatants now came faintly up the hill-side, and hurried those hands that were busily engaged in arming, so that many a buckle was put awry, and many a tag was left to hang loose. The Douglas staid not to complete his harnessing, but sprang into his saddle ere he was half armed, while Lord Moray rode away to his post without discovering that he had forgotten to put his helmet on.

The night still continued extremely dark, and had not Lord Douglas taken accurate note of the ground below him whilst the light of the sun had shone upon it, he must have found it almost impracticable to have led his men on, notwithstanding that his ears were admonished by the din of the distant skirmish, and the discordant braying of at least five hundred bullocks' horns, blown by the varlets and wainmen who were not engaged ; for such were in those days always carried by the Scottish soldiers, and Rory Spears had taken care that all who could not fight should at least blow, that the extent of their force might appear the greater to the enemy.

The Douglas conducted his little army with great silence and circumspection through the skirting brushwood ; and it so happened, that just as he approached the place of action, the full-orbed moon arose to run her peaceful and majestic course through a clear and cloudless sky, throwing a mimic day over the scene. Loud shouts arose from the powerful army of the English, for now they began to comprehend the actual situation of their affairs; and making one bold and determined charge, they burst at once through the whole breadth of the entrenchments, overwhelming all who attempted to stand before them. Now it was that the Scottish Earl gave the word to his men, and just as the English were pushing rapidly on towards the slope of the high ground where the Scottish camp hung glittering in the moonbeam, driving a handful of brave men before them, who were still fighting as they retired, the shout of " Douglas !—Douglas !—Scotland !—Scotland !—Douglas !— *Jamais arriere?*" ascended to Heaven, and the determined Scots poured from their covert out upon the open plain, and rushed against the troops of Piersie.

Confounded by this unexpected charge from an enemy whom they expected to find asleep in their tents, the English army was driven back in considerable dismay. Then might Harry Piersie and his brother Sir Rafe have been seen flying from standard to standard vainly endeavouring to rally their men; but it was not until they had been driven into the open ground that they could succeed in stopping what almost amounted to a flight.

"What, Englishmen—is this your mettle?" cried Hotspur with vehemence. " Fly, then, cowards, and leave Harry Piersie to die. He may not outlive this disgrace on the standards of St. George."

These upbraiding words had the effect of checking their panic, and gave them time to observe the comparatively small body to whom they were so basely yielding. The two brothers quickly restored the battle by their daring example. Deafening cheers arose, shouts of " Piersie " and " St. George" being loudly mingled with them ; and a fresh and very impetuous onset was made, that drove the Scottish troops entirely through their entrenchments. The struggle was now tremendous, and the clash of the Scottish axes was terrific ; but, although the success of the English wavered a little now and then, yet the weight of their mass was so very superior, that the Scottish army lost ground inch by inch, till, after a long contest, the Piersie found himself almost at the Scottish tents.

" Piersie !—Piersie !—The pennon of the Piersie !" cried he, shrieking with the wildest joy, and sanguine with the hope of

29

success ; while backed by a band of his choicest warriors, he
made a bold dash towards the standard of Scotland, that stood
before the pavilion of Douglas, with the pennon beside it.   The
Douglas was at that time fighting in another part of the field,
where the press against his men was greatest.   The Earls of
Moray and Dunbar were bravely striving to withstand the numbers that came against the respective wings they commanded,
supported by Montgomery, Keith, Fraser, and many others.
Assueton, though but half recovered from the bruise he had received at Newcastle, and Halyburton, Lindsay, and some others
were doing their best to resist the tide of the English in those
parts of the battle where fortune had thrown them. Sir William
de Dalzel had been carried to his tent grievously wounded to
the loss of an eye ; and already had the brave Sir Malcolm
Drummond, and the gallant Sir John de Gordon, Lord of
Strathbolgy, fallen, covered by glorious wounds.   Yet was not
the standard of Scotland, nor the Piersie's captive pennon, left
altogether undefended ; for before them stood the dauntless Sir
Patrick Hepborne of Hailes the elder, with his son by his side,
backed by a small but resolute band of their own immediate
dependents.

"My brave boy," cried the elder knight, "trust me there is
nowhere in the field a more honourable spot of earth to die on
than that where we do now stand."

"Then we quit it not with life, my father, save to drive the
Piersie before us," cried his son.

"Piersie—Piersie !—Piersie's pennon !—Hotspur's pennon !"
cried those who came furiously on to attack them.

The father and the son, with their little phalanx, remained
immovable, and, receiving them on the point of their lances, an
obstinate and bloody contest took place.   Harry Piersie and his
brother fought for the fame of their proud house, and their
eager shouts were heard over all the other battle cries, as well
as above the clashing of the weapons and the shrieking of the
agonized wounded, as they were trodden under foot and crushed
to death by the press ; but the bulwark of lion hearts that defended the standard was too impregnable to be broken through.
Piersie's men already began to slacken in their attack, and to
present a looser and wider circle to the Scottish band ; and now
the elder Sir Patrick Hepborne, seeing his time, and eager to
catch his advantage, brandished a battle-axe, and his son following his example, they joined in the cry of "A Hepborne, a
Hepborne !" and charged the enemy so furiously at the head of
their men, that Piersie and his followers were driven down the

slope with immense slaughter. The axes of the bold knight and his son never fell without the sacrifice of an English life. " A Hepborne, a Hepborne !" they cried from time to time, and " A Hepborne, a Hepborne !" was returned to them from those who ran together to their banner; and yet more and more of the English line gave way before the accumulating aid that crowded after Sir Patrick and his son, who went on gradually recovering the lost ground, by working prodigies of valour.

Whilst the Hepbornes were so manfully exerting their prowess in one part of the field, the Douglas was toiling to support the battle where it was most hopeless. The great force of the enemy had been accidentally directed to the point where he fought, although they knew not against whom they were moving. The dense body opposed to him so encumbered him, that his men were unable to stand before it, and defeat seemed to be inevitable. Finding himself hampered on horseback, he retired a little back, and leaping from his horse, and summoning up his gigantic strength, he seized an iron mace, so ponderous, that even to have lifted it would have been a toil for almost any other individual in the field, and, swinging it round his head, he threw himself amidst the thickest of the foe, bearing ruin and death along with him. At every stroke of the tremendous engine he whirled whole ranks of the English were levelled before him, like grass by the scythe of the mower; and he strode over the dead and dying, down a broad lane cleared through the densest battalions that were opposed to him. Terror seized upon the English, and they began to give back before him. On he rushed after their receding steps, reaping a wide and terrible harvest of death, and strewing the plain with the victims of his matchless courage and Herculean strength. From time to time he was hardily opposed for a few minutes by small bodies of the enemy, that closed together to meet the coming storm, unconscious of its tremendous nature. But his resistless arm bore away all before it, until, encountering a column of great depth and impenetrability, the hero was transfixed by no less than three spears at once.

One entered his shoulder between the plates of his epaulière; another, striking on his breast-plate, glanced downwards, and pierced his belly; and the third easily penetrated his thigh, which in his haste had been left without the cuisse. For a moment did the wounded Douglas writhe desperately on the lance shafts, to rid himself of their iron heads, which had so suddenly arrested his destructive progress. But fate had decreed that his glorious career should be terminated. He received

a severe blow on the head ; his muscles, so lately full of strength
and energy of volition, now refused to obey his will, and he sank
to the ground borne down by those who had wounded him, and
who knew not how noble and how precious that life's blood
was, to which they had opened so many yawning passages of
escape.

His brother-in-law, Sir David Lindsay, and John and Walter
Saintclaires, ever the tried friends of the Douglas, and a few
others who had been fighting along with him before he thus
plunged from their sight into the midst of his foes, took advantage of the terror which his onset had occasioned, and followed
bravely in his course, until accident led them to fall in
with the stream of victorious Scots who were pouring onwards
under the triumphant Hepbornes. Recognizing each other,
and joining together with loud cheers they swept away all
that ventured to oppose them. They had cleared the plain
ground of the enemy for several bowshots before them ; the
English battalions had been thinned and dispersed over the
ground, and the Scottish troops were urging after them without
order, when Sir Patrick Hepborne the younger, with Lindsay
and the Saintclaires, who were pushing forward together, saw
before them the brave and good Richard Lundie, sorely wounded,
yet boldly bestriding the body of a warrior, and dealing death
with a battle-axe to every Englishman who ventured to approach
within his circle. Those who still contended with him quickly
fled at their approach, and then, to their great grief, they discovered that it was the noble Douglas that lay weltering in his
blood. He had not fallen alone, for his faithful esquires, Simon
Glendinning and Robert Hart, lay near him both covered with
mortal wounds, and already lifeless, surrounded by heaps of the
slaughtered foe. His gallant natural son, too, the handsome
Archibald Douglas, faithful to the trust reposed in him, though
severely wounded, and bleeding helplessly on the grass, still
held his banner with the grasp of death.

"How fares it with thee, Lord Douglas?" cried Sir John
Saintclaire, overwhelmed with grief at the sad spectacle before
him, and hastening to assist the others in raising him up.

"Well, right well, I trow, my good friends," replied Douglas
feebly, "seeing that I die thus, like all my ancestors, in the field
of fame. But let not the death of Douglas be known, for 'a
dead man shall yet gain a glorious field.' Hide me, then, I pray
thee, in yonder brake; let some one rear my standard, the
jamais arriere of the Douglas, and let my war-cry be set up,
and I promise that ye shall well revenge my death."

By this time the English, who had been driven for several bowshots beyond that part of the field where the Earl of Douglas had fallen, were now rallying under the heroic efforts of the Hotspur, who, aided by his brother, was again cheering them on to the charge. The Scottish troops began again to give ground before their superior force, and were already retreating in numbers past the group who were occupied about the dying hero. They saw the immediate necessity of conveying. him away while the ground was yet clear of the enemy, and Lundie, Lindsay, and the two Saintclaires hastened to obey his injunctions. He uttered not a word of complaint to tell of the agonizing tortures he felt whilst they were removing him. They laid him on a mossy bank among the long ferns, in the closest part of the thicket. Then he took their hands in succession, squeezing them with affection, and when he had thus taken leave of Lindsay and the two Saintclaires—

"Go," said he faintly to them, "ye have done all for the Douglas that humanity or friendship might require of ye; go, for Scotland lacketh the aid of your arms. Leave me with Lundie; 'tis meeter for his hand to close the eyes of his dying lord."

The brave knights looked their last upon him, covered their eyes and stole silently away from a scene that entirely unmanned them. Lundie took out a silver crucifix, and, bending over the Douglas, held it up under a stream of moonlight that broke downwards through an opening in the thick foliage above them.

"I see it, Lundie," said Douglas; "I see the image of my blessed Redeemer. My sins have been many, but thou art already possessed of them all. My soul doth fix herself on Him, in sincere repentance, and in the strong hope of mercy through His merits."

The affectionate Lundie knelt by the Earl's side, and whilst his own wounds bled copiously, his tears were dropping fast on his dying master.

"I know thine inmost heart, Lord Douglas," said he in a voice oppressed by his grief; "thy hopes of Heaven may indeed be strong. Hast thou aught of worldly import to command me?"

"Margaret," said Douglas in a voice scarcely audible, "my dearest Margaret! Tell Moray to forget not our last private converse; and do thou—do thou tell my wife that my last thought, my last word was—Margaret!"

His countenance began to change as Lundie gazed intently

on it under the moonbeam. The weeping chaplain hastily pronounced the absolution, administered the consecrated wafer from
a casket in his pocket, and performed the last religious duties
bestowed upon the dying, and the heroic spirit of the Douglas
took its flight to Heaven.

The grief of Lindsay and the Saintclaires subdued them only
whilst they beheld the noble Douglas dying. No sooner had
they left the thicket where he lay, than, burning with impatience to revenge his death, they hurried to the field. The
younger Sir Patrick Hepborne had already reared his fallen
standard, and shouts of "Douglas! Douglas! *Jamais arriere!—*
A Douglas! a Douglas!" cleft the very skies. At this moment
the English were gaining ground upon the Scottish centre, but
this animating cry not only checked their retreat, but brought
aid to them from all quarters. Believing that the Douglas was
still fighting in person, down came the Earl of Moray, with
Montgomery, Keith, the Lord Saltoun, Sir Thomas Erskine, Sir
John Sandilands, and many others, and the shouts of "Douglas,
Douglas!" being repeated with tenfold enthusiasm, the charge
against the English was so resistless that they yielded before
Scotland in every direction. Bravely was the banner of Douglas
borne by the gallant Hepborne, who took care that it should be
always seen among the thickest of the foes, well aware that the
respect that was paid to it would always ensure it the close
attendance of a glorious band of knights as its defenders. As
he was pressing furiously on, he suddenly encountered an
English knight, on whom his vigorous arm, heated by indiscri-
minate slaughter, was about to descend. The knight had lost
his casque in the battle; the moon shed its radiance over a
head of snow-white hair, and an accidental demivolt of his horse
bringing his countenance suddenly into view, he beheld Sir
Walter de Selby.

"I thank God and the Virgin that thou art saved, old man,"
cried Hepborne, dropping his battle-axe "oh, why art thou
here? Had I been the innocent cause of thy death——"

He would have said more, and he would moreover have staid
to see him in safety. But the press came thick at the moment,
and they were torn asunder; so that Hepborne, losing all sight
of him in the melée, was compelled to look to himself.

And now, "A Douglas, a Douglas!" continued to run through
the field, and the English, thrown into complete confusion, were
driven through the baggage-camp at the place they had first
entered, flying before the Scottish forces. Hotspur alone stood
to defend his brother, who was lying on the ground grievously

wounded. Harry Piersie had abandoned his horse, and was standing over Sir Rafe, fighting bravely against a crowd of Scottish men-at-arms, when Sir Hugh Montgomery, Sir John Maxwell, and Sir William de Keith came up.

" Yield thee," said Sir Hugh Montgomery, "yield thee, noble Hotspur. God wot, it were bitter grief to see so brave a heart made cold."

" And who art thou who would have the Hotspur yield ? " cried Piersie.

" I trust, Sir Harry Piersie, that to yield thee to Sir Hugh Montgomery will do thee as little dishonour as may be," replied the Scottish Knight ; " yield thee, then, rescue or no rescue."

" I do so yield to thee and fate, Sir Hugh Montgomery," said Hotspur ; " but let my brother Rafe here have quick attendance, his wounds do well out sorely, and his steel boots run over with his blood."

" Let him be prisoner to these gentlemen," said Sir Hugh, turning to Keith and Maxwell, "and let us straightway convoy him to the Scottish camp."

The flying English were now driven far and wide, and day began to break ere the pursuit slackened. Among those who followed the chase most vehemently was Sir David Lindsay. Infuriated by the loss of the hero to whom he was so devoted, he seemed to be insatiable in his vengeance. Whilst he was galloping after the flying foe at sunrise, the rays, as they shot over the eastern hill, were sent back with dazzling splendour from the gold-embossed armour of a knight who had stopped at some distance before him to slake his thirst at a fountain. He was in the act of springing into the saddle as Lindsay approached ; but the Scottish warrior believing, from the richness of his armour, that he was some one of noble blood, pushed after him so hard, and gained so much upon him, that he was nearly within reach of him with his lance-point.

" Turn, Sir Knight," cried Lindsay. " It is a shame thus to flee. I am Sir David Lindsay. By St. Andrew, an thou turn not, I must strike thee through with my lance."

But the English knight halted not ; on the contrary, he only pricked on the more furiously, and Lindsay's keenness being but the more excited, he followed him at full gallop for more than a league, until at last the English knight's horse, which had shot considerably ahead of his, suddenly foundered under him. The rider instantly sprang to his legs, and drew out his sword to defend himself.

" I scorn to take unfair vantage of thee, Sir Knight," said

Lindsay, dismounting from his horse, when he came up to him, and throwing down his lance and seizing a small battle-axe that hung at his sadle-bow, he ran at the English knight, and a well-contested single combat ensued between them. But the weight of Lindsay's weapon was too much for the sword of the Englishman; and after their strokes had rung on each other's arms for a time, and that the Scot had bestowed some blows so heavy that the plates of the mail began to give way under them—

"I yield me, Sir David Lindsay," cried the English knight, breathless and ready to sink with fatigue; "I yield me, rescue or no rescue."

"Ha," replied Lindsay, "'tis well. And whom, I pray thee, mayest thou be who has cost me so long a chase, and contest so tough, ere I could master thee?"

"I am Sir Matthew Redman, Governor of Berwick," replied the English knight.

"Gramercy, Sir Governor," said Sir David Lindsay; "sit thee down, then, with me on this bank, and let us talk a while. We seem to be both of us somewhat toil-spent with this encounter, yea, and thy grey destrier and my roan do seem to have had enow on't as well as their masters. Behold how they feed most peaceably together."

"Let us then imitate their example, good Sir Knight of Scotland," said Sir Matthew Redman. "I have a small wallet here, with some neat's tongue, and some delicate white bread; and this leathern bottle, though it be small, hath a cordial in it that would put life into a dead man."

The two foes, who had so lately endeavoured to work each other's death, sat down quietly together and silently partook of the refreshment, and then alternately applying the little leathern flask to their lips, they talked in friendly guise of the result of the battle.

"And now, Sir David of Lindsay," said Redman, "I am thy prisoner, and bound to obey thy will. But I have ever heard thee named as a courteous knight, the which doth embolden me to make thee a proposal. I have a certain lady at Newcastle, whom I do much love, and would fain see. If thy generosity may extend so far, I shall be much beholden to thee if thou wilt suffer me to go thither, to assure her of my safety, and to bid her adieu; on which I do swear to thee, on the word of a knight, that I will render myself to thee in Scotland within fifteen days hence."

"Nay, now I do see, Sir Matthew," said Lindsay archly—

" now I do see right well why thou didst ride so hard from the field ; but I am content to grant thee thy request ; nay, if thou dost promise me, on the faith of a knight, to present thyself to me at Edinburgh within three weeks from the present time, it is enow."

" I do so promise," replied Redman. And so shaking hands together, each took his horse and mounted to pursue his own way.

By this time a thick morning mist had settled down on the face of the country, and Lindsay had hardly well parted from the prisoner ere he perceived that he had lost his way. As he was considering how he should recover it, he beheld a considerable body of horsemen approaching, and believing them to be some of the Scottish army who had pushed on thus far in the pursuit, he rode up to them with very great joy ; but what was his surprise when he found himself in the midst of some three or four hundred English lances !

" Who art thou, Sir Knight ? " cried the leader, who, though clad in armour, yet wore certain Episcopal badges about him that mightily puzzled the Scottish knight.

" I am Sir David Lindsay," replied he ; " but whom mayest thou be, I pray thee ? "

" I am the Bishop of Durham," replied the other ; " thus far am I come to give mine aid to the Piersie."

" Thine aid cometh rather of the latest, Sir Bishop," replied Lindsay ; " for, certes, his army is routed with great slaughter, and he and his brother Sir Rafe are prisoners in the Scottish camp."

" I have heard as much already from some of those who fled," replied the Bishop : " *Quæ utilitas in sanguine meo ?* what good would my being killed do my cousins the Piersie ? Now I do haste me back again to Newcastle ; but thou must bear me company, Sir David."

" Sith thou dost say so, my sacred Lord," replied Sir David, " I must of needscost obey thee, for, backed as thou art, I dare not say thee nay. Such is the strange fortune of war."

Sir David now rode towards Newcastle with the Bishop, and soon overtook the large army which he commanded that was now returning thither. After being fairly lodged within the walls of the town, the Bishop treated him with the utmost kindness and hospitality, and left him to wander about at his own discretion, rather like a guest than a prisoner. The place was filled with mourning and lamentation, and every now and then fresh stragglers, who had fled from the field of Otterbourne, were dropping in to tell new tales of the grievous loss and mor-

tifying disgrace which had befallen the English arms.   Murmurs
began to rise against the Bishop because he had not proceeded
against the Scots, and attempted the rescue of the Piersies.   At
all events, he might have revenged their loss.   The Bishop
himself, too, began to be somewhat ashamed that he should
have retired so easily, and without so much as looking on the
Scottish army.   At last he consented to summon a council of
war, and in it he was persuaded, by the importunity of the
knights and esquires who were present, to order immediate
proclamation for the assembling of his army, consisting of ten
thousand men, to march long before sunrise.

"Verily, our foes shall be consumed," said the Bishop, his
courage rising.   "*Si consistent adversum me castra non time-
bit cor meum.*   Let the whole Scottish force be there, yet will
my heart be bold for the encounter."

After the council of war, the Bishop introduced Sir David
Lindsay to the guests who filled his house.   The Scottish knight,
so closely connected with the Douglas, was courteously received
by the English chevaliers, who, though much cast down in
reality by the failure of the Piersies' attempt, did their best to
assume an air of gaiety before him.   They vied with one another
who should show him greatest kindness.   Many were the questions put to him about the fate of the Douglas, but he was too
cautious to say anything that could lead them to believe that
he had fallen.

The ladies crowded around him to satisfy their curiosity
about the particulars of the battle, and he answered them with
becoming gallantry.   Among those who so addressed him was a
lady in a veil, who hung pensively on the arm of the Bishop,
and whose figure bespoke her young and handsome.   After some
general conversation with him, during which she endeavoured to
ascertain from him all that he knew as to what English knights
had been killed or taken—

"Sir Knight," said she, with a half-suppressed sigh, "I have
heard of a certain brave chevalier of Scotland who did distinguish
himself in France, Sir Patrick Hepborne, the younger of that
name.   Was he in the bloody field? and hath he escaped
unhurt, I pray thee?"

"I do well know him, lady," replied Sir David Lindsay.
"To him, and to his gallant father, was chiefly due the gaining of
the glorious victory the Scots did yesternight achieve over the
bravest army that did ever take the field.   I saw him safe ere I
left the fight.   Proud might he be, I ween, to be so inquired
after by one so lovely as thou art."

"Nay," said the lady, in some confusion, "I do but inquire to satisfy the curiosity of a friend." And so saying, she retreated towards the protection of the Bishop of Durham, who seemed to take an especial charge of her.

Sir David Lindsay, for his part, to avoid being annoyed by further questions, retired within the deep recess of a Gothic window, where he sat brooding over the untimely fate of the Douglas, and weeping inwardly at the blow that Scotland had sustained by his loss. He was awakened from his reverie by a friendly tap on the shoulder.

"Ha, Sir Matthew Redman!" said Lindsay, looking up with surprise.

"Sir David de Lindsay!" cried Redman, with signs of still greater astonishment; "what, in the name of the holy St. Cuthbert, dost thou make here at Newcastle? Hath my cordial bottle bewildered thy brain so, that thou hast fancied that it was I who took thee, not thou who took me? Did I not promise thee, on the word of a knight, to go to thee at Edinburgh? and thinkest thou that I would not have kept my word?"

"Yea, Sir Matthew," replied Lindsay, "I have full faith in thine honour; but I believe there may now be little need that thou shouldst journey so far, or make to me any fynaunce; for no sooner hadst thou parted from me than I did fall into the hands of His Grace the Lord Bishop of Durham, who hath brought me hither as his prisoner; and if ye be so content, I do rather think we shall make an exchange, one for the other, if it may so please the Bishop."

"God wot how gladly I shall do so," replied Redman, shaking him cordially by the hand; "but, by my troth, thou shalt not go hence until thou hast partaken of my hospitality; so thou shalt dine with me to-day, yea, and to-morrow alswa; and then we shall talk anon with the Bishop, after which thou shalt have good safe-conduct for Scotland; nay, I shall myself be thy guard over the Marches, yea, and moreover, give thee hearty cheer in mine own good town of Berwick as thou dost pass thither."

CHAPTER LX.

The Bishop's Army—Sorrow for the Fate of the Heroic Douglas.

THE two brothers, the Earls of Dunbar and Moray, were now

left to command the Scottish army after the afflicting death of
the Earl of Douglas.   Deeply as they grieved for him, they had
but little leisure for mourning, since every succeeding moment
brought them in harassing rumours that the Bishop of Durham
was coming against them with a great army.   During the whole
of the day succeeding the battle, and of the night which followed it, they were so kept on the alert that they could even
do but little to succour the wounded or bury the dead.   The
prisoners, however, among whom were many renowned knights,
besides the two Piersies, were treated with all that chivalric
courtesy and hospitality for which the age was so remarkable.
Sir Rafe was immediately despatched in a litter to Alnwick,
that he might have the benefit of such careful treatment as
might be most likely to cure the many and severe wounds he
had received.

After various false alarms, the second morning after the
battle brought back the scouts, who had been sent to follow the
flying enemy, and to gather what intelligence they might in the
neighbourhood of Newcastle.   By these men they were informed
of the proclamation which had been made in the town, and of
the proposed march of the Bishop of Durham's large army.   A
council of war was immediately held, and the opinion was
unanimous that they should remain where they were to receive
the Bishop in their present position, which they had already
proved to be so favourable for successful defence against superior numbers, rather than march harassed as they were with a
number of wounded and prisoners, and with the risk of being
overtaken in unfavourable ground.   They accordingly hastened
to strengthen themselves in the best way they could ; and, as
they had but little time for a choice of plans, they piled up an
abattis, formed of the dead bodies of the slain, on the top of the
broken rampart that stretched across between the flanking
marches, and defended the entrance to their position.

Before the enemy appeared, a very serious question arose
for the consideration of the leaders.   Their prisoners amounted
to above a thousand, and what was to be done with them ?   To
have put them to death would have been so barbarous that such
an idea could not be entertained for a moment in such times ;
yet, as their number was nearly equal to half their little army,
the danger they ran from their breaking loose upon them during
the fight, and even turning the tide of battle against them, was
sufficiently apparent to every one.   At length, after much debate
and deliberation, it was generally resolved to trust them.   They
were accordingly drawn up in the centre of the camp, and an

oath administered to them that they should not stir from the spot during the ensuing battle, and that, be the result what it might, they should still consider themselves as prisoners to Scotland. After this solemnity, they left them slenderly guarded by some of the varlets and wainmen, with perfect confidence that they would keep their oath.

Then it was that the Earl of Dunbar thus encouraged his soldiers, after having drawn them up behind their lines.

"My brave Scots," said he, "ye who have hardly yet well breathed sith that ye did conquer the renowned Piersies of Northumberland, can have little fear, I trow, to encounter a mitred priest. Verily, though his host be great, it will be but two strokes when both shepherd and sheep will be dispersed, and we shall teach this pastoral knight that it were better for him to be a scourger of schoolboy urchins with birchen rods than to essay thus, with the sword, to do battle against bearded soldiers."

This speech was received with shouts by the little army to which it was addressed, and, "Douglas, Douglas! revenge our brave, our beloved Douglas!" was heard to break from every part of the line. The two Earls had hardly completed their preparations, when the approach of the Bishop of Durham's army was announced. Orders were immediately issued for each soldier to blow the horn he carried, and the loud and discordant sound of these rude and variously-toned instruments being re-echoed and multiplied from the hills, was distinctly audible at several miles' distance. It rung in the ears of the Bishop, and very much appalled him. Had it not been for a spice of shame he felt, he would have been disposed to have gone no farther; but the knights and esquires who were with him were still sanguine in their hopes of successfully attacking, with so large a force, the small army of the Scots, wasted as it was by the recent bloody engagement.

"Verily, it is a sinful thing to trust in the arm of flesh," said the Bishop, growing paler and paler. "Who knoweth what may be the issue of the battle? Trust not in numbers. *Non salvatur rex per multam virtutem;* even the bravery of a Bishop shall not always win the fight. *Gigas non salvabitur in mul titudine virtutis suæ;* even the courage of the greatest of Churchmen shall not always prevail. *Fallax equus ad salutem;* a horse is counted but a vain thing to save a man. St. Cuthbert grant," ejaculated he in a lower tone—"St. Cuthbert grant that our steeds may be preserved."

The Bishop, however, dissembling his feelings as well as he

could, continued to advance in good order until he came within
sight of the Scots ; when, beholding the strength of their position, and the horrible bulwark of defence they had constructed
with the heaps of the dead bodies of the English whom they had
already sacrificed, and listening to their wild shrieks of defiance,
mingled with the increased sound of their horns, his blood froze
within him, and he halted to reason with those who had been so
prone to attack the foe.   But opinions had been mightily
changed in the course of a mile's march.   The knights and
esquires, who had been lately so bold, now listened with becoming patience to the prudent arguments of their reverend leader :
and when, after a considerable halt, and holding a communication
with the Castle of Otterbourne, the Bishop did at last give the
word for his army to retreat, there was not a single voice lifted
in condemnation of the movement.

When it was fully ascertained in the Scottish army that the
retrograde march of the English was no manœuvre, but a
genuine retreat, a strong guard of observation was planted, and
orders were given to proceed with the sad duty, already too long
neglected, of collecting such of the wounded as had lain miserably on the plain, without food or attention, ever since they had
fallen.   Parties were also appointed to bury the dead.

The body of the heroic Douglas had never been deserted by
the affectionate Lundie, who, though himself grievously wounded,
sat watching it by the thicket where he died, until the termination of the battle and the break of day enabled the Saintclaires,
the Earl of Moray, and the Hepbornes, to come to his aid.
Then was his honoured corpse carried to the camp ; but it was
not till after the departure of the Bishop of Durham, that the
Earls of Moray and Dunbar, accompanied by the whole chivalry
of the Scottish army, met together at night in the pavilion of
the Douglas.   There—sad contrast to the happy night which
they had so lately spent in the same place, under the cheering
influence of his large, mild, and benignant eye !—they came to
behold his body laid out in state.   It was attended, even in
death, by those who had never abandoned him in life.   By the
side of his bier lay his brave son Archibald, who had so well
fulfilled his last injunctions.   At his feet were stretched his two
faithful esquires, who had so nobly perished with their master.
Near them stood Robert Hop Pringle, leaning on the Douglas's
shield, who, having been separated from him in the thickest
press, had fought like a lion, vainly searching for him through
the field, and who now looked with an eye of mingled grief and
envy on his comrades.   Richard Lundie too was there, wounded

as he was, to perform a solemn service for that soul with which he had long held the closest and dearest converse. The place was dimly illuminated by the red glare of numerous torches, held by some hardy soldiers, who, though formed of the coarsest human clay, were yet unable to look towards the bier where lay the body of their brave commander, whose fearless heart had so often led them on to glory, without the big tears running down the furrows of their weather-beaten cheeks. Those who were tempered of finer mould, and whose rank had brought them into closer contact with the Douglas, and, above all, those whom strict friendship had bound to him, though they struggled hard to bear up like men, were forced to yield to the feelings that oppressed them. So overpowering indeed was the scene that Harry Piersie himself, who had craved permission to be present, wept tears of unfeigned sorrow over the remains of him who had been so lately his noble rival in the field of fame. "Douglas," said he with a quivering lip that marked the intensity of his feelings, "what would I not give to see that lofty brow of thine again illumined with the radiant sunshine of thy godlike soul ? Accursed be my folly—accursed be my foolish pride ! Would that the curtailment of half the future life of Hotspur could be given to restore and eke out thine ! God wot how joyously he would now make the willing sacrifice. Thou hast not left thy peer in chivalry, and even Hotspur's glory must wane for lack of thee to contend with."

This generous speech of the noble Piersie deeply affected all present. Sir Patrick Hepborne stole silently out of the tent to give way to his emotions in private, and to breathe the invigorating breeze of the evening, that sported among the dewy furze and the wild thyme that grew on the side of the hill. The moon was by this time up. Hepborne looked over the lower ground, that was now widely lighted up by her beams, where the furious and deadly strife had so lately raged, and where all was now comparatively still. The only signs of human life—and they spoke volumes for its folly, its frailty, and its insignificance —were the few torches that were here and there seen straggling about, carried by those who were creeping silently to and fro, over the field of the dead, looking for the bodies of their friends.

Hepborne's heart was already sufficiently attuned to sadness ; and it led him to descend the slope before him, that he might be a spectator of the melancholy scene. As he wandered about from one busy group to another, he met his esquire, Mortimer Sang, who, so actively engaged at the beginning of the battle, had fortunately escaped, covered indeed with wounds of little importance in themselves. His friend Roger Riddel, who had been a good deal hurt, but who had been also fortunate enough to survive an attack where it appeared almost impossible that a mouse could have escaped with life, was with him. They were employed in the pious duty of looking for some of their friends who had not appeared. After they had turned over many an unknown and nameless corpse, and many a body whose face had been familiar to them, on each of whom Roger Riddel had some short and pithy remark to bestow, they at last discovered the well-set form of Ralpho Proudfoot.

" Good fellow, thy pride is laid low, I well wot," cried Roger Riddel, as he held up the head of the dead man to the light of the torch, and discovered who he was.

The same haughty expression that always characterised him still sat upon his forehead in death ; his eyebrows were fiercely knit and his lip curled. His battle-axe was firmly grasped with both his hands, and a heap of English dead lay around him. He had fallen across the body of a Scottish man-at-arms, and on turning him up, Hepborne was shocked to behold the features of Robert Lindsay.

" Ah me !" cried Roger Riddel ; " what will become of thine ould father, Robin."

" Robert Lindsay !" said Sang—" Blessed Virgin !—no—it cannot be—ay—there is indeed that open countenance of truth the which was never moved with human wrath or wickedness. This is indeed a bitter blow to us all ; and as for his poor father, as thou sayest, Roger, Heaven indeed knows how the old man may stand it, for poor Robert here was the only hope and comfort of his life. Let me but clip a lock of his hair, and take from his person such little trinkets as may peraunter prove soothing, though sad memorials, to the afflicted Gabriel."

" Alas, poor Robert Lindsay !—alas for poor Gabriel !" was all that Hepborne's full heart could utter, as recollections of home, and of his boyish days, crowded upon him until his eyes ran over.

The position in which their bodies were found sufficiently explained that Lindsay and Proudfoot had been fighting side by side in the midst of a cloud of foes. Lindsay had fallen first, and Proudfoot had stood over him, defending his dying friend, until, overpowered by numbers, he had been stretched across him, covered with mortal wounds. Near him lay the body of an English knight, and some of those who knew him declared him to be Sir Miers de Willoughby.

Hepborne saw that a grave was dug to contain the bodies of Lindsay and Proudfoot, and he himself assisted the esquires in depositing them in the earth, locked in each other's embrace.

CHAPTER LXI.

The Field of Otterbourne after the Fight.

AFTER Sir Patrick Hepborne had assisted to perform the last sad duties to the remains of Robert Lindsay and Ralpho Proudfoot, his attention was caught by the appearance of a solitary cluster of lights on the distant part of the field, where the slaughter of the English had been greatest. Curiosity led him to approach, when he perceived that they were borne by a party who followed a bier, that was slowly carried in the direction of Otterbourne Castle. Advancing to a point which they must necessarily pass, he saw, as the procession drew nearer, that the bier was supported by some English spearmen, and that it was followed by a group of women.

Hepborne's attention was particularly attracted by a lady in the midst of them, who walked with her head veiled in the folds of her mantle, and seemed to be deeply affected by that grief in which the others only sympathised. She took her mantle from her head, and threw her eyes upwards as if in inward ejaculation. Sir Patrick started, for he beheld that very countenance the charms of which, though seen but by glimpses at Norham, had made too deep an impression upon his heart ever to be forgotten ; but now they seemed to be more than ever familiar to him, as he was disposed to believe, from their frequent presence to the eye of his imagination. He gazed in silent rapture. The strong resemblance between his page Maurice de Grey and the lady now struck him the more powerfully, that he had a full opportunity of perusing every trait ; he was confounded ; the mantle dropped over the alabaster forehead, and the countenance was again shrouded from his eyes. The procession moved on, and he followed, almost doubting whether it was not composed of phantoms, until it approached the gate of the Castle of Otterbourne, where the captain of the place, attended by his garrison, appeared to receive it. Still Hepborne had difficulty in convincing himself that the whole was not a waking vision—a belief warranted by the superstition of his country. It slowly entered the gateway. The lady in

30

whom he felt so deep an interest was about to disappear.   He could bear suspense no longer.

"Lady Eleanore de Selby—Lady de Vere," cried he, in a frantic voice.

The lady started at the sound of it, threw back the mantle from her head, and cast her eyes around in strong agitation, until they glanced on Hepborne's face, when she uttered a faint scream, and fell back senseless into the arms of her attendants, who crowded around her, and hastily bore her within the gateway of the Castle, the defences of which being immediately closed, she was shut from his straining sight.

Hepborne stood for some time in a state of stupefaction ere he could muster sufficient self-command to return to his tent. The abrupt termination of the scene, which still remained fresh on his mind, almost convinced him of the accuracy of his conjecture as to its having been some strange supernatural appearance he had beheld.   He slowly found his way to his friends, his soul vexed by a thousand contending conjectures and perplexities, which he found it impossible to satisfy or reconcile.

Meanwhile Mortimer Sang, who had been earnestly searching for the body of Rory Spears, of whose death he had begun to entertain great apprehensions, was surprised by the appearance of a damsel, whom he saw bearing a torch and bitterly weeping.

"Holy St. Andrew !" exclaimed he ; " Katherine Spears, can it be thee in very body—or is it thy wraith I behold ?   Speak, if thou be'st flesh and blood—for the love of the Holy Virgin, speak."

"Oh, dear Master Sang," cried Katherine, running to him and proving by the gripe that she took of his arm, that she was indeed something corporeal, " the blessed St. Mary be praised that I have met with thee ; thank Heaven, thou art safe at least.   But, oh, tell me, tell me, hast thou seen aught of my dear father?   Hath he 'scaped this dreadful field of death ? "

"Thy father, I trust, is well," replied Sang, much perplexed; " but how, in the name of all that is wonderful, didst thou come here ? "

"I came with an English lady, who is now at the Castle of Otterbourne," replied Katherine evasively.   " But, oh, tell me, tell me, I entreat thee," said the poor girl, earnestly seizing his hand, " tell me, hast thou seen my father sith the fight was over ? "

"He hath not appeared since the battle," said Sang in a half-choked voice, and with considerable hesitation ; " but we trust he may be prisoner with the English, for as yet we have searched for him in vain among the slain scattered over the field. Yes," continued he, in a firmer and more assured tone, as he observed the alarm that was taking possession of her ; "yes, he hath not been found—and as he hath not been found, dear Katherine, it is clear that he must be a prisoner—so—and—and so thou wilt soon see him again ; for as there must be a truce, the few prisoners ta'en by the English must speedily be sent home again."

"Nay, but do they seek him still, Sir Squire?" cried Katherine, but little satisfied with this attempt of Sang's to soothe her apprehension "Alas, I must seek for him."

"Nay, this is no scene for thee, dear Katherine," replied Sang ; "return I pray thee to the Castle, and I will search, and thou shalt quickly know all."

"Try not to hinder me, Sir Squire," replied Katherine ; "I will go seek for my father. I have already seen enow of those grim and ghastly faces not to fear in such a cause."

"Then shall I go with thee, Katherine," cried Sang, seeing her determination. "Here, lean upon mine arm."

When they came into the thickest part of the field of slaughter, Katherine shuddered and shrank as they moved aside, from time to time, to shun the heaps of slain. Sang looked everywhere for his comrade Roger Riddel, and at last happily met him ; but, alas! Riddel could give no intelligence of him they sought for. By this time they had approached the abattis of dead bodies which had been so hastily piled up for defence against the expected attack of the Bishop of Durham.

"Come not this way, Katherine," cried Sang ; "this rampart of the dead is horrible."

Katherine's heart was faint within her at the sight ; she stopped and turned away, when, just at that moment, her ear caught the whining of a dog at a little distance.

"That voice was Oscar's," cried she eagerly. "Oh, let us hasten, my father may be there."

They followed her steps with the lights, and there she beheld her father lying on the ground, grievously wounded, and half dead with want and loss of blood. Luckily for him, poor Oscar had been accidentally let out at the time that Sang and Riddel went forth to search among the slain, and having sought more industriously for his master than all the rest, he had discovered the unhappy Rory Spears built into the wall of the dead. Rory had fallen before the tremendous charge made by the English, when they burst through the line of entrenchment,

where he had fought like a lion himself, and inspired a something more than human courage into those around him. Having lost his basinet, he had received a severe cut on the head,
besides many other wounds, which affected him not. But the
thrust of a lance through his thigh was that which brought him
to the ground; after which, he was nearly trampled to death
by the rush of English foot and horsemen that poured over him.
During the time that had passed since he was laid low, he had
fainted repeatedly, and had been for hours insensible to his
sufferings. Whilst lying in one of his mimic fits of death, he
had been taken up by some of those who were employed in
heaping the slain into a rampart, and who, having little leisure
for minute examination, had made use of him as part of its
materials. Fortunately his head was placed outwards, so that
when he recovered he was enabled to breathe, and consequently
was saved from suffocation. Oscar had no sooner found him
than, seizing the neck of his haqueton with his teeth, be pulled
him gently out upon the plain.

" My father, my dear father !" cried Katherine Spears, running to support him, and much affected by the sight of his wan
visage, the paleness of which, together with his sunken eye,
showed more ghastly from the blood that had run down in such
profusion from his wound, that the very colour of his beard was
changed, and the hairs of it matted together by it.

" What dost thou here, Kate ?" demanded Rory, in a firmer
voice than his appearance would have authorized the bystanders
to have expected from him ; "sure this be no place for a silly
maiden like thee."

" Oh, father, father," cried Katherine, embracing him, and
doing her best to assist Sang in raising him up by the shoulders ;
" the holy Virgin be praised that thou art yet alive."

" Alive !" answered Rory ; " troth, I'm weel aware that I'm
leevin, for albeit that the agony o' my head wad gi'e me peace
enow to let me believe that I had really depairted in real
yearnest, the very hunger that ruggeth so cruelly at my inside
wad be enew to keep me in mind that I was still belonging to
this warld. For the sake o' the gude Saint Lawrence, Maister
Sang, gar ane o' them chields rin and see gif Mrs Margaret
MacCleareye can gi'e me a bit o' cauld mutton or sike like, and
a wee soup yill. Tell the woman I'll pay her for the score o'
yestreen and a' thegither. But, aboon a' thing, see that they
mak haste, or I'll die ere they come back. What sould I hae
done an it hadna been for the gude wife's wee bit supper afore
we fell to !"

Sang immediately despatched one of the camp followers who was standing by, and who quickly returned with the melancholy intelligence that Mrs MacCleaveye's frail hut had been levelled with the earth by the press—that her provender had been scattered and pillaged—that her ale barrels had been rolled away and emptied—and that she herself had also disappeared.

"Hech me," cried Rory, altogether forgetful of his own craving stomach ; "poor woman, I'm sorry for her loss ; aboon a', it erketh me sair that I paid her not her dues yestreen. But, an a' live, she or her heirs shall hae it, as I'm a true esquire. But, och, I'm faunt !"

"Take some of this, Master Spears," cried Mortimer Sang, holding a leathern bottle to Rory's mouth, and pouring a few drops of a cordial into it.

"Oich, Maister Sang, that is reveeving !" said Rory. "A wee drap mair, for the love o' St. Lowry. Mercy me ! Weel, it's an evil thing after a' to be killed in battle (as I may be allowed to judge, I rauckon, wha has been half killed), was it no for the glory that is to be gotten by it. But to be cut down and then travelled ower like a mercat-causey, and then to be biggit up like a lump o' whinstane intil a dyke—ay, and that, too, for the intent o' haudin out the yenemy, and saving the craven carcages o' ither fouk, and a' to keep the dastard sauls in chields that ane is far frae liking as weel as ane's sell—troth, there's onything but honour or pleasure in't to my fancy."

"Uve, uve ! sore foolish speech, Maister Spears," said a voice from the heap of dead bodies. "Great pleasures and high honours in troth, sure, sure."

"Captain MacErchar !" cried Sang. "Run, Roger, and yield him relief."

Squire Riddel hastened to the assistance of MacErchar, and drew forth his great body from the place it had occupied in the bottom of the fortification, where the skilful architect had, with much judgment, made use of him as a substantial foundation. His history had been something similar to that of Rory Spears, and he had not suffered less from wounds. He was brought forward and placed on a bank beside Rory, and a portion of Squire Sang's life-inspiring bottle was given to him with the happiest effect.

"Hech me," cried Spears, looking round with great compassion on his companion in glory and misfortune—"hech me, Captain MacErchar, wha sould hae thought that thou wert sae near ? Had we but kenn'd we mought hae had a crack the-

gither, albeit hardly sae cosy as in Mrs MacCleareye's. Troth,
I was sair weary and lonesome wi' lying, and even the converse
o' the sagaciousome brute there was a comfort to me. This is
but ane evil way o' weeting a squireship. We sould hae done
it in ane ither gate, I rauckon, had the English chields but
defaured a wee. But I trust that neither have you disgraced
your captaincy nor I my squireship. I saw you fighting like a
very incarnate deevil, ay, and sending the Southrons back frae
the rampyre like raquet ba's frae a wa', though it may be pre-
meesed that nane o' them ever stotted again."

"Ouch ay, troth ay," replied MacErchar, "it was a bonnie
tuilzie, Maister Spears. She did her pairts both—both, both.
Ou ay; it was a great pleasures, in troth, to see her chap the
chields on the crown."

"Poor Oscar, poor man," said Rory, patting his dog's head
as he put his nose towards his face to claim his share of his
master's attention; "troth, I maun say that thou didst do me a
good turn this blessed night. I was just thinking as I lay
here that as I must now bear the proper armorial device of ane
esquire, I sould take the effigy of ane allounde couchant beside
his master sejant, with this motto, '*Fair fa' the snout that pu'd
me out.*'"

"How couldst thou think of such things, my dear father,
whilst thou didst lie in plight so pitiful!" cried Katherine
Spears.

"Troth, I had naething else to think o', ye silly maiden, but
that or hunger," said Rory; "and that last, I'll promise thee,
was a sair sharp thought. And, by St. Lowry, it doth sore
sting me at this precious moment."

"Uve, uve! sore hungry—sore hungry," cried MacErchar.

"Nay, then, let us hasten to carry both of them to camp
without further let," cried Sang.

"Come, bestir ye, varlets," said he to a crowd of camp-
followers who were standing near; "lend us your aid."

"Nay," said Katherine, "my father must be carried to Otterbourne Castle."

"Otterbourne Castle!" cried Rory; "what mean ye, silly
quean?"

Katherine bent over him, and put her mouth to his ear to
whisper him.

"Ay—aweel—poor thing!—very right—an it maun be sae,
it just maun," said he, after hearing what she had to say.
"Aweel, Maister Sang, ye maun just tell the Yearl that as I
can be o' nae mair service in fighting at this present time, I

may as weel gae till the Castle o' Otterbourne as ony ither gate to be leeched, mair especially as it is my belief that kitchen physic will be the best physic for me. Tell him that I'm gaun there wi' my dochter Kate till a friend of his, and that he sall ken a' about it afterhend."

Rory was accordingly carried straight to Otterbourne Castle, whither the gallant Mortimer Sang accompanied Katherine. Their parting at the gate was tender—but he could wring nothing from her that could elucidate the mystery of her present conduct.

CHAPTER LXII.

Withdrawal of the Scots Army—Obsequies of the Gallant Dead— The Mystery solved.

ALTHOUGH the morning sun rose bright and cheerful upon Otterbourne, yet were its rays incapable of giving gladness to those in the Scottish camp. The little army of heroes had gained a great and glorious victory, but they had dearly paid for it in the single death of Douglas. There was, therefore, more of condolence than of exultation among them, as they gave each other good morrow. They broke up their encampment with silence and sorrow, and marched off towards Scotland, under the united command of the Earls of Moray and Dunbar, with the solemn pace and fixed eyes of men who followed some funeral pageant; indeed, it was so in fact; for at the head of the main body of the army was the car that carried the coffin of the Douglas. Before it was borne his banner, that "*Jamais Arriere*" which, in the hands of Sir Patrick Hepborne the younger, had so happily turned the fate of the battle; and, in compliment to the gallant young knight, it was his esquire, Mortimer Sang, to whom the honour of carrying it was assigned. Behind it came the fatal pennon of Piersie, which had been the cause of so much waste of human life, and around the machine were clustered all those brave knights who had lately looked up to the hero for the direction of their every movement—at whose least nod or sign they would have spurred to achieve the most difficult and dangerous undertakings, and whose applause was ever considered by them as their highest reward. The life and soul of the army seemed now to have departed. They hung their heads, and marched on, rarely breaking the silence that prevailed, except to utter some sad remark calculated to heighten the very sorrow that gave rise to it.

The last of their columns disappeared from the ground, and when Katherine Spears and the lady on whom she attended cast their eyes over it from the window of the tower in the Castle of Otterbourne, it was again as much a scene of peace as if no such fierce warfare had ever disturbed it. Huge heaps, and long lines, indeed, marked the places under which hundreds of those who had merrily marched thither now reposed, Scot and Englishman, in amity together. The ruined huts and broken-down entrenchments too were still visible ; but the daisies and the other little flowers that enamelled the field, refreshed by the morning dew, had again raised their crushed heads, and the timid flocks and herds which had been scared by the din of arms, had again ventured forth from the covert whither they had been driven, and were innocently pasturing on the very spot where heroes had been so lately contending in the mortal strife. The lady, however, suffered her attention to be occupied with these objects for a brief space only ere she returned to perform her melancholy task of watching by those beloved remains she had so piously rescued from the promiscuous heaps of slaughter that covered the battle-field. She again sought the Chapel of the Castle, where lay the brave old knight Sir Walter de Selby, for it was he who, having met with some less merciful foe than Sir Patrick Hepborne, had been cut down in the melée. The mortal wound now gaped wide on his venerable head, and the beauty of his silver hair was disfigured with clotted gore. The tears of her who now seated herself by his bier fell fast and silently, as she bent over that benignant countenance now no longer animated by its generous spirit. Now it was she recalled all that affection so largely exhibited towards her from her very childhood. His faults had at this moment disappeared from her memory, and as the more remarkable instances of his kindness arose in succession, she gave way to that feeling natural to sensitive minds on such occasions, and bitterly accused herself of having but ill requited them.

The body of Sir Walter remained in the Castle of Otterbourne for several days, until proper preparations were made there and at Norham for doing it the honours due to the remains of so gallant a knight, and one who had enjoyed so important a command. After the escort was ready, the lady parted with much sorrow from Katherine Spears, whose father was yet unable to bear the motion of a journey. She commended both to the especial protection of the Captain of the Castle, and then hastily seating herself in her horse-litter to hide her grief from observation, the funeral procession moved away.

It was long after the sunset of the second day, that the troops of the garrison of Norham, under the Lieutenant Oglethorpe, marched out in sad array to meet the corpse of their late governor. Clad in all the insignia of woe, and each soldier bearing a torch in his hand, they halted on the high ground over the village, and rested in mute and sorrowful expectation of the approach of the funeral train. Lights appeared slowly advancing from a distance, and the dull chanting of voices and the heavy measured tread of men were heard. The coffin had already been removed from the car in which it had hitherto been carried, and four priests who had gone to meet it, one of them bearing a crucifix aloft, now appeared walking bareheaded before it, and chanting a hymn. The coffin itself was sustained on the shoulders of a band of men-at-arms, who accompanied it from Otterbourne ; and after it came the horse litter of the lady, attended by a train of horsemen who rode with their lances reversed. Among these, alas ! no man belonging to the deceased was to be seen, for all had perished with him in the field.

When the procession had reached the spot where the troops from Norham were drawn up to receive it, those who formed it halted, and the bearers, resigning their burden to the chief officers of the garrison, fell back to join their fellows. One-half of the soldiers of the Castle then moved on before the body, whilst the other half filed in behind the lady's litter, and the men of Otterbourne were left to close up the rear of the pageant.

As they descended the hill, the inhabitants of the village turned out to gaze on the imposing spectacle ; and after it had passed by, they followed to witness the last obsequies of one whose military pomp had often delighted their eyes, and the hardy deeds of whose prime were even now in every man's mouth.

Having reached the entrance to the church, the soldiers formed a double line up to the great door, each man leaning upon his lance, in grief that required no acting. The lady descended from her litter. With her head veiled, and her person enveloped in black drapery, she leaned upon the arm of Lieutenant Oglethorpe, and followed the body with tottering steps and streaming eyes into the holy fane. The church was soon filled by the Norham soldiery, ranked up thickly around it, the blaze of the torches pierced into the darkest nook of its Gothic interior, and the solemn ceremony proceeded.

The lady had wound up her resolution to the utmost, that she might undergo the trying scene without flinching. She stood wonderfully composed, with her eyes cast upon the ground, endeavouring to fix her thoughts on the service for the dead, which the priests were chanting ; when, chancing to look up, her attention was suddenly caught by the figure of a Franciscan monk, who, elevated on the steps of the altar, stood leaning earnestly forward from behind a Gothic pillar that half concealed him, his keen eyes fixed upon her with a marked intensity of gaze. Her heart was frozen within her by his very look, and, uttering a faint scream, she swooned away, and would have fallen on the pavement but for the timely aid of Oglethorpe and those who were present. Dismay and confusion followed. The ceremonial was interrupted ; and the bystanders believing that her feelings had been too deeply affected by the so sad and solemn spectacle, hastened to remove her from the scene, so that she was quickly conveyed to her litter, and escorted to the Castle.

The funeral rites were hurried over, and the body was committed to the silent vault, with no other witnesses than the officiating priests, the populace, and such of the officers and soldiers as had been bound to the deceased by some strong individual feeling of affection, and who now pressed around the coffin, to have the melancholy satisfaction of assisting in its descent.

While the remains of Sir Walter de Selby were conveying from Otterbourne Castle, the Scottish Nobles and Knights who had accompanied the body of the Douglas were engaged in assisting at the obsequies of that heroic Earl at Melrose. All that military or religious pomp could devise or execute was done to honour his remains, and many a mass for the peace of his soul was sung by the pious monks of its abbey. The brave Scottish Knights surrounded his tomb in silence and sorrow, all forgetting that they had gained a victory, and each feeling that he had lost a private friend in him whose body they had consigned to the grave.

It was only that morning that Sir Patrick Hepborne had heard accidentally from his esquire the particulars of his unexpected meeting with Katherine Spears ; and this information, added to those circumstances which had so strangely occurred to himself, determined him to proceed to Norham the very next day, where he hoped to unravel the mystery that had been gradually thickening around him. The truce that had been already proclaimed ensured his safety, so that he entered the court-yard of the Norham Tower Hostel with perfect confidence. Although Hepborne and his esquire came after it was dark, the quick eye of Mrs. Kyle immediately recognized them; and, conscious of the share she had had in the treachery so lately attempted against them, she took refuge in the innermost recesses of the kitchen part of the building. But Sang was determined not to spare her, and, after searching everywhere, he at last detected her in her concealment, from which he led her forth in considerable confusion.

"So, beautiful Mrs. Kyle," said he, " so thou wert minded to have done our two noble knights and their humbler esquires a handsome favour, truly, the last time they did honour thy house ? By St. Andrew, we should have made a pretty knot dangling from the ramparts of Norham."

"Nay, talk not so, Sir Squire," replied the hostess in a whining tone; "it was the wicked Sir Miers de Willoughby who did bribe me to put ye all in his power. And then he did never talk of aught else but the ransom for thy liberty; and in truth, love did so blind me that I thought no more of the matter. But I trow I am well enow punished for my folly; for here he came, and by his blazons and blandishments, he did so over-match me that he hath ta'en from me, by way of borrow (a borrow, I wis, that will never come laughing home again), many a handful of the bonny broad pieces my poor husband Sylvester, that is gone, did leave me. Yet natheless have I enow left to make any man rich; and when Ralpho Proudfoot doth return frae the wars——"

"Poor Ralpho Proudfoot will never return," said Sang, inter-rupting her, in a melancholy tone; " these hands did help to lay him in the earth."

"Poor Ralpho," cried Mrs. Kyle, lifting her apron to a dry eye, " poor Proudfoot ! He was indeed a proper pretty man. But verily," added she, with a deep sigh, whilst at the same time she threw a half-reproachful, half-loving glance at Sang, " verily, 'twere better, perhaps, for a poor weak woman to think no more of man, seeing all are deceivers alike. Wilt thou step this gate, Sir Squire, and taste my Malvoisie ? Or wilt thou—"

"What tramp of many feet is that I hear in the village ?" demanded Sang, interrupting her.

" 'Tis nought but the burying o' our auld Captain o' Norham," replied Mrs. Kyle; "I trust that we sall have some right gay and jolly knight to fill his boots. Auld de Selby was grown useless, I wot. Gi'e me some young rattling blade that will take pleasure in chatting to a bonny buxom quean when she comes in his way. I haena had a word frae the auld man for this I kenna how lang, but a rebuke now and then for the deboshing o' his men-at-arms, the which was more the fault o' my good ale than o' me. But where are ye running till, Master Sang?—Fye on him, he's away."

Sang did indeed hasten to tell his master of the passing funeral procession, and Hepborne ran out to follow it. It had already reached the church, and by the time he got to the door the interior was so filled that it was only by immense bodily exertion that he squeezed himself in at a small side door. His eyes immediately caught the figure of the lady, and there they rested, unconscious of all else. The moment she lifted her head he recognized the features of Maurice de Grey and of her whom he had seen on the battle-field of Otterbourne. But her fainting allowed him not a moment for thought. The crowd of men-at-arms between him and the object of his solicitude bid defiance to all his efforts to reach her, and ere he could regain the open air her litter was already almost out of sight.

"Poor soul," said a compassionate billman, who had been looking anxiously after it, "thou hast indeed good cause to be afflicted. Verily, thou hast lost thy best friend."

"Of whom dost thou speak, old man?" demanded Hepborne eagerly.

"Of the poor Lady Beatrice, who was carried to the Castle but now," replied the man.

"What saidst thou?" demanded Hepborne; "Lady Beatrice! Was not that the daughter of thy deceased governor? was not that the Lady Eleanore de Selby, now the Lady de Vere?"

"Nay, Sir Knight, that she be not," replied the man, "nouther the one nor the other, I wot; and if I might adventure to speak it, I would say that there be those who do think that the Lady Eleanore de Selby, now the Lady de Vere, hath no small spice of the devil in her composition, whilst the Lady Beatrice is well known to all to be an angel upon earth."

"Who is she, and what is her history, my good fellow?" demanded Hepborne, slipping money into his hand.

"Meseems thou art a stranger, Sir Knight, that thou knowest not the Lady Beatrice," said the man; "but I can well satisfy thy curiosity, seeing I was with good Sir Walter in that very Border raid during which she did become his. Our men had driven the herds and flocks from a hill on the side of one of the streams of Lammermoor, when, as we passed by the cottage of the shepherd who had fed them, his wife, with an infant in her arms, and two or three other children around her, came furiously out to attack Sir Walter with her tongue, as he rode at the head of his lances. 'My curse upon ye, ye English loons!' cried she bitterly ; 'no content wi' the sweep o' our master's hill, ye hae ta'en the bit cow that did feed my poor bairns. Better take my wee anes too, for what can I do wi' them ?' A soldier was about to quiet her evil tongue by a stroke of his axe. 'Fye on thee,' said Sir Walter ; 'what, wouldst thou murder the poor woman ? Her rage is but natural. Verily, our prey is large enow without her wretched cow.' And then, turning to her with a good-natured smile on his face, 'My good dame, thou shalt have thy cow.' And the beast was restored to her accordingly. 'The Virgin's blessing be on thee, Sir Knight,' said the woman. 'And now,' said Sir Walter, 'by'r Lady, I warrant me thou wouldst have ill brooked my taking thee at thy word. Marry, I promise thee,' continued he, pointing to a beautiful girl of five years, apparently her eldest child, 'marry, I'll warrant me thou wouldst have grudged mightily to have parted with that bonny face ?' 'Nay, I do indeed love Beatrice almost as well as she were mine own child, albeit I did only nurse her,' replied the dame ; 'but of a' the bairns, she, I wot, is the only one that I could part with.' 'Is she not thy child, then ?' said Sir Walter ; 'whose, I pr'ythee, may she be ?' 'That is what I canna tell thee, Sir Knight,' replied the woman. 'It is now about four years and a-half sith that a young lordling came riding down the glen. He was looking for a nurse, and the folk did airt him to me, who had then lost my first-born babe. He put this bairn, whom he called Beatrice, into my arms, and a purse into my lap, and away he flew again, saying that he would soon be back to see how the bairn throve. The baby was richly clad, so methought it must be some fair lady's stolen love-pledge. But I hae never seen him sithence, nor need I ever look for him now. And troth, Robby and I hae enew o' hungry mouths to feed withouten hers, poor thing—ay, and maybe a chance o' mair.' 'Wilt thou part with the child to me, then ?' said Sir Walter ; 'I have but one daughter, who is of her age, and I would willingly take this beauteous Beatrice to be her companion.' The poor woman had many scruples, but her husband, who now ventured to show himself, had none ; and, insisting on his wife's compliance, Beatrice was brought home with us to Norham, adopted by the good Sir Walter, and has ever been treated by him sithence as a second daughter. What marvel, then, Sir Knight, that she should swoon at his burying ?"

Light now broke in at once on Sir Patrick Hepborne. As we have seen in the opening chapter of our story, he was struck, even in the twilight, by the superior manner and attractions of the lady who had lost her hawk, and whose gentle demeanour had led him to conclude that she was the Lady Eleanore de Selby, of whose charms he had heard so much. Having been thus mistaken at first, he naturally went on, from all he heard and saw afterwards, and especially in the interviews he had at Norham, with her who now turned out to have been the companion of the Lady Eleanore de Selby, to mislead himself more and more. He returned to his inn to ruminate on this strange discovery; but be the beautiful Beatrice whom she might, he had loved her, and her alone, and he felt that his passion now became stronger than ever. His mind ran hastily over past events; he at once suspected that his inconsiderate jealousy had been, in fact, awakened by accidentally beholding an interview between the real Eleanore de Selby and her lover, and he cursed his haste that had so foolishly hurried him away from Norham; he remembered the fair hand that had waved the white scarf as he was crossing the Tweed; he recalled the countenance, the behaviour, and the conversation of his page, Maurice de Grey; he kissed the emerald ring which he wore on his finger; and his heart was drowned in a rushing tide of wild sensations, where hope and joy rose predominant. His generous soul swelled with transport at the thought of being the protector of her whom he now adored, and whom he now found, at the very moment she was left, as he believed, in a state of utter destitution. His impatience made him deplore that decency forbade his visiting the Lady Beatrice that night, but he resolved to seek for an audience of her early the next morning.

At such hour, then, as a lady could be approached with propriety, he despatched his esquire on an embassy to the Castle. He had little fear of the result, from what had already passed between them; but what was his mortification to learn that the Lady Beatrice had been gone from Norham for above five or six hours, having set out during the night on some distant journey, whither no one in the Castle could divine.

It is impossible to paint the misery of Sir Patrick Hepborne. Hope had been wound up to the highest pitch, and the most grievous disappointment was the issue. He was so much beside himself that he was little master of his actions, and Mortimer Sang was obliged to remind him of the necessity of returning immediately to Melrose, to join his father, who, with the other Scottish nobles and knights, had resolved to stay there for the space of three days ere they should separate.

The warriors parted, with solemn vows uttered over the grave of the Douglas; and Sir Patrick Hepborne and his son, accompanied by the Earl of Moray, Assueton, Halyburton, and a number of other knights, set out for Hailes Castle. The Lady Isabelle was ready to receive them on their arrival. She sprang into the court-yard to clasp her father and her brother to her bosom ; and although modesty and maiden bashfulness checked those manifestations of love towards her knight with which her heart overflowed, yet, as he kissed her hand, her cheeks flushed, and her eyes sparkled with a delight that could not be mistaken.

Among those who came out to welcome the war-like party was old Gabriel Lindsay. Leaning on his staff on the threshold, he eagerly scanned each face that came near him with his dim eyes.

"Where is my gallant boy?" cried he. "I trow he need seldom fear to show his head where valorous deads hae been adoing ; he hath had his share o' fame, I warrant me. Ha, Master Sang, welcome home. Where loitereth my gallant boy Robin? he useth not to be so laggard in meeting his old father, I wot. A plague on these burnt-out eyes of mine, I canna see him nowhere."

"Who can undertake the task of breaking poor Robert's death to the old man?" cried Sang, turning aside from him in the greatest distress. "Sure I am that I would rather face the fierce phalanx of foes that did work his brave son's death than tell him of the doleful tidings."

"Where hast thou left Robin, Master Sang?" said the doting old man again. "Ah, there he is ; nay, fye on my blindness, that be's Richie Morton. Sure, sure my boy was never wont to be laggard last ; 'twas but the last time he came home with Sir John Assueton that he had his arms round my ould neck or ever I wist he was at hand ; he thought, forsooth, I would not have ken'd him : but, ah, ha, Robin, says I to him——"

"My worthy old friend," said Sang, quite unable any longer to stand his innocent garrulity, so ill befitting the reception of the bitter news he had to tell him, and taking his withered arm to assist him into the Castle, and leading him gently to his chamber—"my worthy friend, come this way, and I will tell thee of thy son—we shall be better here in private. Robert Lindsay's wonted valour shone forth with sun-like glory in the bloody field of Otterbourne ; but——"

"Ah, full well did I know that he would bravely support the gallant name of Lindsay," cried the old man, interrupting him with a smile of exultation. "Trust me, the boy hath ever showed that he hath some slender streams of gentle blood in his veins ; we are come of good kind, Master Sang, and maybe my boy Robin shall yet win wealth and honours to prove it. My great-great-grandfather—nay, my grandfather's great-great——"

"But, Robert," said Sang, wishing to bring old Gabriel back to the sad subject he was about to open.

"Ay, Robert, Master Sang," replied the old man, "where tarrieth he?"

"At Otterbourne," replied Sang, deeply affected. "Thy son, thy gallant son, fell gloriously, whilst nobly withstanding the whole force of the English line as they burst into our camp."

"What sayest thou, Master Sang?" said the infirm old man, who perfectly comprehended the speaker, but was so stunned by his fatal intelligence that his feeble intellect was confused by the blow—"what sayest thou, Master Sang?"

"Thy heroic son was slain," replied Sang, half choked with his emotions. "This lock of Robert Lindsay's hair, and these trinkets taken from his person ere we committed his body to the earth, are all that thou canst ever see of him now, old man."

The esquire sat down, covered his face with his hands, and wept; and then endeavouring to command himself, he looked upward in the face of Gabriel Lindsay, who was standing before him like the decayed trunk of some mighty oak. The time-worn countenance of the old man was unmoved, and his dull eyes were fixed as in vacancy. The wandering so common to wasted age had come over his mind at that moment, sent, as it were, in mercy by Providence to blunt his perception of the dire affliction that had befallen him. Fitful smiles flashed at intervals across his face—his lips moved without sound—and at last he spoke—

"And so thou sayest my boy will be here to-night, Master Sang, and that this is a lock of his bride's hair? It is golden like his own; my blessing be on him, and that of St. Baldrid. But why feared he to bring her to me attence? Ha, doubtless he thought that the joyful surprise mought hae made my blood dance till it brast my ould heart. But no, Master Sang, joy shall never do for me what sorrow hath failed to work. I lost his mother—lost her in a' her youth and beauty, and yet I bore it, and humbled myself before Him who giveth and taketh away, and was comforted; and shall I sink beneath the weight of joy? Nay, even had he died in the midst of his glory, I trust I am soldier enow, though I be's ould, to have borne the news of my son having fallen with honour to Scotland, and to the name of Lindsay; but doth he think that his ould father may not be told, without risk, how he hath fought bravely—how he was noticed by the gallant Douglas—and, aboon a', how he is coming hame in triumph with a bonny gentle bride? And didst thou say they would be here to-night, Sir Squire? Fye, I must gang and tell Sir Patrick—and the brave young knight—and my Lady Isabelle; they will all rejoice in Gabriel's glad tidings. A bonny bride, thou sayest, Master Sang; and shall I yet have a babe o' Robin's on my knee ere I die? But I must away to Sir Patrick."

He made an effort to go. Sang rose gently to detain him. He stopped—looked around him wildly—fastened his eyes vacantly for some moments on the ceiling—reason and recollection returned to him, and his dream of bliss passed away.

"Oh, merciful God!" he cried, clasping his hands together in agony of woe. "Oh, my boy, my brave, my virtuous boy, and shall I never see thee more?"

Nature with him was already spent; his failure was instantaneous; his limbs yielded beneath him, and he sank down into the arms of the esquire, who hastily laid him on the bed and ran for assistance. Sir Patrick Hepborne, his son, and the Lady Isabelle, as well as many of the domestics, quickly appeared in great consternation; but they came only to weep over the good old Seneschal—He was gone for ever.

The death of this old and faithful domestic threw a gloom over the Castle, so that Assueton felt that he could hardly press on his marriage-day. At last, however, it was fixed. The preparations were such as became the house of Hepborne; and the ceremony was performed in presence of some of the first nobles and knights of Scotland.

The Countess of Moray had come from Tarnawa to meet her Lord. Sir Patrick Hepborne, the younger, eagerly sought an opportunity of having private conversation with her, hoping to have some explanation of the strange disappearance of his page. But the noble lady, maintaining the same distance towards him she had so mysteriously used, seemed rather disposed to shun the subject; and it was not until Hepborne had prefaced his inquiry with a full exposition of all he suspected, and all he knew, regarding the Lady Eleanore de Selby and the Lady Beatrice, and that she really saw where his heart was sincerely fixed, that she would consent to betray the secret she possessed. Hepborne was then assured that his page Maurice de Grey was no other than the Lady Beatrice.

Believing that Hepborne loved her, she had looked with joy to other meetings with him; she had been filled with anxiety when she heard of the encounter between him and Sir Rafe Piersie; and she was exulting in his triumph over that knight

31

◢

at the very moment they came to tell her of his departure. She
hastened to a window overlooking the Tweed, where she beheld
the boat that was wafting him to Scotland. It was then, when
she thought herself deserted, that she really felt that she loved.
Almost unconscious of what she did, she waved her scarf. He
replied not to the signal. Again and again she waved, and in
vain she stretched her eyeballs to catch a return of the sign.
The boat touched the strand; he sprang on shore, and leaped
into his saddle. Again in despair she waved; the signal was
returned, and that faint sign from the Scottish shore was to her
as the twig of hope. So intense had been her feelings that she
sank down overpowered by them. Recovering herself, she again
gazed from the window. The ferry-boat had returned, and was
again moored on the English side. She cast her eyes across to
the spot where she had last beheld Sir Patrick. The animating figures were now gone—some yellow gravel, a green
bank, a few furze bushes, and a solitary willow, its slender
melancholy spray waving in the breeze, were all that appeared, and her chilled and forsaken heart was left as desolate
as the scene.

It was at this time that she was called on by friendship to
dismiss her own griefs, that she might actively assist the high-
spirited Eleanore de Selby. By the result of Sir Rafe Piersie's
visit, that lady was relieved from his addresses; but they were
immediately succeeded by the strange proposals of her infatu-
ated father, when deluded by the machinations of the Wizard
Ancient. All her tears and all her eloquence were thrown away,
and so perfect was Sir Walter's subjection to the will of the
impostor that even his temper was changed, and his affection for
his daughter swallowed up, by his anxiety to avert the fate that
threatened. Such coercion to a union so digusting might have
roused the spirit of resistance in the most timid female bosom;
but Eleanore de Selby, who was high and hot tempered, resolved
at once to fly from such persecution; and, taking a solemn vow
of secrecy from the Lady Beatrice, she made her the confidant of
a recent attachment which had arisen between her and a certain
knight whom she had met at a tilting match held at Newcastle
a short time before, when she was on a visit to an aunt who
resided there. The Lady Eleanore informed her friend that her
lover was Sir Hans de Vere, a knight of Zealand, kinsman to the
King's banished favourite the Duke of Ireland, who had lately
come from abroad, and who looked to gain the same high place
in King Richard's affections which the Duke himself had filled.
From him she had received a visit unknown to her father, and it

was the parting of the lovers after that meeting which had so filled Hepborne with jealousy. In the urgency of her affairs she implored her friend to aid her schemes, which were immediately carried into effect by means of the Minstrel.

Having thus been gradually, though unwillingly, drawn to be an accomplice in the Lady Eleanore's plans, Beatrice felt that she could not stay behind to expose herself to the rage of the bereft father. Having assisted her friend, therefore, to escape, she accompanied her, in male attire, to the place where her lover waited for her at some distance from Norham. There she parted, with many tears, from the companion of her youth, having received from her the emerald ring which Sir Patrick Hepborne afterwards became possessed of. Her own depression of spirits, occasioned by Sir Patrick's unaccountable desertion of her, had determined her to seek out some convent, where she might find a temporary, if not a permanent retreat. Under the protection of old Adam of Gordon, therefore, she crossed the Tweed into Scotland. There he procured her a Scottish guide to conduct her to North Berwick, where he had a relation among the Cistertian nuns, and thither she was proceeding at the time she met Hepborne in the grove by the side of the Tyne.

When Sir Patrick addressed her she felt so much fluttered that it was some time before she could invent a plausible account of herself; and when he proposed to her to become his page, love triumphed over her better judgment, and she could not resist the temptation of an offer that held out so fair an opportunity of knowing more of him, and of trying the state of his heart. As to the latter she became convinced, by some of those conversations we have detailed, that she had been cruelly deceived, and that she had in reality no share in it. She heard him passionately declare his inextinguishable love for the lady Eleanore de Selby, and when he said that he had seen too much of her for his peace of mind, she naturally enough concluded that they had met together on some former occasion. She became unhappy at her own imprudence in so rashly joining his party, and was anxious to avail herself of the first opportunity of escaping from one whose heart never could be hers. The Countess of Moray's kindness to her as Maurice de Grey induced her to discover herself to that lady. She earnestly entreated that she might remain concealed, and that Sir Patrick might not be informed. It was the Lady Jane de Vaux who laid the plan for deceiving him about the departure of his page, and she and the Countess of Moray could not resist indulging in tormenting one whom they believed to have wantonly sported with the affections of the Lady Beatrice, and who had consequently suffered deeply in the good opinion of both.

The Minstrel, who, to do away suspicion, had returned to Norham immediately after the escape of the ladies, no sooner learned from the guide the change which had taken place in Beatrice's plans, and that she had gone to Tarnawa, than he determined to follow her thither, under pretence of going to the tournament. Having learned from him that her benefactor, Sir Walter de Selby, had been overwhelmed with affliction for the loss of his daughter, of whose fate he was yet ignorant, and that he had also grievously complained of her own desertion of him, she was filled with remorse, and determined to return to him immediately, and to brave all his reproaches ; but indisposition, arising from the trying fatigue of body and the mental misery she had undergone, prevented her setting out until several days after the departure of the Earl of Moray and his knights for Aberdeen. Hepborne could now no longer doubt of the attachment of the Lady Beatrice. The thought that he had ignorantly thrown away a heart so valuable as that which his intercourse with his page had given him ample opportunity to know, was a source of bitter distress to him. His spirits fled, he loathed society, and he industriously shunned the huntings, hawkings, dancings, and masquings that were going merrily forward in honour of his friend's nuptials with his sister the Lady Isabelle.

But Assueton was not so selfishly occupied in his own joys as not to be struck with the change in his beloved Hepborne. He besought him to unbosom the secret sorrow that was so evidently preying on his mind, and Sir Patrick, who had hitherto generously concealed it, that he might not poison the happiness in which he could not participate, at last yielded to the entreaty, and told him all. Sir John had but little of comfort to offer : the subject was one that hardly admitted of any. He saw that the only way in which friendship could be useful was by rousing him to do something that might actively divert his melancholy.

Sir David de Lindsay having returned from his captivity in England, had lately arrived at Hailes, where Sir William de Dalzel and Sir John Halyburton had remained, to witness Assueton's marriage. They were now about to proceed to London, to make good the pledge given to Lord Welles. Hepborne would have fain excused himself from the engagement he had so cheerfully made with them at Tarnawa, but Assueton contrived to pique his chivalric spirit, and at length succeeded in inducing him to become one of the party. Sir John even offered to accompany his friend, but Hepborne would by no means permit him to leave his newly-married Lady.

CHAPTER LXIII.

The Scottish Knights at the English Court—The wealthy London Merchant—Combat on London Bridge.

EVERYTHING that art could achieve, by means of steel, gold, embossing, embroidery, and emblazoning, was done to give splendour to the array of Sir David Lindsay, and his companions and attendants, that Scotland should, if possible, be in no whit behind England upon this occasion. A safe-conduct was readily granted them by the English court, and they departed, all high in spirits, save Hepborne alone, who seemed to suffer the journey rather than to enjoy it. They travelled very leisurely, and frequently halted by the way, that their horses might not be oppressed ; and they were everywhere received with marked respect.

It was towards the end of the third week that they found themselves crossing a wide glade among those immense forests which then covered the country, lying immediately to the north of the English metropolis, when they were attracted by an encampment of gay pavilions, pitched among the thin skirting trees. A strong guard of archers and well-mounted lances, that patrolled around the place, proved that there was some one there of no mean consequence. Within the circle was a vast and motley crowd of people, moving about in all the rich and varied costumes which then prevailed. There could be descried many nobles, knights, and esquires, some equipt in fanciful hunting-garbs, and others in all the foppery of golden circlets, flowing robes, party-coloured hose, and long-pointed shoes, attached to knee-chains of gold and silver ; and these were mingled with groups of huntsmen, falconers, pages, grooms, lacqueys, and even hosts of cooks and scullions. Many were on horseback, and whole rows of beautiful horses were picketted in different places, and their neighing mingled cheerily with the baying of tied-up hounds and the hum of many merry voices.

It was a spectacle well calculated to arrest the attention of the Scottish knights, and accordingly they halted to enjoy it, and to listen to the trumpets and timbrels that now began to sound. In a little time they observed a party of horsemen

leave the encampment, and they were soon aware that it came
to meet them. At the head was a knight clad in a white
hunting-coif richly flowered with gold, and a sky-blue gippon of
the most costly materials, thickly wrought with embroidery,
while the toes of his tawny boots, being released from their
knee-chains, hung down nearly a yard from his stirrup-irons.
On his wrist sat a falcon, the badge of a knight. He rode a
superb horse, and his housings corresponded in grandeur with
everything else belonging to him.

"Ha!" exclaimed he, as he reined up his steed affectedly
in front of the group, raised himself in his high-peaked saddle,
and, standing in his stirrups, put his bridle-hand to his side, as
if selecting the attitude best calculated to show off his uncommonly handsome person; "ha! so I see that my divination doth
prove to have been true to most miraculous exactitude. My
Lord of Welles must forfeit an hundred pieces, in compliment
to my superior accuracy of vision and of judgment. Sir David
de Lindsay, I knew thy banner. I do give thee welcome to
England, beausir; nay, I may add, welcome to London too,
seeing thou art barely two leagues from its walls, and that the
very spirit of its greatness is here in these sylvan solitudes, in
the person of the Royal Richard, attended as he is by his chivalrous Court."

"Sir Piers Courtenay," exclaimed Sir David de Lindsay,
"perdie, it doth rejoice me to behold thee, strangers as we are,
in these parts."

"Trust me, ye shall be strangers no longer, gentle sir,"
replied Sir Piers, with a condescending inclination of body, that
he now deigned to continue round, with his eyes directed to the
other knights severally, whom he had not noticed until now.
"When I, with singularly fortunate instinct, did assert that it
was thee and thy bandon we beheld, the Lord Welles did wager
me an hundred pieces that I did err in sagacity; but as I parted
from him to ride hither, to bring mine accuracy to the proof, he
charged me, if I were right, to invite thee and thy company to
the Royal camp."

"Travel-worn and dust-begrimed as we are," said Sir William de Dalzel, "meseems we shall be but sorry sights for the
eyes of Royalty, especially amid a crowd of gallants so glittering as the sample thou hast brought us in thine own sweet and
perfumed person, beausir."

"Nay, nay," replied Sir Piers Courtenay, glancing with contempt at Dalzel's war-worn surcoat, and taking his ironical
remark as an actual compliment, "we are but accoutred, as thou

seest, for rustic sport; we are shorn of our beams among the shades of these forests. But let us not tarry, I pray thee; the sports of the morning are already over; the sylvan meal is about to be spread in the grand pavilion, and rude though it be, it may not come amiss to those who have already travelled since dawn. Let us hasten thither, then, for the King doth return to London after feeding."

Under the guidance of this pink of fashion, the Scottish knights advanced towards the Royal hunting-encampment; and long ere they reached it, the Lord Welles, who already saw that he had lost his wager, came forth to meet them, and received them with all that warmth of hospitality which characterized the English people of all ranks even in those early days, and for which they were already famed among foreign nations. He led them through a mass of guards, who, though they appeared but to form a part of the pageantry of the Royal sports, were yet so completely armed, both men and horses, that it was manifest security from sudden surprise was the chief object of their being placed there.

Sir David Lindsay and his companions, after quitting their saddles, were led by the Lord Welles to his own tent, where they soon rendered themselves fit to appear before Royal eyes. They were then conducted to the King's pavilion, which they found surrounded by a strong body of archers, and they had no sooner entered the outer part of it than they were introduced to the Earls of Kent and Huntingdon, half-brothers to the King, who were in waiting. These were now Richard's chief favourites since the late banishment of De Vere, Duke of Ireland, and others. By these noblemen they were immediately introduced into the Royal presence.

The young Richard was not deficient in that manly beauty possessed by his heroic father, the nation's idol, Edward the Black Prince, but his countenance was softened by many of those delicate traits which gave to his lovely mother the appellation of the Fair Maid of Kent. His eyes, though fine and full, were of unsteady expression, frequently displaying a certain confidence in self-opinion, that suddenly gave way to doubt and hesitation. Though the dress he had on was of the same shape as that worn by his courtiers, being that generally used by noblemen of the period when hunting, yet, costly as was the attire of those around him, his was most conspicuous among them all, by the rich nature of the materials of which it was composed, as well as by the massive and glittering ornaments he wore. The gorgeous furniture of his temporary residence too, with the endless numbers of splendidly habited domestics who waited, might have been enough of themselves to have explained to the Scottish knights whence that dissatisfaction arose among his subjects, who were compelled to contribute to expenditure so profuse.

The King's natural disposition to be familiar with all who approached him would of itself have secured a gracious reception to Sir David de Lindsay and his companions, but the cause of their visit made them doubly welcome. Their coming ensured him an idle show and an empty pageant which would furnish him with an apology for making fresh draughts on his already over-drained people. Every honour, therefore, was paid them, as if they had been public ambassadors from the nation to which they belonged, and the most conspicuous places were assigned them at that luxurious board where the Royal collation was spread, and where, much as they had seen, their eyes were utterly confounded by the profusion of rarities that appeared.

The King had been hunting for nearly a week in these suburban wilds, and he was now about to return to his palace in the Tower, which he at this time preferred as a residence to that of Westminster. But the pleasures of the table, seasoned by dissolute conversation with the profligate knights and loose ladies, who were most encouraged at his Court, together with that indolence into which he was so apt to sink, had at all times too great charms for him to permit him easily to move from them. He therefore allowed the hours to pass in epicurean indulgence, whilst he gazed on the wanton attitudes of the women who danced before him, or on the feats of jugglers and tumblers.

At length the camp was ordered to be broken up, and then the whole Royal attention became occupied in the arrangement of the cavalcade, so that it might produce the most imposing effect, and the humblest individuals were not considered as unworthy of a King's notice on so important an occasion. All were soon put into the wished-for order, and Richard himself figured most prominently of all, proudly mounted on a magnificently-caparisoned horse, having housings that swept the ground. A canopy was borne over him by twelve esquires, and he was surrounded by his archers. Sir David de Lindsay and his companions formed a part of this pageant, which they failed not to remark was carefully defended on all sides by well-armed horsemen.

From the summit of an eminence the Scottish knights caught their first view of London, then clustered into a small space within its confined walls.   It seemed to be tied like a knot, as it were, on the winding thread of the majestic Thames, which, after washing the walls of the Palace of Westminster, flowed thence gently along its banks, fringed by the gardens and scattered country-dwellings of the nobility and richer citizens, until it was lost for a time amid the smoke arising from the dusky mass of the city, to appear farther down with yet greater brilliancy.   The sun was already getting low, and was shooting its rays aslant through the thick atmosphere that hung over the town.   They caught on its most prominent points, and brought fully into notice the venerable tower and spire of the then Gothic St. Paul's, and the steeples of the few churches and monasteries which the city contained, together with its turreted walls and its castles.   All between the partially wooded slope they stood on and the gates, was one wild pasture, partly covered with heath, interspersed with thickets, and partly by swamps, and a large lake.

As they drew nearer to the city, they passed by crowds of young citizens engaged in athletic exercises.   Some were wrestling ; others, mounted on spirited horses and armed with lances, were tilting at the quintaine, or jousting with wooden points against each other.   In one place they were shooting with bows at a mark ; and in another, groups of young men and damsels were seen dancing under the shade of trees, to the gratification of many a father and mother who looked on   Besides these, the ground was peopled by vendors of refreshments ; and, in diverse corners, jugglers and posture-masters were busy with their tricks before knots of wondering mechanics.   So keenly were all engaged, that the Royal hunting party, carefully as the order of its march had been prepared, passed by unheeded, or, if noticed at all, it was by a secret curse from some of the disaffected, who grudged to see that Richard had been hunting in that part of the forest which it was more particularly the privilege of the citizens of London to use.   Nor did the haughty courtiers regard these humbler people, except to indulge in many a cutting jest at their expense, which Richard's ready laugh of approbation showed they were thoroughly licensed to do.

"We have seen some such jousting as this before," said Courtenay, with a sly toss of his head, immediately after an awkward exhibition that had accidentally attracted notice.

" Yea, so have I too," observed Dalzel calmly ; " I did once see ane English knight tilt so on the Mead of St. John's."

Crossing the broad ditch of the city by a drawbridge, they

made their entry between the towers of Cripplegate, having its
name from the swarms of beggars by which it was generally
infested, and they immediately found themselves in narrow
streets of wooden houses, uncouthly projecting as they rose upwards, and detached shops, which were already shut up for the
day.   Here and there the windows were decorated with coloured
cloth or carpets, and some few idle vagabonds ran after the
cavalcade crying out, "Long live King Richard!" looking to be
recompensed for their mercenary loyalty by liberal largess.
But the respectable citizens were already enjoying their own
recreation in the Moorfields, those who did remain having little
inclination to join in the cry where the Monarch was so unpop-
ular; and many a sturdy black muzzled mechanic went
scowling off the street to hide in some dark lane as he saw the
procession approaching, bestowing his malediction on that
heartless prodigality and luxury which robbed him and his
infants to supply its diseased appetite.   Hepborne and Halyburton, who rode together, could not help remarking this want
of loyal feeling towards the young English Monarch; and,
calling to mind the enthusiasm with which they had seen the
aged King Robert of Scotland, in his grey woollen hose, greeted
by his people, they began to suspect that there must be faults of
no trifling sort in a Prince to whom nature had given so pleasing
an exterior.

Having got within the fortifications of the Tower, the Scottish
knights were astonished with the immense army of the minions
of luxury who filled its courts.   The King himself signified his
pleasure to Sir David Lindsay and his friends that they should
enter the Royal apartments, where they partook of wine and
spices, handed about in rich golden cups ; after which a banquet
followed in a style of magnificence calculated to make everything they had before seen to be altogether forgotten in comparison with it.   The King honoured them with his peculiar
attention, and even deigned to attend to making provision for
their proper accommodation.   For this purpose, he called for the
Lord Welles, and gave him a list of those persons who were to
be honoured with the expense of lodging and entertaining these
strangers and their people.   With singular contradiction to his
own wish that they should be treated with exemplary hospitality, he chose to select as their hosts certain persons who had
offended him, and whom he had a desire to punish, by thus
exposing them to great expense ; and so the strangers were
thrown into situations where anything but voluntary kindness
might be looked for.

When the King gave them their leave, they found their esquires in waiting for them. Mortimer Sang led Hepborne into the Vintry, to the house of a certain Lawrence Ratcliffe, a wine merchant. His dwelling was within a gateway and court-yard, on each side of which there were long rows of warehouses and vaults extending nearly quite down to the river wall.

It was dark when Sir Patrick entered the court-yard, and as he passed onwards to where he saw a lamp burning within the doorway of the dwelling house, he heard the voice of a man issuing from an outbuilding.

"Jehan Petit," said the person, who spoke to some one who followed him, "see that thou dost give out no wine to this Scot but of that cargo, the which did ship the sea water, and that tastes brackish. An the King will make us maintain all his strange cattle, by St. Paul, but as far as I have to do with them they shall content themselves with such feeding as it may please me to bestow. Let the esquire and the other trash have sour ale, 'tis good enow for the knaves ; and I promise thee it will well enow match the rest of their fare, and the herborow they shall have. Alas, poor England ! ay, and above all, alas, poor London ! for an we have not a change soon, we shall be eaten up by the King's cormorants—a plague rot 'em ! "

By this time Hepborne and his landlord met in the stream of light that issued from the open doorway. Hepborne made a courteous though dignified obeisance to Master Ratcliffe, a stout elderly man, whose face showed that he had not been at all negligent during his life in tasting, that he might have personal knowledge of what was really good before he ventured to give it to his friends. The wine merchant was taken somewhat unawares. He had made up his mind to be as cross and as rude as he well could to the guest that had been thus forced upon him. But Hepborne's polite deportment commanded a return from a man who had been in France, and he bent to the stranger with a much better grace than he could have wished to have bestowed on him.

"I do address myself to Master Lawrence Ratcliffe, if I err not ? " said Hepborne, in a civil tone.

"Yea, I am that man," replied the other, recovering something of his sulky humour.

"Master Ratcliffe," said Hepborne, with great civility of manner, "I understand that His Majesty the King of England's hospitality to strangers hath been the cause of throwing me to thy lot. But I cannot suffer his kindness to a Scottish knight to do injury to a worthy citizen of his own good city of

London. To keep me and my people in thy house, would run thee into much trouble, not to talk of the expense, the which no man of trade can well bear. I come, therefore, to entreat thee to permit me to rid thee and thy house of unbidden guests, who cannot choose but give thee great annoy, and to crave thine advice as to what inn or hostel I should find it most convenient to remove to. By granting me this, thou wilt make me much beholden to thee."

Master Lawrence Ratcliffe looked at Hepborne with no small astonishment. This was a sort of behaviour to which he had been but little used, and for which he was by no means prepared.

"Nay, by St. Stephen, Sir Knight, thou shalt not move," said he at last; "by all the blessed saints, thou shalt have the best bed and the best food that London can furnish; yea, and wine, too, the which let me tell thee, the King himself cannot command. Go, get the key of the trap cellar, Jehan Petit," said he, turning briskly to his attendant; "bring up some flasks of the right Bourdeaux and Malvoisie. Thou dost well know their marks, I wot."

"Nay, send him not for wine, I pray thee, good Master Ratcliffe," cried Hepborne; "I trow I have already drank as much as may be seemly for this night."

"Chut," cried the wine merchant, with a face of glee, "all that may be; yet shall we drain a flask to our better acquaintance. Fly, sirrah Jehan! This way, Sir Knight. Would that Heaven mought send us a flight of such rare birds as thou art; thine ensample mought peraunter work a change on these all-devouring vultures of King Richard's Court. This way, Sir Knight. Have a care, there be an evil step there."

Master Lawrence Ratcliffe ushered Hepborne into a very handsomely furnished apartment, the walls of which were hung round with costly cloths. It was largely supplied with velvet and silk covered chairs, and with many an ancient cabinet, and it was lighted by a small silver lamp. They were hardly seated, when a lacquey brought in a silver basket of sweetmeats and dried fruits, and soon afterwards Jehan Petit appeared with the venerable flasks for which Master Ratcliffe had despatched him. It was with some difficulty that Hepborne could prevent the liberal Englishman from ordering a sumptuous banquet to be prepared, by declaring that repose, not food, was what he now required; but he made up for this check on his hospitality by giving ample directions for the comfort of all the members of Hepborne's retinue, quadrupeds as well as bipeds. The wine was nectar, yet Hepborne drank but little of it ; but Master Ratcliffe did ample duty for both.

"I fear, Sir Knight, that thy people were but scurvily treated ere thou camest," said he to Hepborne; "but, in good verity, I have too much of this free quartering thrust upon me by the Court. I promise thee, King Richard is not always content with his two tuns out of each of my wine ships. By'r Lady, he doth often help himself to ten tuns at a time from these cellars of mine, and that, too, as if he were doing me high honour all the while. It did so happen lately that he lacked some hundred of broad pieces for his immediate necessities. Down came my Lord of Huntingdon with his bows and fair words. 'Master Lawrence Ratcliffe,' said he, 'it is His Majesty's Royal pleasure to do thee an especial honour.' 'What,' cried I, 'my Lord of Huntingdon, doth the King purpose to make an Earl of me?' 'Nay, not quite that,' replied his Lordship, somewhat offended at my boldness, 'not quite that, Master Ratcliffe, but, knowing that thou art one of the richest merchants of his good city of London, he hath resolved to prefer thee to be his creditor rather than any other. Lend him, therefore, five hundred pieces for a present necessity. And seeing it was I who did bring this high honour upon thy shoulders, by frequently enlarging to the King of thy princely wealth, thou mayest at same time lend me fifty pieces from thine endless hoards, for mine own private use.' 'My Lord,' replied I, 'seeing that thou thyself hast been altogether misinformed as to my wealth, thou mayest hie thee back speedily to undeceive the King, else may the Royal wrath peradventure be poured out upon thee, for filling his ear with that which lacketh foundation. I have no money hoards to play the Jew withal.' 'Nay, then,' replied Huntingdon, with a threatening aspect, 'thou mayest look for the King's wrath falling on thine own head, not on mine. By St. Paul, thou shalt repent thee of this thy discourteous conduct to the King.' The profligate Earl was hardly gone when I felt that I had permitted my indignation to carry me too far, and that it would have been wiser to have paid five times the demand, and I soon had proof of this. I judged it best to pay the money ; yet hardly hath a week elapsed sithence that I have not been tormented in a thousand ways by orders from the Court. But, by'r Lady, such a state of things may not last," said he, after a pause ; and then starting, as if he thought he had perhaps said too much, "for what poor merchant's coffers may stand out against such drafts as these? And now, Sir Knight, thou mayest judge why I was resolved to receive thee

so vilely.   But thou mayest thank thine own courtesy for so
speedily disarming my resolution."

On the ensuing morning the Lord Welles came, by the King's
order, to wait on Sir David Lindsay, and to invite him and his
companions to a Royal banquet, to be given that day at the
Palace of Westminster, whither they were to go in grand procession by land, and to return by water to the Tower at night.
The Scottish knights, therefore, joined the Royal party, and
leaving the city by Ludgate, descended into the beautiful country
which bordered the Thames, their eyes delighted, as they rode
along, by the appearance of the suburban palaces and gardens
which lay scattered along the river's bank. Passing through the
village of Charing, they approached the venerable Abbey and
Palace of Westminster, and were received within the fortified
walls of the latter. The entertainment given in the magnificent
hall was on a scale of extravagance perfectly appalling, both as
to number of dishes and rarity of the viands ; and the aquatic
pageant of painted boats was no less wonderful.   It was impossible for the poor commons to behold the money wrenched from
their industry thus scattered in a useless luxury that but little
nourished their trade or manufactures, or at least could not appear to their ignorance to have such a tendency, without their
becoming disaffected ; and, accordingly, every new pageant of
this kind only added to the mass of the malcontents.

The handsome Courtenay had this day outshone all his
former splendour of attire.

" Didst thou mark that popinjay Sir Piers Courtenay ?" demanded Sir William de Dalzel, as they were returning in the
boat ; " didst thou mark the bragging device on his azure silk
surcoat ?"

" I did note it," replied Halyburton ; " a falcon embroidered
in divers silks, that did cunningly ape the natural colours of the
bird."

" Yea, but didst thou note the legend, too ?" continued Sir
William de Dalzel.   " It ran thus, methinks—

> I bear a falcon fairest of flight :
> Whoso pinches at her his death is dight,
>   In graith."

" Ha," said Hepborne, " by St. Andrew, a fair challenge to us
all ; the more, too, that it doth come after the many taunts he
did slyly throw out against Scottish chivalry at Tarnawa.   But
he shall not lack a hand to pinch at his falcon, for I shall do it
this night, lest the braggart shall change his attire."

" Nay, nay, leave him to me, I entreat thee," said Sir Wil-

liam de Dalzel. " He is mine by right, seeing I did first note
his arrogant motto.   Trust me, I shall not leave London without bringing down this empty peacock, so that he shall be the
laughing-stock of his own companions."

On the plea of giving sufficient repose to the Scottish
champion, Richard ordained that yet three more days should
pass ere the joust should take place between Sir David Lindsay
and the Lord Welles ; and the time was spent in divers amuse-
ments, and in balls, masquings, and feastings.

At length the day of the tilting arrived, and everything had
been done to make the exhibition a splendid one.   Triumphal
arches had been erected in several parts of Thames Street ; and
the inhabitants were compelled by Royal proclamation to garnish
their windows with flowers and boughs, and to hang out cloths
and carpets ; while many of those who had houses on London
Bridge were forced by an edict to vacate their dwellings, for the
use of the King and such of his courtiers and attendants as he
chose to carry thither with him.   These houses were wretched
enough in themselves, being frail wooden tenements, arising
from each side of the Bridge, partly founded on it, so as to
narrow its street to about twenty-three feet, and partly resting
on posts driven in to the bed of the stream, so that they hung
half over the water, and were, in some cases, only saved from
falling backwards into it by strong wooden arches that crossed
the street from one house to another, and bound them together.

The Royal procession was to be arranged in the Tower-yard,
and in obedience to the commands of King Richard, the Scottish
knights repaired thither to take their place in it.   The banner of
Sir David Lindsay, bearing *gules*, a fess cheque *argent* and
azure, with his crest an ostrich proper, holding in his beak a
key *or*, appeared conspicuous ; and his whole party, esquires as
well as knights, were mounted and armed in a style that was by
no means disgraceful to poor Scotland, though in costliness of
material and external glitter they were much eclipsed by the
English knights.   Of these Sir Piers Courtenay, who was to
perform the part of second to the Lord Welles, seemed resolved
to be second to none in outward show.   His tilting-helmet was
surmounted by a plume that was perfectly matchless, and there
the falcon, which on this occasion he had chosen as his crest,
was proudly nestled.   His coat of mail was covered with azure
silk.   The belt for his shield, and the girdle-stead for his sword,
were of crimson velvet, richly ornamented with golden studs and
precious stones.   The roundels on his shoulders and elbows
were, or at least appeared to be, of gold.   His mamillieres were

of wrought gold ornamented with gems, and heavy golden chains,
of sufficient length not to impede his full action when using the
weapon, depended from them, so as to attach the hilt of his
sword to his right breast, and the scabbard of it to his left. His
sword and his dagger were exquisite both as to materials and
workmanship; but what most attracted attention was the azure
silken surcoat embroidered with the falcon upon it, and the
vaunting motto—

> I bear a falcon fairest of flight:
> Whoso pinches at her his death is dight,
>   In graith.

Courtenay rode about, making his horse perform many a fanciful curvet, full of self-approbation, and throwing many a significant glance towards the Scottish party, as he capered by them,
evidently with the desire of provoking some one among them
to accept the mute and general challenge he gave, and winking
to his friends at the same time, as if he believed that there was
little chance of its being noticed. The sagacious Sir John Constable and some others said all they could to check his impertinent foolery, but their friendly advices were thrown away on
the coxcomb.

All being prepared, King Richard was becoming impatient
to move off, when it was signified to him that Sir William de
Dalzel, who was to be second to Sir David de Lindsay, had not
yet appeared. The King ordered an esquire to hasten to his
lodgings to tell him he was waited for, when just at that moment a knight appeared attired in a style of splendour that was
only to be equalled by Sir Piers Courtenay himself; but what
was more wonderful, he seemed to be in every respect the very
double of that magnificent cavalier. All eyes were directed
towards him, and when he came nearer, the King himself gave
way to immoderate fits of laughter, in which he was heartily
joined by every one in the court-yard, down to the lowest
groom; in short, by all save one, and that was Sir Piers
Courtenay.

This second edition of the English exquisite was Sir William
de Dalzel, who, having found out beforehand what Courtenay
was to appear in, had contrived, with great exertion, pains, and
expense, to fit himself with a surcoat and appendages exactly
resembling those of the coxcomb; with this difference only, that
his azure silk surcoat had on it a magpie, embroidered with
divers coloured threads, with this motto—

> I bear a pyet pykkand at ane piece:
> Whasa pykes at her I sall pyke at his nese,
>   In faith.

The laugh continued, whilst the square-built Dalzel rode about with his vizor up, wearing a well-dissembled air of astonishment, as if he could by no means divine what it was that gave rise to so much merriment. But Courtenay could bear it no longer. He even forgot the Royal presence of Richard, which, however, was but seldom wont to throw much awe over those with whom he was in the habit of being familiar.

"By the body of Saint George," exclaimed Courtenay, riding up to Dalzel, "thou hast attired thyself, Sir Scot, but in mockery of me. By the Holy St. Erkenwold, thou shalt speedily answer for thine unknightly rudeness."

"Nay, by the body of St. Andrew, Sir Englishman, the which I do take to be an oath that ought to match thine," said Dalzel, with great coolness, seasoned with an air of waggery, "I do in nowise insult thee by mine attire more than thine attire doth insult me. Perdie, on the contrarie, I do but give thee infinite honour, in the strict observance of thine excellent fashion. Didst thou not, with great condescension, bestow upon the Scottish chivauncie at Tarnawa, myself being one, full many a wise saw on the supereminent judgment of English knights, or rather of thyself, the cream of all English knighthood, in matters of dress and arming? Didst thou not discuss it, buckle by buckle? Hither then am I come, in all my clownishness, to profit by thy wisdom; and such being mine errand, how, I pray thee, can I do better than copy thee to the nail—thou, I say, who canst so well teach me to put on a brave golden outside, where peradventure the inner metal may be but leaden?"

"By the rood of St. Paul," cried Courtenay, "thine evil chosen attirement was but small offence, compared to that thou hast now heaped on me by thy sarcastic commentary on it. I will hear no more. There!" said he, dashing down his gauntlet on the pavement. "With permission of the Royal presence, in which I now am, I do hereby challenge thee to combat of outrance, to be fought after the tilting-match."

"Nay, sith that thou wilt fly thy fair falcon at my poor pie," said Dalzel, "and run his head into my very talons with thy eagerness, by the blessed bones of St. Dunstan, I will pinch her as well as ever the monk did the beak of the Evil One;" and saying so, he leaped from his saddle, and taking up the gauntlet stuck it in his helmet.

The procession being now formed, moved off in order and with sound of trumpet by the Tower-gate, and so along Thames Street, towards the bridge, where the Royal party were accommodated in the balconies and windows of the central houses,

32

close to where the shock of the encounter was expected to take
place.   The bridge was then cleared of all obstacles, and the
gates at either end were shut so as to act as barriers to keep out
all but the combatants or those who waited on them.

The scene was now very imposing.   The antique wooden
fronts of the houses, of different projections and altitudes,
approaching nearer and nearer to each other, as they rose
storey above storey, till they came so close at top as to leave
but a mere riband's breadth of sky visible ; the endless variety
of windows and balconies, decorated with webs of various-
coloured cloths, tapestry, and painted emblazonments ; the
arches that crossed from one side of the way to the other, hung
with pennons and streamers of every possible shade ; the Gothic
tower that rose from one part of the bridge, where the banner
of England waved from a flag-staff set among the grizzly heads
of many a victim of tyranny, as well as many a traitor, among
which last that of Wat Tyler was then conspicuous ; and these,
contrasted with the crowds of gay knights and ladies who shone
within the lattices and balconies, the gorgeous band of heralds,
the grotesque trumpeters, and musicians of all kinds, and the
whimsical attire of the numerous attendants on the lists were
objects singularly romantic in themselves, and the effect of
them was heightened by the courtly-subdued whisper that
murmured along on both sides, mingling with the deafened
sound of the river dashing against the sterlings of the bridge
underneath.

It being signified to the King that the knights were ready,
he ordered the speaker of the lists to give the word, "Hors,
chevaliers !" and the heralds' trumpets blew.   The barriers at
both ends of the bridge were then opened, and Sir David
Lindsay entered from the north, attended by Sir William de
Dalzel.   The Lord Welles and Sir Piers Courtenay, who had
purposely crossed into what is now Southwark, appeared
from that direction.   The trumpets then sounded from both
ends of the lists, and the challenge was proclaimed by one
herald on the part of the Lord Welles, and accepted by
another on the part of Sir David de Lindsay, while the articles
of agreement as to the terms of combat, which had been regu-
larly drawn up and signed by both parties at Tarnawa, were
read from the balony of the heralds.   The combatants then
rode slowly from each end until they met and measured lances,
when their arms were examined by the marshal, and their
persons searched to ascertain that neither carried charms or
enchantments about him.   The knights then crossed each other,

and each attended by his companion and one esquire, rode slowly along to the opposite end of the bridge, and then returned each to his own place, by this means showing themselves fully to the spectators. The Lord Welles was mounted on a bright bay horse, and Sir David Lindsay rode a chestnut, both of great powers. But the figures, and still more the colours, of the noble animals, were hid beneath their barbed chamfronts and their sweeping silken housings.

The King now gave his Royal signal for the joust to begin by the usual words, " Laissez les aller," and the heralds having repeated them aloud, the trumpets sounded, and they flew towards each other with furious impetus, the fire flashing from the stones as they came on. An anxious murmur rushed along the line of spectators, eagerly were their heads thrust forward to watch the result. The combatants met, and both lances were shivered. That of Sir David Lindsay took his opponent in the shield, and had nearly unseated him, whilst he received the point of the Lord Welles' right in the midst of his ostrich-crested casque ; but although the concussion was so great as to make both horses reel backwards, yet the Scottish knight sat firm as a rock. The seconds now came up, and new lances being given to the combatants, each rode slowly away to his own barrier to await the signal for the next course.

It was given, and again the two knights rushed to the encounter, and again were the lances shivered with a similar result. Sir David Lindsay received his adversary's point full in the bars of his vizor, yet he sat unmoved as if he had been but the human half of a Centaur. A murmur ran along among the spectators ; with some it was applause for his steadiness of seat, but with by far the greater number it was dissatisfaction. It grew in strength, and at length loud murmurs arose.

" He is tied to his saddle—Sir David de Lindsay is tied to his saddle. Never had mortal man a seat so firm without the aid of trick or fallas. Prove him, prove him—let him dismount if he can !"

Sir David Lindsay soon satisfied them. He sprung to the ground, making the bridge ring again with the weight of his harness, and walking up opposite to the balcony where the King sat, he made his obeisance to Majesty. His well-managed horse followed him like a dog, and the knight, after thus satisfying the Monarch and every one of the falsehood of the charge that had been made against him, leaped again into his saddle, armed as he was. Hitherto the choice breeding of those who were present had confined the applause to the mere courtly clapping

of hands.   But now they forgot that they were nobles, knights,
and ladies of high degree, and the continued shout that arose
might have done honour to the most plebeian lungs.

The combatants now again returned each to his barrier.   The
trumpets again sounded, and again the generous steeds sprang
to their full speed.   But now it was manifest that Sir David
Lindsay was in earnest, and that he had hardly been so before,
was proved by the tremendous violence of the shock with which
his blunt lance head came in contact with the neck-piece of the
Lord Welles, who was lifted as it were from his saddle, and
tossed some yards beyond his horse.   So terrific was the effect
of Sir David Lindsay's weapon that the operation of the lance
borne by the Lord Welles was so absolutely overlooked that no
one could tell what it had been, and so admirably was Lindsay's
skill and strength displayed by this sudden and terrible overthrow of his opponent, that the spectators, with all the honest
impartiality of Englishmen and Englishwomen, shouted as loudly
as if the triumph had been with their own champion, when the
trumpets proclaimed the victory of the Scottish Knight.

The gallant Lindsay leaped from his horse, and, altogether
unheeding the praises that were showering upon him, ran to lift
up his opponent, who lay without motion.   With the assistance
of the seconds and esquires, he raised him, and his helmet being
unlaced, he was discovered to be in a swoon, and it was judged
that he was severely bruised.   A litter was immediately brought,
and the discomfited knight speedily carried off to his lodgings
in the Tower.   Meanwhile Lindsay's attention was called by
the voice of the King.

"Sir David de Lindsay," said he, addressing him from his
balcony, "we do heartily give thee joy of thy victory.   Thou
hast acquitted thyself like a true and valiant knight.   Come up
hither that we may bestow our Royal guerdon on thee."

Lindsay ran up stairs to the balcony where the King sat, and
kneeling on one knee before him—

"Accept this gemmed golden chain, in token of Richard's
approbation of thy prowess," said the Monarch, throwing the
chain over his neck ; "and now thou hast full leave to return
to thine own country when thou mayest be pleased so
to do, bearing with thee safe-conduct through the realm of
England."

"Most Royal Sir," said Lindsay, "I shall bear this thy gift as
my proudest badge ; but may I crave thy gracious leave to
tarry at thy Court until I do see that the Lord Welles is restored to health by the leeches ?   Verily, I should return but

sadly into Scotland did I believe that I had caused aught of serious evil to so brave a lord."

" Nay, that at thy discretion, Sir Knight," replied Richard ; "our Court shall be but the prouder while graced by such a flower of chivalry as thyself."

Lindsay bowed his thanks, and then retreated from the applauses which rang in his ears, that he might hasten to follow the Lord Welles to his lodgings, where he took his place by his bed-side, and began to execute the duties of a nurse, rarely quitting him for many days, that is, until his cure was perfected.

Lindsay was no sooner gone than the gay Sir Piers Courtenay, who had by this time mounted, and who had been all along writhing under the ridicule which Sir William de Dalzel had thrown upon him, now prepared to give his challenge in form. Bringing his horse's head round to front the Royal balcony, and backing him with the most perfect skill, he rose in his stirrups, and made a most graceful obeisance to his King.

" What wouldst thou with us, Courtenay ? " said Richard, with a smile playing about his mouth.

" My liege," replied Courtenay, bowing again with peculiar grace, " I have to ask a boon of your Royal favour."

" Speak, then, we give thee license," replied the King.

" So please your Majesty, I do conceive myself grossly insulted by a Scottish knight ; in such wise, indeed, that the blood of one of us must wash out the stain. May we then have thy Royal leave to fight before thee even now, to the outrance ? "

" Name the Scottish knight of whom thou dost so complain," said the King, with difficulty composing his features ; " thou hast our full license to give him thy darreigne."

" 'Tis he who now rideth this way," replied Courtenay, "Sir William de Dalzel."

" Ha ! what wouldst thou with me, most puissant Sir Piers ? " said Dalzel, who just then returned from riding slowly along the whole length of the bridge, with his vizor up, a grave face, and a burlesque attitude, so as to show his pie off to the greatest advantage, bringing a roar of laughter along with him from the balconies and open lattices on both sides of the way, and who now approached Courtenay with a bow so ridiculous, that it entirely upset the small portion of gravity that the young King was blessed with ; " what wouldst thou with me, I say, most potent paragon of knighthood ? "

"I would that thou shouldst redeem thy pledge," replied Courtenay, with very unusual brevity.

"What, then, Sir Piers," replied Dalzel, "must it then be pie against popinjay? Nay, cry you mercy, I forgot. Thy bird, I do believe, is called a falcon, though, by St. Luke, an 'twere not for the legend, few, I wis, would take it for aught but an owl, being that it is of portraiture so villanous."

"By the blessed St. Erkenwold, but thy bantering doth pass all bearing," cried Courtenay impatiently, and perhaps more nettled at this attack on the merits of his embroidery than he had been with anything that had yet passed. "Depardieux, my falcon was the admiration of the Westminster feast. By the holy St. Paul, it was the work of the most eminent artists the metropolis can boast."

"Perdie, I am right glad to hear thy character of them," replied Dalzel, "for my pie is here by the same hands; nay, and now I look at it again, 'tis most marvellously fashioned. By the Rood, but it pecks an 'twere alive."

"Thou hast contrived to turn all eyes upon me by thy clownish mockery," cried Courtenay, getting still more angry, as the laugh rose higher at every word uttered by his adversary.

"Nay, then," replied Dalzel, with affected gravity, "methinks thou shouldst give me good store of thanks, Sir Knight, for having brought so many bright and so many brave eyes to look upon the high perfections of thee and thy buzzard."

"My liege," replied Courtenay, no longer able to stand the laugh that ran around from window to window at his expense, "am I to have thy Royal license?"

"Go, then, without further let," said the King; "let the heralds of the lists proclaim the challenge."

The usual ceremonies were now gone through, and Sir Piers Courtenay rode off to the barrier lately tenanted by the Lord Welles. Dalzel sat looking after him for some seconds, until he was master of his attitude, and then turning his horse, cantered off to his own barrier, so perfectly caricaturing the proud and indignant seat of the raging Courtenay, that he carried a peal of laughter along with him. But the universal merriment was much increased when the banner of the falcon was contrasted with that of the pie, which was raised in opposition to it. It was silenced, however, by the trumpets of warning, that now brayed loudly from either side of the bridge.

A second and a third time they sounded, and Courtenay flew against his opponent with a fury equal to the rage he felt. Even

the serious nature of the combat could not tame the waggery of
the roguish Dalzel, who, though he failed not to give due attention to the manner in which he bore his shield, as well as to the
firmness of his seat, rode his career in a manner so ludicrous as
altogether to overcome that solemn silence of expectation that
generally awaited the issue of a combat where death might
ensue. The spectators, indeed, were made to forget the proba-
bility of such a consequence, and Courtenay's ears continued to
be mortified by the loud laugh which, though it followed his
adversary, fell with all its blistering effect upon him. Though
much disconcerted, the English knight bore his lance's point
bravely and truly against Dalzel's helmet; but the cunning Scot
had left it unlaced, so that it gave way as it was touched, and
fell back on his shoulders without his feeling the shock ; whilst
his own lance passed high over the head of his antagonist.

This appeared to be the result of accident, and they prepared
to run again. The signal was given, the encounter came, Dalzel's helmet gave way a second time, whilst he with great
adroitness pierced the silken wreath supporting the falcon that
soared over Courtenay's casque, and bore it off in triumph.

"Ha!" exclaimed he, "by St. Andrew, but I have the popinjay!" And so saying, he waited not for further talk, but rode
off along the bridge with pompous air, and returned bearing it
on high, to the great mortification of Courtenay, and the no
small amusement of the spectators.

Courtenay's ire was now excited to the utmost. The trumpet sounded for the third career, and he ran to Dalzel with the
fullest determination to unhorse him; but again the treacherous
helmet defeated him, while he received the point of his adversary's lance so rudely on the bars of the vizor, that they gave
way before it.

"Come hither, come hither quickly," cried Courtenay to his
esquire. "By the blessed St. George, I have suffered most
fatal damage, the which the clownish life of that caitiff Scot
would but poorly compensate."

All eyes were now turned towards him ; and his esquire having released him from his helmet, showed his mouth bleeding so
profusely, that those who were near him began seriously to fear
that he had really suffered some fatal injury.

"As I am a true knight, my liege, I shall never lift my head
again," said Courtenay. "I have lost the most precious ornaments of my face, two pearls from my upper jaw—see here they
are," said he, holding them out, "fresh, oriental, and shaped
by nature with an elegance so surprisingly and scrupulously

accurate, that they were the admiration of all who saw them. What shall I do without them?"

"Nay, in truth, thou must even make war on thy food with the wings of thine army, instead of nibbling at it with the centre, as I did remark thou were wont to do," said Sir William Dalzel, looking over his shoulder.

"Dost thou sit there, my liege, to see one of thy native knights made a mock of? Had not the traitor's helmet been left unclosed, by the holy shrine of St. Erkenwold, but he should have bit the dust ere now. I demand justice."

"Nay, of a truth I did greatly err, most valiant sir," said Sir William Dalzel, with mock penitence. "It was that hawk-shaped nese of thine that my pie would have pyked at."

"Give me but one course all fair, and thou mayest pick as it may please thee," replied Courtenay.

"Nay, I am willing to pleasure thee with six courses, if thou wouldst have them, good Sir Knight of the Howlet," replied Dalzel; "but then, mark me, it must be on equal terms. Hitherto thou hast fought me with a secret vantage on thy side."

"Vantage!" cried Courtenay with indignation; "nay, me-thinks the vantage hath been all thine own, Sir Scot."

"In truth, it must be owned I have had the best of it, Sir Englishman," said Dalzel with a sarcastic leer; "natheless, 'tis thou who hast had the secret vantage."

"Let us be judged then by the Royal Richard," said Courtenay.

"Agreed," said Dalzel. "But let each of us first pledge in the Royal hands two hundred pieces of gold, to be incontinently forfaulted by him who shall be found to have borne the secret vantage."

"Agreed," cried Courtenay confidently.

A murmur of highly-excited curiosity now ran along the lists, and the knights despatched their esquires for the money. Dalzel gave a private hint to his as he went. In a short time the two esquires returned, each carrying a purse on a pole, both of which were put up in the balcony where the King sat. But what surprised every one was the appearance of a farrier, who followed Dalzel's squire, bearing a burning brand in his hand.

"And now," said Dalzel aloud, "I do boldly accuse Sir Piers Courtenay, the knight of the How——, nay, he of the Falcon, I mean, of having fought against me with two eyes, whilst one of mine was scooped out at Otterbourne, doubtless by one of the hot-spurring sons of Northumberland's Earl. I do therefore claim his forfaulted purse.   But as I do fully admit the bravery of the said Sir Piers, the goodness of whose metal is sufficiently apparent, though it be besprent with so much vain tinsel, I am willing to do further battle with him, yea, for as many as six courses, or sixty times six, if he be so inclined, but this on condition that he doth resign that unfair vantage the which he hath hitherto had of me, and cheerfully submit to have one of his eyes extinguished by the brand of this sooty operator."

"Sir Piers Courtenay," said Richard, laughing heartily at a joke so well suited to the times, and which had renewed the convulsions of laughter so severely felt by Dalzel's antagonist, "art thou prepared to agree to this so reasonable proposal?"

But Sir Piers Courtenay was so chagrined that he wanted words.   He hung his head, and was silent.

"Then must we of needscost forbid all further duel, and forthwith decide incontinently against thee.   The purses are thine, Sir William de Dalzel, for, sooth to say, thou hast well earned them by thy merry wit."

"Nay, then, Sir Piers Courtenay," said Dalzel, riding up to his opponent, "let not this waggery of mine cause me to tyne thy good will.   Trust me, I will have none of thy money ; but if thou art disposed to confess that thou hast no longer that contempt for Scottish knights the which thou hast been hitherto so much inclined to manifest, let it be laid out in some merry masquing party of entertainment, the which shall be thine only penance.   When all else, from the Royal Richard downwards, have been so hospitable, why should we have to complain of the despisal of one English knight?   Let us shake hands, then, I pray thee."

"Sir William de Dalzel, though thou hast worked me a grievous loss, the which can never be made good," replied Courtenay, laying his hand on his mouth, "verily I do bear thee no unchristian ill-will ; and sith that his Majesty hath absolved us of our duel, I do hereby cheerfully give thee the right hand of good fellowship."

"'Tis well," said Dalzel.   "Instead of fighting thee, I will strive with thee in that for the which neither eyes nor teeth may be much needed.   I will dance a bargaret with thee, yea, or a fandango, if that may please thee better, and there I shall ask for no favour."

CHAPTER LXIV.

Lady de Vere and her Lovely Guest. Innocence and Purity endangered. The King's Confessor and the Franciscan Friar.

AFTER the spectacle was over, and whilst the homeward procession was forming, Sir Patrick Hepborne was surprised by the wave of a fair hand, accompanied by a smiling bow of acknowledgment from a very beautiful woman in one of the balconies close to that of the King. From the richness of her attire, and the place that had been allotted to her, she was evidently a lady of some consequence. He returned the compliment, but, whilst he did so, he felt unconscious of having ever spoken to her, although, upon re-perusing her face, he remembered her as one whom he had seen at the King's banquets, where he had observed that she was particularly noticed by the Sovereign. Turning to Sir Miles Stapleton, who stood by him, he besought him to tell her name.

"What," exclaimed Sir Miles in reply, "hast thou been at our English Court for so many days, Sir Patrick, and yet knowest thou not the Lady de Vere? Depardieux, it doth much surprise me that she hath not sooner sought thine acquaintance, for, by the Rood, she is a merry madam, and fond of variety. She hath been married but a short space, yet she already changeth her lovers as she doth her fancy robes."

"Is it possible?" cried Hepborne, in astonishment.

"Possible, Sir Patrick!" returned the English knight; "perdie, I am surprised at thy seeming wonder. Are Scottish ladies then so constant to their lords that thou shouldst think this fickleness so great a marvel in the Lady de Vere? She hath been for some time an especial favourite of Majesty; that is, I would have thee to understand me, in friendship, not par amours, though there be evil tongues that do say as much."

"Indeed?" cried Hepborne.

"Yea, they scruple not to say so," continued Sir Miles; "but I, who better know the King, do verily believe that, albeit he is much given to idle dalliance with these free ladies of this licentious Court, there be but little else to accuse him of. Thou needst have no fear, therefore, Sir Patrick, that the dread of Majesty will interfere with thy happiness, if it be her will to receive thee as a lover; so I wish thee joy of thy conquest.

Trust me, I do more envy thee than I do the brave conqueror
of the Lord Welles, much glory as he hath gained."

Sir Patrick turned away, at once confounded and disgusted.
What! the Lady Eleanore de Selby, of whose excellence he had
heard so much, the friend of the Lady Beatrice—was it possible
that the contamination of a Court could have already rendered
her a person of character so loose? He was shocked at the
thought. He turned again to watch her motions, when he
observed the King himself advance towards her as she was
preparing to get into her saddle, and a private conversation pass
between them, that drew the eyes of all the courtiers upon
them ; but Sir Patrick being called away to join the Scottish
party, lost the opportunity of observing the conclusion of their
conference.

Whilst the procession was dispersing in the court-yard of the
Tower, the Lady de Vere entered, riding on a piebald palfry,
richly caparisoned. She was surrounded by a group of gay
chevaliers, with whom she was talking and laughing loudly ;
but she no sooner espied Hepborne than she broke from among
them and advanced to meet him.

"Sir Patrick Hepborne," said she, smiling, "it erketh me
that mine evil fortune hath hitherto yielded me no better than
public opportunity to know him, who, by consent of all, is
acknowledged to be the flower of Scottish chivalry. Trust me,
my private apartments shall be ever open to so peerless a
knight."

"Nay, Lady," replied Sir Patrick, "the title thou hast been
pleased to bestow on me belongeth not to me but to Sir David
Lindsay and Sir William Dalzel, who have this day so nobly
supported the honour of Scotland."

"They are brave knights, 'tis true," replied the lady ; "yet
be there other qualifications in knighthood than mere brute
strength or brute courage. That thou hast enow of both of
these to the full as well as they, we who have heard of Otterbourne do well know. But in the graces of knightly deportment there be few who admit them to be thine equal, and of
that few I do confess myself not to be one."

Hepborne bowed ; but, disgusted alike with her freedom and
flattery, he gave token of approval neither by manner nor words.

"These are my apartments, Sir Knight," continued the lady,
pointing to a range of windows in a wing of the palace. "If
thou canst quit the banquet to spend some merry hours with
me this evening, trust me, thou shalt meet with no cold reception from the Lady de Vere."

This invitation was seasoned by some warm glances, that spoke even more than her words ; but Sir Patrick received both the one and the other with a silent and formal obeisance. The lady turned towards a flight of steps, and being assisted to dismount by an esquire, she tripped up stairs and along a covered terrace. A door opened at its farther extremity, and a lady appeared for a moment. It was the Lady Beatrice ; he could not be mistaken ; her image was now too deeply engraven on his heart. The blood bounded for a moment within his bosom, rushed through each artery with the heat and velocity of lightning, and then, as the thought of the Lady de Vere's character arose within his mind, it returned cold as ice to its fountainhead, and froze up every warm feeling there. He felt faint, and his head grew giddy. He looked towards the door where the ladies were saluting each other with every mark of kindness, and his eyes grew dim as they vanished within the entrance.

Almost unconscious of what he was doing, Sir Patrick turned his horse to go to his lodgings. As he recovered from the stunning effect of the spectacle he beheld, his mind began to be agonized by the most distressing thoughts. It was impossible that the Lady Beatrice, whom he believed to be so pure, could be the willing guest of so vile a woman, knowing her to be such. Yet, though such was his impression, he knew not well what to think. It was most strange that the Lady de Vere should have thus urged him to visit her while Beatrice was with her ; unless, indeed, the latter were privy to it, and that it was on her account. But be this as it might, he liked not the complexion of matters ; and, in a state of great perplexity and unhappiness, he reached the wine merchant's, where, having given his horse to a groom, he slowly sought his chamber, unwillingly to prepare for the banquet.

In going along the passage which led to his apartments, thinking of what so much occupied him, he, in a fit of absence, opened a door, believing it to be his own ; and, to his great surprise, he found himself in a room, where some dozen or twenty persons were seated at a long table, on which lay some papers. His host was there among the rest, and the appearance of the knight threw the whole party into dismay and confusion. Hepborne drew back with an apology, and hastily shut the door ; but he had hardly reached his own, when he heard the steps of his host coming hurrying after him.

"Sir Knight," said Master Ratcliffe, "'twas but some of those with whom I have had money dealings, come to settle interest with me."

As Hepborne looked in his face, he was surprised to notice that it had exchanged its generous ruby red for a deadly paleness ; the wine merchant was evidently disturbed ; but neither this observation, nor the confusion he had occasioned among the party whom he had seen surrounding the table, could then find room in his mind for a moment's thought. He therefore hastily explained that the interruption had been quite accidental on his part, and the wine merchant left him apparently satisfied. It will be easily believed that Sir Patrick Hepborne was but ill attuned for the revelry of the Royal banquet. He sat silent and abstracted, ruminating on the monstrous and afflicting conjunction he had that day witnessed, and perplexing himself with inventing explanations of the cruel doubts that were perpetually arising in his mind. The King broke up the feast at an earlier hour than usual, and Sir Patrick, glad to escape from the crowd, stole away by himself.

As he was leaving the palace, he turned his eyes towards the casements of the Lady de Vere. They were eminently conspicuous, for they were open, and lighted up with great brilliancy, while the sound of the harp came from them. He thought of the invitation he had received, and hung about for some time, weighing circumstances, and hesitating whether he should immediately avail himself of it, that he might ascertain the truth, or whether he should, in the first place, endeavour to gather it by some other means. Passion argued for the first, as the most decided step, and prudence urged the second as the wisest plan ; but whilst he was tossed between them, he was gradually drawn towards the windows by the unseen magnet within. As he got nearer, he ascertained that it was a man's voice that sung the melody and words, to which the instrument was an accompaniment ; and by the time he reached the bottom of the flight of steps, he could catch the remaining verses of a ballad, part of which had been already sung. They were nearly as follows :—

> " And wilt thou break thy faith with me,
>   And dare our vows to rend ? "
> " Hence ! " cried the angry sire ; " with thee
>   My Eda ne'er shall wend.
>
> " Her name doth prouder match demand ;
>   Lord Henry comes to-night ;
> He comes to take her promised hand,
>   And claim a husband's right.
>
> " Then hence ! "—The knight, in woful guise,
>   Turned from the perjured gate ;
> The maiden heard her lover's sighs,
>   All weeping where she sate.

" Now up and run, my bonnie page,
    Fly with the falcon's wing,
Fly swiftly to Sir Armitage,
    And give to him this ring.

" And tell him, when the rippling ford
    Shall catch the moonbeams light,
I'll leave the hated bridal board,
    To meet him there to-night."

The boy he found Sir Armitage
    In greenwood all so sad ;
But when he spied his lady's page,
    His weeping eyne grew glad.

And up leaped he for very joy,
    And kissed his lady's ring,
And much he praised the bonny boy
    Who did such message bring.

" I'll meet my lady by the stream,
    So, boy, now hie thee home ;
I'll meet her when the moon's broad beam
    Comes dancing over the foam."

And now to grace the wedding-feast
    The demoiselles prepare ;
There were the bridegroom, sire, and priest,
    But Eda was not there.

She left her tyrant father's tower,
    To seek her own true knight ;
She met him at the trysted hour,
    Prepared to aid her flight.

" Sir Armitage, with thee I'll ride
    Through flood, o'er fell so steep ;
Though destined for another's bride,
    My vow to thee I'll keep."

" Oh bless thee, bless thee, lady mine,
    That true thy heart doth prove ;
Before yon moon hath ceased to shine,
    The priest shall bless our love."

He raised her on his gallant steed,
    And sprang him to his selle ;
" Keep, keep thy seat, my love, with heed,
    And grasp my baldrick well."

Beneath the moon the wavelets flash'd,
    Struck by the courser's heel,
And through the ford he boldly dash'd,
    Spurr'd by the pointed steel.

High up his sides the surges rose,
    And washed the blood away ;
They lav'd fair Eda's bridal-clothes,
    And fill'd her with dismay.

" Alas, the stream is strong," she cried.
    " Fear not, my love," said he ;
" 'Tis here the waters deepest glide,
    Anon we shall be free."

Behind them rung a wild alarm,
　And torches gleam'd on high ;
Forth from the Castle came a swarm,
　With yells that rent the sky.

Again the knight his iron heel
　Dash'd in his courser's side.
He plung'd—his powerful limbs did reel—
　He yielded to the tide.

Down went both mailed horse and knight ;
　The maid was borne away,
And flash'd the moonbeam's silver light
　Amid the sparkling spray.

His daughter's shriek the father heard,
　Far on the moonlit wave ;
A moment Eda's form appear'd,
　Then sunk in watery grave.

Peace never blest the sire again ;
　He curst ambitious pride,
That made him hold his promise vain,
　And sacred oaths deride.

Still in his eye his sinking child,
　Her shriek still in his ear,
Reft of his mind, he wanders wild
　Midst rocks and forests drear.

But where that cross in yonder shade
　Oft bends the pilgrim's knee,
There sleep the gentle knight and maid
　Beneath their trysting tree.

When the musician had finished, Sir Patrick Hepborne still
continued to loiter with his arm on the balustrade of the stair,
when the door opened, and he heard a feeble step on the terrace
above. He looked upwards, and the light of a lamp that was
burning in a niche fell on the aged countenance of a man who
was descending. It was Adam of Gordon.

"Adam of Gordon !" exclaimed Sir Patrick.

"And who is he, I pray, who doth know Adam of Gordon
so far from home ?" demanded the minstrel. "Ah, Sir Patrick
Hepborne ; holy St. Cuthbert, I do rejoice to see thee. Trust
me, the ready help thou didst yield me at Forres hath not been
forgotten ; though thou didst sorely mar my verses by thine
interruption. Full many sithes have I tried to awaken that
noble subject, but the witchery of inspiration is past, and——"

"But how camest thou here ?" demanded Hepborne, impatiently interrupting him.

"Sir Knight, I came hither with a lady from the Borders,"
said Adam, hesitatingly ; "a lady that——"

"Nay, speak not so mystically, old man," replied Hepborne ;

"I am already well aware of the story of the Lady Beatrice, and heartily do I curse mine own folly for permitting jealousy so to hoodwink mine eyes as to make me run blindly away from mine own happiness. I already guess that it was she whom thou didst accompany hither, and I know that she is now an inmate of those apartments, with the Lady de Vere, the daughter of the late Sir Walter de Selby."

"Nay, nay, so far thou art wrong, Sir Knight," replied the Minstrel. " She to whom these apartments do belong is not the daughter of Sir Walter de Selby. True it is, indeed, that when the Lady Eleanore did leave Norham Castle, she did call the companion of her flight by the name of Sir Hans de Vere, a Zealand knight, kinsman to the Duke of Ireland ; but some strange mystery doth yet hang over this affair, for he who doth own these gay lodgings, and who is the husband of this gay madam, is the identical Sir Hans de Vere I have just described, and yet he knoweth nought of the Lady Eleanore de Selby."

"Thy speech is one continued riddle, good Adam," said Hepborne; "canst thou not explain to me ?"

" Nay, of a truth, Sir Knight, thou dost know as much as I do," said the minstrel. " What hath become of the Lady Eleanore de Selby no one can tell. If he that she married be indeed a De Vere, he is at least no kin to the Duke of Ireland, as he or she would have us believe. There have been De Veres enow about the English Court since this King Richard began his reign, albeit that the day may be gone by with many of them, sith that their chief, the Duke of Ireland, hath been forced to flee into Zealand, where his race had its origin. But of all the De Veres, none doth answer the description of him whom the Lady Beatrice and I did see carry off the Lady Eleanore de Selby from Norham."

"Strange, most strange," said Sir Patrick Hepborne ; "but knowest thou aught of this Lady de Vere? Men's tongues do talk but lightly of her."

"Nay, in good truth, I have begun to entertain strange notions of her myself," replied Adam. "By'r Lady, she would have had me sing some virelays to-night that were light and warm enow, I promise thee, had I not feigned that I knew them not ; and, by my troth, she spared not to chide me for my sober minstrelsy, the which she did tauntingly compare to the chanting of monks. My Lady, quoth I, consider I am but a rude Border——"

" But say, old man," cried Hepborne, impatiently interrupting him, "how did the Lady Beatrice seek shelter with such a woman? Quick, tell me, I beseech thee, for I must hasten to rescue the poor and spotless dove from the clutch of this foul howlet."

"In the name of the Virgin, then, let us lose no time in thinking how it may best be done," said Adam of Gordon earnestly ; "St. Andrew be praised that thou, Sir Knight, art so willing to become the protector of an angel, who—— Yet I dare not say how much thou art beloved. But, hush ! we may be overheard here in the open air. Let us retreat to my garret yonder, where I will tell thee all I can, and then we may, with secrecy and expedition, concert what steps thou hadst best take."

Hepborne readily followed the minstrel to his small chamber, and there he learned the following particulars.

The Lady Beatrice had no sooner recovered from the swoon into which she had been thrown by the appearance of the Franciscan at Sir Walter de Selby's funeral, than she sent for the Minstrel, of whose attachment and fidelity she had already had many a proof, and imparted to him her design of quitting Norham Castle immediately. Without communicating her intention to any one else, she mounted that milk-white palfrey which had been the gift of Hepborne, and travelled with all speed to Newcastle, where she sought shelter in the house of a widowed sister of Sir Walter de Selby. There she lived for a short time in retirement, until at last she adopted the resolution of visiting London in search of her friend the Lady Eleanore, whom she believed now to be the Lady de Vere, that she might communicate to her the death of her father, if she had not already heard of that event, and entreat from her a continuance of that protection which she had so long afforded her. She and the Minstrel, therefore, went on board a ship sailing for the Thames ; but having been tossed about by contrary winds, and even compelled to seek safety more than once in harbours by the way, they had only arrived in the metropolis three days before that of which we are now speaking.

The Minstrel was immediately employed by the Lady Beatrice to make inquiry for the Lady de Vere, and he was readily directed to the lodgings of the lady of that name in the Tower. But he was no sooner introduced into her presence and that of her husband, Sir Hans de Vere, than he discovered that there was some strange mistake. To exculpate himself for his seeming intrusion on a knight and lady to whom he was an utter stranger, he explained the cause of his coming, and told whom he sought for, when, to his great dismay, he learned that no such

33

persons as those he described were known about the Court.
Filled with chagrin, he returned to the Lady Beatrice, whose
vexation may be more easily conceived than described.   She was
a stranger in London, in a wretched hostel, without a friend but
old Adam to advise her, and severed for ever, as she feared,
from the only human being on whom she could say that
she had the least claim for protection.   Despair came upon
her, and hiding her face in her hands, she gave full way
to her grief.

Whilst she sat in this wretched situation, in which Adam in
vain exerted himself to comfort her, a page arrived, with a kind
message from Sir Hans and Lady de Vere, in which they offered
her their house as a home, until she should have time to determine as to her future conduct.   So friendly, so seasonable a
proposal, was not to be rejected in her circumstances, even coming
as it did from strangers, and the Lady Beatrice gladly became
the guest of the Lady de Vere.

So far went the Minstrel's knowledge; but leaving Sir
Patrick to question him as he pleases, we shall ourselves more
deeply investigate the circumstances, as well as the secret
springs of action which produced this event.   It happened that
just after the Minstrel's interview with the Lady de Vere, King
Richard came to idle an hour with her as he was often wont to
do to gather the gossip of the Court.   The lady told him what
had passed, and the Monarch joined with her in the laugh
it occasioned.   The Lady de Vere had extracted enough of
Beatrice's history from the Minstrel to be able to answer the
King's questions.

"And who may this Beatrice be?" demanded Richard.

"A damsel, I believe, whom old De Selby picked up at the
door of a Scottish peasant, and whom he fancied to educate as a
companion to his daughter Eleanore," replied Lady de Vere ;
"doubtless, now that he is dead, she seeks to hang herself about
the neck of the heiress of her patron."

"And sith that she hath so come, might we not find some
other neck for her to hang about?" said the King laughing.
"Pr'ythee, send for her hither ; we should be well contented to
see this stray bird."

The Lady de Vere well knew her advantage in humouring
all the wild fancies that entered the King's head, and accordingly
gave immediate obedience to his wishes, by sending to Beatrice
the message we have already noticed.   Fatigued to death by
her voyage, Beatrice had no sooner complied with the invitation
she had received, than she was compelled to retire to the apart-

ment the Lady de Vere had prepared for her ; and she continued so long indisposed that she was unable to be present at the tilting.

Towards the evening of that day, however, she was so far recovered as to quit her room ; and, accordingly, when the procession returned from London Bridge, she hastened to pour out her gratitude to the Lady de Vere for the hospitable reception she had given her.

Sir Hans went to the King's banquet, but his lady remained with Beatrice ; and the Minstrel was sent for to amuse them with his ballads. There was something free and bold in the manner of the Lady de Vere that was by no means agreeable to Beatrice ; but believing that there was nothing worse in it than an unfortunate manner, she endeavoured to reconcile herself to it, in one who had shown her so much apparent friendship.

They were seated in a luxuriously-furnished apartment, hung with tapestry of the richest hues, and lighted up by silver lamps, when the door opened, and Sir Hans de Vere entered, ushering in a young man, whom he introduced as the Earl of Westminster. The Lady de Vere smiled on the young nobleman, and Beatrice, though she had never heard of such a title, was aware that new lords were created so frequently, that there was little wonder she should be ignorant of it. The young Earl, who was very handsome, seemed to be on habits of great intimacy with Sir Hans de Vere and his lady. He seated himself by the Lady Beatrice, and began to trifle pleasantly with her, mixing up a thousand courtly compliments with the agreeable nothings that he uttered. Spiced wine and sweetmeats were handed round, and soon afterwards a small, but very tasteful and exquisitely cooked supper appeared, with wines of the richest flavour. The Lady Beatrice ate little, and refused to touch wine. The night wore apace. The young Earl of Westminster became more and more earnest in his endeavours to make himself agreeable to Beatrice, who began to find considerable amusement in his conversation, and insensibly permitted him to absorb her whole attention. Suddenly he began, in a sort of half-serious manner, to address her in a strain of tenderness that by no means pleased her. She prepared to shift her place ; but what was her astonishment, when, on looking up, she saw that she and the young Earl were alone. Sir Hans de Vere and his lady had stolen unnoticed from the apartment. Beatrice started up to follow them.

"Nay, stay to hear me, lovely Beatrice," cried the Earl, endeavouring to detain her.

" Unhand me, my Lord," cried she boldly, and at the same
time tearing herself from him.

" Hear me, only hear me," cried the Earl, springing to the
door, so as to cut off her retreat.

This action still more alarmed her. She screamed aloud for
help, and flying to the casement, threw it open ; but the Earl
dragged her from it by gentle force, and having shut it, he was
vainly endeavouring to compose her, when the chamber door
was burst open by a furious kick, and Sir Patrick Hepborne
appeared, with his drawn sword in his hand.

" King Richard !" cried the knight, starting back with astonishment : "Doth England's King so far forget the duty of the
high office he doth hold, as to become the destroyer instead of
the protector of innocence ? Yet, by St. Andrew, wert thou
fifty times a king, thou shouldst answer to me for thine insult
to that lady.   Defend thyself."

The cool presence of mind exhibited by Richard whilst yet
a stripling, on the memorable occasion of Wat Tyler being
struck down by Walworth the Lord Mayor, showed that he was
not constitutionally deficient in courage ; but in this, as in
everything else, he was wavering and uncertain, and no one
was more liable than he to yield to sudden panic.   Seeing Hepborne about to spring on him, he darted into an inner room, the
door of which stood ajar.

" Sir Patrick Hepborne !" cried the Lady Beatrice, her lovely
face flushing with the mingled emotions of surprise, joy, gratitude, and love.

" Yes," cried the knight, throwing himself on one knee before
her, " yes, Lady Beatrice, he who may now dare to call himself
thine own faithful and true knight—he who hath now had his
eyes cleared from the errors which blinded him—he who, whilst
deeply smitten by those matchless charms, believed that in his
adoration of them he was worshipping the Lady Eleanore de
Selby—he who thus believing himself to be deceived and
rejected, did yet continue to nourish the pure and enduring
flame in his bosom after all hope had fled, and who now feels it
glow with tenfold warmth, sith that hope's gentle gales have
again sprung up to fan it—he who will——But whither is my
passion leading me ?" cried he, starting up, and taking Beatrice's
hand ; " this is no time for indulging myself in such a theme,
dear as it may be to me.   Lady, thou art betrayed.   This is no
fit place of sojournance for spotless virtue such as thine.   The
false Lady de Vere is one who doth foully minister to the King's
pleasures.   Lose not a moment, I beseech you.   I have seen

Adam of Gordon, who waits for us without. Fly then," cried he, leading her towards the door, "fly with me; I will be thy protector. Let us haste from the impure den of this wicked woman, who would have——"

Sir Patrick threw open the door as he pronounced these words, and in an instant he was prostrated on the floor by the blow of a halbert.

"Seize him and drag him to a dungeon," cried the Lady de Vere, with eyes flashing like those of an enraged tigress; "I accuse him of a treasonable attack on the sacred person of the King of England. He shall die the death of traitor." The guards obeyed her, and lifting up the inanimate body of the knight, bore him away.

"So," cried the fury, "so perish those who shall dare to insult the love of the Lady de Vere; and as for thee, minion," she said, turning round, "thou art a prisoner there during my pleasure." And saying so, she pushed Beatrice into the room, and locked and bolted the door on the wretched damsel, who fell from her violence, and instantly swooned away.

When the Lady Beatrice recovered, and began to recollect what had passed, she arose in a tremor, and tottering to a seat, rested herself for some moments, throwing her eyes fearfully around the apartment. Everything in it remained as it was. No one seemed to have entered since. The lamps had begun to burn so faintly, that they appeared to tell of the approach of midnight, and this idea was strengthened by the silence that prevailed everywhere both without and within the palace. She tried the bolts of the door, but, to her great horror, she found them fast. A faint hope of escape arose, when she remembered that the King had disappeared by the inner apartment, whence there might be a passage leading to other chambers. She snatched up an expiring hand lamp, and hastened to explore it. But there was no visible mode of exit from the room, and she now became convinced that the King must have returned through the apartment whilst she lay insensible, and that some one had liberated him from without. The recollection of the cruel wound, which she almost feared might have been Sir Patrick's death blow, together with the certainty of his captivity, and the probable issue of it, now filled her mind with horror; and this, added to the perplexity of her present situation, so overcame her, that she sat down and wept bitterly.

The lamps now, one after another, expired, until she was left in total darkness. She groped her way into the inner apartment, and, having fastened the door within, threw herself upon the couch, and abandoned herself to all her wretchedness.

Whilst the Lady Beatrice was lying in this distressing situation, she was startled by a noise. Suddenly a glare of light flashed upon her eyes; she rubbed them, and looked towards the spot whence it proceeded. A man in a friar's habit stood near the wall; he held a lamp high, that its light might the better fill the room. Immediately behind him was an opening in the tapestry, the folds of which being held aside by a hand and arm, admitted the entrance of another shaven crowned head. To the terror of the Lady Beatrice, she recognized in this second monk the piercing eyes and powerful features of the very Franciscan whose dagger had so alarmed her at Lochyndorbe, and the sight of whom had so affected her at Sir Walter de Selby's funeral. She attempted to scream, but fear so overcame her, that, like one who labours under a nightmare, her lips moved, but her tongue refused to do its office, and she lay with her eyes wide open, staring on the object of her dread, in mute expectation of immediate murder.

"Is she there, Friar Rushak?" said he whom we have known by the name of the Franciscan.

"She is here," said the first monk, who bore the lamp; "all is quiet too—thou mayest safely enter."

The Franciscan who followed now stepped into the apartment, and came stealing forward with soft, barefooted tread.

"Give me the light, Friar Rushak, that there may be no mistake," said he, taking the lamp from his companion.

The blood grew chill in the Lady Beatrice's veins as the Franciscan approached the couch where she lay. He held the lamp so as to throw its light strongly upon her face.

"It is she indeed," said he, in a muttering voice, while his features were lighted up by a grim smile of satisfaction, which gradually faded away, leaving a severe expression in his lightning eye.

"She trembles," said Friar Rushak, advancing towards the couch with a terrible look; "conscious of her own depravity, she is guilt-stricken."

"Ay, she may well be guilt-stricken," said the Franciscan.

"Alas, of what am I accused, mysterious man?" cried the Lady Beatrice, clasping her hands together, and throwing herself on her knees before them. "Murder me not—murder me not. Let not the holy garments you wear be stained with the blood of innocence."

"Innocence!" cried Friar Rushak, "talk not thou of innocence ! Why art thou in these apartments if thou be'st innocent ?"

"So help me the pure and immaculate Virgin, I am not here by mine own consent," said the unhappy lady. "Murder me not without inquiry—I am a prisoner here—I was eager to escape—I should have escaped with Sir Patrick Hepborne, had not——"

"Sir Patrick Hepborne," said the Franciscan, with a ferocious look. "Ay, so! The curse of St. Francis be upon him !"

"Nay, nay, curse him not—oh, curse him not!" cried Beatrice, embracing the Franciscan's knees. "Murder me if thou wilt, but, oh, curse not him, who at peril of his noble life would have rescued me from these hated walls."

"Yea, again I do say, may he be accursed," cried the Franciscan, with increased energy and ferocity of aspect. "Full well do we know thy love for this infamous knight—full well do we know why he would have liberated thee."

"But to find thee here as a toil spread by the Devil to catch the tottering virtue of King Richard !" cried Friar Rushak.

"Yea," said the Franciscan, striking his forehead with the semblance of intense inward feeling, "to find thee a monster so utterly depraved, is indeed even more than my worst suspicions."

"What couldst thou hope, minion !" said Friar Rushak sternly; "what couldst thou hope from fixing thine impure affections on the Royal Richard."

"Blessed Virgin," cried the tortured Beatrice, clasping her hands and throwing her eyes solemnly upwards, "Holy Mother of God, thou who art truth itself, and who canst well search out the truth in others, if I do speak aught else than truth now, let thy just indignation strike me down an inanimate corpse. I am here as an innocent victim to the treachery of the Lady de Vere. She it was who inveigled me into these apartments by pretended friendship, that she might make a sacrifice of me. I knew not even the person of King Richard ; and had it not been for Sir Patrick Hepborne, who so bravely rescued me from his hand——"

"Um," said Friar Rushak, somewhat moved by what she had uttered ; "thine appeal is so solemn, and it must be confessed that the evidence of those who did accuse thee of plotting against the King's heart is indeed but questionable. It may be —But, be it as it may, it mattereth not, for thou shalt soon be put beyond the reach of weaving snares for Richard. Yet shall we try thee anon, for thou shalt see the King, and if by word or

look thou dost betray thyself, this dagger shall search thy heart,
yea, even in the presence of Richard himself."

"King Richard!" cried Beatrice, with distraction in her
looks. "Take me not before the King; let me not again behold
the King. Where have they carried Sir Patrick Hepborne? In
charity let me fly to him; he may now want that aid which I
am bound to yield him."

"Nay, thou shalt never see him more," said the Franciscan.

"Oh, say not so, say not so—tell me not that he is dead,"
cried the Lady Beatrice, forgetting everything else in her apprehension for Sir Patrick; "oh, if a spark of charity burns within
your bosoms, let me hasten to him. I saw him bleeding, and on
the ground—I heard him cruelly condemned to a dungeon—oh,
let me be the companion of his captivity—let me watch by his
pillow—let me soothe his sorrows—let me be his physician. If
my warm life's-blood were a healing balm, this gushing heart
would yield it all for his minutest wound." Her feelings overcame her, and she fell back, half fainting, on the floor.

"Raise her head," said Friar Rushak to the Franciscan, who
was bending over her with some anxiety; and he applied to her
nostrils a small golden box, containing some refreshing odour.
which speedily began to revive her.

"Alas!" said the Franciscan, "however innocently she may
be here, as affects the King, her abandoned love for her seducer
hath been too clearly confessed."

"She reviveth," said Friar Rushak; "raise her to her feet.
And now let us hasten, brother; the moments fly fast, and we
have yet to effect our perilous passage through the——"

"Is there no other way?" demanded the Franciscan.

"None," replied the Friar Rushak; "and if the King
should——"

"The King!" repeated Beatrice, with a thrill of dread.

"Ay, Lady, the King," replied the Friar Rushak, with a
strong emphasis and a desperate expression; "but thou must
wear this disguise to conceal thee," continued he, opening out
a bundle containing a Franciscan's habit. "Draw the cowl over
thy head and face; follow me with caution; and whatever thou
mayest see, utter no word, or give no sign, else——Nay, let not
thy breath be heard, or——Come on."

The Friar Rushak now led the way with the lamp, and the
Lady Beatrice, shaking from a dread that even her loose disguise
could not conceal, stepped after him through a spring door behind the tapestry, that led into a passage in the centre of the
wall. The Franciscan followed, and shut the door behind him.

The passage was so narrow, that one person only could advance at a time. It was strangely crooked also, frequently bending at right angles, so as to defy all Beatrice's speculation as to where they might be leading her. A dead silence was preserved by both her attendants, and they moved with a caution that allowed not a step to be heard. Friar Rushak halted suddenly, and turned round; the lamp flashed upon his face, and showed his angry eye; the Lady Beatrice fell back in terror into the arms of the Franciscan behind her. Friar Rushak put his finger to his open mouth, and then told her, in a whisper, to suppress the high breathing which her fears had created. The Lady Beatrice endeavoured to obey. Friar Rushak motioned to her and the Franciscan to remain where they were; he advanced three or four paces with great caution, and, slowly opening a concealed door, listened for a moment; then gently pushing aside the tapestry within, he thrust forward his head, and again withdrawing it, motioned to Beatrice and the Franciscan to advance.

"They sleep," whispered he. "Follow me—but no word, sign, or breath, as thou dost value thy life."

Friar Rushak entered within the tapestry, and the Lady Beatrice followed him into a magnificent chamber, lighted by a single lamp. A gorgeous bed occupied one end of the apartment. Over it, attached to the heavy Gothic ceiling, was a gilded crown, whence descended a crimson drapery, richly emblazoned with the Royal Arms of England, under which lay a young man, his head only appearing above the bed-clothes. She hastily glanced at his features, which the lamp but dimly illuminated. It was King Richard. His dark eye-lashes were closed, but she trembled lest he should awaken. Around the room were several couches, where his pages ought to have watched, but where they lay as sound as their Royal master.

They had hardly stepped into the room, when a little dog came growling from under the King's bed. The Lady Beatrice had nearly sunk on the floor, but the little favourite of the monarch instantly recognized Friar Rushak as a well-known friend, and quietly retreated to his place of repose. The pages showed no symptom of alarm, but the King turned in bed, and exposed his head more fully to view. The Lady Beatrice shook from head to foot as she looked towards him; but her apprehension was excited yet more immediately, when she beheld Friar Rushak at her side, with a menacing eye, and a dagger in his grasp. A sign at once conveyed to her that it was silence he wanted; and though she ventured not to breathe, her heart beat so against her side as she stood, that she felt as if the very

sound of its pulsations would break the slumbers of all around
her.   Again the King was quiet, and Friar Rushak moved on
towards the opposite door.   The Lady Beatrice drew the cowl
more over her face, and, without daring to repeat her glance at
the King, followed with as much caution as her sinking knees
would permit her to use.

The door was opened by Friar Rushak with the utmost
gentleness, and they found themselves at one extremity of a
suite of apartments, the long perspective of which was seen running onwards from one to another, and where they could perceive groups of dozing domestics lying on chairs, and stretched
on benches, in every possible position.   Through one of these
rooms they passed, and then retreated by a side-door into a narrow circular stair, by which they descended to the hall of
entrance, where they found about a dozen archers sitting
slumbering by a great fire.   These men roused themselves on
their approach, and, starting up, sprang forward to bar their
passage with their halberts.   The Lady Beatrice became
alarmed, and, in the trepidation that seized her, dropped the
friar's habit that had hitherto concealed her.

"Ha!" exclaimed one of the soldiers, "a woman and two
monks!   Who may that considerate lord have been who hath
thus taken the shrift with the sin?"

"Silence, Barnaby," cried another man; "that is the holy
Father Rushak, the King's Confessor."

"Let me pass, knaves," cried Rushak.

"Ay, ay, let him pass," said another man; "he hath right
of entrance and outgoing at all hours.   I would not have thee
try to stop him, an thou wouldst sleep in a whole skin to-
morrow night."

The passage was cleared in a moment.   The Lady Beatrice,
overpowered with apprehension, was supported by the Franciscan.

"Come on, brother," cried Friar Rushak.

"She faints," cried the Franciscan.

"Lift her in thine arms, then," cried Rushak.

The Franciscan raised her from the ground, and carried her
half senseless to the door.   At that moment a man entered, and
brushed by them in breathless haste.   He looked behind him
at the group.

"The Lady Beatrice!" cried he.   "Ha, whither do ye carry
her, villains?"

"Answer him not, but run," said Rushak, flying off at full
speed across the court, followed by the sturdy Franciscan,

who carried his fair burden as if he felt not her weight. The steps of many people were heard following them. All at once the noise of a desperate scuffle ensued behind them, and the two monks, who stayed not to inquire the nature of it, pressed on towards a low archway that ran under the river-wall. The air blew fresh from the river on Beatrice's cheek. She revived, and found that he who carried her was standing near an iron gate of ponderous strength, which Friar Rushak was making vain attempts to open.

"Holy St. Francis assist us!" cried he, "I fear that my hands have erred, and that I have unluckily possessed myself of the wrong key."

"Hush," said the Franciscan, "and keep close. The step of the sentinel on the wall above falls louder. He cometh this way."

They drew themselves closer to the wall. The sentinel's step passed onward to the extremity of his walk, and then slowly returning, it again moved by, and the sound of it sank along the wall.

"Try the key again, brother," said the Franciscan; "the man is beyond hearing."

Friar Rushak again applied the key; the great bolt yielded before it; the gate creaked upon its hinges, and the Franciscan deposited his trembling burden, more dead than alive, in a little skiff that lay in the creek of the river running under the vault.

"Thanks, kind brother," said the Franciscan in a low tone of voice, to Friar Rushak; "a thousand thanks for thy friendly aid."

"Hush! the sentinel comes again," whispered Friar Rushak.

They remained perfectly still until the man had completed his turn, and was gone beyond hearing.

"Now thou mayest venture to depart," said Friar Rushak—"away, and St. Francis be with thee!" And so saying, he waved his hand, shut the gate, and quickly disappeared.

The Franciscan got into the boat. A little crooked man, who had hitherto lain like a bundle of clothes in the bottom of it, started up, and began pushing it along by putting his hands against the side-walls until he got beyond the vault. Then he sat down and pulled the oars.

"Who goes there?" cried the sentinel, "who goes there?—Answer me, an thou wouldst not have a quarrel-bolt in thy brain."

The Franciscan minded not, and the little figure went on, pulling with all his might. Beatrice sat trembling with affright.

It was dark, but she heard the sentinel's step running along the wall, as if following the sound of the oars. He halted ; the click of the spring of his arbaleste reached her ear, and the bolt that it gave wings to had nearly reached her too, for it struck with great force on the inside of the boat that was opposite to the man who shot it. The rower pulled off farther into the stream. The sentinel's cry for raising the guard was heard ; but the tide was now running down, and it bore the little boat on its bosom with so much swiftness that they soon lost all sound of the alarm.

"Tell me, oh, tell me who art thou, and whither dost thou carry me ? " cried Beatrice, her heart sinking with alarm as she beheld the walls of the city left behind them.

" Daughter, this is neither the time nor the place for the explanation thou dost lack," replied the Franciscan ; " methinks I do hear the sound of oars behind us. Let me aid thee, Bobbin," cried he, taking one of the oars, and beginning to pull desperately.

The united strength of the two rowers now made the little boat fly like an arrow, and in a short time the eyes of the Lady Beatrice were attracted by five lights that burned bright in the middle of the river, and hung in the form of St. Andrew's cross.

"St. Francis be praised," cried the Franciscan ; "we are now near the bark that is to give us safety. Pull, Bobbin, my brave heart."

The lights grew in magnitude in the Lady Beatrice's eyes, and the water beneath the shadowy hull blazed with the bright reflection.

" Hoy, the skiff ! " cried a stern voice in a north-country accent.

" St. Andrew ! " replied the Franciscan.

" Welcome, St. Andrew," said the voice from the vessel. " Hast thou sped, holy father ? "

" Yea, by the blessing of St. Francis and the Virgin," replied the Franciscan.

The lights, which were suspended to a frame attached to the round top of the short thick mast, were at once extinguished. The skiff came alongside, and the Lady Beatrice was lifted, unresisting, into the vessel, and carried directly into the cabin, and in a few minutes the anchor was weighed.

" So, my brave men," cried the master to his sailors, after they had got the anchor on board, " now, hoise up the mainsail. Take the helm, Bobbin ; we shall drop slowly down till daylight doth appear."

"Art thou sure of shaping thy course safely through all these intricate windings?" demanded the Franciscan.

"Yea," replied the commander, "as sure as thou hast thyself seen me when running between the Bass and the May. What, dost thou think that I have been herrying these English loons so long without gathering sea-craft as well as plunder? And then, have I not crooked Bobbin here as my pilot, who was bred and born in this serpent of a river? By St. Rule, but he knoweth every sweep and turn, yea, and every sand and shoal bank, blindfold. Had I not had some such hands on board, how dost thou think I could have carried off that spice-ship so cunningly, having to steer her through so many villainous eel-knots?"

"I see thou art not a whit less daring than thy sire," said the Franciscan.

"Nay, an I were, I should ill deserve the gallant name of Mercer," replied the other. "Thou didst witness enow of his exploits, I ween, the while that thou wert aboard of him, to remember thee well that he did neither want head to conceive, boldness to dare, nor coolness to execute. Trust me, I lack not my father's spirit; and though I have not the fortune to sail with a fleet of stout barks at my back, as he was wont to do, yet, while the timbers of the tough old Trueman do hold together beneath me, I shall work these Southrons some cruel evil, to revenge the loss of my father and his ships. Haul from the land, Bobbin; haul off, to weather that point. Climb the forecastle and look out there, he who hath the watch."

CHAPTER LXV.

In the Dungeons of the Tower of London.

LET us now return to Sir Patrick Hepborne, and inquire into his fate, as well as endeavour to explain how he was enabled to render so speedy aid to the Lady Beatrice.

After having heard everything from the Minstrel, he resolved to avail himself of the invitation he had received from the Lady de Vere; by doing which immediately, he hoped to have some happy accidental opportunity of seeing and conversing with the Lady Beatrice. He had no sooner presented himself at the door of her apartments, than a page, who seemed to have been on the watch for him, sprang forward, and ushered him into a small chamber, voluptuously furnished, and moderately lighted by a single lamp. In his way thither he heard voices and laughing in another place. The page left him, and in a very short time he heard the light trip of a woman's foot. The door opened, and the Lady de Vere entered alone. She accosted him with an easy gaiety of manner, and, ordering her page to bring in spiced wine, she began to assail his heart with all the allurements of which she was mistress. Sir Patrick, still hoping for an opportunity of seeing her whom he so much loved, mustered up all his ingenuity to keep the lady in play, but his mind was so much employed in thinking of the Lady Beatrice, that he ministered but awkwardly to the coquetry of the Lady de Vere, and met her warm advances so coldly, that she began to think in her own mind that this phœnix of Scottish chivalry was little better than a frigid fool.

It was whilst he was engaged in playing this truly difficult game that the shrieks of the Lady Beatrice reached his ear. He started up at once from the Lady de Vere's side, and, drawing his sword, made his way with the speed of lightning towards the chamber whence the screams proceeded, and, with the force of a thunderbolt centred in his foot, burst open the door as we have already seen. The Lady de Vere, boiling with indignation at being so abandoned by him, called for some of the King's guards, and, arriving with them just in time to hear the language in which he was talking of her to Beatrice, her rage knew no bounds, and the reader is already aware to what a cruel extremity it carried her against the hapless lovers.

The blow which Sir Patrick received, though it effectually stunned him, was by no means fatal. When he recovered from the swoon into which it had thrown him, he found himself stretched on a heap of straw, on the floor of a dungeon. The grey twilight that peeped through a small grated window placed high in the wall, told him that morning was approaching. He arose, with a head giddy from the blow it had received, and found that the axe-wound in his scalp had bled so profusely as to have deluged his hair, and so clotted it together that it had of itself stopped the effusion. The knight then began to examine the place of his confinement, when, to his surprise, he beheld another prisoner in the vault, who seemed to sleep soundly. Sir Patrick approached to look upon him, and he was not a little astonished to discover that it was no other than his landlord, Master Lawrence Ratcliffe. He hesitated for a time to disturb so sound a repose; but at length curiosity to know how he came there got the better of everything else, and he gently shook him from his slumbers. The wine merchant started up—rubbed his eyes, and betrayed, by his look of terror, that he was awakened to a full recollection of his situation, and that he feared he was called to meet his doom ; till, seeing thât it was his Scottish guest whose countenance he beheld, his expression changed.

" So thou hast come to look upon the victim of thy traiterie," said he, with a reproachful tone.

" What meanest thou, my good friend ? " replied Hepborne ; " I am a prisoner here, as well as thyself."

" Ha, ha ! So then, whilst they listened to thy tale, they did begin to suspect thee of having had some share in the treason," said Ratcliffe.

" What treason ? " demanded Hepborne ; " I protest, on the honour of a knight, that I am altogether ignorant of what thou dost mean. Believe me, I am here for no matter connected with aught that thou mayest have done. My crime is the having dared to rescue a virtuous demoiselle from the wicked assault of King Richard. I was on the eve of springing forward to punish him on the spot for his villainy, when he fled. I was suddenly rendered senseless by a blow from the halberd of one of his guards, and I recovered not from my swoon until I found myself on yonder straw. But what, I pr'ythee, hath made thee the tenant of this gloomy dungeon ? "

" And art thou really innocent of betraying me then ? " demanded Ratcliffe, with a strong remnant of doubt in his countenance.

" I have already declared, on the faith of knighthood, that I know not what I could have betrayed thee in," replied Hepborne, a little displeased that his truth should be thus questioned ; " Depardieux, I am not wont to be thus interrogated and suspected."

" Nay, pardon me, good Sir Knight," cried Master Ratcliffe, starting up, and stretching out his hand to Hepborne ; " by St. Paul, I do now most readily believe thee, and I am heartily ashamed of having ever doubted thee for a moment. But thou camest in on us so strangely, as we were in secret conclave assembled, that when my arrest came at midnight, I could not but believe that thou hadst betrayed me."

" What could I have betrayed thee in ? " said Sir Patrick. " I came in on thee and thy friends by an accident, and I neither did know, nor did I seek to know, the subject of your deliberation."

" Nay, trust me, it was matter of no weight, Sir Knight," cried Ratcliffe eagerly ; " simple traffic, I promise thee. Yet men's most innocent dealings be cruelly perverted in these slippery times; and some one, I trow, hath sorely misrepresented mine, else had I not been here. But right glad am I to find that thou art free from such suspicion; for verily the disappointment I felt in discovering that thou wert, as I did then think, a traitor, was even more bitter to me than the effect of the traiterie of the which I did suppose thee guilty. But tell me, Sir Knight," said he, rapidly changing the subject, and speaking with an air of eagerness, "tell me how did King Richard escape thine arm? Methought that arm of thine mought have crushed him like a gnat. Ha! trust me, thou needst have no fear that England should have lacked a monarch, if thou hadst chanced to have rid her of him who now reigns. But, blessed St. Erkenwold, what noise is that I hear? Holy St. Mary, grant that there be not spies about us!"

The door of the dungeon opened, a man entered, and the guards who brought him retreated, after again locking the door.

"Mortimer Sang!" cried Sir Patrick Hepborne; "what, I pray thee, hath brought thee hither? There was at least some spark of kindness in their thus admitting thee to visit thy master."

"Nay, not a whit, Sir Knight," replied Sang; "for albeit I am right glad to have the good fortune thus to share thy captivity, by St. Baldrid, I came thither as no matter of favour, seeing I am a prisoner like thyself."

"A prisoner!" cried Hepborne; "and what canst thou have done to merit imprisonment?"

"I sat up for thee yesternight, until I did become alarmed for thy safety, Sir Knight," replied Sang; "and knowing those who had the guard at the Tower gate, I made my way in, and was in the act of entering the Palace to inquire about thee, when, as I crossed the threshold, I was met by two friars, one of whom bore a lady in his arms. She was disguised in a monk's habit; but my recollection of Maurice de Grey, together with what your worship hath told me, made me recognize her at once as the Lady Beatrice. The Franciscan who carried her——"

"Franciscan!" cried Hepborne. "What! he who came to Lochyndorbe to denounce the Bishop of Moray's threatened excommunication against Lord Badenoch?"

"The same," replied Sang.

"Then," cried Hepborne in distraction, "then hath the hapless lady's murder been made the consummation of their guilt.

That friar was an assassin. He did once attempt her life at midnight. Ah, would I could break through these walls, to sacrifice him who hath been the author of a deed so foul ; would I were led forth to death, for that alone can now give relief to my misery. But," continued he, turning reproachfully to his esquire, " how couldst thou behold her whom my soul adores thus borne to her death, and not strike one blow for her deliverance ? "

" Nay, verily I did rush to her rescue, Sir Knight," replied Sang ; " but ere I could reach her, I was beset by some dozen of the guards from the Palace, and, ere I wist, I was beaten to the earth, captured, and thrown into a vault, where I lay for the remainder of the night, and whence I have been this moment brought hither, being accused of treason, in attempting to enter the Royal Palace at midnight, with intent to kill the King."

Hepborne threw himself down on his straw, and yielded himself up to the full flood of the affliction that came on him with the thought of the Lady Beatrice's fate. He reproached himself in a thousand ways for not having prevented that over which he could have had no control ; and neither his esquire nor Master Lawrence Ratcliffe could succeed in giving him the smallest consolation.

CHAPTER LXVI.

A Ship of Olden Times—Tempest Tossed—Arrival at the Maison Dieu in Elgin.

THE bark which we left threading its way down the mazes of the Thames made a tedious and difficult passage northwards along the coast of England. It was sometimes borne on by favouring breezes, but it often encountered furious contrary blasts that compelled the dauntless Mercer, its commander, to yield before them, and to submit to be driven back for many a league. We must not forget that naval architecture and nautical science were then, comparatively speaking, in their infancy. The hull of this Scottish privateer, or pirate, as she was called by the English, was awkwardly encumbered by two enormous erections. One of these, over the stern, is still recognized in some degree in the poop of our larger ships. Of the other, called the forecastle, although nothing now remains but the name, it was then in reality a tower of considerable height,

34

manned during an engagement by cross-bow men, who were enabled to gall the enemy very severely from that elevated position. The masts were three, one rising from the middle of the vessel, and the others from the two extremities, each formed of one thick short tree, the mainmast being the largest. At the upper end of each mast was fixed a circular stage, walled strongly in with wood ; these were called the round-tops, and were large enough to admit of several warriors being stationed in them. Each mast had but one sail hanging from its yard, and that attached to the mainmast was the only sheet of magnitude.

"Ha ! what sayest thou now, Barnard ?" exclaimed Mercer, slapping on the shoulder his steersman, an old sailor, who had served him and his father before him for some fifty years in the same capacity, and whose back was bent by his constant position at the helm ; "methinks this is the only breeze that hath promised to be steady during these fourteen days of our wearisome voyage. An it do but last for some good hour or twain, we may hope to see the other side of St. Abb's yonder."

"Ay," replied Barnard, casting his eye over his left shoulder, "but I like not yonder wide-flaming cloud that doth heave itself up so i' the sou'-west, Master Mercer. I'm no sailor an it be not big with something worse than aught we have had yet to deal with."

"Come, come, no evil-omened croaking, Master Barnard," replied Mercer ; "should the breeze freshen, we shall speed but the faster."

"Nay, but I do tell thee, there is some cruel ill-nature yonder," said Barnard, sticking testily to his point.

"By St. Rule, but it doth look somewhat angry," replied Mercer. "We must get more under the lee of the land ere the mischief cometh."

"By St. Paul, but it doth come already," cried Barnard ; "seest thou not yonder white-topped waves tripping after us ?'

"By the mass, but it doth come indeed," cried Mercer, jumping forward. "Ha, there goeth the foresail flying through the air like a sea-mew. Down with the mainsail. Come, stir ye, stir ye, my hearts. Out with your long-sweeps, my brave spirits—put her head to the land, Barnard. Pull yarely now, my gallants. There is a lull yonder beneath the rocks."

" 'Tis a lull thou wilt never reach, I'll promise thee, Master Mercer, pull as thou wilt," said old Barnard gruffly. "Better let her drive to the open sea before the storm. See how angry yonder sinking sun doth look. Trust me, no human power may force her against the tempest. But thou art ever for working impossibilities."

"Tush, old man," cried Mercer; " time enow to give in when we shall have tried and failed. I have no fancy for a run to Norway, if by any means we may reach the bonny Frith o' Forth. So put her head more to the land, I say."

In obedience to the command of his resolute master, the old helmsman, grumbling like a bear, put the bark into the course he had ordered, and the mariners, aided by the pike and crossbow men, put their hands steadily to the long oars. The brave Mercer moved actively about, giving life and spirit to their exertions. The storm rapidly increased, and he climbed the forecastle to look out ahead.

"Mercy on us," cried old Barnard, " there burneth a blue flame at the foremast head. 'Tis gone. Some one is near his end, I trow. Run, boy, and tell the master to come down. He is, as it were, mine own son, and I like not to see him yonder after that dismal warning."

The ship-boy carried the steersman's message, but Mercer laughed and heeded it not.

"Here, Peter Patullo, do thou take the helm a bit," cried the old man, becoming anxious. "He is so wilful, I must go to him myself."

Barnard had hardly spoken, when a tremendous wave came rolling on against the head of the ship, and striking the forecastle, a dreadful crash followed, the huge timber tower being swept away like a cobweb.

"Holy Mother of God, he is gone," cried Barnard. "My master—Oh! the boy I nursed, as I may say. Ha, see'st thou nought of Him?" cried the distracted old man, running to the lee-side of the ship, which was drifting broadside on, from the sudden cessation of the panic-struck rowers. "Ha, he's there; I see him; I saw him as he was heaved up on the bosom of the billow. I'll save him, or I'll perish with him."

"Stop him," cried the Franciscan, who had rushed from the cabin on hearing the confused cry; "stop him, he plunges to certain destruction."

But old Barnard was too alert for them all. He was overboard ere any of them could reach him.

"Madman," cried the Franciscan, hastily picking up a rope; and as the sea lifted up the bulky form of the old skipper, who hung for some moments poised as it were on the crest of the wave, he, with great dexterity, threw a coil over him, and Barnard was dragged most miraculously on board, being unwillingly saved from his rash, though generous, but utterly hopeless attempt.

Meanwhile the brave Mercer was borne away, seemingly to certain destruction. Everything was done by the active Franciscan to bring the bark near him. He was seen, now tossed on the high top of a mountainous surge, and now far down in the gulf out of which it had swelled itself. Sometimes he was thrown violently towards them, and again he was whirled far away with the velocity of thought; yet amidst all the horrors of the apparently inevitable death that surrounded him, he struggled with a calmness that showed his undaunted soul, and seemed determined to husband his strength as long as hope remained. A rope with a noose upon it was thrown to him. He had watched the endeavours his friends were making to save him, and he now exerted all his strength and skill to aid them. After many an unsuccessful effort, he at last caught the rope, and, with great adroitness, passed the noose over his head and arms. The Franciscan and the half-frantic helmsman, aided by some of the crew, began to pull him gently towards the vessel. A long rolling wave came and dashed him against the ship's side. He was hastily pulled up—but life was for ever extinct.

The deepest grief fell upon the crew when they beheld their beloved commander thus stretched inanimate before them; and they forgot their own safety and that of the vessel in their affliction for his loss. Poor old Barnard hung over the dripping corpse of his master, and seemed to be utterly unconscious of all that was passing around him.

"Alas!" he cried, looking in his face, and putting back his drenched locks with his rough hand as he said so, "would I had but sunk ere I had beheld thee so. I had never the blessing of wife or of children, but I did esteem thy father as my son; yea, and thou wert as the grandchild of mine old age. Thou didst grow to be a man under mine own especial nurture. I had pride and pleasure in thy gallantry and in thy success. Right cheerfully did I work for thee; ay, and would have worked for thee whiles my old timbers did hang together; but now, sith thou art gone, I have but little tie to this world. I care not how soon I weigh anchor for the land of souls; for what have I, a poor old lonesome man, to do here without thee; Let fresher hands take the watch, for—I—I—" his feelings overcame his hardy nature for a moment, but he recovered himself. "Take care no harm comes over his corpse," cried he, looking sternly round upon his shipmates. "Let it be laid decently out in his own berth—and—and——" His voice again became choked—he coughed—he put his hands to his eyes—and turning hastily away, disappeared into the hole that was his usual place of repose, to bury his emotions in darkness and silence.

After the loss of Mercer, there was an utter confusion and want of system among the under officers and crew, until the Franciscan monk boldly assumed the command. Many of those on board had sailed with him in the days of old Mercer, and being well acquainted with his resolute mind, as well as with his nautical knowledge, they scrupled not to obey him. He was indefatigable in his exertions ; but nothing he could do availed, and he was compelled to allow the bark, crazed as she was, to drift before the wind with every fear of her foundering.

Dreadful was the night that ensued, and anxiously did every soul on board long for morning, but when it came it was like a mimic night. The clouds hung darkly over the sea, as if about to mingle with it. Torrents of rain fell ; and the waves arose like peaked mountains, their whitened tops piercing the black vault of the clouds. The tempestuous wind seemed to shift from one point to another ; and they were so tossed to and fro that they became bewildered, and could not even avail themselves of the imperfect needle then in use. Land they could see none ; and when the second night fell upon them, each man gave his soul to the care of the Virgin or his patron saint, persuaded that there was but little chance of ever seeing another sun.

Meanwhile the hardy Franciscan never quailed, nor did he ever leave the deck. Little could be done to aid the ship, but he ceased not to encourage the mariners, both by his voice and his example.

At last the tempest seemed to yield. The wind became hushed, and although the swell of the sea continued for some hours, yet it diminished every moment, and went on gradually moderating until daybreak. By this time the sky had cleared itself of the clouds that had hitherto obscured it, the sun rose above the horizon in full splendour, and a faint hope arose with it that the vessel might yet be saved. But no land was yet visible. The needle was consulted, and it was determined to hoist the mainsail, and to avail themselves of an eastern breeze, to steer in that direction where they knew the British coast must lie ; and two men, who were placed in the round-top to look out a-head, soon cheered them with the intelligence that the land was visible ; upon which they gave thanks to Heaven,

and, as they scudded gently before the breeze, the blue mountains began to appear in the distant haze, and were swelling
every moment upon their sight.

Now it was that some of the older men in the ship came to
inform the Franciscan that it had been the wish of Mercer,
repeatedly expressed during his life, that wherever he might
die, he should, if possible, be buried at sea; and, since the
cessation of the storm permitted them to have some leisure, the
monk gave directions accordingly to prepare for the solemn rite.
Old Barnard had never appeared since the moment he left the
deck after the catastrophe that befel Mercer, and the struggle
the crew had been maintaining ever since with the angry
elements had hindered any one from visiting him where he had
retreated. He was now sent for; but the sailor who went for
him speedily returned with a face of alarm, to report that he
could get no answer from him. The Franciscan then lighted a
lamp, and went below, followed by several anxious faces. There
lay the old man, wrapped up in a blanket, in his berth. His
head was turned from them. The Franciscan shook him gently,
but he stirred not. He then turned him round, and the light
of the lamp fell upon his face. It was ghastly—the eyes were
glazed, and the rough features fixed in death. He seemed to
have died soon after he had lain down; but whether he had
suffered some fatal injury in his noble attempt to save Mercer,
or whether he had died of a broken heart for the loss of the
brave young man, to whom he was so much attached, it was
impossible to say.

Preparations were made for bestowing upon old Bernard the
same funeral rites as were contemplated for his master. The
religious duties were performed over both by the Franciscan,
and both were consigned together to the deep amidst the tears
that fell from many a weather-beaten face.

The breeze continued, and the distant mountains grew every
moment more and more distinct; but long ere they had
approached the land sufficiently near to enable them to determine what part of the coast they were borne towards, a thick
fog arose, and put an end to every speculation on the subject,
by shutting it entirely from their eyes. The vessel laboured
exceedingly, from her shattered condition, and there was no hope
of safety left for them but to avail themselves to the utmost of
the favourable breeze that still continued to blow. It lasted
them bravely, and carried them cheerily on until sunset, but then
it fell calm; and the mist clearing away, the moon arose, and
showed them a bold coast some miles to the south. Farther on

the land became lower, and thither the Franciscan made the crew pull with all their might. As they neared the land, the Lady Beatrice was brought out, half-dead, upon the deck, to be prepared for disembarking immediately, the frail vessel beginning every moment to show more alarming symptoms of the shattered state to which the continued storm had reduced it. They now beheld the lights in some fishermen's huts on shore, and the distant murmur of the waves, breaking gently on the beach, was the cheering music of hope to them. All at once the vessel struck upon some sunken rock or sand, and instantly began to fill. The confusion was dreadful. The Franciscan approached Beatrice, and quickly made her sensible of her danger. The boat was got out, but it was instantly overloaded—sunk—and all were in the water.

"Hold fast by my cowl, and fear not," cried the Franciscan, who had the wisdom to stick to the vessel, and who now committed himself to the waves, as it went down under them. Where all were men accustomed to the sea, all were necessarily swimmers, and all made lustily for the shore. Thither also did the bold monk press his way, the Lady Beatrice hanging with the gripe of fate to his cowl; and the distance being but short, and the sea smooth, she was soon placed in safety upon the beach, whence he quickly carried her to the fishermen's cottages.

The poor inhabitants of the fishing hamlet did all in their power to cherish the unfortunate people who were thus shipwrecked amongst them, but it was little they could do; and the comfort of a large fire was the utmost that any of the hovels could furnish. The Franciscan eagerly inquired what part of the coast they had been thrown on; and he declared that, since it had pleased the saints to deny them an entrance into the Frith of Forth, where lay their destination, he had reason to rejoice that they had taken land on the eastern coast of Moray. The Lady Beatrice, who had never held up her head during the tempestuous voyage, was grievously weakened by sickness. She sank down exhausted on the wretched pallet that was provided for her, and, eager as was the Franciscan to proceed with her to Elgin, the following day was far spent before she could gather strength enough to undertake even so short a ride. Horses were then procured, and they arrived at the gates of the Hospital of the Maison Dieu, where they were kindly received by the pious brethren and the sisterhood, who administered the hospitalities of the institutions to pilgrims and strangers of the better sort, as well as its charities to the poor.

CHAPTER LXVII.

*The Wolfe of Badenoch again—The Burning of Elgin
Cathedral.*

THE Franciscan left the Lady Beatrice with the nuns of the
establishment, and hastened to present himself before the
Bishop of Moray, who was then at his Palace of Spynie, at
some distance from the town. He found the good man in
deep conference with some of his canons, and he received
him joyfully.

"Blessed be St. Francis that thou art arrived, Friar John,"
said the Bishop aloud, after they had whispered together apart.
"Thou comest right seasonably, seeing we do discuss the endless
theme of the Wolfe of Badenoch."

"What! my Lord Bishop of Moray," cried the Franciscan,
"hath that destroying angel been again let loose, to invade the
holy territory of the Church?—to burn and to devastate?"

"Nay, nay, Friar John," replied the Bishop, "for this time
the news we have to tell thee are good. The King hath sent
a body of troops to dispossess his sacrilegious son from our
Badenoch lands, and they are now again in the hands of the
tenants of the Church. What sayest thou to this?"

"Um," replied the Franciscan, doubtfully shaking his head—
"and do the King's troops tarry in Badenoch, to guard the possessions of the Church?"

"Nay, that I do not believe," replied the Bishop, "but methinks he will hardly try so daring an attempt again."

"Hast thou brought down his proud spirit, then, to entreat
on his knees for the removal of thine anathema?" demanded
the Friar.

"Nay, as well hope to make the eagle stoop to the earth, and
quail before me," replied the Bishop.

"In truth, then, my Lord Bishop," said the Franciscan,
"thou mayest as well hope to reclaim the eagle, so that he shall
sit on thy wrist like a falcon, as look for a peace from the Wolfe
of Badenoch."

"Dost thou indeed think so?" demanded the Bishop. "Methought that after his Royal father's reproof, and this his late
signal interference against him, we might have looked for peace.
Something must be tried, then. To thee, Friar John, we shall
look for counsel, and the sooner we do have it the better. So

shall we straightway ride with thee to Elgin, and summon a Chapter, that we may consider of this weighty matter."

The Franciscan accordingly returned to the town with the Bishop and his attendants, and such of the canons as were within call were immediately summoned. The Bishop then occupied his stall within the Chapter-House, supported by his Dean, Archdean, Chancellor, and Chanter ; and the other members having taken their places, they remained some hours in council. When the Chapter broke up, the Bishop held some private conference with the Franciscan, and then permitted him to go to his lodging in the Maison Dieu, whither he was happy to retire, being overpowered by exhaustion from his late fatigues, and glad to be at last allowed to seek the needful refreshment of a few hours' rest.

The vesper hymn had died away through the lengthened aisles of the venerable Cathedral ; every note of labour or of mirth was silenced within the town. The weary burghers were sunk in sleep, and even the members of the various holy fraternities had retired to their repose. No eye was awake, save those of a few individuals among the religious, who, having habits of more than ordinary severity of discipline, had doomed themselves to wear the hard pavement with their bare knees, and the hours in endless repetition of penitential prayers before the shrine of the Virgin, or the image of some favourite saint. Not even a dog was heard to stir in the streets. They were as dark, too, as they were silent ; for, with the exception of a feeble lamp or two, that burned in niches, before the little figures set up here and there for Popish worship, there was nothing to interrupt the deep obscurity that prevailed.

Suddenly the sound of a large body of horsemen was heard entering the town from the west. The dreams of the burghers were broken, and they were roused from their slumbers ; the casements were opened, one after another, as the band passed along, and many a curious head was thrust out. They moved on alertly, without talking; but although they uttered no sounds, and were but dimly seen, the clank of their weapons, and of their steel harness, told well enough that they were no band of vulgar, peace-loving merchants, but a troop of stirring men-at-arms ; and many was the cheek that blenched, and many was the ejaculation that escaped the shuddering lips of the timid burghers, as they shrunk within their houses at the alarming conviction. They crossed and blessed themselves after the warriors had passed by, and each again sought his bed.

But the repose of the inhabitants was for that night doomed

to be short.   Distant shrieks of despair, mingled with shouts of
exultation, began to arise in the neighbourhood of the Cathedral
and the College, in which all the houses of the canons were
clustered ; and soon the town was alarmed from its centre to
its suburbs by the confused cries of half-naked fugitives, who
hurried along into the country, as if rushing from some dreadful
danger.

"Fire, fire !—murder !—fire, fire !—the Wolfe of Badenoch !"

The terrible name of the fell Earl of Buchan was enough, of
itself, to have spread universal panic through the town, even in
the midst of broad sunshine.   But darkness now magnified their
fears.   Every one hastened to huddle on what garments might
be at hand, and to seize what things were most valuable and
portable ; and all, without exception—men, women, and children
—hurried out into the streets, to seek immediate safety in
flight.   As the crowd pressed onwards, scarcely daring to look
behind them, they beheld the intense darkness of the night
invaded by flames that began to shoot upwards in fitful jets.
The screams and the shouts rang in their ears, and they
quickened their trembling speed ; their voices subdued by
fear, as they went, into indistinct whispers of horror.   No
one dared to stop ; but, urging on his own steps, he dragged
after him those of his feeble parents, or tottering wife, or
helpless children.

Those who were most timorous, halted not until they had
hid themselves in the neighbouring woods ; but those whose
curiosity was in some degree an equipoise to their fears, stopped
to look behind them whenever a view of the town could be obtained, that they might judge of, and lament over, the devastation that was going forward.   Already they could see that the
College, the Church of St. Giles, and the Hospital of the Maison
Dieu, were burning ; but these were all forgotten, as they beheld
the dire spectacle of the Cathedral, illuminated throughout all
the rich tracery of its Gothic windows by a furious fire, that
was already raging high within it.   Groans and lamentations
burst from their hearts, and loud curses were poured out on the
impious heads of those whose fury had led them to destroy so
glorious a fabric, an edifice which they had been taught to
venerate from their earliest infancy, and to which they were
attached by every association, divine and human, that could
possibly bind the heart of man.   In the midst of their wailings,
the pitchy vault of heaven began to be reddened by the glare of
the spreading conflagration ; and the loud and triumphant
shouts that now arose, unmingled with those cries of terror

which had at first blended with them, too plainly told that the power of the destroyer was resistless.

As the Lady Beatrice and the Franciscan were the last comers among the crowd of pilgrims and travellers who that night filled the charitable caravansera of the Maison Dieu, they had been put to lodge in the very uppermost storey of the antique and straggling building. The lady occupied a chamber at the extremity of a long passage, running through one wing that was dedicated to the use of the few sisters who inhabited the Hospital, and their female guests. The Franciscan was thrust into a little turret room that hung from one angle of a gable at the very opposite end of the edifice, being connected with the garrets that lay over that wing occupied by the preaching brethren and the guests of their own sex. There was no direct communication between the opposite parts of the building where the lady and the friar were lodged. The main stair, that opened from the doorway of the Hospital, arose within the body of the house, and several narrow passages branched off from it, having separate stairs leading to the different parts of the higher regions.

The brethren and sisters of the institution, as well as the numerous temporary inmates of its various chambers, were alarmed by the shrieks that arose when the firebrands were at first applied to the Cathedral, and the houses of the clergy connected with it. Neither the permanent nor the accidental tenants of the house had much personal property to remove, and what they had was instantly carried out by a general rush into the courtyard, whence they hastily escaped, each prompted by a desire of self-preservation. Not so the Lady Beatrice and the Franciscan. Both of them had suffered so much from want of natural rest, and the monk especially had undergone fatigue of body so lengthened and so severe during the protracted storm they had lately had to struggle with, that they lay as unconscious of the noise as if their senses had been locked up by the influence of some powerful opiate. The Lady Beatrice, indeed, was half awakened by the din occasioned by the escape of those who were in the house. But she had been dreaming of the ship and of the sea, and the hurry of the retreating steps and the confused voice of alarm having speedily subsided within the Hospital, she turned again to enjoy a more profound repose, believing it was her fancy that had made her imagine she had heard the sound of the waves and the winds, and the bustling tread of the mariners.

Again a noise came that increased and jarred in her ears,

and a vivid light arose that flickered through the casement into the place where she lay, and falling strongly on her face, her silken eyelashes were gradually opened, and, terror seizing upon her, she sprang at once from her couch to the window. Then it was that she beheld the court of the Hospital below filled with mounted men-at-arms, together with numbers on foot, who seemed to be active agents in kindling combustibles, by the employment of which the whole main body of the building was already in flames—as she could easily guess from the suffocating smoke that arose, and the red glare that was thrown over the features of those who, with their faces turned upwards, were watching the progress of the devouring element with a fiendish expression of satisfaction.

Half-dead with fear, the Lady Beatrice began to hurry on her garments, doubtful, in the state of distraction she was thrown into, whether she might or ought to hope to escape from the fire, since she could not possibly do so without exposing herself to the fury of a savage band, whose present occupation was enough to proclaim them enemies of the most reckless description. She was bewildered, and knew not what to do. The towers and spires of the Cathedral were blazing like gigantic torches. The darkness of night seemed to be put to flight, and distant yells arising from time to time, proclaimed the multitude who were actors in this scene of ruin.

But the more pressing danger brought her at last to recollection, and she rushed from her chamber to make an effort to escape. Already were the narrow passages filled with a stifling smoke, which she made some faint efforts to penetrate; but finding it impossible to proceed, she returned to her chamber, and, throwing herself upon her knees, grew faint from despair. Recovering herself in some degree, she grasped her croslet, and began offering up her prayers for that mercy in the next world of which she believed she had now no hope in this; and, as she was so employed, she thought she felt the very boards heating beneath her. She sprang to her feet, and again approached the open casement, that she might breathe more freely. At that moment a loud murmur, rather than a cry, arose in the court below.

"He cometh—'tis he—'tis he himself.—The Earl—the Earl of Buchan—the Wolfe of Badenoch!—Hush!"—And their clamour was instantly silenced.

"Out o' my way," cried the Wolfe of Badenoch, as, armed cap-a-pie, and with his vizor up, he came galloping furiously in at the Gothic gateway, followed by his four younger sons, and some forty or fifty mounted spearmen and axemen. The pavement rattled under the clatter of their iron shod hooves, and their polished mail flashed back the blaze of the flaming edifice.

"Ha, ha, ha! by all the fiends, but the mischief doth work well here too," shouted he laughing wildly as he reined up his steed, with a check that threw him backwards on his haunches; "yet this is but baby's work compared to the blazing towers yonder—ha, ha, ha! The haughty pile on the which the pride of that scurvy Priest-Bishop hath heretofore been so loftily perched, will soon be prostrate amidst its own dust and ashes. Ha! by the beard of my grandfather, but it is a glorious vengeance. What was the brenning of Forres to this?—ha, ha, ha! Not a hole shall these corbies have to hide their heads in. Every nest polluted by these stinking carrions shall be levelled. Such be the fate of those who dare to contend with the Wolfe of Badenoch! But have all escaped from this burning house? I would not have the hair of a human head singed—not a hair of a head, I tell ye. Didst thou see all escape them hence?"

"I did, my noble Lord," replied one of his esquires, who had superintended the execution of this part of his commands; "with our own eyes did we see them, as we arrived, scour from the walls, like an army of mice from a hollow cheese."

"Ha! by my faith, but thou liest, villain," cried the Wolfe, turning hastily round, and levelling the speaker to the earth with one blow of his truncheon; "thou dost lie black as hell. By all that is unlucky, I did even now behold a female form at yonder window. Nay, now the smoke doth hide it; but—see, see—ha! why hath it been so, knaves? Did I not warn ye all that not a life should be tint?"

"Help, help, Lord Badenoch," cried the Lady Beatrice—"help, help, or I perish! The boards burn.—Help, help, for the love of mercy—for the love of the blessed Virgin, save me, save me!"

"By the holy mass, I should know that voice," cried the Wolfe of Badenoch; "nay, 'tis she indeed, or 'tis her wraith I do behold."

"'Tis some evil spirit, father," said Sir Andrew Stewart, who had accompanied his father in this expedition, not willingly, but because the Wolfe of Badenoch had resolved that he should have a share in it.

"Evil spirit!" cried the Wolfe, turning angrily around on him; "ha! 'tis thou who art the evil spirit, son Andrew. Thou darest not to look on her whom thou wouldst have injured. But, by this hand, thou shalt. The damsel shall not perish, if

I can help her. I will go rescue her, and thou, son Andrew, shalt follow me."

"Nay, try not anything so rash, father," exclaimed Sir Andrew Stewart, dreadfully alarmed to find that he was expected to participate in an attempt so desperate ; "the whole body of the house is in flames."

"What, villain," cried the Wolfe indignantly ; "so, thou couldst love the damsel to do her violence, and yet art base enow to shrink from the glorious achievement of saving her life, or perishing in the attempt.   Unworthy whelp of the Wolfe of Badenoch !   Dastard, dismount and in with me, or, by the blood of the Bruce, the spears of my men-at-arms shall goad thee to it."   And saying so, he sprang from his horse, while Sir Andrew Stewart, though half-dead with fear, was compelled to follow him with all the alertness that might have befitted a hero well stomached for the desperate undertaking.

"What, Andrew going thither !" cried Walter Stewart. leaping from his horse ; "by this hand, but I shall in too, then."

"And so shall I," cried James, following his brother's example.

"And by my beard that is to grow," cried the boy Duncan, "but I shall not be left behind."

"Nay, stay, Sir Duncan," cried an esquire.   "By the mass, but he is in after the others ; and what will my Lord say if anything doth befall him ?   He loveth the boy more than all the rest put together.   I'll in after him."   Upon which the man rushed in, followed by a crowd of the others, who were equally afraid of the rage that might fall upon their heads for having permitted the boy to escape from them.

And now a terrible scene ensued.   The crowd who entered soon wedged themselves in the narrow passages just within the doorway, so that they could neither advance nor retreat.   The smoke accumulated about them from the stoppage of its vent. They struggled and crushed, and poured out half-choked curses. Some fell, and were trampled under foot ; and at length the voice of the Wolfe was heard from within—

"Ha ! clear the passage, or I am suffocated ; clear the passage, villains, or I will murder ye all."

The fear of their violent master did for them what they could not before accomplish.   An unusual exertion on the part of those who were outermost extricated them from the doorway, and the passage being now less wedged, the force from within sent them all out headlong into the court, and out rushed the Wolfe, nearly spent by the continued suffocation he had endured.

"By all that is miraculous, I do believe that it was a spirit after all," said the Wolfe, half in soliloquy, as soon as he had gathered breath to speak ; "I did make my way to the chamber where she did appear, and she was not there ; nor was she anywhere else to be seen. Such tricks of fancy are often played by sprites. And how, after all, could she have been there—she who must be even now in Norham ? But, ha !" cried he aloud, "what figure is that I do now behold in yonder hanging towernet that doth blaze so fiercely ?"

All eyes were now directed towards the spot he had indicated, and there, to the astonishment of every one, appeared the form of the Franciscan, brightly illumined by the jets of flame that surrounded it.

"Holy Virgin !" cried his followers, crossing themselves, "'tis a sprite—'tis a devil. Mercy on us, 'tis no monk, but something unholy," cried half-a-dozen voices.

The teeth of the stern Wolfe himself were heard to chatter as he gazed on his old enemy, of the reality of whose present appearance he almost doubted. The keen eyes and strongly expressive countenance of the Friar were now wildly distorted by the alarm which had seized him, on suddenly awaking from the deep sleep he had been plunged in, and finding himself surrounded by all the horrors of the most dreadful of deaths. A red and unearthly light was thrown on his features, and broadly illumined his tonsure, giving him a most terrific and ghastly look. It was, therefore, little to be wondered that even the hardy-minded Wolfe of Badenoch should have for an instant believed that it was the Devil he beheld.

"By all the fiends of hell, 'tis wonderful !" cried he, as he stood fixed in a kind of stupor.

"Help, help !" cried the Franciscan.

"Ha !" cried the Wolfe, recovering himself, "if thou be'st in very deed the chough Friar, bren, bren, and welcome. But if thou be'st the Devil, thou mayest well enow help thyself."

"Help, in mercy help !" cried the Franciscan ; "a ladder, a ladder."

"A ladder !" cried the Wolfe, now sufficiently reassured, and becoming convinced that it really was the very Franciscan in true flesh who had so bearded him at Lochyndorbe, and no phantom nor demon. "Ha ! prating chough, is it thee, in troth? A ladder, saidst thou ? Thou couldst have lacked a ladder but for thy hanging, and now thou needst it not, seeing thou art in the way of dying a better death."

"Help, help!" cried the unfortunate wretch, who seemed hardly to have yet gained a knowledge of those who were below.

"Help!" repeated the Wolfe; "by my trusty burlybrand, but I shall hew down the first villain who doth but move to give thee help. What, did I say that no hair of life should be touched? By the blessed bones of mine ancestors, but there lacked only this accident to make my revenge complete. Ha, ha, ha! did I not swear, thou grey-hooded crow, that as thou didst escape from the pit of water, thou shouldst be tried next by the fire? By my head, I did little imagine that I should thus so soon see thee bren before mine eyes; and bren thou shalt, for no man of mine shall risk the singeing of his beard to pluck thee from the destruction thine atrocious tongue has so well merited."

The monk disappeared for some moments, and soon afterwards, to the astonishment of all, was seen making his way along the roof through volumes of flame and smoke. Every eye in the court below was turned towards him. It seemed impossible that anything but a demon could have clambered where he went. Again he was lost to their eyes, and anon he appeared in the very room which had been lately occupied by the Lady Beatrice. He shrieked out her name; was again invisible; and then, again, was seen in all the upper apartments, one after another. At last they saw him no longer.

"He is either the Devil himself, or he is brent by this time," whispered some of the awe-stricken followers of the Wolfe.

In an instant he again appeared on the top of the turret in which he had been first seen; the flames arose everywhere around him; terrible was his aspect, and an involuntary shudder crept through the silent crowd.

"Alexander Stewart, Earl of Buchan, and Lord of Badenoch," cried he with an appalling voice, whilst he threw his arms abroad, in an attitude befitting the denunciation he was about to pour out—"the red hand of thine iniquity hath again lifted the firebrand of destruction, but as thou hast kindled these holy piles dedicated to God, so shall the wrath of the Almighty be kindled against thee. The measure of thine iniquity is now full, and yonder flaming heavens do bear witness to thy crimes. Seest thou yonder fiery cloud that doth now float over thy devoted head? There sitteth the Angel of Vengeance, ready to descend on thee and thine. Prepare—for instant and direful punishment doth await thee."

The monk again disappeared. The Wolfe of Badenoch looked upwards to the sky, and beheld the fiery cloud that hung as it were over him. Fancy depicted in it a countenance that looked down upon him in terrible ire. He gnashed his teeth, and his features blackened. At that moment shrieks arose from the higher chambers of the building.

"Ha, ha, ha, ha!—let him die," cried the Wolfe, clenching his fists and laughing wildly; "let the villain die, I say."

The shrieks came again, and louder.

"Ha! what voice was that?" exclaimed the Wolfe, in an altered tone, and in considerable agitation.

"Help, help!" cried a voice, and a figure appeared at an upper window, in the midst of the flames.

"Oh God!" cried the Wolfe, in an agony, "my son, my son! —my dearest boy, Duncan? Save him, save him—save my child!"

With the fury of a maniac he rushed fearlessly towards the burning building. His people sprang after him. He had already reached the doorway, when the central stair fell with a tremendous crash within; and had not his followers dragged him back the instant before, he must have been crushed beneath the descending ruin.

"Father, father!" cried a piteous voice from the ground.

"Walter," cried the unhappy Wolfe of Badenoch, running to lift up his son, "what hath befallen thee?—Speak."

"I was knocked down and crushed by the men-at-arms as they rushed outwards," said the youth faintly; "I do feel as if I had tane some sore inward bruises."

"Merciful God!" cried the miserable father, removing his son farther from the danger. "But where is James?" demanded he, looking wildly about him.

"He also fell near me," said Walter.

The attendants now ran forward, and amongst several wounded people who lay on the pavement they found and raised James Stewart, who was only known to be alive by his quick breathing. But the distracted father had little leisure to attend to either of these his wounded sons, and in an instant they were abandoned to the care of those about him; for the boy Duncan, his youngest and his darling child, the pride of his heart, was again heard to shriek from an upper window. The flames were rioting triumphantly within, and every possible approach to him was cut off.

35

"Ladders, ladders!" cried he, in a frenzy; and his people set off in a hopeless search of what he called for.

"Ladders!" cried the Franciscan, with a voice like thunder, as he unexpectedly appeared behind the boy; "ladders! how dost thou dare to call for that help which thou didst refuse to yield to others? Now doth thy fiendish joy begin to be transmewed into mourning, thou accursed instrument in the hands of an incensed God. Already do two of thy lawless brood lie on that pavement, to be carried home with thee to linger and die; and now this child, thy youngest and dearest, shall be lost to thee by a more speedy fate." He caught up the boy in his sinewy arms with a savage laugh of triumph, and held him aloft with a gripe so powerful, that his puny efforts to escape were utterly hopeless. "Ha, ha, ha! now may I laugh in my turn," cried the Franciscan, with a yell that struck to the heart of the Wolfe of Badenoch, and subdued him at once.

"Mercy!" cried he, clasping his hands and wringing them together, and his breath came thick and laborious, so that he could hardly find utterance, as he looked up with stretched eyeballs, expecting every instant to behold the horrible spectacle of his best beloved son's destruction. "Mercy!—fiend!—ha!—Ladders, ladders!—Oh, mercy, mercy!—Oh, spare my boy!—Oh, mercy, mercy—mercy on my boy!" He sank down on his knees, his broad chest heaving to his very cuirass with its labouring respiration, and his lips moving, even after all power of utterance was denied him.

"Ha! mercy, saidst thou?" cried the Franciscan, with a contemptuous smile and a glaring eye; "what, mercy to thee—to thee, who hath no mercy!—mercy to thee, who hath incurred God's highest wrath!—mercy to thee, who hath wrapped all these holy buildings, and these dwellings of God's peaceful servants and people, in impious flames!—thou, who wert but now revelling in the hellish joy of thy daring sacrilege—mercy to thee!—mercy meanly begged, too, from him whom thou didst but this moment doom to the most cruel death! Ha, ha, ha! But my life or death is not in thy weak power to withhold. My life will be preserved by Him who gave it, that it may yet fulfil the purpose for which He did bestow it. Thy fate doth hang in my grasp, and the gripe which I do now hold of this frail fragment of thyself," continued he, lifting up the trembling boy in a terrific manner, "is but a symbol of the power which God hath given me over thee to force thee to repentance."

"Oh, spare, spare, spare!" cried the miserable Lord of Badenoch, bereft of all thought but of his son's fate.

The boy screamed for help, but the ruthless Franciscan laughed savagely, and then sprang backwards with him through the flames.

The wretched Lord of Badenoch remained fixed on his knees, his face still turned upwards, and his eyes fastened on the casement so lately occupied by the figures of the Franciscan and his lost boy. It was now filled by a sheet of brilliant flame. His lips muttered, and "Mercy—oh, mercy!" were still the only words that escaped them. His followers crowded around him in dismay, the whole group being broadly illuminated by the fire, which had now gained complete mastery over the interior of the building.

CHAPTER LXVIII.

The Bishop's Palace at Spynie—The Wolfe gets a Surprise.

THE wretched Wolfe of Badenoch was slowly raised by those who were about him; and he submitted, as if altogether unconscious of what they were doing. His features were immoveable, and his eyes vacant, until they rested on his two sons, Walter and James, who lay wounded in the arms of his servants.

"Where is my son Andrew?" cried he, suddenly recovering the use of speech.

The attendants muttered to one another, but no one answered him.

"Speak, ye knaves," cried he, grinding his teeth, and at the same time springing on them, and seizing one of them in each hand by the throat; "villains, I will choke ye both with my grasp if ye answer me not."

"My noble Lord," cried the men, terrified by his rage and his threats, "we saw him enter the burning building with thee, but none of us saw him issue thence."

"Villains, villains, tell me not so!" cried the Wolfe, shaking the two men from him, and sending them reeling away with such force that both were prostrated on the earth. "What, hath he too perished?—And it was I who did myself compel him thither!" and, saying so, he struck his breast, and moved about rapidly through the court, giving vent to a frenzy of self accusation.

"Ha!" cried he, halting suddenly, as he heard the clang of horses' heels approaching; "who comes there?—Alexander—my son—thou art all that is left to me now;" and springing forward, he clasped the knees of Sir Alexander Stewart, who at that moment appeared, followed by the whole of his force.

"Why tarriest thou here, father?" demanded his son; "depardieux, but I have sought thee around all the glorious fires we have kindled. Little did I think to find thee here in this by-corner, looking on so paltry a glede as this, when the towers of the Cathedral do shoot out flames that pierce the heavens, and proclaim thy red vengeance on the Bishop of Moray, yea, even to his brother-mitred priest of Ross, even across the broad friths that do sunder them.—Come with me, I pray, and ride triumphant through the flaming streets, that our shouts may ring terribly in the craven corbie's ears, and reach him even where he doth hide him in his Palace of Spynie.— But what aileth thee, father, that thou seemest so unmanned."

"Alexander," cried the afflicted father, embracing his son, who stooped over him, "thy brethren have perished; Walter and James are there dying from their bruises, and Andrew and Duncan—my beloved boy Duncan—have perished in these flames."

"How, what! how hath this happened?" cried Sir Alexander, leaping from his horse and running to question the attendants who supported his two wounded brothers. From them he gathered a brief account of the events that had occurred, and for some moments gave way to the sorrow that afflicted his father.

"But why grieve we here, my Lord?" cried he suddenly; "of a truth, whatever woe hath befallen us, hath but come by reason of that ill-starred enemy of our house, Bishop Barr, who has driven us to the desperation out of which all these evils have arisen. He and his accursed flock of ill-omened crows have flown to the refuge of his Palace of Spynie. Rouse, my noble father, and let us gallop thither and seek a sweet revenge by pulling the choughs from their nests."

"Right, son Alexander," cried the Wolfe, his native temper being so far roused for the moment by this speech that he shook off the torpor that had come upon him, and sprang into his saddle; "by this beard, but thou dost say right. 'Tis indeed that accursed Priest-Bishop who hath embittered the whole stream of my life, and hath now been the cause of hurling all this misery upon me. Alas, my poor boys!—But, by the blood of the Bruce, they shall be avenged.—I shall take thy counsel, my son—My son, said I?—Alas, Alexander, thou wilt soon, I fear, be mine only son.—Dost hear, Sir Squire?" said he, turning fiercely to one of his attendants, "See that thou dost take care of my wounded boys. Take people enow with thee, and see that they be promptly and tenderly carried on men's shoulders to Lochyndorbe—Dost thou mark me?—Thy head shall pay the forfeit of thy neglect of the smallest tittle of thy duty."

"Ay," cried Sir Alexander Stewart, "our business, I trow, will soon be sped, and we shall overtake them before they shall have gone many miles of the way."

"Come, then, Alexander, let's to Spynie," cried the Wolfe; and then turning again to the esquire—"But take care of my boys, and see that they be gently borne."

"On, brave spears," cried Sir Alexander; "ye shall have work peraunter to do anon."

Out dashed the Wolfe of Badenoch, gnashing his teeth, as if to wind himself up to desperation, yet rather led than followed by Sir Alexander Stewart, and away rattled about two hundred well-armed and well-mounted men-at-arms at their backs, leaving behind them a sufficient force to escort the wounded youths homeward in safety. There were but few among the troops that would not have willingly stayed behind. They liked not this ungodly warfare, and although they witnessed the execution of the Wolfe of Badenoch's fell fury on the holy edifices, done by a few of the less scrupulous ministers of his vengeance, they felt conscience-stricken at the sight, and this feeling had not been diminished by the denunciations of the Franciscan, the direful fate of the boy Duncan Stewart, and of his brother Sir Andrew, and that which had befallen the youths Walter and James, of whose recovery there seemed to be but little hope.

The Palace of Spynie offered them but a wretched defence against any assailant who might choose to attack it, for it was not till the following century that it was so strengthened as to enable Bishop David Stuart* to defy the proud Earl of Huntly. The buildings, indeed, were surrounded by a wall; but, trusting to that awe which the sacred dignity of the possessor was calculated to inspire, the wooden gate was left unprotected by any portcullis of iron. It therefore promised to be easily assailable by the sledge-hammers which had been found so useful in furthering the work of destruction they had already accomplished.

The Wolfe of Badenoch, hurried on by his son, swept over

---

* Having some debates with the Earl of Huntly, he laid him under ecclesiastical censure, which so provoked the Gordons that they threatened to pull the Bishop out of his pigeon-holes. "I will build a house," said the Bishop, "out of which neither the Earl nor his clan shall pull me," and he accordingly erected that strong tower still known by the name of Davy's Tower. Even the present walls were of date posterior to that alluded to in the text.

the gentle eminence lying between the town and the palace, and as the distance was but a mile, his excitement had had hardly time to expend itself ere he found himself approaching the walls. The lurid red vault of the sky reflected a dim light, which might have been sufficient to enable them to discover the building before them. But, independently of this, the summit of the outer walls was lined by a number of torches, which began to flit about hastily, as soon as the thundering sound of the horses' feet reached those who carried them.

"The place doth seem to be already alarmed," cried the Wolfe of Badenoch, as they advanced, his resolute soul shaken by his recent calamities. "These lights are not wont to appear on the grass-grown walls of these mass-ensconced priests. Thou shalt halt here, son Alexander, and let me advance alone to reconnoitre. I cannot, I wis, afford to peril the life of thee, whom my fears do tell me I may now call mine only son."

"Peril my life?" cried Sir Alexander indignantly; "what, talkest thou of peril, when we have but these carrion crows to deal with? I trow there be garrison enow of them, sith that all their rookeries, grey, black, and hooded, have doubtless gathered there to-night. By my knighthood, but it doth almost shame me to attack them with harness on my back, or men-at-arms at my heels. And see, the lights have disappeared. Never trust me, but those who did flourish them have fled into the deepest cellar of the place, at the very tramp of our war-steeds."

"Nay, but, son Alexander," repeated the Wolfe, "I do command thee to halt; thou shalt not advance until I shall have first——Where hath he vanished?" cried the Wolfe, losing sight of him for a moment in the dark. "Ha! there he speeds him to the gate," and, leaping from his saddle, he launched himself after his son. Sir Alexander had snatched a sledge-hammer from some one near him, and was already raising it to strike the first blow at the gate, when his right arm fell shattered and nerveless by his side, and he was crushed to the earth by some unseen power. The Wolfe of Badenoch reached his son but to raise him up in his arms. At that moment a broad blaze arose on the top of the wall, immediately over the gateway, in front of which the Wolfe of Badenoch stood appalled by the apparition it illumined, and he grew deadly pale when he beheld the figure of the Franciscan, of that very friar whom he believed nothing but superhuman power could have saved from the flames of the Maison Dieu, again presented before his eyes. The attitude of the monk was fearfully

commanding. He reared a large crucifix in his left hand,
whilst the other was stretched out before him. The light by
which he was encircled shot around him to a great distance,
showing the walls thickly manned with crossbow-men prepared
to shoot upon the assailants, and exhibiting these assailants
themselves with their faces turned to what they believed to be
a miraculous vision, which filled them with a terror that no
merely human array could have awakened.

" Alexander Stewart, Earl of Buchan, and Lord of Badenoch,"
cried the Franciscan, in his wonted clear but solemn voice,
" have I not told thee that the Omnipotent hath resigned thee
and thine into my grasp for penance or for punishment ? Go,
take thy wounded son with thee, sith that thou hast sought this
fresh affliction. His life and the lives of those who are now
borne to thy den hang on thy repentance."

A hissing sound was heard—a dense vapour arose—and all
was again dark as before. Some of the Wolfe of Badenoch's
terrified attendants ventured to approach the gate to assist him.
They carried Sir Alexander away ; and the ferocious Earl,
again subdued from the high wrath to which his son's sudden
excitation had for a moment raised his native temper, relapsed
into that apathetical stupor from which he had been roused.
He seemed to know not what he was doing, or where he was ;
but, mechanically mounting his horse, he retired from the walls
of Spynie, and took his way slowly homewards. As the distant
conflagration flashed from time to time on his face, he started
and looked towards it with wild expression—and then elevated
his eye towards his son, who was carried on a bier formed of
crossed lances, by some men on foot ; but excepting when he
was so moved, his features were like those of the stone effigy
which now lies stretched upon his tomb.

The Bishop and the dignitaries of the Cathedral who composed his Chapter, had assembled in fear and trembling in the
Chapel of the Palace, where they offered up prayers for deliverance from their scourge ; and the Wolfe of Badenoch and his
formidable party were no sooner ascertained to have permanently
withdrawn, than they issued forth, bearing some of the most
holy of their images, with the most precious relics of saints,
which had been hastily snatched from their shrines on the first
alarm of the enemy's approach, and began to move in melancholy procession towards Elgin, guarded by the armed vassals
of the Church, who had been summoned to man the Palace
walls. As they rose over the hill, they beheld the flames still
raging in all their fury. The sun was by this time rising over

the horizon, but his rays added little to the artificial day that
already possessed the scene. The smiling morning, indeed,
served to show the extent of the devastation which the flames
had already occasioned; but the cheerful matin song of the
birds accorded ill with the wailings that burst from those who
beheld this dismal spectacle. The pride of the Bishop, if the
good man ever had any, was indeed effectually humbled. As
he rode on his palfrey at the head of the sad procession, the
reins held by two attendants, one of whom walked on each side
of him, he wept when he came within view of the town ; and,
ordering them to halt, he crossed his hands meekly over his
breast, and looked up in silent ejaculation to Heaven.

" *O speculum patriæ et decus regni,*" cried he, turning his
eyes again towards the Cathedral, whilst the tears rolled over
his cheeks. " Oh, glory and honour of Scotland—thou holy
fane, which we, poor wretched mortals, did fondly believe to be
a habitation worthy of the omnipotent and mysterious Trinity,
to whom thou wast dedicated—behold thee, for the sins of us
the guilty servants of a just God, behold thee yielded up a prey
to the destroyer ! Oh, holy Father, and do thou, blessed Virgin
Mother, cause our prayers to find acceptance at the Almighty
throne, through the merits of thy beloved Son—may we, thy
sinful creatures, be humbled before this thine avenging arm :
and may the fasts, penances, and mortifications we shall impose
be the means of bringing us down, both body and soul, unto the
dust, that thy just wrath against us may be assuaged; for
surely some great sin hath beset us, seeing it hath pleased thee
to destroy thine own holy temple, that our evil condition might
be made manifest to us."

Those who formed the procession bent reverently to the
ground as the venerable prelate uttered these words.

" And now, my sons," said he with a sigh, " let us hasten
onwards, and do what we can to preserve what may yet have
escaped from the general destruction."

The first care of the good Bishop was to collect the scattered
townsmen, who had already begun to cluster in the streets ; and
every exertion was immediately used to put a stop to the
conflagration. The Franciscan was there, but his attention was
occupied with something very different from that which so
painfully interested every one else. The Lady Beatrice—was
she safe? At the risk of his life he had clambered over the
blazing roof of the Maison Dieu to seek her in her chamber.
She was gone from thence. He had searched anxiously through
all the upper apartments of the building, and yet he had seen

no trace of her. Full of alarm, he had been compelled to rest on the hope that she might have escaped with others from the flames ; and, with an unspeakable anxiety to have that hope confirmed, he went about inquiring impatiently of every one he met, whether any damsel, answering to the description of the Lady Beatrice, had been seen; but of all those to whom he addressed himself, there was no one who could say that she was known to have escaped.

"Miserable wretch that I am," said he, "have her sins then been punished by so terrible a death—sins for the which I myself must be called to dread account both here and hereafter—I who deprived her of the blessing of a virtuous mother's counsel, and of a father's powerful protection ? Holy St. Francis forgive me, the thought is agony."

He sat him down on a stone in the court of the Maison Dieu, and he was soon joined by sister Marion, the lame housekeeper of the Hospital, who came to mourn over its smouldering ruins.

"Oh, dear heart and alas !" cried the withered matron— "the blessed St. Mary defend, protect, and be good unto us— and there is a dole sight to be sure. Under that very roof hae I been housed and sheltered, come the feast of Our Lady, full forty—— nay, I should hae said fourteen years and upwards, and now I am to be turned out amidst the snares and temptations of this wicked world, to be the sport and the pastime of the profligate and ungodly. What will become of us, to whose lot beauty hath fallen as a snare, and fair countenance as an aid to the Evil One ? Where, alas ! shall we hide our heads that we fall not in the way of sinners? Where——"

"Tell me, sister !" cried the Franciscan, impatiently interrupting her—" tell me, didst thou see the Lady Beatrice, whom I escorted hither yesterday ?"

"Yea, in good verity, did I that, brother," replied Marion.

"Where ?—where and when ?" cried the anxious Franciscan.

"Nay, be not in such a flurry, brother," replied she. "I did first see her in the refectory when thou didst bring her there, and a pretty damsel she be, I trow."

"Nay, but didst thou see her after the fire ?" demanded the Franciscan.

"In very deed, nay, brother," replied the literal sister, Marion.

"Wretch that I am," cried the Franciscan, in an agony of suspense, "hath then no one seen her escape ?"

"St. Katherine help us, an thou dost talk of her escape,

indeed, thou comest to the right hand in me," replied she, "sith that it was I myself who did show her how to escape ; but that was neither before nor after the fire, I promise thee, but in the very height of the brenning, when the flames were bursting here, and crackling there— and the rafters——"

" Nay, tell me, I entreat thee, sister," cried the Franciscan, interrupting her, though greatly relieved—" tell me how and where she did save herself ? "

" But I do tell thee thou art wrong, brother," cried the peevish old woman, "for it was in no such ways, seeing, as I said before, it was I myself that did save her, But thou art so flustrificacious ; an thou wouldst but let me tell mine own tale——"

" Go on then, I pray thee, sister Marion," cried the monk, curbing his ire, and patiently resuming his seat upon the stone ; " take thine own way."

"In good troth, my way is the right way," replied sister Marion. " Well, as I was a-saying, I was sound asleep in my bed, in the back turret at the end of the passage, when cometh the Lady Beatrice to my room, and did shake, shake at me; and up did I start, for luckily for me I had taken an opiate, tincture, or balsam, the which the good cellarer doth give me ofttimes for the shooting toothache pain (but, alas ! I doubt it be all burnt now), and so I had somehow lain down in my clothes ; and then came the cries of the people, and the smoke and flame—and so I did bethink me straightway of the nun's private stair to the Chapel, the which did lead down from my very door. This I did enter, and bid the Lady Beatrice follow me. But I being rather lame, and the stair being fit only for one at a time, she did sorely hurry and hasten me ; and methought we should never hae gotten down to the Chapel.   A-weel, as we were crossing the Chapel to make our way out at the door that doth lead into the garden, who should I see coming down the steps of the main-stair that doth lead from yonder passage on the ground floor into the Chapel, but Sir Andrew Stewart, the son of the Wolfe of Badenoch himself.   Trust me, I stayed not long.   But if the Lady Beatrice did complain of my delay in the way down thither, I trow she had reason in sooth to think me liard enow in leaving it.   I was gone in a trice ere she did miss me ; for of a truth I had no fancy to fall into such hands, since who doth know what——"

" And the Lady Beatrice ?" interrupted the Franciscan.

" Nay, I must confess I did see him lay his hands on her,"

answered Marion ; "and I did see him behind me as I did flee through the garden. But——"

"Then all is well," interrupted the Franciscan, turning away from the fatiguing old woman, and finishing the rest of his speech in grateful soliloquy. "It doth rejoice me much that she hath fallen into the hands of Sir Andrew Stewart ; for albeit the Wolfe of Badenoch hath wrought so much evil, verily I have myself seen that he is no enemy to the Lady Beatrice. And then, Sir Andrew Stewart hath the reputation of being the best of his family—one who is a mirror of virtue and of peaceful gentleness ; a perfect lamb of patience in that ferocious litter of wild beasts. Even our holy Bishop hath him in favourable estimation. He could not choose but take especial care of her. Praised be the Virgin, I may now go about the Bishop's affairs withouten care, being sure that I shall hear good tidings of her anon."

All that day and night, and all the following day, had passed away—the flames had been partly extinguished by active exertion, and had partly expired from lack of further food, and much had doubtless been done by the influence of images and relics. Measures also had been taken to preserve the quiet and peace of the town, as well as to ensure the immediate accommodation and support of such of its inhabitants as had suffered in the general calamity. Penitential prayers had been offered up, and hymns chanted in the conventual churches and chapels which had not suffered. A general penance and solemn fast had been ordered, after all which the Bishop sent for the Franciscan, and held a long conference with him on the subject of the affairs of the Church, which we shall leave them to discuss together, that we may now follow the humbled Wolfe of Badenoch to Lochyndorbe.

CHAPTER LXIX.

Changes at the Castle of Lochyndorbe—The Wolfe tamed— Alarm for the Lady Beatrice.

THE scene within that fortress was materially changed since our last visit to it. The boys, Walter and James Stewart, were laid in beds from which there was but small hope of their ever rising. Sir Alexander Stewart also lay in a very dangerous and distressing state, with a shattered arm and a bruised body, resulting from the heap of heavy stones which had been thrown down

upon him from the wall of Spynie; and the hitherto hardy and
impregnable mind and body of the Wolfe of Badenoch himself,
yielding before the storm of calamity that had so suddenly
assailed him, had sunk into a state of torpor, and he was now
confined to a sick bed by a low, yet rapidly consuming fever. In
so short a time as two days his gigantic strength was reduced to
the weakness of a child.   His impatience of temper had not been
entirely conquered by the disease, but its effects were sufficiently
moderated by his prostration, to render him no longer a terror
to any one; and this feeling was heightened in all around him,
by the conviction that his malady was of a nature so fatal that
his existence must soon be terminated.

The Lady Mariota was one of the first who became aware of
this, and she prudently regulated her conduct accordingly. Yes,
she for whose illicit love he had sacrificed so much—she who
had ever affected so devoted an attachment to him—she who
was the mother of his five boys—she on whose account he had
so resolutely braved so many tempests, and who had been the
original cause of the very feud with the Bishop of Moray which
had led to the commission of excesses so outrageous, and now
produced so much fatal affliction—she it was who, now beginning
to show herself in her true character, sorrowed not for him, but
as her own importance and high estate must inevitably sink in
his deathbed.   Even her grief for her lost sons, and her anxiety
for those whom she feared to lose, arose more from the thought
that in them perished so many supporters and protectors who
might yet have enabled her to hold her head proudly, than from
any of that warm and perfectly unselfish feeling, which, if it anywhere exists, must be found to throb in the bosom of a mother.
Instead of flying in distraction from couch to couch, administer-
ing all that imagination could think of, to heal, to support, or to
soothe, she wisely remembered that, in her situation, time was
precious; and, accordingly, she employed every minute of it in
rummaging through the secret repositories of many a curious
antique cabinet, and in making up many a neat and portable
package, to be carried off the moment that the soul of the Wolfe
of Badenoch should quit his body.   Nor were her active
thoughts bestowed on things inanimate, or within doors only;
her tender care soared even beyond the Castle walls and the
Loch that encircled them; and by means of a chosen few of her
own servants whom she had managed to secure by large bribes
to her especial interest, the surrounding country was raised, and
the cattle and sheep that fed in the lawndes of the forests for
many a mile round, were seen pouring in large bodies towards

the land-sconce, to be ready to accompany her, and to unite their lowings and bleatings to her wailings, when she should be compelled to take her sad departure from Lochyndorbe.

Nor was the knowledge of this base ingratitude spared to the dying man. She had not visited him for the greater part of the day. He called, but the hirelings, who were wont to fly to him ere the words had well passed his lips, were now glad to keep out of his sight, and each abandoning to the rest the unwelcome task of waiting on him, he was left altogether without help. He was parched with a thirst which he felt persuaded the Loch itself would have hardly quenched; and in the disturbed state of his nerves he was haunted with the eternal torture of the idea of its waves murmuring gently and invitingly around him. It was night. A light step entered his room cautiously, and the rays of a lamp were seen. He entreated for a cup of water, but no answer was returned to his request. At length his impatience gave him a momentary command over his muscles, and throwing down the bed-clothes, he sprang on his knees, and opened wide the curtains that shaded the lower end of his bed. By the light of the lamp he beheld the Lady Mariota occupied in searching through his private cabinet, whence she had already taken many a valuable, the table being covered with rich chains of gold, and sparkling gems of every variety of water and colour, set in massive rings, buckles, brooches, collars, and head-circlets; and so intently was she busied that she heard not his motion.

"Ha, wretch," cried the Wolfe of Badenoch, in a hollow and sepulchral voice of wasted disease; "the curse of my spirit upon thee, what dost thou there?"

The Lady Mariota gave him not time to add more, for, looking fearfully round, she beheld the gaunt visage of the Wolfe of Badenoch, with his eyes glaring fiercely upon her; and believing that he had already died, and that it was indeed his spirit which cursed her, she uttered a loud scream, and rushed in terror from the apartment. The Wolfe, exhausted by the unnatural exertion he had made, sank backwards in his bed, and lay for some time motionless and unable to speak.

"Oh, for a cup of water," moaned the miserable man at length, the excruciating torture of his thirst banishing even that which his mind had experienced in beholding so unequivocal a proof of the Lady Mariota's selfish and unfeeling heart; "oh, will no one bring me a cup of water? And hath it then come so soon to this, that I, the son of a King, am left to suffer this foretaste of hell's torments, and no one hand to help me? Oh,

water, water, water, for mercy's sake ! Alas ! Heaven's curse
hath indeed fallen upon me. My dead and dying sons cannot
help me ; and Mariota—ha ! fiends, fiends ! Ay, there is bitterness—venom—black poison. Was it for this," said he, casting
his eyes towards the glittering jewels on the distant table ;
" was it for a heart so worthless that I did so brave the curse of
the Church ? Was it for such a viper that I did incur my
father's anger ? Was it for a poisoned-puffed spider like this that
I did do deeds that made men's hair bristle on their heads, and
their very eyes grow dim ? Did I bear her fiercely up before a
chiding world, that she might turn and sting me at an hour like
this ? Ha ! punishment, dread punishment was indeed promised me ; but I looked not that it should come from her whom
I did so long love and cherish—from her for whom I have sacrificed peace in this life, and oh, worse than all, mercy in that to
which I am hastening." He shuddered at the thoughts which
now crowded on his mind, and buried his head for some
moments under the bed-clothes.

It now approached midnight, and the solitary lamp left by
the Lady Mariota was still burning, when his ear caught a rustling noise.

" Ha, Mariota, art there again ? " cried the Wolfe of Badenoch,
impatiently lifting up his head.

He looked, and through the drapery of the bed, that still
remained wide open, he beheld the Franciscan standing before
him.

" Ha, what ! merciful St. Andrew," cried the Wolfe ; " ha, is
it thou, fiend, from whom hath sprung all mine affliction ?
Devil or monk, thou shalt die in my grasp." He made a desperate effort to rise, and repeated it again and again ; but he
sank down nerveless, his breast heaving with agitation, and his
eyes starting wildly from their sockets. " Speak, demon, what
further vengeance dost thou come to execute on this devoted
head ? Speak, for what fiendish torment canst thou invent that
shall more excruciate the body than racking and unsatisfied
thirst ? or what that shall tear the soul more cruelly than the
barbed arrows of ingratitude ? Hence, then, to thy native hell,
and leave me to mine."

"Alexander Stewart, Earl of Buchan, and Lord of Badenoch,"
said the Franciscan, " I do come to thee as no tormenting fiend.
The seal of death doth seem to be set on thy forehead ; thou
art fast sinking into his fleshless arms. The damps of the grave
do gather on thy brow. 'Tis not for mortal man as I am, to
push vengeance at such an hour. When thou wert in thy full

strength and power I did boldly face thy wickedness; but now thou art feeble and drivelling as the child that was born yesterday, or as the helpless crone over whose worn head and wasted brain an hundred winters have rolled, I come not to denounce aught of punishment against thee; for already hast thou enow here, and thou wilt soon be plunged for endless ages in that burning sea to which it were bootless for me to add one drop of anguish. Forgetting all thy cruelty against myself, I do come to thee as the hand of Mercy to the drowning wretch. I come to offer myself as the leech of thy soul as well as of thy body ; and, as an offering of peace, and a pledge of my sincerity, behold thy beloved son ? "

The Franciscan threw aside the folds of his habit, with which he had hitherto concealed something, and he held up the smiling boy, Duncan Stewart.

" Mock me not, foul fiend," cried the frantic father, believing that what he saw was a phantom; " hence, and disturb not my brain."

" Again I repeat, I am no fiend," said the Franciscan mildly. " I come to tell thee that repentance may yet ensure thee salvation in the next world ; nay, even life in this; yea, and life also to thy sons; and as a gracious earnest of God's infinite mercy, behold, I here restore thee thy best beloved boy, the Benjamin of thy heart, whose life mine hand did save from that raging fire thyself did so impiously kindle."

The Wolfe of Badenoch devoured the very words of the Franciscan as he spake. He gazed wildly on him and on his boy alternately, as if he yet doubted the reality of the scene ; and it was not until the little Duncan's joyous laugh rang in his ears, and he felt the boy's arms fondly entwining his neck, that he became satisfied of the truth of what he heard and saw. He was no longer the iron-framed and stern-souled Wolfe of Badenoch; his body was weak and his mind shaken, and he sank backwards in the bed, giving way to an hysterical laugh.

" Oh, my boy, my boy," cried he at length, smothering the youth with his caresses; " my beloved Duncan, what can I do for so great a mercy ! What—what—but—Oh, mercy, one cup of water, in mercy !—I burn—my tongue cleaveth—Oh, water, water, in mercy ! "

The Franciscan hastened to give him water ; and the thirsty wretch snatched the cup of life from the hand of him whom his unbridled rage had so wantonly consigned to the cruellest of deaths.

"More, more, cried the impatient Wolfe of Badenoch;
"mine entrails do crack with the scorching heat within me."

"Drink this, then," said the Franciscan, taking a phial from
his bosom, and pouring part of its contents into the cup:
"drink this, and thou shalt have water."

"Ha!" cried the Wolfe, darting a glance of suspicion towards
the monk. "Yet why should I hesitate?" continued he, as his
eyes fell upon Duncan. "He who hath restored my son, can
have little wish to hasten the end of a dying wretch."

"And he who might have used the dagger against thee," said
the Franciscan calmly, "would never have thought of giving
thee a death so tedious as that of poison. Drink; there is
health in the cup."

The Wolfe hesitated no longer.

"Now water, oh, water, in mercy!" cried he again, after he
had swallowed the drug.

"Thy thirst must be moderately ministered unto for a time,"
said the Franciscan; "yet shalt thou have one cup more," and
he poured one for him accordingly.

"Why art thou thus alone, father," demanded the boy Duncan; "why is not my mother here? she who doth ever so caress
and soothe thee, if that the pulses of thy temples do but throb
unreasonably. I'll go and fetch her hither straightway."

"Fetch her not hither, Duncan, if thou wouldst not have me
curse her," cried the Wolfe of Badenoch, dashing away the half-
consumed cup of water, in defiance of his thirst. "Oh, that I
might yet be myself again, were it but for a day, that I might
deal justice upon her. Then, indeed, should I die contented."

"Hush," said the Franciscan; "such is not the temper that
doth best befit a dying man; yea, and one, too, who hath so
much for the which to ask forgiveness. It doth more behove
thee to think of thine own sins than of those of others. If it
may so please Heaven, I shall be the leech of thy body; but it
were well that thou didst suffer me to give blessed medicine to
thy diseased soul, for thy life or thy death hangeth in the
Almighty hand, and no one can tell how soon thou mayest be
called to thy great account. Say, dost thou repent thee of all
the evil thou hast wrought against the Holy Church and her
sacred ministers?"

"I do, I do; most bitterly do I repent me," cried the Wolfe
of Badenoch, grinding his teeth ferociously, and with an expression of countenance very different from that becoming an humble penitent. "I do repent me, I say, in gall and bitterness:
for verily she for whom I did these deeds——"

" Nay, talk not of her," said the Franciscan, interrupting him ;
" mix not up thine angry passions with thine abasement before
thine offended Maker. Repent thee of thy sins—make instant
reparation to the Church from the abundance of thy wealth—
resolve to put away all thine abominations from thee—and,
finally, make a solemn vow, that, if it should please Heaven to
restore thee to health, thou wilt do such penance as it may seem
fitting for the injured Bishop of Moray to impose upon thee—
do these things, and all may yet be well with thee. If thou art
willing to vow solemnly to do these things, if Heaven in its
mercy shall yet spare thee, verily I will receive and be witness
to thy serment ; and I do beseech thee to speak quickly, for I
would fain leave thee to that healing repose, for the which my
medicine hath prepared thee, that I may go to give healthful
balsams to thy three sons, that they may yet be snatched from
an early grave."

" Yea, most merciful and beneficent monk," cried the Wolfe
of Badenoch, " thou whom I did believe to be a fiend, but whom
I do now find to be saint upon earth, most gladly do I yield
me to thee. I here most solemnly vow to the Virgin and the
Holy Trinity, that I do heartily repent me of mine outrages
against the Holy Church of God and His holy ministers ; that I
am ready to make what reparation I may ; and that, if it so
please Heaven to rescue me from the jaws of death, I shall do
penance in such wise as to the Bishop and the King, my father,
may seem best."

" Be thy vow registered in Heaven," said the Franciscan,
solemnly crossing himself. " And now, with the blessing of
St. Francis, thou shalt soon be in a state for fulfilling it. But
let me entreat thee to yield thyself to that repose, the which
the healing draught thou hast taken must speedily ensure to
thee ; when thou dost again awake, thy consuming fever will
have left thee, and in two or three days at most thou mayest
be again in thy saddle. Let me now hasten to help thy
sons."

The boy Duncan Stewart had already paved the way for the
Franciscan's favourable reception with his brothers, who gladly
submitted themselves to his directions, and he speedily administered to their respective cases. The domestics now began to be
re-assured of the probable recovery of the invalids, and they
already quaked for the returning wrath of the Wolfe of Badenoch. The Lady Mariota sat trembling in her apartment. The
Franciscan, who had formerly disappeared so miraculously, and
who now re-appeared so strangely among them, was eyed with

36

fear by every one within the Castle, and his orders were obeyed
as implicitly and as promptly as the Wolfe himself, so that he
lacked for nothing that his patient required.   Having done all
for them that art could effect, he had time to think of the Lady
Beatrice, whom he believed to be an inmate of the Castle, seeing
he had no doubt that Sir Andrew Stewart must have brought
her thither.   But he found, on inquiry, that the knight had not
appeared.   He was vexed at the disappointment, but taking it
for granted that her protector had carried her to some other
fastness belonging to his father, he felt no uneasiness, trusting
that he should soon have tidings of her.

Dismissing all thoughts of the Lady Beatrice, therefore, from
his mind, he devoted himself eagerly to the restoration of the
sick, being filled with the idea of the signal service he was about
to perform to the Church, the extent of which would much depend on the recovery of those who now lay in so precarious a
state, that they might appear before the world as living instances
of penitence.   For two days, then, he was indefatigable in his
attentions; and the effect of his care and skill was, that the
Wolfe of Badenoch's cure was rapid.   His disease had been
chiefly caused by sudden affliction, operating on an impatient
temper, and a conscience ill at ease.   The Franciscan's words,
therefore, had happily combined with his medicines to produce
an almost miraculous effect ; and, ere the time promised by the
monk was expired, he appeared in the great hall, haggard and
disease-worn indeed, but perfectly ready to fill his saddle.   The
recovery of his sons, though there was now little to be feared for
them, promised to be more tedious ; and it was well for the
peace of the Castle of Lochyndorbe that it was so, for they
might have made some objections to the decided step which
their father took the moment he again showed himself.

" Ha, villains," cried he as he came stalking through the
opening crowd of domestics that shrunk from him on either
hand—" so the Earl of Buchan, the son of a King, mought have
died for all ye cared.   Ha ! whither did ye all hide, knaves,
that I was nearly perishing of thirst, and no one to give me
a cup of water ?   But 'tis no marvel that ye should have forgotten your master when—Ha ! Bruce—send Bruce, the old
esquire, hither.   What mighty lowing of cattle, and bleating of
sheep, is that I do hear ?"

The domestics looked at each other, but no one dared to
speak.   The impatient Wolfe hurried up a little turret-stair,
from the top of which he had a view over the outer walls of the
Castle, and the narrow strait that divided that from the main-

land. There he beheld the whole of the flocks and herds which the Lady Mariota had so prudently collected together, and which her trepidation had made her forget to order to be driven again to their native hills and forests. He wanted no further information, for the truth flashed on him at once. His eye reddened, his cheek grew paler than even the disease had left it, his lip quivered, and he rushed precipitately down to the hall.

"Where, in the fiend's name, is Bruce?" cried he. "Ha! thou art there, old man. Get thee quickly together some dozen or twain of mounted spears, with palfreys for the Lady Mariota and her women, and sumpter-horses needful for the carriage of their raiment; and let her know that it is my will she do forthwith depart hence with thee for my Castle of Cocklecraig, the which is to be her future place of sojournance."

The esquire bowed obediently, and hastened to execute the command of his impatient Lord. In a little time a page appeared, with an humble message from the Lady Mariota, to know whether the Earl was to accompany her into Buchan.

"Tell her no," replied the Wolfe, turning round on the frightened page, and speaking with a voice that shook the Gothic hall, which he was rapidly measuring backwards and forward with his paces.

Again a woman came to him from the Lady Mariota, most submissively entreating for an interview.

"Nay, the red fiend catch me then!" cried the furious Wolfe, his eyes flashing fire; "I do already know too much of her baseness, ever to trust myself with a sight of her again. 'Twere better, for her sake, that she urge me not to see her. Ha! tell her I have sworn by my knighthood that the threads that hath bound my heart to her worthlessness shall be for ever snapped. Let not the poisonous toad cross my path, lest I crush her in mine ire, and give to my conscience another sin to be repented of.—Away!"

The Wolfe again paced the hall, very much moved. The neighing of horses and the noise of preparation were heard in the court-yard; the warder's call for the boats sounded across the lake; and a wailing of women's voices soon afterwards succeeded. The Wolfe paced the hall with a yet more rapid step; he became much moved, and hid his face from the Franciscan, who was the only witness of his agitation. But at last it became too strong to be concealed, and he rushed up the turret-stair, whence he had before looked out towards the land-sconce. He remained absent for a considerable time; and when he returned, his face was deeply marked with the traces of the strong contending emotions he had undergone.

"How doth thy leech-craft prosper, good Sir Friar?" demanded he at length, evidently from no other desire than to talk away his present feelings, seeing that he had already put the same question more than half-a-dozen times before.

"I do trust that, under God, thy sons will yet be well," replied the Franciscan. "But be not impatient, my Lord; their cure must be the work of time. Meanwhile, be thankful to a merciful Providence, who doth thus restore to thee all those of whom thou didst fear thou wert bereft."

"All!" cried the Wolfe, shuddering, "nay, not all; all but Andrew, and he did perish horribly in the flames of the Maison Dieu, whither I did myself enforce him. Heaven in its mercy pardon me!"

"Andrew!" cried the Franciscan, with surprise; "trust me, my Lord, Sir Andrew Stewart is safe."

"Safe!" cried the Wolfe, clasping his hands together in an ecstacy—"then thanks be to a merciful God, who hath saved me from the torturing thought of having been the cause of working my son's death. But where, I pray thee, was he seen?" demanded the Wolfe eagerly.

"He was seen in the Chapel of the Maison Dieu with a lady, whom he did thereafter lead through the garden of the Hospital," replied the Franciscan.

"What, the Lady Beatrice!" demanded the Wolfe; "for that is all the name I did ever know her to bear as a woman, albeit I do well recollect her masculine appellation of Maurice de Grey."

"The same," replied the Franciscan.

"Then hath Andrew preserved her life," replied the Wolfe. "By the beard of my grandfather, but I do greatly rejoice to hear it. There is still some virtue in the caitiff after all. My efforts to save the lady were vain; I did even gain her chamber, but I found her gone; from which I was compelled with grief to believe that she had surely perished. But whither hath my son Andrew conveyed her?"

"Nay, that I have not yet discovered," replied the Franciscan; "but Sir Andrew Stewart saved not the Lady Beatrice from the flames. One of the sisters of the Hospital did teach her how to escape; and as they crossed the Chapel together, Sir Andrew Stewart, who had fled thither for safety——"

"Ah, coward," cried the Wolfe; "so, after all, he was the craven kestrel. By my beard, I thought as much. And so thou sayest that thou art yet ignorant where the Lady Beatrice hath been bestowed."

"Nay, my good Lord," replied the Franciscan; "but with a knight of his good report she is sure of protection, and——"

"What sayest thou?—good report, sayest thou?" interrupted the Wolfe. "Though he be a brauncher from mine own nest, yet must I, in honesty, tell thee, Sir Friar, that a greater hypocrite presseth not the surface of the earth. Protection, saidst thou? By St. Barnabas, but she hath already hath enow of his protection."

"What dost thou mean, my Lord?" replied the monk, in astonishment.

"Why, by my knighthood, but I am ashamed to speak so of mine own son," replied the Wolfe; "yet am I bound to treat thee with candour, and so thou shalt e'en have it." And he proceeded to give the monk a short history of the infamous treachery of Sir Andrew Stewart towards the Lady Beatrice.

"My Lord of Buchan," cried the Franciscan, with an agitation and earnestness of manner which the Wolfe of Badenoch could by no means explain, "if I have found favour with thee, lend me thine aid, I entreat thee, to recover the Lady Beatrice from thy son. She is destined to take the veil, and in giving me thine aid to reclaim her thou wilt be doing a pious duty, the which will assuredly tell for the good of thy soul, yea, and help to balance the heavy charge of thine iniquities."

"Right joyfully shall I give thee mine aid," replied the Wolfe of Badenoch; "the more that she was the lady of the gallant Sir Patrick Hepborne, with whom she was here, in the disguise of a page. Ha, ha, ha, ha! But wherefore doth she now take the veil?"

"'Tis fitting that she doth atone for a youth of sin by a life of penitence," replied the Friar, unwilling to speak more plainly.

"So," said the Wolfe of Badenoch, with a significant look, "after all her modest pretence, and after all Sir Patrick's cunning dissembling, 'twas as I did suspect then, after all?"

"Thou didst suspect, then?" said the Friar; "alas! I do fear with too much reason. Yet let us not tarry, but hasten to recover her, I pray thee."

"Squires, there—what, ho, within!" cried the Wolfe, "hath no one as yet heard aught of Sir Andrew Stewart?"

"No one, my noble Earl," replied an esquire who waited.

"By the holy mass, then," said the Wolfe, "but the caitiff hath taken refuge in some of my strongholds. But 'twill be

hard an we ferret him not out. Ha! knaves there, let fifty
mounted lances be ready in the lawnde beyond the land-sconce
ere I can wind my bugle."

The Wolfe of Badenoch was restored to all his pristine
vigour by the very thought of going on an expedition, even
though it was against his own son. The court-yard rang with
the bustle the Castle was thrown into, and all the boats were
put in requisition to ferry the horses across. Everything was
ready for them to mount at the land-sconce in an incredibly
short space of time ; but, however short the delay, still it was
too much for his impatience ; nor was his companion less restless than the Wolfe, till he found himself in saddle. When all
were mounted, the monk showed, by his forward riding, that
there was little risk of his being a drag upon the speed of the
furious-pricking knight, and the Wolfe of Badenoch exulted to
behold his horsemanship.

"By the mass," cried he, pulling up a little, "but thou art a
prince of friars ; 'tis a pleasure, I vow, to have a stalwarth
monk like thee as a confessor ; wouldst thou be mine, thou
shouldst ever ride at my elbow. Where hadst thou thy schooling, Sir Friar ?"

"I have rode in the lists ere now," replied the Franciscan ;
"yea, and war have I seen in all its fashions. But it doth now
befit me to forget these vain carnal contentions, and to fight
against mine own evil passions, the which are harder to subdue
than any living foe. And in this let me be an ensample to
thee, my Lord, for verily the time is but short sith that I was
as violent and tempestuous as thyself ; and hard it is even yet
for me, frail man as I am, to keep down the raging devil that is
within me. May the blessed Virgin increase our virtuous resolution !" said he, crossing himself.

To this pious ejaculation the Wolfe added a hearty "Amen;"
and they again pushed on at the same rapid pace at which they
had originally started.

CHAPTER LXX.

Bishop Barr at Lochyndorbe Castle— Reception by the Wolfe.

THE Wolfe of Badenoch and the Franciscan had hardly reached
the end of the lake, when they descried a mounted knight approaching them.

"By all that is marvellous," cried the Wolfe, halting suddenly.
"but yonder doth come my very son Andrew !"

" Is it indeed Sir Andrew Stewart ? " said the Franciscan ; " methinks he cometh as if he had little fear of blame about him."

" By'r Lady, but his coming home thus at all doth look something like honesty," said the Wolfe ; " but do thou let me question him, holy father, nor fear that I will deal over gently with him. So, Sir Andrew," cried he, as soon as his son was near enough to hear him, " I do rejoice to behold thee again. Whence comest thou, I pray thee ? "

" From Elgin straightway, my noble father," replied Sir Andrew Stewart.

" Marry, and what hath kept thee there so long, then ? " demanded the Wolfe ; " methought that thou hadst seen enow to teach thee that no whelp of mine could be welcome guest there."

" In truth, I did so find it indeed," replied Sir Andrew Stewart.

" Then what a murrain hath kept thee there ? " demanded the Wolfe sternly. " Come, thou knowest I am not over patient. Thy story—thy story quickly. What befel thee after thou didst enter the blazing Spital of the Maison Dieu ? Didst thou rescue the damosel—the Lady Beatrice ? "

" I did," replied the unblushing knight ; " verily, I rushed to the upper chamber through the fire and the smoke, and I did snatch her from the very flames, and bear her forth in safety."

" There thou liest, caitiff," roared out the Wolfe ; " thou dost lie in the very threshold of thy story. By the mass, but we shall judge of the remainder of thy tale by the sample thou hast already given us. But go on, Sir Andrew. What didst thou with her after thou didst save her, as thou saidst ? ay, and tell us, too, how thou didst escape ? "

" But first, where is she now ? " demanded the Franciscan, breaking in.

" Nay, Sir Friar, be not impatient," cried the Wolfe of Badenoch ; " thou wilt gain nothing by impatience. Interrupt him not, I entreat thee ; but let him go on in order. Proceed, sirrah."

" I retreated with the Lady Beatrice, through the Chapel of the Maison Dieu," replied Sir Andrew Stewart, now assuming greater caution as to what he uttered.

" Well, Sir Knight," exclaimed the Franciscan keenly, " what hast thou done with her ? Speak to that at once."

" Nay, Sir Friar, why wilt thou thus persist in taking speech ? "

demanded the Wolfe testily; "thou art most unreasonably
hasty. By the beard of my grandfather, but impatience and
unbridled passion doth ever defeat itself. Dost thou not see
that I am cool and unflurried with this knave's face? Answer
me, villain," roared he to his son, "answer me, thou disgrace to
him from whom thou art sprung—thou child of thine infamous
mother—answer me, I tell thee, quickly, and to the point, or,
by the blood of the Bruce, I shall forget that thou hast any
claim to be called my son."

"Be not angry with me, father," said Sir Andrew, trembling ;
"verily the lady is safe, for all that I do know of her ; and——"

"Where hast thou bestowed her, villain?" shouted the
Wolfe ; "speak, or, by all the fiends, thou shalt never speak
more."

"I will, father, if thou wilt but suffer me," replied the terrified Sir Andrew Stewart.

"Why dost thou not go on then?" cried the Wolfe yet more
impatiently ; "where hast thou bestowed the lady, villain! An
we be not possessed by thee of the whole of thy story, and
of the place where thou hast confined her, in less time than the
flight of an arrow doth consume, by the blessed house of my
ancestors, I shall cause hang thee up, though thou be'st called
my son."

"The lady is not in my hands," replied Sir Andrew Stewart
in terrible alarm ; "she fled from me in the garden of the Maison
Dieu, and I did never see her more."

"Hey—what?—but this may be all of a piece with the
beginning of thy tale, which we know was false as hell," replied
the Wolfe.

"Nay, we do indeed know so much as that thou didst never
save her," cried the Franciscan ; "we do know right well how
she was saved ; yea, and we do know, moreover, that thou
didst seize her as she did pass through the Chapel, and thou
wert heard with her in the garden. Tell me speedily whither
didst thou carry her, and where is she now?"

"Ay, where is she now," cried the Wolfe ; "out with the
truth, if thou wouldst escape hanging. Be assured that every
false word thou mayest utter shall be proved against thee ; so
see that thou dost speak truth."

"Have mercy on me, father," cried the wretched Sir Andrew
Stewart, throwing himself from his horse, and dropping on his
knees between the Wolfe and the Franciscan ; "have mercy on
me, and I will tell thee all the truth. To my shame I do
confess that vanity and the fear of my father's wrath against

my cowardice did prompt me to utter that which was false; and ——"

"Ha! where is she, then, villain?" cried the Wolfe, interrupting him.

"Distraction! where hast thou concealed her?" cried the Franciscan.

"Verily, I know nothing of her," said the knight.

"Wretch, dost thou return to thy falsehood?" cried the Franciscan.

"Nay, what I say in this respect is most true," said Sir Andrew Stewart; "it was in saying that I did rescue the Lady Beatrice that I spake falsely. I was too much daunted by the fierceness of the flames to venture aloft; but having been once upon a time a guest in the Maison Dieu, I well knew its various passages, one of which did lead from the bottom of the main staircase of the building directly into the Chapel, whence I was aware that a retreat into the garden was easy. As I entered the Chapel I beheld one of the sisterhood of the Maison Dieu hobbling away with the Lady Beatrice. Mine ancient passion returned upon me, and——"

"Villain! thou didst carry her off," cried the Franciscan, interrupting him.

"Thou lying caitiff, where hast thou concealed her?" cried the Wolfe.

"I did straightway attempt to lay hands upon her, when she fled before me into the garden, and escaped among the trees and bushes, where I instantly lost all trace of her."

"But where hast thou been all this time sithence?" demanded the Wolfe fiercely; "answer me straightway to that."

"My Lord Earl," replied Sir Andrew Stewart, "as I wandered in the garden I did encounter the old gardener, who, under the light of the burning, did remember me for one of thy sons. He instantly seized me, and having snatched my sword from my side, he did swear potent oaths that he would put me to death if I dared offer to resist; and with these threats he forced me through the garden, and plunged me into a deep vault at its farther extremity, where I was immured without food for two days."

"Ha! and by the Holy Rood, thou didst well merit it all, I ween, thou most pitiful of cowards," cried the Wolfe, angrily gnashing his teeth; "what, thou the son of the Wolfe of Badenoch, to be frayed and captured by an old doting unarmed gardener! By all the fiends, but thou dost deserve to wear a kirtle and petticoat, and to have a distaff to handle. But what more hast thou to tell, thou shame to knighthood ? "

" When I was nearly spent by hunger and thirst," continued Sir Andrew, " the gardener came, with some of the brethren of the Maison Dieu, to take me from my prison, and I was led before the Bishop of Moray."

" Ha ! and how did the Bishop treat thee ?" interrupted the Wolfe.

" He received me with much mildness and gentleness," replied Sir Andrew Stewart ; " and he did severely chide those who so cruelly left me without food, and ere he would allow a question to be put to me, he did straightway order my hunger and thirst to be forthwith satisfied ; and, when I had well eaten and drank, he ordered an apartment to be instantly prepared for me, that I might enjoy the repose the which I had so much need ; and verily I was right glad to accept of the proffered blessing. The Bishop did keep me with him until a messenger came to him from Lochyndorbe, after which he entertained me rather as his favoured guest than as his prisoner."

" Nay, so far he speaketh truth," said the Franciscan ; " that messenger was mine ; he was the messenger of peace."

" I do indeed speak the truth in everything now," replied Sir Andrew Stewart, " the which thou mayest soon learn from the Bishop himself, for I am sent before him to announce a peaceful visitation from him, and he will be here anon."

" Ha ! if thou hadst but listened, Sir Friar," cried the Wolfe, " if thine impatience had but suffered thee to listen, we had saved much time."

" Yea, much time mought have indeed been saved," said the Franciscan ; " but, sinner that I am, what hath become of the Lady Beatrice ?   Her disappearance is most mysterious, if what Sir Andrew Stewart hath told be indeed true."

" But didst thou not say that the Bishop was coming hither, son Andrew ?" cried the Wolfe of Badenoch ; " what force doth he bring with him ?"

" He bringeth not a single armed man with him," replied Sir Andrew Stewart ; " nay, he hath not above some fifteen or twenty persons in all his company."

" Had we not better hasten us homewards ?" said the Wolfe to the Franciscan ; " had we not better hasten to prepare for receiving my Lord Bishop, sith that he doth honour me so far ?"

" Thou art right, my Lord," replied the Franciscan, starting from a reverie into which he had fallen ; " it may be that my

Lord Bishop may peraunter have some tidings to give me of her about whom I am so much interested."

The Franciscan had little leisure to think more of the Lady Beatrice at that time. They were no sooner within the Castle walls than he found that he had a sufficient task to fulfil in preparing the fierce mind of the Wolfe of Badenoch for receiving the Bishop with that peaceful humility which became a sincere penitent. It was so far a fortunate circumstance that the Wolfe himself was already very greatly touched by the prelate's generous conduct towards his sons Duncan and Andrew, whom fortune had placed at his mercy.

" By the Rood," exclaimed he, " but the Bishop hath shown kindness where, in truth, I had but little reason to expect it at his hands. He might have hanged both my boys, taken, as I may say they were, red-handed in a manner. Then his coming thus doth show but little of that haughtiness of the which I did believe him to be possessed. By this hand, we shall muster out our garrison and meet him on the land-sconce with all our warlike parade, that we may do him all the honour that may be."

" Nay," replied the monk mildly, " not so, I do entreat thee, my Lord. Let us appear there with all the symbols of peace and humility, and——"

" What," interrupted the Wolfe hastily, " wouldst thou have me put myself in the power of the prelate?"

" Nay, thou needst hardly fear that, if thou rememberest what thy son Sir Andrew did say of the unarmed state of his small escort," replied the Franciscan; " and, in truth, meseems that if the peaceful Bishop doth adventure so far as to entrust himself and his people unarmed in thy stronghold, it would speak but little for the bold heart of the Earl of Buchan to go armed, and attended by armed men. Nay, nay, my Lord; of a truth, this is a bold act of the Bishop of Moray, when all that hath passed is well considered. He hath indeed been generous, and now he doth prove himself to be dauntless. Let him not have to boast, then, that he hath outdone thee either in generosity or fearlessness. I need not call upon thee to remember thee of thy vow, the which I did witness, and which is now registered in heaven. Show that thou art truly penitent and humble, and remember that thine abasement before God's minister is but thine abasement before God, who hath already shown thee such tender mercy, and who will yet show thee more."

After listening to this exhortation, the Wolfe of Badenoch became thoughtful, and the Franciscan gradually ventured to propose to him the manner in which it would best become him to receive the Bishop. The countenance of the ferocious warrior showed sufficiently how painful the humiliation was to his feelings; but he submitted patiently, if not cheerfully, and the necessary preparations were accordingly made.

The warder who was stationed in the barbican blew his horn to announce the first appearance of the Bishop's party, who were seen winding like black specks through the scattered greenwood at the farther end of the lake. The colony of herons were scarcely disturbed by their slow and silent march. The little fleet of boats clustered under the Castle walls was manned, and the Wolfe of Badenoch and his whole garrison were rowed across to the land-sconce, where they immediately formed themselves into a procession, and walked onwards to meet those who were coming.

First went fifty warriors, unarmed and with their heads bare. Then followed the Wolfe of Badenoch himself, also unarmed, and wearing a black hood and surcoat. At his side was the Franciscan, and behind him were his sons Andrew and Duncan, after whom came fifty more of his people. The Bishop approached, mounted on his palfrey, surrounded by some of the dignitaries of his diocese, and followed by a few monks and a small train of attendants. The Wolfe of Badenoch's men halted, and, dividing themselves into two lines, formed a lane for the Bishop and his party to advance. The Wolfe moved forward to meet the prelate; but though his garb was that of a humble penitent, his eye and his bearing were those of a proud Prince.

"Ah, there is the good Bishop, who was so kind to me at Spynie," cried little Duncan, clapping his hands with joy; "he did teach me to play bowls, father, and he gave me so many nice sweatmeats. Let me run to him, I beseech thee."

The boy's innocent speech was enough; it brought a grappling about the heart of the Wolfe of Badenoch; he hastened forward to the end of the lane of men, and made an effort to reach the Bishop's stirrup, that he might hold it for him to dismount.

"Nay, nay," said the good man, preventing his intention by quitting his saddle ere he could reach him; "I may not allow the son of my King so to debase himself."

"My Lord Bishop," said the Wolfe, prompted by the Franciscan, "behold one who doth humbly throw himself on the mercy and forgiveness of God and thee."

"The mercy of God was never refused to a repentant sinner," replied the Bishop; "and as for the forgiveness of a fallible being like me, I wot I do myself lack too much of God's pardon to dare refuse it to a fellow-sinner. May God, then, in his mercy, pardon thee on thy present submission, and on the score of that penance to which thou art prepared to submit."

"My Lord Bishop," replied the Wolfe, "I am ready to submit to whatsoever penance it may please thee to enjoin me. Thy mercy to my sons, and in especial that to my boy Duncan, hath subdued me to thy will. But let me entreat of thee that, sinner though I be, thou wilt honour my Castle of Lochyndorbe with thy sacred presence. There shall I learn thy volunde, the which I do here solemnly vow, before the blessed Virgin and the Holy Trinity, whom I have offended, to perform to the veriest tittle, were it to be a pilgrimage to the Holy Sepulchre itself. Trust me, thy tender mercy towards me and mine hath wrought more with me than all that thy power or thy threats could have done."

"Let us not talk more of this matter at this time, my Lord," replied the Bishop; "I do hereby take upon me, in the meanwhile, conditionally to remove from thee the dread sentence of excommunication, seeing thou hast made all the concession as yet in thy power, and that thou art ready to make what reparation thou canst for what hath passed, and to do such penance as may be required of thee; and so shall I cheerfully accept thy hospitality for this night."

The Wolfe of Badenoch's men stared at each other, to behold their fierce master thus become the peaceable companion of the very prelate and monk against whom the full stream of his fury had been so lately directed. They shrugged and looked wise at each other, but no one ventured to utter a word; and the two processions having mingled their truly heterogeneous materials together, they turned towards the land-sconce, and peacefully entering the boats, crossed the Lake to the Castle, where the chief personages were soon afterwards to be seen harmoniously seated at the same festive board. But before they were so assembled, the Franciscan had a conference with the Bishop in his private apartment.

"Thou hast indeed well served the cause of the Church, Friar John," said the prelate to him; "yea, thou hast done God and our holy religion good service, by having thus so miraculously tamed this wild and ferocious Wolfe. Thou hast tilled a hardened soil, that hath heretofore borne but thistles, thorns, and brambles, that did enter into our flesh and tear our very hearts. But thy hand must not be taken from the plough until thy task be complete. Thou must forward with the Earl of Buchan towards Perth to-morrow. 'Twere well to take him

while his mind is yet soft with the meliorating dews of penitence. I have spoken to him apart sith I did come hither.
Already hath he agreed to make over to me certain large sums
in gold, to be placed at the disposal of our chapter, as alswa
divers annual rents springing from a wide extent of territory,
to be expended in the restoration of our Cathedral. Moreover,
he hath declared himself ready to perform the penance I have
enjoined him, the ceremonial of which thou wilt find detailed in
this parchment, after which he will be absolved by the godly
Walter Traill, Bishop of St. Andrews, in the Blackfriars
Church of Perth. To thy prudence and care do I commit the
proper ordering and execution of all that this parchment and
these directions I have written do contain, seeing there be none
other who could do it so well."

"I must obey all thy commands, my sacred Lord," replied
the friar; "yet is my mind ill attuned to the task, seeing it is
distracted because of the uncertain fate of the Lady Beatrice.
I beseech thee, hath any tidings of her reached thee?"

"Nay, I heard not of her," replied the Bishop, "save what I
gathered from Sir Andrew Stewart, who parted with her in the
garden of the Maison Dieu. Yet did I not cease to make
inquiry—and, in truth, I do greatly fear that she hath availed
herself of her liberty to flee towards the south, to join herself to
him with whom she did once so scandalously associate, and for
whom thou sayest she hath unblushingly confessed her inextinguishable love. I hear our Scottish champions have returned
from the English expedition, and doubtless Sir Patrick Hepborne the younger is by this time at the Court of King Robert,
at Scone, if he hath not been detained in the Tower, to answer
for his outrage. From what thou hast told me there must have
been some secret concert between the knight and Beatrice.
She must, therefore, have been well possessed of all his intentions—and if so, she was well prepared to avail herself of
any chance of escape, that she might fly to join herself to him
again. Hadst thou any talk with her on the subject of Sir
Patrick Hepborne?"

"Never, my sacred Lord, sith the night when Friar Rushak
enabled me to take her from the Tower," replied the Franciscan.
"Nay, save some short dialogue between us after the ship
weighed anchor, when, to quiet her fears and compose her mind,
I did tell her the secret in which she was so much interested,
and explained to her by what right I so assumed control over
her—the stormy voyage, and the fatigues that followed it, left
me no leisure to hold further converse with her. But thou art

right, my gracious Lord Bishop.   She hath doubtless fled to her paramour, who seems to carry some love enchantment about him that he hath so bewitched her."

"The King hath lately removed to Scone," said the Bishop; "so, I do verily think that, on going to Perth on this errand of the Church, thou shalt have the best chance to recover her who hath fled from thee; at least, thou wilt hear of Sir Patrick Hepborne; and where he is, there will she be also."

"I do verily believe so the more I turn the subject in my thoughts," replied the Franciscan; "nay, it can be no otherwise. Trust me, I do gladly give thee thanks for this hint, as well as for all thy friendly actings towards me.   I shall go hence with Lord Badenoch to-morrow.   My heart shall first of all be given to the service of the blessed Church, the which I do yet hope to see raise her head but so much the higher from these her late calamities.   That accomplished, I shall seek for and find Beatrice, though her foul seducer should conceal her in the bowels of the earth."

The hot feud had so long subsisted between the Wolfe of Badenoch and the Bishop of Moray that each had for many years viewed the other through a false medium.   The eyes of the ferocious Earl had been specially diseased, and now that the scales had been removed from them, he was astonished to discover the mild and unpretending demeanour, and the forgiving disposition of the man whom he had believed to be his proud and implacable enemy.   This induced him to overwhelm the Bishop with all that the kindness of his native hospitality could devise, and so a mutual re-action took place between them, which the politic Franciscan took every opportunity to improve. The Wolfe even listened with tolerable patience of countenance, and altogether without offensive reply, to the Bishop's remonstrance on the subject of his misconduct to his wife Euphame Countess of Ross; and, strange as it may seem, he solemnly vowed that the first step he should take after doing penance, would be to receive that injured woman again to his bosom.

Preparations for an early march next morning were made with that expedition with which all his orders were generally executed by his well-disciplined people; and when the time of departure came, the Bishop and he set out cordially together, and afterwards separated, each to pursue his respective way, with a friendly regret that can only be comprehended by those who are well conversant in the whimsical issues of the human heart.

CHAPTER LXXI.

The Scottish Knights in London—Father Rushak's Tale.

ALLOWING the Wolfe of Badenoch and his friend the Franciscan to proceed on their journey, we must now return to inquire into the fate of Sir Patrick Hepborne. We left him lying on the straw in his dungeon, giving way to a paroxysm of grief for having been so cruelly rent from Lady Beatrice, tormenting himself with fears for her safety, and refusing the comfort which his esquire Mortimer Sang, and Master Lawrence Ratcliffe, were in vain attempting to administer to him. Whilst he was in this state of bitter affliction, the door of the dungeon was again opened, and a number of guards entering, silently approached him. Believing that they were about to lead him to immediate execution, he rose to meet them.

"I am ready," said he recklessly ; " my life is now but of little value to me. The sooner it is over the better. Lead on, then, my friends."

Mortimer Sang sprang forward to prevent their seizure of his master, but he was speedily overpowered, and Sir Patrick was led passively away.

He was conducted through a long dark passage, and finally lodged in a cell, to which he ascended by a short circular flight of steps. He questioned his conductors as to what was to be his fate, but they retired without giving him any reply. His new prison, though small, was less dark and gloomy than the larger dungeon from which he had been taken ; and though sufficiently strong, it had an air of greater comfort about it ; yet would he willingly have exchanged it for that he had left, to have been again blessed with the society of his esquire and the wine merchant. He seemed to be now condemned to solitary imprisonment, and he anticipated the worst possible intentions from this seclusion. The survey he took of the four walls that enclosed him left no hope of escape. There was indeed another small door besides that by which he had entered, but both were so powerfully fenced with iron as to be perfectly impregnable. He viewed this second door with an eye of suspicion, and the idea that through it might enter the assassins who were privily to despatch him, presented death to him in a . shape so uninviting, that, ready as he had been to lay down his life but the moment before, he now resolved to sell it as dearly as he could, although he had no other weapon but his hands to defend himself with.

He sat down on a stone bench in a niche in the wall opposite to this suspicious door, and, fixing his eye on it, he fell into a reverie, from which he was roused by the sound of footsteps, as if descending towards it. He sprang up, that he might be prepared for action. The door opened, and a young man in the garb of a lacquey, and altogether unarmed, appeared at the bottom of a very narrow spiral staircase. He made an obeisance to Sir Patrick, and silently, but respectfully beckoned him to follow ; and the knight, resolving to pursue his fate, immediately obeyed. He was conducted up several flights of steps, until at length, to his great surprise, he was brought into a little oratory, where he was again left alone.

He had not waited long, when a pannel in the wall, behind the altar, opened, and a Franciscan Friar appeared. The knight regarded him with a calm and steady look. It was Friar Rushak, the King's Confessor.

" Sir Patrick Hepborne," said the monk mildly to him, " I come to thee on private embassage from the Royal Richard. Thine intemperance in breaking in upon his privacy as thou didst, hath led thee to be accused, by some who are more zealous than prudent, of having made a premeditated attempt to assassinate His Majesty. But this hath been done without the Royal sanction ; for albeit that appearances do of a surety most powerfully array themselves against thee, yet he doth acquit thee of all such traitorous intent. But thou hast been led by blind fury to lift thine hand against the Sovereign whose hospitality thou dost now enjoy, and that, too, in defence of one against whom he did mean nothing dishonourable, though circumstances may have wrought up her fears to believe that he did."

" What ! " cried Hepborne, with a strong expression of doubt in his face ; " so King Richard doth deny all dishonourable intention against the Lady Beatrice ? But what availeth it if he doth so ? Hath he not sithence devoted her to certain destruction, by giving her up to one who hath already proved himself to be her enemy, yea, an assassin, who would have murdered her ? "

" Sir Knight," said Friar Rushak, after some moments' thought, " trust me, the King had no hand in the disposal of her. He did never see the lady after that moment when thou didst force him to retreat before thine inconsiderate rage. But, an assassin—a murderer, saidst thou ? How canst thou so accuse a brother of St. Francis ? "

37

" Because I have good reason to know that he did once steal
into the chamber of the Lady Beatrice at the hour of midnight,
armed with a dagger," cried Hepborne impatiently ; " and had
she not saved herself by flight——"

" Thou must suffer me to tell thee that this strange tale is
difficult of credence with me," said Friar Rushak, interrupting
him ; " the more, too, that it cometh from the very knight
whom report doth accuse of having taught the damsel to stray
from the path of virtue, and to whom she oweth her present
infamy."

" What mean ye, friar ? " cried Sir Patrick Hepborne, with
mingled indignation and astonishment. " Who hath so foully
and falsely dared to charge me and the Lady Beatrice—she who
is pure as an angel of light—Who, I say, hath dared to prefer
so foul and false an accusation ? "

" The Franciscan whom thou——"

" Villain !" cried Sir Patrick, interrupting Friar Rushak, and
giving way to a rage which he was quite unable to control ;
" villain, black and damnable villain ! I swear by the honour
of a knight, that this charge is false as hell. Pardon me,
holy father, for my just ire. I do beseech thee, tell me what
thou dost know of this wretch, of this assassin, who doth so
foully stab reputation too, and who hath so imposed on thy too
easy belief—What, I pray thee, dost thou know of him ? "

" Nay, I am ashamed to say, I know not much," replied Friar
Rushak, already shaken in his opinion of the Franciscan by the
solemnity of Sir Patrick's asseverations ; " yet what I do know I
was about to tell thee, when thou didst break in on my speech.
Being yesterday at the Franciscan Convent in the Newgate
Street, a stranger brother of the order did claim a private audience
of me, when he entreated mine aid to recover a damsel of good
family from the house of the Lady de Vere. He stated his
belief that she had come hither for the purpose of meeting
with thee, with whom she had once lived in lawless love, hid
in the disguise of a page, a connection which both were impatient to renew. He said that it was intended to bury her
disgrace in a convent. Fearing, for certain reasons, that the
King might see her at the Lady de Vere's, and so be misled to
take up with one so light, I resolved to do my best to assist in
her removal, and to this I was afterwards the more spurred on
by hearing that Richard had gone expressly to meet with her,
as I did believe, by her own especial consent. Availing myself
of my private knowledge of the palace, I did enable the stranger
Franciscan to take her from the apartment, where she succeeded

in convincing me that she was no willing captive; and the King's confession of this morning, the which I am so far permitted to impart to thee, hath satisfied me that I had weened too gravely of the matter as it did regard him, and that the whole of his share in it did but arise from a harmless piece of humour."

"And whither hath the Lady Beatrice been carried by this villain?" cried Hepborne, in all the agony of apprehension for her safety.

"He took her hence by water," said Friar Rushak, "and Scotland did seem to be the object of his voyage. But, of a truth, mine intercourse with the foul deceiver was so short that I had little leisure to question him."

"Fiend!" cried Sir Patrick Hepborne, his rage overpowering his grief. "If St. Baldrid do but speed me, I shall find him though he were to flee unto the uttermost parts of the earth. Meanwhile, may God in his mercy, and the blessed Virgin in her purity, protect the lady Beatrice!"

"Amen! my son," said the father confessor. "Verily, I do grieve for thee and for her; and of a truth I do bitterly reproach mine own facile credence, the which hath led me to be the innocent author of this misfortune. Thou shalt have my prayers. Meanwhile, let us return to the object of my mission. Richard did send me to tell thee that he doth freely forgive thee thine indiscreet attack on his sacred person, seeing it was committed under a delusion. Thou and thine esquire are forthwith liberated, under his word as a king, and yours as a knight, that all that hath passed shall be buried in oblivion by both sides; and further, that thou, on thy part, shalt fasten no quarrel on Sir Hans de Vere for what hath passed."

"Nay," replied Hepborne; "meseems that His Majesty doth ask too much in demanding of me to withhold punishment in a quarter where it is so justly due."

"Yes, and where it would be so well merited, Sir Knight," observed the Friar Rushak. "But yet must thou yield for peace's sake."

"Thou mayest tell the King, then," said Hepborne, "that as a mark of the high sense I entertain of his hospitality, he shall be obeyed herein, and that Sir Hans de Vere shall find shelter under it from my just indignation."

"And now let me show thee forth, Sir Knight," said Friar Rushak.

"Ere I go," said Hepborne, forgetting not the misery of others amid his own affliction; "ere I go hence let me entreat thee to use thine influence with His Majesty for the liberation of mine host, Master Lawrence Ratcliffe."

"Knowest thou aught of this same Ratcliffe, Sir Knight?" demanded the Friar after a pause, during which he endeavoured to read Hepborne's countenance.

"Nay, nothing further than that I have experienced his hospitality by His Majesty's good will," replied Hepborne.

"And how may he have treated thee and thine?" inquired Rushak, resuming a careless air.

"With a kindness for which I cannot sufficiently express my gratitude," replied Hepborne.

"'Tis well," replied Rushak. "Then may I tell thee in confidence that he hath been for some time suspected as a malcontent, and after thine attempt of yesternight against the King, he was taken up by the officious minions of power, as the most likely person to have set thee on. But I may now promise for his liberation. Thou shalt forthwith see him at his own house, and he shall know, ere he goeth, that it is to thee he oweth his liberty."

Sir Patrick Hepborne now hastened home to his lodgings, whither he was soon afterwards followed by his esquire and Master Lawrence Ratcliffe. The former was all joy, and the latter all gratitude. By and by he was joined by Adam of Gordon, who wept bitterly for the fate of the Lady Beatrice. Hepborne, much as he wanted comfort himself, found it necessary to administer it to the good old man, whom he immediately took into his service. He was now impatient to begin his quest after the Franciscan, and he would have quitted London immediately could he have easily procured a safe-conduct for himself individually; but this could not be granted. Sir David Lindsay, however, having witnessed the perfect recovery of the Lord Welles, on whom he had been unceasing in his attendance, he readily yielded to Hepborne's impatience, and the brave band of Scottish knights departed, leaving a sweet odour of good fame, both for courtesy and deeds of arms, behind them.

Their journey was speedily and safely performed; and they were no sooner in Scotland than Hepborne hastened to Hailes Castle, whither he was accompanied by his friends. Thence he was eager to pursue his way northwards to Elgin, where he believed that the Franciscan had his abode, and whither he thought it likely that he had conveyed his prisoner. But Sir John Halyburton, to whom he had been much attached ever since their first acquaintance at Tarnawa, and with whom his friendship had been drawn yet tighter by the intercourse he held during their late expedition, had already extracted a promise from him that he would be present at his marriage with the Lady Jane de Vaux, a promise from which he felt it impossible to rid himself by any excuse he could invent. But this, he hoped, would occasion him but small delay, for the Lord of Dirleton, with his lady and daughter, were understood to be with the Court at Scone; and thither Sir John Halyburton resolved to proceed immediately, in the hope that the consummation of his happiness would not be long deferred. Delay to Hepborne was distraction; but it was at least some small comfort to him, that at Scone he would be so much nearer that part of Scotland whither his anxiety now so powerfully drew him.

The whole party then hastened to Scone, which the residence of the Court had already made the general rendezvous of the great. There Sir Patrick Hepborne had the happiness to find his father, and there he also embraced his happy sister Isabelle, and her Assueton. The Lord of Dirleton and his lady expressed much pleasure in again enjoying his society; but, to the great grief of Sir John Halyburton, and to the secret mortification of his friend Sir Patrick, the Lady Jane de Vaux was not with her father and mother, for, not being aware of the so early return of the knights from England, they had permitted their daughter to accompany the Countess of Moray from Aberdeen to Tarnawa, whence that noble lady was daily expected to bring her to Scone.

The venerable King Robert received the knights who had so nobly supported the honour of Scotland on the bloody field of Otterbourne with distinguished cordiality and condescension. Sir Patrick Hepborne was among those who were most highly honoured. To him was granted the privilege, only extended to a limited number of courtiers, of entering the Royal presence at all times; and Robert, pressing his hand with a warmth which kings seldom permit themselves to show, told him that the more frequently he availed himself of the power of approaching him, the more he would add to his satisfaction. This flattering reception from his aged King, together with the gratifying notice bestowed on him by the Earl of Fife and Menteith, now the Regent of the Kingdom, might have made him well contented to prolong his residence at Court, and little regret the delay of Halyburton's marriage, had it not been for the thought, that never forsook him, of the mysterious fate and probable misery of the Lady Beatrice. His mind was ceaselessly employed in fancying a thousand improbable things regarding her, and he was generally abstracted in the midst of those gay scenes which the politic Regent took care should follow one another with the greatest rapidity, that he might the better keep his hold of the fickle hearts of the nobles. In vain were the fairest eyes of the Court thrown upon Sir Patrick Hepborne : their warm glances were invariably chilled by the freezing indifference by which they were met.

Day after day passed away, and still no appearance of the Countess of Moray and her lovely companion; and Halyburton's loudly-expressed impatience was only to be equalled by that which affected Hepborne in secret. The two knights had nearly agreed to proceed northwards together, a plan proposed by Hepborne, and listened to by Halyburton with great grati- tude, as he considered it a very strong proof of his friend's anxiety for his happiness. But, happening to recollect that the party from Tarnawa might reach Scone perhaps a few hours only after they should leave it on this doubtful expedition, and that the long-wished-for meeting with his beloved Jane de Vaux might thus be much delayed, instead of hastened, Halyburton, to Hepborne's very great grief, abandoned the scheme as unwise. Soon afterwards came the intelligence of the burning of Elgin, which, whilst it threw a gloom over the whole Court, filled Hepborne's mind with fresh apprehensions and anxieties.

CHAPTER LXXII.

At the Scottish Court—The Penitential Procession—Sir Patrick and the Friar.

It happened one day that Sir Patrick went to pay his duty to the King, and understanding, as he passed through the ante- room, from those who were in waiting, that His Majesty was in the apartment he usually occupied as a private audience-cham- ber, he approached and opened the door. To his unspeakable astonishment, he beheld the very Franciscan whom he was so anxious to go in search of, standing beside His Majesty's chair, and in conference with him. They were alone. Holding a letter and parchment carelessly folded in his hand, His Majesty seemed to have been much moved with what had been passing between him and the monk, and he was so much occupied in listening, that Sir Patrick's entrance could have hardly been observed, had not the opening of the door startled both of them.

Sir Patrick was so petrified with what he beheld, that he had neither self-command enough to retreat, as he ought to have done, nor to apologise, as the interruption demanded.

"Another time, Sir Patrick Hepborne," said the King, nodding him away. But His Majesty was compelled to repeat the hint ere the knight had so far regained his self-possession as to take it, and when he did retire, it was with a face overwhelmed with confusion, and with a heart boiling with rage against the monk.

"Ha!" said he, at length, in soliloquy; "at least I am now nearer the object of my anxious quest than I did think I was. The friar must be a fiend, who can thus so soon catch the King's ear. But, fiend or mortal, he shall not escape me. How malignant was his eye-glance, shot at me the moment that he heard my name uttered. But, by St. Baldrid, were he a basilisk I will seize him by the throat. He shall tell me where he hath hid her who is the idol of my soul; yea, he shall disgorge all that his black heart doth contain, even though the monarch himself should endeavour to protect him. What if the Lady Beatrice may be here? Oh, misery! so near me, and yet am I denied the delight of hearing that voice, the which did so soothe mine ear when it came from the lips of my faithful page—or of beholding that eye, which did so beam upon me with looks that nothing but love could have explained. But the monk at least shall not escape me this time. I shall station myself here, and watch his approach, albeit he should tarry within till doomsday."

After thinking, rather than uttering, all this, Sir Patrick mingled with the crowd in the ante-room, where he waited patiently for the greater part of the day, until the King came forth to get into his litter to take the air. His Majesty appeared unattended by the friar, and then it was that Sir Patrick Hepborne began to recollect, what his agitation had made him overlook before, that the Franciscan must have been admitted, and allowed to retire, by a private passage, only accessible to those who received a very particular confidential audience of His Majesty. Hepborne threw himself as much in the King's way as he could, and made a very marked obeisance to him as he passed; but Robert, who usually received all his advances with peculiar kindness and condescension, now turned from him with a certain distance of manner that could not be mistaken, and which chilled Sir Patrick to the heart. At once it flashed upon him that the Franciscan, who had so strangely possessed himself of the King's ear, must have poisoned it

against him, as he had formerly done that of Friar Rushak.
His rage against the monk grew to tenfold strength, and, in the
agony of his distraction, he resolved to risk His Majesty's displeasure by seeking his presence again, rather than not gain his
object. He determined to accuse the Franciscan to the King,
as he who had stolen away, and perhaps murdered, the Lady
Beatrice, and this in defiance of all consequences.

Sir Patrick again tried to catch the Royal eye, as the King
returned from his airing, but again he had the mortification to
observe that he was shunned and neglected. His Majesty
appeared not at the banquet, where, indeed, he had not been
since the news of the burning of Elgin had reached him ; and
when Hepborne thought on this, a faint hope came over him
that the King's neglect might perhaps proceed from no par
ticular feeling against him, but might arise from the vexation
that must naturally fill the Royal breast on this unhappy occasion. But then again he remembered, with incalculable
chagrin, that although the sunshine of the Monarch's smiles
had been eclipsed towards him, it had fallen with all its wonted
cheering influence upon some who were near him, and who had
hitherto been considered as planets of a much lower order, and
of infinitely less happy influence than himself.

But Sir Patrick now became so impatient to get at the truth,
that he threw aside all that delicacy which might have otherwise swayed him. He resolved to make an attempt to obtain
an audience of His Majesty at his hour of couchée ; and,
accordingly, entering the ante-room a little before the time, he
made his enquiries for that purpose.

"The King hath given strict orders that no one be admitted
to him," replied the Lord-in-waiting, to whom he addressed
himself. "He doth hold private conference. And between
you and me, Sir Patrick Hepborne, I do verily believe that it is
with his son, the furious Wolfe of Badenoch, who hath so besieged the Bishop of Moray, that he is to hold parlance."

"What, hath the Earl of Buchan arrived, then ?" demanded
Sir Patrick.

"Yea, he is here," replied the nobleman with whom he
talked. "Hast thou not heard that to-morrow the streets of St.
Johnstoun will see a sight the like of which hath not been seen
in Scotland before ? for there the fierce and proud Wolfe of
Badenoch is to walk in penance from the Castle, where he now
hath his lodging, to the Church of the Blackfriars."

"And how dost thou know all this ?" demanded Sir Patrick
Hepborne, who had probably heard the report, but who had

been too much occupied with his own thoughts to attend to anything extraneous, however interesting it might be to others.

"The news hath already gone fully abroad," replied the nobleman; "but, moreover, all manner of preparation hath been already made for the ceremony; yea, and all the world do make arrangement for witnessing so great a miracle. I, for one, shall assuredly be there."

Sir Patrick Hepborne retired. As he passed by the entrance to the King's private staircase, a portly figure brushed by him, and entered it hastily. He called to mind that he had encountered the same as he left the King's presence at Aberdeen. It was indeed the Wolfe of Badenoch, but he had passed Sir Patrick Hepborne without observing him.

King Robert was at this moment seated in a large antique chair, placed close to the chimney corner, somewhat in the same dishabille as we have described him to have worn on a former occasion. His foot-bath stood ready prepared, and his attendant Vallance, who waited at a respectful distance, ventured more than once to remind His Majesty that the water was cooling. But the old man was deeply absorbed in serious thought. His eyes were directed to a huge vacuum in the hinder part of the chimney, amidst the black void of which the play of his ideas went on without interruption. A gentle tap was heard at his private door.

"We would be private, Vallance," said the King, starting from his reverie, and pointing to his attendants to quit the apartment.

When they had withdrawn, Robert arose feebly, and propped himself on a cane. The knock at the private room was repeated. The old Monarch tottered towards the middle of the room. The knock was heard a third time, and with more impatience.

"If it be thou, son Alexander, come in," said the King.

The door opened and the Wolfe of Badenoch entered, with a chastened step, and a mien very different from that which usually characterised him. He made an humble obeisance to his father. He spoke not, but his eyes glanced unsteadily towards the King, as if yet half in doubt what his reception might be. He beheld the old man standing before him struggling with emotions that convulsed his face and threw his whole frame into a fit of trembling. He saw that a great and mortifying change had taken place on his father since the last interview, and his conscience at once struck him that his own disobedience and outrageous conduct must have largely contributed to produce the decay which was so evident. He was smitten to the heart.

"Oh, my father, my father!" cried he in a half-choked voice; "canst thou forgive me? When all have forgiven me, canst thou refuse me pardon?"

"Son Alexander," said Robert, in a voice that shook from agitation as well as debility, "all others may pardon thee, and yet it may be the duty of thy King, albeit that he is thy father, to put on sternness with thee. Nor have we been wanting in performance of the severe duty of a King towards thee; for ere we did receive the godly Bishop of Moray's letters regarding thee from the hands of the good Friar John, we had issued orders for the arrestment and warding of thy person in the nearest and most convenient of our prisons. Nor did we ever spare to meet thee with harsh reproof whilst thou wert headstrong and rebellious; but now that thou dost come before us as a penitent and afflicted son, saying, 'Father, I have sinned against Heaven and in thy sight;' when thou comest as one willing to submit thee to all that the Church may demand of thee in reparation or in penance for thine outrages, we can no longer remember that we are a King, but we must yield us to those feelings which do now so stirringly tell us that we are a father. Oh, Alexander, my son, my son!" cried the old man, yielding to those emotions which he could no longer restrain, and bursting into a flood of tears, whilst he threw his aged arms around the manly form of the Wolfe of Badenoch; "the joy of this thy repentance doth more than recompense for all the affliction thou hast occasioned me during a long life. For thee, my son Alexander, have all my nights been sleepless; yea, and for thee have all my prayers been put up. Blessed be the holy Virgin, that they have not been put up in vain. Verily, I do sink fast into the grave; but thanks be to the Almighty King of kings, I shall now die in peace and with joy, sith that it hath pleased Him to bring thee to a due sense of the enormity of thy guilt."

"Alas, alas!" cried the Wolfe of Badenoch, deeply affected by his father's wasted appearance, and sobbing aloud from remorse; "alas! I do fear that thy life hath been amenused by mine iniquities. Oh, father, I could bear all but this, the bitterest punishment of all. Thou hast sadly drooped sith that I did last behold thee. Would that I had then listened to the voice of thy wisdom, when it did so eloquently speak. But a devil hath possessed me; and, fiend that I was——"

"Speak not so, my son," cried the old King, who had now

sufficiently recovered himself to be able to talk calmly. "Self-accusation, except in so far as it is used as an offering before Heaven, is but a vain thing. Let thy whole heart be given up to that contrition the which is between thee and thy God alone, through the medium and mediation of the blessed Virgin and her Son ; and let the seemliness and sincerity of thy public penance be an earnest of the amendment of thy future life."

"I will, I will, my father," cried the Wolfe of Badenoch, much moved. "Would that ages of my penance could but add to the number of thy peaceful and righteous years ; cheerfully would I wander as a barefooted palmer for the rest of my miserable days. Yet fancy not, my father, that I have lacked mine own share of punishment. The viper for whom I did risk thy wrath and that of Heaven, hath stung me to the heart. Ha! but 'tis over now. The good Friar John hath taught me to keep down the raging ire which her black and hellish ingratitude did excite within me. May the holy Virgin grant me aid to subdue it, that my whole heart may be in to-morrow's work ; for, sooth to say, 'tis cruel and cutting, after all, for a hardy, haughty soul like mine to bend me thus beneath the rod of the priesthood. Ha! by the bones of my ancestors, a King's son too—thy son ! Nay, 'tis that the which doth most gall and chafe me ; to think that thou shouldst thus be brought into derision by the disgrace which befalleth me. Thou, a King who——"

"Son Alexander," said the venerable Monarch, calmly interrupting the Wolfe of Badenoch, as he was gradually blowing up a self-kindled flame of passion ; "think not of us—think not of us now. Thou shouldst have thought of us and of our feelings before thou didst apply the torch of thy wild wrath to the holy temples of God and the peaceful habitations of his ministers. Robert was indeed ashamed of a wicked son, glorying in his mad and guilty rage ; but Robert never can be ashamed of a son who is an humble penitent. No, Alexander ; thy penance will be a crown of glory to us. Further, we would have thee remember that the priesthood are but the ministers of the justice of a greater King than any upon earth ; and we would have thee to bear in mind how the Son of that Almighty King did, in all His innocence, submit Himself to the scourge and the cross, to infamy and cruel suffering, that He might redeem such sinners as thou and I. Let this humble thy pride and tame thy temper, if, indeed, pride or violence may yet remain with thee. And now haste thee homeward, that, by a night spent in conversation and prayer with the holy Friar John, thou mayest fit and prepare thyself for to-morrow's duty, the which ought

588

to be rather esteemed a triumph than a trial to thee. We shall
be at the Castle of St. Johnstoun by times to give thee our best
comfort ; till then take with thee a father's blessing."

The Wolfe of Badenoch bowed his head to receive the benediction of the good old King, who wept as he gave it him, and
throwing one arm round his son's neck, he patted his head with
the other hand, kissing his cheek repeatedly with all the
affection of a doating father, who abandons himself to the full
tide of his feelings and who is unwilling to shorten the transports he enjoys.

The news of the intended penitential procession of the King's
son, the terrible Wolfe of Badenoch, spread like wildfire through
the town of St Johnstoun, as well as throughout the surrounding
country, and produced a general commotion. The Bishops of
St. Andrews, Dunkeld, and Dunblane, had already arrived at
the Dominican Convent, each having separately entered the
town in great pomp, attended by all the high dignitaries of
their respective dioceses. It was a proud triumph for the
Church, and secret advices had been accordingly sent everywhere, that it might be rendered the more imposing and im-
pressive by the numbers and importance of those religious
persons who came as deputations from the different monastic
houses which were within reach. Of the canons regular, there
were the Abbots of Scone, Inch Colm, and Inch Mahome, with
the Priors of St. Andrews, Loch Leven, Port Moak, and Pitten-
weem ; of the Trinity, or Red Friars, were the Ministers of the
Hospitals of Scotlandwell and of Dundee ; of the Dominicans or
Black Friars, the inmates of the Dominican Convent of Perth,
where the ceremony was to take place, with the heads of the
Convents of Dundee, Cupar in Fife, St. Monans, and St.
Andrews ; of the Benedictines, the Abbot of Dunfermline ; of
the Tyronenses, the Abbot of Lundores ; of the Cistertians, or
Bernardines, the Abbots of Culross and Balmerinoch ; of the
Franciscans, or Grey Friars, the head of the Convent of Inver-
keithing ; and, lastly, a numerous body of Carmelites, or White
Friars, from the neighbouring Convent of Tullilum. All these
heads of houses were largely attended ; and if the crowd of
these holy men was great that of the laity and vulgar was tenfold greater. The houses of the place were unable to contain
them, and many were glad to encamp on those beautiful
meadows stretching to north and south of the town, thankful
to huddle themselves under any temporary shelter they could
procure. The Black Friars Monastery, which was to be the
scene of the humiliation of the Wolfe of Badenoch, was all in a

ferment, and many there were who, knowing the formidable character of him they had to deal with, muttered secret ejaculations that all were well over.

The King left his Palace of Scone early in the morning, and entered Perth in his litter, attended by the Regent and the courtiers, being desirous to get as quietly as possible into the Castle. The King's body-guard were drawn out to line the street from the Castle to the Church of the Dominican Convent. The distance was short, but the crowd contained in that small space was immense. The murmur was great, and the eyes of the spectators were constantly directed towards the gate of the Castle, whence they expected the procession to come. Every motion among the multitude excited an accession of impatience.

At length the King's litter appeared, attended by the Regent, and followed by the crowd of courtiers. They came without order, and the litter hurried into the Church amidst the loud shouts of the people. All was then eager expectation, and nothing interrupted the low hum of voices, save the noise occasioned by those who made way for the different religious deputations, who approached the Church from different directions.

All these had passed onwards, and some time had elapsed, when a general hush ran through the crowd—a dead silence ensued—all eyes were directed towards the Castle gate—and the Wolfe of Badenoch appeared. He was supported on his right hand by his confessor, the Franciscan Friar, and he was followed by his two sons Andrew and Duncan, and by a very numerous train of attendants, all clad in the same humiliating penitential garb, walking barefooted. The Wolfe of Badenoch had no sooner issued from the Castle gateway than he appeared to be astonished and mortified at the multitude of people who had collected to witness his abasement. Anticipating nothing of this sort, he had prepared to assume a subdued air ; but he was roused by the sight, and advanced with his head carried high, and with all his usual haughtiness of stride, his eyes flinging a bold defiance to all round, and their glances travelling rapidly from countenance to countenance, as they surveyed the two walls of human faces lining his way, as if he looked eagerly for some one whose taunting smile might give him an apology for breaking forth, and giving vent to his pent-up passion by felling him to the earth. He went on, biting his nether lip, and still he scanned them man by man ; but everywhere he encountered eyes that quailed before his, and peaceful, gaping faces, filled with vulgar wonder, perhaps, and indicating much of fear, but nothing of scorn to be seen. The Franciscan was observed to whisper him; he seemed to listen with reverence, and, as he approached the entrance to the Church, he adopted a more humble gait and look. As for his men, they hung down their heads sheepishly from the first, like felons going to execution.

When the procession had reached the great door of the Church, which was closed against it, the Franciscan approached, and knocked slowly and solemnly.

" Who is he who knocketh for admission into the Church of God?" demanded a voice from within.

" Alexander Stewart, Earl of Buchan, and Lord of Badenoch, son of Robert, our most pious King," replied the Franciscan.

" We do know right well that there once was such an one as thou dost name," replied the voice; " but now he hath no existence. The great sentence of excommunication hath gone forth against his hardened obstinacy, and the Holy Church knoweth him no longer."

" He cometh here as an humble penitent, to crave mercy and pardon of our Holy Mother Church," replied the Franciscan.

" Is he ready to confess his sins against God and man, then?" demanded the voice. " Is he prepared humbly on his knees to declare his penitence, and to implore that mercy and pardon, the which must of necessity be extended to him ere he can again be received back into the bosom of that Church which he hath so greatly outraged?"

" He is," replied the Franciscan.

" Then, if such be his sincere professions," replied the voice, " let him and all understand, that albeit she can greatly and terribly punish, yet doth the Church delight in mercy, and it is ever her most joyful province to open her doors wide to her sincerely repentant children."

These words were no sooner uttered, than the folding doors were thrown wide, and the populace were dazzled with the grandeur of the spectacle that presented itself. The verse of a hymn, that burst from a powerful choir within, added to the sublimity of the effect, whilst it gave time for the spectators to feast their eyes without distraction on what they beheld. In the centre of the doorway stood Walter Traill, the Bishop of St. Andrews, arrayed in all the splendour of his pastoral robes. Within his left arm was his crosier, and in his right hand he raised aloft a large silver crucifix. On his right and left were the Bishops of Dunblane and Dunkeld, behind whom were the whole dignitaries of the three sees in all their pomp of costume.

The Church had been darkened that it might be artificially lighted by tapers, so as to present objects under that softly diffused and holy kind of illumination most favourable for the productions of strong impressions of awe. By this was seen a long train of Abbots and Priors, with Monks and Friars from all those religious houses we have already particularised. The sight was grand and imposing in itself, and picturesque in its grouping and disposal. The Franciscan Friar John whispered the Wolfe of Badenoch, and he bent down with a rigid effort until his knees were on the pavement. His sons and his followers imitated his example.

"Alexander Stewart, Earl of Buchan, and Lord of Badenoch," said the Bishop of St. Andrews, in a full and sonorous voice, when the music had died away, "dost thou earnestly desire to be relieved from the heavy sentence of excommunication which thy manifold crimes and iniquities have compelled the Church to issue forth against thee?"

"I do," replied the Wolfe in a firm voice.

"Dost thou humbly confess and repent thee of thy sins in general," demanded the Bishop; "and art thou willing to confess and repent thee of each sin in particular at the high altar of this holy temple?"

"I do so repent me, and I am willing so to confess me," replied the Wolfe.

"Then arise, my contrite son," said the Bishop, "and humbly follow me to present thyself at the holy altar of God."

The three Bishops with their attendants then turned away, and being followed by the Wolfe of Badenoch and his long train of penitential adherents, they moved in slow procession up the middle of the church towards the high altar, before which the penitents kneeled down, with their stern leader at their head, the monks of the various orders closing in behind them. The most perfect silence prevailed, and the soft fall of the footsteps on the pavement, and the rustling of draperies, were the only sounds heard.

"Alexander Stewart, Earl of Buchan, and Lord of Badenoch," said the Bishop of St. Andrews, "dost thou confess that thou hast greatly sinned in thine abandonment of thine honourable and lawful wife Euphame Countess of Ross, and dost thou repent thee of this thine offence?"

"I do repent me," said the Wolfe in an humble tone.

"Dost thou confess that thou hast greatly sinned in taking to thy bosom that foul and impure strange woman, Mariota Athyn?" demanded the Bishop; "especially thou being——"

"I do so confess, and I do most sincerely, yea, cruelly repent me," cried the Wolfe, breaking in impatiently, and with great bitterness, on the unfinished question of the Bishop, and shouting out his answer in a tone that re-echoed from the Gothic roof.

"And art thou willing, or dost thou purpose to put this strange woman far from thee?" demanded the Bishop.

"I have already turned her forth," shouted the Wolfe, in the same furious tone; "yea, and before God, at this His holy altar, do I swear, that with mine own will these eyes shall never see her more."

"And wilt thou take back thy lawful wife?" demanded the Bishop, now willing to be as short as possible.

"I will," replied the Wolfe.

"And now, dost thou sincerely acknowledge and repent thee of all the outrages thou hast done to our Holy Mother Church, as well as to God and His ministers?" demanded the Bishop.

"I do," replied the Wolfe.

"Then do I, God's servant, proceed to give thee and thine absolution, and to remove from thee the excommunication which was hurled upon thee by the Church in her just vengeance," said the Bishop, who immediately began to pronounce the form of absolution prescribed by his ritual, as well as that for removing the excommunication.

Miserere was now sung by the choir, after which a mass was chanted, and the impatient Wolfe of Badenoch, tired twenty times over of a ceremony which would have worn out a much more submissive temper, tarried not a moment in the church after it was concluded, but, attended by the Franciscan, forced his way without any delicacy through the crowd, which yielded him a ready passage, and made a hasty exit from the church door. Having gained the open air, he strode along the lane of the guards, with an air that might have led a bystander to fancy that he gloried in his strange attire.

He was about to enter the Castle-gate, when a loud voice, calling "Halt!" came from behind him. He stopped, and turning loftily round, he beheld an armed knight, who came rushing through the abashed and scattered ranks of his men, who were straggling after him. In an instant, the mailed warrior made an effort to grapple the Franciscan by the throat; and he would have succeeded, had not the friar sprung nimbly aside to avoid him.

"Ha!" cried the Wolfe, in a voice like thunder, and at the

same time snatching a formidable Scottish axe from one of the guards, and planting his unprotected body firmly before the Franciscan; "ha! who art thou that doth thus dare to attack the father confessor of the Wolfe of Badenoch? Dost thou think that I have tyned my spirit in yonder church? By all the solemn vows I have made, I will split the skull of any he who may dare to lay impious hands on this holy Franciscan."

"Is this possible?" cried the knight, raising his vizor, and showing himself to be Sir Patrick Hepborne the younger; "can it be that the Earl of Buchan will thus defend the very friar whom mine ears have so often heard him curse as a fiend? But let me pass to him, my Lord; I do beseech thee to provoke me not, for, of a truth, I am mad, utterly mad, at this present."

"Mad or sober, Sir Patrick Hepborne," cried the Wolfe, "for now I do perceive that thou art indeed Sir Patrick Hepborne, and much as I do love thee, I swear, by the beard of my grandfather, that neither thine arm, nor that of any created man, shall reach the friar save through this body of mine."

"Wull she wants her helps? wull she wants her to grip him? wull she cleave the Wolfe's crown?" said Duncan MacErchar, who now stepped out from the ranks, and spoke into Sir Patrick's ear. "Troth, she wull soon do that, though she be twenty Wolfes, and a hundert Badenochs."

"Stand aside, Duncan," cried the knight, now somewhat sensible of his apparently unwarrantable violence, and altogether confounded by the Wolfe of Badenoch's unlooked-for defence of the Franciscan. "By St. Baldrid, my Lord of Buchan, I should have as soon looked to have seen the eagle defending the owl who hath robbed her nest, as to see thee thus stand forth the protector of that accursed priest, that foul-mouthed slanderer, and remorseless assassin. Let me secure him. He is a criminal who must be brought to justice."

"Thou shalt not touch the hem of his garment," roared the Wolfe of Badenoch.

"Nay, give him way, my noble Lord of Buchan," said the Franciscan in a taunting manner; "let this brave knight have way to use his poinard, or his sword, against the defenceless body of a friar. But," continued he, snatching a long spear from one of those near him, whilst his eyes flashed a fiery defiance against Hepborne, "let him come on now, and he shall find that beneath this peaceful habit there doth beat as proud and determined a heart as ever his bosom did own. As for his

38

villainous and lying charges, I do hereby cast them back in his teeth as false."

"Caitiff," cried Sir Patrick, "I should gain but little credit, I trow, by attacking a vile friar. I did but intend to prevent thine escape from the justice thou dost merit; and if I were but sure of seeing thee again in fitter time and place, when and where I could bring forward my charges, and prove them against thee, I should let thee go for this present."

"Nay, fear not, I will promise not to shun thee, Sir Knight," said the friar; "and thou, too, dost well know what charges thou shalt have to defend. The Earl of Buchan here will answer for my presence in the Castle when it shall be wanted; but who shall answer for thine?"

"I will," said Sir John Halyburton, who chanced to come up at that moment.

"Sir John Halyburton!" exclaimed the Franciscan, with an air of astonishment. "Um—'tis well; and trust me, Sir John Halyburton, thou wilt find that thou hast more interest in his being forthcoming than thou dost at this moment imagine, and so the sooner he doth appear the better."

"Nay, I will follow thee now," replied Sir Patrick; "by all the holy saints, thou shalt not leave my sight."

"Come on, then," replied the Franciscan, with a bitter laugh; "and yonder cometh the King's litter, so thou shalt have little time to wait, I wis, for ample justice."

The monk then entered the Castle, followed by the Wolfe of Badenoch, who still brandished the long Scottish axe, and looked sternly around from time to time upon Sir Patrick as if suspicious that he might yet meditate an attack upon the friar.

"Hoit oit," cried Duncan MacErchar, "and has the Hepbornes lost their spunks sith the battles o' Otterburns? Who would hae thought that ony ane o' her name would hae ta'en the boast yon way even frae the Wolfes o' Badenoch hersel? Huits toots, Sir Patrick—uve, uve!"

"Pshaw," replied Sir Patrick, much mortified to find that MacErchar had attributed his forbearance to want of spirit, "Wouldst thou have had a Hepborne attack a monk, or a man half naked, and at such a time as this too!"

"Ou fye! faith an' it may be's," replied Duncan, somewhat doubtfully; "but she might ha' gien him a clour for a' tats. But can she do nothing to serve her honour?"

"Yea," replied Sir Patrick, "plant thyself here; let not that Franciscan Friar leave the Castle until I have questioned him."

"Ou, troth, and she'll no scruples to gie him a clour," replied Duncan.

Hepborne hastened into the Castle, and Captain MacErchar mechanically took his stand, nor did even the approach of the King's litter, and the bustle that came with it, dislodge him from his post.

CHAPTER LXXIII.

Accusation made in presence of the King—The Challenge.

SIR PATRICK HEPBORNE, accompanied by his friend Sir John Halyburton, made his way into the hall of the Castle, burning with impatience to bring the Franciscan to a strict account, and half dreading that he might yet escape, by that mysterious power which had already so marvellously availed him. The Wolfe of Badenoch had hurried to his apartments to rid himself of his penitential weeds; and the Franciscan having disappeared also, the two knights were left to pace the hall for at least two hours, until Sir Patrick began to suspect that his fears had been realized. Rushing down to the gate, however, he found Captain MacErchar as steady at his post as the walls of the fortress; and, having questioned him, he learned that no friar had passed outwards. When he returned to the hall, he found the King seated on a chair of state, and his courtiers ranged on either hand of him, forming a semi-circle, of which he was the central point.

"Sir Patrick Hepborne," said the King, with a high and distant air, "we are here to listen to thine accusation against the holy Franciscan Friar John, whom, we do understand, thou hast dared to malign."

"My liege," said Hepborne, "the thirsty steed panteth not more for the refreshing fountain than I do for audience of your Most Gracious Majesty, from whom I would claim that justice the which thou dost never deny to the meanest. of thy subjects."

"And we shall not refuse it to thee, the son of our ancient and faithful servant," replied the King; "to one who hath himself done us and our kingdom of Scotland much good service. Yet do we bid thee bear in mind, that the best services may be wiped away by !the disgraceful finger of polluted iniquity. Speak, Sir Patrick, what hast thou to say ?"

"Nay, my liege, I would stay me until mine adversary doth appear to meet my charge," said Sir Patrick.

" 'Tis so far considerate of thee," replied the King; " but thou mayest say on, for he will be here anon."

" I come here, then, to impeach this Friar John of having feloniously carried off a damsel from the Tower of London, where she did then abide," said Sir Patrick Hepborne, violently agitated; "a damsel whom he did once before attempt to murder, and whom he doth even now secrete, if he hath not already cruelly slain her."

" Friar John is here to meet thy charge, Sir Knight," cried the Franciscan, who had entered the hall in time to hear what had fallen from Hepborne, and who now came sternly forward, attended by the Wolfe of Badenoch, the Lord of Dirleton, and some others; " Friar John shall not shrink from whatever tales thine inventive recrimination may produce against him; he too shall have his charge against thee; but let thine be disposed of first, whereby the incredible boldness of thy wickedness may be made the more apparent to all."

" What sayest thou?" demanded Hepborne, with considerable confusion.

" I do say," replied the friar, " that conscious guilt doth already stagger thee in the very outset of this thine infamous attempt against an innocent man, whom thou wouldst fain sacrifice to hide thy foul deeds. Guilt doth often prove its own snare, and so shall ye see it here, I ween."

" Villain, wretch, fiend?" cried Sir Patrick Hepborne, who forgot in his resentment the presence in which he stood; " mine emotions, the which thou wouldst have others so misjudge, have been those only of horror and astonishment at thine unparalleled effrontery. My liege, this fiend—this wicked sorcerer—for so do I believe him to be—this assassin——"

" Ha! by the ghost of my grandfather," cried the Wolfe of Badenoch, who stood by, now restored to all his knightly splendour—"by the ghost of my grandfather, but I will not stand by to hear such names hurled without reason on my holy father confessor. As he is here to answer thee, Sir Patrick Hepborne, and as I would not willingly seem to interfere with justice, say what thou wilt of calm accusation, for I fear not that he will cleanse himself, whosoever may be foul. But, by all the holy saints, I swear that, friends though we have been, I will not hear the holy man so foully miscalled; and I am well willing to fight for him to the outrance, not only in this world, but in the next too, if chivalry be but carried thither."

" Silence, son Alexander," said the King; " speak not, I pray thee, with lips so irreverent. And do thou, Sir Patrick Hep-

borne, proceed with thy charges, withouten these needless terms
of reproach, the which are unseemly in our presence, and do but
tend to inflame."

"My liege," said Sir Patrick, making an obeisance to the
King, "I shall do my best to restrain my just indignation.—
The Lady Beatrice, of whom I do now speak, did accompany me
to Moray Land in the disguise of a page; and——"

"Ha!" exclaimed the King, starting with an air of surprise,
and exchanging a look with the Franciscan and some others,
that very much discomposed Sir Patrick; "so—dost thou confess this?"

"I do confess nothing, my liege," replied Sir Patrick; "I do
only tell the truth. When we were guests for some days to thee,
my Lord of Buchan, at Lochyndorbe, this friar did enter the
apartment of the Lady Beatrice armed with a dagger, and had
she not fled from him to save her life, she had surely been murdered by his villainy. Already have I told that he did snatch
her from the Tower of London, by means of false representations
made to Friar Rushak, King Richard's Confessor, and thence he
did carry her by ship to Scotland, as I do know from Friar Rushak himself. I do therefore call on him to produce the damsel
straightway, if indeed his cruelty hath not already put it beyond his power so to do."

"Hast thou aught else to charge him withal?" demanded the
King.

"Nay, my liege," replied Hepborne, "but I require an immediate answer to these charges."

"Before I do give a reply," said the Franciscan, assuming a
grand air, "I, on my part, do demand to know by what right
Sir Patrick Hepborne doth thus question me."

"Right, didst thou say?" exclaimed Hepborne; "I must
answer thee by simply saying, that I do question thee by that
right which every honourable knight hath to come forward in
the cause of the unfortunate. But I will go farther, and say
before all who are here present, that I do more especially appear
here against thee for the unquenchable love I do bear to the
Lady Beatrice."

"Ha! so," replied the Franciscan, with a bitter expression,
"thou hast so far confessed that thou didst entertain the Lady
Beatrice in thy company in male attire, and that thou dost
cherish an unquenchable passion for her? Then, my liege, do
I boldly accuse this pretended phœnix of virtue, this Sir Patrick
Hepborne, of having stolen this damsel from the path of honour
—of having plunged her in guilt—of having so bewitched her

by potent charms, that she did even follow him to London, whence, with much fatigue and stratagem, I did indeed reclaim her, yea, did bring her to Scotland in a ship. But she was not many hours on land when she so contrived as to flee from me; and no one can doubt that her flight was directed to him who hath thrown his sorcery over her, and to whom she hath made so many efforts basely to unite herself again."

"Friar, thou hast lied, grossly and villanously lied," cried Sir Patrick Hepborne in a fury, "But now let me, in my turn, demand of thee what hast thou to urge that mought have given thee right so to control the Lady Beatrice?"

"All have right to prevent the commission of wickedness," said the Franciscan. "But I do claim the right of parentage to control the Lady Beatrice. I am her uncle. Hath not so near a parent some right to control the erring daughter of his brother? Speak then; tell me where thou hast hid her, Sir Knight?"

"Can this be true?" exclaimed Sir Patrick Hepborne, petri-fied with astonishment at what he heard; "canst thou in very deed be the uncle of the Lady Beatrice? But what shall we say of that tender uncle who doth enter the apartment of his niece at midnight with a dagger in his hand? Villain, I observe thee blench as I do speak it. Thou art a villain still, let thy kindred to her be what it may. Thou hast murdered my love, and thou wouldst shift off suspicion from thyself, by an endea-vour to throw guilt upon me. Wretched hypocrite! foul stain to the holy habit thou dost wear—say where, where hast thou bestowed the Lady Beatrice? Is she dead or alive?"

"Nay, foul shame to knighthood that thou art, 'tis thou who hast secreted the Lady Beatrice—thou who hast poisoned her mind—thou who hast disgraced her—thou who dost hide her from the light of day, that she may minister to thine abandoned love. Tell, tell me where thou hast hid her, or, friar as I am, I do here appeal thee to single duel."

"Ha!" said Sir Patrick, "And right willingly, I trow, shall I do instant battle in support of mine unsullied honour—in support of the honour of her who hath been so foully calumni-ated; but with a friar like thee!"

"Nay, let that be no hindrance, Sir Knight," cried the Franciscan, whilst his eyes darted lightnings; "now indeed I am a friar, but, trust me, I was not always so. In me thou shalt have no weak or untaught arm to deal withal; and if I may but have dispensation——"

"Talk not so, Friar John," said the King; "thou shalt never

be suffered to peril thy life. Thou must seek thee out some
cham——"

"Nay, seek nowhere but here," cried the Wolfe of Badenoch,
slapping his right hand furiously on his cuirass. "If the good
Friar John doth bestir himself to save my soul, 'tis but reason,
meseems, that I should rouse me to save his body. I am in
some sort a witness to the truth of part of what he hath asserted.
So, by the blood of the Bruce, Sir Patrick——"

"Nay, nay, my Lord Earl," cried the old Lord of Dirleton,
now starting up with an agitation that shook every fibre, and
with a countenance in which grief and resentment were powerfully blended; "verily I am old ; but old as I am, I have still
some strength ; and my heart, at least, hath not waxed feeble.
It shall never be said that a De Vaux did suffer a son of the
Royal house of Scotland to risk the spilling of his noble blood,
to save that which hath already been so often shed in its defence,
and the which shall be ever ready to flow for it, whilst a drop
of it may remain within these shrivelled veins. Here am I
ready to encounter the caitiff knight, on whose smiles, when an
infant, I looked with delight as the future husband of my very
daughter Beatrice, and who did so gain upon me lately by the
plausible semblance of virtue. Base son of thy noble sire, full
hard, I ween, hath it been for me, an injured father, to sit silent
thus so long listening to thy false denials, and thy vile recrimi-
nations against my brother John. But now do I give thee the
lie to them all, and dare thee to mortal combat."

"My Lord, my Lord," cried Sir John Halyburton, going up
to the Lord of Dirleton in great astonishment, "calm thy rage,
I beseech thee. What is this I do hear ? Of whom dost thou
speak ? For whom dost thou thus hurl mortal defiance against
my dearest friend Sir Patrick Hepborne? Daughter, saidst thou?"

"Ay, daughter, Sir John Halyburton," exclaimed the old
man ; "my daughter Beatrice—she whom I have discovered to
be yet alive, only that I may wish her dead. Oh, I could bear
the loss of mine innocent infant—I could forgive a sinning and
now repentant brother—but to forgive the villain who hath
robbed my sweet flower of her fragrance—no, no, no, 'tis impossible. The very thought doth bring back all a father's rage
upon me. Give me my daughter, villain !—my daughter. Oh,
villain, villain, give me my daughter !" The aged Lord of
Dirleton, exhausted by the violence of his emotions, tottered
forward a step or two towards Sir Patrick, and would have sunk
down on the floor had he not been supported to the seat he had
occupied.

"Sir Patrick Hepborne," said Sir John Halyburton, sternly advancing towards him, after he had assisted the father of his future bride, "we have been warm friends, yea, I did come in hither to stand by thee to the last, as thy friend ; but my friendship did sow itself and spread its roots in that honourable surface with the which thou wert covered. 'Tis no wonder, then, that it should dry up and wither when it doth push deeper into the less wholesome soil, which was hitherto hid from my sight. The Earl of Buchan, the Lord of Dirleton—nay, all do seem to know thy blackness, and I do now curse myself that we were ever so linked. We can be friends no longer; and sith that it has pleased heaven to deny a son to that honourable but much injured Lord, it behoveth me, who look soon to stand in that relation to him, to take his wrongs upon myself. We must meet, yea, and that speedily, as deadly foes. My liege," continued he, turning towards the King, and making his obeisance, "have I thy gracious permission here to appeal Sir Patrick Hepborne to single combat of outrance, to be fought as soon as convenient lists may be prepared ?"

"Thou hast our licence, Sir John Halyburton," replied the King ; "to-morrow shall the lists be prepared, and on the day thereafter this plea shall be tried."

"Then, sith that I have thy Royal licence, my liege," cried Sir John Halyburton, "I do hereby challenge Sir Patrick Hepborne to do battle with me in single combat of outrance, with sharp grounden lances, and after that with battle-axes, and swords and daggers, as may be, and that unto the death. And this for the foul stain he hath brought upon the noble family of De Vaux, of the which I am about to become a son, and may God defend the right, and prosper the just cause ;" and with these words, Sir John Halyburton threw down his gauntlet on the floor.

"I will not deny," said Sir Patrick, as he stooped to lift it with a deep sigh, "I will not deny that it doth deeply grieve me thus to take up the gauntlet of challenge from one whom I have so much loved, and one for whom I should much more willingly have fought to the death than lifted mine arm against him. But the will of an all-seeing Providence must be obeyed ; that Providence, who doth know that I wist not even that the Lady Beatrice was aught else but the page Maurice de Grey, until after she did flee from me. Twice did I afterwards behold her ; once in the field of Otterbourne, where she had piously sought out and found the body of her benefactor, Sir Walter de Selby, and once within the Church of Norham, where she did

assist at his funeral rites ; but on neither of these sad occasions
had I even speech of her. A third time I did behold her but
for an instant in the house of Sir Hans de Vere, in the Tower
of London, and then did I save her, at the peril of my life, from
what I then conceived to be a base assault of King Richard of
England against her, for the which I did pay the penalty of imprisonment. On these three occasions only have mine eyes
beheld her, sith that we parted at Tarnawa. If to love her
honourably and virtuously be a crime, then am I indeed greatly
guilty ; but for aught else——"

"Thou hast told a fair tale, Sir Patrick," said the King,
shaking his head.

"Nay, 'twere better to be silent, methinks, than thus to try
to thrust such ill-digested stories on us," cried the Franciscan.
" But 'tis no wonder that he should be loth to appear in the lists
in such a cause. Conscience will make cowards of the bravest."

" Nay, let God judge me then," cried Sir Patrick Hepborne,
turning fiercely round, and darting a furious glance at the friar.
" Conscience, as with thee, may sleep for a time ; but trust me,
its voice will be terribly heard at last. Then bethink thee how
thou shalt answer thine, when thy death-bed cometh. Coward,
saidst thou ?—By St. Baldrid, 'tis the first time—But Sir John
Halyburton, thou at least will readily acquit me of aught that
may have so disgraceful a savour. I do accept thy challenge ;
I am thine at the appointed time ; may God indeed defend the
right ! Then shall mine innocence appear, while the transcend-
ent virtue of the Lady Beatrice, whom I do glory to proclaim
my lady-love, shall shine forth like the noonday sun."

By one of those unfortunate accidents which sometimes
occur, it chanced that the elder Sir Patrick Hepborne had been
gone for some days on private business to his Castle of Hailes.
Had he been present, this unfortunate feud might have perhaps
been prevented ; but he could not be now looked for at Scone
until after the day fixed for the duel ; and if he had been
expected sooner, things had already gone too far to have been
arrested, without some living proof to establish the truth. Sir
John Assueton was present during the scene we have described,
but he had been too much confounded by all he had witnessed
and heard to be able to. utter a sentence.

" My dear Assueton," said Sir Patrick, going up to him, and
taking him aside after all was over, " my friend, my oldest, my
best-tried, my staunchest friend, thou brother of my dearest
affections, from thee, I trust, I may look for a fairer judgment
than these have given me ?"

"Thou mayest indeed, Hepborne," replied Assueton, griping his friend's hand warmly. "Trust me, it doleth me sorely to see such deadly strife about to be waged between thee and one whom we both do so much love. Yet are the ways of Providence past our finding out. But may God do thee right, and make thy virtue appear."

"Thou canst not have been astonished at the tardiness I did show!" said Hepborne. "Alas! my heart doth grieve to bursting; perplexed, lost in a maze of conjecture, the whole doth appear to me to have been delusion. So the Lady Beatrice proveth to be the long-lost daughter of the Lord of Dirleton! and the Franciscan—ha!—the Friar—he then is that John de Vaux who did so traitorously steal his brother's child!—and hath the word of such a villain had power to face down mine? Oh, monstrous! Nay, now do I more than ever fear for the safety—for the life—of her whom I do love to distraction. And then her pure fame blasted, mine own good name tarnished, and no other means left for the cleansing of mine honour and her fame, but to lift the pointed lance, and the whetted sword, against the life of him whom, next to thee, I do of all men account most dear to me! May the holy Virgin, may the blessed Trinity, aid and sustain me amid the cruel host of distresses by the which I am environed!"

"Most hardly art thou indeed beset," replied Sir John Assueton; "yet hast thou no other choice but to put thy trust in God, and to do thy best in this combat for the establishment of thine own honour as a knight, and the pure fame of thy lady-love, leaving to Providence the issues of life and death."

After this conversation, Sir Patrick Hepborne and Sir John Assueton prepared to leave the Castle. As they were passing through the gateway, Hepborne, who was deeply absorbed in his own reflections, was gently touched on the arm by some one.

"She be'e here, Sir Patricks," whispered Duncan MacErchar; "troth, she hath catched the friars, and troth she be's a strong sturdy loons. Uve, uve, but she had a hard tuilzie wi' her."

"What? whom?" cried Sir Patrick.

"Troth, she did tell her to stand there till Sir Patricks come," said MacErchar; "but she would not bide; and so, afore a' was done, she was forced to gie her a bit clouring. Would she no likes to——"

"What?" cried Sir Patrick, now beginning to comprehend him, "thou dost not talk of the Franciscan? I do hope and trust thou hast not hurt the Franciscan?"

"Phoo! troth, as to tat, she doth best ken hersel the friars," replied Duncan ; " but hurts or no hurts, she be's in here," continued he, pointing under the gateway to a low vaulted door, " and she may e'en ask the friars hersel."

" Holy Virgin ! " cried Hepborne, " thou hast ruined me with thy zeal. Open the door of this hole, and let me forthwith release the friar. Though he be mine enemy, yet would I not for kingdoms lie under the foul suspect of having caused him to be waylaid."

" Troth, she shall soon see her," said Duncan, opening the door of the place—" Ho, ho, ho ! there she doth lie, I do well wot, like a mockell great grey swine."

There indeed, in an area not four feet square, was squeezed together the body of the Franciscan. He had a considerable cut and bruise upon his tonsure, from which the blood still - oozed profusely. He seemed to be insensible ; but he was no sooner lifted into the open air, than it appeared that his swoon was more owing to the closeness of the hole he had been crammed into than the wound he had received. He quickly began to recover and Sir Patrick raised him up and assisted him to stand.

" To thee, then, I am indebted for thy villainous traiterie ? " cried the Franciscan, looking wildly at Sir Patrick, and shaking himself free from his arms as he said so. " Oh, shame to knighthood, thus to plant an assassin in my path ; but rivers of thy blood shall speedily flow for every drop that doth fall from this head of mine."

With these words he darted into the Castle ere Sir Patrick could speak, leaving him stupified by this unfortunate mistake, which had brought a fresh cause of shameful suspicion upon him.

" May she leave her posts noo ! " demanded Duncan MacErchar with great coolness."

" Leave thy post ! " cried Hepborne in a frenzy ; " would thou hadst been in purgatory, knave, rather than that thou hadst wrought me this evil."

" Oh, hoit-toit ! " cried Duncan. " Spurgumstory ! Uve, uve ! and tat's from Sir Patricks ! "

" Forgive me, Duncan," cried Hepborne, immediately recovering his self-command, and remembering whom it was he had so wounded, " forgive my haste. I do well know thy zeal. But here, by ill luck, thou hast fortuned to carry it farther than befitting. It will be but an evil report when it shall be told of Sir Patrick Hepborne that he did plant a partizan to assail and wound the friar with whom he had feud. But thou art forgiven, my friend, for I do well know that thine intention was of the best."

" Phoo-oo-o !" cried Duncan, with a prolonged sound, " troth, and she doth see that she hath missed her marks, fan she did hit the friars a clour. But troth, she will see yet and mend the friar's head ; and sith she doth ken that she hath a feud wi' her, och, but she will mak her quiet wi' the same plaisters that did the ills."

" On thy life, touch him not again," said Sir Patrick, " not as thou dost love me, Duncan. Let not the friar be touched, else thou dost make me thy foe for ever."

" Phoo, ay, troth she's no meddles mair wi' her," said Duncan ; " ou ay, troth no, she'll no meddles."

CHAPTER LXXIV.

The missing Lady Beatrice.

WHILST preparations are making for the duel, it may not be improper to relieve the reader's mind regarding the Lady Beatrice, who had thus unwittingly become the subject of a feud likely to terminate so fatally. After having providentially effected her escape, first from the flames of the Hospital of the Maison Dieu, and then from the base and treacherous protection of Sir Andrew Stewart, she fled through the garden, and, being bewildered by a complication of terrors, she ran she knew not whither, and unwittingly taking the direction of the town, rushed wildly through the streets. Terror-struck by the blaze of the Cathedral and the shouts of those who were engaged in its destruction, some of whom her fears led her to imagine had joined in the pursuit which she believed Sir Andrew Stewart still held after her, she darted onwards with inconceivable rapidity, until she passed quite through the town. A little beyond its western entrance, she beheld a light at some distance before her, and believing that it proceeded from the casement of some cottage, she sprang towards it with renewed exertion. To her great disappointment, it turned out to be one of those lamps kept burning within a shrine of the Virgin that stood by the wayside. She sank down exhausted before the image it contained, and clasping her hands together, implored protection from her whom the figure represented.

While she was occupied in devotion, she heard the distant tramp of a horse. At first she was doubtful of the reality of the sound, confounded as it was with the far-off shouts of the Wolfe of Badenoch's people; but it soon became too distinct to be mistaken. It came not very quick, however, and she had yet time to flee. Filled with fresh alarm, she again sprang to her feet; but, alas! their strength was gone. Her limbs refused to do their office, and, tottering for a step or two, she again sank down on the ground, under the half shadow at the base of the little Gothic building. As she fell the horseman came on. He halted in doubt whether that which he beheld sink so strangely was corporeal or spiritual. His horse, too, seemed to partake of his alarm; for when he tried to urge the animal to pass by, he snorted and backed, and could not be persuaded or compelled to advance by any means the rider could use.

Meanwhile, the Lady Beatrice, believing that the man who rode the horse had halted for the purpose of dismounting, lay trembling with apprehension that Sir Andrew Stewart was about to seize her. Fear robbed her for some moments of recollection, from which temporary stupor she was roused by feeling her waist powerfully encircled by two arms of no pigmy size or strength, upon which she screamed aloud and fainted away.

When the Lady Beatrice regained her recollection, she found herself seated on the saddle, and travelling at a good round pace. She was held in her place, and supported by the same sinewy arms, which were also employed in guiding the reins, and pressing on the steed.

"Mercy, mercy, Sir Andrew Stewart," shrieked she; "oh, whither dost thou carry me?"

"St. Lowry be praised that thou hast gathered thysel back frae the warld o' sauls, my leddy! Of a truth I did greatly fear that thy spirit had yode thither."

"Merciful Providence, Rory Spears!" cried the Lady Beatrice, almost doubting the evidence of her ears. "The holy Virgin be praised, if it be thee indeed!"

"Yea, in good truth, it is assuredly me, Roderick Spears, esquire, at the humble service of thy leddyship," replied Rory.

"Then thanks be to the blessed Virgin, I am safe!" replied Beatrice.

"Safe!" cried Rory; "yea, as safe as the bold heart of ane esquire can make thee. Trust me, they sall take measure o' ane ell and ane half o' this lance that hangs ahint me here, that may essay to do thee aught o' harm between this and Tarnawa, whither my shalty Brambleberry shall speedily convey us."

"May the saints unite to shower their blessings upon thee,

Rory, for thy timely aid !" cried the Lady Beatrice ; "but how, I pray thee, didst thou chance to rescue me from the power of Sir Andrew Stewart ?"

"What !" cried Rory, "so that ill-doing, misbegotten fumart hath been besetting thee again with this accursed traiterie. By St. Lowrie, but I did ance tak measure o' him afore."

"Yea, he encountered me as I did escape from the flames of the Maison Dieu, and he pursued me to the shrine of the Virgin, where he was in the act of laying his impure hands on me, when I did faint away."

"Na, troth, my leddy," said Rory, "the hands that war laid on thee war my hands ; and, though I should speak weel o' that the which be's mine ain, I do boldly avow that they are purer than the scartin' claws o' that mouldwarp, although they hae handled mony a foul fish, and I wad be sair ashamed an they waur no teucher. It was me that took haud o' ye, my leddy, and I made bauld to do that same (being ane esquire) that I might succour ye, distressed damsel that thou wert, by lifting thy dead body into the saddle, that wi' a sair heart I mought bring thee aff to Tarnawa, where, an thou didst not recover thee, thou mightest have had ane honourable yirdin'."

"But tell me, I pray thee, how thou didst chance to come there ?" demanded Beatrice.

"I'll tell thee," said Rory. "My master, the Yearl, did send me to Aberdeen wi' a flight o' falcons he had promised till the King's Majesty ; so I hae been there, yea, and did behold his Royal Grace afore he depairted for his Palace of Scone. I wot he was weel pleased wi' the birds, and he did show me the fair side o' his Royal favour for bringing them, partly, nae doot, for the sake o' my noble master the Yearl o' Moray, and partly, I do opine, because I am noo an esquire admitted and acknowledged, the which the King himsel did alswa most graciously confirm out o' his ain mouth. For, says he to me, 'Squire Rory,' says he, 'are the falcons well mewed, and hast thou reclaimed them to purpose ?' To the which I did answer, 'Try ye them, my Royal Liege, and ye'll see gin there be ony Royal hern that'll mount wi' them. Trust me, my Lord King, that they have a wing that will carry them up to the very riggin' o' the lift, an ye can find a hern that 'ill gang there before them.' The king gied a most gracious laugh thereupon, and so I did laugh too, and the Lords did laugh. At length the King telled ane o' his fouk to see that Squire Roderick Spears was well feasted ; and so I was in good troth, yea, and got handsome gurdeon I rauckon alswa. So, as I was on my way back from Aberdeen, I stopped late yestreen at the Spital o' the Mason's Due ; but I had not lain long asleep until I was startled to my legs by the cry o' fire, and the flames bursting out. I hurried on some of my garments, and grupping the rest in my hands, I made the best o' my way to the stable ; but there I could not get in for lack o' the key. It was firm fast, and I had hard wark, I wis, till I could get something to break it open wi'. Then did I ride through a' the town to see what destruction the Wolfe o' Badenoch was doing. But as I was but ae man, and that it would ill become me to find faut wi' the son o' the King or the brother o' my leddy Countess, I cam aff hot foot to tell the Yearl. So seeing thee moving in the light yonder, I maun just say, that, at the first, I did opine that thou wert something not o' this warld ; and had it not been for Brambleberry here, who would by no means pass thee by, and whose good sense therein did gie me time to see that thou were nae ghost, verily thou mightst ha'e lain there still for me."

Under the protection of the faithful Rory Spears, the Lady Beatrice arrived safely at Tarnawa, where she was joyfully received by the Countess. Her converse with the Franciscan had been enough to inform her of the pleasing fact that she was indeed the daughter of the Lord of Dirleton ; and the happy Jane de Vaux learned this much from her with a rapture that melted Beatrice's heart with emotions of delight she had never before experienced. To her, who had grown up without knowing aught of the affectionate regard of a near relation, how soothing must have been the pure embrace of a sister, of a sister too who had already shown herself to be the kindest of friends. But the joy of Jane de Vaux and the Countess of Moray, who had fully participated in the felicity of her young friend, was converted into extreme anxiety about Beatrice, who was seized with a severe illness, the effect of the fatigue, shipwreck, dread, and agitation to which she had lately been exposed. To add to their distress, the Earl of Moray had been gone from home for some days. It is no wonder, then, that the Countess and the Lady Jane de Vaux should have been too much occupied with their patient to think of making inquiry about her uncle the Franciscan ; nor was it until the Earl returned that he did what they should have done before ; and then it was they learned from the Bishop of Moray that the friar had gone on his important mission to the Wolfe of Badenoch.

CHAPTER LXXV.

The Ordeal of Battle.

HAVING thus seen the Lady Beatrice safe into the hands of friends, we must leave her to be recovered by their affectionate care, whilst we give some account of the preparations which were making for the duel between Sir Patrick Hepborne and Sir John Halyburton.

The Lord of Dirleton, after some moments of cool reflection, began to regret that his feelings had so hurried him away, as to make him forget that his family honour could gain but little by the cause of the duel being made public.   He therefore lost no time in beseeching the King that the lists might be erected in some situation where the vulgar, at least, could be excluded; and, in compliance with this request, a spot was fixed on, in the meadow below the Palace of Scone, and there workmen were employed in immense numbers to ensure their erection against the time fixed on.   Even during the night they worked unceasingly, and the lights were seen flitting about, and the hatchets, saws, and hammers were heard in full operation, so that by the morning of the appointed day a rudely-constructed amphitheatre of combat was prepared.

The morning was beautiful, and although all about the court knew that the day must end in a tragedy, yet nothing could be more gay or brilliant than the prologue to the scene.   The King's pavilion was pitched close to the outside of the lists, and a private door and stair led up from it into a balcony over the centre of one of the sides of the enclosure, where the King took his seat, with the Regent, the Lord of Dirleton and his lady, together with the Franciscan and some others.   Between the outer and the inner lists, a wide space extended all around on both sides, from one gate to the other, which was dedicated to the nobles and knights who sat on horseback, there to witness the combat.   There were barriers in the inner circle of palisadoes, one opposite to each side of the gate.

The two knights arrived at the outside of the lists, each attended by his esquire, and armed at all points, both horse and man; and each of them waited at a different gate, that he might be admitted with all the ceremony of chivalry.

After the King was seated, the Constable, Marshal of the lists, and the heralds took their stand in the places allotted for them below. Then appeared Sir John Halyburton, attended by his esquire, at the east gate ; which circumstance being formally announced to the Constable and Marshal, they went thither to receive him.

"Who art thou, and for what purpose art thou come hither?" demanded the Constable.

"I am Sir John Halyburton," replied he ; "and hither am I come, mounted and armed, to perform my challenge against Sir Patrick Hepborne, younger of Hailes, and to redeem my pledge. Wherefore do I humbly desire this gate to be opened, that I may be suffered to perform mine intent and purpose."

"Thou shalt have way hither if thou be'st indeed he whom thou dost set thyself forth to be," replied the Constable. "The Moor's head proper on thy crest, and thy golden shield with those three mascles on a bend *azure*, do speak thee to be him whom thou dost say thou art. Yet must we behold thy face. Raise thy vizor, then, Sir Knight."

Sir John Halyburton did as he was desired, and his identity being acknowledged, he was led into the lists, and placed opposite the King, where he was to remain until the defendant should appear.

He had to wait no longer than the nature of the ceremony required, when the Constable was called to the western gate to receive the defendant, who, on being formally questioned, declared himself to be Sir Patrick Hepborne, younger of Hailes.

"We do indeed behold the couped horse's head with bridled neck on thy crest," said the Constable; "and on thy shield *gules*, the chevron *argent*, with the two lions pulling at the rose, but we would have other proof that thou art in very deed Sir Patrick Hepborne. Raise thy vizor, Sir Knight, that we may behold thy countenance. Ay, now we do indeed see that thou art the very defendant in this duel. Enter;" and he was accordingly led into the lists, and placed by the side of his challenger.

Then were the weapons of each examined. These were a lance, a battle-axe, a sword, and a dagger. The lances were measured, and everything was adjusted in such a manner that neither should have any undue advantage over the other. The Constable next besought His Majesty's pleasure, to know whether he would in person take the oaths of the combatants, or whether he would empower him and the Marshal to do it ; and having received orders to proceed, they first addressed Sir John Halyburton, and demanded of him what were the terms of his challenge.

39

"I do appear as champion for William de Vaux, Lord of Dirleton," replied Sir John ; "he being of an age which doth render it impossible that he can take arms in his own person ; also for John de Vaux, his brother, a friar of the order of St. Francis, to do battle against Sir Patrick Hepborne, younger of Hailes, whom, in their name, and upon their credit, I do accuse of having wronged them in certain matters well known to His Majesty, as also to the defendant, and to compel him to own his guilt, or to clear it by his arm."

"Thou dost swear, then, on the holy Evangelists," said the Constable, "that this is the true cause of thy coming hither, that thou dost thyself believe the averments of those for whom thou dost appear, and that thou art prepared, if it be God's will, to support the same with thy life."

"I do swear," replied Sir John Halyburton.

"And thou, Sir Patrick Hepborne," said the Constable, "dost thou comprehend the charge that is brought against thee ; and if thou dost, what hast thou to answer ?"

"I do comprehend the charge," replied Sir Patrick ; "and I do deny it solemnly in all its parts. I do deny that I have ever done injury to the Lord of Dirleton, or to any person or thing of his ; and I do declare, that both to him and to his I have borne, and do still bear, the strongest love. This do I swear on the holy Evangelists ; and God so help me as I do speak the truth."

Then the second oath—that they had not brought with them other armour or weapon than such as was allowed, nor any engine, instrument, herb, charm, or enchantment, and that neither of them should put affiance or trust in anything other than God and their own valour, as God and the holy Evangelists should help them—being solemnly sworn by both, each was led off to the barrier opposite to the gate he had entered by, where his banner and blazon were set up ; and whilst both were in preparation, the usual proclamation was given forth by the heralds.

The lists were then cleared of every one save only of two knights and two esquires, one of each to wait upon the Constable and the Marshal. The knight who was assigned to the Constable was Sir William de Dalzel, and he who was appropriated to the Marshal was Sir John Assueton. To each was given a headless lance, and they sat mounted immediately before the place occupied by the Constable and the Marshal, and directly under the King's balcony, that they might be ready to part the combatants, if it should so please the King.

When all was in readiness, the bugle-note of warning sounded from both barriers, and, after a short pause, the King issued the usual command, "*Laissez les aller !*" and, the signal being given by the heralds' trumpets, the knights flew together. Halyburton and Hepborne had been, nay, were at·that moment, warmly attached to each other, but his individual honour as a knight was dearer to each of them than even friendship. Whatever had been their feelings of regret, or unwillingness to engage in mortal strife, each now only remembered him of his own name and that of his lady as he spurred ; and, throwing the blame on unhappy fate, which had thus doomed them to this unnatural struggle, each thought but of working the death of his opponent, as if it had been but the winning from him of some gaudy trophy in a tournament. The collision was tremendous ; the clash resounded far and near, and a murmur of admiration burst from the assembled knights. Both lances were shivered, and both steeds were thrown so much back on their haunches, that, for the fraction of a second, it seemed to the spectators as if it were impossible that they could again recover themselves.

But the horses regaining their legs, the riders lost not an instant in seizing the battle-axes that hung at their saddle-bows ; and then the fight became dreadful indeed. Their blows fell so thick and fast upon each other's head and body, that the sound resembled that which may be supposed to come from the busy forge of an armourer ; and desperate were the dints made in the plate-mail both of the horses and their riders. The noble quadrupeds reared and plunged, and, dexterously guided by the rein, leaped forwards and backwards, and from side to side, with as much precision, while the strokes were dealing, as if they had been but parts of the animals that combated on their backs. But this equestrian battle was not of long duration. A heavy blow from the axe of Sir John Halyburton fell upon the head of Hepborne's favourite war steed, Beaufront, and, in defiance of his steel chamfront, the noble animal was so stunned by it that he staggered, and measured his length on the sod. But as his horse was sinking under him, Sir Patrick made his battle-axe tell heavily and loudly on the helmet of his opponent, who had leaned forward to give his stroke more weight, and he beat him fairly down from his saddle.

Sir Patrick extricated his feet from the stirrups with great agility as his horse was falling, and leaped on the ground. His antagonist, having taken some seconds to regain his legs, was completely in his power. But here friendship came into operation. Although he might, with perfect honour, have taken full advantage of Sir John Halyburton, he only brandished his battle-axe over him for an instant to mark that advantage, whilst the spectators shuddered, in expectation of the blow that was to put an end to the combat, and then dropping his arm harmlessly by his side, he retreated a few paces, to wait until his antagonist should be again equal with him. The King, and the knights who looked on, clapped their hands in sign of approbation.

And now the combatants again approached each other, and desperate was the encounter. The armour of both knights was battered so tremendously, that their helmets were soon shorn of their proud plumes and crests, which hung down in tattered fragments about their heads. Soon afterwards, the lacings of their head pieces were cut, and each, in his turn, lost his bassi-net. Their surcoats were cut to shreds, and some of the fasten-ings of the most important defences of their bodies being also demolished, the plates dropped away piecemeal, and the persons of both were left comparatively exposed, having nothing to resist the blows but their hanberks and hauquetons. Still they fought with their battle-axes, until both becoming unable longer to wield them, they seemed to throw them away by mutual con-sent, and, drawing their swords and daggers, began to cut and stab, aiming at those places where their former weapons had opened breaches, through which they hoped to extract each other's life's blood.

And now, indeed, the combat assumed the character of a deadly strife. The most experienced warriors present declared, that so perfectly matched a contest had never before been wit-nessed, and a very general opinion prevailed, that, instead of one of them only being slain, the death of both the knights would probably be the result of this fierce and desperate duel. De-spairing of the life of her champion, the Lady Dirleton had already fainted, and had been borne out to the King's pavilion. The poor old Lord of Dirleton also began to picture to himself the melancholy scene which must take place on the return of his daughter, the Lady Jane de Vaux, to weep over the cold and bloody corpse of him whom she expected to find warmly waiting to salute her as his bride. As for John de Vaux the Franciscan, he inwardly regretted that he had not been his own champion; the apprehension of evil fortune that naturally arises where there is a doubt, having already led him to fear that Halyburton had much the worst of the combat. As for Assueton and Sang, they each sat silently in their saddles, in the places where they were posted, doubtful and unhappy. Their eyes being more turned

upon Hepborne than upon his adversary, they trembled to
remark each new wound he received, and each reeling step
which the successful blows of Halyburton occasioned. His
growing faintness was anxiously and fearfully noticed by them
in secret, and every moment made an accession to their anxiety
and their fear. The minstrel, Adam of Gordon, who was seated
among the attendants behind the King, trembled, clasped his
hands, groaned, and moved backwards and forwards on his place;
and as Duncan MacErchar, who was there with his company of
Guards, and who as yet knew little of the usages observed at
such duels, it was with the utmost difficulty that he was prevented from rushing to Hepborne's assistance, and he was at
length only hindered from doing so by being seized by the order
of the Marshal of the lists.

The combat was raging, though both the knights were
evidently growing fainter and fainter, when a bugle sounded at
one of the gates, and one of the marshalmen being sent to
ascertain the cause, brought a message to the Constable that
an esquire waited there who craved immediate admittance to
the King; and the circumstance being signified to his Majesty,
leave was granted to the stranger to enter. He no sooner appeared within the gate than he was seen to push his horse
furiously along behind the drawn-up ranks of the mounted
knights who were looking on, making directly for the stair that
led up from thence to the King's gallery. Some who recognized the face of this esquire knew him to be Rory Spears.
Leaping from his froth-covered horse, he left him to pant, and,
springing up the steps to the King's gallery, he was seen to
throw himself on his knees before His Majesty. What he said
was known only to those who were near the Monarch's person;
indeed the sudden appearance of this messenger carried away
the eyes of the spectators for a few moments only from the
combat, which now appeared to be approaching nearer and
nearer to that fatal termination which so many experienced
heads had anticipated. Already both knights staggered and
grew giddy with their numerous wounds and their loss of
blood; and those generous bosoms who surrounded the lists
cursed the interruption which the King's attention was receiving, being persuaded, that if it had been still directed towards
the combatants, he could not possibly have allowed the duel to
proceed to the extinction of two such brave lives. They
trembled with dread that he should not look and act until his
interference would be of no avail; for it seemed as if every
moment would see both the heroes extended dead upon the

sod, that had been already rendered slippery with the blood
they had spilt.

All at once a great confusion seemed to have taken place in
the King's gallery. His Majesty himself appeared to be much
agitated, and a signal was given, in his name by the Regent to
the Constable and Marshal, to stop the combat. Their two
knights assistants, who had both been in misery for the fate of
their friends who were fighting, gave their horses the spur, and
darted forward like arrows, with their headless lances extended,
to separate the combatants. The two champions, breathless
and hardly able to support themselves, were yet not approached
by any one, save by those who divided them by their lance-
poles, for in this stage of the affair the duel was only stayed;
and as it might yet be the King's pleasure that they should renew their strife to the death, the law required that they should
be left precisely in the same state, that if the combat should re-
commence, it might do so with each champion in the same
circumstances, with relation to his adversary, as he had been in
when the King had interfered. Faint, and ready to drop, therefore, they supported themselves on their well-hacked swords;
and whilst the blood poured from many a wound, they panted,
and silently surveyed each other's grim and gory features, at
the short distance by which they were divided, as if each read
his own death legibly written in the death-like face of his
opponent.

Female shrieks were now heard coming from the King's
pavilion without the lists, and all was commotion in the King's
gallery. Robert himself was seen moving away, supported by
some of his people; and, in defiance of propriety, many were
seen rushing out before him by the way that led down to the
pavilion. In a few minutes the gallery was cleared.

Meanwhile the combatants still stood gazing with fixed and
ghastly look at each other; and their two friends sat like equestrian statues, with their lance-shafts crossed between them, but
uttering no word, and giving no sign; and, while they were thus
grouped, a messenger came to announce to the Constable the
King's pleasure that the duel should be forthwith terminated
and ended without further bloodshed, he having taken the
quarrel into his own hand, and that he was prepared to decide
it in his own pavilion, where the combatants were ordered
immediately to attend him; that the two knights should be led
forth of the lists, each by his own gate, the one by the Constable, and the other by the Marshal, and that both should make
exit at the same moment, by signal from the heralds' trumpets,

that neither might suffer the disgrace of being the first to quit them.

The King's command was no sooner made known than a loud shout burst from the brave and noble hearts who had witnessed this obstinate and sanguinary duel. His Majesty's orders were punctually obeyed, and Sir Patrick Hepborne followed the marshalman with tottering steps, whilst Halyburton went staggering in the opposite direction, and as if he was groping his way in the dark after the Constable. The trumpets sounded, and they disappeared from the gates. Hepborne, supported by his guide and his faithful esquire, made the best of his way round to the external entrance to the King's pavilion; but thither Sir John Halyburton never came, for he swooned away the moment he had crossed the threshold of the gateway. As Hepborne was entering the pavilion, a lady, frantic with grief and despair, rushed by him, and made her way towards the eastern gate, followed by several attendants.

Sir Patrick made his obeisance to the King, immediately upon coming into the pavilion, and His Majesty, with the Regent, came kindly towards him, to praise his valour and to inquire into his safety. A crowd, among whom he recognized the Lord and Lady Dirleton, the Earl and Countess of Moray, and the Franciscan, surrounded a lady who seemed to be overwhelmed with affliction.

"He is safe," cried half a dozen voices to her immediately on perceiving him; and the circle opening at the moment, he beheld the Lady Beatrice de Vaux. At one and the same instant she screamed aloud when she saw him, and he sprang forward to throw himself at her feet, where he fainted away.

CHAPTER LXXVI.

The Friar's Tale—The Two Combatants—Lady Eleanore's explanation—All is well that ends well.

It was not wonderful that a sudden ecstasy of joy, such as that which burst unexpectedly on Hepborne, coming after so much mental wretchedness, and when his bodily frame had been so weakened by fatigue, wounds, and loss of blood, should have thrown him into a swoon, from which he only awakened to show symptoms of a feverish delirium. He passed some days and nights under all the strange and fluctuating delusions of a labouring dream, during which the angelic image of her he loved, and the hated form of the Franciscan, appeared before him, but in his delirium he knew them not.

It was after a long and deep sleep that he opened his eyelids, and felt, for the first time, a consciousness of perfect calmness and clearness of intellect, but combined with a sense of great exhaustion. He turned in bed, and immediately he heard a light step move towards it from a distant part of the room. The drapery was lifted up, and the lovely, though grief-worn countenance of Beatrice looked anxiously in upon him.

"Blessed angel," said Sir Patrick, clasping his hands feebly together, and looking upwards with a heavy languid eye, that received a faint ray of gladness from what it looked upon; "blessed angel, is it a fair vision that deceives me, or is it a reality I behold? I have dreamed much and fearfully of thee and of others; tell me, do I dream still, or art thou in truth Beatrice, the lady of my heart?"

"Hush, Sir Knight," replied the lady, a smile of pleasure delicately blending on her countenance, with a rich blush of modesty; "I am indeed Beatrice. It joyeth me much to hear thee talk so calmly, seeing that it doth argue thy returning health; but quiet and repose are needful for thee, therefore must I leave thee."

"Nay, if thou wouldst have me repose in peace, repeat again that thou art Beatrice, that thou art mine own Beatrice," cried Sir Patrick feelingly. "Say that thy beauteous form shall never more flit from my sight; and that we shall never, never part."

"Do but rest thee quietly, Sir Patrick," said Beatrice. "Trust me, thine own faithful Maurice de Grey shall be thy page still, and shall never quit the side of thy couch until health shall have again revisited those wan and wasted cheeks."

"'Tis enough," exclaimed Sir Patrick, rapturously snatching her hand and devouring it with kisses; "thou hast already made me well. Methinks I do almost feel strong enow to quit this couch; and yet I could be ill for ever to be blessed with such attendance."

"Nay, thou must by no means think of rashly quitting thy sick-bed," said the Lady Beatrice, withdrawing her hand, and looking somewhat timorous at his impetuosity, as she dropped the curtain.

A stirring was then heard in the apartment, then a whispering, and immediately Assueton and Sang appeared, with anxious looks, at his bedside.

"My dearest friend, and my faithful esquire," said Hepborne, with a face of joy, and with so collected and rational an expression, that they could hardly doubt the perfect return of his senses; though they soon began to believe themselves deceived, for his features suddenly became agitated; "but what eye is that which doth glare from between you? Ha! the face of mine arch enemy—of that demon, the enemy of the Lady Beatrice. Doth he come to snatch her from me again? Seize him, my beloved Assueton—seize him, my faithful esquire—let him not escape, I entreat thee, if thou wouldst have me live."

"We have been in terror, my dearest Hepborne," said Assueton, calmly, after having ascertained that it was the Franciscan, who had been looking over his shoulder, that had excited Hepborne's apparent fit of frenzy; "this Franciscan, this friar, John de Vaux, hath now no evil thought or wish against thee or the Lady Beatrice. He was worked upon by false impressions, which were not removed until that Providential discovery, the which did put a stop to thine unfortunate duel with Sir John Halyburton. But sith that all is now cleared up, the holy Franciscan hath made good reparation for all the evil his misjudgment did occasion thee; for sith that thou wert laid here, he hath never ceased day or night to watch by thy bedside, save when called to that of another; and to him, under God, do we now owe the blessed hope of thy speedy recovery."

"Strange," cried Hepborne; "but didst thou not say unfortunate duel? I beseech thee speak—Hath my beloved friend, Halyburton, against whom fate did so cruelly compel me to contend—oh, say not, I beseech thee, that aught hath befallen him! What, thou dost hesitate! Oh, tell me not that he hath died by my hand, or happiness shall ne'er again revisit this bosom."

"He is not dead," said the Franciscan, "but he is still grievously sick of his wounds; yet may we hope that he will soon recover as thou dost."

"Thank God, he is not dead," cried Hepborne with energy; "thank God, there is hope of his recovery."

"Nay, this good Friar John will keep him alive, as he hath done thee," said Assueton.

"Strange," said Hepborne, "to see thee, my truest friend, Assueton, thus in league with the man whom I did esteem my bitterest foe; wonderful to learn from thee that he hath exerted himself to recall me from death. Of a truth, then, I must of needscost yield me to conviction so strong, and pray him and God to forgive me for the hatred I did harbour against him."

"Nay, Sir Knight," said the Franciscan, "of a truth much hatred and misjudging doth need forgiveness on both our parts, and I do grieve most sincerely and heavily for mine, as well as for the mischief it hath occasioned."

"But I do earnestly entreat thee to clear up my way through this strange wilderness of perplexity in which I am still involved," said Sir Patrick.

"That will I most readily do for thee, Sir Knight," replied the Franciscan; "but anxiety for thy certain and speedy return to health would lead me to urge thee to postpone thy curiosity, until thou shalt have gained further strength."

"Nay," said Sir Patrick, "of a truth I shall have more ease and repose of body after that my mind shall have been put at rest."

"In truth, what thou hast said hath good reason in it," replied the Franciscan; "then shall I no longer keep thee in suspense, but briefly run over such circumstances as it may be necessary for thee to know.

"My brother, the Lord of Dirleton, hath told me that thou art already possessed by him of the story of the loss of his first-born infant daughter. It was I, John de Vaux, his brother, to whom he did ever play the part of a kind benefactor and an affectionate father—it was I who repaid all the blessings I received from him by robbing him of his child. My mother ('tis horrible to be compelled thus to allow it) was the worst of her sex. I was young and violent of temper, and not being at that time aware of her infamy, I was hurt by the neglect with which she was treated, and, instigated by her, I boldly attempted to force her into the hall of my brother's Castle, then thronged by all the nobility and chivalry of the neighbourhood, to witness the ceremonial baptism of the little Beatrice. My brother was justly enraged with mine impudence; he did incontinently turn both of us forth with disgrace, and in doing so he struck me a blow. Stung with the affront, I gave way to the full fury of my passion, and vowed to be revenged. My mother wickedly fostered mine already too fiery rage, till it knew no bounds. She urged me to watch mine occasion to murder the child; and although my young soul revolted at a crime so horrible, yet did her proposal suggest a plan of vengeance, which, with less of guilt to me, should convey as much of misery to my brother, and especially to his wife, against whom we had a peculiar hatred.

" It was long ere a fitting opportunity offered for carrying my purpose into effect. At length, after frequent watching, I did one evening observe the nurse walking in a solitary place, with the babe in her arms. With my face concealed beneath a mask, and my person shrouded in a cloak, I came so suddenly on her, that I snatched the child from her arms before she was aware. Ere I could flee from the woman, she sprang on me like a she-wolf robbed of her young—pulled the mantle from the child in a vain attempt to reach her, and clung to me so firmly as I fled, that, to rid myself of her, I was compelled to wound her hand deeply with my dagger. My horse was at hand, and, to put the child equally beyond the reach of the affection of its fond parents or the cruelty of my mother, I wrapt it in my cloak, and, riding with it over to Lammermoor, consigned it to the care of a shepherd's wife. To avoid suspicion, I returned home immediately ; but conscious guilt would not permit me to remain long near those I had injured. I withdrew myself secretly, and entered on board the privateer of the brave Mercer, where for six or eight years of my life I encountered many a storm, and bore my part in many a desperate action. I was a favourite with the old man, and did gain considerable wealth with him ; but my proud spirit would not brook command, so I quitted the sea-service, and travelled through foreign lands as a knight, when I did share in many a stubborn field of fight, and won many a single combat. Yet was I not always successful ; and, having been overthrown in a certain tournament, I was so overwhelmed with mortification at the disgrace that followed me, that I became soured with the world, and straightway resolved to exchange the helmet and the cuirass for the Franciscan's grey cowl and gown, vainly hoping to humble my haughty temper by the outward semblance of poverty. But my towering soul was not to be subdued by a mere garb of penance.

" From the foreign convent into which I entered, I chanced to be sent to England, and, having been recommended as a proper person for confessor in the family of the Earl of Northumberland, mine ambitious and proud heart did again begin to show itself. Sir Rafe Piersie, to whom I was more especially attached, made me large promises of future promotion in the Church ; and, having set his affections on the Lady Eleanore de Selby, he did employ me to further his suit. To effect this, I bribed a certain villainous pretender to necromancy, who was well known to have much influence over the old knight. But the villain deceived me. Sir Rafe Piersie had a flat denial, as well from the father as the daughter, and this did I partly attri-

bute to the traiterie of the impostor, whose services I paid for,
and partly to the interposition of Sir Walter de Selby's adopted
daughter, whom I did not then know to be my niece, the Lady
Beatrice.   Sir Rafe Piersie, believing that I had been playing
the cheat with him, drove me indignantly away.   I burned to
be revenged against those who had occasioned this overthrow of
my hopes, and soon afterwards I had nearly glutted my rage
against the Ancient by a cruel death, from which he most narrowly escaped.   I did then journey northwards to the Franciscan
Convent at Elgin, where I arrived at the very time the Bishop
of Moray was sorely lacking some one bold enough to beard the
Wolfe of Badenoch.   It was a task quite to my mind, and I
accordingly readily undertook that, the which all others did
most anxiously shun.   Thou, who wert present at Lochyndorbe,
mayest well remember how mine attempt was likely to have
ended.   As they dragged me from the hall I did detect the
companion of the Lady Eleanore de Selby under her page's
disguise, having seen her by accident at Norham.   One of mine
old scamates, who chanced to be among the number of Lord
Badenoch's men, procured me admission to the Castle, and he
it was who effected mine escape from the horrors of the Water
Pit Vault.   He would fain have had me flee instantly, but,
much against his will, I did insist on his showing me the page's
chamber ; and I went thither, determined to question closely
her whom I did then only know to be the companion of the
Lady Eleanore de Selby, as to what share she had in persuading
her friend against an union with the Piersie.   I sought her
chamber with my mind rankling with the remembrance of my
disgrace, inflamed and full of prejudice against her, and,
Heaven pardon me, it is in truth hard to say how far my blind
rage might have hurried me, had she not fled from me at the
sight of my dagger.

"It was soon after this that my brother, William de Vaux,
came to Elgin.   The remembrance of my ingratitude to him
came powerfully upon me.   I contrived to bring him, at night,
into the Church of the Franciscan Convent, and then it was I
discovered that his heart, instead of being filled with a thirst of
revenge against me, was full of charity, compassion, and forgiveness.   This discovery so worked upon my soul, already beginning to feel compunction for mine early wickedness, that I
should have confessed all to my much-injured brother, had not
some one, accidentally approaching at that moment, unluckily
interrupted the conference and compelled me to retreat.   But I
went straightway to the good Bishop of Moray, with whom by

this time I stood in high favour for my bold service, and to him did I fully confess my sins against my brother, of the which, until now, I had but little thought, and had never repented. I did then forthwith solemnly vow to do all that might be in my power to restore his child to him, if that she did yet live. In this good resolution the Bishop encouraged me ; yea, and he did moreover lend me ample means for effectuating the purpose I had in view. I hastened to the South of Scotland, to find out the woman with whom I had left the baby. From her I learned that poverty and my neglect had induced her to part with Beatrice to Sir Walter de Selby. Then did I shudder to think of the scene at Lochyndorbe, where, but for the providence of God, I might have murdered mine own niece, and I secretly blessed a merciful Being who had snatched her from my hands.

"But now another cause of affliction took possession of me. Believing, as I did, that Beatrice was the unworthy partner of thy journey, and that thou hadst taken her with thee, by her own guilty consent, from Norham, where I did well know thou hadst been, I cursed my villainy, which had removed an innocent babe from that virtuous maternal counsel and protection, the lack of which, I believed, had been her undoing. My suspicions were confirmed when I beheld thee among the crowd at the funeral of Sir Walter de Selby in Norham Church. I doubted not but thou hadst come thither to meet with Beatrice, and by her own consent to carry her off. Her eyes encountered mine as I stood near the altar, and, as they were full of severity from the impressions then on my mind, it is little marvel that the sight of me should have produced the fainting fit into which she fell. That night I was deprived of all chance of an interview with her ; and when I sought for one in the morning, I found that she had departed, no one knew whither. After seeking her for many days, I at last returned to Dunbar in despair, where I did by chance meet with the son of mine old sea captain, Mercer, and from him I learned that she had been sojourning for some time at Newcastle, but that she had sailed for London. Having heard of the expedition of the Scottish knights thither, I readily believed that her errand was for the purpose of meeting him who had so won her heart from virtue. My soul boiled within me to rescue her from so base an intercourse, and mine old sea-mate having offered to carry me to the Thames in his ship, I did accept his aid, and did take her from thence, as thou dost already know, Sir Knight; but instead of making the port whence we had sailed, we were driven northward by a storm, and, after much tossing, we suffered wreck on

the eastern coast of Moray Land, whence I conveyed Beatrice
to the Hospital of the Maison-Dieu at Elgin, on that night the
place was burnt by the Wolfe of Badenoch. As I was well
assured that the lady had escaped from the fire, and that I
could nowhere hear tidings of her, it was no wonder that I
believed she had fled to thee ; for our stormy voyage had left
me no leisure to undeceive myself by the discovery of her
innocence."

The Franciscan then went on to give Sir Patrick such other
explanations as his eager questions called for. But his patient
seemed to be insatiable in his thirst of information. Afraid
that he might do himself an injury, the learned leech forbade
him further converse, and, having ordered some proper nourish-
ment for the invalid, desired that he should be left quiet. Sir
Patrick accordingly fell into a deep and refreshing sleep, from
which he next day awakened, with pleasing dreams of future
happiness.

Sir Patrick Hepborne the elder had not yet returned to
Scone. The younger Sir Patrick saw less of the Franciscan
after he became convalescent; but his friend, Assueton, was
indefatigable in his attendance on him, and Mortimer Sang did
not even permit his love for Katherine Spears to carry him
away from the affectionate duty he paid his master. It was not
surprising, then, that his cure went on rapidly, being so carefully looked to. As he got better, he was visited by many.
The King sent daily inquiries for him ; the Regent came himself ; and the Wolfe of Badenoch, though his impatient temper
would never permit him to make his visit long, generally called
three or four times a day to see how he did. But the grateful
Duncan MacErchar lay in the ante-room, like an attached dog,
from the moment that Hepborne was carried into the Palace,
and never quitted the spot save when he thought he could run
off for something that might do him good or give him ease.

Hepborne was a good deal surprised, and even a little hurt,
that, amongst all those who came to see him in his wounded
state, he had never beheld the old Lord of Dirleton, who had
ever shown so warm a heart towards him until the late unfortunate misunderstanding. The Franciscan, too, came but to dress
his numerous wounds, which were fast healing up, and then left
him in haste. But when some days more had passed away, and
he was enabled to quit his bed, he learned intelligence that
explained this seeming neglect of the De Vaux, and filled him
with grief and anxiety. It was the anticipation of its producing
this effect upon him, indeed, which had occasioned the conceal-

ment of it, as the Franciscan feared that his recovery might have been retarded by the communication. Sir John Halyburton's case had been much less favourable than Hepborne's. His life still hung quivering in uncertainty. The Lord of Dirleton, his lady, and the unhappy Lady Jane de Vaux never left him; and the Franciscan, who had been the unfortunate cause of bringing it into its present peril, was reduced to the deepest despair.

No sooner had Sir Patrick learned those doleful tidings, than, calling to his esquire, he put on his garments, and demanded to be instantly led to the apartment of Sir John Halyburton, where he found those who were so deeply interested in him sitting drowned in affliction, believing that they should soon see him breathe his last. Sir Patrick mingled his tears with theirs; but he did more—he spoke the words of hope, comfort, and encouragement; and the Franciscan and the others being worn out, and almost rendered unserviceable with watching, he took his instructions from the learned leech, and then seated himself by the wounded knight's bedside. It seemed as if a kind Providence had blessed the hand which had inflicted the wounds with a power of healing them. From the moment that Sir Patrick sat down by his friend's couch, he had the satisfaction of finding his disease take a favourable turn. He never left his patient, who continued to improve hourly. In less than a week he was declared out of danger, and in a few days more he was able to join Hepborne and the two happy sisters, Beatrice and Jane de Vaux, in their walks on the terrace of the Palace.

The reader may easily fancy what was the subject of conversation that gave interest to these walks. It was during one of them that the Lady Beatrice de Vaux was suddenly met by a woman of the most graceful mien, who, standing directly in her path, threw aside a mantle that shrouded her face. Astonishment fixed Beatrice to the spot for an instant, when, recovering herself, she sprang into the arms of the stranger, exclaiming—

"Eleanore—my beloved Eleanore de Selby!"

The meeting was overpowering, and Hepborne hastened to conduct the two friends into the Palace, where they might give full way to their feelings without observation. After their transports had in some degree subsided, the Lady Beatrice eagerly inquired into the history of her friend.

"Proud as thou knowest me to be, Beatrice," replied Eleanore, "I do here come to thee as a suppliant, nor do I fear that I come in vain; albeit I have peraunter but ill deserved a favour at thy hands, since I did deceive thee into being the

propagator of a falsehood, by telling thee that he with whom I
fled from Norham was Sir Hans de Vere——"

"Ah! if thou didst but know into what wretchedness that
falsehood had nearly betrayed me," exclaimed Beatrice; "but
who then was thy lover?"

"Thou dost well know that my poor father was early filled
by a wicked and lying witch with a superstitious dread of the
union of his daughter with a Scottish knight, the cunning
fortune-teller having discovered his prejudice, and fostered it by
prophesying that such a marriage would lead to certain misery.
So he did ever study to keep me from all sight of Scottish
chevaliers. But, when visiting my aunt at Newcastle, I did
chance to meet with Sir Allan de Soulis, who had fled from Scotland for having killed a knight in a hasty brawl, and to him
did I quickly resign my heart. 'Twas this which made me
despise the splendid proposals of the proud Sir Rafe Piersie,
and which rendered the thought of the horrid union with the
Wizard Ancient, if possible, even yet more insupportable. I
agreed to fly into the arms of Sir Allan; but, to effect mine
escape, thy connivance was indispensable, nay, without thine
aid it would have been impossible to have carried my scheme
into execution. I did well know thine attachment and devotion
to my father, and I felt how difficult it would be to shake thee
from what thou wouldst conceive to be thy duty to him. I
saw, however, that I had thy full pity for the unwonted harshness I was enduring; yet I feared that if thou shouldst discover
the country of my lover, thou wouldst never consent to keep my
secret, far less to become my accomplice in an act that would
tend to make Sir Walter so unhappy. I was therefore compelled to resort to falsehood. I did introduce Sir Allan to thee
as Sir Hans de Vere, one who, from being kinsman to King
Richard's favourite, De Vere, Duke of Ireland, was likely to rise
to high honours. By doing this, I hoped to weaken thine
objections to the step I was about to take. Nor was I wrong
in my conjecture, for thou didst at last kindly agree to facilitate
my flight."

"And whither didst thou fly, then?" demanded Beatrice.

"First to Newcastle," replied the Lady de Soulis, "and then
to Holland. Being banished from his own country, and dreading to remain in England, where he, too, could not tarry during
war without proving himself a traitor to Scotland, we were compelled to retreat beyond sea for a time. It is not long since
that the sad news of my father's death did reach me. I was
struck with deep remorse for my desertion of him. We hastened

back to Norham. There I found that some low-born kinsmen of my father's, trusting that I should never return, had seized on the greater part of his effects and divided the spoil. The small remnant that was left me was saved by the fidelity of the trusty Lieutenant Oglethorpe. There doth yet remain for us Sir Allan's paternal lands in Scotland, the which have not yet been forfaulted ; but without the Royal remission he dare not return to claim them. To thee, then, my Beatrice, do I look to use thine influence with the merciful King Robert in behalf of the gallant De Soulis, that he may be restored to his country, his estates, and the cheering countenance of his Sovereign."

We need push the conversation between these two friends no farther. It is enough to say that the united entreaties of Hepborne, Halyburton, and the two Ladies de Vaux, soon prevailed in moving the clemency of the good old King, and the happy Lady de Soulis flew to England to be the bearer of her own good news to the brave Sir Allan.

The joy of the old Lord of Dirleton and his lady in contemplating the happiness that awaited their children may be imagined ; and it will also be readily believed that the delight of the elder Sir Patrick Hepborne was no less, when he returned to Scone, and found that he had lost his share of the general misery, and had arrived just in time to have full enjoyment in the unalloyed pleasure that spread itself throughout the whole Court.

The King resolved that the double nuptials should be celebrated in his presence, with all the splendour that he could shed upon them. The Bishop of Moray came from his diocese, at His Majesty's particular request, to perform the marriage rites ; and the Wolfe of Badenoch, to mark his respect for the good man, actually made one of his rapid journeys into Buchan, to bring thence his neglected spouse, Euphame, Countess of Ross, that she might be present with him on the happy occasion. So magnificent and proudly attended a ceremonial had not been witnessed in Scotland for many a day. Old Adam of Gordon, who was now a member of the younger Sir Patrick's Hepborne's household, composed and performed an epithalamium that put all the other minstrels to shame; and as for Squire Rory Spears, and Captain MacErchar, of His Majesty's Guards, their joy was so totally beyond all restraint, that, much to the amusement of the company, they performed a bargaret together—a sort of dance of these days which antiquarians have supposed to have borne some resemblance to the fandango of Spain, or the saltarella of Italy.

40

If the two knights who thus married the co-heiresses of Dirleton were friends before, they now became attached to each other with an affection almost beyond that of brothers, and Sir John Assueton was united with them in the same strict bonds. Sir Patrick Hepborne being aware that the unexpected discovery of Beatrice had diminished the prospect of wealth which would have eventually accrued to Halyburton, had Jane de Vaux been the sole heiress of her father, privately influenced the old Lord to leave his Castle, and the larger part of his estates, to his brother-in-law. On the death of William De Vaux, therefore, Sir John Halyburton became Lord of Dirleton. For the descendants from these marriages, those who are curious in such matters may consult "Douglas's Peerage," vol. i., pp. 223 and 687.*

We must not forget to mention that Rory Spears and Captain MacErchar were called on soon afterwards to repeat their dancing exhibition which had met with so much applause; and this was on occasion of the wedding of Squire Mortimer Sang and the lovely Katherine Spears. Many a happy hour had Squire Roderick afterwards, in teaching his grandson the mysteries of wood and river craft, whilst the youth's father, the gallant Sir Mortimer, was gathering wreaths of laurel in foreign lands, whither he travelled as a valiant knight.

One of the last acts of King Robert was to bestow a small estate in the valley of the Dee upon the veteran MacErchar. Thither he retired to spend a comfortable and respectable old age, and, having married, became the head of a powerful family.

It has always been a very common belief in Scotland that, when a wicked man becomes unexpectedly good, the circumstance is a forewarning of his approaching death. It was so with the Wolfe of Badenoch, for he lived not above two or three

---

* The reader, on consulting the second reference of our text, will find that Douglas has run into much confusion in regard to the Halyburtons. The Sir John Halyburton who married the co-heiress of Dirleton, he kills at the battle of Nisbet in 1355. Now, by consulting the first reference, p. 223, it will be found that Sir Patrick Hepborne, younger of Hailes, who married the other sister, was killed at the battle of Nisbet in 1402, at which time Sir Patrick Hepborne, sen., was alive. This we know to be true, and perfectly according to history; but to suppose that Sir Patrick Hepborne's brother-in-law could have been killed in 1355 is a glaring absurdity. The inconsistency is easily explained, however, for there were several Sir John Halyburtons, and two battles of Nisbet. There was a Sir John Halyburton killed at the battle of Nisbet in 1355, and there was a Sir John Halyburton taken at the battle of Nisbet in 1402. On this last occasion Sir Patrick Hepborne commanded. It is therefore quite natural that his brother-in-law should have had a share in this expedition.—Vid. FORDUN, II., p. 433.

years after the reformation that was so surprisingly worked in him. The Franciscan, who still continued with the Earl as his confessor, gained a great ascendancy over his ferocious mind ; and his endeavours to subdue it to reason had also the good effect of enabling him the better to command his own proud spirit, which he every day brought more and more under subjection. The happy effects of this appeared after the demise of him to whom he had been so strangely linked ; for, despising that Church advancement which was now within his grasp, he retired into the Franciscan Convent at Haddington, where he subjected himself to the penance of writing the Chronicle from which these volumes have been composed ; and those who have suffered the tedium of reading the produce of it, may perhaps be judges of the severity of this self-inflicted punishment. That the Wolfe of Badenoch had not failed to make good use of the remnant of his life, in wiping off old scores with the Church by making it large donations, we may well guess, from the following epitaph, which may yet be read in well-raised, black-letter characters sculptured around the edge of the sarcophagus in which his body was deposited in the Cathedral of Dunkeld ; but where now, alas ! there remains not as much of the dust of ALISTER-MORE-MAC-AN-RIGH as might serve to make clay sufficient for the base purpose to which the fancy of our immortal dramatic Bard has made his moralizing Prince of Denmark trace a yet mightier Alexander, and an Imperial Cæsar,

> To stop a hole to keep the wind away.

The Epitaph is :—

Hic Jacet
Dominus Alexander Seneschallus
Comes de Buchan et Dominus de Badenoch,
Bonæ Memoriæ,
Qui Obiit xx Die Mensis Februarii,
Anno Domini MCCCXCIV.*

* This monument is still in tolerable preservation, though it suffered mutilation by a party of Cameronians about the time of the Revolution.

THE END.

GLASGOW : ROBERT MACLEHOSE, PRINTER TO THE UNIVERSITY.

New Books and New Editions.

THE WOLFE OF BADENOCH. A Historical Romance of the Fourteenth Century. By SIR THOMAS DICK LAUDER. Complete unabridged edition. Thick Crown 8vo. Price 6s.

This most interesting romance has been frequently described as equal in interest to any of Sir Walter Scott's historical tales. This is a complete unabridged edition, and is uniform with "Highland Legends" and "Tales of the Highlands," by the same author. As several abridged editions of the work have been published, especial attention is drawn to the fact that the above edition is complete.

THE LIVES OF THE PLAYERS. By JOHN GALT, Esq. Post 8vo. Price 5s.

Interesting accounts of the lives of distinguished actors, such as Betterton, Cibber, Farquhar, Garrick, Foote, Macklin, Murphy, Kemble, Siddons, &c., &c. After the style of Johnson's "Lives of the Poets."

KAY'S EDINBURGH PORTRAITS. A Series of Anecdotal Biographies, chiefly of Scotchmen. Mostly written by JAMES PATERSON. And edited by JAMES MAIDMENT, Esq. Popular Edition. 2 Vols., Post 8vo. Price 12s.

A popular edition of this famous work, which, from its exceedingly high price, has hitherto been out of the reach of the general public. This edition contains all the reading matter that is of general interest; it also contains eighty illustrations.

THE RELIGIOUS ANECDOTES OF SCOTLAND. Edited by WILLIAM ADAMSON, D.D. Thick Post 8vo. Price 5s.

A voluminous collection of purely religious anecdotes relating to Scotland and Scotchmen, and illustrative of the more serious side of the life of the people. The anecdotes are chiefly in connection with distinguished Scottish clergymen and laymen, such as Rutherford, Macleod, Guthrie, Shirra, Leighton, the Erskines, Knox, Beattie, M'Crie, Eadie, Brown, Irving, Chalmers, Lawson, Milne, M'Cheyne, &c., &c. The anecdotes are serious and religious purely, and not at all of the ordinary witty description.

DAYS OF DEER STALKING in the Scottish Highlands, including an account of the Nature and Habits of the Red Deer, a description of the Scottish Forests, and Historical Notes on the earlier Field Sports of Scotland. With Highland Legends, Superstitions, Folk-Lore, and Tales of Poachers and Freebooters. By WILLIAM SCROPE. Illustrated by Sir Edwin and Charles Landseer. Demy 8vo. Price 12s. 6d.

" *The best book of sporting adventures with which we are acquainted.*"—ATHENÆUM.

" *Of this noble diversion we owe the first satisfactory description to the pen of an English gentleman of high birth and extensive fortune, whose many amiable and elegant personal qualities have been commemorated in the diary of Sir Walter Scott.*"— LONDON QUARTERLY REVIEW.

DAYS AND NIGHTS OF SALMON FISHING in the River Tweed. By WILLIAM SCROPE. Illustrated by Sir David Wilkie, Sir Edwin Landseer, Charles Landseer, William Simson, and Edward Cooke. Demy 8vo. Price 12s. 6d.

" *Mr. Scrope's book has done for salmon fishing what its predecessor performed for deer stalking.*"—LONDON QUARTERLY REVIEW.

" *Mr. Scrope conveys to us in an agreeable and lively manner the results of his more than twenty years' experience in our great Border river. . . . The work is enlivened by the narration of numerous angling adventures, which bring out with force and spirit the essential character of the sport in question. . . . Mr. Scrope is a skilful author as well as an experienced angler. It does not fall to the lot of all men to handle with equal dexterity, the brush, the pen, and the rod, to say nothing of the rifle, still less of the leister under cloud of night.*"—BLACKWOOD'S MAGAZINE.

THE FIELD SPORTS OF THE NORTH OF EUROPE. A Narrative of Angling, Hunting, and Shooting in Sweden and Norway. By CAPTAIN L. LLOYD. New edition. Enlarged and revised. Demy 8vo. Price 9s.

" *The chase seems for years to have been his ruling passion, and to have made him a perfect model of perpetual motion. We admire Mr. Lloyd. He is a sportsman far above the common run.*"—BLACKWOOD'S MAGAZINE.

" *This is a very entertaining work and written, moreover, in an agreeable and modest spirit. We strongly recommend it as containing much instruction and more amusement.*—ATHENÆUM.

PUBLIC AND PRIVATE LIBRARIES OF GLAS-GOW. A Bibliographical Study. By THOMAS MASON. Demy 8vo. Price 12s. 6d. net.

A strictly Bibliographical work dealing with the subject of rare and interesting works, and in that respect describing three of the public and thirteen of the private libraries of Glasgow. All of especial interest.

THE LIFE OF SIR WILLIAM WALLACE. BY JOHN D. CARRICK. Fourth and cheaper edition. Royal 8vo. Price 2s. 6d.

The best life of the great Scottish hero. Contains much valuable and interesting matter regarding the history of that historically important period.

THE HISTORY OF THE PROVINCE OF MORAY. By LACHLAN SHAW. New and Enlarged Edition, 3 Vols., Demy 8vo. Price 30s.

The Standard History of the old geographical division termed the Province of Moray, comprising the Counties of Elgin and Nairn, the greater part of the County of Inverness, and a portion of the County of Banff. Cosmo Innes pronounced this to be the best local history of any part of Scotland.

HIGHLAND LEGENDS. By SIR THOMAS DICK LAUDER. Crown 8vo. Price 6s.

Historical Legends descriptive of Clan and Highland Life and Incident in former times.

TALES OF THE HIGHLANDS. By SIR THOMAS DICK LAUDER. Crown 8vo. Price 6s.

Uniform with and similar in character to the preceding, though entirely different tales. The two are companion volumes.

AN ACCOUNT OF THE GREAT MORAY FLOODS IN 1829. By SIR THOMAS DICK LAUDER. Demy 8vo., with 64 Plates and Portrait. Fourth Edition. Price 8s. 6d.

A most interesting work, containing numerous etchings by the Author. In addition to the main feature of the book, it contains much historical and legendary matter relating to the districts through which the River Spey runs.

OLD SCOTTISH CUSTOMS: Local and General. By E.
 J. Guthrie. Crown 8vo. Price 3s. 6d.

*Gives an interesting account of old local and general Scottish
customs, now rapidly being lost sight of.*

---

*A HISTORICAL ACCOUNT OF THE BELIEF IN
 WITCHCRAFT IN SCOTLAND.* By Charles
 Kirkpatrick Sharpe. Crown 8vo. Price 4s. 6d.

*Gives a chronological account of Witchcraft incidents in Scot-
land from the earliest period, in a racy, attractive style. And
likewise contains an interesting Bibliography of Scottish books on
Witchcraft.*

"Sharpe was well qualified to gossip about these topics."—
Saturday Review.

*"Mr. Sharpe has arranged all the striking and important
phenomena associated with the belief in Apparitions and Witchcraft. An extensive appendix, with a list of books on Witchcraft
in Scotland, and a useful index, render this edition of Mr.
Sharpe's work all the more valuable."*—Glasgow Herald.

TALES OF THE SCOTTISH PEASANTRY. By
 Alexander and John Bethune. With Biography
 of the Authors by John Ingram, F.S.A.Scot. Post
 8vo. Price 3s. 6d.

*"It is the perfect propriety of taste, no less than the thorough
intimacy with the subjects he treats of, that gives Mr. Bethune's
book a great charm in our eyes."*—Athenæum.

*"The pictures of rural life and character appear to us re-
markably true, as well as pleasing."*—Chambers's Journal.

*The Tales are quite out of the ordinary routine of such litera-
ture, and are universally held in peculiarly high esteem. The
following may be given as a specimen of the Contents:—" The
Deformed," "The Fate of the Fairest," "The Stranger," "The
Drunkard," "The Illegitimate," "The Cousins," &c., &c.*

---

*A JOURNEY TO THE WESTERN ISLANDS OF
 SCOTLAND IN* 1773. By Samuel Johnson, LL.D.
 Crown 8vo. Price 3s.

*Written by Johnson himself, and not to be confounded with
Boswell's account of the same tour. Johnson said that some of
his best writing is in this work.*

THE HISTORY OF BURKE AND HARE AND OF THE RESURRECTIONIST TIMES. A Fragment from the Criminal Annals of Scotland. By GEORGE MAC GREGOR, F.S.A.Scot. With Seven Illustrations, Demy 8vo. Price 7s. 6d.

" *Mr. MacGregor has produced a book which is eminently readable.*"—JOURNAL OF JURISPRUDENCE.

" *The book contains a great deal of curious information.*"—SCOTSMAN.

" *He who takes up this book of an evening must be prepared to sup full of horrors, yet the banquet is served with much of literary grace, and garnished with a deftness and taste which render it palatable to a degree.*"—GLASGOW HERALD.

THE HISTORY OF GLASGOW: From the Earliest Period to the Present Time. By GEORGE MAC GREGOR, F.S.A.Scot. Containing 36 Illustrations. Demy 8vo. Price 12s. 6d.

An entirely new as well as the fullest and most complete history of this prosperous city. In addition it is the first written in chronological order. Comprising a large handsome volume in Sixty Chapters, and extensive Appendix and Index, and illustrated throughout with many interesting engravings and drawings.

THE COLLECTED WRITINGS OF DOUGAL GRAHAM, "Skellat," Bellman of Glasgow. Edited with Notes, together with a Biographical and Bibliographical Introduction, and a Sketch of the Chap Literature of Scotland, by GEORGE MAC GREGOR, F.S.A.Scot. Impression limited to 250 copies. 2 Vols., Demy 8vo. Price 21s.

With very trifling exceptions Graham was the only writer of purely Scottish chap-books of a secular description, almost all the others circulated being reprints of English productions. His writings are exceedingly facetious and highly illustrative of the social life of the period.

SCOTTISH PROVERBS. By ANDREW HENDERSON. Crown 8vo. Cheaper edition. Price 2s. 6d.

A cheap edition of a book that has long held a high place in Scottish Literature.

THE BOOK OF SCOTTISH ANECDOTE: Humorous, Social, Legendary, and Historical. Edited by ALEXANDER HISLOP. Crown 8vo., pp. 768. Cheaper edition. Price 5s.

The most comprehensive collection of Scottish Anecdotes, containing about 3,000 in number.

THE BOOK OF SCOTTISH STORY: Historical, Traditional, Legendary, Imaginative, and Humorous. Crown 8vo., pp. 768. Cheaper edition. Price 5s.

A most interesting and varied collection by Leading Scottish Authors.

THE BOOK OF SCOTTISH POEMS: Ancient and Modern. Edited by J. Ross. Crown 8vo., pp. 768. Cheaper edition. Price 5s.

Comprising a History of Scottish Poetry and Poets from the earliest times. With lives of the Poets and Selections from their Writings.

*** These three works are uniform.

A DESCRIPTION OF THE WESTERN ISLES OF SCOTLAND, CALLED HYBRIDES. With the Genealogies of the Chief Clans of the Isles. By SIR DONALD MONRO, High Dean of the Isles, who travelled through most of them in the year 1549. Impression limited to 250 copies. Demy 8vo. Price 5s.

This is the earliest written description of the Western Islands, and is exceedingly quaint and interesting. In this edition all the old curious spellings are strictly retained.

A DESCRIPTION OF THE WESTERN ISLANDS OF SCOTLAND CIRCA 1695. By MARTIN MARTIN. Impression limited to 250 copies. Demy 8vo. Price 12s. 6d.

With the exception of Dean Monro's smaller work 150 years previous, it is the earliest description of the Western Islands we have, and is the only lengthy work on the subject before the era of modern innovations. Martin very interestingly describes the people and their ways as he found them about 200 years ago.

THE SCOTTISH POETS, RECENT AND LIVING.
By ALEXANDER G. MURDOCH. With Portraits, Post 8vo. Price 6s.

A most interesting resumé of Scottish Poetry in recent times. Contains a biographical sketch, choice pieces, and portraits of the recent and living Scottish Poets.

THE HUMOROUS CHAP-BOOKS OF SCOTLAND.
By JOHN FRASER. 2 Vols., Thin Crown 8vo (all published). Price 5s.

An interesting and racy description of the chap-book literature of Scotland, and biographical sketches of the writers.

THE HISTORY OF STIRLINGSHIRE. By WILLIAM NIMMO. 2 Vols., Demy 8vo. 3rd Edition. Price 25s.

A new edition of this standard county history, handsomely printed, and with detailed map giving the parish boundaries and other matters of interest.

This county has been termed the battlefield of Scotland, and in addition to the many and important military engagements that have taken place in this district, of all which a full account is given,—this part of Scotland is of especial moment in many other notable respects,—among which particular reference may be made to the Roman Wall, the greater part of this most interesting object being situated within the boundaries of the county.

A POPULAR SKETCH OF THE HISTORY OF GLASGOW: From the Earliest Period to the Present Time. By ANDREW WALLACE. Crown 8vo. Price 3s. 6d.

The only attempt to write a History of Glasgow suitable for popular use.

THE HISTORY OF THE WESTERN HIGHLANDS AND ISLES OF SCOTLAND, from A.D. 1493 to A.D. 1625. With a brief introductory sketch from A.D. 80 to A.D. 1493. By DONALD GREGORY. Demy 8vo. Price 12s. 6d.

Incomparably the best history of the Scottish Highlands, and written purely from original investigation. Also contains particularly full and lengthened Contents and Index, respectively at beginning and end of the volume.

THE HISTORY OF AYRSHIRE. By JAMES PATERSON.
5 Vols., Crown 8vo.   Price 28s. net.

The most recent and the fullest history of this exceedingly interesting county.   The work is particularly rich in the department of Family History.

MARTYRLAND: a Historical Tale of the Covenanters.
By the Rev. ROBERT SIMPSON, D.D.   Crown 8vo.
Cheaper Edition.   Price 2s. 6d.

A tale illustrative of the history of the Covenanters in the South of Scotland.

TALES OF THE COVENANTERS. By E. J.
GUTHRIE.   Crown 8vo.   Cheaper Edition.   Price 2s.
6d.

A number of tales illustrative of leading incidents and characters connected with the Covenanters.

PERSONAL AND FAMILY NAMES. A Popular
Monograph on the Origin and History of the Nomenclature of the Present and Former Times.   By HARRY
ALFRED LONG.   Demy 8vo.   Price 5s.

Interesting investigations as to the origin, history, and meaning of about 9,000 personal and family names.

THE SCOTTISH GALLOVIDIAN ENCYCLOPÆDIA
of the Original, Antiquated, and Natural Curiosities
of the South of Scotland.   By JOHN MACTAGGART.
Demy 8vo.   Price raised to 25s.   Impression limited
to 250 copies.

Contains a large amount of extremely interesting and curious matter relating to the South of Scotland.

---

*THE COMPLETE TALES OF THE ETTRICK
SHEPHERD* (JAMES HOGG).   2 vols., Demy 8vo.

An entirely new and complete edition of the tales of this popular Scottish writer.

GLASGOW : THOMAS D. MORISON.
LONDON : HAMILTON, ADAMS & CO.

www.ingramcontent.com/pod-product-compliance
Lightning Source LLC
Chambersburg PA
CBHW021931110726
47901CB00003B/796